DUET OF PERNICIOUS EELS

PALADINS OF THE HARVEST: BOOK TWO

KADEN LOVE

SVETLING PRESS

ALSO BY

Also by Kaden Love:

Beastcall: a Paladins of the Harvest novella

Elegy of a Fragmented Vineyard

CONTENTS

For the Break-ins

Scott Palmer, Joshua Walker, Adrian M. Gibson, Z.S. Diamanti, Isaac Hill, Louise Holland, Francisca Liliana, Jonathan Weiss, Nicholas W. Fuller, Rob Leigh, Sam Paisley, Bryan Wilson, Andrew Watson, Aaron M. Payne, Calum Lott

Thank you for being the best group of supporting authors a boy could ask for.

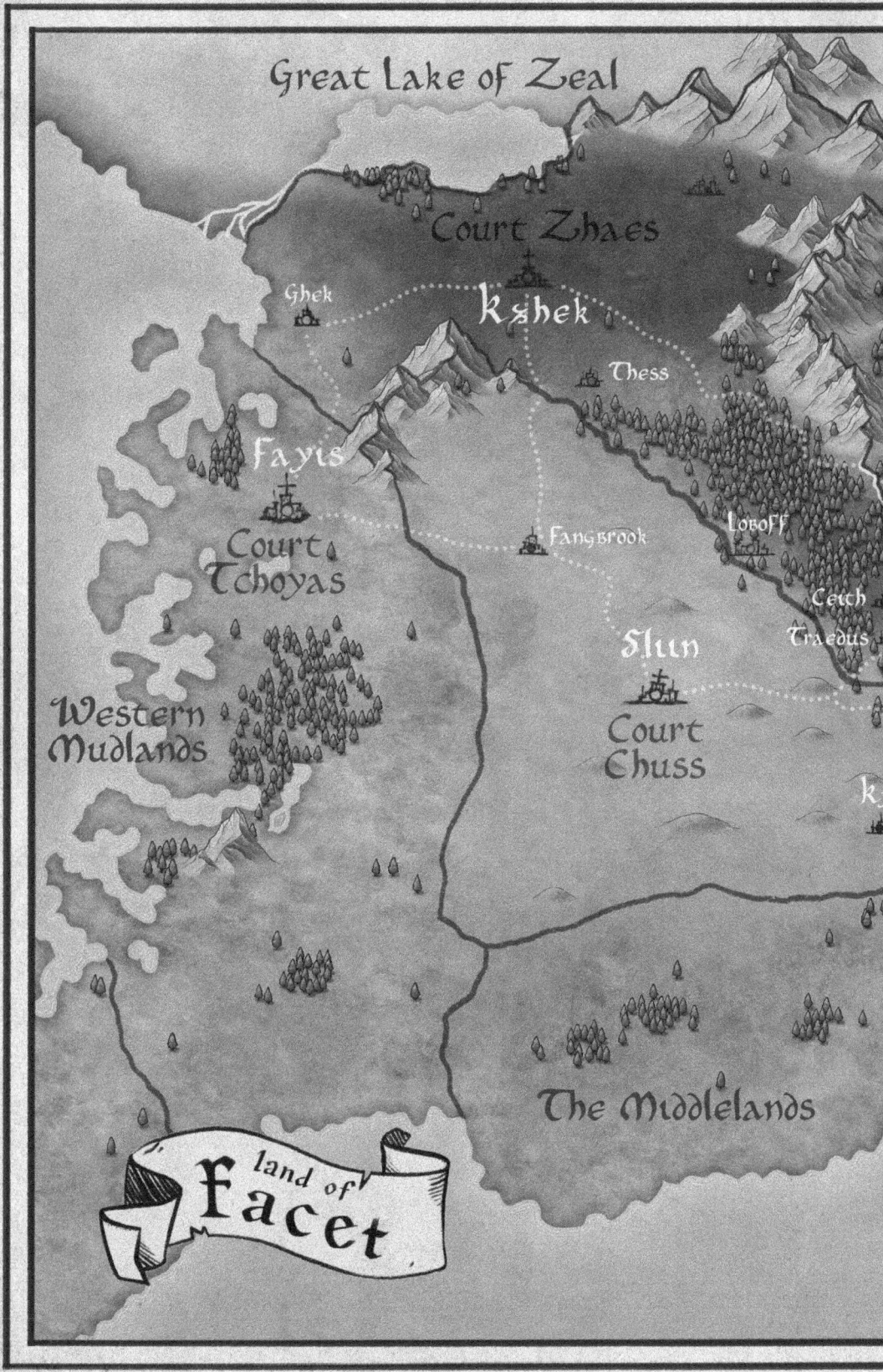

Great Lake of Zeal

Court Zhaes

Ghek

Kshek

Thess

Fayis

Court
Tchoyas

Fangbrook

Loroff

Ceth

Traeous

Slun

Court
Chuss

k

Western
Mudlands

The Middlelands

land of
Facet

Northern cliffs

Gruth
Sea

Ekscomos

Court
Priess

Paiell

Court
Sleff

kellford

dotrift

Bruten

doot

Thusk

ul

Court
Gruth

Seas of the Beyond

THE STORY THUS FAR:

Phenmir:

Phenmir, a Chuss surgeon, has just finished his last harvest. No longer will he participate in the extraction of endowed organs from infants. When learning that the Chuss Krall has accepted a graft, he returns to his Court's capitol to be with his wife–Meira–and son–Hir–in a time of political upheaval.

Upon his return, Phenmir witnesses the assassination of his Court's Krall by the hands of a man named Sleffman Colrig. Colrig introduces himself as the leader of the Harmony Allegiant, a coalition that hopes to overthrow harvesting in the six Courts. As the pro-harvesting Courts Zhaes and Sleff face anti-harvesting riots, the sound of revolution is heard.

After meeting with the Chuss nobility, Colrig and the Thanes decide to elect Phenmir as the Chuss Thane of Harmony to represent their Court in this war. Phenmir agrees and leaves his Court to travel with Colrig to Court Tchoyas, another anti-harvesting Court.

The Allegiant meet with the Tchoyas nobility, including Krall Trhet, his Thanes, and the young Shiftling Voln, who leads the Tchoyas Endowers.

After a meeting with the Krall, Phenmir joins Voln, another Shiftling Endower named Kaela, and a Sleff scouting company to search for potential allies in Kzhek.

The company of Phenmir, Voln, Kaela, Port, and the other Sleff scouts witness the riots in Kzhek's center before ending their night in an inn. The innkeeper learns of their plans and brings in his own company to oppose them. They fight and the loyalists kill a Sleff scout and injure Voln. Phenmir tends to Voln's wounds by sneaking into the Zhaes Canton of Haleness before returning to Fayis.

They return and the Harmony Allegiant soon after departing to ambush Kzhek and join with the rebels there after learning from Aerhee that the Zhaes Thanes plan to destroy the Zhaes rioters in a trap.

The war in Kzhek ensues, ultimately leading to an Allegiant victory. They establish their base in the city and Phenmir returns to Sliin to help reorganize his government and to meet with Kaela, after she was sent to organize the Chuss Endowers, as had been done in Court Tchoyas.

Aerhee:

Aerhee serves as the Caser of Court Zhaes, working closely with the Thanes and Krall of her Court. After a meeting attended by her scribe, Fheo, she learns of the Sleff anti-harvesting riots. She discusses this with Thane Lettre, who informs her about a lack of Endowed in Court Tchoyas. Riots run rampant in Kzhek, but Aerhee safely meets with Thane Sheath Leisa, after a fruitless search in the Athenaeum of Kzhek.

Aerhee and Sheath seek the guidance and records of Thane Gromm, despite Aerhee's derision for the Patriarchy of Scholars. They learn that the previous Zhaes Caser, Felta Zhil, had ties to Thane Sorn of the Canton Endowment and dealings with Court Sleff Endowers. Upon visiting her, they learn that Zhil and Sorn opposed harvesting and worked to horde Sleff Gorgers in a northern Sleff colony for a future rebellion.

They return to inform the Zhaes nobility of this treason, noting that Thane Sorn has gone missing in the collapse of his Canton. Royss decides to expedite quelling the rebellions in Kzhek, which will require a massacre as a show of Zhaes power. Aerhee wants to preserve as many lives as possible and flees with her scribe Fheo to try to coerce the Tchoyas Krall into a peace treaty to prevent mass destruction.

Aerhee arrives in Court Tchoyas, surprised to find the rebel leaders. She tries to meet with their leaders to discuss peace, but the Zhaes plans are read from her mind by a Tchoyas Endower. She is then locked in the Tchoyas palace with Fheo while the Allegiant armies head to Kzhek to join the rebels there with a knowledge of the Zhaes strategy.

While captive, she learns that Krall Trhet would rather have things as they were rather than a complete revolution. The Krall agrees to let her send Fheo to the Zhaes nobles to let them know of his desires to seek peace under different terms.

Captivity gives Aerhee time to reflect upon her past as a Priess refugee who fled to Kzhek with her parents. They faced prosecution and ultimately the death of her father under the hands of the Patriarchy of Scholars. She grows resentful of war and injustice and wants peace and life for all. She considers the Chuss Ideal, "Care is the Creed."

The Zhaes Thanes flee defeat and meet Krall Trhet under peaceful terms. In a surprising turn, Krall Trhet murders his Thanes out of their loyalty to the Harmony Allegiant and states that he wants to direct the Court under his own terms and power, detaching himself from the Allegiant radicals.

Aerhee escapes after a change of heart to join with the Harmony Allegiant to prevent the injustice wrought by Trhet and those who prefer power over mercy.

Yetrik:

Yetrik, a curious Gruthman is assigned by his preceptor, Thane Fortik Gett, to accompany a Shiftling named Semi on an expedition to Court Zhaes. Thane Gett has organized a deal to obtain Zhaes Bronze and needs Yetrik to finish the agreement with the Zhaes Thanes. The purpose of the bronze is not disclosed, nevertheless, Yetrik is eager to leave to explore the world.

Semi and Yetrik face dangerous rebels in Sleff en route and are then told to skip a stop in Priess to make sure they arrive in Kzhek before the rebellions grow even more dangerous. They meet with Royss, Thane Lettre, and Thane Gromm, who bring them into their fold to quell the rebellions rather than focus on Thane Gett's request. Royss utilizes them as Gruth connections to ensure loyalty as the Courts grow more divisive. Semi is wary of Royss' extremism, while Yetrik follows, hoping that he can do his best for the masses. Semi works with Royss to gather the Gorgers needed to control the rebels, though the Thane finds more success by other means.

Yetrik joins Runith and the Zhaes Beastlings to capture two kaesan, who are to be used against the rebels, should the battle turn dire.

He returns and meets with Royss and discusses his interest in the middlemen. Royss promises to look into using them after peace returns to Kzhek. Royss then shows him the brutality of the rebels, fighting some on their way to the Canton of Diplomacy to meet Sheath Leisa. Sheath has helped quell Semi's fear, deciding to send her back to Gruth to establish formal relations as the war has now officially begun.

Soon after Semi's departure, Kzhek is raided by the Harmony Allegiant. Yetrik is captured, but later freed by a Shiftling spy who brings the Gorgers into central Kzhek, freeing many of the Zhaes Thanes. The few escaped Thanes gather for a solution. Fheo arrives and tells them of Krall Trhet's offer. As the city falls, they flee with Fheo, hoping to reorganize in Fayis with a new influential ally.

Krall Trhet greets them with a feast, after which he murders his Thanes. Yetrik is shaken but continues to obey.

He joins a small party to the middlelands, while some head to Priess to establish relations. They arrive and greet the middlemen, learning that the Endowers have an innate skill that allows them to speak with middlemen, regardless of their power alignment.

GLOSSARY

Beastling: Endowers who can speak with animals.

Canton: A building and institution led by a Thane under their respective responsibility.

Caser: High administrator that serves alongside the Thanes of a Court to serve the Krall and populus. Counted among the nobility.

Cloven Gleff: Center of Facet's mining. Site of export for Zhaes bronze, among other metals. Located near Kzhek.

Court: One of the six fiefdoms that make up the continent of Facet.

- Court Sleff

    ○ Banner: Yellow banner with a black spinerat

    ○ Salute: Place the heels of the palms on the temples and extend the fingers upward

    ○ Ideal: *Pious is the Giver*

    ○ Values: Humility, meekness

    ○ Scripture: The Tome of the Meek

    ○ God: Heitt

- Court Tchoyas

- Banner Blue putle on a light gray banner

- Salute: Interwoven fingers covering the mouth

- Ideal: *Steadfast is the Honor*

- Values: Loyalty, honor

- Scripture: The Tome of Piety

- God: Klen

- Court Zhaes

  - Banner: Bronze Kaesan on a dark gray banner

  - Salute: Steepled fingers over the face, pointing upwards

  - Ideal: *Whole is the Holy*

  - Values: Obedience, perfection

  - Scripture: The Tome of Measure

  - God: Laeih

- Court Gruth

  - Banner: Green leviathan eel on a teal banner

  - Salute: Elbows against the torso, bent at ninety degrees, fists clenched, as if bracing for a strike to the abdomen

  - Ideal: *Firm is the foundation*

  - Values: Endurance, strength

- Scripture: The Tome of Stability

- God: Deilf

- Court Chuss

  - Banner: Crimson ghete on a white banner

  - Salute: Hands creating a circle and placed over the center of the chest

  - Ideal: *Care is the creed*

  - Values: Love, charity

  - Scripture: The Tome of Charity

  - God: Cheric

- Court Priess

  - Banner: White land eel on a maroon banner

  - Salute: Right ear cupped as if trying to hear, left arm raised in a fist

  - Ideal: Mighty is the free

  - Values: Pride, liberation

  - Export: textiles

  - No scripture or god

Currency:
- Base coin: Petiir

- 12 Zhon = 1 Petiir

- 10 Petiir = 1 Jame

- 15 Jame = 1 Maeth

Endower: Children born with an additional intestine, granting them a "god-sent" ability. The cardinal sign is a second umbilical cord at birth. Reports state that many do not survive past their first year of life. Four of the six Courts harvest these organs to be grafted into an adult Endowed.

Endowed: An individual who has received a graft from an Endower in order to gain their congenital ability.

Eurythrin: Endowers who can halt blood flow, regenerate, and help heal.

Facet: Continent composed of six Courts. Its boundaries do not include the Middlelands or nations beyond the northern cliffs.

Feelman: Endowers who can read people's emotions by identifying their bodily functions, correctly predict their next move, and almost read their mind.

Foreteller: Endowers who can analyze possibilities to predict the future.

Ghete: Reptilian steeds that share are described as "a large cat with green scales and no ears."

Gorger: Endowers with increased growth of the mind and muscle.

Harmony Allegiant: Coalition of political opposers to harvesting.

Harvest: The medical process of removing an Endowed intestine from an Endower at birth. This intestine will then be grafted into an adult, making them an Endowed.

The Induction: The year in which harvesting was implemented, five years after the Year of Manifest - C.E. 327.

Kaesan: Elusive beasts said to dwell in caves. Their depiction can be seen on the Zhaes banner. They are described as having large, muscular bodies capable of standing on their hind legs. Their abdomen is bare of fur and reaches only to the neck of their ferocious elk-like head topped with large antlers. Myth tells that they are sent to cleanse the plain of humankind from sin through violent purging.

Krall: Monarch of a Court.

The Pact of Province: The agreement upon which harvesting was accepted.

Patriarchy of Scholars: A Scholarly society that is not deterred by Court boundaries. They are said to promote unity and societal growth, though they are very exclusive and do not reveal their works to those outside of their ranks.

Putle: Amphibious creatures, similar to bipedal toads, with large rib cages and sizable nostrils. Their skins are often harvested for water repellent wear.

Pressist: Endowers who can control others through supernatural coercion

Seasons:

- Thaust - thawing of ice, second to third month of a year

- Vestning - blooming of buds, fourth to fifth month of a year

- Letur - peak of seasonal heat, sixth to seventh month of a year

- Ousell - death of the leaves, eighth to ninth month of a year

- Holdae - transition from warmth to cold, end of harvest, tenth to eleventh month of a year

- Zeemer - freezing of the land, final month of a year to the first month of the new year

Shiftling: Endowers who can manipulate their vocal cords to match any other person's voice, and can shift skin pigments like a chameleon.

Sprouten: Endowers who can control, speak with, and manipulate plants and their growth

Terpel: Endowers who are unable to experience exhaustion.

Thane: An elect individual that serves over a specific office of a Court. The only office higher than a Thane is that of a Court's Krall. Members of the nobility.

- Offices include the Thanes of:

  - Utilities: Technological advancements, engineering

  - Veneration: Religious practices and law

  - Haleness: Medicinal practice and health promotion

  - Diplomacy: Diplomatic matters with foreign Courts

  - Scholarship: Represent the Patriarchy of Scholars and all scholarly pursuits

  - Agriculture: Livestock, metals, crops, and all other natural materials

  - Progress: Politics, anthropology, and innovation

  - Endowment: Harvesting and Endowed in Courts that permit the process. Courts who oppose harvesting manage Endower growth, usage, and study.

Year of Manifest: The year credited for the first Endower birth - C.E. 322

Dramatis Personae

Aerhee Kleeh: Caser of Court Zhaes.

Avra: a zlatog.

Besh Plath: Krall of Court Gruth.

Calss Gromm: Zhaes Thane of Scholarship, member of the Patriarchy of Scholars.

Chenn Hult: Leader of the Chuss Endowers, son of the Chuss Thane of Diplomacy

Coln Tywing: Zhaes Thane of Haleness.

Colrig Fesst: Sleffman, founder of the Harmony Allegiant.

Deene Kelm: Gruth Thane of Scholarship.

Dhera Kost: New Krall of Court Chuss

Dessen: Sleff soldier in Port's company.

Derlik: Aerhee's father.

Dumek: Hir's preceptor in the Patriarchy of Scholars.

Faeth: Aerhee's mother.

Fennta Trhet: Tchoyas Thane of Progress, eldest granddaughter of Krall Trhet.

Fortik Gett: Gruth Thane of Utilities.

Fuih Lettre: Zhaes Thane of Veneration.

Garen Renss: Chuss Thane of Haleness.

Golma: Tchoyas Endower Beastling. Wears a mask of a hawk.

Gorrhin Vheen: Krall of Court Zhaes.

Hir Stolk: Son of Phenmir.

Horrah: Alchemical healer that often accompanies Runith's party of Beastlings.

Kaela: Tchoyas Endower Shiftling. Wears a mask of a serval.

Kenth Keersh: Gruth Thane of Endowment.

Kevlen Phanos: son of the Priess Krall, Beastling, captain of the Priess zlatog riders.

Khenna Lonik: Chuss captain.

Khoga: Kelvin's zlatog.

Kollra Holmn: Tchoyas Thane of Endowment.

Kuid Trhet: Krall of Court Tchoyas.

Lele: Runith's putle companion.

Lhaen Pensa: Krall of Court Sleff

Meira Stolk: Phenmir's wife.

Peval Phanos: Krall of Court Priess, "the Boated Krall."

Phenmir Stolk: Chuss surgeon, proficient in harvesting.

Port Kamen: Sleff Thane of Harmony.

Roill Lehket: Tchoyas Thane of Veneration.

Royss Belik: Zhaes Thane of Agriculture.

Runith: Head of the Zhaes Beastling corp.

Sairee Phemus: Priess Thane of Haleness, Erythrin.

Scholar Sokov: Chuss member of the Patriarchy of Scholars.

Semi Ershif: Gruth Shiftling.

Sheath Leisa: Zhaes Thane of Diplomacy.

Shome Keff: Gruth Thane of Agriculture.

Taer: Tchoyas Endower Gorger. Wears a mask of a Beaver.

Telsa Serish: Gruth Thane of Diplomacy.

Terin Trosh: Priess Thane of Diplomacy, Gorger.

Tick: Sleff soldier in Port's company.

Voln Zertef: Tchoyas Endower Shiftling. Wears a mask of a wolf.

Yetrik Kloff: Gruth scribe that works close beside Thane Fortik Gett.

Zeir Kleeh: Aerhee's husband.

"War has its necessities...and I have always understood that. Always known the cost. But, this day, by my own hand, I have realized something else. War is not a natural state. It is an imposition, and a damned unhealthy one. With its rules, we willingly yield our humanity. Speak not of just causes, worthy goals. We are takers of life."

—— **Steven Erikson,** *Memories of Ice*

PROLOGUE: BRONZE TONGUE

HOURS BEFORE KRALL TRHET'S TREACHEROUS FEAST

S in is easier to tolerate when one forces another to commit the crime.

"You Zhaesmen do not disappoint." Krall Trhet sank into his cushioned chair, one not unlike his throne, matching the lavish silver and blue decor in the chamber. "Thank you for the timely arrival on such a short notice."

Did we have a choice? Royss thought. "Anything for a new ally. Do you mind if I close the door?" It took some coercion to find time for a private meeting, but that was no difficulty for the Thane of Agriculture.

The Krall responded with a nod, one slowed by fatigue. Royss wondered how the Krall was able to see at all. The eyeholes in his owl mask were slits compared to most, and he kept the room dim with candlelight rather than large lamps. Court Tchoyas felt like it lived in perpetual dusk with its cloud coverage and humidity more dense than anywhere in Court Zhaes.

He sat across from the Krall and adjusted himself with no recoil from the cushion. Had the Krall taken this perding excuse for comfort from the marshes? He scanned the room for a drink. Even mead would do after the too-sour wine. The musk of the marshes was still strong, even in the finest of chambers, but at least the room was accented by a lavender aroma.

"I am a trusting man," said the Krall, "but why would you request a *private* meeting? Are we not all allies, as you declared?"

"Before we complicate this alliance, I felt it best to put the leaders of our companies together. Two voices can come to an agreement easier than a crowded council."

"*Leaders*? Are you not the Thane of Agriculture? Where is your Krall?"

"Held in the city, alongside the other Thanes. Kzhek is under the control of the dissenters and their allies."

"Excuse my frankness, Thane Belik, but are you not then the ones in debt? We offer you sanctuary while your capital falls to rebels. What do you offer us?"

Royss tensed his eyes, not so much as to squint, but to draw his focus. He took a moment to breathe, biting his cheek.

"I too am a trusting man, Your Grace. What can you offer *me?*"

The Krall forced a dry laugh. "Is this a jest? Need I repeat myself? You are in debt–"

Receive my words. Listen. Follow. Submit. Royss tightened his chest, sitting with perfect posture. "*What will you give us? Show us your loyalty, Your Grace.*" He hissed out the final word like a boa encircling his prey.

The tension in the Krall's shoulders fell. "What can I offer you, Thane Belik?"

Exhale. The Krall was not under Royss' control, per se, but had become more so *willing* to comply with the words of the Thane. Royss offered a nod of gratitude but felt as if he thanked himself.

"Your Grace, how have your Thanes received your pledge to restore Facet to its former tranquility?"

"Three of my Thanes joined the raid on Kzhek." He spoke with reluctance.

"And *the others*?" He had counted on the Krall resisting. The best rulers constantly juggle right and wrong to appease their people. Royss had no moral predicament that prevented him from pressing further. He only had to be sure to avoid pushing so much that the Krall would recognize it as such.

"The other Thanes remain here in the city, mingling with my people and the rebel extremists."

Royss had seen the extremists' excitement upon their arrival to Fayis. He was not surprised to learn that the Tchoyas Thanes were fond of the movement against harvesting.

He did not rejoice in what he would have to do. It was his duty, an essential step to peace. It was what Laeih would desire.

"How unfortunate for them. *You* are the Krall, the supreme authority in Court Tchoyas. *Perhaps you should seek new Thanes who would be willing to establish order. We must not allow enemies in our midst.*"

"Most certainly." Krall Trhet spoke free of opposition, like a child conditioned to obey.

"See that it is taken care of swiftly. Our presence in this city might be unwelcome by the likes of them. Take care and we will worry about the denizens and foreigners in the coming days. This Court will be *yours*, Krall Trhet."

The Krall nodded with more conviction. "I will gather them to feast with you and your fellow Thanes this evening. I will immediately send invitations."

Royss forced him further with a stare.

"I will ensure that they know that this is not a gathering to dismiss."

"You swear that they will be out of our wake before the end of the night?"

"On my honor as a Tchoyasman, it shall be done."

That will do. Royss stood with his chin held up. "I look forward to it. Have your servants prepare the feast and I will gather my fellow Zhaesmen."

He stood and dismissed himself, leaving the Krall to his thoughts.

The organ was the best perding gift that he had ever received. It was one too precious to expose to those outside of his most inner circle. He was yet to meet another person who possessed his ability, besides the High Scholars and the few Endowers they had removed from society. Still, the Scholars could not see all that happened in Facet, contrary to their belief. He was glad that was Gromm's responsibility, not his. Maybe others were wise enough to keep it hidden. The best advantages are those unknown to one's enemies. He was the great Royss Belik, Thane of Agriculture, Endowed - *Pressist.*

CHAPTER ONE

THOSE WHO SUFFER

"**M**istress Ershif, excuse my delay." A panting messenger ran in through the doors of the Canton of Utilities.

Semi turned, paused and turned mid-way up the stairs.

He handed her a worn envelope, wrinkled and dried from rain. "We searched the entire Endowed Guildhouse until a kind Gorger led us here."

"I tend not to frequent the Guildhouse," she replied, tearing at the envelope's corners.

"Where might we find you, should more messages come from the Zhaes nobility?"

She had dismissed the bronze wax seal, but now took note of the kaesan crest. "Have them sent to Thane Gett. I visit him often enough." She dismissed him with a Gruth salute, flexing her arms and placing her elbows at her hips.

Privacy was not the trouble, but residency was. She was not homeless but saw herself as a nomad. Most Endowed employed by the Court lived likewise. Her parents would be willing to offer her a bed, but she would never have time to rest in it. The Endowed Guildhouse was, in fact, that–a *house*. It was one accommodated to host more than fifty Endowed, but often held much less. Few Endowed finished their day in the center of Thusk. During her extended stay in Thusk, now her fifth, Thane Gett was polite enough to offer a secluded room in the Canton of Utilities.

Semi held to the side rail of smooth marble to read, relieved that the ink on the note was not too smeared. Red cheeks grew with a smile as she recognized the poor penmanship.

Mistress Shiftling,

Sorry, I don't know how to formally address you. Thane Gett never required me to write any official letters. How have you been? Have you arrived? I assume that you have if you are reading this. Royss did not require me to send this. If you receive a second letter, I cannot say that it will be the same. I know I tend to ramble. I'm usually an organized man, you know.

I hope to hear from you soon. I don't need to tell you what to do once you arrive in Thusk. I trust you have already accomplished much by now. I only hope this does not arrive late.

In the few days since her arrival, she had spoken with Thane Gett, informing him about the proposal from the Zhaes nobility to join the harvesting loyalists in a union, but was yet to present the offer to the Krall. She had been on her way to meet Thane Gett before a formal council with the Krall and the other Thanes. She took a deep breath, aiming to forget the heavy responsibilities in the coming hours, and read on.

I only wish you were here for me to tell you what has happened. I know you will have questions, but I plead that you trust my words and the direction of our leaders.

Krall Trhet has pledged loyalty to our cause. He does not wish to bring harvesting to his Court, but merely to return Facet to its pre-war state. Royss trusts him, and I suppose I do too.

Thane Leisa left to establish a stronger alliance with the Priessmen in Ekscomos.

Lastly, though you may doubt it, we've found and have begun to communicate with the Middlemen. I write to you after having spent a few days in the Middlelands. I pen this in Fayis after returning from our first contact.

I assume you heard that Kzhek fell to the extremists. We have settled in Fayis for the time being, which you might know. Aside from losses and difficulties, some of us will return to the Middlelands in the coming days with a company of Endowers. Oddly enough, no Beastling was initially capable of speaking with the crop people, but the Endowers spoke with them as if it was their mother tongue.

I'll set down my pen now. There is so much to tell you, but I do not know how to write it all. I hope to see you soon. I miss you, Semi.

Firm is the Foundation,

Yetrik

She left the staircase swiftly, avoiding any who passed. Anxiety over the news and a blush from the final line caused her skin to go as red as if she changed it to match a crimson Chuss banner.

Semi sat on a divan down the corridor from Thane Gett's study. She made sure she would not be disturbed while taking a moment to contemplate Yetrik's words. Should anyone attempt to enter her corridor, she would shift her face to match that of a noblewoman and banish them from the premises.

She opened the letter once again, scanning it to confirm what she had read. Rumors had circulated of Kzhek's fall soon after her departure, yet it shook her to hear it confirmed by a trusted friend. She wanted to deny it as propaganda, but Yetrik was likely in the city when it occurred. She was relieved to hear that he had found a haven yet remained disheartened. *How could Deilf allow such an atrocity? How could Laeih allow it to occur? Are the gods at war as well?*

She let the thoughts simmer in her mind. She wanted to feel terror, wanted to force it on her, but could not bring herself to such sorrow. Could it have been caused by the brash decisions of a Zhaes Thane who neglected to counsel with his Krall? She tried to avoid blaming Royss, but wondered what would have happened if Thane Leisa was given control. Regardless of her opinions, the events had passed. Yetrik was safe and seemed optimistic about the future. Then again, when was he anything but an optimist?

She focused on the few words that he shared about his encounter with the Middlemen. It was odd that only the Endowers–the natural born Endowed–were capable of communicating with them. Was this due to their purest form of the endowed abilities? What did Yetrik hope to gain? He was obsessed with them, but what would the crop people want in a human conflict?

Questions continued to fill her thoughts, but only paved endless trails. She would not see these resolved in the coming days, if ever. Such answers were not hers to obtain. She was to fortify an alliance between the Gruthmen and the vagabonds of Zhaesmen in Fayis. *Firm is the Foundation. Ignore everything else and serve your duty. That's the best thing to do, right? Perd. Ignorance will kill us all.*

No one had disturbed her, much to her relief. She folded Yetrik's letter into a palm-sized square, tucked it in her worn leather travel satchel, and approached Thane Gett's door with a knock.

"Semi," he said with an amiable grin, "I was expecting you."

"Your Foreteller's humor grows more stale each time you utter that line."

He began to laugh and she couldn't help joining as he stepped out and locked the door behind him.

It felt good to jest with an old friend. Yetrik claimed she feared the nobility. What a poor misunderstanding. She merely *revered* those with authority. Royss had caused her to question her respect for *all* Thanes. The man had the reverence of a tavern braggart. If she were to be casual with any Thane, it would be Thane Gett. She still kept his title and only opened up to him further upon her return. She had even visited the Thane and his wife for an evening meal. Deference was due when warranted, but they were now alone.

"Shall we?" He gestured with an open arm as if he was a young man accompanying her to a grand ball. In truth, it was more like a favorite grandfather escorting her.

"We shall."

The harsh Gruth sun beat on them with a warm blanket of humidity pulling even more sweat from every gland. The sizzling sounds and alluring scent of fried oysters reminded her that she had forgotten to eat. Though the circumstances of their meeting with the Krall were dire, she was sure they would find the council room tabletop covered by a bounty of food. Funeral or wedding, a Gruth gathering required copious refreshments. If Gruthmen were not so adamant about manual labor, it would be a land of blubber and immobile giants. Opposingly, their frequent feasts only worked to create men and women that could rival a Gorger from another Court.

Their conversation began casually, but her anxiety forced her to focus on more pressing matters. One could only discuss the weather so much when war had begun in the west.

"I..." Semi reached for the letter in her satchel. The edges of the envelope were torn beyond redemption as the letter fell right out. "I received this just before meeting you."

"And?"

"Yetrik wrote to me. He said that the rumors regarding Kzhek are true, and the–"

"He wrote to me as well. I figure he wanted us both prepared to meet the Krall with clear expectations."

He wrote the Thane? Was his letter just a routine gesture? Surely the Thane's letter wasn't as detailed. She reread the final line. *"I miss you."* Her anxieties were laid to rest.

"Oh, how fortunate." She saw the slight hint of a smirk on his face. "What do you make of it?"

"Royss told you why I sent you, did he not? I have been expecting this for some time. I will not deny that it feels surreal to be on the brink of a war."

"You know, we were never able to procure that bronze for you."

"I think that is obvious, seeing that Kzhek is no longer under the control of the Zhaes nobility. I assume that those who remain in the city are captives to these radicalists."

"But..."

"But my vision never came to fruition?"

She nodded.

"My visions were true. War has come. Conflict has returned to Facet. I received the warning but did not reap the rewards of early preparation. The fields of grain grow and fall. My vision was not tied to bronze. If Royss led you to believe otherwise, I apologize. Regardless, I do not regret sending you to Kzhek. The city's fall was inevitable. Yetrik is faring well through adversity and you are growing to become a greater diplomat and noblewoman. We have much to prepare for."

"Are you confident in my career?"

"I expect much from you, Semi, but that is not the preparation that I speak about."

"Have you had another vision?"

"Many." He huffed out a nervous laugh. "But one that particularly haunts me, recurring nearly daily."

"What...what was it...sir?"

"My vision of the fields was enigmatic, yet decipherable. I regret to inform you that this one is beyond me. I saw a cobblestone square, not unlike Thusk's center, with a corner covered in vines. Storm clouds obscured the distance. Before rain fell with their approach, the ground was scattered with seeds. The storm came and passed, causing the seeds to sprout. Most grew into weeds, but others became vines, which approached the square. As the distant vines met each other, one vine rose above the others, growing thick sprouting leaves that covered the other plants. The new vines tried to grow towards the larger but were blocked or perished in the way of smaller tree saplings, whose base was covered in bronze. I will have you know Semi, I am not the Thane of Agriculture for a reason. I do not enjoy botany, neither do I understand the persistent presence of bronze. Not all of my visions tell of the growth and death of plants, only the most perturbing. I expect that it is from no other than Deilf himself."

"Those sound like visions from the god of the Middlemen."

"If they even have one, I suppose Yetrik will tell us."

Semi nodded but kept her gaze on the ground, where no vines grew. She was no philosopher, but she could not remove her thoughts from the Thane's odd visions. Perhaps it was the novelty of his allegory, but it was the only thing that kept her mind away from Yetrik.

Semi had visited the Krall's palace but had never spoken to him directly. As she sat across from him in his lavish council chamber, she felt her timidity towards the nobility return.

Krall Besh Plath's heavy brows furrowed as he stared at her with pale blue eyes. He stroked his short beard that hinted of graying but was still preserved by his youth. He was nearing the fourth decade of his life and had the attitude of one ten years younger. His personality reminded her of Royss, though more diligent. He wore the marine circlet, a green ring of emerald shaped after seaweed, around his short cut sides as the top of his hair was swept to the right. Clam shells of bronze, each the size of an open palm, covered each shoulder.

Semi appreciated his fanciful wear but wondered what the cost of those bronze shells entailed. Such adornments were not purchased from the Zhaesmen by coin, but by intimate relations. He wore them with purpose, making an implied statement for those who would question his loyalty. She would present the offer from the Zhaes nobility for an official alliance, but she knew that he had already made the decision.

"Shall we begin?" Krall Plath turned his gaze away from Semi.

What had he been trying to see? Surely he is no Feelman. I would have known that.

"Your Grace," began Thane Gett, "how can we begin when you have only three of the Thanes here? Surely we must wait for the rest before proceeding."

The Krall eyed the Thanes on either side of him.

Shome Keff, the Thane of Agriculture sat on his left two heads higher than the Krall even while slouching.

Telsa Serish, Thane of Diplomacy, was nearly as large as Thane Keff, but had filled out by excess feasting rather than forming labor.

A tall, leaner man who was reminiscent of an aged Yetrik sat to Thane Gett's left. Kenth Keersh, Thane of Endowment. She knew Thane Keersh just as well as Thane Gett, having labored close beside him with the other Endowed.

"We have enough. Semi informed me that Thane Belik of Zhaes requested this meeting." The Krall faced the burley Thane. "Thane Keff is his close associate." He turned to the woman on his other side. "Thane Serish will oversee the diplomatic manners of this council." He then directed his attention to the man beside Thane Gett with an open palm. "Thane Keersh will oversee any of the needs of the Endowed. I will have the other Thanes informed of the results of this meeting. For now, their voice is not my concern. *I* am Gruth's monarch, not them."

"Very well." Semi forced confidence to placate Thane Gett, who continued to watch the door for the absent Thanes. Should she be concerned about his distrust for the Krall? She had heard that he was an occasionally brash, impulsive ruler beneath his charismatic facade. "Hearing that you mentioned Roy–Thane Belik, I assume you were able to read my preamble prior to arrival?"

"How else would I have known that you requested a meeting?" He chuckled, elbowing Thane Keff.

Semi dug her thumbnails into her index fingers. "I have been informed that following my departure from Kzhek, the city was seized by the anti-harvesting radicals. A trusted associate of mine has informed me that the free members of the Zhaes nobility have fled to Fayis to join in an alliance with Krall Trhet."

"The Tchoyasmen?" guffawed the Krall. "Why in Deilf's name would those masked conservatives join our cause? Were they not a part of the rebellious alliance that stormed Kzhek?"

"Some did, but more remained behind. My associate suggested that the Krall does not wish to eliminate harvesting, only to return autonomy to the Courts, letting them direct harvesting as they please. Perhaps the Tchoyasmen generally oppose the matter, but it seems that the Krall is more neutral than most. Maybe the Tchoyasmen are divided over harvesting?"

The Krall folded his arms and leaned against the back of his seat.

"The Sleffmen are divided," Semi continued. "It was their contention that led to the riots throughout the Courts. Zhaes faced similar circumstances. Have any uprisings begun here?"

"Not in Thusk, but rumors have circulated of some northern cities following the trend. Doot faced some protests but quelled them by enforcing social order before their supporters could congregate. Priess remains loyal to harvesting without any opposition and Chuss remains against it in totality, more so since the death of their Krall. Besides these two, each Court has some degree of division."

"That's a relief," sighed Thane Keff.

"I would argue that it is less than ideal," countered Thane Serish. "I would prefer that our Court remained loyal."

"Well, of course!" Thane Keff returned. "I only meant that we have not yet lost hope. Priess still remains loyal to the cause. I would have never thought the Priessmen to be the most righteous among us." His nervous laugh was put to shame by silence in the room.

Thane Serish glared at him as if he were an unfaithful lover. "Politics do not entail piety, even if their political status aligns with ours."

"Thane Laeisa of Court Zhaes has left to attempt rekindling an alliance with the Priessmen." Surprised glares turned to Semi.

"What other choice do we have?" offered the Krall. "It is time we overcome our differences with the Priessmen."

"Still," said Thane Serish, "we cannot deprive ourselves of our resources to aid Court Priess while we have our own people to look after."

"I do not suggest that we do." The Krall turned to Keersh with a grin. "Let the Zhaesmen focus on the Priessmen. Thane Keersh and I have discussed our tactics, should war arise. I think it is time that we enact them, Kenth."

Thane Kenth kept his brows low, a cocktail of victory and disgust. "The Endowed are the reason for this war. Likewise, they are the way to triumph. The anti-harvesting fanatics are not the only ones capable of building an army."

"We have all heard about the Sleff Gorgers who joined the extremists. Copying their tactics would only make us equals, not superiors." Thane Keff folded his arms.

"Terpels. You have enough of them. Am I mistaken, Thane Keff?"

Thane Keff's lie was a thin spider web. "I do not know what you speak of."

Thane Serish nodded. "Yes, yes. *This* is what we need." She condemned Thane Keff with a glare. "We all know about them. Hiding it does not eliminate the immorality of it, Keff."

The Krall sat, pleased with himself despite the Thanes' contention.

"I don't know what you are talking about," remarked Semi.

Thane Serish turned to her, sucking air through clenched teeth.

Semi turned to Thane Gett, who held his head low. "I am as responsible for them as you, Thane Keff."

"Do not cast guilt on me," Thane Keersh said. "I just did as you asked."

"Could you please speak clearly?" Semi held herself back from shouting.

Thane Gett turned to the Krall. "Sir, may I–"

"She deserves to know. Look at who she is sitting with. Go ahead."

"But you said it would only be known by the nobility!" contested Thane Keff.

"She is nobility already in my eyes," said the Krall. He adjusted the seaweed crown. His chest rose. "Our monopoly on food production has not come without a price." He looked to his Thanes and received nods. "I am sure that you have been told that many Gorgers are used as laborers."

Semi nodded. "Their strength and endurance makes—"

"–them the ideal laborers and they are worth ten standard humans. Yes, we have all heard it. True, some Gorgers aid in construction, but they charge more than ten standard laborers would and have no greater endurance than any other individual. What *does* provide hours of quality work, or rather, who does? The Terpels."

She drew her eyes to slits.

"I figured you hadn't heard of them. Those who know about them believe them to be Gorgers of a smaller size. These Endowed never fatigue. Their bodies do not produce the humors that cause one to tire. Feed one enough and they could run to the far western ends of the Tchoyas mudlands. Additionally, they are remarkably quick, faster than a land eel."

Semi turned to Thane Serish, who replied with a delicate nod. "How have I never met any of them?"

"You may have without knowing," said Thane Serish, "but they are not employed by the Court in the same manner as you are."

"There is no pleasant way to say it and no use hiding it." The Krall sat back with a sigh. "They are cheap laborers. We provide them with grafts and they are property of the Court, laboring without end."

"Slaves?" Gasped Semi. "You traffic Endowed!"

"It is for the people! We–"

The Krall held up a hand. "No need to justify it, Thane Keff. They are little more than property. Do we celebrate this? No, but it keeps us affluent and in control of our food trade. All Terpel organs since the Pact of Province have been given to us. Agriculture is not a one-Court ordeal."

Royss. "We did not need such an abundance of food before the Endowed!" Semi clenched the armrests of her seat.

"You should know that the extra organ in your body demands twice the amount of food as a standard human. You are only a Shiftling, Endowed are more demanding. Terpels are the same, though they provide more with their labor than they take from our resources."

She looked at Thane Gett, whose gaze was cast beyond the teal-stained glass windows. "Do you kidnap street urchins and force the organs into them? And what about the Terpel Endowers? Surely I would have heard of them."

"Are you too insolent to believe that we know about all the organ strains?" remarked Thane Serish, his nose up. "Shiftlings, Gorgers, Feelmen, these are all terms given by us to describe the organ tendencies. We know but a *fraction* of what exists. You may be a *Shiftling*, but that does not determine the extent of your ability. You may have a skill that some other Shiftling does not possess."

Thane Serish opened to speak again, but was placated by the Krall, who knocked his ringed fingers against the table. The monarch smiled, the kind one would offer to a dull child. "While Thane Serish is correct, you have reason to ask such a question. Recognize that you do not know all the Endowed that our Court has under its control. We can only suppose that the Terpel Endowers are seen as insignificant. The Chussmen and Tchoyasmen who deal with their Endowers likely recognize that some of their young are quite resilient. I suppose the Eurythrins that read organ patterns upon birth are not familiar with this strain, besides those with whom we labor in Zhaes. What we do know is that Terpel births have increased drastically since harvesting began. Why this is, I do not know. Without such an increase, we could not have the monopoly on exports that we do. Regardless of any possibility, we invest in our secrecy. The other Endowed who know about this ensure its confidentiality. We trust that you will as well."

"Alright," Semi said, "but that does not answer my question. How do you *own* them?"

The Krall's grin fell flat. "We offer payment for extensive periods of labor. Those trapped in poverty are more than willing to offer themselves."

"*How* extensive?" Semi asked.

"Don't you see, girl?" hissed Thane Serish. "We *lie*. We are not Tchoyasmen sworn to truth. They are told that they will be compensated for days of labor. We tell them that this will be their escape. We take them in and deny escape. Those with familial obligations are cut off, false letters are sent to sever ties. It is morally undesirable, but necessary to maintain our agricultural production."

Semi caught in an awestruck stupor. She could not argue, for they had already condemned themselves. Any further condemnation would be accepted by them for some hope of a *greater good.*

Thane Serish turned his head with a slight grin. She knew he had recognized her defeat.

"*But,*" began the Krall, "we have received enough for some to be released and fulfill their roles as Endowed elsewhere. Conscripting laborers from allied Courts during this conflict will allow us to send an excess of Terpels into combat training. Five years of recruiting has left us with hundreds of them. We will conscript an elite force of warriors consisting of no less than three hundred Terpels. Using stratagems and combat expertise from historical tomes, these Endowed will be made into elite, tireless assassins. Worry not, we will ensure their loyalty. Thane Serish has formed an elite training program. By the time this so-called *war* reaches our Court, we will have a peerless legion of warriors, the likes of which have never before been seen."

CHAPTER TWO

CHOOSE THIS DAY WHOM YOU WILL SERVE

P *uff sniff sniff puff puff puff.*

The Middleman's eyes grew wide. It crouched and bore its viney fingers into the soil, palming a large clump of it. With the speed of an archer, it threw the earth at Runith's chest before running away.

Taer fell to the ground with laughter.

"What did I do?" Runith asked, looking at the beaver mask of the Gorger Endower. The Tchoyasboy was a ten-year-old, one of the first endowed-born, and measured to Runith's shoulders. "I only told it that I admire its roots."

"Might as well have asked it to mate with you."

Runith cheeks were burning. "I think I have had enough of them for today."

"Come on, Runith!"

"No, apologize to them if you see them again. We need to start cooking, anyway."

Runith's ears caught another disturbance towards the camp. Large reeds divided like a splitting log before him, drawing closer with a bounding thump. The reeds stood up to his knees, obscuring the bouncing blue creature.

"What is a putle doing here?" asked Taer.

Runith smiled as the amphibian stood to his waist. "I ran upon her during one of our visits to Fayis before returning with more Endowers." The frog-like creature stood, revealing its enormous ribcage with an inhalation and opening nostrils the size of fists upon exhaling. Webbed feet waddled towards Runith.

"But why is it here?"

"She and I had some nice conversations and..." Taer's eyes opened through their holes nearly as wide as the putle's black orbs. "Nothing of that sort! *Perd me!* She wanted to see beyond Tchoyas, and I figured maybe she could be of some help. With a chest as large as hers, she must be capable of some great breathing patterns. Maybe she could talk to the Middlemen."

Taer laughed. "I'm famished. Let's return to camp."

It was odd to hear the boy's refined diction, though they had spent a few days together. The Gorgers' extra organ helped fuel their muscles, but it was important to remember that their mind grew likewise. The boy had the strength of a kaesan and the mind of an aged scholar.

Runith turned to the putle, speaking in its tongue. "*Time to head back, Lele.*"

"*I came all the way out here to find you, just to return?*" Her nostrils flared.

"I never asked you to come out here." He said.

Her ribcage clenched like a brawler's fist.

He chuckled. *"I'm sorry. What did you want out here, anyway?"*

She wrinkled her nose twice, something he had taken to be a shrug.

Runith chuckled, attempting the same gesture which caused him to sneeze. *"I don't know why I'm here, either. I'm only following the orders of the Thanes."*

"Why do you value their words? They are mere humans, not great spirits."

Even the creatures of the land recognized the spiritual side of life. Had he been neglecting his faith for the direction of flawed men? Was that not obedience? Heeding the law of those greater than you? Was this not what a Zhaesman was to strive for?

Why are you toying with your faith over the words of some large amphibian?

Runith lifted his head to Taer, who hopped with a loud gurgling. "Are you choking, lad?"

"Just thought I would try to join in on your conversation," Taer said.

He may be smart, but he still seeks attention like any ten-year-old.

"I'll leave you to speak with the boy. I can handle the silence. I'll see you at the camp." Lele ran in a hop with the speed to rival a prized racing ghete.

Runith jogged forward to walk beside Taer. He laughed through his nose, shaking his head. *Caught between the pleads for attention from a giant child and a cheeky swamp dweller.*

"You wanted to talk," Runith swung his arm over the boy's shoulders, "let's hear it."

"Why are we here?" Taer's voice was barren of joy. "Why are *you* here? What do you Zhaesmen want with us?"

Runith scowled but tried to maintain his smile. "We want allies. Why else? You Tchoyasmen are–"

"I am not talking about my Court." Taer glared at Runith's abdomen, despite the clothing covering his Endowed scar. "What do you want with the Endowers? War is raging because of us. Some of our Endowers left to join the fight in Kzhek. What do you organ thieves wish from us?"

Runith lost his smile. "Your Krall wants to end this conflict in his way. We're merely cooperating."

"That shriveled kulf has held his throne for too long. I know there are things happening behind our backs. You better thank your god that I am no Feelman." His brows settled beneath his mask. "I'm sorry, Zhaesman. It is hard to trust *your kind* at this time. I know you likely had nothing to do with the child who gave you your organ, but the fact of it eats at me. I just... I cannot help but feel lost out here. Too many of our Endowers labor aloof without an understanding of politics. You Endowed have the upper hand there, I will admit to that. I wish Voln were here to offer a sound, stern voice."

Taer's hands trembled but grew still the more he talked. Runith could not find anything to say. *By Laeih, he doesn't even know that Krall Trhet killed his own Thanes?* What could one say to a child, not unlike the one killed to give him his own organ? He could not admit that they were fighting to enforce harvesting. Runith was as honest as the most pious Tchoyasman, but he had to find a way to placate the beaver-masked Endower.

"Why did the old fool send us here?" asked Taer. "Shouldn't we be with the other Courts that went to Kzhek?"

"What happened there is over. Krall Trhet is working with us to stop the violence before it grows worse."

"And he hopes to find some *mystical* solution with these crop people?"

Runith shrugged. "I suppose that is what we are here to learn."

Runith pulled the tent flap back as he entered to join Royss and Thane Lettre beside three Tchoyasmen that had come with the second expeditionary group.

"This region was more difficult to transverse, but I–"

"Runith! Any luck this time?" Royss interrupted the squid-masked Tchoyasman to welcome Runith into the circle.

"I insulted one of them. Perding Endowers continue to make a fool of me."

"In due time it will come," said Lettre. "It is miraculous that you can communicate with them at all. Maybe one of our other Endowed back home will be able to work beside you to find a better way to learn their language."

"What home?" Royss said.

"Well, I... surely Kzhek isn't all–" Lettre said.

"Unlikely," said Runith. "This is something beyond Endowed. I don't know how to explain it, but I can feel it. I only have a glimmer of communication because of my Beastling experience, but I can feel resistance on their side. The Endowers... they just get it. I've tried to understand them explain it, but they struggle to do so themselves. It's something with their *natural* organs."

"More to learn. How exciting." Lettre turned back to the squid-masked Tchoyasman. "Forgive the interruption, Sen–" He turned back to Runith. "Oh, Runith, you must come and meet our cartographer Senell. He is most–"

"Pleasure," said Senell as he drew his attention back to a large sheet of parchment rolled across the table.

Runith approached the table. Upon further inspection, the parchment was an unfinished map. The drawings were professional, but it was little more than a collection of four regions, connected by a few paths each.

Senell circled the left side of the map with his finger. "The western region had the most Middlemen, though it had fewer huts than the eastern regions. This would lead us to believe that their nomadic–"

"Nomadic?" questioned a Tchoyaswoman whose mask was of a human face with a third eye. "I must have traveled further west, or north, than you. I recall some of the western stone formations that you mentioned, but they had more than huts. They had buildings."

"How do you define a building?" Senell asked.

"You must have found a village with huts in the east, because I saw what looked like a marketplace. Large tents and domed buildings. It reminded me of a Chuss city."

Royss chucked. "I'm glad our anthropologist was able to find what she needed. Well done, Byra. Senell, it looks like you have some exploring to do."

Senell shook his head and stood back from the table to fold his arms.

"Proctor Thurn," Thane Lettre asked the last Tchoyasman with the mask of a smiling man with oversized cheeks. "Find anything of interest for the Canton of Utilities?"

"Most certainly," he replied.

How does he feel about the death of his Thane? thought Runith. *Does he know or was he fed a lie? Do the Tchoyasmen know about the feast? Or is he just another sycophant looking to advance as far up the ladder as he can by nuzzling the Krall's wrinkled ass?*

It sounded like the Middlemen were quite advanced, but Runith had no interest in technology. He enjoyed how things were in the wild. Natural and undisturbed by man-made solutions that rendered human skills useless when accomplished by some metal and wood. Runith turned to whisper to Royss as Thurn rambled on about cogs and switches.

"I saw these three come back with you from Fayis a couple of days ago, but who invited them?"

"I did," said Royss.

"And you trust them?"

The humor drained from Royss' face. "They *will not* betray us."

"You know, not all Tchoyasmen are loyal to their Ideal," Runith smirked.

Royss did not share his smile. "They are under my supervision. They will not betray us."

Runith nodded with a sigh. "So, they came to wander? I thought that was my job?"

"You have your assignment. They have theirs. We need professionals. A cartographer to give us a reliable guide to the area, an anthropologist to study the Middlemen, and a servant of the Canton of Utilities to assess how advanced of a society they are. Each one goes on expeditions just like you, accompanied by an Endower or two for translation."

Runith checked on the group. The Proctor tried to draw some contraption on a sheet of parchment that looked like a blade attached to a box by a rope.

"I thought I was the one assigned to speak with the people. If the three eyed Tchoyasman has that covered, what is my assignment?"

Royss glared at Runith for a moment, then turned to interrupt the group. "Yes, Proctor, very interesting, but we can speak about...whatever that is later. Runith, are any of them ready to head back to Fayis? Are they...aware enough to fight?"

"Royss?" Runith glared at him as if he were reading a convoluted tome. "You can't expect us to conscript them all, especially not yet. We are still working on building *any* relationship. We cannot approach them just to draft troops."

"But can we take one back to speak with Krall Trhet, Gromm and I?" asked Royss.

"Well, if you expect some diplomat or leader, we cannot help there. It would be a random pick. We have the *faintest* idea of how their society works." He pointed to Senell with a chuckle. "This kulf didn't know they lived in anything greater than huts until now!"

"Well, I assure you–"

Runith waved Senell away, not paying him a glance. "We can *try* to see if one would be willing to join you in Fayis, but we have so much more to do before we can even *consider* asking them to join our political pursuits."

"Great!" said Royss. "Grab some water for it to plant its feet in for the journey back and–"

"Royss!" Runith shouted. He looked at the others, calming himself. "Just take a *perding* breath! You proved my point! We don't know if they need water, by Laeih, we don't even know if they can survive outside of the Middlelands. These are *people,* not weapons."

Royss inhaled deeply, closing his eyes for a moment. "I will worry about these *people,* when mine are not dying under the control of our enemies in *our perding Court*!"

"Then what do you want?" Runith shouted. He and Royss were the only two not stepping back from the table.

"I want you to think about yourself and your people. There is more than nature to care about. Remember that, Beastling. You've been here for a couple of weeks. These *things* are not Zhaesmen."

Runith scowled, clenching sweaty fists.

"You have three days. All of you, Tchoyasmen included. I want you to explain to whoever has influence among them that we need one of them to come with us to Fayis." Runith stormed towards the tent door shaking his head and paused before leaving. "I am returning to Fayis at the end of the week and by Laeih's holy name, you will find a Middleman to join me."

CHAPTER THREE

SELF-PROCLAIMED IMPOSTER

Tears fell from Thane Fennta Trhet's mask.

Aerhee felt she should cry but could not. She wanted to feel for the fallen Tchoyas Thanes. Their murder was one of the most horrendous events in Facet's history. She hated the Krall for it and her hatred was too loud to let sorrow through.

Thane Trhet stepped forward, the last to lay a large gray feather on the pyramid of spears. They stood in a cobblestone courtyard behind the Zhaes palace. The Thanes' bodies were likely tossed by the Krall to feed the buzzards, but that did not mean that the remaining Thanes could not honor their memory.

Colrig passed by the final Tchoyas Thanes, lighting their torches with his. He then extinguished his own in a muddy puddle. Only family was permitted to light the pyre. The remaining Tchoyas Thanes were the closest thing to a family in their current circumstances.

The four symbols of the fallen Thanes burned at the base of the pyre. A beetle, a portrait of a crying man, a stork's feather, and a day-old fish carcass each burned to represent the respective masks of the fallen Thanes.

Thane Trhet stepped forward, turning her face toward the heavens. "May the Lord Klen accept you into his embrace. Each of you served with piety. May you remain loyal to our Lord in the realms beyond. Steadfast is the Honor!"

"Steadfast is the Honor!" Everyone joined to shout the Tchoyas ideal.

Thane Trhet turned back, saluting them with interwoven fingers over her mouth.

Aehree joined the others in mimicking the salute. Silence fell as the pyramid of flames danced with the rage that burned in their hearts.

The camaraderie warmed her chest, yet it felt somewhat forbidden to join in a non-Zhaes salute.

Is this a sin?

No, cast off your past self. Cast off Zhaes imperialism. That is not Laeih's desire.

She lowered her hands, watching Tchoyasmen, Chussmen, and Sleff-men embrace. *This is Laeih's desire, a perfect union.* They were all only a hint of perfection, but this was the dawn of a new era. Resentment for opposing faiths still ate at her, but she knew that *this* was right, not her feelings. She had to deny Zhaes policy to embrace Zhaes, the truth so long forsaken by condescending Zhaesmen. *Condescending supremacists just like me.*

Thane Trhet placed her hand on the shoulder of a Zhaesman, nodding as he spoke. The other Thanes were vehement when Aerhee had informed them of the Krall's treachery, but Thane Trhet took it worse. Her tears were louder than any shout. Today was the first time that she seemed anything more than distraught. She had spent nearly a week in seclusion. If she had gaunt cheeks, they were hidden behind her mask, but near starvation showed in her disinterest and lethargy.

The influx of Tchoyas refugees seemed to improve the attitudes of the Tchoyas Thanes. It was a relief to see that once the Krall's actions were made public, that many still held true to their Allegiant pledges. Though the leaders of the Harmony Allegiant rejoiced over their migration, Aerhee could not help but worry about their dwindling resources. The city was yet to return to functioning. Mills, markets, and other trades were just beginning to resume production. There had not been a single food shipment from Gruth since the fall of Kzhek and most of the Kzhek farmers were preoccupied with the revolution. Phenmir had sent only a few messages back to Kzhek since his arrival in Sliin, none of which mentioned any influx of Tchoyasmen into the Chuss capital. They needed to spread their roots rather than grow a large tree in Kzhek.

A hand squeezed Aerhee's shoulder. She turned from the dwindling embers to see Colrig at her right. "Head inside, Caser. We have a letter from Sleff."

"Port?"

Colrig nodded. "Tell the other Tchoyas Thanes to join us. When they are ready, of course. The Sleffmen and Chussmen are already on their way. I'll go talk to Trhet. She could use someone with a more *delicate* touch."

Aerhee scowled, making Colrig's smirk grow more pronounced. "And the Zhaesmen?"

Colrig pointed to her left as he walked away. A bronze direwolf prodded the leaders of the Zhaes rejectionist towards the palace, nipping at a few, who struggled to turn away from the pyre. The so-called 'Tchoyas Thane of Endowers' had adopted the bronze shade since Colrig said that the boy deserved a medal for his contribution to the Allegiant's victory. When Colrig had no medal to offer, the boy made himself into one.

He was a cocksure child, but one of the best living arguments against harvesting.

Have you convinced yourself yet that harvesting should be abolished? Is that what you are here for, or is it for some vainglorious crusade to change Zhaes into what you think it should be?

"'—I fear we are ill-equipped for a battle here in Sleff that would make what happened in Kzhek seem like a minor dispute,'" Colrig concluded, looking out to the silent council as he lay Port's letter on the table.

Colrig pulled his shoulders back. "We have to expect delays. I have already warned that this was not the time to focus on Court Sleff. Well, if this is what you all want, so be it."

"You say you were against focusing on Sleff, yet you encouraged Port to go there once he volunteered?" accused Thane Holnm, her teethed mask making her comment more menacing.

"I did, because I believe in my people. Still, there are risks in all that we do. Nevertheless, Port wanted to see this through and has taken too many of our troops for us to shirk off this opportunity to gain the entirety of Sleff."

"What about the rioters in Sleff? The members of the Allegiant? Can they not help him?" asked Thane Lehket, stroking his goat mask's chin.

Voln laughed, gesturing to the Sleffmen.

"Yes, Voln is right," said Colrig.

The boy arched his back, exaggerating his posture.

"He is partially right. Most of the Allegiant members are with us in Kzhek or already in the army with Port. Sure, we left rioters to cause unrest, but as I have stated before, *Sleff was not our focus*. Most of the Sleffmen of worth came to help take Kzhek. Perd me, even the Gorgers are here, at least those that survived the battle." Colrig placed his palms on his temples, extending his fingers upward to salute the fallen Endowed. The others joined. "If I was not clear, Allegiant Sleffmen will not win us the war."

"Surely the Sleff loyalists cannot be that fortified?" argued Thane Holnm.

"Rumors speak that some of the free Zhaes Thanes have already established an alliance with the Priessmen. We've arrested plenty of Priess recruiters," said Aehree.

Thane Mortriff whispered to his fellow Chuss Thanes with a scowl.

"What do you mean, Priess recruiters?" argued one of them.

"Priessmen and some Zhaes loyalists flooding the streets with anti-Allegiant propaganda. They're offering large bounties for informants and insight into our strategies. I have been working with the Tchoyas Thanes to apprehend them. How do you not–you're not in league with them, are you Chussmen?"

A Chuss Thane guffawed. "Me? How characteristic of a Zhaes *noblewoman* to target a Chussmen when your problems arise!"

"My problems? This is not a personal matter!"

"And you insist on making it one!"

"I will–

"You need to–"

"Enough!" Shouted Colrig. "*None* of us are traitors."

"I object." Aerhee stood. "Forgive me, Chussmen. I do not want to blame you, but there is someone to blame."

"And who might that be?" asked Thane Frent.

Aerhee returned to her seat. "I don't know."

"Then why make accusations?" asked Colrig.

Aerhee looked to Thane Trhet, then back to Colrig. "It's been five months since the battle of Kzhek. The Zhaes loyalists have had enough time to forge an alliance with the Priessmen. Someone must have divulged our plans to return to Sleff so quickly after your capture. Priessmen had to have joined with the Sleff loyalists to defend their Court. Just as Thane Holnm said, Sleff could not defend itself on its own. We did not send a large army, but our forces were strong enough to capture a city in a weaker state than Kzhek."

"Priessmen with escaped Zhaes Thanes are sending their people to defend my Court?" Colrig asked. "Is this some joke?"

"No." said Thane Trhet.

"Now *you* believe her? How–"

"I've had more visions."

Colrig gasped and stared around the table, losing his sense of surprise as everyone else remained straight faced. "They know?"

"They know," Thane Trhet nodded. "We are at war, and I have nothing to hide from my allies. However, if Caser Kleeh insists on a traitor in our midst, perhaps I should be more reserved. I may not be the best Foreteller, but this vision is proving true."

"And why did you not tell us?" asked Colrig.

"Her visions do not always prove true," said Thane Holnm.

Colrig eyed Thane Trhet with an arched brow.

"It's true."

"Then how can we trust *this* one?"

"The future is not always set. The stronger visions are tied to more likely occurrences. When I led Thane Stolk to you during the battle of Kzhek, I knew that would occur. It was a *complete* vision. This one... I was not so sure about, but it seems to be proving true."

"Can you check again?" asked Colrig.

She shook her head. "Some of the Endowers can force visions, but that has not been my case."

"But you trusted Caser Kleeh?"

"Well, I... yes."

"Why her?" He turned to Aerhee, offering an apologetic smile.

She was not offended. She had come to join them on a whim.

"She is the most honest of anyone here." Thane Trhet turned to her fellow Tchoyas Thanes. "I do not doubt the loyalty of anyone present, but neither did I doubt the loyalty of my grandfather. What has our Court come to when a Tchoyaswoman cannot rely on her Court's Ideal when dealing with her own people? Caser Kleeh, however, *defied* her own people to pursue what she knew to be the will of her god. I have never met a Zhaeswoman so true to her Ideal. She forsook temporal law for the higher law."

Aerhee nodded. Thane Trhet was delicate, but she was proving to be the finest of her new allies.

"We do not have time to worry about betrayal right now," said Aerhee. "We can focus on the traitor once we have a *specific* plan to strengthen our forces in Sleff."

"And if the traitor is among us?" asked one of the Chuss Thanes.

"That is a risk we must take," said Colrig. "The Caser is right. Sleff needs our attention now." He turned to his side. "Voln?"

The wolf boy gave up trying to shove an entire turkey leg between the teeth of his mask and surrendered to sawing it down with a fork and knife. "Yes?"

"We need a Beastling."

"For?" he grunted as he continued to try to saw through the bone with the already dull kitchen knife.

"Raven."

"Fine." He set the utensils down with a sigh. "Hand me the letter and I'll have one of my Beastlings tell the raven where to go. Where is he?"

"He should be in Paiell, or near the city," said Colrig.

"Corvids are a particularly clever avian family," noted Thane Lehket. "If you have a Beastling, tell the messenger to look for the captain of a Sleff army. It should be able to locate him."

"Thank Laeih for Endowers," chuckled Voln, chunks of meat expelled from his too-full mouth. "What do you want in the letter?"

"I will pen it myself. After all, he is my second in command and the Sleff *Thane of Harmony*. Members of the Allegiant, feel free to correct me, but I believe that we need Port to pull back until we can send further reinforcements."

They all nodded.

"Captain Shoge?"

"Yes, Sir Colrig?" The Sleff gorger stood, anvil-strong arms pressed tight at his sides.

"I want you to lead fifteen of your Gorgers east. We have already sent some with Port, but we need the rest here to help rebuild the city, not including your fifteen. I will have Port pull south from Paiell to Bruten. The duke there is unlike any other nobleman, but I trust his direction. He should provide a temporary safe haven while they wait for reinforcements. Voln?"

Voln grunted, fingers reaching in to pry the meat stuck between his teeth.

"I want another letter sent to Sliin. Thane Stolk's last letter led me to believe that the city has calmed down enough for our order to prevail. We'll have him send some forces of his newest recruits to join Port in Bruten. With a complete army, in addition to the small troop with port, and more soldiers from Chuss, we should be able to take Paiell without difficulty."

Voln nodded as he chewed and swallowed.

"Anyone have anything to add? Any objections?"

"Do I get to go?" Voln pushed his plate away and slouched in his chair, rubbing his stomach.

Colrig struggled to answer. Aerhee smirked. The Sleffmen often disagreed with the radical Shiftling's ever-present desire to help on the front lines. This time, however, he struggled to disagree. Their relationship was comedic, yet heartfelt. She wondered where his parents were in all of this. If Voln needed a father figure, Colrig was not a bad substitute.

"The Priessmen might have Beastlings in Sleff," noted Thane Trhet. "Do not forget the catastrophe with the Kaesan. We would have surely lost without the Endowers."

"But Voln is not a Beastling," said Colrig.

"I know that," Trhet replied, "but he has a way with the others."

Colrig scratched his mouth with a subtle grin. "If we send a substantial crew of Beastlings, I guess they would not be complete without their captain."

"Great," replied Voln. "I'll be ready by the morning."

Colrig held up a hand. "We still need to settle the logistics. I'll take you and Shoge to the barracks after this and we will figure out the plan from there." Colrig lifted a worn ledger from the table, skimming a couple of pages before returning his attention to the council. "Caser Kleeh, how has your work been in the city?"

Better than I could have ever wished for. "Central Kzhek is nearly back to full working order. Four out of the five surrounding villages have pledged to support the Harmony Allegiant, while the fifth remains peaceful, though in opposition by policy."

"An improvement since last month," said Colrig. "How many were previously pledged?"

"Two, sir."

Colrig clapped. "This! This, members of the Allegiant, is the news we strive for. For each setback, we have two steps forward. Well done, Caser. Congratulate Zeir for me, as well."

"I could have never done it without him. You would have thought *he* was the member of the nobility in our family."

Colrig shrugged. "With a new order in Court Zhaes, there are bound to be openings."

She smiled. There were difficulties, more that she could fathom, but her circumstances earned a moment of bliss. Joy was a childhood fantasy that she was learning to believe in once again.

Surprised was not the best work to describe how she felt about Zeir accepting her decision to join the Allegiant, more *relieved*.

"Zeir, this is against all that I have pledged for..."

"But it is what you must do to 'be a better Zhaeswoman.' Am I wrong?"

"No."

"It's what your father would want."

"Yes."

"I know, Aer. You know. I never doubt you. I never doubted that you would return to my side once you figured things out. True, I have my own opinions, but you know I was never a man for politics. Harvesting is a law decreed by men, not by Laeih."

"You speak my thoughts better than I ever could."

"We fared without harvesting before. We will again, if that is what you believe."

"You think so?"

"Perhaps, but that is for us to find out. What matters is that I trust you."

"Zeir–"

"I'm with you Aer. No need to defend yourself anymore. Now, what can I do?"

"And the Thanes?" asked Colrig. His voice pulled her focus back to the council.

"Still vehement that I am contributing to the fall of humankind." Aerhee chuckled, shrugging it off. "Perding stubborn Zhaesmen, aren't we?"

"You said it, not me."

"We've moved them to private rooms, not unlike the one Krall Trhet kept me in. Perhaps a change of scenery will help them rethink their stance."

"And Krall Vheen?"

"I have arranged to see him following this meeting."

"Excellent, Caser." Colrig scratched his eye. "I cannot express enough gratitude for your service. I would have never thought to gain aid from a Zhaes noble at this point in our campaign."

"The first of many."

"I hope so."

"What about the opposition?" demanded Thane Holnm. "Some of our interrogators have captured people who claimed loyalty to some 'Holy Reapers.' I've heard of them gathering in Peakbridge and more in The Pinnacles." She looked for a sign of recognition and furrowed her brow. "Am I the only one who has heard about this? Thane Trhet?"

Thane Trhet shook her head.

"I've heard rumors, but little else," said Aerhee.

"I've been working with the Zhaes Shiftlings. Some of us have run into a few of their recruiters." Voln spoke as if it was no more eventful than seeing mud on his boots.

The group faced him, astounded.

He lifted his head, mask imprints left on his fists from holding his chin up.

"And what did they say?" asked Colrig.

"Some chain of lies, saying that harvesting is from Laeih, others that Facet needs a new order greater than the Courts. Poor kulf thought I was a Zhaesboy. Sure, I'm a Shiftling, but my acting is better than any Endower. They talked about meeting in the Pinnacles. They were almost as bad as the Patriarchy with their secrets and such."

Colrig grinned and approached him with folded arms.

"What?"

"You know what I'm going to ask. Sorry, but you will have to wait to go to Court Sleff."

Voln shrugged. "Zhaes is better anyway. Too many ugly faces like yours in Sleff."

"You can investigate for me, then?"

"I guess you need help from the best Shiftling there is."

"Kaela's not here."

"Hey! I'm–"

"Good enough for the job. Let's talk tomorrow. I think we could all use some sleep."

"What about Fayis?" asked Thane Trhet.

Aerhee knew the question was coming. Worse for her, she knew she was the best lead they had on the escaped Zhaes Thanes. *What would Sheath think of me now?*

"Have any of your scouts learned anything, Caser?" asked Colrig.

"I'm afraid not," Aerhee said. "I haven't heard from any of them yet."

She turned to Thane Trhet with an apologetic frown. They had built a friendship, or what she had thought was one, over the past few months. Regardless of her efforts, she had been a poor friend. As she had been to too many other people. She helped organize the memorial service for the Tchoyas Thanes but had only done so when it worked for *her.* Their service was conducted *months* after their deaths. It was moments like this that made her glad that Thane Trhet's disappointment was hidden behind a mask.

"Refugees continue to flee Fayis to stay by the Allegiant's side," said Thane Lehket. "I would assume that things are only growing worse in the Court."

Colrig hung his head and shook it. "We will continue to hope that our scouts return, but what else can we do, Tchoyas Thanes?"

Kill the Tyrant and take back their land. Did Thane Trhet still hope there was a chance of redeeming her grandfather? Surely, he could not have betrayed them in a more conniving way.

"What is the point of capturing another Court when we cannot even hold one of our own?" asked Thane Holnm. "How much power can a single man have? Without the Thanes, our Krall is a decrepit nobleman who dreams of his youth and the power he could hold with fewer years weighing him down."

"He has the Zhaes Thanes." Aerhee almost mumbled.

"And?" asked Thane Holnm.

"The Thanes that we have captured here are the *least* influential in my Court. Thane Royss Belik is a serpent of a man and can manipulate anyone. Thane Sheath Leisa has more connections across Facet than anyone I know. Thanes Lettre and Tywing should not be ignored, but Thane Gromm is one of the highest ranking members of the Patriarchy of Scholars."

"How high?" asked Thane Lehket.

"I—its more than—he—"

"How is she supposed to know?" Colrig winked at her, his demeanor stern. "How are any of us supposed to know if we know *nothing* about the Patriarchy? I think Caser Kleeh is trying to warn us that even though Thane Leisa may have connections, the connections that Thane Gromm has may run deeper. We are bold, but I do not think we are ready to take on the Patriarchy just yet."

"Are there any brothers of the Patriarchy in the Harmony Allegiant?" asked Thane Trhet.

"Not that I know of," replied Colrig.

"Hir," spoke Thane Renss, "Thane Stolk's son was just assigned his preceptor in the Patriarchy."

"A member soon enough," said Colrig.

Thane Renss nodded. "Yes, if he stays allied with our cause."

"I don't care about the perding Patriarchy!" Thane Holnm slammed a fist on the table. "I care about *my* people. It is *quite* difficult to focus on the Sleffmen while our people are in danger."

"Those who are in most immediate danger are here with us, Thane Holnm." Thane Lehket placed a wrinkled hand delicately on his fellow Tchoyas ally's shoulder.

"You want to just ignore the others then, Lehket?"

"Not ignore but wait. The large influx of refugees is evidence enough that we have the support we need. They have their sanctuary here in Kzhek while we focus on maintaining a strong center of operations. We Tchoyasmen loyally refute the Pact of Province. We pledged our stance to our Lord Klen, not to any monarch."

"Then why aren't they rebelling like the Zhaesmen?"

"They are afraid, just as you and I. Do not fear that the hearts of our people will change. We need to focus on Facet as a whole, as Sir Colrig directs. Should problems arise, or should we hear from Caser Kleeh's messengers that they already have, we can intervene. The Zhaesmen seem focused on working with the Priessmen and, I assume, the Gruthmen."

"You want us to wait?"

"I am afraid so."

Thane Holnm sat back with a sigh and eyed Thane Trhet. "And you?"

"The Zhaes Thanes are the larger problem. If they are feeding power into Priess and Gruth, as Thane Lehket suggested, we should let it sit."

Thane Holnm shook her head, took a shot of Middleman's Bane, and held out her glass for a cupbearer to bring her another.

"Are you sure, Thane Trhet?" asked Aerhee.

"We are already spread thin, rebuilding this city, working in Sleff and Chuss. I trust that Klen will preserve our people until we are prompted to intervene."

By the time our gods prompt us to intervene, it may be too late. "I pray that Laeih blesses us as well."

CHAPTER FOUR

THE BATTLE FOR PAIELL - PART 1

"Forgive me Sle–" Port winced, holding his screams as the ribcage of a perished ally crunched beneath his boot. An explosion ahead caused him to stumble. *He must have fallen earlier with an injury to the chest. I couldn't have stepped that hard, could I?*

He searched for his hand spear to no avail, picking up an enemy sword. He took a deep breath, praying with the little focus that he could obtain over the cacophony. *Heitt preserve me. Preserve us.*

He cursed himself for being too much of a coward to fight on the front-lines. He clenched his fists as he marched forward with heavy steps, cursing himself for fighting close to the front-lines when he was supposed to be commanding.

The Sleffmen of the Harmony Allegiant trudged onward. They were nearing the Tower of Alms and would claim it as their own if the tide of battle did not reverse.

Regardless of the victories, if reinforcements did not arrive, they would perish within a week. Port *had* to find a solution. *Had* to pull back, yet they had won in Kzhek through perseverance. *One* more battle would be worth the effort.

Would it be worth it for the tens, hundreds of soldiers that die on this battlefield for a single point of control? He had to convince himself that the Tower of Alms was worth the effort. If he failed to do so, he would be as guilty of murdering his allies as his enemies were.

A hill rose to the tower's base. Priessmen surrounded it to protect the ultimate vantage point that was the tower. The Allegiant Sleff legion pressed onward, but only through the light forces of Sleff loyalists. Port had already seen a few acquaintances among the loyalist troops, but those relationships were not enough to deter him from his purpose.

Victory had been a guarantee, or so they believed. The Priess aid was an unexpected terror, striking them like a lightning bolt sparking a fire in a forest of dead trees.

Port fell to his left as a comrade landed on him. A row of Allegiant soldiers fell likewise, some tossed above the crowd.

A pair of Priess Gorgers charged through the Sleff lines.

Port stood and raised a hand, ready to call the troops to his left to help eliminate the Gorgers but held it as sunlight shone through smoke to glimmer on the full suits of armor worn by the Gorgers.

"Shield wall ready!" shouted Port.

A swarm of ten soldiers pulled from the left flank to join Port. He stood behind the formation of large rectangular shields with the Zhaes sigil of a kaesan emblazoned on the front. Not only had the Allegiant forces gained experience from the battle of Kzhek, they had become equipped with the best armor and weapons from the fallen and captured elite of the Zhaes city guard. Port, as captain of this campaign, had been surrounded by those with the best equipment, as well as being equipped himself to participate in the shield wall. Traveling with carts of heavy armament was proving to be worth the effort.

"Brace and hold," Port commanded, waiting for the Gorger to charge.

"Coming, four in from the right flank!" shouted an Allegiant skirmisher, peering just beyond the right edge of the shield wall. "Two in line!"

"Heavies!" Port held his hand up.

"Lifting and holding!" shouted a chorus from behind.

"Divide, right four and five!" The shield wall split at Port's command between the respective units. "Charge!" Port dropped his hand.

"Allegiant forward!" Four heavy units charged through the shield gap holding a tree-sized bolt from one of the enemy's ballistas. With two men on each side, they charged the bolt forward like a jousting lance, meeting the unsuspecting Gorgers in their blood-raged pursuit. The first Gorger was hunched over as she charged with her shoulders forward and was impaled by the bolt from the center of her chest and out her lower back. The second Gorger followed close behind but was knocked onto his back with a tear in his chest leathers.

"Drop the wall and finish!"

The right and left flanks held their shields to defend the forward charge. Four soldiers held the Gorger down while the others stabbed him with their hand spears, making his body look like an overused archery target. Two Gorgers would not win them the Tower, but it was a chunk out of the Priess and Sleff loyalists' wall. It was cause for a minor celebration, yet no opportunity would be granted. This was war, not a thing to be celebrated.

The soldiers who were finishing off the fallen Gorger were consumed with the success of their strategy. Loyalist soldiers met their distraction with swords, bringing a swift end to their valiant efforts.

"Hold back and stay in line!" Port shouted. He felt a coward for taking a few steps back from the frontline. He shook his head. *What makes you think your life is greater than theirs?* He embraced his cowardice and ran back twenty paces behind the frontline.

The Sleff banner held by the Allegiant fell but was raised again by a new bearer. The flag danced in the cold Zeemer breeze. Their defense against the Gorgers was proof that their training had paid off, but had been a distraction? Regardless of their efforts, the Tower was no closer.

"Captain Port!" A firm hand shook Port's shoulder. "Port!"

"Wha–" he turned to see Treg, commander of the third of four legions. "I–"

"Focus, Sleffman! We are losing momentum. What can we do?"

"We–I–"

"I've lost most of my legion. Corth's legion is either dead or scattered. Prossa can't even–"

"I don't know!" He threw Treg's arm back and paced forward. He stepped atop a cracked crate to see above the clashing armies.

"What do you mean you *don't know*?" Treg continued to follow.

"I–" He turned back.

Allegiant corpses lay fallen and mixed with those of their enemies. Their convictions were gone with their spirits, pointless ideals that would not matter in the eternities. The loyalist line continued to press them further from the Tower.

Port squinted back and ran to stand atop another crate not far behind him.

"Do you see something, Captain?" Treg asked.

"Southeast. Come here." He pulled Treg up, pointed out, and turned his ally's head. "Do you see that?"

"What? The carts?"

"Those aren't carts, Sleffman, those are trebuchets."

"They abandoned them because they were too easy to dodge. We're fighting men, not fortresses."

"Do you think they still work?"

"Captain, they're useless! Two of them are broken anyway. You can see the scattered pieces."

"But the third one on the right is worth a try."

"It will kill three, maybe five at best. Port, I think it might be time to retreat."

"Not *yet*." Port pointed towards the Tower of Alms. "We don't need it to kill a couple of soldiers. We need it to take down the Tower."

"But captain, that is why we came!"

"We came to take Sleff, not the monuments. The tower is filled with archers. You can see by their armor that most of them are Priessmen. If we cannot take it, we will not leave it to be used against us."

"Do you know how to operate it?"

Port shook his head. "No, but the scrappers who came to help us destroy them were familiar with their mechanisms."

Treg gave a slow nod. "Do you think it will work? What if we *can* take the Tower?"

"Our banner falls further from the Tower by the minute. We can't take it. Not without something like this."

"I trust you."

"Thank you, Treg."

"I'll alert the scrappers. Last time I checked they were with the medics."

"If they can repair a second trebuchet, have them do it. We will probably need a couple of shots to take it down. Its fall should kill enough of their people to startle them."

"Exactly, Treg. Their archers have plenty of explosive arrows. Taking it down may be more catastrophic than we can hope for. After the scrappers do their job, we can see if they retreat or hold strong."

Treg gave Port the Sleff salute and ran back to fulfill his duty.

All they could achieve was a small victory. Until then, they had to continue to hold off their opponents as much as possible.

Port ran, still holding back from the frontlines where he hoped to find one of the other commanders. They had served him with unquestioning loyalty, but the size of their army was too small. Colrig insisted on four legions. Had Port known that Priessmen would be involved, he would have insisted that Colrig send a better captain.

The memory of Colrig naming him the Sleff Thane of Harmony was still a vivid fright. He had abided by Phenmir's orders before and during the battle of Kzhek. To be appointed to an equal level as Phenmir by Colrig was an initial joy that became tinged by dread as he recognized the lives that rested in his hands.

Port's four commanders took his word for law, as if he had spoken from *The Tome of the Meek*. In truth, his words were no greater than the impulses of a frightened man. *"Fear is not a sin, but do not let it control you,"* Phenmir had told him before his departure. *"If harnessed, it will make you a conqueror of your own inhibitions."* "Prossa!" he shouted. "Corth! Theeta!" With Treg–head of the third legion–focused on directing the sappers, he cried for the aid of the respective leaders of the first, second, and fourth legions.

Pulling back to await the aid of the Gorgers had worked in Kzhek. Shouldn't it work here while we await the trebuchets?

Port understood little about warfare, despite his scrupulous studies, but he *knew* that he could always weaponize the pride of his enemies, even if some of their opponents were Sleffmen. *Sleffmen by blood, but their actions show otherwise, especially beside Priessmen.*

He continued to shout for the commanders, gradually losing hope as he failed to find any sign of them. "Prossa! Corth! Thee–"

"Captain Port!" someone shouted behind him. He turned to see an Allegiant trooper running towards him with half of her face covered in blood and a dent in her helm.

He nodded, waving her forward.

"Commander Prossa was killed."

"How did—was she your commander?"

"No, commander Theeta is."

Is. "And is she alive?"

"Yes, but her condition is deteriorating. A ballista bolt hit her in the right thigh. It tore the rest of her leg off."

"Then who is leading her legion?"

"I-I'm not sure, sir." She struggled to maintain eye contact. "We just fight. We press forward."

He sighed, glancing at the battlefield. The Sleff banner was still standing yet drew closer to him.

"Can you still fight?" He pointed at her face.

She touched the blood there. "This is not mine."

"And your helm?"

"The dent? It's uncomfortable, but as far as I can tell, I have no injury."

"But can you still fight?"

"I believe so."

"Then you are the new commander while commander Theeta is cared for. Focus on defense. Hold up shield walls, dodge, hold tight, do whatever you need to endure."

"Being defensive will only prolong our suffering. We came to take the city back, didn't we?"

"Just listen to me and do as you are told unless I command otherwise!"

"Yes sir!" She ran off to legion and disappeared into the crowd.

He hated the force of his tone. It was nothing like the commands Phenmir had given. Phenmir was a Chussman, but that was not an excuse for Port to banish any sense of kindness and care for others.

"Facet is best when all of us embrace each other's Ideals," Phenmir had told him. *"Except for the Priessmen. No one needs pride and you, Port, are evidence of what humility can accomplish."* He had not become prideful with his position. He held onto that much, yet he struggled to maintain the calm of a captain. He did not worry that his troops would disobey him because of unkind words. It *was* war, but he worried that his lack of self-control would cause others to doubt that he deserved the title of Thane.

Near the back of the second legion, one of the fallen trebuchets rose again. The one behind the first legion still stood tall, but the others remained broken.

He held hope, for there was nothing else he could do. He could not return to combat to become another casualty. *Not yet.* He tried to focus on his breathing, hoping to clear his mind for a plan after the Tower fell, but nothing came. Swords and spears continued to clash in an unholy chorus accompanied by battle cries of glory and death. He tried to focus his gaze on the Tower but could not avert his eyes from the clashing tides between the front lines of each army.

Too many Priess soldiers held their swords high to celebrate each kill, only to be impaled before their focus returned to battle. Even with their haughty deaths, their troops pressed the Allegiant lines further away from the Tower of Alms.

Sonorous creaking, like that of a boat pushing off of a dock, drew Port's attention to the two trebuchets, each one being pulled to launch.

Large stones set aflame by the sappers flew like comets into enemy territory. Tension pulled at his heartstrings as he choked with anticipation. His eye held on to the closest flaming stone. He grunted as if punched in the abdomen as the shot was miscalculated and landed too far to the right, but still caught a few of their opponents.

With a thunderous clamor from the second stone, Port's eyes shot to watch the Tower.

A perfect hit at the Tower's base took out the front wall, but it was not enough to fell the tower. If their claim that combustibles filled the building held true, they struck the wrong floor.

Again. Again. By Heitt's preservation, please do it again.

The battle slowed with the distraction but continued.

Port remained above the crowd atop his crate. Hope and fear paralyzed him. Minutes had passed with only the screams and clashing to ring in his ears.

The creaking of old wood returned as the trebuchets began to launch their second shot. The closest of the two creaked louder, then cracked as its right side collapsed under poor repairmanship. Its boulder launched, still aflame, but did not fly beyond the allegiant lines. No less than five Allegiant soldiers provided a landing pad for the boulder, its base now painted red with blood.

Port ignored the tragic mistake. He forced himself to dismiss it and focus on the more distant shot. A captain could not overwhelm himself with every loss. Doing so would cost him his mind. Like a saving bolt from the gods above, the second shot hit right above the last on the Tower.

Sword clashes grew sloppy and armies lost focus as a stone giant fell. Priessmen archers toppled from the balcony as the Tower shook, then fell towards the trebuchets. The Priessmen and Sleff loyalists gave up the will to fight and ran into the allegiant territory. Conglomerations of bricks fell onto groups of soldiers. The Tower began to empty its contents in its fall, tossing more bricks and barrels of explosives into the crowd.

Bricks, walls, and combustibles hit the ground, exploding again to toss the Tower's bricks in any random direction, taking out more troopers.

Port ran back, jumping off his crate, and over abandoned supplies in the Allegiant territory, then hid behind an abandoned ghete carriage.

Their ploy had worked, but only time would tell if it worked in their favor. He was sure that all the Tower's occupants had perished with its brutal fall, along with all who fell under its ultimate collapse, but the explosions were a deadly game of chance. The explosions continued for what seemed like ten minutes, many of the explosions triggering others on both sides of the battlefield.

As the stones began to settle, Port could not tell if the clashing of swords had resumed or if his ears were ringing from the havoc wrought upon them.

He stood, peeking behind the carriage to see what was left of the battle. His hearing grew clearer, shouts and groans now audible alongside the occasional sword and shield collision. Smoke and dust hid most of the field, yet he saw something above, dancing in the wind.

He stood, relieved to be uninjured, and ran forward to catch a clearer glimpse. Like a beacon of hope, the Sleff banner stood farther than it had been before the fall of the Tower of Alms.

"Rise and march, Harmony Allegiant!" he shouted. He was sure that they had lost legions of soldiers, especially those who ran forward to blitz the enemies between the attacks on the tower.

The battle resumed. The Sleff banner continued to wave, though they had farther to go to reach most of the Tower's rubble.

Praise Heitt. Praise his preservation. Praise–

The Allegiant banner fell back. It did not fall back a couple of steps but flew back towards the Allegiant base in retreat. *Preserve us.*

The dust continued to clear. Large silhouettes fell from the clouds. Golden horns, as if fresh from a crucible, curled on the sides of hideous faces with sword-like teeth coming from a bat's snout.

The demons descended, tearing through legions of Allegiant troops with talons sharper than an elite claymore. Their wings spanned the size of a house, aiding them to descend and attack with grace.

Five zlatogs had joined the enemy's side mounted by armored Priessmen. They could be nothing else than elite Priess Beastlings.

Port dropped his sword, his focus devoured by the V formation of zlatogs as they circled back to land atop the rubble of the Tower of alms.

Confused by what he thought he saw, Port ran forward, though still behind the battle lines, to see the zlatog riders. One of the riders did not wear the dark purple leather with his silver armor. The outlier removed his helm, confirming Port's suspicions beside the rider's green leather.

No longer was this a battle between Sleffmen and Priessmen. A Gruth Beastling had joined their battle.

CHAPTER FIVE

GOLDEN HORN

2 MONTHS PRIOR TO THE BATTLE FOR PAIELL

Yetrik grimaced with fear and disgust at the young calf speared by a spit as it screamed over a fire. He had heard that the Priessmen customs were an abomination to the ideals of the other Courts, and this sight was not a pleasant welcome to Ekscomos, their capital city.

"Want a slice?" asked the Priess butcher at the screaming calf's side. He sharpened his knives, rubbing the grease from past cuts across a black cloth.

He feared the smell of cooking meat would be forever spoiled. "But, it's...alive." His eyes grew wider, and he stepped back. The calf rotated to face him, staring with too-human eyes.

The butcher looked up from his knives and wiped his hand across a blonde goatee, staining it with grease and a hint of dark blood.

"Ah, a Gruthman." he chuckled. "You know, they are better cooked this way. Young and *alive*. I'll bet you ten petiir it will be the best steak you ever try."

He wanted to scream at the man for torturing the animal for a meager pleasure. The Zhaes Thanes Leisa and Tywing had taken him to the central market less than an hour after his arrival in the city and he already knew that the rumors of Priess hedonism were no exaggeration.

"No, please, I–"

"It's on me." The butcher stabbed the calf with prongs and began to slice a chunk from its right thigh. The left was already missing. The calf screamed even louder, making the butcher laugh as if he had the best work in the world.

How has it not died yet?

He held out the prongs with a thumb-sized slice of the calf. "Trust me, I'm an Eurythrin. Using my organ is the only way to keep a calf alive and aware while I cook it. You are losing money if you don't try it."

Yetirk's eyes kept returning to the calf's eyes like a curious child to a flame. *What would Runith think of this?*

"I'm not a–big–uh–meat–type of–thanks." Yetrik left and weaved in and out of the rows of vendors, fearing to look back and notice the disappointed look on the butcher's face.

"Yetrik! Have you found anything to eat?"

Yetrik turned to the right. The two Zhaes Thane's approached him with kind faces, growing concerned with his obvious discomfort.

"Are you alright?" asked Thane Tywing.

Two Priess Thanes stood on Tywing's right. One, a tall woman with a round face, brown hair curled with precision. The other a man half his size. Yetrik would have thought he was fourteen if not for the face that aged him over forty.

"Yeah, I just–"

"Are our dishes not good enough for your palette?" the tall Priess-woman asked with a haughty chuckle. "Even *Zhaesmen* can handle our delicacies."

Thane Tywing held a small plate of steak. Yetrik couldn't bear to look at it.

"Leave him alone, Phemus." the other Priess Thane remarked, his face disgruntled as if he fought back pain.

"*Thane* Sairee Phemus, please, Thane Trosh. We are in a public setting and this Gruthman is no Thane."

Thane Trosh grumbled.

"He is as much a nobleman as any of us," Thane Leisa said as she adjusted the black band that spanned her head and covered her missing right eye. "Find something to eat, Yetrik, then meet us back in the Canton of Diplomacy. Do you remember where it is?"

Yetrik nodded, though he knew the gesture lacked confidence.

Thane Trosh placed his hand on Yetrik's shoulder. "I'll find something to suit his palate and escort him back to the Canton. When you arrive, my study should be unlocked, and no one will trouble you."

"Can you handle the banter of two Thanes of Haleness at your side?" Thane Phemus asked Thane Laeisa.

"Surely our conversations are not that dull." chuckled Tywing.

"You're in good hands, Yetrik." said Thane Leisa, nodding to Thane Trosh as they left the market.

Yetrik had not yet been given time alone with the Priess Thanes. He had arrived after Thanes Leisa and Tywing had already rekindled old relationships with the Priess nobility. Common ground was not hard to find with the current conflict.

Before he had been given time to settle, they had taken him to the market to see the heart of Priess culture. It was not a time of festival or holiday, yet all days were worthy of celebrating the Court that prided itself on hedonism.

He was surprised that Thane Leisa had requested his presence in Court Priess, more so because she knew how invested he was in the Middlemen. He had expressed a desire to stay and search the Middlelands with Runith, but Sheath insisted that he would be a valuable asset for strengthening Priess relations. After Semi had left for Thusk, he was the only Gruthman who had experienced the political catastrophe that was the battle of Kzhek.

He felt for a sheet of parchment in his satchel, hoping that he would remember to write Semi again after arriving in Priess. After speaking with the other Priess Thanes, he was sure that he would have plenty to share.

"A lot on your mind, Gruthman?" Thane Trosh asked. He walked with a goateed chin up, more so in a confident manner than the haughty expressions shown by Thane Phemus.

"Nothing really."

"You're hungry, I take it?" He turned to Yetrik with a raised eyebrow.

"Not really, but I should eat."

"You saw the calf, didn't you?"

Yetrik nodded.

"Not my preferred dish, either. Too many Priessmen rely on fatty meats and excess sweets. I prefer to cook for myself."

"Really?"

"What? Surprised to meet a Thane that does not rely on his servants? Just because we have luxuries does not mean that we have to live as shrines to be worshiped."

Yetrik struggled to form a response.

"Let me guess, you thought all us Priessmen were the same? Lousy heathens that don't know how to enjoy anything that doesn't give instant gratification?"

"I haven't been outside of Gruth much."

"Figures, but there is no need to feel bad. Very few understand us. Even most Priessmen do not understand each other. It's too easy to live as you wish and assume that others believe the same as you do."

Thane Trosh stopped before a smaller booth with no customers and fewer decadent decorations than most of the other booths. He pulled a few coins from a pouch on his belt and handed it to the vendor. "Grechta, one bowl, please."

"Cream?" she asked as she filled a bowl with brown, rice-like grains.

"Have you ever had *real* Priess grechta?" he asked Yetrik.

"Never heard of it."

"Plain and natural," Thane Trosh told the woman, taking the bowl and handing it to Yetrik

"You don't need cream. I want you to taste pure Priess grechta for the first time."

Yetrik took a spoonful and began to chew on the small brown grains. The taste was reminiscent of clove and rye. "It's...quite simple."

"It's sustainable and will leave you feeling energized, unlike most of the dishes here."

Yetrik nodded, taking more and growing accustomed to the natural spice. "So, what *do* you believe?"

"About what?"

"You said that all Priessmen might not believe the same things. If that is true, what do you believe in, if not the gods of Facet?"

Thane Trosh bid him forward, away from the market. "I would not say that I believe *in* something, rather I am open to believing that something exists. I feel that there is a greater order to our existence, but I am hesitant to define what it is. Not all Gruthmen are so strict to their traditional beliefs, am I wrong? What about you? Do you prescribe to *Deilf's* teachings?"

"Most assuredly."

Thane Trosh was taken aback by his rapid response. "As per tradition, I see."

"Yes, but it is more than tradition. I've had experiences."

Thane Trosh pointed towards a staircase that led up to a tall building. "And those might be?"

"When I exercise my prayers and try to understand the *Tome of Stability*, words become thoughts and thoughts become experiences. I do not expect to see an angel, nor Deilf himself, but I hold firm to what I feel."

Thane Trosh smirked.

I told you my innermost feelings and you take it as something to mock? "What is it?"

"Don't worry, Gruthman, I think your beliefs are fascinating, but–"

"But what?" Yetrik clenched his fists, noticing that he had raised his voice.

"But why *not* believe in godly visitations? This is a strange era for Facet. We've heard of your ordeals with the Middlemen, which I look forward to hearing more about. Nations turn against each other and themselves. If the gods, or a god, were to make themself known, now would be the time. I think it is best to tread with an open mind, as will I."

Yetrik felt his muscles still, trying his best not to judge this Thane too quickly.

Thane Trosh slowed as they approached the door to a tall yet relatively thin, pyramidal building not far from what sounded like the city center to the east. Two guards stood at each side wearing light armor and helms with large eyes imprinted on each side. With the opening for their eyes and the mouth guard up, they were reminiscent of the creature on the banner that blew in the wind above them. The land eel was not an uncommon sight in the dryer climates throughout Facet but was renowned as a symbol of quick wit and versatility among the Priessmen.

The guards opened the double doors, each one then saluting Thane Trosh and Yetrik as they entered by raising their left arms in a fist and cupping the area over their right ears with the other arm.

"Mighty is the Free!" they chanted.

Thane Trosh invited Yetrik forward, dismissing them with a nod and an unenthusiastic wave.

"Need a place for your coat?" the Thane asked.

Yetrik shook his head, rubbing his hands across the scaled pattern of leather on his arms. "It's not much warmer in here, so I would rather keep it with me."

"Priess is no sunny seaside and it will only get worse as Zeemer continues to roll in. Best buy yourself a thicker coat if you plan on staying long." He waved Yetrik to follow him up a spiral staircase in the pyramid's center, each level with walkways branching out to reach rooms against the angled walls.

How long did Thanes Leisa and Tywing expect him to stay? Their plans had been unclear. To be fair, they had to fight for clarity and hope since the fall of Kzhek. If Courts Gruth and Priess had not offered aid, though they were still settling on the extent of what that *aid* would be, they would have been victims of the rebels' whims like the other Zhaesmen. He wanted to help in the Middlelands, but no one knew where that would leave them. And he had yet to hear from Semi. The other Thanes spoke little of what was happening in Fayis. He assumed the worst after what the Krall had done to his people. It would be best for him to listen and follow at this point. Even if the Thanes had plans, no one knew where their spread endeavors would lead them.

They left the staircase one level before reaching the peak of the pyramid and met the other Thanes outside Trosh's study. They spoke with a young Priesswoman, who saluted Thane Phemus and left before they met the others.

"Was it locked?" Thane Trosh reached for the gilded door handle. "I could have sworn that I left it open." He turned it and pressed the door open, gesturing for the others to enter.

"Oh, it was open," said Thane Phemus, "and we spent some time in there. Really a dreary place, Thane Trosh. I know plenty of artists who could touch it up for you."

"It serves its purpose." He waved for them to enter again.

She shook her head and turned to the Zhaes Thanes with a smile. "We have guests, Priessman. We *must* entertain."

"They are here for matters of war and peace, not entertainment, *Preisswoman*."

"Why not show them the city?"

"Because they've seen it. These two have been here for weeks."

"Yes, but what has this *Gruthboy* seen?"

People thinking of him as a child had grown so old that it no longer bothered him. Let her think as she wished. He already had a poor opinion of her.

"Forgive my impertinence." She placed her hand on Yetrik's shoulder. "Thanes Leisa and Tywing have told me about some of your achievements. Perhaps you would like to see our Beastlings? Let us see how they compare to the ones you have worked with." She turned to Thane Krosh with a wide grin. "We are leaving this instant. These two may have seen the city, but we are yet to show them Endowed Row."

Thane Trosh rolled his eyes. "Sairee, this is serious. If you want to go to your pleasure houses, you can do that on your own. Now, come in."

Thane Laeisa offered Thane Trosh a pitiful grin, her gaze jumping between the Priess Thanes.

She's reading them. There was no better advocate for peace than a diplomat who could read the will of two conflicting parties and pick the best possible solution based on her clairvoyant assessment.

"I would not mind seeing this 'Row,'" said Thane Leisa.

"What is it?" asked Thane Tywing.

Thane Trosh grumbled, clenching his stomach and squinting. He let out a slow breath from pursed lips and closed his door, approaching Thane Tywing. "Endowed Row is the pinnacle of Priess hedonism. A business street with the sole purpose of exploiting Endowed abilities."

"You *know* it is more than *that*," said Thane Phemus, her voice even more pompous. "What kind of Priessman are you? Do you want to go Sleff and suffer for your humility?"

"Standing beside you is enough suffering." He squeezed the side of his abdomen, practicing more pursed lip breathing.

Thane Phemus turned away. "Endowed Row is living evidence of the glory of the Endowed. While they are crucial to societal progression, that does not negate their occupational value."

"*Entertainment* value," Thane Trosh muttered.

While Thane Trosh was a contradiction to the general Priess stereotypes, Thane Phemus embraced them and wore them as a crown, letting her beauty and value be gorged upon by all who knew her. *How sadistic must one be to kill a child and give an adult their organ purely for entertainment? Where was the line between entertainment and necessity?*

"Thane Leisa," continued Thane Phemus, "we recognize that you are a Feelwoman, so it would be best to avoid wasting time in their guilds of silent fornication."

Thane Leisa nodded. If she thought the same as Yetrik, neither of them wished to know what 'silent fornication' guilds entailed, especially for Zhaesmen in Priess.

"You can find something to suit everyone in the Row. Plenty more Eurythrin roasters if you enjoyed the calf cuts. They even have seafood if that better suits your palate, Gruthman. Just as they preserved the rotisserie calf, they keep fish alive as they are cooked the same way. The fish feel as if they are suffocating, but they roast well. I know we just ate, so let me assure you, there is more to offer from the Eurythrins, I should know better than most."

"No need to boast," said Thane Trosh.

"I'm not *boasting* but *appraising* my fellow Eurythrins." She turned and grinned at Yetrik, savoring his surprise. "Cosmetic modifications that would not be possible without the aid of a Eurythrin. Drinks and all the brush you could smoke with Eurythrins at your side to prevent the consequences of exceeding the body's natural limit of any substance."

She turned to Yetrik. "Beastling pleasure houses, helping you in *any* way, shape, or form you desire." She winked, causing him to quiver. "If you are looking for something intimate and more aggressive, our Gorger fighting rings are well renowned. With Eurythrins at their side, there is no limit to the brutality."

"*Perd me, Sairee.* Are you so obsessed with your flaunting? These people do not need a guide, they need allies. How *idiotic* are you to suggest they go watch Gorgers beat the *shit* out of each other when they just watched the same perding thing happen in the capital of their Court?"

"Really"—Thane Laeisa held up a hand—"no offense taken. I understand she wanted to help us feel comfortable."

Thane Phemus's pale face was growing red, but she held a smile. "Perhaps you are the offended one. I should have known a man like you would hate seeing other Gorgers fight where you cannot."

Thane Phemus continued to insist on offending, not even apologizing to the Zhaes Thanes. If Thane Leisa had not been so emotionally intelligent, finding middle ground with this Priesswoman would be impossible.

"You know I jest, Terin." She reached her hand down and rubbed Thane Trosh's shoulder. He shrugged it off and shook his head with a smirk. "If all else is too extreme for you, Zhaesmen, there is always the Beastling menagerie to visit."

"That sounds splendid," Thane Leisa was quick to say. "Light spirited enough for us to speak openly."

"I would not say the menagerie is *light spirited*," said Thane Trosh. Thane Phemus scowled at him. "Just trying to be honest. I didn't mention the theater productions that make jest at their religious practices."

"On to the Row, then!" Thane Leisa spoke before anyone else voiced opinions.

Thane's Leisa and Tywing lingered behind Thane Phemus once they reached the street. Yetrik gravitated towards Thane Trosh, who struggled behind, rubbing his fist against his stomach.

"Is everything alright, Thane Trosh?" asked Yetrik.

"Yes," Thane Trosh hissed between his teeth. "Really, it's nothing. Don't worry about me, you can go walk with the Zhaesmen. We–" he grunted. "We Priessmen are a bother to you, anyway."

"You are no bother, Thane–"

"Call me Terin."

"Terin."

"See, doesn't sound too bad, eh?" He sighed, no longer clenching his abdomen. "Just don't call Thane Phemus by her first name, at least to her face. Don't worry about offending me, though. I recognize how hard-hearted some of my people can be, and I do not claim to be any more perfect than they are."

Thane Phemus turned over her shoulder. Her eyebrows were tented with exaggerated concern as she drifted back to interject herself between Thanes Tywing and Leisa.

Yetrik stared at Terin's abdomen.

"What? You want to see the scar?"

"Is that why you keep squeezing it? Does it hurt? Wait... Thane Phemus said something about *other Gorgers*, but–are you–"

"I'm a sad exception. The scar is not the reason that I have cramps and colic pains. It's just part of who I am, no reason to feel sorry for me. *What about the scar?* Yes, I'm an Endowed. Yes, I am smaller than you. I have had abdominal issues my entire life and once harvesting was discovered, we thought that a graft might resolve whatever *this* is. So they cut me open, told me that my large intestine's walls were as thick as a fortress and that the inner lining looked like a cobblestone street. They gave me the organ, patched me up, and nothing changed with my cramping and diarrhea. You've asked, boy, so I will not hide any of the dirty details. I embrace it even though it leaves me on the toilet too often."

Yetrik offered a pitiful smile.

"Ah come on, don't feel bad for me, the organ wasn't wasted. Sure, I cannot digest as well as most people, hence my shorter stature, but I am still stronger than any natural warrior. My strength is less than the average Gorger, but don't forget that a Gorger's mind grows as well as their muscles. I may speak as an ignorant pessimist, but I can outsmart any other nobleman in this Court." He turned to Yertik and winked. "Which is not too high an accomplishment."

❦

Endowed Row was as wide as two normal streets put together and spanned Ekscomos.

Yetrik had heard mention of it in the past, but most non-Priessmen tried to avoid speaking of the 'Court of Pride'.

They entered through a gateway with a large sign of gold and silver that proclaimed the street's name. Buildings were pressed against along either side of the street, with few alleys to divide them.

Children were slain for Priessmen to receive pleasure here.

Terin stepped ahead of the group, keeping Thane Phemus behind. "Come on, no need to get lost in debauchery. We have things to see."

Thane Phemus was too set on flaunting the city while Terin tried to combat her lackadaisical attitude with a clear direction.

The air smelt of mulled wine, but later adopted the stench of burnt hair and cloves. When smoked by a user, brush was horribly pungent and much more addictive than tobac or any other herb. He wondered if the Eurthyrins did anything to prevent the risks associated with smoking it.

The Shiftling district was much less pungent, but he was more so unsettled by the seductive glares and nude solicitors. Thanes Leisa and Tywing kept their eyes down and covered them while Terin pressed them forward. Yetrik felt guilty for glancing up. Nudity was not uncommon in Gruth, especially on the coast, but it was never seen as something sexual. Shiftlings of all shapes and sizes flaunted the most provocative parts of their bodies, speeding towards anyone who showed the slightest interest.

Terin shouted for Thane Phemus to follow, after seeing her giggle as Shiftlings changed themselves to appear catlike and flirted with her. She could not be so dull to think that they were interested in anything more than payment for her most carnal indulgences, yet she savored any attention she received, regardless of its authenticity.

Cheers and shouts sounded from above.

"We've passed the Shiftlings," said Terin. "Keep to the right side of the street."

Yetrik looked above to see a cage with a latticed platform and walkways leading to the roof. Blood dripped from the platform, falling from two Gorgers locked in a fight in the cell. Audiences cheered from the surrounding roofs. Thane Leisa starred in disgust at the dried blood splattered all on the street that had accumulated over hours of fighting.

"End of the second round!" an announcer shouted from above with volume that could only be produced by a Shiftling who enlarged their vocal chords. "Heal time! Five minutes. Bring out the Eurythrins!"

Smaller fights were conducted in the other buildings, but the combatants were no more than average Priessmen.

Yetrik looked at the merchants, entertainers, and events, but Terin trudged forward with focus.

The cobblestones were filled with dirt between the cracks. The new scent was farmlike, with a hint of manure. After a minute, a pleasant aroma of fresh grass and blooming flowers replaced the musk..

Thane Leisa inhaled and sighed.

Thane Phemus copied her. "Add enough greenery and flowers and the smell of beasts is gone. This may be the Beastling district, but the Sproutens have done well to make this area bearable. Am I wrong, Zhaes Thanes, to believe that Sproutens are uncommon in your Court."

"No, you are correct," said Thane Tywing. "Our wet climate does not make it difficult for plants to thrive, so they are not as necessary. Sproutens are better off here, where they can beautify your Court or in Gruth where they can cultivate the crops."

"Beastlings are more exciting" attested Thane Phemus. "In my humble opinion."

"Is anything that comes out of your mouth humble?" grumbled Terin.

"I'm sorry, Thane Trosh, did you say something?" Thane Phemus asked. "I said we should start with the tamer beasts, where our conversations will not be inhibited by roars and howls."

"Then why don't you lead us?"

"Gladly." He waved the group forward. "No need for zlatogs yet. Let's go to the ponds."

The group followed him down a street, through an alley, and onto a vast plain of architectural feats to rival the coliseums of Gruth.

"Keep straight ahead," instructed Terin. "The large dome to your right is the aviary and further to the right are the hanging cliffs."

The dome was almost made completely of glass, only thin metal lines divided it. The hanging cliffs were like the floating isles in the flying lands beyond the Gruth sea, if they had been given a giant stem of a pillar to hold them down. He had seen the top as they came into the city, but he had dismissed it for a mountain. It reminded Yetrik of a flat-topped mushroom. He wondered how one reached the top with no staircase to access it.

"To the left and beyond the stone gate," Terin continued, "are the predatorial plains. Safe with a Beastling guide, but entrance is forbidden without one."

A vast turquoise lake spanned before them. Priessmen walked in groups, some in pairs, around the lake, which was the size of a small village.

Not all who strolled around the lake were involved with anything more than each other, but many were led by guides, Beastlings who called animals and creatures from the water for show. Regally dressed Priessman rode in the center of the lake on decadent boats, providing a luxury experience as their Beastling guides brought them face to face with schools of flying fish, lake serpents, and even large crustaceans.

"Let me fetch a ferry. There is no better way to experience the lake." Thane Phemus tried to leave the group but was held back by Terin.

"We can see plenty from here. If you wish to be our guide, so be it, but we are going to stay ashore for now."

She folded her arms and scowled.

"No? Then I will *gladly* lead."

Terin waved the group forward and paced beside Thane Leisa as they took a left to begin circling the lake. "Thane Leisa, my fellow Thane of Diplomacy. Do tell. What has occurred since we last spoke of the war?"

"The so-called *Harmony Allegiant* has invaded court Sleff?"

"And this surprises you? The Sleffmen seem to be the ones who instigated this rebellion. It only makes sense that they would return to their home Court to ensure that they are in control of it."

"So you already knew about it?" Thane Leisa asked.

"I have ears in every Court."

She squinted at him.

Perd, can she not read him? Yetrik knew a confused face well, having worn one too often. He did not know how far-reaching her Feelman abilities were, but he assumed that blockades were inevitable. *Assumed,* but did not *know.*

Terin smiled. "Tis' duty of a Thane of Diplomacy to have a wide reach."

She shrugged. "I wonder what they want to gain from it? There is obvious value in Kzhek, but Sleff is less than profitable."

"And we Priessmen are?"

"We both know that, Thane Trosh."

He smirked. "It took us war to realize that there is more to life than religious debates. So, I take it you have an interest in helping the Sleffmen loyalists?"

She nodded.

"When this began, the first riots were reported in Sleff. I would have assumed that they were the first city to be captured."

"It seems that there is more to them than we know."

"What *do* you know about them?"

She stared at the lake.

"Tywing?" he asked.

"They are simple-minded rebels. What else is there to know?"

Terin chuckled. "That is where you are, my friend. Regardless of how foolish your enemy may be, you are the fool if you excuse their actions to be simple-minded pursuits. Tell me, why give thought to the Sleff loyalists when you could focus your efforts on the capital of your Court?"

"We need to understand their motives," said Thane Laeisa. "Because we know too little about them, they took the largest city in Facet in two days."

"You, Gruthman?" asked Terin. "What do you know about them?"

"Nothing more than they do." He recalled the Sleff riots that he and Semi had seen before their arrival in Kzhek.

"You, Thane Phemus?" he asked with a sardonic smile.

"Those religious zealots–"

"Exactly, nothing as I assumed. So, we have been given a chance to ensure that the harvesting prevails in Court Sleff." He turned to the Zhaes Thanes with a frown. "You two have already lost your city, so there is little else to lose. Riots are unheard of in Gruth and Priess, as far as I know, and you still have the loyalty of most of the Sleff nobility. Now is the time to pause and think."

"What good will waiting do?" asked Thane Tywing. "The Harmony Allegiant continues to pillage regardless of how we feel."

"I never said to wait, but to *pause and think*." He stared at them with wide eyes. "Have you taken a breath? Pulled the poles from your asses? Especially yours, Phemus. It's been far up there ever since we met. Are you ready to talk about what *matters*? No whining or judgment of each other's opinions? Great. Now we can have a real conversation. Thane, Leisa."

"Yes?"

"What is your goal?"

"Secure our harvesting rights."

"Vague, but acceptable. What does that look like to you?

She turned to Thane Tywing, who offered no help. "I want Zhaes back under our authority."

"And what will you do with the rebels who helped the *Harmony Allegiant*?"

"Punishment as per the law dictates."

"And when another rebellion rises?"

Yetrik watched her clench her fists behind her back. "We will be prepared this time."

"*This time*, yes." He grinned. "If you want to make an impact *this time*, there will be no *next time*. What you need is power and domination. What you need is a permanent solution. Sovereignty."

"What about you, Priessmen?"

"I do not suggest that you dominate Facet, but that we put differences behind us. Uniting not to become allied Courts, but a greater union."

"You want to dissolve the Courts?"

"Not dissolve, exactly, but create a high council to oversee all that occurs in Facet. A single unifying power that will ensure peace and prosperity."

"A new ruling class?" she asked.

"A higher government," Thane Phemus attested, drawing near.

"Ponder this," said Terin. "This is a permanent solution to a lasting peace. You will understand soon enough that this is a better solution than returning Kzhek to its former power, only to fall again."

The Zhaes Thanes exchanged concerned looks.

Terin turned to Yetrik. "The future should not be limited to past comforts. Why dwell on Facet's silver era when a golden one lies ahead? People evolve as far as society is willing to evolve with them. Which leads us back to Sleff, Thane Leisa. We are going to help the Sleffmen not because the nobility agrees with your stance on harvesting, but because they have control. I, a Priessman, turn to you, a Zhaesmen. With my Court at your side, how would you wish for us to contribute?"

"If the Sleff loyalists are under attack, we need to supplement them with troops."

"How large are the rejectionist forces?"

"Reports suggest a much smaller army than the one that invaded Kzhek," said Thane Tywing. "With the Harmony Allegiant supposedly originating from their Court, they must have people in the Sleff system. It would be wise to assume that they are staging an attack to finish cleaning up the Court."

"As you said, we know too little about them to form such conclusions," said Thane Phemus. "We can offer aid, but more is needed than just sending troops. We need scouts, inquisitors, Endowed if we must, to ensure that the Sleffmen remain under the Zhaesmen as they have for centuries."

Thane Leisa scowled.

Thane Phemus rolled her eyes. "Oh, perd me. Everyone knows Court Sleff serves as a harlot to Court Zhaes."

Terin forced down a smile. "What she is trying to say is that we will ensure that Sleff remains pledged to our cause, and wherever we take Facet in the future, but we must utilize this opportunity. Once we help to defend against the rogue Sleffmen of the Harmony Allegiant, we can utilize our resources to learn more about their organization so that we can strike at their center and dissolve them before they overthrow Facet."

"But–"

Terin reached up to squeeze Thane Tywing's shoulder. "But killing them will only make martyrs? I know. It's the same reason that your plan to punish the rioters in Kzhek failed. Take a moment to separate your yourself from harvesting. Yes, it may have caused this war, but we are dealing with a *greater* dilemma. These rebels are undermining a system of separate governments to unite under one flawed idea. They value preserving individual lives over the life of an entire civilization. To stop them from destroying Facet, we need unity. I fear that the days of separate governments are coming to an end. Where there is division, there are separate ideals that cause arguments, selfishness, and war. It is an eternal cycle that can only be prevented by a greater union. Do you see now why I am trying to get you to see a greater picture? Yes, we will send troops and burn those perding rebel kulfs to the ground, but we will do this not to help a friend in aid, but to help a dying nation."

Terin's voice grew in volume as he spoke and had left them in stunned silence as he was shouting by the end of his monologue.

As it had occurred with most of the Thanes that Yetrik had met, he was intimidated by Terin's enthusiasm. He was much like Royss in that sense, but Royss was focused on a single battle. A single people. His people. His Court. Terin laughed at Royss' vision and pulverized it, hoping that he would see a vast mosaic rather than a poor caricature. Terin focused on the greater war. He focused on more than his people. He focused on all who would become his people. Still, his vision was limited. He saw the Courts as different policies, rather than different faiths. What would he have of their religions in this 'greater union?' Where would the Middlemen fit into his image? Would they be another commodity burnt by his passion?

Thane Tywing nodded. "We understand. We see what must be done."

Do we? Is a union of all Courts what would bring peace or would it dissolve the autonomy that makes our cultures? What would become of a land free of differences?

"As soon as you arrived, Thane Phemus and I tried to assess your failure in Kzhek, learning how to improve upon it. There is no shame in asking for help, but we knew that if we were to pledge our people to join your cause, we would not lose."

"And what knowledge did your assessments bring?" asked Thane Leisa.

"I had Beastling messengers send ravens to follow witnesses and learn more about what happened at the core of the battle in Kzhek. There were two major points that turned the battle's favor towards the Harmony Allegiant, besides the sheer number of soldiers."

He turned to the Zhaes Thanes, ensuring that they were focused. "First, you lacked the Gorger coordination that they had. We still do not understand how they had so many, especially noting that they were Sleff Gorgers. The Beastlings and their kaesan were responsible for most of the loss."

"Loss?" Thane Tywing guffawed. "They killed more rebel soldiers than any individual trooper."

"Killing just as many Zhaesmen," Sheath replied. "Did you ignore Runith when he told us how their contact was infiltrated?"

"No, I–"

"Yes," Terin smiled, "*infiltrated*. Your imperfect command of kaesan caused them to be distracted by mere Beastling Endowers. From what I could conclude, it does not seem that the Endowers were able to control the kaesan. The Endowed held onto that much. Still, the young Endowers managed to distract and enrage the kaesan, sending them into a frenzy."

"So we need to eliminate the Endowers? See that any rebel Endowed is killed as well?" Thane Tywing shook his head. "Only Laeih knows *why* they would rebel against their own kind."

"You need beasts that will only respond to one Beastling," said Yetrik. "Like a jockey with their ghete."

"Exactly." Terin waved them off of the path that surrounded the lake. "I have something for you to see, Gruthman."

He directed them away from the main fanfare of exotic creatures and the wealthy spectators who paid their guides extra to see a trick performed. They passed down a corridor of greenery to meet a line of the most regally dressed Priessmen Yetrik had seen. At the end of the line stood a collections office with a porter behind the desk.

"Thane Trosh!" the porter exclaimed as they approached. "And Thane Phemus." He waved the other Priessmen to the side as if they were flies. "Here for a ride with your... guests." The last word fell flat. The porter seemed the type of man who would shout expletives at Zhaesmen if they were not accompanied by Priess Thanes. Nationality and power go a long way in the mind of a bigot.

"Put us on your next lungden flight." Terin ordered, paying five maeth for each member of their group. Yetrik's eyes grew as wide as moons as more money than he made in a year back home was placed on the counter.

"Enter right away!" The porter commanded a guard to open an arched black gate that led farther into the forested corridor. "You are just in time for the midday group. Five others are at the lungden's side, ready to depart."

Terin pointed back with the flick of his wrist. "Send them back. We travel alone."

"But sir, the customers will be most frustrated with my services. I must–I cannot–"

"Better to have the populus frustrated with your service than the nobility."

"Indeed." The porter nodded. "Helmin!" he shouted at the gatekeeper. "Guide this party to the lungden and bring the others back. Tell them they will be in the afternoon group with drinks and brush on us."

The gatekeeper nodded and bid the group forward.

Yetrik turned back to disappointed faces that forced pleasantries as Thane Phemus bowed with a sneer.

The forested corridor opened and gradually lost its greenery as it led them to a well-trodden dirt plain twice the size of Royss' courtyard behind the Canton of Agriculture.

A wooden stairway on wheels stood beside what looked like a tortoise the size of a small building. Its face was flattened, making its tortoise beak look avian, though it still retained a reptilian glare. Its six feet were the size of giant tree trunks, each with four claws protruding from each side of the circular feet like arrows on a compass. Yetrik had heard mention of lungdens but had never seen an accurate representation of what they were. The crowning oddity was the gelatinous platform on its back. Where one would expect to find a shell was a lump of green, translucent gel with a flat top. A Preissman stood atop it and shouted in loud grunts, his feet stuck into the gel up to his waistline.

"Midday group?" he shouted, then squinted. "Thane Trosh, a pleasure, as always."

"The pleasure is all mine, Falrin. I did not know that you were working as a lungden pilot. A pleasant change of scenery?"

"One can only corral so many ghete. I needed something more freeing."

Thane Phemus stepped before the group and ascended the stairwell. "Coming? Surely this is not your first time."

"Thane Leisa?" Thane Tywing asked, shaking his head.

"Never," she replied. "I've never seen one in our Court."

"Why aren't they more common among the Courts?" asked Yetrik. "They fly, don't they?"

"After a manner," said the Beastling Falrin, waving for the group to follow Thane Phemus as she trudged through the creature's gelatinous back. "You'll see soon enough. They are mighty creatures but can only travel short distances. A schedule of three trips a day to the hanging cliffs exhausts them enough. If you wanted to travel across Facet with one of these, you would be better off with a ghete, maybe even on foot." He patted the gelatin like still water and caused it to sway. "They're slow, but great for large groups on a scenic tour."

Thane Tywing was hesitant to step forward, while Thane Leisa waved Yetrik to go ahead of them.

Terin stood in the gelatin, which rose in a green line up to his -torso. He reached out a hand to steady Yetrik as he stepped into the green of the lungden's back.

He expected it to feel wet, but he only felt a cold embrace. It was thicker than water but was not too difficult to tread through. He reached the far end and stood by Thane Phemus. The treaded paths behind him closed and embraced his legs.

Thane Tywing was the last to join, raising his hands to avoid touching the gelatinous back.

"All here?" Felsin turned, counted each of them on his fingers, and nodded. He started to speak to the creature with a deep bass, like the throat singers of northern Gruth. The lungden responded, though its call caused the gelatin on its back to vibrate and pulse.

"Crouch and leave only your head exposed!" Felsin shouted.

They plunged themselves deeper into the cool gel, except for Thane Tywing who groaned as if he'd been asked to eat it.

Felsin shouted at the creature again. As it rumbled another reply, the gel grew darker and hardened around them. It was not as thick as stone but rather waxlike.

"Relax," Felsin said. "It will soften once we land on the cliffs. It will only take a few mintues." He shouted louder at the lungden, and it jumped to the height of a mountain.

From above, Yetrik not only could see the hanging cliffs halfway down from them, but the entirety of the city. The few people he could see were no larger than specs. It was the most magnificent sight he had ever beheld. It was not the pride and scorn attached to the name Priess. He saw buildings, fields, feats that testified of what a unified people could create. Large statues of former rulers and artisans stood in triumph, more alive than the pieces of stone he had seen up close while looking at the cracks in their aged stone. Perhaps this was how the gods saw humanity. A marvelous beauty, most unexpected, when compared to their inner flaws. It was difficult to breathe, more so as his breath was taken away.

"Do not panic," Felsin shouted. "Take deep breaths. We'll be down soon enough."

Despite the titanic weight of the lungden, it descended and glided through the wind like a falling leaf with a clear goal.

Their descent took five minutes, though it felt shorter. The lungden landed on one of the hanging cliffs with grace. Felsin called, and the lungden responded, returning its waxy back into a malleable state.

Thane Tywing was the first to leave and shook himself as if he had jumped from a frozen lake.

"We shouldn't be too long, Felsin," said Terin, the last of the group to descend from the lungden's back.

"No rush," the Beastling Shrugged. "It's more peaceful up here anyway. Enjoy the golden horns."

Terin led the crew around the lundgen, whose stomach was pressed to the ground with legs out. Before they passed by its head, it had already fallen asleep.

With the edge of the isle visible in every direction, it was easy to forget that the plain was held up by a giant stone pillar. It was not a grassy field, nor was it filled with any greenery, as he had expected. Clustered rock mounds sprang up like waves in a storm. A central platform stood with flat pavement and a walkway extending to reach the isle's rims. Terin bid them forward, and they continued on the path to the center.

The hanging cliffs were greater when seen from below when left to one's imagination. The cliffs themselves were no architectural feats, but a plain of rock mounds. Despite Yerik's initial disappointment, the winged beasts that roamed over the rock mounds were the true treasure of the isle.

A single figure stood in the central platform adorned with silver armor and purple leathers, the same armament worn by those who mounted the twenty or so creatures on the rocks.

The Priessman in the center doffed his helm and called to the other Priessmen with a screech that sounded like forks dragged across porcelain plates. His cape billowed in the wind. The Priess sigil of the land eel shimmered with golden highlights. He turned to face their party as the other armored Beastlings flew to the platform's edge, surrounding them with bat-faced drakes with curling golden horns.

"Thane Trosh," the man said, approaching them as he pressed golden curls away from his face. He looked no older than twenty-five.

"Captain Kevlen, I'm glad to see that you are not missing any limbs."

"We know how to control the zlatogs well enough." The captain chuckled. "These are the Zhase Thanes I have heard so much about?" He approached Thane Leisa and kissed her hand with a slight bow. "*Whole is the Holy.*" He winked and offered a gauntleted hand to Thane Tywing. "Haleness and Diplomacy. And who might you be, Gruthman?"

"Yetrik Kloff."

"You look young to be with the nobility."

"I could say the same for you."

Terin placed his hand on Yetrik's shoulder. "Yetrik was present during the battle of Kzhek. He played a part in the procurement of the kaesan."

"Kaesan? A Beastling?"

"Well, not entirely," said Terin.

Not entirely? Not even close. Last time I checked, I had no scar on my abdomen.

The captain nodded. "Well met. I'm the Beastling captain for the Court. Captain Kevlen works, or Captain Phanos. Honestly, I never cared for titles. Kevlen is fine."

"*Phanos?*" Yetrik asked.

Kevlen smirked. "Yes, son of *Krall* Phanos. My father leads the Court and I, the Beastlings. Best to focus on me for now. His shadow can be a bit of a burden." Kevlen nodded to Yetrik. "Is *he* the one that…"

"Yes," said Terin, "but we have to explain to our Zhaes comrades before we address his role."

"You want to send these zlatogs into battle?" asked Thane Tywing. "What makes them better than the kaesan?"

"Allow me to show you." Kevlen then screeched with a ringing slightly lower pitched than a bat's call. A riderless zlatog pressed itself between two of the other mounted beasts and turned its left side towards the edge of the platform. Kevlen mounted it and patted on its back in a rhythmic pattern, causing it to move with him towards the party.

Thane Tywing stood back, nearly falling, but Thane Leisa stepped forward with a glare.

"Move closer, Yetrik," Terin commanded.

He did so with childish awe.

"Did you see how I patted her back?" asked Kevlen. "Their bat-like snouts with large ears are not misleading. They are indeed a distant, superior relative to the cave bats we are all familiar with. While their sight is impeccable, they have another sense beyond our usual five. So far as we can tell, it is adjacent to hearing, though it is more reliant on pulsations, like echolocation."

"So you speak to them with rhythmic drumming?" asked Thane Leisa.

"Yes, but there is more than rhythm. It relies upon location, tone and...many other aspects of their language that only a Beastling can understand. Yes, you saw me speak to them with their screeches, but percussion is their second, more intimate language, if you can call it that. When Beastlings speak to other creatures, they are more open to suggestion and influence. Speaking to zlatogs does no such thing. Trying to persuade them with screeches is akin to a beggar shouting at the Krall to promote him to the nobility. These percussions–which can only be done by a rider–forms a bond, allowing us to speak with them in screeches from far away, if necessary."

"Only their rider can control them," attested Terin. "They cannot be deterred by any Beastling or Endower not bound to them, unlike the kaesan. Don't worry, if a zlatog rider were to be killed, they would not form a bond with a new rider unless they were willing. As far as we can tell, these creatures are loyal, even after the death of a rider."

"You've had riders die?" asked Yetrik.

"Only one," said Kevlen. "And that was due to an unrelated disease that took him a year ago. His mount seems ready for a successor. We've spoken with the zlatog and she is willing to take another rider."

Terin turned to Yetrik, Kevlen already staring at him with determination. "You and the Zhaes Thanes were promised troops to help defeat the Harmony Allegiant in Sleff. We will send them in three days, but not before this new rider is ready."

It cannot be.

"I do not make these plans on a whim. I already told you the extent that I went to once I heard of the fall of Kzhek. Since the arrival of Thanes Leisa and Tywing, I have had time to prepare for your arrival, Gruthman. I've heard much about you and your contribution to the efforts against the Harmony Allegiant. Not only was your arrival well planned, but this entire day was plotted by me, whether Thane Phemus recognized that or not. I wanted you to learn of the *higher* problem that we face. You *do* understand what must be done to ensure that peace prevails, yes?"

No. I can't agree with you, but what choice do I have? We need Court individuality. Still, without an end to war, how can we ever see peace again? "Yes."

"Then we must be on our way to the Canton of Benefaction. Tonight, you receive a graft to become a Beastling. Our Eurtythrins will ensure that you have a quick recovery and you will join these riders and their zlatogs to defend Court Sleff."

CHAPTER SIX

PARENTHOOD

"Will we let foreign dictates trample upon our faith?"

"No!" The crowd shouted their approval of the Krall's platitudes.

"Will we let foreign dictates trample upon the Sleffmen who plead the cause of the Harmony Allegiant!"

"No!"

"The Thane of Harmony pleads your aid. Will you allow him to go unaided?"

"No!"

The Krall smirked at Phenmir. "Anything else you want to be said?"

He shook his head.

She turned to the crowd. "If your hearts so desire that our Court pledges fealty, let it be heard!"

They shouted approval.

She gripped the rails of the palace's balcony like a lion ready to jump and roar. "Is it approval that I hear?"

The tumult of their excitement rivaled only the greatest of Zhaes thunderstorms.

"Let it be known that I, Dhera Kost, Krall of Court Chuss, declare that the nobility and people of this Court belong to the Harmony Allegiant!" She formed a circle with her fingers and placed them over her heart. "Care is the Creed!"

"Care is the Creed!" they returned.

She waved them away and turned to join Phenmir and Meira who stood near the balcony's exit.

"A little ostentatious for my taste," Meira noted. They embraced.

Phenmir had known Dhera, the novel-elect Chuss Krall, as long as he knew Meira. He was pleased with his wife's choice of monarch and her sway to bring Dhera to the Throne. It had taken months of plotting, but Meira's appointment of Dhera found ground with the other Thanes when Phenmir returned and stood by her.

"I do what must be done," replied Dhera. "Time was due for an official declaration of our Court's stance."

"Well done," noted Phenmir. "You seem comfortable on the throne and did not fear losing your head. The last Krall who stood in your place was not so fortunate."

She replied with a shrug. "It's not my first time in front of a crowd. Regardless, the Sleffmen are with us now and I'm nothing like that coward of a traitor."

"Why did you need a formal declaration?" asked Meira. "With Phenmir's departure alongside some of the Thanes and the others remaining in support, I would have supposed that our Court's stance had already been declared?"

"Implied, perhaps presumed, but I have a duty to fulfill as the Krall. We needed an official declaration so all might know that this is more than some rebellion. The Harmony Allegiant is part of Chuss. I will not be a dictator, but a mouthpiece for the people, unlike the late Krall who perished on this balcony for rejecting the will of the people."

Phenmir smiled. "*Krall Kost*, do not forget your humility. Serving as a mouthpiece for the people, moving with their will and not what you believe to be best, requires more humility than most Sleffmen could ever dream of." He laughed. "You sounded like a jousting announcer before the crowd."

"Must be the old calling slipping through my noble visage. Training the Endowers with the intensity of one of your commanding officers did not make me a calm woman. Especially the Gorgers. Those children are as stubborn as a wild ghete."

The guards standing on each side of the door pulled it open for them to enter the palace.

The palace, though Chuss in every aspect, reminded him of his travels in the other palaces and Cantons that he had visited. The white rugs and orange stone walls seemed but a small difference to the gray stone walls and the black rugs that adorned the Cantons in Kzhek. Those memories were not without difficulty and sorrow, yet he felt a longing to return to the sides of his commanding comrades in Kzhek. He wanted nothing more than to stay with his family but knew that he would return to plot with the Allegiant leaders before the month's end.

"Now that you have a higher responsibility, who will take your place as the Procter of Endower training?" asked Meira

"The Canton of Endowment had plenty of worthy replacements, but your husband found a better solution."

"All that time you spent with Kaela and the Endowers finally paid off?" Meira asked.

Phenmir nodded. "Her leadership skills are remarkable. If she would have been a Chussgirl, she would be my first choice. The experience of working with Voln to gather and lead the Endowers in Tchoyas contributed to her prowess, but we have a remarkable troop of Endowers. You did well, Dhera, but Kaela has established an elite force of them that would rival the Patriarchy of Scholars in loyalty and efficacy."

"Who leads them?" Dhera asked.

"Chenn Hult."

"The Thane of Diplomacy's son?" asked Meira.

"The very same."

"Sounds like nepotism."

"Perhaps that had some influence," noted Dhera, "but I am not surprised to hear that he was chosen. The boy is quite humble. I doubt Kaela even knew who his father was when she made the decision. With early lessons in diplomacy, paired with his Feelman identity, I would have felt inclined to choose the boy myself. He's not even one of the oldest. Only nine years of age and can hold as well as any adept member of the Canton of Diplomacy."

They reached the end of the hall lined with past Kralls and descended the marble stairwell to the third floor of the palace.

"Are your Proctors here?" Dhera asked.

Phenmir shrugged. "They were just outside the palace during your address. Unless they have left, they should already be pouring wine in the council room."

He gestured for her to lead the way, then locked arms with his wife. She giggled like a smitten Chussgirl as they locked eyes. His departure had only brought them closer. He knew that reunions were often the sweetest of meetings, but he did not want another one. He wanted to forget all the cares of the world and spend the rest of his days at her side.

But now was not his time. Effort wasted on himself would only cost the lives of soldiers as they fulfilled their duty. He savored these moments, no matter how short, with Meira. He would return to battle, but not now. Even though they entered a council room to center their attention on the war, these moments were for Meira. All of it was. His fight was for her and for Hir.

The Proctors of Harmony stood as they entered, saluting Phenmir and Dhera with circles placed on their chests.

"Thank you." The Krall waved for them to sit.

"Congratulations on the loyalty pledge, Your Grace," one of the Proctors said with a bow.

Phenmir had forgotten that the title of Thane came with an office to uphold, that is until he returned from Kzhek. He was comfortable with his captains and commanders, but the new Krall insisted that he be given a Canton and Proctors to help progress the cause of the Allegiant from Sliin. With Fayis in the grip of Krall Trhet and Paiell in contest between the warring Sleff parties, Sliin and Kzhek had become the firmest bases for the Harmony Allegiant. His canton was no more than a repurposed municipality building, but it provided solid ground to fulfill Dhera's promise to immerse Court Chuss in the Allegiant's plight.

"How many did you decide to send to Sleff?" asked Phenmir.

One of the Proctors sighed and stood to face Phenmir. "Recent reports tell that Beastlings caused the retreat of Captain Port's forces."

"How many were sent?"

The proctor winced. "Twelve legions."

Phenmir cleared his throat.

"Thane Stolk, surely–"

He swiped his hand. "We do what we must. We need their Court pledged to the Allegiant."

"The Endower commander sent twenty Beastlings with them, but only those older than seven years were permitted to join."

Older than seven. No child is too young to become a warrior.

Phenmir had seen the cost of war and feared that the sting of guilt would never lessen. He sent children to their deaths while he stood behind a table and conversed. It was thoughts like this that made him recognize that perhaps he was better away from Sliin. Every moment spent in council intensified his guilt at being so distant from the battles.

"That leaves plenty to protect us, should Sliin be attacked by other Beastlings. They were Priess Beastlings, I presume?"

The Proctor nodded.

"So they *have* joined the loyalists," said Dhera.

"But the Gruthmen are yet to react," said the Proctor.

Phenmir nodded, staring at the table in silence for what felt like a minute. "*Twelve* legions." He turned to the Proctors. "And the recruitment?"

"Slow."

"Krall Kost's address should enliven some Chussmen, but we need more. If Gruth comes our way, our remaining forces are too few to protect the city. Have your adepts, scouts, and anyone willing to serve the Krall's message to distant villages. Arm any who will fight. I'll speak with the other Thanes to have their Canton members do the same. Have them form Allegiant chapterhouses so that the whole Court might be prepared to leave and fight or stay and protect in the case of an invasion. Any who are willing to leave their homes can receive the best treatment we can offer here in Sliin."

"We have some scouts focusing on the most proximal villages, but I will see that our efforts are extended."

"What about the *other* chapterhouses?" Dhera asked.

"The Patriarchy?" Meira asked.

The Krall nodded.

Phenmir nodded to his wife. They both stood. "Thank you for your time, Proctors. Excuse our short visit. We have matters to deal with at home."

They left the Proctors to plot their excursions and invited Dhera to join them in the hall.

"How long has he been with them?" Dhera asked after the door clicked closed.

"He's been an apprentice for two months," said Phenmir.

Dhera smiled. "You should be proud. Neither of my sons is anything close to a scholar."

"Are you coming?" asked Meira. "He speaks of them very little with us, but I hope that Hir would be willing to share some of his knowledge of the Patriarchy if the Krall made a personal request."

❧❧❧❧❧ ❧❧❧❧❧

The northern chapterhouse in Sliin was a fifteen minute carriage ride from the palace. Phenmir had grown used to not having Hir at home, but he found Meira staring at their son's bedroom occasionally.

He and Hir had always been close. They still were, but his involvement with the Patriarchy placed a wall of secrecy between them. Phenmir understood that the Patriarchy had its reason for confidentiality, yet the barrier caused an emotional rift.

"We'll have to be brief," said Meira. "We will have at least an hour, if necessary, but chapterhouse closes to visitors soon."

Dhera nodded. "Do we just enter?"

Phenmir chuckled and shook his head. "This is one of the few places to deny the Krall sovereignty, that and the other Patriarchal institutions." He pointed to the left side of the building. "The dining hall or the courtyard are the only two open to visitors. Choose a location and I'll have one of the brethren call for Hir."

"The courtyard will do," said Dhera.

Meira bid for a Scholar to retrieve Hir once they reached the back side of the chapterhouse. The courtyard was as one would expect for those who spent their day studying. A mellow stream cut through red sandstone, cacti and sage sprang up on both sides of the bank. Marble benches and tables were spread across the area, though more Scholars returned indoors as the sky became more golden and pinker. While they awaited Hir, they sat at an unoccupied table in the shade of the building-high yuccas.

"What do you hope to gain?" asked Phenmir.

Dhera scowled.

"Lighten up, Phen," Meira started to scratch his back.

Dhera matched his tone. "As dissent continues to create fissures between Courts, I wanted to know how the Patriarchy is holding together. Are they experiencing similar divisions?"

Phenmir chuckled. "That is the problem with the Patriarchy. You never know what holds them together, what they strive for, or what they do. As I become more involved with politics, I become more frustrated with the Patriarchy's secrecy. The Scholars of this chapterhouse are Chussmen. Their highest priority should be to Cheric and his people, not to some temporal sect."

"Phen is just frustrated that he has to let Hir go on his own for once. Knowing that our son has a life of his own is eating at him."

"It's okay, Phenmir," said Dhera. "We have to accept that we are growing old. Your son living his own life should be a milestone, not a sign that your grave is being prepared."

"Tell me you feel the same when your sons leave."

"The Krall herself graces me with her presence." Phenmir already faced his way, but Dhera and Meira turned back to see their son approaching the table. "It is good to see you, Dhera."

"You as well, *Brother*."

Phenmir moved to make room for his son to sit at his side.

"Still an apprentice," Hir replied.

"Still more than any of us will be. This is the first time I have seen you since you were accepted. You look well, but are you eating enough?"

He chuckled, scratching the shaved side of his head, then running his fingers through his tight platinum curls. "Yes, plenty."

Phenmir had seen Hir three times since he left to reside in the chapterhouse but was yet to grow used to seeing his son in the white and gold-embroidered robes of a Scholar.

Phenmir placed his arm around Hir. "You know I'm proud of you."

Meira rolled her eyes. "And you tell him this every time we visit."

"Thank you, Father. I mean it. I couldn't have made it here without your support. It sounds hollow, but I mean it sincerely."

His child was no longer his. Hir was a man of his own. Free to change the world or let it change him.

"So, what's the occasion?" Hir asked.

"Facet continues to grow more divisive," said Meira.

"Yes," Hir chuckled. "I'm not as secluded from the world as you might believe. I'm probably more involved with it than you are." He pointed to Phenmir and Dhera. "Well, you two may be the only exception, but you understand what I mean."

"And that is why I have come to speak with you," said Dhera

"If you expect me to share the secrets of the Root Lord, I will tell you as I tell anyone who asks. I know very little, and I am limited in what I can speak about."

Root Lord was such an ominous name for the grand leader of the Patriarchy of Scholars. Their existence seemed little more than a rumor. Curiosity pestered Phenmir like a forbidden room in one's home. The only solution to still one's mind was the bliss of ignorance.

"I understand that much. One does not become the Krall without a little bit of common sense. Our Scholar, Thane Prence, has left for Kzhek, and I cannot trust his Proctors at this time, but I *know* you, Hir. As you have said, you have been involved with the conflicts this year. What has happened to the Patriarchy since the battle of Kzhek? They are supposed to be one of the few things that transcends Courts and meager politics. Have you noticed any *division* in the Patriarchy?"

"Not that I am aware of." He smiled, but his expression was tight. It was the same face that Phenmir had seen when he caught his son hiding a book under his pillow after he was told to sleep.

Dhera bit at her lip, then let it loose to speak. "Hir, your loyalty is to your people, yes."

"Of course. Care is the Creed."

"Is there anything...anything that we should be concerned about?"

Hir rubbed his thumb and forefinger together. "I am a Brother of the Patriarchy. The core of the Patriarchy is aligned with the will of Cheric." He looked side to side, then leaned in to whisper. "I have to be aware of more than ears and eyes observing me. There is no division in the Patriarchy, since the Bronze Seers broke off. Some believe that they still have a hold over certain members of the Patriarchy. I have even heard that some of the Zhaes Thanes deal with the Seers. These facts are well known." He leaned back with a smile. "It has been great to see you. Especially you, Krall Kost. Please, visit again."

Phenmir could hear his heartbeat. Hir gave them very little information. He did not expect that any would punish Hir for telling them of such rumors. He had heard similar rumors in passing, but hearing the words solidified by his son changed them from curiosities into concerns.

"You two go," said Phenmir. "I'll escort him back to the doors. Meira and Dhera nodded and left.

Meira placed her hand on Dhera's back and pressed her towards the front courtyard.

Phenmir smiled, placing his right hand over his heart with half of the Chuss salute. Meira completed the salute with her left hand over her heart as she left.

"Father, I love you, but you know that your prying only makes my life more difficult."

Phenmir pulled Hir closer with his arm around his son's shoulders. "I know, but rumors of Scholars traveling more during a time of war only complicate my role. I would not insist on your help if it was not paramount to maintaining peace."

"Why? Are you afraid they will side with the harvesters to destroy the Harmony Allegiant? I assure you, their role in Facet is more complex than choosing a side in a war over a single policy."

Phenmir pulled Hir to face him as they stood behind a wide sandstone monolith near one of the chapterhouse's less frequented entrances. He had seconds, perhaps a minute or two, if he was fortunate.

"Then tell me, Hir, what does the Patriarchy do?"

"Learn, teach, bind the Courts–"

"No. I won't accept any of these empty explanations. Lann, Thane Prence would not tell me what he was about before leaving for Kzhek. I trust that he has the best in mind, but the Patriarchy is too important to ignore."

"You have no idea, but I fear I know little more than you. Trust me. I will never forsake Cheric's will."

"What *is* Cheric's will to you?"

Hir stared into his father's eyes with more maturity than Phenmir had ever seen. "I'm doing this for you. Please. Let me fulfill my role. I will do more for the Harmony Allegiant than you could hope for, but I must stop this conversation here. I must stop *you* here."

"I love you, Hir."

"I know and will never forget." He embraced Phenmir and left him to enter the chapterhouse.

Phenmir returned to the front to meet Dhera and Meira. *I will do more for the Harmony Allegiant than you could hope for.* Leaving Hir on his own had been one of the greatest leaps of faith he had ever taken. He was a master sculptor, leaving his magnum opus to the elements of the wild, letting time test his efforts. One could only do so much to nurture their offspring. It was time to let Hir free.

"As far as the Patriarchy is concerned in this conflict, we must wait," said Phenmir. "Wait and hope."

CHAPTER SEVEN

FRAIL IS THE HONOR

The rumble of carriage wheels on cobblestone streets was a pleasant welcome back to civilization.

Runith wondered how the two Middlemen were handling the journey in the wagon behind theirs. Royss had insisted that they ride in their own cart, but Runith would have appreciated the chance to practice speaking with them with Golma at his side. Although he had lost that battle, he had convinced Royss to allow Lele to join them in their carriage. *Thank Laeih she isn't secreting this week.*

The carriage pulled to a stop. Shouts echoed from outside the doors.

"Riots?" asked Runith.

Royss shook his head, stepping outside. "Krall Trhet is better at controlling the activists than we were. He imprisons any who have connections to dissenting sects."

"But this whole Court is against harvesting. You cannot imprison an entire city."

Lele jumped out before Runith. He followed and stretched his back, then offered his hand to help Golma down.

"Only those in opposition are punished. Tchoyasmen can stand on either side of the conflict as they wish. They are punished for acts of rebellion, not personal opinions."

It didn't work for us and I can't work for him. "And he has enough Tchoyasmen on his side who are willing to betray their own people?"

"Those who oppose the Krall are the only ones who betray their own people, but no, he is yet to gain the support of many Tchoyasmen. A fair amount of obsequious Proctors and noblemen serve him in the hope of advancing up the political ladder, like our guests in the Middlelands, but much has changed since you were here." He waved him forward. "Come, you have plenty to see."

"And the Middlemen?"

"I'll have someone fetch them. We need to make sure the Krall and Gromm are ready to receive them before we barge in. You might have grown used to them by now, but to most people, they are as alien as the Wilderfolk of the Northern Cliffs.

"Perd you, Zhaesmen!" A heron-masked woman shouted as burly Zhaesmen pulled her away from a tavern. Guests left in haste while other bystanders stopped to stare at the two guards who escorted her to a carriage. The city fell still as they shouted back and forth but resumed activity as soon as she was shut away.

Loyal to each other until they are threatened. Ignorance, the great peace-keeper. Runith wondered if he would have the strength to stand up for injustice if his people were pulled from taverns by foreign powers. Zhaesmen policed the supposed activists, but was this Krall Trhet's doing or a dictate from Royss? Runith was pleased to see that the city had not erupted into anarchy after the death of so many Thanes but wondered how the cracks of trust had been patched. He was glad that Krall Trhet had sided with them, but how much could one trust a monarch who acted against his people? The Chuss Krall had been assassinated. Was the same fate coming for Krall Trhet? *Ignorance is the great peacekeeper*, he reminded himself, walking towards the palace and pleased that he was on the side of power. *A poor time to be a Tchoyasman.*

They started to cross a wooden bridge towards the palace's courtyard, but Lele insisted on holding Runith back by jumping off the walkway and into the murky pond beneath.

A hum vibrated from her puffed-out throat.

"*Returning home. Pure bliss*," she said.

"*I long for the same. At least you have bogs here and in the Middle-lands.*"

"*You have villages wherever we go.*"

"*Yes, but it's not the same.*"

"*Why not?*"

"*Because people are different.*"

"*You humans are too complex and self-interested.*"

She was right. Humans were a single species, creating conflicts that lead to bloodshed over differences of opinions. In a perfect world, he could have a drink with a Priessman or Chussman as if they were one of his own, but it would never be so, at least in this era of harvesting. As long as people were unwilling to give up their conveniences to try the opinions of another, the world would be filled with pride that bred hatred. He hoped that someday, the gods would help all to see their imperfections. As of today, he was pressured to fight for his will, or the will that others told him was his. He was an Endowed, therefore, an advocate of harvesting. He was a Zhaesman, therefore, a servant to the will of the government. There was no other way.

"*Are you coming?*" he asked Lele. Royss had entered the palace without him.

"It might be a while until I have another chance to swim with all of your traveling. I think I will stay here."

"I don't know how long we will be."

"The longer, the better."

"Are you coming, Runith?" Golma shouted from the doorway.

Runith croaked a farewell to Lele and ran to enter the palace.

Golma smiled through the open beak of her hawk mask. She was home, but did she feel like it? The Beaver-masked Endower Taer had argued with him about the Zhaes influence, but was Golma aware of what was happening in her Court? Runith concluded she must be, yet he knew that there were things beyond his awareness changing the land as he had known it. Perhaps Golma had found bliss in ignorance.

"Good to see you again, Runith." He turned to his right after entering the palace. Nearly two heads beneath him stood a Zhaeswoman in dark robes. Her face was one he thought he would never see again. Since Kzhek's fall, he stopped hoping for reunions, but sometimes, some hopes never die.

"Horrah." The words fell from his mouth in a near whisper. "When–how–" they rushed into each other's arms.

"In a time like this, we should all embrace each other as the Chussmen do. You never know when you will see someone for the last time."

"Why did you come? Isn't Kzhek safe?"

"Why did you come here?"

"Convenience? Royss?"

"Because you believe in a cause?" she asked.

Because I had nowhere to run in a war against my kind. "Something like that."

"Most of the Zhaes Endowed heard about what happened and thought it would be better under the authority of Royss and Gromm rather than being commanded by the Harmony Allegiant. I assume you arrived with Royss?"

"Yes, I haven't been back here for weeks, maybe months. You lose track in the Middlelands."

"I look forward to hearing about *that*, but you have a lot to catch up on."

"Tell me in short."

"Most of the radical Tchoyas followers of the Harmony Allegiant fled to join them in Kzhek, while many other Zhaesmen came with me here. You might have seen some of the Zhaes loyalists out there, keeping order."

"So Fayis is stable?"

"I suppose, but everyone says things run smoother when Royss is here to help Krall Trhet." Her eyebrows tightened as she spoke his name.

"You heard about what the Krall did?"

She shifted, then nodded. "A lot of rumors try to illustrate the story to defend what he did. Regardless of his reasoning, it was a cruel act. But what do I know? I'm no Thane."

"You have more sense than some of them."

"If you think that, maybe you are just as oblivious."

She chuckled. Her laugh was sweet. She pushed her hair out of her face, letting it fall down the side of her head. He smiled. She stepped closer to him, looking up to him with hazel eyes that saw into his soul.

"Out of the hall!" a Zhaes guard shouted with a hand on the bronze hilt of the sword at his side. "Everyone is to leave the palace for the remainder of the day."

A second guard approached Runith. "You are to meet Royss and the Krall's party in the Throne room at once." He looked down on Golma. "You come with me."

Horrah looked at him, intimacy replaced by a casual glare. She shrugged. "I suppose I will see you soon enough."

"Just come along. I'm sure Royss wouldn't mind."

She shook her head. "I have other matters to attend to." She laid her hand on Golma's shoulder. "And I look forward to meeting you sometime. If you can keep Runith on a straight path, you must be one tough girl."

Golma giggled. "I *am* a Beastling, so I know how to deal with monsters like him."

Horrah ran her hand down Runith's arm. A warm pulse shot up his arm. She was a Eurythrin and had done something to his blood. He didn't need to know what it was to want more of it. "Whole is the Holy."

Runith walked towards the throne room but was in no rush to do so. He attended gatherings of the nobility when necessary but tried to limit torturous bureaucracy when possible.

Murals of masked, yet simplified, Tchoyasmen spanned the walls. Their masks all featured the same concerned look of a man or woman. They held hands in a long line, one of a shared identity. He had heard that the mask varieties had come about only some few decades ago. What had spurned their change? What had changed with his people during that same time period? He believed that they still worshiped Laeih as their ancestors had, but surely some changes were made in prayer form and scriptural recitation.

He never thought he was the most pious Zhaesman, but he worshiped as he had been taught. Courts were bound to their religion. They were more than mere beliefs, but the identities of the people. As Facet grew more divisive and citizens intermingled with changed loyalties, what further changes would happen to the Courts' belief systems?

Puff sniff sniff puff puff. Golma led the two middleland diplomats towards the throne room. Golma knew very little of the Krall's intentions. The Middlemen knew even less what they were entering. Runith had fears of his own regarding the treatment of their southern guests, but he was little more than a single point in the Krall's plan.

They did not proceed down the hall as commanded but stopped, noting the intricacies of the architecture and various displays of carved oak. The masks of former Kralls stood on pedestals in a small alcove near the entrance, which they were drawn to like children to shiny insects. Although they were an alien species made almost entirely of vines, their curious mannerisms were familiar. They extended the vines that made their fingers to trace them along the older masks.

Runith approached them with caution, waiting until they noticed him.

Perd me, you can do it this time. He took in a slow breath. *Puff sniff sniff puff sniff.*

One of them replied. *"You are"* sniff puff sniff puff *"here?"*

"Runith!" Golma ran to his side. "That actually made sense!"

He chuckled, surprised. "I thought so, but I didn't understand the middle of its question."

"She asked if you are the high vine here, which translates to head of household. I think she means the Krall."

He chuckled and shook his head.

Golma informed them that he was not and invited them forward.

They followed behind, though still took time to touch the textures of tapestries and other handicrafts foreign to their land.

The Middleman he had spoken to approached him closer than any previous Middleman had permitted. He had tried often to speak to them from afar in their land but had never had the opportunity for such a close encounter. Even the Endowers, who spoke fluently, tended to keep their distance.

The Middleman reached her hand out, touching Runith's overcoat and tracing her fingers down to his stomach before pulling away.

He avoided touching her, lest he upset yet another Middleman, but was allowed to stare at her. Her face seemed less a marble mask with eyeholes, but was membranous, reminding him of a peeled boiled egg that still retained its outer membrane. He did not touch it, but knew that it was soft, just as he knew human skin was. Although there was no color to the ovular face, she had a mouth and nose with less prominence than on a human. As he observed closely, the sounds of breathing seemed to come from the chest itself rather than the nostril. Before he took his eyes away, he found himself staring into the piercing yellow eyes with the smallest pinpoint of a pupil.

She stepped away. The ever shifting vines that made up her body moved with her like a bucket of worms.

"Let's go," said Golma. "You've seen them enough, so quit staring. It's weird."

"They'll only get more of it when we enter the throne room."

"That will be a nice break for you."

"What do you mean?"

"You will no longer be the strangest thing in the room."

He smirked and pressed her forward. It was a quip, nothing to laugh at, but he felt reassured that she was comfortable with him. They were at war, many of his people against hers over the organs that they each had, yet this was no reason for division between them. Neither of them were at fault. Each was a game piece to their superiors.

Golma led the way past the entrance but told the Middlemen to stay back by Runith. He held his gaze forward, not wanting to make them any more uncomfortable than they already were. *Was comfort a concern of theirs? Besides appearance, how else do they differ from humankind?*

The throne room was less crowded than he had expected. The Krall sat atop the throne with a swan-masked underling at his side. Royss and Thane Gromm stood on each side of the Throne's base. Beside the noblemen, four other Tchoyasmen stood beside Thane Gromm, each one with the pale robes of a Brother of the Patriarchy.

The Krall began to descend the stairs from the throne, his back hunched to glare at his guests with his aging eyes. "These are they? The beings of bards' tales and journeymen boasts?"

"The very same." Thane Gromm was the first to approach them. His inspection did not show that he was surprised or impressed, rather as if he were reading an old and dusty tome.

The Middlemen stepped backward with the elegance of deer, their eyes narrowing at Thane Gromm.

"Tell them to come here, Golma," said the Krall.

"I can tell them, but I can't force them, Your Grace," she replied. "It's not like talking to a beast. Talking to them is the same as talking to you."

"Very well." He stepped off of the bottom step and drifted towards Royss. "What are we to do with them?"

"Gromm wanted them," said Royss.

Gromm glared at him and shook his head, forcing Royss to remain silent.

Few people could influence Royss, but Thane Gromm was one of them.

Runith knew little about Thane Gromm and cared less to learn more about the reclusive Scholar.

"Scholars?" asked Thane Gromm.

The four Tchoyas Scholars approached the Middlemen, though remained more cautious than perhaps the Middlemen themselves.

Golma spoke to them, pointing at the Scholars. Runith still struggled to understand her but heard her mention the words "trust" and "safe." They gave into her pleading and approached the Scholars with Golma between them.

Runith wanted to offer help, but knew he would only complicate the matter.

Gromm joined the group, watching the Tchoyasmen with squinted glares.

"Endower," he commanded, "translate."

"They want to know who you are."

The Scholars turned to Thane Gromm as he stared into the distance, searching for a strategic response.

"Well?" Golma asked. "Do you want to tell them why they are here?"

"To ask for their assistance in exchange for ours," Gromm replied.

"And what might that be?"

Gromm replied with silence once again.

"What do you know about them, Thane Gromm?" asked a Tchoyas Scholar with the face of a crying man.

"Enough to know that they are the key to winning this war."

"I thought Yetrik was the one who proposed that we go to the Middlelands?" asked Runith.

"True, he was the one who spoke the suggestion but was not the reason we went to the Middlelands."

"Is this about their connection with the Endowers?" Gromm raised an eyebrow as Runith pressed him with another question. "We *are* your allies. You know that, right? Can you speak clearer?"

In the moment of silence between his question and Gromm's reply, he wondered if Gromm *was* his ally. Was he striving for some goal of his own?

"This is not an interrogation for me, but an initial meeting between the Krall, the Middlemen, and *me*."

Runith scowled. "You would have never had them without me! I deserve a place in this."

"You are a commodity. Perhaps even a distraction."

The Middlemen's vines shifted faster as contention grew between Gromm and Runith. They started to move away, but Golma held onto them.

"Enough," Royss groaned. "Gromm, continue your inspection. Runith, I will escort you out if you continue to disrupt this."

Runith wanted to yell at Royss. The man treated him as a child, and it was not the first time. He was on the brink of storming out until one of the Middlemen stared at him and touched his shoulder with a finger vine. At once, he felt more peaceful than if he sat alone on a mountain peak eating roasted nuts.

He looked to Gromm, whose glare maintained its haughty disdain. The Scholar had noticed nothing, yet Runith felt everything.

"Forgive me, Thane Gromm."

Gromm nodded and returned to face the Middlemen. "Tell the one on your right that I am going to approach it," he told Golma.

She breathed a translation. The Middleman replied.

"He allows it."

Gromm pulled a white-hilted knife with a curved bronze blade from his belt.

The Middleman reached forward and clenched the bronze blade, though its motion seemed reserved. He seemed more interested in holding the blade for himself, only hoping to touch the polished bronze. He did not try to defend himself or take the knife from Gromm, only wishing to touch it.

Gromm tightened his grip. Before he could pull the knife back, the Middleman touched his shoulder, stilling him as he had calmed Runith. He breathed a sigh of relief, as if he had just taken his first drink of water after days in the desert.

The Middleman shuddered as it held the blade.

"Tell him to let go."

Golma did as ordered, and the Middleman remained. "He wants the metal."

Gromm scowled.

"I don't care, just tell him to let go and I will give him some *metal* later."

Golma breathed the translation, and the Middleman let go.

Runith peeked over to see the Middleman's hands and saw that despite his tenacious grip, there was no damage to the vines of his hand.

Gromm opened his left palm and cut a deep laceration down the center. Everyone else gasped and cautioned him to stop, but the Middlemen stood still, staring at the wound.

"Thane Gromm!" A fish-masked Scholar rushed to his side, waving his hands around Gromm but avoiding touching him.

"Stand back, Scholar." Gromm stepped towards the Middleman and returned the dagger to its sheath.

"Do you want me to tell him to do anything?" Golma asked.

"No, I want to see what his reaction is." He pressed his hand closer, but still maintained a short distance.

What did the Scholar want from giving a bloody hand to the Middleman? Runith was sure that he had some bare scratches and wounds while working with the Middlemen but had never seen them react to it. If Gromm expected healing or condolences, he would not receive it.

"*Give.*" Gromm hissed.

Runith felt compelled to follow his words and give something himself, but the Middleman did not react.

"No? Very well." Gromm pulled his hand back, giving a small hiss at the pain. "Golma, find me a Eurythrin Endower. I don't want this wound to bother me for the rest of the week."

"Most of them are in the Canton of Endowment," said Krall Trhet.

"How are you going to speak to them while I'm gone?" asked Golma. "It will take me a while to get to them."

"I can translate," said Runith. He kept his gaze away from Golma, knowing that she would doubt his prowess.

"No need," said Thane Gromm. "You can take them to the menagerie on the bottom floor. I am done with them. At least for now."

"Is that the best place you have for them?" asked Runith. "They are people, not beasts."

Gromm chuckled.

"Beasts, animals, any other creatures, talking to them is all the same as Beastling. These people were not the same. They are something more than beasts. They have a civilization of their own and technology unlike ours."

"Oh, enough advocacy," moaned Gromm. "Krall Trhet, do you have a better place for them to stay?"

"That depends on how long you will need them here."

"I expect a couple of weeks, maybe months. I am going to send for High Scholars from all the Courts to come and council here regarding our contact with them."

"Months?" Runith shook his head. "We never told them they would be away from the Middlelands for months. We don't even know if they can survive away from their usual environment for that long."

Gromm continued to speak. "Golma, I want you and some of the other Beastlings to bring me some ravens to send messages to the other Courts. You can take care of that after you find me a Eurythrin."

"Is that the wisest choice at this time, Gromm?" asked Royss.

"What would make it unwise?"

"You are the Scholar, I shouldn't have to explain it to you." Gromm stared at him. "We are at war, Zhaesman. How can you expect to convince the Chussmen to come here? What about the rebel Zhaesmen and Sleffmen? What if they come only to sell our intrigue to the Harmony Allegiant? I thought you wanted the Middlemen to come here to help *us* win the war."

"The allegiance of the Patriarchy is not tied to politics or bound by public policy. The Patriarchy transcends this *war on harvesting*. I want to invite them for a mere scholarly pursuit. They need not know our intentions. Should they grow concerned with our usage of them, I will settle that myself. I am higher in the Patriarchy than any Krall in his or her own Court."

"You're one confusing kulf, you know that?" remarked Royss. Coming from anyone else, Gromm would have exploded in fury. He chuckled instead.

"I suppose I can find an appropriate place for them to stay," said Krall Trhet. He coughed and cleared his throat. "Golma, forgive our endless list of requests, but I will need an Endower escort to remain with our southern guests. Have we had enough here, Thane Gromm?"

Gromm nodded.

"Very well. Golma, follow me."

As Krall Trhet departed, Gromm waved for the other Scholars to leave, only lingering to speak with Royss. "Anything significant to report about their civilization?"

Royss sighed. "Nothing conclusive yet. The Tchoyas Proctors continue to accommodate themselves to the culture of the Middlemen. I suppose they will have something to share soon."

Gromm turned to leave. "Runith, make sure those Tchoyasmen remain loyal. We can always replace them. Do not let them forget that."

He felt relieved, a feeling never felt following words from a brother of the Patriarchy, that he would be permitted to return to the Middlelands.

Being with the Middleman felt better than the solitary embrace of an empty mountain trail. Speaking with them was not awkward, at least to him, despite the difficulty. They breathed tranquility. They were nature itself, speaking with the breath of the wild. He had difficulties in his assignments as a Beastling, but he felt like an object used for the convenience of his superiors. Speaking with the Middlemen was a challenge, but there *was* progress. He had a purpose beyond Royss' assignments. By speaking with the Middlemen and attempting to understand them, he built a bridge between diverse cultures, harboring peace. The opposite effect of war. Peace is never eternal, it always requires the efforts of the righteous to remain. As a peacekeeper, there was endless progress.

"Are you lost, Zhaesman?" Royss patted Runith on the shoulder.

"No," he said with a chuckle. "Just thinking."

"About what?"

"You know, Gromm... the Endowers."

"No. I'm afraid I don't."

Runith shrugged and started towards the exit. He had no trouble talking with the Middlemen or most people. Royss was his friend. A close friend. Yet a distance had grown between them.

"Why don't you explain?" Royss followed him. "What about the Middlelands? Are you upset to be returning to the Middlelands?"

"Much better than spending the day with condescending Scholars."

"Are you still finding it difficult to trust Thane Gromm?"

"Do you trust him?"

"Of course."

Runith gave a frustrated chuckle, standing at the doors but not leaving. "How can you trust him when everything he says is so cryptic? When everything he does means nothing to anyone but himself? I don't think the man has ever offered a direct statement."

"I suppose he can be difficult."

"*Can*? What about the whole thing with Yetrik? How could he have influenced the Gruthman to take us to the Middlelands when he had prior interest in them?"

"We needed someone to stand as the *reason* for going there. Yetrik was vocal about it and was a fine representative. Once we learned about his interest, it was easy for Gromm to lay seeds. When I extended the offer, Yetrik took it with glee, not knowing that his thoughts had been read by one of our Feelmen. If everyone knew it was Gromm's idea, we would have had complications."

"Complications? Do you not hear yourself, Royss? He wants to invite the other Scholars from all around Facet to see the Middlemen."

"*Scholars*, not noblemen. This is all well within our expectations. You are not finding any problems that we have not already fought ourselves."

"But how does that explain Gromm's influence over Yetrik? The boy hardly spoke with the Scholar."

"Gromm is an Endowed. What do you expect?"

"'He's an Endowed' is not the answer to everything, Royss. I know you think that I might be thickheaded, but I need more of an explanation. Yetrik was no beast that would listen to a Beastling, and last time I checked, making someone do something wasn't an arrow in the quiver of Feelmen or–"

"Listen to me! *Enough. Obey.*"

While speaking with the Middlemen, he felt the extent of his abilities pressed beyond their usual threshold. He felt his additional intestine work harder than before. It felt like a cramp; not painful but somehow pleasant. He had spoken with the Endowers who mentioned feeling the same feelings as their abilities grew. He felt that now as Royss commanded him. There was something in his words that made Runith want to obey, regardless of his frustrations.

"What was that, Royss?"

"What do you mean?"

"You commanded me and I felt something. Is that what Gromm did to Yetrik?"

"*Stop.*"

"You perding kulf, you did it again."

For once in his life, Royss was at a loss for words.

"Why won't you speak to me clearly, you perding coward? I know I am no part of your sect of Thanes, but that does not diminish the trust between us. The trust we once had."

"Runith," he forced a laugh, "you're being irrational."

"I see. You were always conceited, but you have only grown worse since you decided to lead us when Kzhek fell."

"I'm trying."

"*I'm trying* to see why you trust that murderous Krall? This was supposed to be about righteousness and the pursuit of good, not power and influence."

Royss gave up trying to hide his feelings with feigned humor.

"If you ever want to have a real conversation, I'll listen. Until then, perd you."

Runith hated how he felt about abandoning a friend as he left the palace to find a tavern. He did not know when he would leave for the Middlelands or with whom he would travel, but he needed time to sit and dispel his thoughts. Royss had been one of his closest friends. He hoped that he still could be, but it was hard to harbor a relationship with someone who held secrets. Powerful secrets. Vile secrets.

He entered a tavern alone for the first time in his life. He enjoyed nature and time alone, but drinking was a sorrowful business without someone at your side. Tchoyasmen filled the tables and no Zhaes loyalist refugees were in sight. The least crowded table sat two Tchoyasmen, a burly one with the mask of a mouse and a smaller one who could barely bend over the table with the mask of a putle. They were locked in conversation and he hoped they would remain so. After the contention with Royss, he found himself longing for silence.

He waved to order a stein of highland mead and handed the barkeep enough coins for at least five more rounds. He didn't know how long he would be, but did not care. The only thing waiting for him the next day would be a long carriage ride back to the Middlelands. Being hungover wouldn't be as bad as some of the rocky roads in the carriage. Neither would bring him any peace.

After the barkeep left him with the drink, he raised it to the Tchoyasmen who shared his table, noting their beady stares through the holes in their masks.

"You come from Kzhek like the rest?" asked the putle-masked Tchoyasman.

"Sure do." Runith sighed as he drank the thick foam from the head of his mead.

"Those Allegiant kulfs are that much of a bother, eh?" The mouse-masked Tchoyasman removed the mouthpiece from his mask and took a large bite from some kind of meat. Dark juice ran down the side of his mask.

"Don't know. Never met them."

The Tchoyasman set down his meat on a stained wooden plate. "But aren't most of you fleeing to avoid their dominance? I don't support harvesting, but I was bothered when they came into our Court, thinking they owned the city. They weren't delicate, but at least it wasn't as bad as yours."

"Oh, I see. I wasn't a part of that big group. Sorry if they have been a bother. I came before."

He started to eat again. "Oh, they're no bother. They just want safety, not control."

"You're with the noblemen?" asked the putle mask.

"Yes. How *fortunate* am I?"

The Tchoyasmen turned to whisper to each other.

Perding fool. They probably think you had something to do with the death of the Thanes.

"You were there for it, weren't you?" said the mouse mask.

"Yes. It was just as unpleasant as you would imagine."

"A shame they had to die," said the putle mask. "To think that our Thanes would try to murder the Krall for attempting to sign a peace treaty with the Zhaesmen?" He shook his head. "Even though he went against the backs of the rebels, he only had the best in mind."

"At least the guards who killed them to save the Krall were of sound mind," said the other. "Klen must look down upon us with disappointment to see the Court of honesty so ridden with lies."

He had wondered what the Tchoyasmen believed, or what they had been told. Seeing how the Krall had killed those loyal to him helped Runith recognize the Krall was not a man of his own Ideal. He was thankful that the treachery had been to advocate the cause of the Zhaes loyalists, yet his opinion of the Krall was no greater than that of the vilest assassin.

He had harbored this opinion since that fateful night, but this day had caused his mind to wander. To question. Thane Gromm and Royss played a part in dictating Yetrik's will to send them to the Middlelands. Where else had their influence played a part in their crusade?

CHAPTER EIGHT

STOICISM AND SUFFERING

"Get up, Chussman."

His vision clouded. Buzzing and ringing. A hand touched his bare back.

"Get up, Chussman!"

Hir was shaken back to reality. His preceptor stood before him.

The Eurythrin pulled away from him. Her healing touch was complete, but the pain was far from diminished.

Hir stood. His ribcage had been shattered moments ago but was now repaired. He wished the Eurythrin had left him incapacitated. The only time he felt he could rest was when he was unconscious.

He spat blood onto the ground to his right. The Zhaeswoman Eurythrin continued to smile. He tried to return a bloody grin, but his jaw hurt too much.

"Stolk, focus."

His preceptor approached him, his bound fists still dripping with Hir's blood.

"Do you hear me now?"

Hir nodded.

"Zhaeswoman, give him another breath."

His preceptor walked towards the other side of the sparring square, folding his arms. Dumek was only three years his elder, yet he treated Hir as a child incapable of throwing or taking a punch. Hir wanted to hate him yet knew that he had the best in mind. They were both Scholars on their way to whatever that entailed. He had but a small glimpse of the organization's purpose and wondered if Dumek knew more.

"You're doing better than most, Chussman." the Eurythrin whispered as she drew on his back with her fingers. Each stroke felt like hours of rest. He did not know why a Zhaes Endowed worked for the Patriarchy, especially noting the war beyond the chapterhouse. He felt like he should care more but didn't. She served him. Gratitude was the only feeling he felt. Gratitude and slowly diminishing pain.

"Thank you," he whispered. He stood, whipped his arms around, then pulled into a stance with fists raised.

"Ready?" Dumek asked, unphased by the few strikes that Hir had managed to land.

Hir nodded and ran towards him. He pulled his fist back to strike and was knocked back down.

"Again." Dumek commanded before he lost consciousness.

Hir awoke, unable to breathe. He was falling, but it was a slow descent. He opened his eyes to darkness. Only a light shimmered from above. It was colder than anything he had ever experienced. He tried to move, but his arms were slower than a snailhound.

He wanted to surrender to whatever fate tried to pull him down, but an inner force pressed him onward. *Cheric save me.*

He sprang up with the gasp of a phantom, flailing his arms around atop the water's surface. He was disoriented, his eyes were blurry, but he saw a shore and swam towards it.

"Three days remain until you leave for your Crucible and you fight poorer than a drunken Priessman."

He wiped the water from his eyes and wiped his face. Dumek stood above him, stepping back from the water to avoid Hir's splashing.

"I'm trying my–" Hir coughed, lungs exasperated. "I'm trying my best." He coughed again and stomach acid burned the back of his throat.

"The best you can give is not worthy of the Patriarchy's standard." Dumek threw a freshly laundered robe atop a wooden railing. "Go eat. You have an hour before curfew and still need to study. I'll see you at dawn in the sparring square, but do not come before you have finished your morning studies."

Dumek left without waiting for a reply. Hir stared at the empty hallway. Dumek's absence mocked him. He treated Hir like a hound being trained for the city guard.

He pulled himself from the water and onto the ground. It was cold and ridden with red dirt, but he didn't care. He savored the respite and let his mind empty.

He lay prone for ten minutes before forcing himself to stand. After he left the lower levels of the Chapterhouse, he walked towards the feast hall. Only the moonlight shined through the windows. His preceptor had kept him working past sundown. He slowed his pace, giving up hope anyone would be left in the dining hall.

"Hir, working late again? I expect nothing less from you."

Hir lifted his hanging head to see an older Chussman Scholar, his silver locks draping down his sides.

"Scholar Sokov, I–"

"No need to defend. I know your preceptor well. Dumek is one of the tamest preceptors for this year."

Hir wanted to laugh, but he knew it was true. He had heard stories from the other Scholar apprentices that made him grateful to Cheric for the little differences he had.

"Still, he could use a lesson in time management."

Hir nodded, looking the Scholar in his eyes.

"Take your food from the dining hall and head directly to your chambers. Study while you eat and get some sleep. You need as much rest as you can get leading up to the Crucible of the Dunes. You will be lucky to have more than an hour a night during that week."

Hir nodded, no hint of enthusiasm showing—not even the feigned enthusiasm that he had shown for his parents. He was in pain and the feelings were forced to manifest themselves in their most natural form.

"This suffering is not without purpose. I do not need to ask you, Hir. I know you have what it takes to become a Scholar."

Hir's eyebrows tented, struggle and fear beginning to slip through his crumbling visage.

"We are alone, Hir. There is no need to hide."

Hir bit his bottom lip and wept, muffling his sobs as he bit down harder.

"You will become an *astounding* Scholar. But you must know that as you progress in the Patriarchy, you will grow hard. You will find it easier to walk through life with numbed feelings, but do not give into that temptation. Do not let that hardness stunt your growth. Grow mentally and physically. Only then will you grow spiritually."

Hir nodded.

"Thank you, Scholar Sokov."

"Thank the Root Lord."

The next morning came unwanted. He estimated receiving three hours of sleep after eating a camel steak with stale rye bread and studying ancient Chuss and Zhaes lore for three hours. Lore might not have been the best word for his assigned studies, but he knew not what else to call it. He would have guessed that they would have him study medicine, law, or even something relatively political or bureaucratic. In place of the knowledge applied to most standard occupations, he studied legends of unknown creatures, nomadic rituals, alchemy, and other seemingly useless topics that he assumed were alternative forms of breaking him down to become whatever they were going to make of him.

He lit a bedside candle, joining the other apprentices in the room at their desk for the morning's rituals. His back was sore, as was the rest of his body. He leaned down to pull a tome from his study chest and laid a copy of *The Strategist's Dilemma: the writings of the Lord Noh Detti,* beside a sheet of parchment and an inkwell. Detti's words were nothing near a pleasurable read, yet the contents of his writings felt much more applicable than anything he had studied the night before.

He wondered if this tome had been assigned prior to the battle in Kzhek. If it had, it had just escaped from decades of being obsolete. Though war raged beyond the world of the Patriarchy of Scholars, everything within felt at peace, despite the brutality of his training. There was unity between Courts within the walls of the Patriarchy. Endowed from all Courts served in the Chapterhouse and no one seemed to think anything of it. It was all as if they had united under a single faith, serving a single leader.

Is the Root Lord a god to them? To us?

The door flew open and a Scholar barged in with a lantern held high. "Apprentices! Out to your respective trainings!"

The room erupted in a clutter of shutting books and crumpling scrolls.

Hir flung his bag around his shoulder and ran from the room, relieved that he was not one of the last this time. He descended the stairwell to the lower levels and heard the fierce reprimands of the Scholar at the apprentices who were a few seconds slower than him.

A sigh of relief flew from his mouth as he made it to the sparring square before his preceptor. He stood with legs planted firmly and his hands pressed to his side as he awaited Dumek.

He had forgotten how boredom felt, learning to appreciate each moment of stillness as one for contemplation. Trying to review his studies proved worthless, as he concluded that there was nothing in those texts worthy of remembrance. Frustration returned, a feeling that never completely left him.

What do these Scholars want? What do these perding sadists hope to gain with their twisted excuses for training?

He remained still, channeling his rage into his strikes to be used against his preceptor, even though he would beat Hir until forced to moan his surrender.

He had been an apprentice for months already yet was no closer than any outsider to understanding the purpose of the Patriarchy of Scholars. He told his father that he had secrets that he could not divulge, but he had none he could share, even if he wished to.

His body ached. Each joint felt overused and stiff. Each muscle was tense, like it was on the edge of tearing.

He could endure physical pain. They had taught him that much without his choice, but his mind hurt on a deeper level. His emotions were rent like parchment in a Zhaes storm. He forced away sorrow and loneliness, only embracing feigned bravery and determination. Everyone else, even the apprentices, acted like they understood the Patriarchy and the endless prescriptions of ancient texts. He would have been convinced they were lying their way to understanding as much as he was, if they had not spoken so wisely of the content of their studies during seminars and councils. His mind was a stuffed sack, spilling out memories and recollections as he forced in new knowledge that seemed as useless as the violent training he endured.

A Zhaeswoman walked into the room, one much older than the previous Eurythrin. He wished the other one was present. Having healed him so many times, she seemed the only one in the chapterhouse to know his pain. He was disappointed, yet not surprised. The Patriarchy took any pleasure and tore it from his bloody palms before he could grow lax or form an attachment.

The Zhaeswoman greeted him. He returned a nod.

Before joining, he had thought it odd that there were no female Scholars, regardless of the word '*Patriarchy*' in the organization's title. He had been one of the smartest younglings in Sliin, but was surpassed by many Chussgirls that made him feel like he should abandon any hope of joining the Patriarchy. True, he was yet to meet any female Scholar in the traditional sense, but every female Endowed seemed just as much a Scholar. Some of the head Scholars in the other Courts were bound to be Endowed, but in a Court that banned harvesting, the only Endowed he had met in the Sliin chapterhouse were females from other Courts.

The door opened again, and his preceptor entered with another young Scholar. He thought he knew the other apprentices in his cohort, yet he could not recall ever seeing that hair style before. He looked like Hir except his silver hair was shaved on the sides and most of the top, only leaving a finger-wide strip in the center.

"You have a new opponent, Hir." Dumek gestured for the other apprentice to take his place opposite Hir.

"You want me to fight another Apprentice?" asked Hir. The other boy smirked.

"There is no sense in pitting you against opponents equal to your skill. You are a brother of the Patriarchy. Mediocrity is a vice. This is Kovesh, a newly *accepted* Scholar."

An accepted? Hir stopped breathing, recognizing that he was being forced to face someone with months, perhaps years, more experience than him.

Hir's muscles had grown in size because of the rigorous training, yet he still looked like a child compared to his opponent. He learned early on that Scholars' robes often hid bodies that rivaled those of Gorgers. Every assumption that the public had about the reclusive Scholars proved to be wrong with more complicated answers than one could ever guess.

"Remember last night, Hir," said Dumek. "Correct those mistakes. Focus on finding vulnerabilities. Counter when possible."

"But he knows all that I do and more!"

"And I know more than both of you combined, yet we fought yesterday. I do not expect you to win, only to last longer with him than you did with me. Learn from his technique."

"I–"

"No arguments, Hir. You have two days until the Crucible and the beings you will face out there are many more powerful than I am. Ready stance."

Hir nodded, arms held to fight and feet ready to run forward.

"Begin."

They ran towards each other, clashing with blocks that would leave Hir with more bruises to add to his already bluing body.

Hir suffered his first unblocked strike with a punch to his right ribs. He coughed and stepped back to catch his breath, but Kovesh was already on him. Kovesh kicked him back and Hir rolled with the momentum, shredding his bare back on the rough clay surface of the square's terrain.

He was slow to stand.

Kovesh paced with a smirk.

If this was what Hir would be expected to do, he wondered if he really wanted to become a Scholar. What was the purpose of fighting in a Court that glorified pacifism? *Glorified no longer. War had changed that.* Could anything good come from forcing men to fight their allies, never questioning the cost?

"Engage, Hir! If I wanted you to practice defending, I would have jumped into the ring. Strike him!"

Kovesh's sneer made him want to strike him more than anything. Rage built within. He was yet to land a powerful strike on Dumek, but Kovesh would be a fine stand-in. *Rage? Hatred? A desire to inflict pain? What am I becoming? Would my father be more disappointed to see me fail, or to surrender to their violent ways?* He charged with a pouncing ghete stance, letting rage blind him.

Kovesh laughed, knocking him down with a high kick to his head.

He shook his head, blackness dissipating only fast enough for him to see Kovesh on top of him, pounding him with a heavy rainfall of punches.

⋙⋙ ⋘⋘

He woke up as the same failure he had been. Hope continued to dissipate and anger agitated his frustration further. The Zhaeswoman pressed her hand against his head and pulled back a bloody palm. He was disappointed, not in himself for failing, but disappointed that he woke to the perpetual torture that had become his life.

He wanted to give up.

He wanted to, but he would not. *Cheric lift me again to become what I must.*

The cycle of incapacitation and awakening repeated three times until he was permitted to leave. He had finished the day's sparring routine, but that did not entail the end of his pain.

Nothing did.

He passed through the familiar halls, legs hurting more than the previous day. The Eurythrin "healings" helped less than he had hoped. He had heard that some Chuss Endowers were more adept and could actually heal wounds, but the Zhaeswoman's repairs only prevented detrimental conditions. The pain and aches were ever present.

"Learn to hide that limp better." He turned to the open room on his left. "No one here is eager to offer pity or sympathy, only respect for those who need it." Scholar Sokov waved him in. "But I know when rest is due."

Hir entered and sat across from Scholar Sokov, who finished writing a line on a fresh sheet of parchment then placed his quill in an old inkwell. Sokov's study was unkempt, filled with worn tomes and unorganized stacks of parchment.

"Tea?" he offered. "It's Zimint. A little mint could help cool you down."

"But it's still hot."

Scholar Sokov shrugged, sipping from his own cup. The thick Scholarly robes were horrible enough in the Chuss climate and he did not need to make matters worse, especially after sweating himself dry.

"What did you want?"

"What did *I* want, apprentice? Why so short? Cannot a mentor sit with his favorite pupil?"

"Since when have you been my mentor?"

"Mentorships need not be written into existence. Do you deny that I have helped you during your stay? I thought so. I know I tend to offer little more than a distracting conversation, but I wanted to be sure that you are prepared for the Crucible. You have only two more nights in the Chapterhouse until that solemn week."

Hir scratched his index fingers with his thumbs, catching the Scholar's attention.

"Every Scholar must pass through it. You will return a changed man. I know this may sound like yet another useless platitude, but it is true."

"Why are you telling me now? Can't this wait until tomorrow when I have more time to prepare? If you haven't noticed by my eyes that have almost swollen shut, I took a rather fierce beating over the past few hours."

"I will not be here tomorrow."

"Traveling again for Scholarly business? Let me guess, *leisures await those who endure.*"

"I would call it the furthest thing from leisure."

Hir stared at him, not interested in prying. Scholar Sokov was a relatively humble man but was far from a Sleffman. He was one of the Scholars who liked to be asked questions, flaunting the enigma that was the Patriarchy.

"And why might that be?"

"I'm heading to Fayis to meet with other high ranking Scholars."

Hir scowled. "*Fayis?*"

"Yes. I am well aware of what the Harmony Allegiant believes to have occurred there, according to the Zhaes Caser. Your father was adamant on making Krall Trhet's supposed actions known."

"Supposed? Do you not trust my father?"

"I trust him, but I question the Caser who dropped everything that she was known for to join the Harmony Allegiant. I have not met her myself, but she carries a stern reputation for being the most Zhaes of all Zhaeswoman."

"So you believe the rumors that the Tchoyas Thanes died trying to assassinate the Krall? Doesn't that sound like a loyalist excuse?"

"It seems plausible. The Krall is an honorable man. I am not picking one party's statement over the other. I just think that we must remember how polarized these two parties are. The truth is often found somewhere in the middle."

"Regardless of that, the Zhaes Thanes are there."

"And they are more reliable than the Caser? We know their stance on this. They are leading the front against the Harmony Allegiant."

"They may be, but Thane Gromm was the one who extended this invitation."

"And he is somehow more reliable than the others? He is *still* a Zhaes Thane. Was he not one of the contributors to establishing harvesting as law in most of the Courts?"

"Those are his plights, not the Patriarchy's. This is a matter of the Patriarchy, not the war. You should have learned by now that the Patriarchal loyalties run deeper than any political ties."

He thought of the Zhaeswoman Endowed, the younger one that had helped him the day before. She smiled like a Chusswoman, inspired by selflessness rather than the self-interest that was often tied to the Zhaesmen.

"This is not a debate, Hir. You should know by now that you have more to learn than you could imagine."

"Then why share this with me? Why tell me about some secretive meeting?"

"There is nothing secretive about it. You must understand something about the Patriarchy. There are no *secrets*, only bits of knowledge that are not granted until certain concepts are understood. The Patriarchy of Scholars is not a veil of hidden knowledge, but an ever-ascending staircase that provides you with newer, higher knowledge as you progress. Still, you ask why I share this with you?"

Hir sighed and shrugged.

"I want you to understand that I am granting you perhaps the most valuable thing that I can. Trust." His smile melted away as he leaned towards Hir. "The Patriarchy's ties run deeper than politics, but some have a different understanding of the purpose of the Patriarchy. I am going to this gathering not only to learn, but to observe. As the world grows ever divisive, so does our organization."

"Yes, I know, the Bronze Seers. You've warned me before."

"The most pivotal members of their group will be in Fayis, and I intend to learn about their desires for this *finding* of Gromm's. They labor high"—he pointed to himself—"and low"—pointing at Hir. "As division splits the land, their efforts grow ever more persistent. If they manage to conscript apprentices like you with their insidious tentacles, the Patriarchy will become a cult that abandons the core of our organization."

Hir didn't even know what that core was, but he continued through pain and trial, knowing that someday he would. Hoping that he would. If he could become a man so revered as Sokov, it would be worth it.

Are you doing this for glory? Praise? Power?

"Observe your fellow apprentices. Take note of their connections. Whom do they respect? What do they wish to gain in the Patriarchy? The haughty and prideful are likely part of the Seers or are soon to be their next recruits."

"Why? Are they run by Priessmen?"

"It is possible, but there is much yet to learn."

"Then what do you know? Forgive me, Scholar. I trust you, but I find it hard to be motivated to seek out members of an organization about which I know nothing. Why should I fear them?"

"Because I *fear* that they are responsible for harvesting. The Endowers were meant to be born. It was part of Cheric's grand plan, but we were never supposed to taint the divine gift. Whoever instigated harvesting, did it to give themselves power, not the people. They carry that same goal; to make themselves gods, bringing all to fear the power of the Patriarchy. We were never meant to be feared, but revered. We are servants to Facet, but they want to change that. They must not taint the dictates of the Root Lord."

He felt as if his heart had stopped. He had to know what else Sokov knew. Sokov's knowledge was greater than the finest Zhaes bronze, yet he had to hold back his curiosity if he ever hoped to taste it. *A question for another day.* "Very well."

"Their members wear bronze circlets, but they are often hidden or removed in public settings. Beware anyone who is not discrete enough to hide any trace. An imprint from a headband, a red line from a bracelet, even pierced earlobes on those who do not wear jewelry may be a sign of one in their order."

"Why bronze? Now you make me wonder if they are Zhaesmen."

"Bronze has more significance than its ties with Court Zhaes. Its ancient value traces back to the times of prophets and crusaders. Too often we forget the deeper significance of something due to its monetary value."

Hir clenched his teeth, widening his eyes as he held in a yawn.

"We can discuss this more when I return. I am confident that you will survive the Crucible, but there is more to it than that."

I gave up on hoping that the Patriarchy cared for my life after two days of training. He held his bitter remark back, knowing that this was perhaps the only Scholar who cared for Hir.

"It is about learning and transcendence."

"How is surviving alone to complete some unexplained task any way a transcendental experience?"

"Not all learn more than survival, that is true, but the difference depends on those who seek, rather than hide. How one reacts to difficulties determines if they will become a servant or a Scholar."

CHAPTER NINE

EVOLUTION

LESS THAN TWO MONTHS PRIOR TO THE BATTLE FOR PAIELL

Yetrik focused on calming his quivering hands. He removed his tunic and sat on the thin black cloth atop the metal table.

Terin smiled at him. He tried to remain positive while looking at the Thane after accepting his gift.

A gift that cost the life of a newborn.

He was taken aback by the jarring thought. It was not the first time he had faced it, nor would it be the last. No one seemed to share his fear, not even the jovial Chuss surgeon who stood at the edge of the table.

Terin stepped in and patted the Chusswoman on the shoulder. "Did you expect them all to join the rebels? Meisha is the best surgeon in Facet. I know many others would argue, but she's handled the grafts for our Court's best."

"Did you flee the Court after the death of your Krall?" Yetrik bit his tongue, wondering if his question would've been better left to unanswered curiosity.

"I've been living here for years." She said. "Traveling across the continent for jobs wasn't worth my time and the Priessmen know how to treat those loyal to them well. Sure, I'm still a Chusswoman, born and trained by Chuss practitioners, but I see no reason to hold to tradition. Tradition is what is causing this war."

Yetrik nodded. "Do you... still..."

"Live by my religion? Of course! Just because I live away from any organized Chuss churches, I still hold true to who I am."

"But—"

"But I'm not a good Chusswoman because I'm not joining their fight?"

"I didn't mean that. I just... I thought you might prescribe to their choice of side in the war."

"Chuss is not the Harmony Allegiant. If you ask me, *they* are the unfaithful ones. Chussmen should be pacifists, for this is what Cheric's disciples have preached. My people may worship the same god as I do, but that does not mean that we interpret the *Tome of Charity* the same way. I don't need to ask you to know that your Court has its fair share of religious division. We can all worship the same god and still see that being as a different person."

"Exactly! I think that is why I–" He looked at Terin. "Sorry."

"Why? Just because I do not prescribe to your beliefs doesn't mean that I'm not interested in theology. Faith and gods in this war bring up a plethora of fascinating discussions, but we have something of a greater note to settle here."

Yetrik hoped they hadn't noticed the sweat marks left by his hands on the tablecloth. He was excited to receive an organ, but had never undergone surgery.

Two Priessmen entered.

"These will be the Eurythrins assisting me," Meisha said.

"This is a safe procedure, right?" he asked.

The Chusswoman took a step towards him; her smile weakening. "I will do everything within my power to see that you receive the best care. Medical practice has come a long way since the implementation of Eurythrin stabilization. I have succeeded countless times, but that does not eliminate the inherent risks."

"And those are?"

"Organ rejection, infection, perforation of a surrounding organ, excessive blood loss, incontinence, paralysis, and death."

He stared at her with an open mouth.

She placed her hand on his knee. "*Every* surgery carries risks. I am not perfect, but I know what I am doing. Not only are you counting on me, but the entire Priess nobility and my competence is weighed by the success of this procedure."

"You'll be fine, Gruthman," Terin said. "Just because she has to state these risks by law does not mean that anything will happen to you."

"Still–" she began.

Terin patted her arm to stop her from talking. "She is the *best* in the business. You'll wake up having gained everything and lost nothing. Do you understand?"

Yetrik nodded.

"Now, can we start?" Terin asked.

"Not without explaining the procedure," she said.

"I'm going to be asleep for all of it, right?" Yetrik asked.

She nodded and pointed to the Eurythrin on her right. "He will monitor your sedation, no herbs or intoxicants needed. It's all a part of the ability." She laid her hand to rest on the shoulder of the other Eurythrin. "He will prevent blood loss, keeping the flow where your body needs it, but stopping it at the points of incision. Once the organ is inside of you, he'll redirect the flow to the new intestinal portion and you'll wake soon after. Expect some abdominal pain over the next few days, but the Eurythrins will repair as much as they can before leaving the rest of the recovery to you. The organ should make the entire process last only a few days."

"Then it's off to train with the Beastlings," Terin said. He looked at her. They shared a nod, and he turned back to Yetrik. "See you soon, *Endowed.*"

He nodded, only managing to maintain a smile for two seconds.

Terin departed and two more Priessmen entered, wearing white robes, gloves, and cart with a tray of blades and other tools.

He looked at the assortment of scalpels, forceps, and other intimidating devices as they pushed the cart to the edge of his bed.

"Any questions?" she asked.

He shook his head.

She smiled and gestured to the table. "Lie down. We'll put you to sleep and handle the rest. I'll be with you soon after you wake up to answer any questions you might have."

He shuddered as his head touched the pillow. He clenched his fists, though it did nothing to help calm them.

"How long will it take? Should I expect to feel different after–well, of course I should, but *how* different should I expect to feel? How much pain is normal? Do you usually have two Eurythrins? Should you bring another to help just in case? I–"

He stopped as she squeezed his clenched fist and smiled at him. "Relax, Gruthman. Questions after. It'll be easier for you to focus once it has passed."

He clenched his eyes shut and nodded. "Yes, yes. I'm ready."

She chuckled. "Yenin, Roken, take your positions."

Images passed through his mind. Childhood. Time with the loyalists. Royss' trust. Thane Gett assigning him to travel to Kzhek. Meeting Semi.

Traveling with Semi. Talking with her. Worrying with her. Laughing with her. Crying with her.

Logic told him that he would not die, but the creature that was his worry forced him to believe otherwise. Semi had survived. Why couldn't he? Countless people had died from failed procedures. Why couldn't he?

"Enjoy the rest," the surgeon said.

He felt the cold leather of her gloves touch his hips and he lost consciousness.

꙳꙳꙳꙳꙳ ꙳꙳꙳꙳꙳

Heart pounding, Yetrik shot up from the surgeon's table. Two Priessmen grabbed him before he could throw himself from it. He lost the will to fight as a sharp pain burned his lower abdomen. He hunched over and tried to pull his arms free from their grips.

"Yetrik! Yetrik, calm down! Don't touch it! The incision is still fresh!"

"Should we put him out again?"

"No, he needs to wake up."

He moaned and twisted. "Please, please. It hurts. Stop it please!"

"Should we grab a brush pipe? A shot of Middleman's bane?"

"No." A soft hand touched his bare back. Meisha.

He looked up, eyes blurry. "Please do something."

"Roken, hand me the poultice."

"Yes, Chusswoman."

She squeezed Yetrik's fist, let go, then touched his stomach with a wet hand. He opened his eyes for but a second to look down at her hand, spreading a teal mush across the incisions that had been closed by a thin string. He hunched over, wincing again as the cooling sensation from the poultice turned to a searing pain. Crying out again for relief, he tried to focus on his breathing, which slowed without any effort.

He opened his eyes. It no longer hurt but itched.

"Better?" Meisha asked.

"A lot."

"I'll leave you with a jar, but I don't expect you to need it much longer."

He followed her gaze to note that one of the Eurythrins still kept a hand on him.

"Thank you," Yetrik said.

The Eurythrin nodded.

Yetrik turned back to the surgeon. "How long do I have to stay here?"

"You don't *have* to do anything, but I would advise a few more minutes." She laughed at the shock in his eyes. "All we need is stability. I'll have some herbs and elixirs sent to wherever you are staying. Terin will probably want you to begin your training with the Beastlings in a day or two."

Yetrik looked down and touched the stitches on his incision, surprised that it didn't hurt.

"We can take those out once the cut is completely sealed. Come back tonight and it should be fine."

He was awestruck. He knew, as did everyone, that Endowed and Endowers healed faster than any human. When paired with a Eurythrin, the process was supernatural. He *knew* this but was finally coming to believe it.

"Ready to go?"

His attention turned to the door. Terin stood just past the doorway with Captain Kevlen and another armored Beastling in tow.

"Now?" Yetrik asked.

Terin looked at the surgeon. "Has he had enough time to recover?"

"Humors are stable, incisions are sealed. Yes, he is technically ready, but I would suggest a little more time for him to rest. Where are you taking him?"

"To see his steed."

Yetrik wanted to rest, but the child within him was not so dead that he would let pain hold him back from seeing his creature partner. "I can handle it."

She shrugged. "If you feel ready. Terin, bring him back here if he starts to have a fever, bleeding–"

"I know, I know."

"How long ago was the procedure?" Kevlen asked.

"We finished three hours ago."

He chuckled. "Come on, Gruthman. I was up an hour after mine."

"Really?"

He nodded, but the surgeon did not look so sure.

"Go down a level, would you? We have a few wheelchairs in the second wing. Push him around a while longer to avoid straining the incisions."

Kevlen nodded and waved for the other Beastling to follow.

Terin walked closer, holding his arms behind him. He looked up at the surgeon. "Still no hope of helping the paralyzed?"

She frowned. "Perhaps someday. I'm sorry, Terin, but you have to remember that we have only had the Eurythrins in medicine for a few years."

"I know."

"Is your brother well?"

"If he didn't have the occasional pressure sore, I don't think I would ever hear a complaint from him. The chair is a part of him now, not an obstacle." He patted his lower abdomen. "As is my ailment. I suppose the occasional cramp is better than paralysis."

She smiled at him and offered a chair, which he politely declined.

He stepped up to Yetrik. "Kevlen will want you to start training to-morrow, but you still need time. Once you bond with your zlatog, you will likely have the same desire. You will have the rest of your life to worry about training and flying. If you want any of that to work, you need to let the organ work within you. Even though you just had the procedure, the connection should be strong enough for you to at least speak with the beast. Give it a few more days and you'll be a changed man."

He smiled, not wanting to overwhelm Terin with every question he had. Childish joy filled him hearing even *hints* of what the organ could help him accomplish.

Kevlen and the other Beastling returned a few minutes later, out of breath, as they pushed the chair through the door.

"Perding chair weighs more than my father!" Kevlen grunted as he laughed, setting it down with a loud thud.

The bulky wooden chair creaked as it rolled towards his bed with wheels that looked as if they had been taken from a worn carriage.

Kevlen waved for him to take a seat.

"Careful, Gruthman." the surgeon said. She pointed to the Eurythrins to help him move to the chair. They let go as he sat down.

"How does it feel?" she asked.

"Fine."

"I'll have one of the Eurythrins follow in case you need them, but I think your body can manage the rest of it healing on its own."

"Can we take him now?" Kevlen asked.

"Careful with him," she said.

"*Firm is the Foundation*, right? He should be fine."

She bid them farewell with a faint smile.

Yetrik gripped the armrests as Kevlen rolled him down the hall, his wrists burning with tension. The other Beastling helped Kevlen carry the chair down the steps before returning to the bumpy ride that made every crack in the ground shake the chair.

"How far away are the zlatogs?" Yetrik asked as they left the Canton of Haleness.

Kevlen slapped his shoulder as he pushed the chair forward. "Not long. We'll get you back to your bed soon enough."

They curved around the side of the building and left the pavement for a large field of grass so green that it had to have been cared for by a whole team of Sproutens. Kevlen didn't seem to mind ruining their work as the wheelchair crushed the grass beneath the worn wheels, but that was a minor inconvenience compared to the damage done by the class of the three zlatogs ahead of them.

"I figured it would be easier to bring your steed to you."

Pain fled in the presence of wonderment. Two of the zlatogs screeched at each other, while the third looked directly at him. "Does it know me?"

"We've told her about you."

"And?"

"You'll have to earn her trust."

"Do I get to name her?"

Kevlen laughed. "Only if she gets to name you!"

"Come on, he's new, Kev," the other Beastling said. "Once you start beastcalling, Gruthman, the line between human and beast will disappear."

"Then what is her name?" Yetrik asked.

"Ask her yourself," said Kevlen.

Yetrik's hands gripped the chair once again as they neared the zlatogs. The one who they said would become his steed stared at him with huge brown-black eyes from its bat face. It wrinkled its nose, bearing teeth the size of large daggers. Goat-like golden horns reflected the setting sun. Second only to the kaesan, it was one of the most terrifying beasts he had ever seen.

Yet, it was beautiful.

Kevlen pushed his chair right up to the zlatog. Yetrik reached a hand out, instinct triumphing over inhibition, and touched the side of its head.

The beast hummed, and he ripped his hand back.

"No," Kevlen said, "don't do that, you kulf. Keep your hand on her."

He followed. She hummed and he felt thoughts surge from his fingers to his hand.

"*Why are you touching me like that?*"

He laughed. "I heard her!"

"It'll take you a bit longer to speak to her. Screeches first, then percussion. Let me know if you get this. Kevlen screeched in the zlatog language, yet he understood. "*He's yours, if you'll have him. He's new but will learn to speak soon.*"

"Yeah, I did!"

Kevlen patted Yetrik's shoulder. "Touch her horn. It's more polite. If she tells you your name, she's interested in bonding. Regardless, you'll have to prove yourself. Don't be scared."

Yetrik placed his hand on her horn as she lowered her head to his reach.

She hummed. "*You are new. You are not like these callers here. I can sense that. I like that. Stop looking at me like I'm a servant.*"

He looked back at Kevlen, who smiled and nodded.

He looked back at the zlatog, into her brown eyes, and felt their hearts beat in sync.

"*I am not yours. You are not mine. If we proceed, we shall be as one.*" Her eyes squinted in such a human manner that he felt chills. His new organ burned, yet he embraced it, feeling a new part of him come to life.

He screeched out, not knowing what he said, only that it entailed agreement.

She mimicked his cry and hummed her name.

"*Avra.*"

CHAPTER TEN

RISING TIDE

T he green banner of Court Gruth flew high. The sigil of the leviathan eel billowed in the wind atop the fortress wall. It did little to cool Semi from the cloudless sky. She still preferred it over the Zeemer snow that fell in the western Courts.

Semi stared out over the Eastern Sea. Salty air reminded her of simpler times when the ocean entailed relaxation rather than war. Frolicking in the water with other Gruth children who became her best friends after an hour of knowing each other. The only pain being sore fingers after poking washed up jellies.

Thanes Serish and Keff stood on either side of Krall Plath. He looked down to his left at Deene Kelm, the Thane of Scholarship. All waited for the Scholar's presentation.

Kelm kept to himself. While others found value in medicine and linguistic theory, he spent his time studying ancient stories of valor and legendary beings who saved their people from unholy beasts.

His eyes bulged as they shifted back and forth between the sea and the company. He acted like an artist waiting to unveil his greatest creation, hardly keeping in his smile. They all knew why he had invited them but knew little of what that invitation entailed.

"So." Krall Plath slapped the edge of the fortress wall that stood up to his abdomen. He pivoted on his scaled leather boots to face Thane Kelm. "Are the Terpels going to fly in on sky serpents? March in from the east? Or are we here for something else?"

Thane Kelm scowled at the Krall, then leaned over the wall and shouted, "The Krall grows impatient. They have waited long enough!"

They moved toward the wall to see a tall Gruthwoman approach the shore. She knelt and wiped her hand across the water as she stared out at the horizon. Ripples in the distance moved towards her. She stepped into the water, letting the tame waves reach her waistline.

"Again, Deene?" the Krall groaned. "I don't want to be entertained by a school of fish surrounding a Beastling. I'm sure there is some 'great significance to their pattern of human to fish interaction.'" He spoke with a finger pointed up and with a higher pitch voice.

Thane Kelm looked as if he was going to spit at the Krall's face. "You perding fool! Why don't you look over the edge again? You have the patience of a starving imp!"

Krall Plath's trembling lips tried to utter a rebuttal, but Thane Kelm reached up to shove him forward to look back at the sea.

A school of fish had surrounded the Beastling Gruthwoman. She knelt and waved her hands forward as the fish swam outward in every direction, stirring the sea's surface like a boiling pot.

Semi looked at the Scholar, who kicked the floor with the tip of his foot as he awaited the Krall's reaction. She tried to hide her smile and held her mouth shut by resting her chin in her hands with elbows on the edge of the wall.

Thane Kelm nodded with more energy than a Gruthboy seeing his first leviathan eel.

Black dots advanced toward the shore on the sea's surface. Some spread out like jellyfish with tentacles flowing out, though they became dots with the others as they approached the shore. They were not floating debris, nor were they any sea creature. The dots became heads as black hair fell down the sides of a thousand or more faces as Gruthmen and Gruthwomen rose from the sea and marched to line up on the shore.

Their musculature was immaculate, but they were not as large as Gorgers. They were the size of a standard human but were refined to appear like the limestone statues that lined the halls of the Krall's palace.

"Quite the show, Kelm," the Krall sighed.

"You do not understand, *Your Grace*–"

"You do not understand that I came to see an army like no other, not whatever *that* was."

"This *is* an army like no one has ever seen. I wanted to show you what their endurance entails. These Terpels are the embodiment of the Gruth ideal."

"What is that supposed to mean?"

Thane Kelm grinned. "They have been waiting *underwater* for this moment for *two full days*."

"Did His Grace ask you to torture them?" Thane Keff threw his hands up. "You could have killed the greatest labor force in the Court for some"—he waved his hands trying to find words—"senseless spectacle!"

"Quite the lackluster spectacle," said Krall Plath.

"No, no, no." said the Scholar. "You misunderstand. They would have left the water if they knew they were going to drown. Even in the worst case, we know Eurythrins can save people from drowning if they work fast enough."

"Fast enough."

Thane Kelm flung his hand at Thane Keersh. "We know they can work days on end, but this shows you that they can accomplish things beyond your expectations. All Endowed require more food than any standard human, but these Terpels survived without feeding–" he held a hand out to stop the Thanes from arguing. "They survived without breathable air for two days. These Endowed are more than great *endurers*. They are Deilf's gifts for domination. Do you see how well they subject themselves to my command?"

"The persuasiveness of a Scholarly brother," noted the Krall.

"*We both know there is much more to it than that,*" he whispered, but Semi had no problem hearing. "Would you like to meet them?"

"If it would make you happy, Kelm," the Krall said, winking at Semi. She giggled as Thane Kelm stormed towards the fortress' staircase.

The fortress seemed to have no purpose other than being an observation deck for the sea, but she knew it had a rich past. Histories intertwined with war and bloodshed. How much were the politics of the modern day reflecting the past? What was it in people that drove them into cycles of ceaseless contention? Peace would come following the war, but conflict was bound to return.

"Is Yetrik well?" Thane Keersh asked, walking beside her as they descended the stairs.

"I would assume so. You knew him?"

"No, but I feel like I do. Thane Gett likes to boast about him. It sounds like you two had quite the bond."

"I would not call it a bond."

"Then what would you call it?"

She tried to hide a smile. "Ask him when he returns."

"If he returns." He paused. "Sorry, I didn't mean to–"

"No, it's fine." The realization that he could be dead hurt, but she banished the thought before it could grow. It was not the first time it had crept into her mind.

"Many will perish before this ends," said Thane Kelm.

"That is why we have this army," said the Krall. "If they live up to your boasting."

Thane Kelm remained silent, pressing the company to the shoreline.

The army of Terpels stared at the fortress wall, unwavering.

"Forward strike!" The army shifted their stance, fists forward, at Thane Kelm's command.

"Defensive brace!" They gathered into a tight bunch, the outermost Terpels prepared to block.

"How much do you value that old fortress wall, Krall Plath?" asked Thane Kelm.

"What can you do?"

Thane Kelm sneered. "Forward barrage!"

The army rushed to the fortress' wall and bombarded it with strikes faster than any standard human could punch. The portion of the wall crumbled to rubble within five seconds.

The Krall chuckled and gave a slow clap. "Impressive, Kelm."

"When are we sending them out?"

He placed his hand on Thane Kelm's shoulder. "You know, dear Scholar, you surprised me. I didn't expect them to be combat ready. Are they?"

Kelm nodded.

"Semi, what have you heard about the others?"

"The Priessmen are aiding the loyalist Sleffmen to hold their Paiell while the rebels try to capture it as they did Kzhek."

Since the nobility had learned about her relationship with Yetrik. their letters became the central route of communication with the loyalists.

She was, however, disappointed with his most recent letter, which only included three brief sentences.

Heading to Sleff with the Priessmen. Talk soon. Too much to write.

"So you want us to join the Priessmen in Sleff?" asked Thane Keersh.

The Krall adjusted his crown. "How far are we committed to their coalition?"

Thane Kelm started to pace, kicking up the white sand. "Quite committed, Your Grace. As you can see by my efforts to organize these Terpels, we must not dawdle."

The Krall crouched and scooped up a handful of sand, letting it fall between the cracks of his fingers. "But what is the use of exhausting our most elite in *this* dispute over a poverty ridden land?"

"Your Grace," Thane Keff's voice grew concerned. "We cannot abandon them."

"Who is to say that they do not eventually join the rebels? So many already have. The Priessmen are offering their aid. I say it would be best to defer this fight to them. More pride for the prideful. More rest and preparation for us."

"But if we intervene, we can prevent greater losses." Semi clenched her back muscles, holding in her frustration. "And you cannot base your argument on some Sleffmen joining the rebellion. True, it may happen, but all of us are just as likely to become traitors."

"Do you doubt our cause, Semi?"

"Not your cause, but how you are choosing to execute it. This is not a fight for a single Court against another. It is our duty to stand and aid our allies, regardless of their nationality."

"Then do not forget yours, Gruthwoman. We are Gruthmen. Firm is the Foundation. Ours will crumble if we expend our efforts on a dispute already underway. Did Yetrik ask that we send aid?"

"No."

"Then it is unnecessary." He clapped. "Thane Kelm, thank you for the demonstration. Ensure that they are ready when we need them, though I expect we will keep them until we need to recapture Kzhek or take Sliin."

"*Sliin*?" scoffed Semi. "When was that part of the plan?"

The Krall chuckled and shook his head. "Do you want to let these zealots run free after taking Kzhek, the center of harvesting? Justice must be served. Peace will not return until we pave its way."

Peace will never prevail when one rules with domination and power.

Krall Plath shook his head. "As I was saying, Thane Kelm. See that the Terpels are cared for. They are no longer slaves, but as good as noblemen. You say that they do not need to be fed, but I am sure they would appreciate a good meal."

The Krall bid his company of Thanes forward, ignoring Semi. His actions spoke more than any description of him could.

Thane Kelm remained, eyes staring at his army and hands fidgeting, likely wondering how he was going to feed so many people.

Semi left him to himself and walked towards the sea. She stepped into the water, letting the slow tide wash the sand from her sandal straps. It was colder than she expected, but it felt refreshing under the open sun.

Fins rose above the water in the distance. The beasts and fish swam, living their lives free of conflict. She smiled at the notion but lost her smile as she thought of the largest sea creatures feeding upon the weak.

Will we become prey if we remain still?

She left thoughts of the sea behind and returned to the shore. Thane Kelm seemed to have calmed himself but stood in a similar reverie. The Terpels lost their solidarity and conversed as humans, not as the statues they had seemed to be.

"Finally gave them free will?" she asked.

"I never took it from them."

"How do you do it?"

"What, command them?"

She nodded.

"Slave soldiers listening to this poor imp of a Scholar? Is it that unbelievable?"

"I wouldn't say–"

"I would." He laughed. "The Krall recognizes it, and so should you."

"Each time I spend more than ten minutes with him, my respect diminishes."

"He's not a bad man. He is just set in his way."

"His foundation is *too* firm."

Kelm laughed. "He cares about his people."

"So, the Terpels?"

"Commanding them? Best to leave it as a trick of the Patriarchy."

"I've heard that answer too many times," she grumbled.

"These tricks will be revealed soon enough. That or they will be the downfall of our organization."

"What do you mean?"

"Another question for another day, you have better things to focus on." He faced her. "Why are you still here?"

She tried to avoid his glare but was drawn to it. His eyes were bloodshot globes nested into large sacks that suggested days without rest.

"Why are you staring at me, Gruthwoman? Are you disheartened to see a Krall treat his most trusted Scholar like a disappointing heir?"

"I was interested in the Terpels." She neared him. The sides of his thinning black hair were growing gray.

He chuckled, though it sounded more like a squeak from the throat of one who thought smoking a pipe was the best way to break a fast. "It seems all the Courts are now being forced to take an interest in military and combat. You do not seem to care for Krall Plath. What did you hope to gain here?"

"Nothing, I just came to fulfill my duty."

"Oh, by Deilf's strength, no one would spend time with that man out of pleasure. I know who you are, Semi. I know every Thane more than they could ever fear. Likewise, I know that your duty is to be but a simple messenger between the Zhaes nobility and ours. You have fulfilled your role and continue to linger." He turned to her with a smirk. "I know that much, and I am not even a Feelman. Relying upon natural instincts is neglected in our day. Have you come hoping to advance in the hierarchy because of your first-hand experience with this so-called *war*? No, you do not want that. You revere Thane Gett and Keersh among others, but there are some that you are less than fond of. You do not want a title, but a position. You want to influence the Court from its foundation, never toying with dictates and policy. I wish I would have followed a path like yours. Even living as a simple Scholar would have allowed more freedom than chaining myself to the title of *Thane*. So does that thing that your heart desires."

Her wide-eyed gaze was stuck on his omnipotent glare. His cracked lips were turned up in a vile grin.

"*How? How can this grotesque imp of a man know my deepest intentions?* There is no need to ask how. You already know my title. Let that be warning enough to not trample on our ways. Toy with the Krall. Make *him* your pawn, if you will. Now that we have demolished doubts and questions about why you linger, your next question might be to see what I can do for you."

She had no choice but to follow. He believed she was capable of something. More than she believed herself. Capable of turning bitter people away from brutality to find peace some other way. They had already entered war. She had to begin at their level. Work as they willed until she could do something with her voice.

She avoided his gaze for a few moments longer, knowing that turning back to him would force her onto a new path.

Will that path make me feared or loved?

The Terpels conversed with one another. Life had returned to them.

Thane Kelm had commanded them as puppets, but they were not objects to be used for another's power plight. If he offered hope to her, what had he offered them? She had never been a slave like them. Her future was uncertain. For that, she was glad. Now was her chance to jump into a different future. Only time would tell if it would be beautiful or destructive, but for once in her life, she was willing to gamble.

"Help me."

He grinned, though not as he had before. He no longer seemed a serpent with his words, but an honest man trying to lend a hand. "You see trails dividing before you. Who you will become and what you accomplish depends on your choice. Will you become a warrior or a pawn?"

"A Warrior"

"You will train and rise above your enemies not like these soldiers, but as a heroine to fill the histories. Commit yourself to my generous hand and I will see that your name will have power. Let this be more than the promise of a man, but the *guarantee* of a Scholar." He placed his elbow against his hips, straightening his crooked back, and raised his clenched fists as if bracing for a strike.

Semi repeated, signing the agreement with the Gruth salute.

CHAPTER ELEVEN

PAINFUL REMINISCENCE

A erhee spread a poultice on her ribs, its dark green blended with fresh blood. She hissed at the pain of the antiseptic as it covered the open laceration. "It smells like a Tchoyas bog."

"I assume that is why they use putle secretions," said Colrig. "Was it one of them?"

"The Holy Reapers?"

Colrig nodded.

"I don't know. It's hard to tell which ones are the organized rebels and which ones are crazed street urchins."

"Perhaps it is time for you to work with Voln."

She scowled, hissing more as she touched her ribs.

"He has a ... notable personality but is wiser than he would lead you to be."

"Just because he uses the language of an adult barbarian does not mean that he is worthy of an adult role."

"Aerhee," Colrig grabbed a roll of cloth, "you still harbor some of the Zhaes self-righteousness that you swore to rid yourself of."

"You are not wrapping that around me. I can do it myself."

"You Zhaeswomen are too cautious about modesty. You need help with that wound."

She seized the roll from his only remaining hand. "You've seen my bare back already. This is not about modesty, it's about independence."

"And refusing to work with the finest Endower is a matter of independence as well? Or is that an old bias for Endowed over Endowers slipping through?"

She pulled her clothes back over her torso and turned to glare at him. "Is this what you want from me, Captain? For me to spend my time with some child?"

"I think it could be a humbling experience for the both of you."

Her eyes rolled up as she shook her head. "Has he found anything since our last meeting?"

"He knows the Reapers use Endowed to terrorize the Zhaes members of the Allegiant."

"And that surprises you?"

"No, it just confirms our suspicions. From what we can gather, they have no connection to the escaped Zhaes Thanes or to any other loyalists. They seem to be the enemy's equivalent to the early Zhaes rejectionists who killed noblemen to make themselves seen. Are four of the five surrounding municipalities still standing in favor of the Allegiant?"

"Recent reports say that this *loyalist* movement has convinced some of the northern region of Zenth to *reconsider* their alliance with us."

"Three out of five. That is still a majority."

"But a decline nevertheless."

"What about the other Thanes?"

"Still adamant about remaining loyal to harvesting, though I expect it is because of their loyalty to the Krall more than to the policy itself."

"More Zhaesmen making 'the law their god'."

She smirked. "You thought that was quoteworthy?"

"It's not the only thing I have quoted from you, Caser. You are as wise as your reputation claims."

"I will not argue that. We all see ourselves as the wisest living person. That is the downfall of the prideful."

Colrig smirked.

"Yes," she sighed, "and that is why I should humble myself to work with the wolf-child."

"Argue as you will, but I think you two would have quite the remarkable relationship. Do you have any children of your own?"

"No, Zeir and I have tried before, with no success. You?"

He nodded, though he lost his smile. "I'll let Voln know you are interested"

"Do you want me to leave the five municipalities in the hands of someone else?"

"No. You don't need to spend all your time with Voln. Just help him out a little. Do you know the Pinnacles well?"

"I have only visited once or twice. Mountainous regions are not my favorite, and the Pinnacles are the worst in the area."

"Maybe I will join you. I like to think of myself as an outdoorsman. But we shall see. I have much to do."

"As do I. As do we all."

She turned to him with a guilty smile. The question had eaten at her like the guilt that accompanied it. "Of course you had Zhaes members before the fall of Kzhek, but... how did you... did you have any Thanes with you like you did in Chuss and Tchoyas?"

He smiled. "You know that answer, Aerhee. If we had any, they would have helped us. But I know what you are trying to reach."

She raised her eyebrow.

"You know I do my research. I don't blame you for what you did to Caser Zhil, rather, what was done to her. I was not the man I am now before the Allegiant. She did her share of the work and her fate was a result of the Zhaes nobility, not your actions alone."

If he forgives so freely, what past has he hidden? Perd you, Aerhee, learn to forgive. If you deserve it, so does he. "So she was a member of the Allegiant?"

He nodded. "As was Thane Sorn, as you might have guessed. Their sacrifices are greater than any I have offered. Don't let their deaths weigh you down but inspire you to do good as the woman you have become."

Perd me, this is all too good. Forgive me, Laeih, for what I have done. Aid me that I might repay the debt.

"Your wounds shouldn't bother you for a while. I enjoyed this conversation, but I best let you be free. I've heard plenty about the Krall of your Court, but I have never had the pleasure of meeting him myself."

"Pleasure? It is quite the opposite."

"Caser, are you sure you do not want us to join you?"

She gave a small bow of gratitude to the Sleff guards who stood outside of the Krall's chamber on the highest floor of the Canton of Veneration. "Krall Vheen is a civil man, never the kind to assault anyone. He prefers to leave the unwholesome tasks to assassins."

"Klen—Laeih be with you."

"May they both be with you as well, Sleffmen."

He unlocked the door and pulled it open, watching her as she entered the dim chamber.

It was not a prison cell, but a well-furnished room. The Krall had committed no crimes other than remaining loyal to what he believed best.

The vilest of tyrants always serve what they believe to be the greater good.

He was not the greatest man, nor was he a *great* man by her standards. Krall Trhet had treated her well during her imprisonment, but she counted him among the worst people she had ever known. If she were to overcome the biases and intolerance of her past, she had to learn to treat even the worst with kindness.

"Sit, I have guards at the ready."

The Krall turned from the window as he watched the last light of day passing beyond the distant mountains. He sat in a well-cushioned leather chair. "Caser, a man cannot bite the hand that feeds him."

He swept black hair behind his ears, though most of it was too short to stay. He wore the same clothes he had during his capture, refusing to change from his royal regalia. His crown remained, but his disheveled appearance and malodor made him seem a mummer that could never find a role.

"I would be more comfortable if you listened to my requests."

"No, *'Your Grace'*? Are we beyond formalities? I suppose you have done away with order, hearing how you treat the so-called 'loyalists'."

She stared at him, perplexed.

He smiled "Don't worry, I haven't left my chamber, but I hear enough about the state of the Court."

"From whom?"

"Why don't you take a seat, Caser? It would be better to have a conversation rather than an interrogation."

"Maybe for you." She hated sitting and was growing tired of incessant pestering to relax when serious matters needed all that her attention could offer.

"Might I have some wine?"

She shook her head.

He shrugged. "You were one of the best, one of my favorites among the nobility."

"What are you aiming to gain, Zhaesman?"

"*Zhaesman*? Have you already given my throne to another? Is there no justice in this Court?" He chuckled as if he were having a casual conversation with a friend in a tavern.

"The nobility as we knew it is no more."

"Why not? Why can't we join once you recognize the errors of your ways?"

"Your words are evidence enough themselves. You know that this–"

"Let me guess," he interrupted, "you want to feed me with more Sleff propaganda? You are not the first to try, and I am no closer to buying into your rebel sect for a shallow promise of freedom. Let us have a more meaningful conversation, Aerhee. Tell me about your childhood."

Her brows furrowed and her fists clenched behind her back.

"No? Then what about your family? What about *your father?*"

"I can punish you for reasons other than *physical* assaults."

"No need to threaten. This is a *conversation, Priesswoman.* Surprised that I know about your past? Don't be. I know about all of my subordinates. I chose my diverse cast of noblemen for a reason. Your unique history is one of the many reasons that I chose you for Caser, but don't worry, I am not as bigoted towards Priessmen as are most Zhaesmen. I might even know more about your father's trial than you do."

She stepped closer, her distrust unwavering.

"I know how to capture an audience." He remained silent, flashing eyes between her and the seat across from him.

She clenched her jaw and sat with perfect posture.

"Now we can have a civil conversation."

"How–"

He raised a hand to stop her. "Patience, *Aerhee.* I will withhold my secrets until you allow us to have a conversation."

"You never cared to speak with me before all of this." *I know the loneliness that chokes you.*

"A man can change. Isn't that the purpose of imprisonment? Let us go back to that day when the statue was created. Why do you stay?"

"What do you mean?"

"You know very well what I mean. Why did you stay in Zhaes? Why not return to Priess when our Court rejected you?"

Did his voice hint at sincerity? The last thing she expected was an honest conversation with the Krall.

You came to speak to him about a compromise. Do not let him control the conversation. "Personal matters," she replied.

"Avoid it and I will avoid your father's trial."

"Great, I would rather not revisit my past"

"Let the secrets of the Seers rest." He smirked, noticing her eyes opening wide as he mentioned the Seers. "Yes, the Bronze Seers."

She forced herself to focus. "We need your cooperation to restore Zhaes to its full glory."

"Oh, come on, Aerhee. No interest in learning more about your past? I have–"

"Why are you so captivated by my *personal* history?"

He lost his smile.

"You're acting like a tavern drunkard trying to coerce me into buying you another drink! You must have at least ten years on me, yet you act like a child. What could you possibly gain from talking about my deceased father's suffering? Talking about the statue as if it is some scandalous piece of gossip only makes me want to pour molten bronze on you myself! Perding under realms, Gorrhin, is nothing sacred? People are dying because of a perding disagreement. *Our* people, not some foreigners that you can ignore. If we cannot resolve this, you and I will die with the Courts. Is that what you want? Do you want to continue to patronize me until I succumb to your cruel games until you know my weaknesses? You want to see me break character? Oh, how *mighty* the Zhaes Krall! The man who made the concrete Caser cry over her broken past!"

As she had hoped, her rebuke had purchased the Krall's silence.

"You hear me now, *Your Grace*? Thank Laeih. This is *my* conversation."

"Then what do you want? Fayis? I fear I cannot help you there. You saw how Royss dominated the room. I am sure that the man would have nothing to do with me now that he is free from my authority. If I am silent, his voice is unhindered. But you *do* know Sheath. She could be of value to our side."

"*Our*?"

"Of course, Aerhee. This conversation may have begun undignified. I ask your forgiveness. Laeih knows I want nothing to do with the goals of the Harmony Allegiant, but I would like to see an end to this madness as much as you do."

She stared at him, holding her mouth closed, but her eyes open.

"What did you expect? That I would rejoice? Regardless of one's beliefs, death is a tragedy. Because of Royss and his pursuits, we are stuck with a madman ruling Tchoyas and a tyrant leading the Zhaesmen."

"Do you have a solution?"

"You need your close friend at your side. Thane Leisa, Sheath, has the charisma and the relationships to help bind alliances that are crumbling. She is trying to steer Royss back to reason."

"But she is just one person. This is a conflict of nations."

"And nations are composed of people. One person initiated a rebellion and joined like-minded people to create a movement, a movement that is becoming a nation of its own."

"What do you want?"

"What do I want, Aerhee? I could ask the same of you. I want Facet to return to what it was a year ago."

"That is what Krall Trhet sought."

"And so I fear my desires will not come to fruition. I want the best outcome. Forgive my initial approach to our conversation, but we must return to where we began. Sheath is not the only valuable asset. We need Thane Gromm. Royss annoys me, but I *fear* Thane Gromm. He may not want to join us, but I do not need a Foreteller to show me that Gromm's side will prevail."

She had feared that they would be involved. Her pain continued to circulate back to the Patriarchy. Hearing the Krall's fears made her doubt any remaining hope that the Patriarchy was insignificant in this war. Their hand had not yet revealed itself, but the day would come. For all she knew, this could be their war, not the people's.

"Is he one of the dissenters?" she asked as she rubbed the folds of her dress.

"The Seers? I have reason to believe either way. He is not the Root Lord, I know that much."

"Then what do you know?"

He tilted his head to look at her with a gaze that seemed to say, *you know where this is going.*

"I will listen as long as you swear honesty under Laeih."

"I swear it."

"Then you have my permission to speak."

"Very well. I will not patronize you as a child or a plebeian. Your father's crime could not have been committed at a worse time. Even if you deny his involvement with those who lent him the coins, all who took part in his trial saw him as a Seer. I have read these reports well. What do you recall from his trial?"

"Just the Seer title being mentioned during the trial. I was young and remember little else. I know they condemned us as Priessmen, but my mother always told me that they had another excuse for his incrimination. Where did you learn of this? Gromm?"

"Laeih's mercy, no. Most of it was through the Canton of Veneration and less reliable Scholars."

She would have laughed if Gromm did not intimidate her. She held a respectful distance from Thane Gromm when possible, though it was more out of vast differences of opinion. Was her low regard for the Thane of Scholarship enough? Should she *fear* him as much as the Krall did? *Did I make a mistake by turning to him early on in the Sleff Endowed investigation?* His opinion of her was worse than hers for him. Her hateful departure from Fayis was sure to condemn her as his enemy.

"Less reliable? What do you mean?" She sat down on a wooden chair near the Krall but retained a comfortable distance.

"Less reliable to other Scholars. Some take their vows less seriously. Their willingness to speak of their own sacred oaths proves that they would be a poor ally, but that does not discredit the intrigue they are willing to share, especially if you make the right offers. Do not forget that the least loyal of your enemies make poor allies, but great informants."

"And the worst of your enemies make the greatest allies. Is that what you wish to be done with Thane Gromm?"

"I would not count him as an enemy. I don't know where he stands in the Patriarchy, whether it be with the Bronze Seers or the true Scholars, but I recognize his influence. Enough about him."

"My father," she almost whispered, "and the Bronze Seers."

"And you can't remember him dealing with them or anyone discreetly in Priess?"

She tried not to take that as an insult to her father's memory. "No."

"Well, your father's incident occurred when the Patriarchy began to recognize a division in their order. Years before, they alerted the Kralls of their concern, knowing that a compromise in their organization would endanger the livelihood of Facet."

"How so?"

"I am not sure."

"But what do they do that makes the Patriarchy so frightened?"

"Does anyone know what the Patriarchy does?"

She shook her head.

"All I know is that peace never faltered until the Seers rose. As time passed, the name, *the Bronze Seers,* came up. They were a sect within the patriarchy that wanted to direct the Patriarchy's power for their gain, not 'as the Root Lord desired.' Perhaps the Root Lord is a tyrant." He shrugged. "We don't know."

"We trust in blind obedience."

"Exactly."

"But the Bronze Seers have gone public, are they not?"

"The criminal organization that names itself Bronze Seers is not the organization itself, but one of the public tenants of their organization. The only *true* Seers are members of the Patriarchy of Scholars. Again, that does not dismiss the credibility of the contraband merchants and assassins that claim the title.

"Your father was found to have a connection to the Seers before their public representatives were permitted to exist. He was found at the height of the hunt and was executed. I trust you if you do not think him to be a member of their societal branches. If that is so, he was an unfortunate dove flying between two enemy archers. An honest man caught in a crossfire."

I have always known that. Regardless of their excuse, he was an innocent victim in a war between greater powers. "You said they '*were permitted to exist.*' Are you saying that you have allowed these sycophants to traitorous Scholars to conduct crimes? Even under the title of Bronze Seers?"

"They are monitored by a member of the nobility."

"By whom?"

He was reluctant to speak.

"It's not Gromm, is it?"

"Royss."

"The man is almost a criminal himself!" She forced a laugh.

"He monitors their work. I know referencing the public Seers and the Scholar Seers might seem convoluted. What you must recognize is that the public '*Seers*' focus on creature trade, addictive substances, and some other questionable methods of profit. I believe that they are mere servants to the Scholar Seers, who do much more than we realize. Royss managed to remove forgery from the public Seer agenda, but we are sure that they take part in the organ market regardless of their denial."

The Organ Market. Laeih damn them to the under realms.

She had stomached the sacrifice of children for the betterment of society, but stealing those organs to make the snakes grow in power was the greatest sin she could imagine.

"Then what am I to do with this information?" she asked.

"I thought the information would help you find closure. With your disdain for the Patriarchy set aside, you can utilize them to help us find peace. I do not suggest that you seek Gromm, but there are many Scholars who would be willing to help inside and outside of our Court."

"What could they do for us?"

"I told you, their power is greater than that of the Courts. I am allowed autonomy, but I believe that some of the other Kralls are puppets for their Thanes of Scholarship."

"I'm sorry to say that I am more lost than I was before you started to explain this. You encourage me to seek peace and to find help within the Patriarchy, but you still do not know what they do. Aside from that, I am even more sure now that I cannot trust the Scholars. I cannot tell the difference between a Seer Scholar and a true Scholar. This cyclic conversation is leading nowhere and my greatest concern is that I do not understand what you want from it. You speak of peace yet offer no clear way to achieve it."

"Because I do not know where to find it. I simply recognize that division in Facet became more insidious as the Seers grew in power. Their influence reached a peak right before the Courts nearly went to war over the Pact of Province. Now that war has come, and I fear that their will is progressing. Whether they caused the rebellions–"

"Or discovered harvesting."

He nodded. "I can offer little assistance while imprisoned, but I suppose the sum of my advice is to be wary of those you trust. Hold the trustworthy closer to you than your most prized possession. Is Gromm a Bronze Seer or a loyal Scholar? Has Royss learned anything by observing their public representatives? Are any other Thanes involved? You trust Sheath, so reach out to her. *This* is what I ask of you. A true friend is never too far. You are bound to this Aerhee. Your Father died because of the Bronze Seers. If you do not want his sacrifice to be in vain, we must hasten. It is time for the Patriarchy's will to be revealed. I fear that a greater war than ours is happening in their sects."

"But what about harvesting?"

"Do not be so myopic. Can you not see that the dispute over harvesting is a mere tenant of a greater problem? Our ancestors did not go to war over lines drawn on a map, but that their will might prevail. We jest about Court Priess appraising themselves with their prideful Ideal, but the sobering truth is that we are all prideful towards our own definition of benevolence. Humankind's desires will always be corrupt as long as they hold on to their own will over that of the gods. Every battle that was ever fought or will be fought *is* a holy war."

What *was* she to do? Colrig wanted to send her to the Pinnacles with the wolf Endower to investigate yet another rebellion. Now Krall Vheen wanted her to seek the help of her fellow Zhaesmen to investigate the Bronze Seers. Both enticed her, but perhaps for the wrong reasons. The Pinnacle rebellions granted her the opportunity to force her idea of Zhaes righteousness on them, when she wasn't even sure her stance was in line with Laeih's will. The offer to return her focus to the Patriarchy fueled her long-enduring rage.

"This is a lot to consider, Aerhee, but I hope something I said will make a difference. There are few with whom I would discuss my personal philosophies. Consider it a victory, Caser."

"I never expected our conversation to lead beyond empty pleas and dissonant arguments."

"It has been a pleasure." He smiled and reached for a drink that was not there and shrugged. "Return as you please, and I am not saying that because I grow lonesome. Whoever dictates my imprisonment has been surprisingly humane."

"I am sure the time will come when I will need some *sound* advice. Know that is a great compliment from me."

"One of the few I have ever heard from you. If only things were different in the world, we could see each other under different circumstances, you and your husband across from me and my family at the dining table."

"You never seemed to care for that before."

"Being humbled makes one reflect upon the insignificant pleasantries that–in fact–are the most valuable. Tell me, do you know anything about the whereabouts of my wife and children?"

"I am afraid not."

He nodded. His grin was frail. "As I expected."

"Do you want me to look for them?"

"No, it is best that we leave them out of this. My wife loathed politics, but *perd,* she was brilliant. I am sure I will see them when we take care of this. Pray for them, if you will."

"I will pray for you as well, Your Grace."

"It is more than I deserve." He stood and adjusted his belt a loop smaller. "I am always here if you need a break from the Chussmen and Sleffmen. We may not agree on everything, but it can be a relief to talk to another Zhaes nobleman from time to time. Now, off with you, do what you must. You have given me enough pity for the day." He walked over

to a bookshelf, skimming through the same ten volumes for what must
be the hundredth time.

"Whole is the Holy, Your Grace."

"Whole is the Holy, Caser."

Aerhee closed the door softly as she left and gave both of the guards a
nod in passing.

She had no further business to conduct in the Canton of Veneration.
All the other imprisoned Thanes were kept in the Canton's outposts.
The Canton felt uncomfortably empty without Thane Lettre present.
He was one of the few who had escaped after the fall of Kzhek. Where
was he now? Was he still a piece in Krall Trhet's depraved game?

All the Cantons were left nearly empty. Even though most of the
Proctors were likely somewhere in the city, they feared returning to a
place under control of foreigners, regardless of their stance on harvesting.
The city's image had been repaired since the battle, but the underlying
infrastructure was still a ruin of social unrest. Aerhee had much to
accomplish. She wanted to avenge her father but was caught by her obligations as a Zhaes citizen. She was the only free Zhaes noble in the city.
The only one capable of preserving their crumbling civilization. Colrig
had become too focused on harvesting, but Krall Vheen had helped her
see that it was a mere piece in the conflicts that shook the core of Facet.
The public seemed to be like a man who was concerned that his steak was
being overcooked, ignoring the fact that his whole house was set aflame.

She proceeded down the hall, onto the staircase and began her descent
to the main level to leave for... *for what*? Where could she begin? She felt
encumbered by the weight of her Court but knew that she could do very
little herself. She needed aid. A friend.

Sheath.

She needed her closest friend.

A guard stood near the door and opened it as she left. The night was
rolling in with familiar mist. The light rainfall was a beautiful reminder

that she was home, though its charm was overshadowed by the unsettling presence in the doorway.

"Colrig said we are to work together. Hope you have a sense of humor, Zhaeswoman." Voln spat thick phlegm on the Canton's wall.

CHAPTER TWELVE

THE BATTLE FOR PAIELL - PART II

"*Strike the largest first.*"

Yetrik could speak the word "*kill.*" It was not a problem with the percussive language of patting his zlatog, but he did not want to admit that he was ending the lives of his opponents.

He could speak to Avra with screeches, but the percussion was more intimate. Likewise, she responded to his pats with a humming that was only detectable when he placed his hands on her.

"*Sighted ahead, dropping now.*"

He braced himself for the rush of wind. He had trained for less than two months, not nearly enough time to become as skilled as Runith, yet he looked forward to sharing his talent with his fellow Beastling.

She dove. He pressed against her like a startled boy to his father. His face pressed against the thick fur that circled her neck and upper torso. He had handle holds on his harness, but she did not mind him pulling on the fur. With the side of his face against her, he could smell her rich, stoney scent that reminded him of a rainy mountainside covered in sagebrush and pine. Her predatory screech was muffled with the fur covering his ear, yet the tone was made clearer with his head pressed tightly against her.

He shook, imagining being with his father fishing on the eastern sea. The shaking of her wings and rush of wind felt like an enormous wave striking the boat's bow, though he knew it was the rattle of her claws grabbing the Gorger that he had targeted. Her claws and teeth tore the enemy apart as they ascended again. The less he thought about it, the better he felt. He knew he was a coward for turning away from the consequences of his actions, but this was his first battle. He wanted to banish his guilt until he was ready for it, yet never wanted to forget. Guilt keeps one moral. If he were ever to shrug off the cost of a life, he would be no greater than his worst enemies.

It was too easy to ignore the pain, but he did so as he commanded her to choose another target.

As he learned to communicate with beasts like Avra, he learned that each had their own personality. Each was their own being, just like any human. She seemed to like him, but he was still trying to understand her expressions. Not only was their language different, but they were a different species with a culture of their own.

She hummed as she tossed the torn remains of her victim over the enemy troops, showering them with the gore of yet another comrade. *"Is this all you want me to do? Shred their soldiers until they retreat?"*

"I don't think they will retreat soon."

"That last one was small. One of the others finished off the other large one."

I should have known a Gorger would be tougher. "Your voice is louder than mine. Call Khoga."

"Do you want Khoga or her rider?"

"Ask her to ask Kevlen what we should do now. Their troops are diminished and the Priessmen have advanced beyond the fallen tower."

Avra screeched her call, which found Khoga on the left flank. She relayed the command.

He did not hear Kohga's reply but knew that Avra had heard her with her extraordinary ears.

"Kevlen wants us on the right flank. The Priessmen are struggling and need our help. He is going to hit the right flank with a sonar sweep and wants us to do the same on the right."

A month of their combat training was not enough to make him a warrior, but he was determined to make the best of their investment.

"I am with you, Yetrik. Firm foundation."

Had she *heard* the vibrations of his fear? Were his emotions so obvious to her?

"Right, firm foundation." She was a creature born of Court Priess but was more free than any of the Courts' citizens. He did not want to bind her to any human politics, but she was involved in war, robbing her of that choice. If she were to be attached to a culture, he made sure that she recognized the ideals of his culture as he tried to accept hers.

Avra stopped mid-air, flapping to stay up, and called back. Yetrik heard the faint reply of one or two more zlatogs.

"Thii is joining Khoga and her rider. Hothel and his rider will be joining us."

"Will there be enough of us?"

"I know as much as you do."

Seeing how comfortable the zlatogs were in combat caused him to forget that this was a new experience for them as well. They were predators, but never had they been forced to fight armies. He was comfortable with humans. It was other Beastlings that he feared. Gorgers were the only problem, but he had not forgotten what had happened in Kzhek. Even if the zlatogs could not be controlled by anyone other than their riders, he worried that enemy waves would invite larger beasts to challenge the zlatogs. His battlefield prowess was insufficient. His allies were no better than him. He would disappoint, hurt, or even kill others.

"Dropping for ground advance," hummed Avra.

He had no choice. Avra had killed the others with her claws.. These would fall to his blade. He would kill those who never wronged him with the chosen weapon of the Priess zlatog riders.

"Firm foundation, Yetrik. I will be at your side."

"And I, at yours, Avra." Was this the kinship of siblings reunited? One of trust, unwavering and familial love unbreakable? Avra was the greater embodiment of his soul. She had become a new limb, one so ingrained in his very being that losing her would cause him to perish. Two months of time, but a connection stronger than an eternity

"Twenty paces out," she screeched as they landed.

Twenty paces was but a breath of time to plan his initial attack. Avra's boat-sized wings blocked his vision until he dismounted.

Before him stood the essence of his worst anxieties. The line of enemy Sleffmen took a step back as Avra landed but stood their ground as Yetrik dismounted.

His pulse pounded. He focused on each breath. *Frighten them into a retreat.* The Priess commanders decreed that they were to slay any rebels, diminishing their greater forces with all the brutality that they could muster. Yetrik, however, bent that command. He would obey it enough to serve his purpose but would do his best to prevent as many senseless deaths as he could. *Victory is not founded on the anguish of others, but in the peace offerings of the victors.*

To entice such a retreat, he had to engage in combat.

Avra hissed at the approaching line of Sleffmen and lowered her head to touch her right golden horn against his side.

"Take it."

The tip of her horn bent the length of Yetrik's forearm, a straight line deviating from the spiral. The straight portion differentiated itself furthermore from the golden horn, for it was a shaft. He gripped it with his right hand and twisted it out from her horn, revealing a golden sickle that had been sheathed in her horn. The double-edged blade was a weapon of the finest craftsmanship.

Yetrik glanced to his left, noticing that the other Beastling had removed her hornblade. She was distant enough to face her own army, but Yetrik felt a breath of reassurance that he would not be facing the bulk of the enemy's flank alone.

The line of rebels ran at him, spears raised. Yetrik inhaled, stood in a power stance, and gave Avra his signal by slamming the flat of his hornblade twice on his left gauntlet.

Avra let out a booming screech. Yetrik focused on the tone, utilizing his beastcalling ears to brace himself from the sonic attack. He remained standing, but still felt the pulsations of her screech that left a line of Sleffmen inebriated, even falling some as they clenched the sides of their helmets. He felt the strength of her call, but it did not rattle him. Beast and rider, they were in tune.

He sprang forth, banishing inhibitions as he swung the hornblade across any vulnerable gaps between their armor. Avra followed behind to trample upon and finish the fallen soldiers while he took the stunned and startled. The crescent of his blade swung his enemies to the floor as he sliced through their necks and pulled down, leaving them to bleed out. Some Sleffmen rushed him, but he spun his blade around to strike them down. His might was outmatched by any Gorger, but the organ within him still gave him a distinct advantage over the soldiers that rushed him.

His strikes were often imprecise, still wounding his enemies, but not finishing them. Avra helped where she could with more screeches and claws but remained back while Yetrik faced the more resilient Sleffmen. She was mighty, but not impervious to the blades that did little but dent Yetrik's elite Priess armor.

"Perd you Priessman!" A berserker rushed with a large rectangular shield. Avra tried to blast him with a sonic assault, but he stood impervious, shouting as if he were triumphing over a crippling headache.

Yetrik stepped back.

He did not know how he would stop the Sleffman but was sure that he would not be beaten. Deilf had willed him to fight, and the Priessmen stood with him, their troops not too distant.

Hold strong, side dodge, swing in a–

Yetrik was tossed ten paces back as the Sleffman slammed him with a shield nearly as tall as he was. He could not stand. Fear shook his every nerve. Hatred for himself and anxiety for the future left him in a cowardly paralysis.

He was the central character in his story and could not fall. Things were supposed to work out in his favor, just like they always had.

Yetrik rolled to the left as the Sleffman's axe fell on him. He was not quick enough to dodge. The axe blade clipped the edge of his hornblade and knocked it away, though it remained in his grip.

The Sleffman advanced again, holding his shield at his side as he rushed to strike Yetrik again.

Yetrik held his blade up, feigning a block but dropped and lunged with his good leg to hook his enemy's leg with his hornblade, pulling him down with another sideward roll.

His left leg pulsed. Burning sensations crept up his thigh.

He caught himself and stood to jump on the fallen Sleffman with a mighty two-handed strike into the exposed skin between his enemy's cheek-guards. Shimmering gold fell in the center of the fist-sized gap of the Sleffman's helmet and split his face like a hatchet.

He pried the blade side to side, spreading the face further apart in mashed pieces, eventually freeing it from the dark red crevice that had once been a face.

Yetrik's left leg collapsed under the weight of his trembling body. He feared losing consciousness and pulled the Sleffman's shield to cover himself.

The moment was stolen from him as a Sleffman kicked the shield in the air.

A vile smile met Yetrik's cowardice. "Perding chi–"

The Sleffman's body flew away before he had a chance to finish his insult. Before anyone else could swarm him, a sonic screech shook the ground.

Avra flew in, exposing herself to knock down lines of Sleffmen like a ghete running rampant through a hall of statues.

"Mount" she hissed.

He wanted to argue for the sake of bravery, insisting that he could stand, but he knew that was the poorest of lies.

He pressed up off of the ground, using his hornblade for stability. Two Sleffmen, smaller than the berserker, rushed him with frantic swings of their hand spears. *Deilf help me hold.*

Yetrik had little confidence in his remaining strength but took advantage to use skill over their uncalculated rage.

He did not want to risk another roll, not knowing what it would do to his leg. He kept his weight on his right leg out front while the left was loose in the back. Riding Avra had helped him improve his balance, yet he still worried that even a small fall would ensure his demise.

Avra roared at more oncoming Sleffmen. He was alone.

He wanted to shout, proclaiming his actions to be dedicated to the people of his Court or to his god. His desires fell unfulfilled to fatigue as he let out a loud groaning shout as the Sleffmen approached him.

They raised their spears, each tip the length of a shortsword for a downward strike characteristic of their furious combat maneuvers.

Yetrik raised his hornblade, swinging it from the left and catching their blades in a sideswipe with the crook of the brade's ark. He had underestimated the sharpness and power of the hornblade and was pleasantly surprised when it cut the first hand spear in half and knocked the other from its wielder's hands with a large notch cut in its side.

Their surprise left them stunned, caught between a decision to retreat or attack with their bare fists. Before they could act, Yetrik spun the hornblade in his hand, bringing the crook of it back towards the Sleffmen with a swift swipe.

His right abdomen surged with the strength of his new organ paired with an adrenaline-fueled rush. The strike decapitated the soldier and landed the blade deep in the other's neck. His suspicions of Beastlings strength were confirmed, though he knew he could have swung through the necks of three or more soldiers if he had the organ of a Gorger.

His left leg shook, and he fell to his right knee, pulling the limp Sleffman forward with him with his hornblade still halfway through his neck. He ripped it free, and the Sleffmen fell into his lap. He screamed and scrambled back from the dead-eyed stare.

Before any other Sleffmen could capitalize from his collapse, Avra pulled him back with her wing. He climbed atop her as his left leg dangled with dead weight. She ran back from the battle and took off in flight.

Yetrik readjusted himself on the leather mount, then laid his head against her thick fur. He knew she would have something to say, but all he wanted was a moment to breathe with no one pursuing him.

"Be more cautious next time," she warned.

Next time.

The assurance of returning to combat spoiled his moment of relaxation. The Sleff troops fell by the masses, but he knew it would not be the end. He would once again be forced into the slaughter before he could prepare himself.

Prepare. He hoped that he never felt *prepared,* for the day when he had to murder. Regardless of his hesitancy, he no longer had a choice in the war over harvesting. He had become one of *them.* He was an Endowed. This war was fought to preserve *his* kind.

"I will try." He replied by patting her side.

"Aside from your initial injury," she hummed, *"your kills were remarkable."*

"I still have much to learn."

"We all do. Such is life."

"Where are you taking me?"

"Eurythrins. While you finished those last two, I called to the others. They told me we could find the healers near the Tower of Alms. Did you not hear me?"

He remained silent. Staring off her side at the dilapidated field below with the same dead stare he had seen on the half-decapitated Sleffmen.

"I suppose you were distracted. The battlefield is deafening."

"Does it hurt your ears?" he asked.

"Size does not determine sensitivity. I can hear better but I am not burdened by overstimulation."

Avra began her descent beside a billowing tower of smoke. He could hear at least two other zlatogs below and their riders' calls. Yetrik had learned to recognize the distinction between a Beastling's imitation and the call of a beast. It was like that of two bards playing the same song. Each hit the right notes, but they varied in pitch and pacing.

Avra's wings beat faster, but her landing was like a feather landing on a lake. Two zlatogs were locked in conversation, perched on the broken walls of the remains of the Tower of Alms. Avra lowered herself to ease Yerik's dismount. His leg pulsed with each heartbeat as he stepped down. The pain constricted his thigh and numbed his lower leg.

"Hey, Eurythrin, get over here!" a familiar voice shouted.

Yetrik squinted and clenched his teeth as his vision started to fade.

Someone lifted him up, draping his arm around their back.

He turned to see Kevlen, dripping red sweat as he rushed Yetrik forward.

Semi, you look splendid today. Me? I am well. I am more like you now. I understand the pain and pressure of such a calling. I know I have much to learn. How are you? Is it as sweet as you imagined to be back in Thusk?

"Yetrik! Open those eyes!"

I wish I could be at your side. Some of the Priessmen are fine people, but I struggle to trust others. I struggle to trust anyone in this endeavor. I miss having a reliable Gruthwoman at my side.

"He is almost there. Keep holding!"

I will come to you, I promise. I will be at your side. Soon, Semi.

"Open your perding eyes!"

"Push his pulse, Eurythrin."

Soon.

Yetrik came to himself with a gasp, feeling like he could grasp reality again as it had slipped away. Hot blood rushed through his veins.

Kevlen and another Priess Beastling looked over him while a Sleff Eurythrin closed her eyes and rubbed her hands across his bare leg.

"There's our valiant bastard!" Kevlen chuckled.

"I–"

"No, not yet." Kevlen laid a hand on Yetrik to keep him down. "She is still working on your leg."

"Did I lose too much blood?"

They turned to the Eurythrin, who shook her head and opened her eyes, hands still on his leg.

"No, you'll be fine."

He tightened his abdomen to sit up and looked at his leg. It was bound in a cloth wrap, a red line seeping through.

"It's in better condition than it was minutes ago," said the Eurythrin. "The blade barely penetrated your armor, but most of the damage will be from the blunt force of attack. I mended the bone's fractures, but you will be sore and bruised for the coming days."

"Good enough for him to stand?" asked Kevlen.

"Yes, but–"

"Come on up, Gruthman." He lent his hand down to help Yetrik stand.

The pain was pestering, but much less than it had before he collapsed. Kevlen chuckled. "When did you last eat?"

"Yesterday." Yetrik replied as he rubbed his eyes.

"Too much time without nourishment for your new organ. I know it is only midday, but you are fortunate to have lasted this long before collapsing. Remember that we Endowed require much more sustenance than others. You always need something to fuel the extra organ, especially if you are using it as much as you did today."

"So it wasn't the leg that caused this?"

"I already told you it was not," grunted the Eurythrin as she returned various vials to a traveling chest. She removed a dark brown sphere the size of a large fist and handed it to him. "Eat this."

"What is it?" He grabbed with the tips of his fingers, observing it like a child holding a seeping slug.

"Picky? You have been with Zhaesmen for too long. It's made from nut paste, oats, seeds, and some honey for sweetness."

"Enough to keep a man fed for a day," said Kevlen. "Keep beastcalling and you'll need another by dusk, and that's not even including your usual meals."

"I was always told I should put on some muscle to look like a true Gruthman." He took a bite, it dried his mouth and was as thick as overcooked steak, yet more relieving than sleep after a week of dreamless nights. A bite of pure cinnamon complemented the nutty conglomeration, leaving his stomach satisfied and his jaw exhausted.

"That should help the healing as well," said the Eurythrin, enjoying her own nut ball.

A Priessman ran to Avra and tossed a full pike into her mouth. He did not envy those who were tasked with carting all the food for the zlatogs into Court Sleff. At least the cold helped preserve the fish.

Yetrik limped alongside Kevlen, each step becoming easier as they neared Khoga. "Why are you here already? Were you injured as well?"

Kevlen breathed a pompous laugh. He was as Prideful as any rumored Priessman, yet was not condescending. His blatant tone seemed somewhat of an irony, as if he were insulting his own people.

"We caused the left flank to retreat before we could kill twenty of their troopers."

How many did I defeat, three? And the other Beastlings at my side? Why am I concerned with my murderous statistics? Shouldn't I feel proud of doing less harm?

And this is only the beginning.

Deilf preserve my piety.

"Don't worry about it, Gruthman, there's always next time."

Don't remind me. "Should I head back to finish off the right flank?"

Yetrik worried Kevlen would laugh at him. Instead, he smiled as he stroked Khoga's mane. "Two others saw you struggling and jumped in to finish them while you came back to heal."

"And the center?"

"All of them retreated." He patted Yetrik on the back and swung himself up onto Khoga's back.

"Wait—so it's over?"

"Come on, you should know that these *Harmony Allegiant* fanatics like to return with a second wave. Time to recuperate and prepare for the worst." Kevlen grabbed Khoga's reins.

"Then where are you going?"

"Not far. We need to remain in the city to protect, should the Sleffmen return.. The Krall wants to speak with the Priess Endowed. As far as I am concerned, I am the head Endowed. Are you coming?"

"Do you need me?"

"No, but I am starting to see why the Zhaesmen enjoyed having a Gruthman at their side. Hearing that you were so willing to return to battle was not anything I would expect to hear from these other Beast-lings. Let's see you prove that Gruth Ideal even further."

Yetrik nodded. "I'll follow you on Avra, if, of course, she is willing."

"I don't see why not. Khoga listens to whatever I command her to do."

Yetrik started towards Avra but paused to turn back to Kevlen. "So we are sure that the Sleff Krall stands with us over this matter?"

"*This*? The war? Of course, why would you think otherwise?"

"I," he thought of Krall Trhet, "I never know who to believe. Conflict polarizes people. There is no mediator. If we are not sure the Krall is with us, this may be Allegiant trickery."

"I doubt it. Hasn't each Krall and Thane decreed their stance?"

"Perhaps that was how this all began, but riots and zealots have complicated things. Who wanted us to meet with the Krall?"

"Terin."

Terin seeks his own desires.

Yetrik turned back, not noticing that the Sleff Eurythrin was approaching. She took Kevlen's hand and sat behind him on Khoga's back.

"Follow quickly. I'm hoping the Krall can serve her guests well, even if she is a–" He turned back to smile at the Eurythrin, who gave him a spiteful grin. "Just hurry."

Yetrik ran, but slowed to a limp as the throb returned to his thigh. Avra lowered herself, eager to fly.

"*Missed me?*" He patted Avra and rubbed her mane. He checked to ensure that his hornbalde was secure, knowing that it was a wasted check. It was secure, as were most things in his life, yet most of his worries perpetuated. He had never been able to cast them off or ignore their presence, for they had become a part of him. Learning to accept that had been one of the greatest reliefs he had ever tasted. Recognizing their inevitability did not grant them control, it only diminished their power.

"*Hunger was enough of a distraction.*" She replied.

"*So you did miss me? And you admit it?*"

She emitted a rhythmic clicking and her tongue swiped across her fangs. One of the most pleasant aspects of being a Beastling was learning to understand how others expressed joy.

He reached up to grab onto the mount's handles. She pulled her wing back to help lift him up. His leg hurt, but he did not need the assistance. What he needed was to know that someone cared for him. Even if that someone was what others perceived as a nightmare incarnate, it felt good to be valued.

"*Follow Khoga. Time for us to meet the Sleff Krall.*"

CHAPTER THIRTEEN

ABANDONED HOPE

"Perd me to death!" Port shouted as he ran from the battlefield.

He had pushed the troops too far and waited too long to retreat and cursed himself for not pulling back as soon as they had arrived.

He tried to shout words of encouragement as he ran past limping Sleff troopers, but he had not the mind to offer words of hope when he had no hope to offer. He glanced back. Despite his hopes, the Priess and Sleff loyalist were not pulling back despite the retreat.

Perding kulfs taking any opportunity they have to bleed us further.

If it was a simple retreat, he would have had hope but going south to Bruten complicated matters. Going across the Court would leave their corpses scattered along the roadway. Without carriages, the injured would have no chance at survival. He was grateful for the retreat letter from Kzhek, having been too long without guidance, but feared that it had arrived too late.

"Captain," a voice panted at his side, "will Heitt forgive me if I end my suffering here?"

"What?" he coughed.

"I don't want this anymore." The Sleffman slowed.

"Keep going! We need you!" Port stopped for a moment, staring at the tears welling in the Sleffman's smiling eyes.

"Heitt take me." He opened his arms wide and slowed to a stop.

Port did not know the man. Would it be unjust to let him surrender when they had so much to fight for? The man had made his decision. It was Port's duty to respect his ally's last wish.

"Godspeed, Sleffman. Pious is the Giver!" Port gave the man a farewell with the Sleff salute.

"Pious is the Giver!" The Sleffman's shout grew increasingly quiet as Port ran onward, leaving the man to the enemy army.

Port felt as if some giant squeezed his ribs. His hunger was weighing on him. He couldn't continue at this pace for more than an hour.

The expansive field ended. Dying acacia trees and large stones gave way to the entrance of the mountainside forest.

Port coughed. He worried that his sputum would be little more than blood. *Was that Sleffman's choice so unwise?*

No. I have promises to keep. Colrig. Phenmir. The Endowers.

He had made a promise to *his* people and *his* god.

They ran into the thick of the forest and reached an open plain, closed in on either side by mountain walls.

Most of the retreating army ran ahead of him. He was more relieved to see so many capable of continuing than worried about his own fate. Still, he knew he was far from the last. As they ran into the narrowing canyon, the troops beside Port began to slow. Those behind him nearly stopped.

"Keep going!" He wanted to reassure them with some hope of refuge or a goal within proximity, but he was not willing to lie. They would have further support, but Bruten was days, if not weeks, to the south.

He turned to gallop sideways. More Sleffmen slowed to walk as they conversed with one another. Those who had weapons removed them and fixed their posture with a newfound sense of duty.

"What are you doing?" Port cried.

Their faces were at ease, faint smiles with tired eyes.

Is this it? A victory in Kzhek to return and lose our own Court?

"You can't just surrender! Please!" Some troopers continued to run past him, while more joined the others, who stood with weapons ready.

"You can't." the words were a whisper. He saw their desires just as any Feelman would. He understood them. They did not want to fight any more. They were surrendering for peace for themselves and their comrades. He hated them for it and loved them just as much. Regardless of their noble desires, he could not join them. Even if he were not a captain, he would not have the will to stand against certain defeat.

"For the Harmony Allegiant!" a soldier shouted.

"For the Endowers!" a soldier replied as she adjusted her gauntlets and unsheathed her sword.

"For you, Sleffmen!" another shouted. More remained, enticing others to join their last stand.

He wanted to rebuke them, offering more empty words of encouragement. Just as the surrendering soldier let the enemies overcome him, they had made their decision. Theirs was not one of cowardice, nor was it that of capitulation.

He offered the Sleff salute, though this was more meaningful than any he had previously given. The signal of crowned hands meant union and humility under Heitt. It meant brotherhood and sisterhood. The greatest form of submission, the very essence of the Sleff Ideal was to surrender one's needs for the others.

"Pious is the Giver!" he shouted.

Their replies, repeating the ideal, came from all around as more Sleffmen joined their armored line. He had too little time to thank them before enemy forces reached their human barrier. He had to run onward, lest their sacrifice be in vain. Onward to never forget the price they paid. They would not withstand the enemy barrage, but the wall of self-sacrificing Sleffmen would keep them off of the others long enough for them to survive.

We will make it to Bruten. We must. For them.

Distant shouts grew closer, though he was yet to see any beasts in the sky. He turned and ran, struggling to breathe in the cold air amidst sobs of gratitude and sorrow.

⚜ ⚜

Port sat among the surviving Sleffman atop a cliff. Most of the retreating army had gone beyond into the canyon, safely distant from the loyalists.

It was cold enough to warrant a fire, but they dared not risk being seen by Priess and Sleff loyalists.

Port had watched the slaughtered flesh wall on the rocky overlook. It was not close enough to see the suffering on their faces, much to his relief. The sacrificial Sleffmen lasted but for a brief time, enough for the others to flee up the mountainside and away from the loyalists' view. As he had hoped, the loyalists traveled down the trail, only to return with no added blood on their weapons. Port prayed that waiting until dawn would be long enough for the final lingering loyalists to return to Paiell.

"What now, sir?" asked a Sleff trooper, his voice worn like a creaking door.

Port turned away from the corpses below. Thinking that they would become food for wolves was little comfort.

The trooper seemed an insignificant member of their group but had an unforgettable face. *No one is insignificant*, he reminded himself. Now recognizing the value of any ally, regardless of apparent value or rank. His visage was not torn not only by war, but the vilest consequences of Sleff poverty. He had few teeth remaining and a permanent yellow-black stain on those remaining that told of his extensive history of brush smoking. His name was Tick, or at least that was what he had become known as after the sound his jaw made whenever he laughed or shouted. His clothes were filled with burn holes and he smelt like fermented fish, fitting in with the rest of the group. Port was no nobleman, but had seen himself as above those of this man's class. Regardless of the Sleff law to give away more than a week's wage, differences in affluence still existed. A week of labor for a peon was much less than that of a Proctor's assistant.

Despite their differences, the mud and blood that colored their tattered clothes and dented armor made them appear as equals.

Other troopers turned to Port for their command.

"To Bruten. We have nowhere else to go." Port's response was as dry as the dirt in which he traced circles with a stick.

"But, how..." Tick hesitated.

Since when have I been intimidating? "We walk."

He knew everyone questioned the likelihood of surviving the trek. Too many were injured and even the most hale among them would likely collapse halfway to their destination. The small group of Sleffmen numbered no more than thirty. Most of the Sleff Allegiant army would arrive in Bruten without issue.

Tick laughed, the sound fulfilling his namesake.

Port couldn't help but laugh along. Their situation was a poor joke made by Heitt himself. "Do you have any better ideas?"

Tick shrugged. "I thought you were the one paid to have ideas, being the captain and all."

"I'm paid the same as you are."

"I'm not paid anything."

"My point exactly." Port prepared to throw the stick, then caught himself. He set it down, glad that he had not given into the impulse to throw it down where they had last seen the loyalists. "Does anyone have an idea? I guess mine aren't good enough."

"Did you consider the river?" a Sleffman asked. The *S* came out as a *TH*.

"Do you have a map?"

"No, but I've traveled south enough to know that this river runs near Bruten, finishing up at a lake on the Court's southern border."

"I don't see any river here," mumbled Tick.

"It's just over that peak ahead of us." He leaned forward from a stump to the left of Tick to peek across the canyon. Port was ashamed for judging the man based on his voice, but soon saw his missing front teeth. The Sleffman had a fresh slash from the bottom of his right eye down to his chin. His bottom lip had a slight split, as if he had cracked it from spending too much time in dry Court Chuss. His upper lip was much worse, split into two separate pieces that left the gap in his teeth fully exposed.

"Do you have a boat? A dinghy? A raft?" asked Tick.

Port turned to the split-lipped Sleffman, interested in hearing his reply.

"Why should I be the one to have anything when we left it all behind? Learn to use your hands!"

"You want us to make a boat?" asked Tick, on the edge of laughing again.

"We have enough that could help. Our choices are limited and you don't seem eager to offer one of your own. If you have an option, I would be happy to oblige."

"I'm interested," said Port, "but who are you?"

"While you sat in Kzhek safety *commanding*, I was with the other Sleffmen here trying to maintain order. This isn't the first attempt by the loyalists to control us. My name is Dessen, but why should that matter to you? I'm just another soldier that was forced to learn to improvise to keep our efforts going."

Port felt no anger, despite this man's ungrounded accusations, only disappointment. If these men saw him as another careless nobleman, he had failed as a leader. Unlike Colrig. Colrig was of the people. He was directly involved with every conflict. Port had tried to follow him, but were his efforts not enough?

"Perd you, you blind kulf!" Tick hissed. "Captain Port has done more than you, more than I, more than anyone for Sleff, save Colrig. I was with him in Kzhek and saw what he did. Heitt curse you for thinking so little of our captain. You probably left the battle after receiving that cut from your own blade, not knowing how to wield it, while Captain Port faced legions of loyalists."

"It's fine, Tick." Port placed a hand on the man's shoulder, placating him until he slowed his breathing.

Dessen looked down. "Forgive me–"

"No, think nothing of it. Forgive me if I act like such a poor leader. I am giving this my all, but we have room to improve." Port pointed at Tick. "Even you. Now, are we settled to hear what Dessen has to offer?"

Tick nodded. Some of the surrounding Sleffmen joined. Their faces were obscured by the daylight depleting behind the mountainous horizon. A fire would be a warm welcome, yet he was still worried that loyalists continued to scout below.

"Thank you," continued Port. "Let's say we follow this idea, Dessen. How would we go about making anything to take us down the river? The acacias here are sparse and frankly too large to be cut down by our swords and hand spears, unless you have an axe hidden."

"We will need some weapons, though nothing to chop down these trees. When trying to hold on to Paiell, we learned the importance of scavenging. When we needed to get away from the city, we would come up this canyon. If you walk downstream for about twenty minutes, you will find some dilapidated fishing shacks and a shed that we never looked into. I say we take our weapons and break those shacks down. Their walls aren't thick enough to make you feel protected in a storm. Tear those down, find some other materials inside and in the shed, and I think we can work our way into building a makeshift boat, maybe even two, to help us travel down to Bruten."

"Perd me!" scoffed Tick. "Even if we manage to make those, there is no way they can survive the rapids down south."

"So you've traveled the river?" asked Dessen.

"No, but I've heard the stories of failed bridge-builders. Dotrift and Kellfold sit right across from each other. Their respective citizens can practically see each other, but any bridge that they build directly across from each other falls to the unpredictable rapids. If you want to walk from Dotrift to Kellfold or the other way around, you have to travel an hour or so upstream for the next best bridge."

Dessen waved his hand, scoffing at the old man. "I don't buy it. If we can build those cathedrals in Paiell, I don't think our Court's architects would struggle with something like a bridge."

"But Dotrift and Kellfold are mere villages, far away from any major city. They do not have the architects that we do in Paiell."

Dessen forced a laugh. "We live in an age of domesticated ghete and carriages. I am sure if they needed help, they could get it."

"Are there rapids or not, Dessen?" asked Port.

"The old man had some ground. Some bridges continue to fall, but I would blame that on past disputes between the two villages. Proximity does not always entail peace."

"But there are rapids?"

"Yes," Dessen sighed. "I wouldn't worry about them until we reach them. In the worst case, we can pull to shore and travel the rest of the way on foot, finding some other way to carry the injured."

"Why not just catch up with the rest? The injured can remain here."

Port glared at Tick. "I have let too many die under my command and I will not give up on those who need a little help. I know that if they hobbled back into the city, they would be killed on sight, dressed in their wares and bearing the wounds of a warrior. It is too cold for them to march back naked and I am sure that they have loyalist guards stopping any who enter the city. They are coming with us. If there is any chance that the Chussmen send an Eurythrin Endower to meet us in Bruten, it will all be worth it. You can head back if you want, Tick, but I'm going with Dessen and the injured to Bruten."

Tick traced circles in the dirt.

Dessen offered Port a nod, seemingly out of gratitude, but would admit no such thing. Port would gain this man's trust. It would take time, but he would not let himself be seen as a sitting captain. He would become like Colrig, one of the people.

"Who else is with us?" Port asked the others, who sat in a misshapen circle.

One by one, they offered the Sleff salute. Port returned it and glanced beyond their group, seeing that the others had laid themselves for a much deserved rest. They would have no difficulty falling asleep after days of sleepless battles.

"We'll speak with the others in the morning," said Dessen. "Any loyalist followers should be gone by dawn. We can take the healthy with us and head to the shacks before sunrise. Tick can stay back with the other injured to explain it to them while they await our return."

"*Other?*" scoffed Tick. "I'm not one of the injured."

"You will be if you continue to argue with my ideas, old man."

The morning's trek was colder than their night's sleep beside the cool mist of the street-wide river. It was not severe enough to leave them frostbitten, but that time would soon approach. The sides of Port's pants were wet as they had trekked through frost covered sage, but he held onto hope that the rising sun would bring quick relief.

As far as he knew, no one in the party had food. Dessen was not worried, telling him that there were plenty of edible plants along the way. When banished from the city on occasion during the uprising, he had found other means to feed himself when merchants and bakers were forced to turn him away. The other villages were distant enough from the loyalist nobility that Dessen counted on their help to provide more sustainable meals than pale cacti, bitter leaves, and the occasional berries.

Although they had planned on others joining them to see the fishing shacks, no one else agreed to come until they had proof that their plan would work. Dessen grumbled, but Port made sure to impress upon him that it was still worth their time.

"I suppose the walk was longer than I remember, but here we are." Dessen led Port to the first of the abandoned fishing outposts, which were in an even worse condition than he had imagined. Rot had eaten away large holes in the planked walls, giving way to cracks and warped wood.

He patted Port on the back. "I told you they were dilapidated."

Port nodded, his faith in Dessen's plan wavering.

"The furniture inside might be better, but we can layer some of the porous planks if needed."

Port followed Dessen towards the first of the cabins. Dessen reached for the handle, but was knocked back as the broken planks of the doorway flew out in an explosive burst. Port rolled to the side and was hit by a few pieces of wood, though nothing large enough to injure. He arose with shaky legs and reached back to grab his hand spear from his back sheath.

Port would have never assumed that the fiend before him had the strength to tear through the door. Although it was a head taller than either of them, it was as gaunt as the most starved beggar in the Court. It was bald and gray, reminiscent of an imp but more human in its complexion. A tangle of tentacles fell from its stomach.

Dessen stood with his hand on his forehead. The creature turned to Dessen's movement and ran to pounce.

Port knew he would not reach Dessen before the creature, but he had to do something. He was ready to prove to Dessen that he was no mere *observant officer.*

Dessen cried out every curse imaginable as the creature's piercing claws tore at his leather chest pad, slicing deep enough to draw blood.

Port rammed his handspear into the creature's ribs and threw his weight into the maneuver to drive the blade in. He struggled to press it further, but he felt that it was caught between the other side of the ribs.

Its vile face turned to him. He froze with his hand on the shaft. Its pale eyes had the mere shadow of small pupils, like the sun behind thick smoke. Its cheeks were sunken in and seemed like they would be too easily pierced by its finger-length teeth. It hissed and groaned, eyes becoming more antagonistic towards Port.

Dessen pulled his knees to his chest and kicked the creature off of him as it stared at Port. It stumbled back, catching itself with the grace of a cat. With a screech that made Port want to scream, it ripped the spear from its side. The puncture remained in its chest open like a pierced tent flap from which nothing leaked. The spear tip was dark with an oily substance, though it was far from what Port would call blood.

Port jumped closer to let the creature run at him, giving Dessen another moment to recover.

The creature was still a few paces away from Port, giving him time to grab a fist-sized stone from the ground before it jumped on top of him.

He pressed the creature's boney chest off of his while he swung at its head with his stone. He landed a single hit, which only caused the beast to blink, before it ran its impish clawed fingers down his forearm, causing him to drop the stone. Its gums were exposed in a vehement scream that caused Port to join in with one of his own.

Dessen ran behind the fiend to pull its arms back into a tight hold.

Port continued to press against its chest and spared a glance down to its abdomen. The abdominal tentacles hung limp but soon revealed their true nature.

They were not tentacles at all, but withering intestines the length of a forearm. Port kept his left hand up but reached down to pull the largest of the entrails with his right. As soon as he gripped it, the organ squeezed his hand with the strength of a Gorger.

Port screamed, flailing his legs to try to kick the creature, which only grew more enraged. His hand cracked as the organs squeezed tighter.

Dessen pulled the creature's arms up from behind, bending them in a position that would break those of any human. They popped through the rotation and slipped free, uninjured to attack Port, sinking devilish fingers into his biceps like knives.

Dessen jumped onto mount it with legs locking around its abdomen, knocking Port's broken hand free from its grip. While it remained focused on Port, Dessen plunged his hunting knife into its mouth and stabbed the roof of it. It struggled and wailed, but he continued to thrash and spin the knife which must have reached its brain. He roared in pain as his arm was shredded by its long teeth.

Their cries diminished as he pulled a bloodied hand free, the knife still stuck in the now limp fiend's head.

Port's hand pulsed with pain, but it was still intact. He ripped off a piece of his rent coat and ran to Dessen's side. Dessen's right hand had its fair share of cuts, but his forearm looked like a shredded roast that was far too raw.

"Perd perd perd, *ah* perding underrealms," Dessen cursed as Port wrapped it tight. Blood soaked through in an instant. He tore more strips of cloth from his clothing and wrapped it with a second and third layer.

"What was that?" Port sat back against a rock, exasperated, with eyes open in a panicked stare.

"Do I look like a perding Scholar?" Dessen hissed as he held his wrist and rocked back and forth. "Shouldn't you know what they are? Knowing the dangers that we should face, *Captain?*"

Port approached the fiend's corpse, clenching his wrist and rotating his hand. Dessen joined him to stare as a gray ichor seeped from its mouth. "Was it human?"

Dessen shrugged. "Why would you think that? Look at those claws and teeth. It's naked and has no parts down yonder to let us know if it is, or was, male or female." He kicked it and let out an exasperated sigh. "Too dead to answer any questions, but from what I could tell, it was not eager to speak with us even if it could."

Why would I think it once was human? Port looked up, searching for some distant memory. Had he heard stories of them in the past? The feeling ate at him. This was no standard monster of the wild. There was something more.

"What should we do with it?"

Dessen turned to him as if he had just confessed love for it. "Why would we do anything with it? We have more to do than care for a fiendish corpse."

"But... doesn't it concern you? What if there are more of them?"

"I don't intend to find out. You're the captain. I shouldn't be the one to tell you to focus on your duty. How's the hand? Those tentacles had quite a grip."

"It hurts, but I think it should be fine. I felt some popping, but I don't think that it broke much. Also, those weren't tentacles."

"Don't care."

"What about your arm?"

Dessen opened and clenched his arm and touched the bandages with the other hand. "The hand is fine, and the wrist seems to be doing better since your bandaging, but by Heitt's holy name, it stings. Maybe we'll pass through some frozen parts of the river, some ice might help. Enough whining. Can you still help tear some of this shack apart? I say we stick to this one just in case another one of those *freaks* is waiting inside another."

"Should be fine."

Dessen nodded and waved for him to follow. He checked the inside of the shack with a glance, then entered.

Holes throughout the walls and in the roof provided ample sunlight to see in the modest yet quaint shack. It was as large as the bedchambers that Port had seen in the Zhaes Cantons. The shack slept two people comfortably and had ample space for a table, that being one that had collapsed with two standing legs. No fishing gear remained, but an axe and saw leaned against the far wall.

"Ah ha!" Dessen walked across the creaking wood and lifted the axe to inspect the blade. "Dull, but it will do." He swung it into the corner between two walls and wiggled the blade once it hit in place.

He turned back to stare at Port. "Are you going to help?"

"What do you want me to do?"

"Take this," he handed Port the axe, "and finish off that wall. I'll look around for something we can use to fasten the pieces together."

"You just want me to tear this building apart."

"Yes."

Port nodded, feeling the weight of the axe in his hands. Just heavy enough to do the job.

The first swing startled him as a shock ran up his wrist and injured hand. He ripped off another piece of his already-torn clothing and wrapped the axe's handle to give it a buffer against the pain. Each strike ached, but he continued. He continued to fight on as he had with each battle in the war.

You will not stop us.

Strike.

We will not yield.

Strike.

I *will not yield.*

He grunted as the strike hit a foundational point in the wall. The blade barely stuck into the thicker portion of wood.

Never yielding to beasts.

Strike.

Never yielding to enemies.

Strike.

Never yielding to my weaker self!

He swung through the wall.

"Split the larger boards apart from each other but try to keep them intact lengthwise."

Port ignored Dessen's comment and moved to the next corner. He swung as if each strike was a new battle to overcome, for there would be many more.

After three hours of work, they had an array of planks cut for the boat and nails pried from the remaining furniture in the shack. Dessen organized the planks in piles of smallest to largest. Port helped him carry the last pieces from the shack's second wall into the area before it and sat on a flat stone for rest. It was muddy and nearly the same as sitting on the floor, but it would work. He gave up on comfort the day he left Kzhek.

"So, do you have a shape in mind?" he asked Dessen.

Dessen folded his arms and combed the piles with his gaze. "Have you ever seen a Gruth drifter?"

Port shook his head. "I haven't seen Gruth yet."

Dessen raised an eyebrow, seemingly preparing another remark regarding what *"a captain should see"* or *"know,"* but pressed it off with a huff.

"I spent some time on the eastern coast back when I had a job other than soldering."

"What were you?"

"That's a conversation for another time." His face hinted at suppressed anger. "Gruthmen use drifters for sightseeing along the coast to see the smaller islands and such. They are not as practical as even the smallest fishing vessels, but their design is much simpler and should suffice for our journey."

Even in the rapids? Port held back his inquiry, finally giving Dessen the trust he deserved. Port was a commander in war, not in expeditions. Even though he had little experience in the former, he recognized the worth of delegating.

Dessen knelt to draw a rough outline of the drifter in the dirt, though it was moist enough to clump up and leave the shape even rougher. "These will use half of the wood as any other boat and will take half the time if we do it right."

Port leaned over to inspect the rectangular outline.

"One we–"

"Praise Heitt's holy name! Praise the lord of humility that I found you!"

Port shifted to the side on his rock, and Dessen stood from his crouch to see the source of the shout. Port struggled to talk, even to breathe, as he saw a bloody vagabond with a gruesome pit for his right eye.

"Tick, you perding kulf, what happened?" Dessen approached him with a glare battling between fear and concern.

Port stood to follow. Large scratches of four parallel lines traced down Tick's arms and his tunic was torn as if it was spare meat tossed to a rat's den. *It cannot be. It* must *not. Heitt, when will our reverie come? Is this our demise? Where is thine aid?*

He knew his suspicions would be confirmed, but to what degree? He could only listen.

"Big perding–beast–imp–perding nightmare of fiend."

"Gray?" Dessen asked as he clenched Tick's shoulder, trying to get him to focus. "Looked like a gaunt madman with long fingers and–"

"Yes! Yes, the fingers!" he pointed to the mushy pit where his right eye had been.

Dessen nodded. "Where are the others?"

"I couldn't help them."

"You perding coward." Dessen threw Tick's shoulder away. "Did you really leave them?"

"I had to! The gray kulf would've killed me. It stabbed into their heads and stomachs like a perding farmer with a pitchfork! Oh, the blood was everywhere! I almost–"

"Tick!" Port demanded. "Did any of them make it?"

"I–I told you, I couldn't stay."

"Answer his question, you kulf!"

"No, all of them were–they were–oh, Heitt's mercy!"

Dessen pushed Tick. "You should have died with them."

"I couldn't have done anything else. It's not like I didn't try!"

"Just you and I now, Captain." Dessen returned to the woodpile. "Let's get to work. We should be able to make it down the river an hour before dusk."

"What about me?" asked Tick, his ticks becoming more prominent with each plea.

Dessen moved the panels and began to assemble the base.

"You're coming with us." Port reached down to help the old Sleffman stand.

"I will not have a leech tag along."

"Who says I can't help!"

Dessen laughed, never looking back at Tick.

"Dessen."

"You're the captain on the battlefield. You can direct me when we are back fighting the enemy, but I am my own man here."

"You contradict yourself. You insist on punishing him for abandoning the injured, but he is one of them. You are no better than him if we leave him."

"He is better off on his own."

"None of us are. We are all fighting the same battle and that does not end on the battlefield."

Dessen turned to stare at Tick. "If you don't listen to any command, we will leave you in the river."

"Oh yes, you can be sure that I will do what you need!"

Dessen returned to his work, beginning to hammer the base boards together with the back of the axe that they had found.

Port looked at Tick and shared a smile. It was sure to be an arduous journey, yet nothing in the past months had been anything but arduous. Despite the difficult circumstances and the terrors that were sure to return, Port was pleased to see a glimmer of future friendships to come.

CHAPTER FOURTEEN

A SERVAL AMONG GHETE

Phenmir would never admit it to Voln, but Kaela was already proving to be the more organized and efficient Endower leader.

"Shiftlings, adapt!"

At Kaela's command, twenty of the Endowers in the room vanished. Phenmir was astonished as he leaned over the balcony to search for their presence.

Kaela smiled . "You have a minute to hide. Once I call for you to stop, you must remain in your place. Off with you!"

Footsteps clapped against the floor, down the hallways to each side, and up and down the corresponding staircases. Phenmir laughed, astounded that he could not see even a blur in the wide area.

"Stop where you are!" Kaela shouted. She cleared her throat and spoke with her usual volume. "Feelmen, use your telelocation to target a Shiftling's thoughts and find them. Once a Shiftling is found, you can no longer follow them. Each of you Feelmen needs to find your own Shiftling. Return when you have found one. Begin!"

The Feelmen Endowers ran every which way, some stopping to concentrate and changing their directions.

"Thane Stolk, always a pleasure to have you here." Kaela looked up and approached the balcony with a smile.

"I've heard about your training programs, but this is impressive, though–" he paused.

"They seem like games for children?"

Phenmir replied with a laugh. "So I'm not the first to say it?"

"We cannot forget that they–we–are children. There is a fine balance between hard work and knowing how your students learn."

"You seem to have found that balance."

"Yes, but I have as much to learn. Come and stand next to me. I would rather not shout for all to hear."

Phenmir proceeded down the marble stairway. Its pristine steps and railing were contrasted by the red clay dust of the inner courtyard. The walk to meet Kaela was less than half of a minute, yet two Feelmen Endowers had already returned with their Shiftling counterparts.

"Well done, Falik and Draeka." Kaela said as she walked by the Feelmen. She then faced the Shiftlings. "But that means you two, Bogan and Kevik, need to improve."

Kaela continued past them to reach Phenmir.

"They say that the best players of table games make the best strategists. Perhaps that is why I am such a poor captain." They shared a laugh. To know that Kaela laughed at his self-deprecation made him feel accomplished. He did not rely upon the opinions of others, but it was always sweeter than honey to learn that people thought he was a formidable leader.

"They should be just a few more minutes," Kaela said, nodding to another pair of Endowers as they returned to the center of the courtyard.

"If I would have known that you Shiftlings could make yourselves invisible, I would have utilized that during our first trip to Kzhek."

"One of the Chuss Endowers taught us how to do it."

Phenmir raised his eyebrows.

Kaela smirked. "We know *so little* about what our abilities can do."

"Any recent discoveries?"

"Nothing in Sliin, but there is supposedly an Endower in Korth who can persuade anyone to do what he wants."

Phenmir scowled. "Persuade or force?"

She shrugged.

"Either way, that is concerning."

"Which is why we chose a Feelman as the head of Chuss Endowers. Once the Terpel's ability was discovered, we had to ensure that this child was closely observed." She seemed eager to avoid the topic and jumped back to focus on her trainees. "We will be working with the Gorgers and Terpels next."

"You—*we* have Terpels?"

"You should have organized the Endowers years ago, Thane Stolk. Organization uncovers forgotten treasures."

Her wit was astounding. The Endowers were still children in personality but were ever more the adult in their intellect. He could only wonder what else she hid behind her Serval mask.

"Are you having problems with the Endowers here as a Tchoyasgirl?"

"What do you mean?"

"Well, your—"

"My mask?" She forced a laugh. "Judging others because of where they were born is a problem invented by adults to make themselves feel more important. If you can't see that they love me here, I will let you know that plenty of them have told me they wish they had a mask of their own."

She turned to count the Endowers' heads, whispering the numbers. "That should be all. Draeka, you can direct the next exercise. The midday meal is going to be served in an hour. I'll meet you all there." She waved for Phenmir to follow her.

"Did the Krall come with you?" she asked. He had to skip steps to keep up with her pace up the stairwell.

"She is waiting for us in your study." He smirked.

"What? Is that funny to you?"

He shrugged, trying to tame his smile. "I have nothing against you having one. I am astounded to find someone so young with their own study in a Canton."

"It's not *technically* mine. Chenn Hult is the Endower captain in your Court and he doesn't care to use it much."

"Still, you are both so young."

"Times are changing, Thane Stolk. You should see as well as I do that each day our world becomes something new."

"For the better and the worst."

"If the gods are with us, I trust it will only be for the better."

He hoped her words held true. He had felt Cheric guide him yet recognized that the will of the gods was not conditioned to please humankind.

"Never forget that, Kaela." Their gods were different, but their plight was similar. She would know pain, but she did not need to know a loss of faith.

"Your Grace." Kaela bowed at Dhera, who stood before her door. "It is always a pleasure to be in the presence of the Krall."

"I am even more honored to be in the presence of such a renowned Endower. You may be a Tchoyaswoman, but you are always welcome in Court Chuss."

Phenmir gestured for them to enter the study. "Yes, we know how pleasantries work."

Kaela offered him a regal bow and led them in.

"If only I had come here before the war," Kaela invited the Krall to sit near her on a crimson divan. "From what your Endowers say, I understand you were the best trainer in the Court. It is too bad you had to leave them to be burdened with the entire Court's responsibilities."

"I would come back to the Canton if the Court did not adore me so."

Phenmir rolled his eyes as he sat across from them on a chair painted to appear like marble, though it was fashioned from a much less expensive wood. The chair was shorter than what he was used to, matching the desk that was just as short, but was just as wide as any standard Canton desk. Two shelves were barren except for a worn copy of the Tome of Piety. The room smelt like plaster and dust. He noted it had been newly renovated to accommodate her needs, which were quite humble.

"That doesn't mean you are unwelcome," said Kaela.

"Perhaps I should make my rounds more to my *old* throne." She winked at Kaela, then adjusted her posture. "Now, Kaela, while I would love to converse more about Endower training, we have more pressing matters to discuss. You mentioned receiving some messages from the Tchoyas Endowers?"

Kaela's smile remained, but Phenmir noted her eyebrows fell into concern through her mask's eyeholes. "Yes."

"And? What might that be?" Phenmir asked. "Has Krall Trhet done anything to them?"

She took a moment. Her eyes wandered to find the right words. "He hasn't *done* anything, as far as I can tell. Nothing physically. I've been sending a couple of messages with our Beastlings, via ravens, but I have had a difficult time locating them."

"Have they left Fayis?" Phenmir leaned in closer to stare into her eyes. "Or has he sent them against our forces in Court Sleff?"

"No, they aren't in Sleff, but he has sent some of them south. A lot of them were confused about the Zhaes and Tchoyas relations. Most of what they know about the Krall's assassinations came from rumors."

Phenmir held up a hand to stop her and took a moment to breathe. "You said *south*."

She nodded.

"How far south."

"Some Gruthman convinced the Zhaes Thanes and Krall Trhet to contact the Middlemen."

"*Perd.*" Phenmir hissed through his teeth as he leaned back against his chair and stared at the ceiling.

"When did this happen?" asked Dhera.

"The Endowers that I spoke with said that they left Fayis only a few days after the Zhaesmen arrived."

"What do they want with the crop people?"

"They want another way to cut off our resources," grunted Phenmir. "What else could they gain?"

"Our imports from the Middlelands are insignificant," said Dhera. "Though if you are so concerned with the trade, perhaps they lead by the same assumption."

"How much has trade with them changed? I remember nearly reaching a Court-wide famine years ago because of a reported drought in the Middlelands."

"Another fear spawned from rumors. I discussed this very topic with the Proctors in the Canton of Agriculture mere days ago. Recognizing that a Gruth embargo of imported goods is inevitable if the war becomes more insidious, I asked them if we could rely upon our own goods and the middleland imports. They informed me that we would be in dire circumstances to merely rely upon the Middlelands. They provide sustenance for some of the southern villages and cities, but Sliin and most of our other major cities rely upon Gruth imports and even Zhaes imports for the northernmost cities. Trading concerns are quite significant, but we need to place our attention on the reason for our gathering."

"The Krall is right, Thane Stolk. Trade is not their focus," said Kaela.

"Then what is it?" asked Phenmir. "Are they hoping to conscript the crop people to join them in battle?" He scoffed but became serious as Kaela sat still. "They cannot–"

"I am not sure, but that may not be far from the truth."

"How would they recruit the Middlemen if they cannot speak their language?" asked Dhera.

Kaela stroked the bottom of her serval mask. "They *can* speak with them."

"How?" Phenmir and Dhera both asked.

"The Endowers. First, they thought it was through the Beastlings, but that ability has nothing to do with it. As far as my reports tell, the Endowers can speak to the Middlemen as if it were a natural gift."

"So...what...can," Phenmir stopped and ran his fingers between his thickly rolled silver locks. "*Perd*, what are we going to do, Dhera?"

She remained silent, pressing her fingers against her temples.

Phenmir sighed as if he just dropped a weight from his back. "If they are using the Endowers to recruit the Middlemen, how can we trust them? Forgive me, Kaela, but if this is true, they are using Tchoyas Endowers for their plans."

"But maybe this can be a good thing! I can have them trick the Middlemen into serving us."

"I don't think it will be that simple," replied Dhera. "I think Thane Stolk was correct in questioning their loyalty."

"But why not question their loyalty to the Krall? They sent me this message to ask for help."

"What *exactly* did they say?" Phenmir moved his chair closer to Kaela. "In a war of words, the smallest inconsistency or hint can hold more information than the words themselves."

"I...I don't remember. I received multiple messages."

Phenmir sighed, trying to settle her with false relaxation. He had flustered her and could not tame his inner panic but could put on a mask of tranquility. "I'm sorry, Kaela. We've talked over you. Please tell us what this is about."

"They want to be free from the Krall. It is not only those in the Middlelands, but all the Endowers. They feel used, and it has only become worse since they learned what the Krall did. I think a lot of them are torn between doing what they believe to be right and loyalty to their Court. Thane Trhet tells them that this is the will of our god, but I know it is not our god's will to strike down our Thanes."

Who could know the will of their god? Who could know the will of any god? Phenmir did not want to contradict her with ancient scriptures that told of the gods slaying nations when required. Such thoughts often diminished the faith of those whose beliefs were not rooted in a deeper understanding of the will of the gods. Phenmir knew and *accepted* that the gods, even Cheric, had slain the wicked on occasion so that the righteous might prevail. Killing, when seen through a moralist's scope, was never righteous or evil, but something that dwelt in between the two. War was evidence. He did not think the Thanes died at the hands of the Tchoyas god, but he would not lose his faith in deity if that were true. If one is ever to understand the nature of a god, they must understand how limited the feeble human mind is in comparison to that of a holier being.

Kaela continued. "From what the Endowers can understand, Krall Trhet is forcing camaraderie to have the Middlemen help them win the war. They have sent many noblemen from Fayis to try to *understand* their culture, but I am sure that it is all part of the Krall's plot to find what they can use."

"Is there anything valuable there besides the food imports?" Phenmir asked Dhera.

"Perhaps that is a question for the Proctors of Agriculture."

"Why don't you strengthen that contact? I can lead a troop of your Endowers and join them with mine in the Middlelands, where we can strengthen your relations with them, converting them to the side of the Harmony Allegiant."

The Krall shook her head. "These are living creatures, Kaela, not tools."

"Wait, Dhera, she may have a point. Perhaps we could focus on strengthening that relationship rather than *using* them."

Dhera furrowed her brow. "I am sure Krall Trhet had a similar way of defending his recruitment. But if you insist, I will speak with the Proctors of Agriculture myself. Just as Kaela said, this could be beneficial for our Endowers."

Phenmir raised his eyebrow. "I thought we wanted to not engage in conflict with Krall Trhet and his underlings?"

"The Middlelands are big enough. What if we were to keep contact with the other Tchoyas Endowers all while leading an expedition of our own to another part of the Middlelands? I can have a message sent to ask them where they are settled, and we can settle our camp far enough away that we could strengthen your connection with other Middlemen outside of the loyalist camps."

"What if, should we succeed, the Middlemen communicate to one another that they have been working with two opposing human parties?" asked Phenmir. "I do not want to force them into their own war."

"Then we cannot go with a mindset of recruitment as have Trhet's company," said Dhera.

Phenmir knew it would eventually come to that. He did not want to bring the Middlemen into the northern war, but he would use any resource he had if it meant saving his Court. *If trees must fall to protect our young, so be it. Perd, what am I thinking? What kind of Chussman am I to have such thoughts?*

"Are you willing to lead an expedition of Endowers to the Middlelands?" he asked Kaela.

"As long as we have others to support, then yes."

"We would never send you alone. If the Krall desires, I would even go with you myself." Dhera tightened her eyebrows. "But I recognize that I have other responsibilities here."

"Even if we do not send you with her, I would like your help, Thane Stolk. I've mentioned the Proctors of Agriculture enough for you to recognize that they might have some valuable information regarding the Middlemen. Until now, they were the only humans in contact with them."

"I thought all exchanges were done without contact?" asked Phenmir.

"From what I can glean, that is just another groundless rumor. Nevertheless, they are not so keen to speak of the Middlemen freely. Some of them treat the interactions as sacred as any holy ceremony in the temples of clay. Perhaps this is why so many people assume it to be a contactless exchange."

He leaned over to scratch his back. The chair was designed for long periods of comfortable rest, but his back insisted otherwise. His chronic pain had grown worse the more meetings he partook in. Whether it be the Middlelands, Sleff, or Kzhek, he did not care. He was ready for new scenery and movement.

"We live in an age of confusion." He pressed up on the desk to his side to stand. "Find some Endowers for the expedition. I'll come back and see you once I have more information from the Proctors of Agriculture."

"I will get right to it." Kaela stood to walk with them out of the study.

"And I would ask that you both keep me well informed."

"Of course, Your Grace," Kaela bowed.

"Do you even use this study?" asked Phenmir.

"The divan is not too bad to sleep on. Sometimes I like to invite other Endowers in for a meeting."

Phenmir scowled. "You don't always sleep in there, do you?"

"No, I still have a room in Thane Mortriff's estate. He and his wife are more than hospitable, but sometimes a girl needs some space for herself."

"Never forget that, even when you're married." Dhera laughed.

"I already know how bad it will be living with Voln." Phenmir could see the red rise behind her mask. He continued to talk before she could defend herself. "Enough, I have to be a burden now and bring an end to my wife's private time."

"Give her my regards, Phenmir."

"Mine too!" said Kaela.

He bid them farewell with the Chuss salute.

Phenmir fell onto his bed, empty of thought.

"What's bothering you?" Meira lowered her book onto the covers to look at her husband.

He returned his eyes to the ceiling after sparing her a glace. In the dim light, he found shapes in the wood that lead his mind into thought other than those that burdened him. It would have been so easy to tell her that nothing was bothering him, but even the best of liars could not make her believe that. She had told him he carried too much of the Court and he was starting to believe her.

She picked up her book again.

He knew she craved his attention, as he did hers, but sometimes it was too obvious.

He sighed. "I have so much to think about, so much to do. Tomorrow there will be more and the following day..."

"I don't know why you do it."

"I don't know how you focus on the logistical side of politics."

"You command, and I do the work in the background. Neither of us would want the other's position, yet we work well together."

"We do."

She moved closer and leaned on her elbow to look him in the face. "Is it our Court or the others that are causing your distress?"

He turned his head, laying the right side on her leg. "All of them, I suppose."

"Then I cannot offer any help, Phen. We cannot change the world to match our desires, but we can influence others to make such a difference. Have you heard anything about the Sleff campaign?"

He smiled and stroked her cheek with his palm.

She almost giggled but held it in with a soft smile.

"Can we leave politics out of the bedroom?"

She returned the gesture, running her nimble fingers across the side of his trimmed beard. "What would you like to talk about?"

He wanted more than a conversation but had learned patience in her preferences. She had taught him how to value time with another. Time spent with her was more valuable than any rank, currency, or possession.

"Zeemer is approaching."

She lost her smile. "You will sleep in the cold weather if you insist on talking about it. The time you discuss weather is with strangers and with people that do not matter to you."

"A genuine conversation," he laughed, staring into her eyes. She would have something to say. She always did. It was easy for him to confess his concerns, but she required prying. Ever the stoic, only yielding to the few whom she loved. He did not mind the silence. Meira was content. Despite the fears harbored by everyone else in Facet, she could enjoy that moment and was happy at his side.

"How does it feel to be a proud father?"

"Joyous, beyond explanation, yet painful."

"How so?"

"I see myself as young but I am reminded that I'm not whenever I see him."

"I know how you feel."

"Do you remember when we were younger, how *different* adults that are now our age seemed? As a twenty-year-old, you cannot even fathom having a child until that day comes. It comes as a gift, one that I would never trade my life for, but it shatters that illusion of the past. Gone is that feeling that adults are something beyond yourself when you become one."

She nodded and stroked his cheek again. He smiled at her subtle plea for him to shave.

"Do you remember what changed for you to decide that you were ready to have a child?" he asked.

"When we had enough of an income."

He knew there was more that drove her, but she wanted his answer, asking for it with those piercingly large eyes.

He rubbed his eyes and yawned. "I remember working with an abundance of patients, around the time of the dust plague."

Her lips flattened. She was likely recalling the same memories that he had of those three years.

"More patients died than lived. Even though I was just an apprentice, I still felt the pain of what I thought to be wasted efforts when their health continued to decline. I'm sorry to talk about that again. Cheric knows how many times you have heard it. What I mean to say was that I recognized the joy of birth. I noticed that my preceptor made sure I was able to participate in some births. Even when those patients were sick, their joy perpetuated seeing life begin when all around them seemed to end. I knew then, and know more so today, that a child is that perpetuating joy that I needed."

She smiled again, her eyes grew blurry.

"A child is a light amidst the gloom."

"You don't mean–Phenmir, I am not–"

He laughed and sat up. "No, perd me, no. We are too old. Well, maybe not too old."

Her glare stabbed him.

"Now is not the time and I think Hir is enough for our family. I startled you, didn't I?"

She laughed. "The world may be in gloom, as you said, but I cannot think of a worse time to have a child."

"If we were young and without Hir, I would still want one."

"But how could you? Even though we are in Chuss, there is no telling how all of this will unfold for the Endowers. I do not mean to doubt your plight, Phenmir, but a time of war is not when a child will thrive."

"If I have learned anything in these past few months, it is that there are no certainties in life. Well, there are some. A child brings joy to those who welcome it. Pain and trial are sure, regardless of what the child becomes, but joy is ever present."

"And that is why you give yourself to the Allegiant. You want to secure that joy."

"I suppose that *is* why. Perhaps I am too much of an optimist."

"Let us hope that remains so."

She knew he had not thought fondly of the Patriarchy. He had offered them a new consideration, giving them another hypothetical opportunity once his son had chosen to become one of them.

"Regardless of what he becomes, I will never lose the love I have." *I cannot, for this is all for him. Without Hir, would I have ever left that harvesting behind in Zhaes?*

CHAPTER FIFTEEN

A FAILED SCHOLAR

The moon and sparse stars were the only light in the otherwise dark Chuss desert.

Hir sat alone on a stone whose sharp ridges hurt as much as the loneliness. Were he with his parents or at the chapterhouse, he would have feigned a smile. That same false happiness would show as it always had. Alone, he need not worry about drying his tears. The desert would do that for him.

The Crucible of the Dunes had begun. He could not return until he had slain a demon. He trembled to learn what that meant, so instead, he dwelt upon self-pity.

In the desert, he had no friends at his side, yet neither did he have any to run to upon his return. He had plenty who he would claim as friends, though he questioned if they would do the same.

Would Sevit be at my side in the Patriarchy if I had not been such a poor friend?

His mind stuck to his childhood: years spent running through Sliin with Sevit, play-fighting, and talking about what ten-year-olds thought made a difficult life.

He laughed at the thought, yet he was anything but happy. Those memories were gone. Sevit lived his own life.

Their parents were close, and Sevit planned to train for Scholarship with Hir. He was a year younger than Hir, yet they were as close as twin brothers.

He is still my brother, no matter the distance.

Sevit later lost interest in study. He spent time with other Chussmen who preferred drinking rather than study. Hir had heard that Sevit no longer cared to worship Cheric. He became one who lived by Chuss principles on the outside, but not within.

Hir wanted to ask Sevit's parents for forgiveness.

I could have led him in by my side. He knew they had been disappointed in Sevit, for they treated Hir as the older, responsible son. *I'm closer to them than I am to you, Sevit. We could have been in this together. You and I. Scholars. Forgive me for being distant. I'm sorry we never talked about your struggles. When you were depressed, I only talked about studying. I should have been better. I should have exemplified the Ideal I preach.*

Sevit was gone. Anyone Hir would call a friend was gone. His parents were gone. He was alone, not even a teacher at his side. This was already enough of a crucible, but it would only grow more difficult. He wanted to shout his emotional agony, but remained silent, lest he attract lurking dangers.

"Go north, along the trail," was all they told him. They failed to mention that the trail would split.

Hir stood, pressing himself up from the ground with the help of his staff. His back ached from training. He began to walk under the stars in the cloudless sky.

There was no reason to dwell upon his assignment. Even Scholar Sokov denied him any hints. Dumek laughed when Hir asked for advice, only showing him the thick scar across his back as a warning.

The droning of the cicadas was the only sound around. It relieved Hir that there were no sounds of settling sands or cracking rocks. He knew that snakes and molehounds lurked throughout the desert, but something more insidious awaited him at the end of the quest.

He sighed, thanking Cheric after seeing the first stake in the ground after what felt like an hour of aimless walking. He was on the right path, rather *a* path.

His eyes turned to the bronze line that swirled around the staff from top to bottom. Everyone had always told him that bronze was a symbol of the Zhaesmen. His experience with the Patriarchy led him to believe otherwise. Bronze was a sign of Scholarship. A sign of superiority and piety.

Memories of Sevit left him, but the Zhaeswoman Eurythrin returned to his mind. Not the old one who had ridiculed him worse than Dumek, but the young one. She was one of the few who treated Hir as a friend, yet he could not recall her name. *What would she think of my self-pity? I give the training my all, but here I sorrow like a–*

Hir's focus returned to his path. He saw that the faint path that he tread led into a small, forested area of acacias. It was still a dry area of the desert, but more cacti sprung up beside the trees to hide what moved beyond.

The sound of sliding sand caused Hir to tense and clench his staff with already sweaty hands.

He tried to suppress each breath, shuddering as they escaped. A golden glimmer ahead reflected the moonlight. Something stood within the gathering of trees.

He forced himself onward. Fear was ever present, something he had been coping with his entire time training to be a Scholar.

Most of his training had been with fists. Dumek had taught him to use a staff, but the knowledge had not yet applied itself to his muscles. He did not fear pain, rather failure.

The forested alcove was much less dense within. He discovered it was a shaded clearing within a wall of trees. The clearing was as wide and long as a dining hall.

At the end of the clearing stood a rock mound with an open cave mouth. No light shined within. The golden light that he had seen outside was from a rod that stood five paces before the mouth of the cave. Atop the rod was a bronze sphere the size of his head.

Hir approached it. The rod stood to his chest. He peered over and into the cave. A staircase descended, but nothing else was visible. He had no torch nor means of creating a fire, yet knew he was supposed to enter.

Casting his concern aside, he touched the bronze sphere.

A faint line traced around its equator. He touched it and felt small rises and falls as if a lightning bolt had been traced around it. *The Scholars tongue. They cannot expect me to understand it. I haven't even had my first lesson. Is this a puzzle or a distraction?* Hir clenched his teeth, trying to calm himself and direct his focus to the task rather than on frustration.

He stepped back and paced around the clearing. There was no sign that anyone had ever been there except for the rod.

He laughed at himself. They expected too much.

Perd you, Scholars.

He was more frustrated than he had been when forced to read Sleff philosophy for an entire day and expected to recite each doctrinal tenant a week after. His mind hurt from stuffing it with more information than was held by the books in his father's study.

Is this their desire? Do they want to humble me?

The orb hissed. Hir almost fell on his back in startlement. His hands shook, and he felt each heartbeat. He couldn't tell if it was loud or if he was just so used to the silence. Even a whisper would have seemed like a shout in the windless clearing.

He approached the orb. Its hissing reminded him of the faint roar of ocean waves. There was no indication as to how the orb was making such a noise.

The sound began again but came from the cave.

Perd.

He had no choice but to investigate.

The passage was as wide and tall as a doorway. Large enough, but still tight.

Cheric guide me.

He knew that the *Tome of Charity* had some passage about trusting the light when all once can see is the dark, but anxiety clouded his memory.

He began his descent with one hand on the wall and the other taking using the staff to feel the steps below. The process continued only for ten steps until the tunnel flattened out. He dared not turn back, lest the glimmer of light seem too inviting, causing him to retreat.

This is my trial. I will embrace it. A Scholar is patient, mighty, and sure.

Everything was black except for a faint glimmer of green. The glow grew larger as he continued down the corridor. He was not even sure it was a light, yet it was a contrast to the overwhelming black.

Hir's heart dropped as he fell, scraping his hands across the rough ground. Something had tripped him. His palms stung. He had grown too comfortable walking blind, not using his staff to check for obstacles.

He brushed his hands free of dust as he stood, finding his staff just steps ahead. His head continued to face forward, but he swept the ground behind him with his staff. The staff stopped against a lump on the ground. He crouched to feel it and found that it stretched halfway across the width of the passage.

It was thick, yet soft to the touch. He pressed on it, finding it somewhat flexible, and traced his hand further along it.

A root? No, a vine.

He followed it to the end where it led into the corner. He felt ahead and along the walls as he stood, noticing other vines, but most were smaller.

"A Scholar seeks an explanation for everything," Scholar Sokov had said.

This area can sustain life. Moreso, life for greener plants that need more water than desert dwelling plants. This is more than an abandoned cavern. The tunnel was not made from bricks, nor were the stairs placed. Everything besides the bronze orb seemed natural, yet Hir knew that the place had been created for some purpose.

He swung the staff before him, not finding another vine for ten more paces. A vine grew on the right wall. Hir felt it with the staff in his hand and almost stumbled again when the bronze line emitted a faint glow as it touched the vine. In broad daylight, he thought he would not notice a change in the bronze, for the glow was so faint, like that of a distant star that seemed to disappear when focused upon.

Hir let out a relieved laugh. For the first time since his departure, something made sense. What the glowing bronze entailed, he hadn't the faintest idea. It was not a straightforward answer, but a beginning. Some connection existed between the vine and the bronze.

CHAPTER SIXTEEN

THE NAME OF THE VINE

Runith's anger towards Royss had dissipated, yet he was still grateful to be far away from the man. The Thane of Agriculture had chosen to remain with Gromm and Krall Trhet, two people Runith would be fine never seeing again. He did not see himself as a negative, hateful man, but deceit and manipulation had angered him more than any vile beast. Emotions can build and destroy relationships if let free.

Golma followed Lele out of the carriage, Runith walked behind them and took a deep breath to enjoy the clean air of the Middlelands. It was still humid, but nothing like Court Tchoyas. The temperature was like that of Letur, a pleasant contrast to the Zeemer snow that fell upon the northern Courts.

Lele touched her underarms and rubbed strings of mucus across her face.

"*Already too dry for you?*" Runith asked the putle.

Her ribs expanded twice their size with what seemed to be a sigh. "*I wouldn't mind finding a lake or pond.*"

"*We will. Let's tell the others that we've returned before venturing out too far.*"

He noticed Golma listening to their conversation and had almost forgotten that she too was a Beastling. "Thank you again for coming back with me, Golma."

She looked at him as they walked towards a gathering of large tents and pavilions. He could see the smile in her eyes behind the hawk mask.

"I am as relieved as you to be away from the nobility."

Does she know what her Krall did? Regardless, she held firm in her duties. *Doing what she must to survive. Isn't that what all of us are doing?* The Krall had asked her to stay, but she insisted that the other Endowers would serve him well enough. It would take them only a few moments to understand the Middlemen.

"But why me?" she asked.

She had been one of the few Beastlings to return to Fayis after Kzhek's fall. She had been on the opposite side of the battle, even helping to break the will of the kaesan. To anyone else, such a relationship would have built enmity. Runith saw it as an opportunity for camaraderie. Both understood the toll the war took on nature. She came to the Middlelands with the second group and had taken a liking to Runith, for which reason he could not fathom.

He shrugged. "You seem to know what you are doing."

She chuckled. "I am not sure that any of us do."

Lele remained outside, hopping through the tall reeds in search of grasshoppers to eat, while Runith and Golma walked into the central tent in the loyalist expeditionary camp. The others who had joined them on the carriage ride followed them, but Runith didn't care to pay them any attention. They were Zhaesmen and Tchoyasmen loyal to Krall

Trhet, who tried too hard to hide their sense of awe when seeing the Middlemen artifacts and studies on tables in the tent. No Middlemen were in the tent. Runith expected the new guests would soil themselves upon their first encounter with the crop people.

Horrah had denied his request to come along with them. Runith understood her responsibilities, yet remained disappointed. He tried to avoid self-pity, but the only people he felt comfortable talking clearly with were the Endowers. The Tchoyasmen were servile in fear or to gain the Krall's favor. The Zhaesmen were the same towards Royss. Since Yetrik left, Runith found himself talking to the Endowers, beasts, and himself.

"—a rather remarkable method of design, though I struggle to see the point when our methods are more advanced."

Runith walked towards the tightest gathering to hear the Tchoyasman with the smiling mask, Proctor Thurn, pontificating on his knowledge of Middleman technology. Runith doubted they had found anything significant since his departure.

The Endowers were willing to tell Runith everything they learned about the Middlemen, but they held the truth from those who came to gain power over the crop people. Runith tried to avoid dwelling on it, but he knew that some had resorted to painful methods of interrogation to obtain full cooperation from the Endowers.

He did not want to hear more from the Tchoyas Proctor, nor did he care to hear from the Tchoyas anthropologist, though he would not mind some direction from the squid-masked cartographer. He needed to find Taer, the Gorger Endower. His report on what they had found would be more reliable. If the boy had not grown sourer towards Runith, they could work with Golma and the other Endowers to find something of worth in the Middlelands. *Something worthy of peace, not of power.* Runith was no traitor, but he was intent on serving the Middlemen rather than using them as Royss and Gromm so desired.

Runith lifted Golma out of his way and walked towards the left side of the tent.

"What are you doing?" She asked.

"Going to the cartographer. People have seen that we have arrived, so we don't need to involve ourselves with them."

"Then why are you going to the cartographer?"

He shrugged. "Maybe they have a better idea of what the Middlelands look like by now." He leaned down to whisper. "After this I want to go with you and the Endowers to spend time with the Middlemen–away from all of this."

"You're sure you want to talk with the Middlemen more?"

He smirked. "Can't be worse than before."

"Taer told me about last time."

He chuckled. "I don't think I can get any worse than courting a Middleman. Then again, a man can only be lonely for so long." He winked.

Runith pressed Zhaesmen and Tchoyasmen aside, nearing the table to look over scattered sketches that covered its surface.

From a glance, it was clear which ones Senell, the squid-masked cartographer, had drawn, and which ones his understudies had attempted to draw. They had gone from scattered patches of mapped land to a single map the size of a city, though one much smaller than Kzhek.

"Is there a legend?" Runith asked.

A Zhaesman passed him a sheet of parchment. Runith held it so Golma could see, though she had to stand on her toes to see most of the map.

Either the anthropologist's expedition had earned them little knowledge about the Middleman communities or they failed to communicate with the cartographers. Blocked areas marked two large hubs of Middlemen civilization with smaller groups scattered on the distant hills. The larger hubs were connected by a system of rivers that lead to a lake on the west border of the map. It was interesting enough to spark Runith's curiosity, yet he wanted to validate their findings himself.

Runith pulled one of the better maps from the table and rolled it up.

"What do you think you are doing with that?" a Tchoyasman asked, his mask that of swine.

"Thane Gromm needs it. Argue with him if you want."

The man was silent. He would learn that Thane Gromm never came on the expedition, but that was not Runith's problem. Runith handed the map to Golma and pointed towards the tent's exit. He pressed her forward with a hand on her back, rushing her before anyone would recognize him and ask questions. He didn't know if any Thanes were still at the camp and he didn't care to learn.

"Endowers?" she asked.

He nodded, and she led the way through the camp. He called for Lele to follow, but she was busy resting in a barrel of liquid. Water to drink or wash with, what that barrel contained was not his concern. Part of him felt he should regret his ignorance of others, but it felt right to treat them as they sought to treat the Middlemen. *Nature's justice is the most righteous of all judgment.*

They came upon a lively tent with shouting and shaking edges to testify of its occupants.

Golma giggled and ran to greet her masked friends as soon as they passed through the entrance flaps.

Runith smiled and stood with arms akimbo as he looked over the crowd of the Tchoyas children. It was not a tranquil atmosphere, yet their minds were at peace. Outside of the tent, war perpetuated and manipulation of the weak ran rampant. Inside, they were brothers and sisters, free of control. Free to act as they want. Free to live the childhood that had been taken from them, if but for a brief moment.

"Back again?" The beaver-masked Endower approached Runith and gave him a punch in the shoulder. Runith was relieved that the Gorger's resentment had dissipated. Even though Runith was not responsible for the injustice wrought upon them, he knew it was difficult not to blame him.

"I have work to do." Runith said. He rubbed his shoulder. The boy was still learning to hone his strength. "Training?"

Taer turned back to look at the sparring Gorgers. "Killing time."

"Gather a couple of your best. I want to head out to their center."

"The center of their village?"

Runith nodded. "We still have most of the day left."

"But–"

"You've been there, right?"

"Well, not to the very center."

"Like I said. Gather a couple and we'll leave when you're ready. I'm sure Golma will come along."

Taer nodded and stepped back, but Runith grabbed his shoulder before he could leave. "Do you know if any of the Foreteller Endowers have had any visions?"

Taer laughed. "The usual gloom and terror you would expect at a time of war." He left Runith to ponder on his words. Runith never believed that Foretellers were anything noteworthy until they first arrived in the Middlelands. They had become like oracles. Predicting the future and speaking cryptic words that often warned of dangers to come.

Runith left to speak with Golma and some whom she counted as allies. After discerning which Endowers were not servile towards their captors, they left the camp.

Runith, Taer, Golma, and Lele were accompanied by three other Tchoyas Endowers. The first was a boy of around seven years of age named Thren, a Foreteller, with a mantis mask. The second was a girl of ten named Zae, a Eurythrin should any injury occur, with the mask of a panther. The last was a girl of six, a Shiftling named Retha, who wore a putle mask. Her affection for Lele was immediate. Runith only wished she were a Beastling to have a better connection with the creature whose face she wore.

Taer walked alongside Runith and Lele, while Golma told the others about their time in Fayis. She told them of his frustration, which he would deny to the nobility themselves, but these were children. Pure in heart. He felt like a Tchoyasman, willing to tell them his secrets, knowing that they would be kept hidden behind their masks.

The map led them in the right direction, but the proportions were poorly estimated. They expected a twenty-minute walk north to their destination but found that it took more than an hour to find any gathering of Middlemen.

The atmosphere and landscape of the Middlelands was as unique and captivating as the beings that dwelt there. Staring at the sky that became purple and green as they traveled further from their encampment, Runith wondered if he would ever want to return to Kzhek. *What causes such a change in the sky? Why isn't it like this back at the camp?* The sky's hues danced with each other like an artist slowly mixing paints. Endowed organs were science, that much Runith accepted, but the Middlelands were beyond science. He could see it. He *felt* it in his grafted organ. This was a place of magic.

Despite how unhuman they seemed, the Middlemen still had homes of their own and streets beside them to make a grid. As they walked along a street with ten Middlemen watching, most of the crop people in the wake of Runith's company.

He paused, but the children continued to walk. With Golma and Taer now leading, the Middlemen began to approach. Golma veered towards a pair on the left side of the road. One held a basket, like he had seen them carrying when the company had first arrived in the Middlelands, but this conversation was much more comfortable. Golma spoke to them as new neighbors and extended her palm towards one of them.

Runith took slow steps forward, sighing when the Middlemen did not startle.

As if giving a peace offering or some gesture of welcoming, one of the Middlemen stepped forward, extended a finger like a growing vine, and stroked from the heel of Golma's palm to the tip of her middle finger. He struggled to understand their conversation but understood her expression of gratitude.

The supernatural feeling within his organ returned. Runith *wanted* the Middleman to touch him as well. He did not feel left out. He had moved past wanting to belong long ago. Something deeper compelled him to be touched by the viney fingers.

The other Daeti stepped forward to receive the Middleman's touch, yet Runith stood back.

"What are they doing?" asked Lele.

"I'm trying to understand."

"I can feel their language."

Runith shot her a shocked glare.

Her thin-skinned chest expanded to twice its usual size. She breathed out in a pattern, but neither the Endowers nor Middlemen took note of it. *"I can't understand it but I can feel it, like music."*

What is music to an animal? Am I a prisoner to some odd dream?

Runith's attention snapped forward as Golma grabbed his wrist. "It's your turn."

He nodded and followed. He did not want to stare at the plant creature, but he could not resist it. It was his first time seeing one so close, close enough to touch it.

Never have I seen such a magnificent sight.

He had a brief period of smoking brush in his youth but gave it up within a month. Nothing had ever been so addicting, so forceful as to remove his agency. His *need* to be one with the creature felt like a flashback to those times. It was more than dependency. It was a spiritual need for connection. He felt a pounding heartbeat in his graft. *Is this what compels me? Is this the connection the Endowers have?*

"*Rasteen,*" Runith said. He had spoken their language. Not by practice, but by a connection to them through his graft. He knew what it meant without having to think further. He had spoken the true name of their species.

CHAPTER SEVENTEEN

WIND AND WOLF

*Y*ou *need to understand, Sheath, that I am not alone in many endeavors. Our Krall is between our parties. You–*

Aerhee lifted her quill. She wanted to blame Royss. She wanted to
villainize Gromm more than she ever had, but now was not the time for
blame. Both parties were guilty. She continued to write.

*–need to hear what I have to say. We need to meet. All grows worse, but
we–*

She nearly dropped her quill at the bang and roar of laughter outside
of the doors to her study. Breathing out, she honed her focus and set to
finish her letter.

*–have to find a place, somewhere neutral. Find a Beastling to have a
raven send your reply as soon as possible. Trust me. I trust you. I always
have.*

She wondered if that last sentence was a lie. She had trusted Sheath until that trust had been tested.

Aerhee.

She folded the letter after signing her name and slid it into an envelope. She tucked it into her satchel and opened the door. The laughter was even louder than before.

Aerhee forgot to breathe as she stared out into her living room to see Zeir sitting across from *herself*. It *was* her, but shorter. She had almost forgotten who she had invited or had been *inclined* to invite to her house. It had taken years to grow used to standard Shiftlings, those who could merely change the color of their skin and manipulate only a few parts of their body. The *advanced* skills of practiced Endowers were a completely different beast.

"By Laeih's holy name!" said her miniature self.

"Swear by your own god's name. Enough mocking, Voln."

"As you command, Caser." Voln bowed and revealed his true self.

"You think this is humorous?" she asked Zeir.

She could tell that he held back a laugh but showed a shameless smile.

Aerhee let out a laugh through pressed lips. They all joined in. Laughter, even joy, was something she felt unworthy of. This was a time of preparation. *Each moment should be spent planning, helping, fighting –*

Aerhee looked at her arm, seeing Zeir caressing it. She focused on him.

"It's good to see you relax a bit, Aer."

I can only do so much. Savor the beautiful moments while you have them. She thought of the likelihood of loss and death but banished it like a pestering fly.

"It's good to see you two are getting along well," Aerhee said.

"It's not often you meet a Zhaesmen with a sense of humor," said Voln. She had been with the boy for a few hours, though most of those hours comprised her duties while he followed and complained. He was growing on her, but it was still an acquired taste. Colrig was not wrong in saying that he was more than a child, but she still would not count herself a friend to many cynics and braggarts.

"Ready to go?" Voln asked.

If he continued to complain as much as he had, his taste would be much more difficult for her to acquire.

"Voln tells me you two are going to the Pinnacles?" said Zeir.

Voln nodded. "You have had enough of a problem trying to control the loyalists here. I think I'll be able to help fix that."

How? What makes you think a child can resolve insurrections because you have a gift? Aerhee rubbed the fabric of her pants between her fingers. *Hold yourself.*

The pants were a pleasant change from the courtly dresses that had seemed to be synonymous with her skin ever since she became the Caser. Oddly enough, one does not need to worry about personal appearance as much when their government is in turmoil.

She held up the letter. The silver wax seal of the Zhaes Caser faced Zeir.

Vol stirred. She tightened her grip. She could tell he was holding back the urge to seize it and tear it open.

"I have a different direction in mind for today," she said.

Zeir's eyebrows arched.

What was the best way to proceed with a stranger in the house? She had to tell Zeir what the Krall had told her about her father. His story's ties to the Bronze Seers were significant, but not something she felt comfortable sharing with Voln. It had taken her years to tell her husband that she was a Priesswoman by birth. That was not a detail she would freely share.

Zeir's peaceful countenance reminded her of the night when she had told him about her childhood. Not about the fable she told others, but about the story of her immigration. The pain, the joy, all of it. She expected him to take it well, but he knew more than she had expected. He knew that she was a Priesswoman and had a hidden past, but he did not pry. He trusted her when she would not trust him. When she explained the entirety of her childhood, he only responded with gratitude and acceptance. Voln deserved to know about the meeting's significance, but that would be reserved for Zeir.

"And?" Voln asked.

She blinked to pull herself from her reverie. "This is for Thane Leisa."

"You know where she is?" asked Zeir.

"Who?" asked Voln.

Aerhee let her hand drop and rested the letter on her lap. "The Zhaes Thane of Diplomacy, one of the Thanes who fled after the city's capture." She told Voln about her Krall's request. "I don't know where she is now, but I hoped that you could have a Beastling reach out to the other Endowers in Court Tchoyas. She was one of the Thanes that fled there after the fall of Kzhek."

"But Colrig wants us to focus on the loyalists here in Zhaes," said Voln. "The Holy Reapers–"

"Whatever they call themselves, they can wait."

"Are you sure, Aerhee?" Zeir asked. "We lost the Zenth region days ago and rumors suggest one of the three remaining municipalities wants to side with the loyalists."

Are you sure you want to turn away from the directions of your new captain in favor of your old ruler? Choose a side, Aerhee. This is no time for middle ground. "We need her on our side."

"Why?" asked Voln.

"I'm not saying that we should abandon the municipalities to the whims of the loyalists, but–"

"You want a friend at your side, Zhaeswoman? I thought you were the adult here?""Sheath–Thane Leisa–has better diplomatic connections than anyone I know. I am not saying that the Krall is right in all that he wants, but he understands that Sheath would be an invaluable asset in helping bring peace."

"But she is an Endowed," said Zeir.

"We have plenty of them on our side," said Aerhee.

Zeir sighed. "Sheath is inflexible. She may *understand* the perspectives of others, but she is set in her way."

"Just send the perding letter," said Voln. "If she agrees to help, she will reply, but we do not need to change our direction to wait for a response."

"Just–" Zeir scraped his teeth on his lower lip. He had always been reluctant to express his opinions, especially those that contradicted hers, but the war had caused something to change within him. "Just be careful what you tell her. If she doesn't agree with you, she could use our knowledge to her advantage."

One of the benefits of long-distance communication with a Feelman. She would have a conversation with Sheath via letters with no Endowed power giving Sheath an advantage. If she agreed to meet, that would change.

She pointed at the letter in her lap. "I am just asking for a conversation on neutral ground. I trust her."

"I don't know her as well as you do."

"You should know her enough that she is a friend. All politics and policy aside, she respects our relationship." She thought of the times Sheath had invaded her mind with her ability. "I trust her enough to give us a chance to try to find middle ground."

Voln scoffed. "Middle ground isn't an option. My existence is proof of that. I may have been born before harvesting began, but the principle still stands."

Aerhee held back her complaints and nodded.

Voln reached out his hand. "Give it. I'll hand it to one of the Endowers."

Aerhee held it and furrowed her brow.

"Don't forget, Zhaeswoman, that you also have children in your Court who were born before the Pact of Province. With all the scorn they received for what they were, it was not hard to connect."

"So you organized them like the Endowers in your Court?"

He nodded. "Never forget that there is more going on around you than what you see."

"We'll take it to one of them together. Colrig wanted us to work together, so I might as well follow you to see your accomplishments."

He smiled through the jaws of his mask. For once, Aerhee felt comfortable calling the child her ally. She had always assumed that the so-called "advanced intellect" of the Endowed was just a rumor used to justify their livelihood. She struggled but was coming to accept some misconceptions used to manipulate her people into accepting harvesting. The more she worked with the Harmony Allegiant, the more she learned that her Court had to be cleansed of past manipulations.

"So," Voln knelt by the short table before them and studied the map of Kzhek, "what are we going to do while we wait for her response?"

Humility. It was the first time the boy had been willing to listen.

"What does Colrig want you to do?" she asked.

"I don't know. The perding kulf expects perfection from me but just tossed me to you."

Frustration. Vulnerability.

Aerhee turned to Zeir, checking his response to see if she should push the boy further.

"We've been working on maintaining the infrastructure of the five municipalities," said Zeir. "Colrig wants us to strike the loyalist movements at the core. It only makes sense he would send a Shiftling to work with us."

Voln's cold eyes stared at her through his mask. *If only I were a Feelman. Perd, we need you, Sheath.*

Aerhee knew she was stubborn. She had been given a distinct assignment yet tried to find a way around it. Sheath distracted her. The Krall distracted her. Now, the boy.

"Why did Colrig choose you?" she asked.

"I don't *perding* know!"

Even she shook at his shout. "Does Colrig–"

"Perd Colrig! I'm here to work with *you*. Leave him behind."

"Voln." She waited until he seemed calm enough to proceed. "I want you to tell me—"

"I want you to focus on your perding duty! You're not my mother!"

His eyes were bloodshot. She had heard how stoic this boy was, but something had happened. She triggered something all too fresh in his mind.

Not now, Aerhee. She nodded. *But by Laeih, I will learn what that boy has against the Sleffman.* She had no children but would try to imagine Voln as–*no. Too odd. End that thought there and focus on your duty.*

Zeir bounced his leg on the floor. She placed her hand on his thigh and he stilled.

"Let's show you what we have learned so far," she said. She kept her eyes on the documents that covered the table. Voln was embarrassed enough and did not need her prying eyes right now.

She pointed to a sheet of notes on the right side of the table. "We are dealing with two parties. Both seem the same on the outside, but one is more calculated. *They* are the true threat. The others are mindless sycophants."

Zeir leaned forward and pointed to one of the five municipalities. "This area is occupied by said sycophants. These Zhaesmen only want to sustain harvesting because it is what they have been told to do. Their morality and allegiance depend on blind obedience."

His finger shifted to another region. It was larger than the previous and had a line drawn to a mountain range with *The Pinnacles* written atop the peaks.

Zeir looked at the boy's eyes, then back at the map. "This area is of more concern. Imagine if Colrig wanted to enforce Sleff law upon all people. A tyranny of policy. That is what we believe these 'Holy Reapers' are. They do not care about harvesting as much as domination. What is worse is that they do not seem to be affiliated with the loyalists. They are a sect that is trying to utilize a time of disorder to assert their dominance."

"From what we can surmise," said Aerhee, "it is a sect of Zhaes extremists that has been insignificant in the past. They are utilizing the disorder in the Court to recruit people to their cause. These are not harvesting extremists, but *Zhaes* extremists."

Voln sniffed. "So they don't even care about harvesting?"

Zeir shrugged. "While it is not the focus of their efforts, they are using it as a tool to recruit people who do not agree with the Harmony Allegiant."

"They sound like more of a danger to your Court than to the Allegiant."

"Yes," said Aerhee. "While that is true, the Allegiant strives for international unity. Any threat to one of our Courts is a threat to all of them."

Zeir sat up straight, making his posture emit more confidence. "Even if we were to win the entire Court over to oppose harvesting, the Holy Reapers would remain a threat."

"You Zhaesmen are already extreme enough with your Ideal of obedience. What difference does it make if some sect goes a step further?"

"Faithless worship, a secular regime."

Voln stared at her.

She sighed and leaned closer. "The title *Holy Reapers* is a misnomer. They want to make the law their god rather than god their law."

"Like the Priessmen," Voln said, almost as if speaking to himself.'

"I suppose so," Aerhee said, "but with more structure, and with more force. This is all based on assumptions from the little intel that we have. We could be wrong, which is why we still need to investigate them."

"Makes sense, I guess." Voln leaned against the back of his seat and looked up.

Zeir leaned back as well. "It's a lot to process, but you'll see soon enough. We should have assumed that someone would take advantage of war."

Voln stood, joviality breathed back into him. "To the Pinnacles, then?"

Aerhee wanted to calm the boy and had the urge to argue for the sake of control, but she let such feelings go. It was freeing. Humility, once understood, alleviates one from the burden of pride. "Are you coming, Zeir?"

He nodded.

She smiled at Voln. "Find us a Beastling to deliver the letter. We'll find a carriage to the Pinnacles after that.

Voln shifted, turning his skin pale and his mask into the face of a Zhaesboy. "Now we need to find a way for you two to hide your identities. You're still the perding Caser."

CHAPTER EIGHTEEN

SUFFERER

S emi wondered if the Terpels felt pain the same way. They stood firm when struck with a bowstaff. She fell with almost every strike and had lost consciousness twice already.

She stood, feeling the mark the rough wood had left on her already-bruised cheek.

"Are you sure you still want this?" chuckled Thane Kelm. One of his eyes twitched as he smirked.

No, I'm more lost than anyone. Semi spat blood on the hot sand at her feet. She tightened her grip on her staff and crouched.

Thane Kelm's lips turned up even more, but Semi's Terpel opponent only became more concerned.

"Don't hold back," Semi hissed through clenched teeth. Her words betrayed her innermost wishes.

Hesitation captured the Terpel. Semi was ready to attempt a roll and strike, but her opponent held still, shaking.

Semi knew that pain. The Terpel's lips remained tight, but her eyebrows had a slight arch as if she were pleading for help. *As if she were pleading for an escape.*

Semi knew they would fight but would not instigate it. She was not the most adept fighter, but her best fights always began by her reacting to her opponent's first move.

"*Fight already!*" Thane Kelm shouted. Both she and her opponent attacked, their staffs meeting in a clash. Semi was not surprised that her opponent had lost her inhibitions. She also felt compelled by the Thane's words. It was as if attacking was the worst itch she had ever experienced and obeying Thane Kelm's command was the only solution.

Semi landed a strike across her opponent's leg, causing her to stumble.

The Terpel corrected her stance and returned the strike.

Semi rolled, but had mis-predicted her opponent's strike, rolling directly into an attack. The Terpel raised her staff, but Semi held up a hand.

"Do not yield so early, Semi." scoffed Thane Kelm.

She tried to stand, but fell back as a cramp seized her thigh, and her knee buckled.

The Terpel reached over a gauntleted hand and offered help to her stand. Semi took it and stood.

They were all armed with light metal gauntlets to protect their hands but wore little else. Leather pads covered their most vital areas. Their leather helms would provide insufficient protection from a striking greatsword. She hoped they would be better equipped in an actual battle.

In battle.

Those words made her question where she had lost her direction. She was no warrior, and a voice whispered that she never would be. She was stubborn, but this time, that flaw had become a virtue. She would prove her doubts wrong.

She held her staff and crouched but fell back and held onto the staff as she slid back down to the ground. Her head pulsed and her vision faded to black. Consciousness remained, but it was slipping. She clenched her fist. The gauntlet dug into her skin. She focused on the pain. As long as it remained, she was conscious.

"Enough," said Thane Kelm.

She kept her gaze on the floor as color returned to her vision and nodded. Now was not the time to be stoic. Her mind had the will to continue, but her body had given up two rounds ago.

The Terpel helped her stand and slung Semi's arm around her neck. Thane Kelm stared at her with a crooked sneer, his arms behind his back.

"I mustn't forget that you are the only one here that can tire."

"I don't care. I still want to fight with them."

"No." He chuckled and shook his head as he approached. His blood-shot eyes met hers from only a step away. "You are still a Shiftling. A warrior you may become, but not one of these foot soldiers. I have better intentions for you if you remain stalwart." He waved towards the tents. "Take her back, Terpel. I think we have fought enough for now. We need to feed you so you can stay fueled for the night run."

Semi took part in every training that she could, regardless of her inferior stamina. She took part in everything, save the night runs. Terpels did not need sleep or rest, only food to sustain them and their third bowel. As an Endowed, Semi already ate twice as much as the average person, but the Terpels doubled her requirements. While she slept to save energy for the next day, the Terpels would spend the six hours running. She had wondered why they needed to work on their endurance, but Kelm informed her that the runs focused on speed.

Thane Kelm wandered throughout the training ground, barking commands, while the Terpel helped Semi back to the feast tent.

"I think I can walk on my own now."

The Terpel held on but left Semi after a moment of struggle.

"I will still accompany you, Lady Semi."

Semi held in a laugh. Thane Kelm treated her like fish innards but demanded that the Terpels treat her like royalty. Telling them to get rid of the "Lady" or "Mistress" was a wasted endeavor. One might agree to drop it, but that was what felt like an endless amount of Terpels. Even though she had worked with this Terpel for most of the day, she had not tried to build a friendship. The Terpels were like flesh golems, emotionless tools for their masters.

Despite their dead personalities, kindness was never a worthless endeavor.

"Are you holding up well?" Semi asked. "I landed a couple of strikes."

"Nothing that I could not withstand," the woman said. Her voice wavered.

Semi turned her head faster than a ghete in search of prey to confirm her suspicions. The Terpel faced forward, but Semi could still see her eyes.

Bloodshot and wet.

"Gruthwoman, what is wrong?" Semi asked. Had one of them broken free from the emotionless vice of Thane Kelm's control?

"I must see that you rest," replied the Terpel.

Tears ran down her cheeks. Her stone facade remained. Her voice was still.

"What about you? You seem–"

"I am well," the Terpel said, almost shouting. Her lip hinted at a frown.

Should I keep pressing? Will I break her if I try? What will break? Her will or the chains that bind her? She felt bad, but the thought thrilled her. The first hint at humanity was a glimmer of hope.

They were the first to enter the feast tent for the last meal of the day. Semi hoped that they would have some time before another wave if soldiers came to feast. Two Gruth cooks cut bread and laid out dishes at the far end of the tent. Semi felt confident that she and the Terpel would be left alone, if only for a moment.

"What is your name?" Semi whispered as she pointed for the Terpel to sit.

She obeyed but shook her head as Semi sat across from her. "Gruth is the name I live by."

Semi let out a slow sigh, trying to ease her frustration. She had managed to see some emotion from the Terpel, but the woman remained in her shell of obedience. This was not the first time she had asked one of them their name. Each time she tried, she received the same answer. Even though this Terpel had reacted as expected, Semi felt she was close to a true response.

"Tell me how you feel."

"A Terpel does not feel."

"You are crying," she hissed.

"A Terpel is unwavering."

What a poor response. I'm close. Keep pushing. "Tell me how you actually feel."

No answer. She wasn't even looking at Semi.

"Who were you before?"

"A laborer."

Had her memories been purged? "Before your graft?"

She clenched her jaw. Semi sat on the bench across from her. It was old and appeared as if it was made of driftwood.

Servants on the far side of the tent caught Semi's attention with banging pots and dishes as they made haste to prepare the rest of the food for the inevitable rush of Terpels.

"Tell me who you were." The Terpel stared past Semi.

"Who are you?" Semi asked.

The Terpel's breathing trembled.

Semi wished she were a Feelman. "Where is your family?"

"Help me," the Terpel's voice trembled.

"Yes!" Semi tried to contain her excitement. "How, what can I–"

"I want to leave. I have no choice."

"Why? Are they holding your family hostage?"

The Terpel shook her head.

"Why do you obey?"

"We must."

Semi tried to calm herself. "How can I help you?"

"I–"

She stopped speaking as Terpels began to flood the tent. She stood until they lined their respective tables. Thane Kelm followed the last of the soldiers.

"Firm is the foundation!" he shouted as he made the Gruth salute.

"Firm is the foundation!" the others repeated.

Thane Kelm passed through and waved a hand, allowing them to sit.

Semi remained seated the whole time, as did the wavering Terpel, who returned to her emotionless state.

You brought yourself into this. You requested to become a warrior. What *had* inspired her to make such a bold decision to join them? She did not want to fight them in war. She did not want to become another casualty. *Am I here to free them?* Her allegiance was lost in a sea of confusion and fear. She had imprisoned herself because of pride. Some pride that she would appease by becoming the warrior others had wanted her to be.

Servants laid the food before them, each proportioned to share. Large fish were roasted whole and were the size of a shark. Roasted potatoes, yams, and other root vegetables sat in mounds next to a pyramid of dark bread loaves. Semi saw fruits, other meats, and rice among plenty of other options, but ate the options she had directly before her.

The Terpel who had sparred with her ate half of a bread loaf before beginning on the fish. Semi wanted to learn more about her but would gain nothing through direct questions about her past. Her attempts to learn her name proved just as fruitful. As far as she could tell, the Terpels were not forbidden from speaking their names, but only saw themselves as Terpels. They were treated as objects and believed that they were nothing more.

"Trainer, what are we doing tomorrow?"

The Terpel did not seem to hear her.

"Trainer!"

The Terpel looked at Semi and raised her eyebrow as she wiped fish oil from her lips.

"Yes, you."

"I am not your trainer."

"Well, you won't give me another name. I appreciated working with you today. We'll work together again tomorrow."

"We are not allowed to choose our opponents."

"Thane Kelm will grant my request."

The one she had taken to calling trainer slowed her chewing.

Spending enough time with one Terpel was sure to reveal something. Semi was anxious to uncover trainer's history but knew it would be a long journey.

She took her first bite of fish, its savor worthy of a small victory.

❧❧❧❧❧ ❧❧❧❧❧

A bell woke Semi from her small sleeping pad. She sat up to see one of Thane Kelm's servants in the crack of the tent's flaps.

"The Terpels will be back from the run in ten minutes."

Semi nodded and waved for him to leave.

She stood, muscles aching from the previous day's training. Boxes and piles of training supplies lined each side of the tent. She was the only one in the army who needed a place to sleep. Thane Kelm and his servants had tents planned for them when the army formed, but Semi was a late entrant.

Thane Kelm had given her rules to follow, but she wondered how binding her deal with his military was.

She avoided questioning him, but still wondered how the Thane would react if she were to deny a request or a command. He had invested time and effort into her, but what would happen if she were to defect? Would she be counted as a traitor? She had no plans to leave, at least not within the coming days, but still questioned her freedom.

She adorned her training gear and left the tent to meet the army. She heard them in the distance but knew that she still had time before they arrived.

They needed replenishment after an entire night of running. She was expected to join them before her first training session, but she had other expectations for herself. She could join them late. If she caught them during the last few minutes of their meal, she could manage to fit some food in.

She ran toward the beach. She wished the impulse to swim would have hit her before she had adorned her combat gear.

Her mind could be filled with regrets, both large and small, but she let them free as she dove into the brisk water. The morning was warm, but her determination distracted even more from the water's temperature.

Her impulse rejuvenated her, for that is what her past few months had been, a series of impulses to prove to herself that she mattered.

She could not endure the night runs, but that did not diminish her need to train harder than any opponent. She swam with all her might. Even though she knew she could never be as great as a Terpel, she invested all she could.

Each stroke brought her closer to her goal. What that goal was, she was yet to discover. She trained to become a soldier, but did not know if she had the blind determination needed to kill her opponent in battle. She did not *want* to battle and trembled at the thought of killing even the worst person she could imagine. Killing was an abomination, yet the lords of Facet insisted that it was the only way to preserve their vision of righteousness.

She was lost but came to an epiphany that she felt comfortable accepting. She was not training for the Gruth army. The training was not for Thane Kelm. She wasn't even training for Yetrik's approval.

She was training for herself.

The world was a hurricane of politics, bloodshed, and bigotry. Its torrent was ceaseless, yet the constant rhythm of the sea's waves let her forget the world's ills. The pain of exhaustion and the brisk water were but small inconveniences in the grand scheme of her life. The pains had become welcome distractions, like a frightening fireside story.

Pain brought her bliss. Exhaustion brought her pleasure. She swam, trusting in the one being that never wavered.

Lord Deilf guide me.

❧❧❧❧❧ ❧❧❧❧❧

The hypnotic rhythm of the crashing waves was disrupted by a shout from the shore. Semi initially ignored it but stopped when she heard her name. Treading waters, she neared the shore and spotted Thane Kelm beside two of his guards.

Semi wanted to continue and convinced herself that she would have if it was not for the exhaustion. She did not know how long she had swum. She had taken her time for bliss, but like all great pleasures, the joyous peaks of life are not eternal.

"Semi!"

The Thane's call was as strong as any of her personal impulses.

She reached the shore. The sticking sand would grow bothersome, but she did not care. The bliss from the sea remained, though it was wearing off in the Thane's presence. As he and his guards turned away, she knew he was no native to Thusk. Nudity was not taboo among the folk who dwelt on the seaside. She did not feel ashamed because of her nakedness, for she had known nothing of it being odd until she left the bubble of childhood, meeting Western Gruthmen. It had felt nice to be free of the dirty clothing and restrictive combat gear.

"You can look now," she said, approaching the Thane. With sandals in hand, she felt the sand squish between her blistered toes.

He smiled with an uncomfortable grin, as if she smelt of rotten fish. "Where have you been? You missed the morning feast."

She gestured to the sea and he stared back with an empty glare. "Training."

"That is not a part of your regiment."

"I decide my own regiment."

"Then you will fail. Without direction, you will not achieve anything." He shook his head and wiped his eyes. "Combat training, let's go."

"I want to be with the same Terpel that I was with yesterday."

"How do you expect me to remember which one that was? Come now, Semi. Don't lose yourself."

"I can find her."

"No need. We will find you a partner to train with."

"I decide–"

"What have you come here for, Semi? If you do not want to comply, what do you hope to gain?"

How can I answer the very question I ask myself? "I came to serve my people."

His reply sounded like a groan. "As does every soldier here." He waved for her to follow and walked towards the camp. "Enough of this. Come."

She followed, not walking beside the Thane, but a few steps behind.

"Act like a child and you will only make your circumstances worse. *I* have invested time and attention in your success. Please make my efforts worth it."

Semi stepped closer, standing with the Thane and his guards.

"They began without you," he said.

Semi lost her smile.

"But you are more valuable than them."

That should have made her feel better, but she could not rejoice over the Thane's view of the Terpels. She did not want to argue with him over his reason for keeping a slave army, even if he insisted that they chose to serve him. They were both Gruthmen, yet that did not mean that they agreed on every dispute. Even the closest allies do not agree on everything.

"Too many concerns are burdening you, Semi. I can tell."

"Are you a Feelman?" she asked.

He smiled and shook his head. "Even without the ability, you are easy to read."

She knew very little about Thane Kelm besides his role in the nobility and membership in the Patriarchy. Her time with him had confirmed that he had *some* ability, *some* gift to control the Terpels. She would learn soon enough, but did not want to push him any further than she already had. Still, she grew more irritated with him and his claim to know her. She loathed the condescension of those who thought themselves all-knowing. The man was a Scholar by title, but the more she learned about the Patriarchy of Scholars, the less she was inclined to believe that their focus was on Scholarship. If she did not know herself in this situation, there was no chance that this man did.

"Then what have you learned?" she asked.

"It was you who asked to join the Terpels because you felt worthless. You wanted to inspire a change as the world fell around you. You must understand by now that becoming a soldier in an army will yield you nothing."

Make my despair even more pernicious, why don't you?

"But you came to me," he said. "Your aim was not clear, but I will help you direct it."

There is nothing more characteristic of a brother of the Patriarchy than cryptic statements that force you to ask for clarity.

"Do not burden yourself with inadequacy. These Terpels are Endowers *made* to endure, made to fight and labor. Your organ was never aimed at allowing you to fulfill their role. You deserve more delicate assignments. Nevertheless, you can fulfill your desire to serve in our military."

He stopped and turned to face her. "Whether you recognized it, you joined the army to infiltrate and attack from within the enemy territory. With a little more training, you will be prepared to assassinate the leaders of those who call themselves the Harmony Allegiant."

CHAPTER NINETEEN

BROTHERHOOD

Y etrik laid his head against Avra as she flew towards Palace Hill.

He felt the rhythm of her breathing and almost fell asleep, though he credited most of that to his fatigue. He had only participated in a single battle, but what a battle it had been.

Khoga flew to the right, Kevlen swung his hornblade in the air. Yetrik felt less accomplished. He had given a fraction of the effort that Kevlen had and gained none of the glory. Self-doubt and envy crept into his mind, but he banished them by closing his eyes and listening to Avra's rhythmic respirations.

"*I understand you, Yetrik,*" Avra hummed.

He patted a reply. "*Are you reading my thoughts?*"

He felt a vibrating growl. *A laugh.*

"*Am I wrong?*"

"*I can't hear what you think, but I can sense, even feel, your emotions.*"

Yetrik received a graft, expecting to be able to speak with animals. *How myopic was I?* He gained a companion. Not someone to replace a future spouse. Not a close friend. Avra was something greater. His organ had forged a connection closer than any previous relationship he had experienced. They had worked together for such a small sliver of his life, yet she became a part of him. One that if severed, would leave him shattered beyond repair.

Descending on the hill, he lifted his head to see that the building was no spectacle. The palace was nothing greater than a modest fortress in Gruth. Where they had little to make it stand out from the other buildings, its position atop a hill gave it the small amount of respect it deserved.

What respect does a building deserve? What makes these monarchs worthy of luxury any more than the common people? Laws were created by humans, not by gods. These rulers have no right to hold their throne. No one is entitled to glory.

Yetrik did not see himself as a patriot. He fought for ideals, for lives and beliefs, not for a selection of land. He had seen how division brought hatred. Difference was not the reason for division. People could believe and live as they pleased, but where rulers create divisions on maps, tolerance perishes. Court Gruth was his home. He loved the land and the people, but that was all it was. When people turn their nation into their god, they become as corrupt as any idol worshiper.

He tightened his grip on Avra as she landed. Even though she descended into a graceful trot, he braced for a rough landing. He trusted Avra, but not himself. As they grew closer, he learned more about himself than he had ever anticipated.

"*Khoga, Avra,*" Kevlen called. "*Remain nearby. You can roam, but do not go far enough that you could not hear our call.*"

The two zlatogs screeched their agreement.

Avra lowered herself for Yetrik to jump down. Kevlen walked ahead of him towards the modest palace. Yetrik shook himself loose and ran after the Priessman.

The guards standing before the palace entrance had already moved aside. Yetrik wondered if they moved because they recognized them, or if they moved in fear of the zlatogs. With a slim stature and a face that made him look younger than twenty, he never had an intimidating presence. Even in armor he doubted that he looked intimidating. Their timidity did not make him happy, but relieved. He did not want to seem domineering or threatening, but this was war. Fewer questions asked and more privileges given only helped him achieve his goals.

"Have you met the Krall before?" Yetrik asked Kevlen as they entered.

Kevlen shook his head. "That was my father's business. I never wanted to be a diplomat."

"Then what do you want?"

Kevlen shrugged. "I am still trying to find that answer, but I suppose everything depends on the outcome of the war."

The same sobering realization caused Yetrik to question his future.

Without being told, he would have never guessed that he had entered a palace. Even though he saw the guards out front to testify of its role, he still wondered if they were in the wrong building.

He had heard Kevlen jest about Sleff poverty, but even he lost his smile as they stood on the stained and cracked tile pathway. The entrance hall was empty of occupants except for the occasional passing Sleffman. It felt as if they had entered an athenaeum days before its condemnation. Tapestries with the Sleff sigil of the spine rat hung on the walls, but they were dark and dusty with frayed bottoms. The wooden furniture and railings should have been revarnished a decade ago, and the rugs had lost any softness over years of careless trampling. The smell of dust and old wood clouded over the hints of old mead. If it was an old tavern, Yetrik would feel more inclined to be impressed.

They passed down the main corridor and entered into a larger chamber with more entrances to new hallways. A small part of the second story was visible with a wooden railing that he would not trust to lean on. A group of three Sleffman stood by the railing but left in haste after seeing the foreign guests.

None of the palace's occupants were interested in welcoming them. Yetrik hoped the Krall would be more hospitable.

They continued forward and reached two large doors with polished wood and silver studs. The make was much nicer and more impressive than any other doorway in the building. It was old but had been taken care of well.

A Sleff guard in heavy armor opened the door for them and they entered.

"It is nice to finally meet you, Your Grace." Kevlen said as he walked ahead of Yetrik towards a heavily padded chair in the back of the room. His voice echoed through the chamber with his characteristic charisma.

Yetrik quickened his pace to reach Kevlen, who stopped a few paces before the step that lifted the chair, or what he assumed to be the throne. It was nothing compared to the height of the Tchoyas Krall's staircase to his throne, yet it was still a slight sign of superiority.

"What do you mean? Who let these barbarians enter?" exclaimed the Krall.

Kevlen said that Terin sent us to meet with her. Had the Thane not communicated this with her before?

The Krall's face grew from confusion to anger.

She was dressed nicer than any Sleffman he had seen. She did not wear a dress as did most noblewoman but had tight black pants and a robe over her tunic. Despite her anger, she was beautiful, with looks to rival Semi. Her hair had been braided into two locks that hung near the base of her neck. Aside from her sneer, she had a cleft lip that revealed her right incisor. He had heard that Krall Lhaen Pensa of Court Sleff was an intimidating and stern woman, but he never would have guessed so based on her appearance. Nevertheless, her reaction suggested that the rumors were true.

"Pardon me," said Kevlen, trying to lighten the mood with a chuckle. "We were under the impression that you were informed—"

"Informed that my Court would erupt into chaos because of some dispute over a policy? Who are you?" She waved for her six guards to come closer. Each one unsheathed a claymore.

Yetrik's heart dropped. Every instinct told him to retreat, but that was not the response of an Endower. Regardless of his inhibitions, he would have to overcome them to fulfill his calling. He forced himself to push forward and overcome his timidity.

Kevlen can handle this one.

Doubts triumphed. He had failed again.

"Kevlen Phanos, Captain of the Priess Beastlings, son of Peval Phanos, Krall of Court Priess." His voice demanded respect and was free of humor.

Krall Pensa smiled, the cleft in her lip rising as she bore more of her teeth. "Son of the Bloated Krall?"

"Do not mock my father." Kevlen demanded.

"Oh, I do not mean to mock, *Priessboy*. If it wasn't for your father, we would never have learned the consequences of Endowed hedonism. As it turns out, we were not designed to have a *fourth* bowel implanted. I hope your people have learned from his mistake."

Yetrik spoke, hoping to diffuse the growing tension. "I don't know if you have been informed, Your Grace, but the Sleff loyalists are victorious."

"And who might those *loyalists* be, Gruthman? Heitt only knows why you are here. What makes those who oppose or support *you* any more loyal to *my* Court? You zealots have only divided my people. What have I done to deserve such cruelty?"

"Cruelty?" Kevlen stepped forward. Yetrik had seen the Priessman's anger, but he knew how to contain it when necessary. "We *saved* your people! This presumed cruelty is their fault. If you allow people to rebel against order, cruelty is what you will breed."

"None of this was my doing."

"But it was your people who instigated it. The rebellions began here! Right in your Court."

She shook her head. "Civil unrest rises and passes like any other natural disaster. What we did not need was your Courts intervening."

Kevlen laughed. "You think that order would have returned to your Court if you left the people to dwindle? Burn down a few buildings, kill a couple members of the nobility, then it solves itself? You would have nothing left! You Sleffmen–"

"We understand your frustration, Your Grace." Yetrik interrupted. *Perd, Kevlen. Don't live up to the hateful stereotypes that your Court carries.* "None of us want to govern the other's Court." *Except for Terin, who wants to oversee them all.*

Kevlen stepped back.

She leaned forward, resting her head on her palms. They remained silent for a moment until she lifted her head with bloodshot eyes. "What a *perding* disaster. Forgive me. When you two walked in, I finally had someone to pin it on, but alas, we are just pieces in a game. A perding cruel one at that."

"Hopelessness is–" Yetrik said.

Her scowl returned. "I am far from hopeless." She took a deep breath and scratched her eyes with her palms. "Frustration is an emotion I can live with. My Thanes may be self-proclaimed harvesting loyalists, but all of this is just a huge veil for power. You think that so many people would die to continue to harvest organs from children? The ethicality of the practice is not my concern. Those in power want to stay in power."

"You think this is a conspiracy?" asked Kevlen.

"Discounting the zealots who claim that harvesting is a gift from the gods, yes. Regardless of the issues it fixes, it is still an abominable practice. I don't believe in the high mortality of Endower births, either. Did I support the Pact of Province? Can a Krall oppose her Thanes when they all stand in favor of some coup?" She laughed and shook her head. "We are, and will always be, the whores of the Zhaesmen. Maybe your father is guilty, Priessboy, maybe he bought into their harvesting ploy. I don't quite care either way. What I cannot stand is that people die for others to receive glory. *My* people are dying for some Zhaes or Priess 'loyalists' who only advocate their leader's dreams of supremacy. The other half die for some other zealot army that thought it was wise to raid Kzhek. I'm sure the Patriarchy is happy with all the chaos."

"You think–"

Yetrik placed his hand on Kevlen's shoulder to stop him.

The Krall had fixed her mind on conspiracy and found internal satisfaction through blaming others. Yetrik believed that there *was* more to the war than harvesting but did not believe the extremes professed by Krall Pensa. He came to help find peace and middle ground. Not to press the paranoid Krall's beliefs.

Her words were convincing, but he knew how to defend himself against convincing speakers. Kevlen respected his beliefs, but he met a few Priessmen while in Court Priess who tried to convince him that his belief system was comprised fables. Faith was something he had worked for, something he would not surrender. Still, part of him wondered how much more she knew about the desires of the other Court rulers.

How were they to bridge an alliance with her and a man who wanted to dissolve Court boundaries? One who very well might be campaigning for the conspiracy that she feared? Although Yetrik was not a devoted nationalist, he respected those who were so devoted to their native lands.

The room was not comfortable, making it more difficult for the situation to feel anything less than an interrogation. It was only the size of a

Canton council room but lacked the furniture. A window on the right side of the stone and wood chamber helped lighten up the room beside the two torches that hung on each wall, yet it was still dim.

Ignoring the discomfort, Yetrik acted to dissolve the contention in the room. He sat on the ground, not able to cross his legs as well as he had hoped in the armor and looked at the Krall as if they were gathered around a campfire.

Kevlen arched his eyebrows, then sat next to Yetrik.

"What is this?" Krall Pensa guffawed.

"We are here to help as people, not as pieces of the government," said Yetrik.

"Whether you recognize it or not, you are a part of the government's plan."

"Oh," Yetrik nodded, "I am aware of that. I *am* with a Priessmen, after all."

They shared a laugh. An anxious one, but it was a start.

Yetrik sighed and brought his eyes up to meet hers. She remained tense, but was not as unbreakable as before. "Forget them. The Kralls and Thanes, the other military leaders. We are two men and a Krall discussing a suffering city. The anti-harvesting troops have fled the city. I cannot make promises about the future but right now, the city is still. People are injured, suffering, or dead, but there is no fighting. We have to hasten. Kevlen and I have zlatogs and other Beastlings at our side. Politics aside, what can *I* do *right now* to ease some of that suffering?"

His countenance was still, but Yetrik's heart pounded and his hands hurt from clenching his fists.

She smiled.

"Aiding the injured and the homeless because of the destruction is a start." She stood and walked to sit before them. "What concerns me is the inevitable return of battle in my city. I am sure it wages on in the other cities in my Court as we speak."

Her pessimism and complaints made it difficult to find an actual start to their efforts. They needed a bridge.

"I understand our differences in opinion, but would you be open to a meeting with some Thanes from my Court?" Kevlen asked. "You can plead for change, but we cannot reach a resolution—one that would dissolve the violence throughout Facet—without agreements between Courts."

"Which Thanes?" she asked.

"Namely Thanes Terin Trosh and Sairee Phemus."

Yetrik recalled his experience in Ekscomos as their faces played across his mind.

"That depends on their purpose. I do not want them to come here hoping to convince me to join their side."

"So you oppose us?" asked Kevlen.

She shook her head. "I did not say that. I stand with the Sleffmen. They are split, but as their monarch, I am responsible for seeing that I can preserve as many lives as possible."

"Then how do you plan on doing that?" Yetrik asked.

"How do these Priess leaders plan to save my people?"

Yetrik then saw beyond the confident visage forced by the Krall. She looked as young and vulnerable as he was.

She was lost and distraught. Yetrik rarely prided himself on his skill to read others, but he felt the fear in the Krall's words. She denied their offers yet cried out for help. She was a hysterical mother trying to find a salve for her suffering children and had grown tired of fruitless solutions offered by those around her. *We need something promising, but where is promise in a time without peace?*

He hated the realization that crept into his kind, but knew it was the only way that they could capture her attention and cooperation. He would suffer the consequences of lies when they called for payment.

Until then, he made a promise, one that he could not guarantee. He lied for convenience and gain, tossing morality aside for a moment of hope.

"Agree to meet with these Priess Thanes and I can assure you that your Court will have the support of Court Gruth."

"I already told you that I am not interested in this war."

"Not mere political support, but support for your people. Gruth support in the form most characteristic of my people. Food, support, *protection*. If you are willing to let us help, we can help heal your Court."

It was not a lie. If he was fortunate, the promise would be fulfilled and the loyalists would triumph.

"What would you gain?" she asked.

"Camaraderie."

"Under whose authority do you make this claim?"

Thus a hopeful promise becomes one supported by a lie. Firm is the Foundation. The words of the Gruth Ideal resonated in his mind. The words that he had betrayed. A foundation built upon lies is destined for ruin.

"Krall Plath and Thane Gett below him."

Kevlen turned to him with a furrowed brow.

Thane Gett would be willing to comply if their goal was oriented towards peace, but the Krall's intentions were unknown. Yetrik. never thought of himself adept in political maneuvers, but he had surprised himself with the Zhaes Thanes. With Thane Gett, he was sure that they could reach an agreement, should the need arise.

"Very well, then. I will accept your offer. I'll meet with the Priess Thanes *in* Court Gruth. Krall Plath himself needs to promise that he will resolve the conflict in my Court. Not political or militaristic support, but aid for my people."

"Well, I can see–"

She held her hand up to stop Yetrik and continued. "Escort me to Thusk to meet with your Krall." She turned to Kevlen. "If your Thanes insist on meeting with me, we can gather there. I am sure they too would benefit from a meeting in Court Gruth, seeing that you are allies."

Her calm, calculated appearance was a lie. This woman's wishes were as wild as a feral ghete.

Kevlen's eyes were wide, but he sighed to control himself. "Thusk would be twice as far a journey for my Thanes."

He glared at Yetrik as if to ask him where his bold claims had come from. Courts Gruth and Sleff were technically allies, not bearing the implied antagonism that each Court had towards Court Priess, but their alliance was nothing akin to Court Sleff's ties to Court Zhaes.

Thane Plath's cooperation, as Yetrik had promised, would require convincing, but it was not an outlandish hope. The war had caused the loyalists to bond closer than ever before. That much was evident as Yetrik looked at the Priessman next to him and counted him not only as an ally, but a friend. He only hoped that he had not tarnished their trusting relationship with his bold move. If he had, perhaps the friendship was not as rooted as he had hoped.

Yetrik nodded. "Forgive me, Your Grace, but it would be more convenient to meet here in Paiell. It is the middle point between Thusk and Ekscomos, and you wouldn't have to leave your city."

"I *want* to leave the city. When the anti-harvesting armies return, I will be their target. Isn't that what happened in Zhaes?"

Not exactly, but I understand. Yetrik kept his thoughts to himself and continued listening.

The Krall continued. "You promised protection. Courts Gruth and Priess seem to be the safest Courts on your side of this conflict. I would rather turn to Gruth, which I would hope to be the most durable between the two."

"So you want to abandon your people?" asked Kevlen.

"If we gather in Thusk, you may be safe, but your Thanes will nevertheless remain vulnerable," said Yetrik.

"They can hold my Court until we have the promised reinforcement from your Court, Gruthman. Most of them already take part in the chaos. There is a chance that some have perished in battle. *I don't know.* You can see how ruin has swept my land. Order and nobility are but memories of better days. Regardless of its current state and my pessimism, I'll leave the few Thanes that have any sense to avoid throwing themselves into battle under the protection of your other Beastlings."

Kevlen looked as if he was going to shout, but she continued.

"I'll fly to Thusk with one of you. The other will follow. The other riders can stay to defend." She pointed at Kevlen. "Speak to some bird to have a message sent to your Thanes that will meet us in Thusk. I'm sure they have a way to speed up their travel."

Yetrik glared at Kevlen. They shared a silent conversation before turning back to the Krall.

"When would you like to depart?" Yetrik asked.

"Give me the rest of the day to tie up matters here. We can leave at sunrise." She stared at each of them. "Will that be ample time?"

Kevlen turned to Yetrik, his eyes less frustrated, but with eyebrows raised.

"May we have a moment to discuss this?" Yetrik asked.

"By all means," said the Krall.

Her focused glare suggested that she believed she was victorious. Yetrik understood Kevlen's concern, but the victory was more so theirs. The Krall agreed—though under more difficult terms than they had expected—to work towards unity. He had to remind himself that he was not responsible for the choices of the nobility. He was only responsible for leading those responsible for such decisions to each other on peaceful terms. By all means, this was *his* victory.

Yetrik bowed before the Krall, while Kevlen waved for him to follow him outside of the room.

"Please be brief. I am a monarch, after all," she said as they left.

Kevlen started to laugh and shake his head, ruffling his hair as they walked away from the closed door. He turned his back to the nearest wall and slumped against it, lowering himself to the floor.

He ran his forefinger and thumb across his eyes as he pinched the bridge of his nose. Yetrik sat beside him.

"Perding Sleffwoman."

Yetrik stayed silent.

Kevlen turned towards him. "Perding *Gruthman.*"

Yetrik stared ahead, watching a small group of Sleffmen pass by, purposely ignoring him and Kevlen.

"Does none of this bother you?" asked Kevlen

"We have what we wanted."

"Oh, you're so fortunate. You can return home. Bend to her will. It doesn't matter."

"She's the Krall. What did you expect?"

"Not... that."

Yetrik chuckled. "I admit, she was quite eccentric."

"Just a little." Kevlen held his forefinger and thumb close together.

"She was particular, but we at least have what we want."

"But we lose time."

"Doing what? Dying in another battle?"

"Is that what you want, Yetrik? You want to retreat?"

"This isn't a retreat. I'm sorry, Kevlen, but I am lost. I don't understand why you're so frustrated. You keep tossing out insults and complaints, but none of them are landing on me. You said that Terin wanted to meet with her. She agreed to meet. It's a longer journey than he probably expected, but we *have* what we wanted."

Kevlen stared at the floor with wide eyes.

Yetrik elbowed him, forcing out a light laugh. "Still here with me, Priessman?"

The rise and fall of Kevlen's chest quickened. His breathing was shallow, and he started to move his fingers.

"Kevlen?" Yetrik placed his hand on the Priessman's shoulder.

Kevlen buried his head in his hands and started scratching at his head. His fingers scraped deep and Yetrik worried he was drawing blood.

"Kevlen!" Yetrik shook him until his head stopped scratching. Yetrik was always soft in his approach, but he felt Kevlen needed direct attention. He cupped Kevlen's chin and pulled it to force Kevlen to look at him.

Tears fell from the Priessman's eyes and he bit his lower lip until it bled.

The Priessman was stricken with panic, one that Yetrik knew well when his anxieties felt unbearable.

"*Perd me.*" Kevlen hissed, shaking his head as he covered his face."*Pe rding* fool. *Perding* weakling."

"I'm sorry," Yetrik said.

"It's not you, you kulf."

"Terin is going to *kill* me."

Yetrik worried that Kevlen's words were not an exaggeration.

"Is that what this is about?"

Kevlen didn't answer. Yetrik didn't pry for one. He stared ahead, listening to Kevlen sob. Guilt stung him, but he had no salve.

Ten minutes passed until Kevlen stopped and turned to sniffing.

Kevlen wiped his nose. "I'm sorry about that, Yetrik, I shouldn't have–"

"I get it."

"No, it's just–"

"Do you feel choked by your fears? Feel like you are dying even though you know you are alive?"

Kevlen looked at him and nodded.

"I've had panic attack me plenty of times. Battle is horrible, but sometimes mental anguish strikes even harder."

Kevlen smiled, looking at Yetrik not as a friend, but as a brother. "You spoke my mind."

He smirked.

Kevlen scratched his head. "I think I just needed some time."

"As one does. Now, break down that fear. Maybe Terin will be frustrated, but I doubt he will hold anything against you for trying."

Kevlen lost his smile.

"Stay strong," Yetrik said. "Let me hear what you have to say."

"My father may carry a frightening legacy, but Terin is worse than anyone in the Court."

"He seemed kind to me."

"He knows how to play the game of politics, both high and low."

"Then let *him* handle this. Send the invitation. If he decides to come to Gruth he will. If he thinks it a poor idea, he will stay and we can focus on the Gruth nobility."

"But we came to help him, not your people."

Yetrik shook his head. "We came to help the Sleffmen, the loyalists. Forget the Courts. This is about preserving humanity. This is more than just Terin's war."

"You're right, *perd* him. Let's go."

"Have you ever seen the sea?"

Kevlen shook his head.

"It's a great place to let your worries drift away."

He smiled. "You're sure we can trust this Sleffwoman?"

Yetrik laughed. "Not at all, but I'm desperate. I trust my Court's nobility, though. Seeing what is happening here in Sleff hurts. There's already too much suffering."

"And there will be until this war ends."

Yetrik thought about that, then about Terin. Terin believed that peace would only come once Court division was dissolved. His word seemed reliable, yet Kevlen was terrified of the man. What was it about the Thane that caused Kevlen to panic at the thought of disappointing the man? He would have to pry later, but Kevlen was not in the mind to talk about it. The more he learned about Thanes and Kralls, the less he felt he could trust any of them. Aside from his doubts, Thane Gett was always reliable. Gett could help.

"Perd it," Kevlen said. "I'm feeling as eccentric as the Krall. Let's fly to Thusk."

Yetrik smiled.

Kevlen stood, his eyes still red, and lent Yetrik a hand. "But the Krall is flying on Avra with you, Gruthman."

Yetrik chuckled. He never expected to count a Priessman as a brother, but the past few months made that manifest.

He led the way back into the throne chamber, holding the door open for Kevlen to follow.

"Heloath, boys," she greeted. Yetrik understood they were young, but she too was young for her office and could not have been older than thirty. "The verdict?"

Kevlen slapped his hand on Yetrik's shoulder. "This Gruthman has the pleasure of escorting you to Thusk."

CHAPTER TWENTY

THE IMP SLAVES

"Row harder on the right, you perding kulf!" Dessen shouted.

"I'm trying!" Tick lifted his oar too early with each stroke, despite Dessen's reprimands.

"Switch sides with him, Port!"

Port jumped to the right side of the scrap boat and shoved Tick to the left, only rocking the boat a little more as they returned to balance. The weight distribution would no longer matter if Port could not row them out of the rapids before they were thrown into the rocky shore on the right. Rocks stuck out like teeth in the water with edges to rival a leviathan eel's fangs.

Dessen stuck an oar into the water on the left side of their boat to help pivot. He pulled it out before losing it to the rushing water. Port knew that if their boat survived, they would only hear more complaints from Dessen that he was worthless because of his injured right arm. They had wrapped it with rags found in the abandoned shacks. Still, Port feared the arm shredded by the fiend's teeth would soon leave Dessen with an insidious infection. They still had a long journey to Bruten, but they were moving swiftly.

"Keep rowing, Tick!" Port shouted as he continued to give each stroke all that he could. The oars were no artisan's prize, but a poor makeshift tool from supplies that they had found in the shacks. The weight of the oar was wearing on Port and he feared that Tick was even closer to surrendering.

"Perd!" Dessen shouted. The front of their boat was on course for a cluster of rocks that looked like a cramped cemetery with too many headstones. He twisted into an awkward position to help Port row with his one good hand and the wrapped hand to brace it.

Port shouted as he pressed through the water, fearing that his muscles would tear if the oar did not break first.

"Keep rowing, Tick!" Port screamed at the Sleffman, who stared at their efforts in fearful awe.

Port's eyes stung with sweat. His hands seized with cramps. He clenched his teeth.

"Stick it in on the left!" Dessen commanded.

Tick obeyed, and the head of the boat cleared the outermost rock.

Port slid forward in the boat and hit the rock with the tip of his oar, saving the tail of the boat from a collision. The rock's sharp edge took a chunk out of the oar as it collided at a high speed, but the boat remained intact. They rowed at a controlled pace away from the rapids and shot into the left side of the river, which held them at a safe distance from the devilish rapids on the right.

"Keep us steady." Dessen laid on his back with a cough and a sigh and held his injured arm close to his chest. Red seeped through the cloth in small patches.

His eyes looked up, catching Port's concerned gaze. "It's fine. Just keep us on the right path. Tick, row harder."

"I'm trying, sir!"

Port saw Dessen grin. The man had not even looked at Tick.

They continued on for an hour until Dessen called for them to take a rest on a sandy bank. The river was calm, but worry told Port to remain ready for more rapids.

Port tried to tell himself that he was fine with Dessen leading them, but he offered no help and had no rank. Port should have been the one leading. He should have decided when to rest. Colrig had chosen him, not Dessen. He sat up, ready to confront Dessen, but the man had fallen asleep and snored with an open mouth.

Tick leaned over the edge of the boat and dragged his finger through the water in meandering circles. Port felt worse for feeling jealous of Dessen's control. If Port wanted to, he could reprimand Dessen for insubordination and force the injured man to row. He wouldn't, but he felt a touch of satisfaction at the thought.

It was clear that Dessen thought Tick was a burden and a coward, but Port felt otherwise. He was misunderstood. He was the embodiment of the common Sleffman. Despite his circumstances, Tick remained humble, never questioning, only listening and offering occasional words of gratitude when Dessen was not shouting at him.

"Any idea how much longer?" Tick asked, sitting up after cupping water into his mouth.

Port clenched his fist, worried that Tick's question would earn him another rebuke from Dessen for impatience, especially for waking him.

Dessen grunted and cleared his throat. "We should make it there by tomorrow, maybe tonight, if we rush it." His stomach growled and he clenched it with his unbandaged hand.

"Are you ready to get back to it?" Port asked.

Tick reached for another drink. He wiped his mouth, shook his hands dry, and nodded.

Dessen sat up with a grunt and arched his back.

With Dessen's bloody wrap and adamant need to rest it, Port had forgotten about Tick's injuries from his attack. Tick had his flaws, but did not complain about his missing eye or the torso that had been torn by claws. With a finishing jacket to cover his rent tunic and a bandage over his eye, one would never guess that the man was so recently injured. He kept the pain to himself, only complaining about trivial matters.

Tick squinted and his jaw muscles tightened as he retook his rowing position. After seeing Tick's humble resilience, Port felt ready to reprimand Dessen. Port was a captain. Colrig had made him the Sleff Thane of Harmony. He had every right to force Dessen to contribute, yet he remained silent. He did not want to turn Dessen against him and did not want to insult Tick.

Dessen faced forward and waved for them to start rowing.

"Thank you," Port whispered, pointing at his eye and all over his chest.

It took a moment for Tick to understand, but he responded with a smile and a nod.

"I'm glad you could join us."

Tick jumped into the water beside the boat, pushed them off of the sandy bank, and jumped in when they were adrift. He laughed and his jaw clicked. "It beats battle."

"Anything does," said Dessen.

Port grew increasingly frustrated with Dessen the more he thought about his prejudice towards Tick. He was glad that the self-proclaimed captain faced away from them while they rowed.

"Captain Port," Tick said with a determined smile, "how did the last battle compare to Kzhek?"

"I was more involved here in Paiell, so I can't–"

"Paiell was worse," Dessen grumbled.

"You were in the battle of Kzhek?" Tick asked."I think I've told you plenty of times."

"Where were you?" asked Port.

"In Kzhek? Rightmost flank. I was fortunate to fight beside a Sleff Gorger."

"Makes sense that it was easier for you there."

Tick laughed through closed lips. He clenched his jaws to silence the clicking.

"It was still horrible." grumbled Dessen.

"I never said that it wasn't."

"Where were you in Paiell?" asked Port.

"Everywhere. I don't mean to insult you, Port, but Kzhek was more organized."

"We also had three armies in Kzhek, four if you count the Zhaes rejectionists."

"I know, but there was still a clear lack of order."

Port felt anger burn within. He flexed his calf until it cramped, forcing him to focus on the pain instead. "We also had most of the Harmony Allegiant in Kzhek. We had multiple captains, whereas in Paiell we had *my* poor guidance and the help of a select few. Losing the Tower of Alms–we didn't have a surprise influx of Gorgers–I'm nothing compared to Colrig–we were assaulted by Beastlings with no way to counter them–I just, *perd*, I can't–"

"I appreciate what you did." Dessen paused. "Captain, we're entering a new era. It's a perding poor era that forces great young men like you to become something they never wanted to be. You're doing what none of us could ever do, even with your rank. I'm sorry if I said anything that insulted you. It is an unspoken fact that we are all miserable and frustrated. We're all suffering, but we're trying our best to make something of it. Pain should never be wasted, only used to make us better."

"Aye," Tick attested, eager to make himself relevant.

Port felt comfortable back in his rowing pattern. He looked at Tick. "And where were–" Port shook his head. "We'll all be back in the fight soon enough. No need to keep talking about it. Does anyone have a lighter topic to discuss?"

"What?" said Dessen. "We settle after an argument and bond over our trials. Now you think we can banter like friends?"

They shared a laugh.

"I don't mean to return to darker topics," muttered Tick, "but I think we should mention those *things* that attacked us."

"We've moved past petty accusations," Port said. "You survived. Let us rejoice over that."

Tick nodded. "Either of you have the faintest idea *what* those ugly kulfs were?"

A tense silence arose. Dessen was the first to break it. "Are you boys well versed in the *Tome of the Meek*?"

Tick shook his head. "No, but I'm a humble enough Sleffman to admit that much."

"Port?"

"I like to think that I am. I was studying to become a monk before Colrig recruited me."

"A monk in training, and you only claim to '*think*' that you know the book?" Dessen chuckled. "You, my friend, are truly living the Sleff Ideal. I bet you could recite most of the *Tome.*"

Port smiled. He appreciated the praise, but memorization was never his strong suit. He knew the principles and lessons in the book well but was poor at recalling the minute details. In previous circumstances, he kept his past hidden. Those outside of the innermost circles of faith mocked monks for giving their entire life to something was a mere activity for others. Worship was no activity for Port, but what he strived for with each action. "Why do you ask?"

"The final book in the *Tome* warns of the unholy fissure that would arise when Heitt's children succumb to pride and division."

Tick scratched the bandage around his eye. "I know that much, at least."

Dessen looked at him for a moment, then returned his focus to Port. "I don't know what you believe. You probably have a better understanding of that apocryphal section than me, but I always took that warning to be more literal. Facet has gone to—well, it feels like the under realms. The more people turn away from the gods, especially noting the division in our Court, the more we shall be punished."

"I never imagined Heitt to be a vindictive god," said Port.

"It is less his condemnation and more our fault. Enmity breeds demons."

"You think those pale freaks were demons?" asked Tick.

Dessen shrugged. "I was never the type of man to believe that demons looked like they do in tapestries and paintings. Horns and forked tongues are too simple a design for all the evil that lurks out there. Still, if our hatred has torn a rent in the world, opening our world to the under realms, the creature may be a sign of the times."

Tick lost his smile. "I always thought those teachings were more figurative. When contention and pride inspire men to act, they become demons themselves."

"And I never said that they were demons," said Dessen. "I'm only saying that it was a curious thought. You two should have learned by now that most of what I say is far from wise."

Both of them remained silent. Port couldn't have agreed more, but he did not want to make the man feel foolish. Foolish did not feel like the right word. Dessen was dogmatic. Correct or mistaken, he spoke as if his words were doctrine. *Nothing is more dangerous than a man believing that everything he knows and does is right. Demons still see themselves as angels.*

"I think it's a fair point," said Tick.

Dessen had lightened up, but even when he was spiteful, Tick tried to appease him to ensure his spot as a member of the crew.

"What do you think, holyman?" asked Dessen.

Port laughed. "Demonology was never a part of my studies. Most of what people talk about is nothing more than mythology. Cursed spirits and dark magic exist if one digs deep enough into the unwholesome lore, but like I said, I try to focus on becoming better rather than worse."

"Doesn't hurt to know how to protect yourself," said Tick.

Port shook his head. "Spending your time in unholy places does not make you any more protected. If anything, it makes you more vulnerable to slipping away from the holy truths that we should abide by. The most hateful cultists were once the most pious saints."

"I think I've had enough theology for the day," said Dessen.

"But you were the one who brought it up," said Tick.

"Just keep rowing," Dessen growled.

Port was happy to see Tick's broken teeth in a wide smile.

Tick was the last to exit the boat and tripped out of it as he exited, falling into the water and sinking even deeper as he jumped after the boat before it drifted away.

Dessen clenched his stomach as he laughed. Port only felt bad for Tick but clenched his stomach as well. The hunger pains were no longer a tight grip, but a painful vice. Each day on the road , river, and at war, he learned to better appreciate his seemingly insignificant life before joining the Harmony Allegiant.

Dessen caught his breath by the time Tick stood ankle deep in the water. Only his shoulders remained dry.

"Pull it onto the shore in case we need it later."

"Why would we?" Port asked Dessen.

"You see what's happening to Facet. There isn't much we can count on anymore. I have no plans to use it, but it would be a shame to waste such a beautiful creation." Dessen and Tick shared a laugh, and Port joined in. He was astounded that it carried them the whole way, despite looking like a chest made by a failed carpenter's apprentice. They had to scoop water from the boat with their shoulder guards during the ride but survived without any major leaks.

Tick pulled it ashore and Dessen waved them onward.

"Should be nearby," said Dessen

"This is it?" Tick asked.

Dessen nodded.

Port turned to him. "How do you know we are close?"

"Have either of you been to Bruten before?"

Port shook his head.

"I've been to some of the cities to the east," said Tick.

"Doesn't count." Dessen hissed as he scratched his bandaged arm. "Bruten is unlike any other Sleff city."

"Of course I know about the imp slaves," Tick said.

"Be careful with what you believe," said Dessen.

"So they aren't slaves?"

"Not quite."

"What do you mean?" asked Port.

"You can't call them slaves if they are the ones who offer themselves. Perhaps *volunteers* is a better term, even though the imps treat them like slaves."

"What do you think about their devotion, Port?" Tick asked.

"Do I think we should all follow them, becoming humble enough to subject our city to become tools for some imp cult?"

Tick looked worried that Port was going to convince him to do that very thing.

"By Heitt's holy name, no!" Port laughed. Dessen joined in and Tick did after an uncomfortable pause. "There is a difference between humility and subjugation. Regardless of their efforts to be humble by serving the imps, our humility should be directed towards our god, not towards manipulative imps."

"He's right," Dessen said. "Besides the imps being selfish kulfs, their cult does not advocate our faith. I doubt their rituals and sacrifices do anything, but if they appease some deity, it is not a holy being. You wanted to know how I knew we were near Bruten?" he pointed at a tree, then to two others.

Port squinted but could not see what Dessen was talking about and saw that something had been attached to the trees. He stepped closer. Tick followed a few steps behind.

"Perding—!" Tick lost the end of his exclamation as he looked down from the tree with his hand on his head, on the edge of fainting.

Port turned his concern away from Tick and focused on the macabre display nailed to the tree. He had become desensitized by war, especially by seeing the most extreme of Zhaes rebels who stuffed organs into the throats of murdered guards, but this display was beyond pleasant.

A spinerat, the same creature that was on the Sleff sigil, had been stretched with arms and legs spread wide and nailed to the tree. It was a young spinerat, the size of a typical rat and not yet the dog-size that it would reach. Its head was stretched upward with a river eel shoved through the mouth and out of a slit in the chest.

"What in Heitt's name is that supposed to mean?" Port exclaimed.

Dessen placed a finger over his lips. "We don't want to disturb them."

"Why?" Tick looked up. "We have to enter the city, anyway."

Dessen smiled. "I suppose I am nervous, too. Best that we approach them first rather than scaring them with shouts. Enough looking, keep walking."Port helped Tick to his feet, and Dessen led the way.

"You didn't answer my question," Port said. "What was that–I mean, I know what it was–but why would they do that?"

"Why do some of our Sleffmen shove children's organs into their guts?" Dessen shrugged. "We are all abominations."

"Must be some unholy ritual," said Tick. "Most imps are into incantations and the like."

Port never received a straightforward answer from Dessen. He took it to mean that the man was as lost as he was but was not willing to admit it. Without an explanation, he was left to search for one himself.

Forest imps were the size of a child and plain imps were even smaller. If a race of imps enslaved Sleffmen, they had to be of a substantial size and much more intelligent that the smaller races that would lose in a game of wits to a swine. Port knew too little about imps to draw any conclusions. He was only confused as to why the different imp races were still called imps when some were no closer to another than humans and the Middlemen.

"Feeling better?" Port put his hand on Tick's shoulder. The man smelt like stale urine. Port did not expect to smell any better but was only struck with the realization of how rancid they all must appear.

"Good enough. Those kinds of things rarely bother me. Perd, the battle in Paiell was much worse. There was just something *wrong* with that spinerat."

"You mean that it looks like a clear insult to our people?"

"No, I was never the type of man to die for my land."

Port squinted at him. "But you fought in Paiell."

"That was for the *people*. Not the land, not the government. Just the people. I... right, we were talking about the spinerat. I don't know what my problem is. Maybe it was just hunger. No food, dirty water, I have too many problems to count. Hey, Dessen. Do you think they will have any food to share?"

"Imps don't seem the generous type to me."

"But these imps might be willing to help," said Port. "The message that commanded us to go to Bruten also stated that the duke is willing to help the Harmony Allegiant."

Dessen turned to him with a glare. "Why would that imp get involved with our politics?"

"The duke of Bruten is an imp?" guffawed Tick.

"Does that surprise you?" said Dessen.

"I suppose not, it's just..."

"Different?" Port said.

"I guess that is a word for it. Everything is different now."

"Get used to it," Dessen grumbled.

Port sighed, then laughed when the first living sight in Bruten was a Chussman. He expected to see other Sleffmen that retreated from Paiell, then remembered that the river moved much quicker than an exhausted army.

The Chussmen were jovial, helping the sorrowful Sleffmen smile and the imps grumble. The imps would have been more intimidating if he met them alone in the forest, but they felt less threatening with the armed Chussmen. Still, Port wasn't eager to meet the imps, though he was sure he would be well acquainted with them by the end of his stay.

Dessen was not held back by such inhibitions and walked towards an imp who shouted at a trio of Sleffmen to return to work on the side of a stone building.

"Where's the duke?" he asked an imp. Most of the imps looked similar, but breasts gave distinction to their sex. This one appeared to be a male and was a head taller than Dessen, much taller than any imp race he had previously heard of. It was gaunt and had the light green skin tone of lichen. Similar to other imps, it had earlobes that pointed down sharply, the reverse of a goblin's ear. Its lips were dry and cracked, covering teeth with a slight point.

The imp turned to Dessen and stared at him with yellow eyes that had star-shaped pupils. It scratched its thin strip of black hair with nails twice as thick and long as a human's. "Who are you to make such a request?"

"I'm here to help relieve you of these." Dessen pointed to the clusters of Chessmen.

Port stepped forward. "We are members of the Harmony Allegiant, here to–"

"Do you think that means anything to me? These desert-folk tell me the same thing, like I'm supposed to bow down before them."

Dessen put his hand on Port's shoulder and moved him to the side like a father stepping in to help his son. "Please show us to the duke. The sooner we see him, the quicker you can get rid of all of us."

Port was surprised. He never expected Dessen to be so tame towards the stubborn imp.

"I don't know. Ask someone else."

Dessen sighed. Port was happy to see the man holding his temper back. He put his hand on Port's back and started to push him away from the growing gathering of curious imps and Chuss soldiers. "Let's find one of the Chuss captains. We can worry about the Duke later."

"Aren't you hungry?" Port asked.

"Of course I am, but we've come a long way after eating leaf stems. I would rather wait to see what the Krall has to offer us to eat rather than relying on some poor imp's stew."

"You trust an imp's cooking?"

"If he's a duke, he at least will have something with a rich taste."

Port turned to see that Tick had not followed them and instead approached the imp that had turned them away.

"Tick, come along now," Dessen groaned.

Tick gave him a quick look and turned back to the imp.

"What do you want?" the imp asked.

Port grabbed Dessen's arm to stop him. He was surprised that the imp did not insult him for approaching.

"Why do you nail the spinerats to the trees?" Tick asked. He sounded like a curious child rather than a condemning inquisitor.

"Why do your people subject themselves to us?" the imp replied. "Why do you give away your wealth and spend time before your altars? We are not the same. We do not worship your god nor do we worship a god of man."

"Then what do you worship?"

"Do you wish to patronize me or join our order?"

"I'm curious."

The imp's tolerance expired, but he lasted longer than most people with Tick. "Go ask a shaman." He left to command the Sleff laborers.

Port waved for Tick to follow and he did so with reluctance, taking a few glances back at the imp.

Port patted him on the shoulder. "Don't worry, I'm sure you will have plenty of opportunities to speak with imps while we are here."

"Why are you interested in their occult sacrifices, you sick kulf?" asked Dessen.

Tick shrugged. "The thought of that poor creature nailed to the tree bothered me. I can't get that image, can't get that *feeling* that I had when I saw it out of my mind."

"The world is filled with unsettling things," said Port, "now more than ever. It's best to ignore what is out of your control."

"I never wanted to control anything, I just want to know what–"

Dessen interrupted, "Keep searching for an explanation and you'll find yourself sacrificing with them."

"Dessen is right, Tick. Curiosity down dark paths never takes you to a good place. Best ignore it."

Tick nodded.

Dessen led their trio towards the small city square and gravitated towards the first Chussman who appeared to be a higher rank than the others. While all of them dressed in similar armor–light metal plates over white leather–they found one who had a golden Chuss sigil on the center of his breastplate.

"Are you the captain here?" Dessen asked.

Chussman turned to Dessen. He had a short platinum beard, but it was thin and patchy. He was young, only a few years older than Port. "Close enough."

"I want the *head* of your company."

The Chussman squinted at him.

Before he could speak, Dessen grabbed Port by the bicep and pulled him forward. "This is the Sleff Thane of Harmony. He is on the same level as your Thane Phenmir Stolk. Unless he is here, Port–Thane Kamen–outranks any of you."

The Chussman struggled to find an apology.

"Just take me to whoever perding brought you here."

The Chussman nodded and told his companions to wait behind while he led the Sleff trio to a large, but well-aged, farmhouse on the edge of the town.

They entered the building, and the Chussman followed close behind.

Port saw remnants of a family who used to own the place. Amateur paintings and tablets hung on the wall inscriptions of the *Tome of the Meek*. The floorboards were cracked and dirtied and the windows were almost completely clouded over. The stench of rotting meat stained the air. It would have been a nice home, but was neglected since the imps took over to use it for reasons Port would rather not think about.

"—it is the best that I can offer." a high, yet hoarse voice said as they entered the dining room. "If you insist on prolonging your stay, we are going to require some assistance with labor."

The speaker was an imp with a golden cap and was the size of a fifteen-year-old boy, though his wrinkles implied that he had more decades than his stature suggested. Across from him stood a Chusswoman whose chest piece had the same golden sigil as the other high officer, though hers had an obsidian ring around it. She was a head taller than Port, with the stature of a true captain, unlike him. Her platinum hair was braided into tight rows reaching the base of her neck.

She noticed the Sleff trio entering but turned her attention back to the imp across the table. "Don't worry, we plan on departing the day after our forces arrive." She gestured to the Sleffmen. "Judging by our new arrivals, I would assume that the last of them are now joining us."

"Not quite, Chusswoman," Port said as he greeted with the Chuss salute. "Heloath."

She returned the gesture with the Sleff salute. Any inhibitions he had in her were dispelled. "Heloath to you as well. Are you the captain?" she asked.

I'm the Sleff Thane of Harmony and you will address me as such. Port was afraid of the prideful command that nearly pressed through his lips. He never had to worry about staying humble, for he had nothing to be prideful about. Now that he was trusted with a new position, one that had sway over others, he felt the toll that humility required for one eager to boast.

He nodded. "And you are the head of this Chuss company?"

"I am. Captain Khenna Lonik." She reached out and shook Port's hand with a grip much tighter than his.

"How many have you brought?"

"Twelve legions."

Perd me. They are giving all they can to ensure victory. Bless them. Let's hope this doesn't leave them vulnerable elsewhere. "Well, I am glad to hear that we have so many."

"And twenty Endowers. Beastlings, to be precise."

More children brought to fight a war. Despite his hatred of their involvement, he was grateful to have something that gave him hope against the Priess Zlatogs. "Excellent, just what we need to repeat the triumph in Kzhek."

"Precisely. Where are the rest of the arrivals?"

"We took the river." Dessen stepped up beside them. Tick still stood near the entrance of the room. "The rest are on foot."

"Why did you part ways?"

Port did not push Dessen out of the way, nor did he give the man a punishing glare. He looked at Dessen with kind eyes, earning his silence with friendship. He thought of a passage from the *Tome of the Meek*: *"Even in power, with the might of the world in mine palm, I remain with the lowliest of my brethren. Mine glory doth shine in unity."*

Dessen stepped back.

"We had to retreat in haste from Paiell. While some companies fled into the forest, others were pursued across the plains and into the hills."

"Tell her about the demons," Tick said from across the room.

Khenna started to smile but it dissipated like snow falling into steaming tea when she noticed that Port did not seem to think it was humorous.

"We were ambushed, but there is more to it." Port scratched his eyes. They felt heavy and dry. His stomach felt like it was digesting itself. His knees and back throbbed. "We can discuss this later. We have eaten nothing substantial in days."

Khenna walked toward him and turned him around with a clap on the back. "An unfed soldier is no better than a corpse. These Sleffmen do not have near enough to feed us and I don't want to think about sharing food with the imps." She turned back to glance at the duke. "No offense to you, sir."

She waved for her Chuss companions to follow as they left the building. Dessen stayed with the group, but Tick remained paces behind. Port tried to catch his attention to bring him forward, but he was otherwise occupied speaking with the Duke.

Khenna continued to talk as they walked. "I sent a hunting party out a few hours ago. If their success continues, we should have plenty of deer, frogs, maybe even some boar for all of us. If you can wait a while longer before resorting to stale bread or shriveling vegetables. We would be happy to hear about your journey over supper."

"I couldn't be more grateful." Port's tongue flooded with saliva.

"I'll have some of my troopers work with the imps to find you a place to sleep for the next few days. You deserve some rest, Sleffman. I've heard terrible things about the battle in Paiell. Was it as bad as they said?"

In conversations with Dessen and Tick, he found it easy to ignore the gruesome details of the battle. It was an event, but thinking about it next to Khenna made him recall the *experience* that it had been.

Visceral pain. Loss and hope frayed like a rope, thread by thread. His body was decorated with scars and his soul adorned with wounds of trauma. He was still learning to accept and actualize what he had lived. He wasn't ready to face the totality of it, including the guilt of killing fellow Sleffmen, but knew he would one day be forced to confront the atrocities. That day was approaching and would come without warning. He focused on returning to Paiell with reinforcements but accepted that battles could arise at any point along that road.

"It was," he replied. "Have you seen battle yet?"

"Of course. How else would I have gained my position? I was in Kzhek."

He nodded. There was no need to compare the brutality between Kzhek and Paiell again.

Khenna looked at him with a sad smile. He was glad that she did not probe further.

After fifteen minutes of conversations that avoided the topic of war, Khenna's officers arrived to lead the Sleff trio to their temporary residency.

Anticipating the eventual influx of Sleffmen, the Bruten Sleffmen had cleared out a street of old homes to quarter the troops. Port was initially surprised to see how many abandoned buildings there were, figuring that many Bruten Sleffman had escaped the control of the imps. He spoke with some of the Sleffmen to learn that the imps were indeed honest in stating that their Sleff servants were not hostages. Those who served the imps did so according to their decision to humble themselves. Many Sleffmen left Bruten years before when the city pledged itself to the imps, leaving space for imps to dwell and plenty of buildings for storage.

Dessen fell on the first bed he saw when they entered their residence. "You two can find another room. I'll keep this one to myself."

"For now," Port chuckled, "but you might not have that privilege when the others arrive."

Dessen sat up and nodded. "I'll still take it for as long as I can."

Port smiled. It felt good to have a moment of comfort and security. He recognized and accepted that the bliss would soon dissipate, but he tried not to focus on the entropy. Too often, the present was spoiled by a fear of the future. Dessen's smile reflected that he too relished in the brief peace that they had. Thoughts of a great feast that evening made their hope extend beyond that single moment.

Port felt a crack in his joy as he turned back to see Tick sitting against the wall in the hallway.

Port walked towards him. "Did you find a spot that suits you, Tick?"

He shook his head.

"Best find something soon, Sleffman," Dessen said. "I'm not sharing this bed with you."

Port smiled, but didn't hold it as Tick remained serious. He walked closer and put his hand on Tick's shoulder and whispered. "Is something wrong?"

"Just... thoughts."

"Hunting party's back!" someone with a Chuss accent shouted from the open front door.

Dessen stood and walked towards them. "Let's go eat, boys. We've earned it."

Port nodded, gave Tick a friendly smile, and led the group down out of the building and towards the farmhouse where the Chessmen would hold their feast.

The other two walked behind Port, but he kept a brisk pace ahead. His legs ached, but hunger overpowered fatigue. As they neared the old building, he turned back and noticed that although Dessen was a few steps behind, Tick had left their small company.

CHAPTER TWENTY-ONE

ENTROPY ON A SILVER PLATTER

"Are you sure about this, Chussman?"

Phenmir nodded.

The Proctor of Trade scoffed and shook his head with a smile. "Who am I to judge the perding rebel captain?"

Although the Proctor jested, Phenmir felt the condescension in his voice. Phenmir would never call himself a rebel captain. He had a greater role, one more complex than commanding soldiers. Or perhaps that was one of the many lies he told himself to justify what he had done to see his Ideal prevail.

"When do you plan on departing?" the Proctor asked.

"This evening."

"Well, I've given you most of what we can offer."

Next to nothing. Phenmir was not surprised that the Canton of Agriculture's knowledge regarding the Middlemen was just as limited as everyone assumed. They traded goods without any contact. The Chussmen sent bronze alloys and native seeds while the Middlemen sent the most revered vegetables and fruits in the Chuss culture. If the Canton had any valuable information regarding the Middlemen, it had been lost over years of increasingly distant contact with the crop people.

"Are you sure this is the best time for you to leave on some fool's journey, Phenmir? Don't you have more of a significant role in this war than becoming a diplomat with the Middlemen?"

"The Endower ability to speak with them—"

"I know. I never said it couldn't be a worthwhile endeavor, but this hardly seems the time for such an expedition."

Now you value my role? Pick a side.

"We have captains abroad leading attacks and defense elsewhere. Sliin is protected. Remember, Proctor, that I am not a captain, nor am I just a general. I was appointed to lead the heart of the Harmony Allegiant in Court Chuss, not the Court itself, but as far as you are concerned, this effort is the heart of our operation. Let the Krall and her Thanes manage everything else."

He lifted his hands up as if in surrender. "I see, I see."

Phenmir stared at him until the Proctor lost his smile.

"Is there anything else I can provide?"

"Bronze."

"Our last trade was a month ago. We've already given them some from our Court reserves. Besides, you know that the mining in Zhaes has not been very active over the past few months."

"I'll take whatever you have. We must meet them on good terms."

"As if your charm wasn't enough."

Phenmir smiled. His attempts at humor were enraging, but Phenmir recognised he was close to finishing his business with the man.

"Anything else, Thane Stolk?" Before Phenmir could continue, the proctor interrupted him again. "You are taking ample protection with you, I presume?" He started to laugh. "I hear the crop men have thorns–"

"Do you insist on treating me as *perding* child?"

Phenmir's retort silenced the proctor.

He tried to stave off the anger from patronizing comments, but his exacerbating joint pain only contributed to his shriveling will. "Of course I am going to protect my people, you kulf!" He scratched his face. "Learn to keep your pitiful humor to yourself. Cheric help me contain myself! If I were not bound by our Ideal, I would–" he clenched his fists and hissed through clenched teeth until the tension fled. "Just give me some of your histories and I will leave."

The proctor ran to the shelf against the wall and removed a thin book with a black leather binding.

Phenmir took it and stood. "I'll have someone return it after I leave." He turned his back on the proctor and pushed the chair away, nearly knocking it over.

"Forgive me, Thane–"

"Care is the *perding* Creed, Chussman." He slammed the door as he left.

⊱⊰

He was not happy to see Dhera in his home when he arrived with rage still burning. Meira sat next to her on their divan and was a saving grace that helped him forget the rest of his built-up tension. His temper was a rabid hound, but one that he would never unleash on Meira or Hir. They were his everything.

"Is everything set for tomorrow?" the Krall asked.

Phenmir nodded and held up the book. "It would have been a worthless meeting if not for this."

Dhera raised an eyebrow.

"A brief history of our interactions with the Middlemen."

"The Proctor of Trade was less helpful than we hoped?"

"Have you met the man?" Phenmir asked.

Dhera shook her head.

"Then you have been spared."

"Phen, was he so terrible?" Meira asked.

He swiped his hand in the air and sat down across from them. "Enough negativity for the day. Let's move on."

Meira smiled. He was not the best at avoiding conflict, but he was trying, trying for her.

Two children walked in from outside, holding roasted slices of deep-blue pineberries on sticks. The girl held two hand-sized slices, while the boy held one and an empty spear, his lips blue.

Phenmir looked back at Meira.

She smiled. "They deserved some reward for their hard work."

Kaela took a bite from one of her slices, only shredding it a little on the teeth of her serval mask. The other child was a Chussboy, one Phenmir had seen at noble gatherings, but was yet to meet in person.

Phenmir gave the boy the Chuss salute and felt his anger repelled by the boy's soft smile.. "Don't worry about saluting me. You have your hands full. You must be Chenn."

The boy nodded and took a bite from his pineberry slice. His platinum hair had been cut as short as possible. Phenmir imagined the boy had likely grown tired of Kaela rubbing her hand against it. He was as tall as Kaela with a slim build and skin as dark as any average Chussman. His sleeveless red robe suggested they had recently been training.

"I'm glad to finally meet you. Your father is an admirable man."

Chenn nodded and smiled, then wiped blue juice from the corner of his mouth.

"This is Thane Hult's son?" asked Meira.

Phenmir nodded.

Meira saluted Chenn. "He is the best Thane of Diplomacy that we have ever had."

Chenn swallowed, then nodded with a timid smile.

"But is more than just some nobleman's son," said Kaela. She stepped closer to the Chussboy. "He is the captain of the Chuss Endowers."

"As I have heard," Phenmir said. "I can already tell that he is more humble than our dear captain Voln."

"And he knows how to listen," Kaela said.

Meira took the empty wooden spears from Chenn. "What do you mean?"

Kaela handed her one of her spears. "He's the only Feelman Endower that I have met that doesn't interrupt you even when he knows what you are going to ask or say. He can use his ability as well as any other, actually better than most other Feelman, but you would never guess that he was an Endowed if you didn't pry it from him. Chenn is even polite enough to not read others unless he needs to or is asked to, for the most part. He's still a boy." She giggled.

Chenn looked at the floor, maintaining his shy smile.

"Well," Phenmir said, "we are glad to have him. Are both of you ready for tomorrow?"

"Mostly," Dhera said. "Chenn, have you chosen the Endowers that will be joining you?"

"I think so," he replied, looking back at the smoking grill pit outside the open door.

"Do you want more?" Dhera asked.

He shrugged.

Phenmir held back a smile, knowing that Chenn had read Meira to learn how to get more pineberry without asking.

Dhera smiled and took two slices from the kitchen and placed them on the grilling pit. She stepped away to stand in the doorway. "How large is the company?"

"In total?" asked Dhera. "Phenmir will travel with Kaela and Chenn, alongside three others in a smaller carriage. The other Endowers will accompany them in a second carriage. Two more larger carriages will follow them with armed guards."

"Are you putting these children in danger, Phen?"

Chenn walked towards Meira and shared her concern.

"Meira." *You know that you can't promise safety. You are at war and you are leading these children into an uncharted land that is occupied by mythical beings and enemy Zhaesmen.* "Of course, we are aware of the danger, but the guard forces will see that we have a safe journey. Right, Dhera?"

"They will enter the Middlelands away from loyalist territory. Any beasts along the way should not be a problem with the ghete leading the carriages. Their company will have Gorgers and Beastlings should anything dire occur."

"I know, but it's never easy to see your husband leave on a long journey."

Phenmir walked towards Meira and stroked her arm. "At least you have an idea of where we are going. We are just going south and will return before we go anywhere else."

She nodded and rested her head on his shoulder. She spoke to him in a soft voice. "You know I trust you."

"Of course." He kissed her forehead.

"I have stayed long enough." Dhera stood.

"The Krall must be about her business," Meira said with a smile. "I don't think I will ever get used to that."

"You think I'm comfortable with people thinking that I own the Court?" Dhera tightened her headdress. "Cheric be with you, Thane Stolk."

"Care is the Creed, Your Grace."

Dhera waved them farewell and left forthwith.

Meira took the pineberry slices from the pit and handed them to Chenn. The boy thanked her and handed one to Kaela. Phenmir thought he saw her blush beneath her mask. It was difficult to read the Tchoyasmen, but he was beginning to notice the small mannerisms like clicking their fingernails and tapping on the side of their mask.

Kaela put her second spear on the table and took a bite from the slice. "I'll walk Chenn home and be back before dark."

"What do you mean?" Phenmir asked.

Meira smiled. "She's spending the night with us."

He nodded.

Kaela took Chenn's hand. "Hurry, Chenn. Let's walk back with the Krall. You live close to the palace, don't you?"

He shrugged and closed the door behind them.

"Remind you of anyone?" Meira asked.

"Hir?"

"Exactly. I hope he breaks from his shell before too long."

"I'm sure he will." He put his hand on her back and led her to their bedchamber. "Was he that quiet before I arrived?"

She nodded. "I wonder why they chose *him* as the captain."

"We'll make something out of him on the road."

"Don't forget that you are working with children."

"I know, I know, but we can't forget that they are *more* than just children."

"Still–"

"You trust me, Meira, right?"

"Always, but sometimes my anxiety speaks louder than trust."

"Just try not to dwell on it too much. We have a lot ahead before this is over, but it *will* end. Cheric is with us. I have faith in a better future. Please, just don't lose hope."

⁕⁕⁕

Phenmir appreciated Chenn's docile nature. His example caused the other Endowers in the carriage to behave well. Despite their maturity and self-control, he knew he would spend most of his social time on the journey with the guards, who followed them in a separate carriage. It was going to be a long journey and did his best to choose the officers that he could rely on as leaders and friends.

"You said you worked with my father," Chenn said. The other children spoke with one another, but Chenn had only muttered a few words since their departure.

Phenmir straightened his shoulders and pressed his back against the seat. The cushioning had become as hard as stone. His lumbar spine throbbed. "I have, even more, since I was chosen to become the Thane of Harmony."

"My father chose you?"

"Your father?" he chuckled. "No, a Sleffman did, of all people. Kaela and the Krall have told you about this, right? The Harmony Allegiant? The anti-harvesting campaign?"

Chenn nodded.

Perd, this journey will force him into an expedited adulthood. "Is something wrong?"

Chenn's gaze focused on the floor of the cabin.

"Just because they call you the 'captain' doesn't mean that you need to understand everything."

Chenn nodded, but his lower lip protruded and his eyes welled with tears.

Years ago, Phenmir had faced similar circumstances with Hir's anxiety. He learned through regretful experiences that telling a boy to 'brush off' his worries and 'ignore what he can't control' did not help. Mental ailments, as well as physical wounds, do not heal through ignorance. Using his hands as a surgeon to administer care and compassion was not enough. He had to use his words as well.

Phenmir tapped the thigh of the Chussboy on his right. "Switch seats with Chenn, please."

The Endowers swapped and sat, each one nearly falling as the carriage rode on rough terrain. Phenmir let the boy sit and cope with his emotions before prompting him to speak.

He put his arm across Chenn's shoulders. "Let it out if you need to. Your father might not be here, but I am."

The Chussboy who now sat in Chenn's seat closed his eyes and laid his head on the slumped Chussgirl next to him, trying to join the other sleeping Endowers.

Chenn turned his head towards Phenmir and pressed it against his ribs to hide the tears that fell. He felt guilty for the boy's sorrow, yet he was warmed by the need to stand as a father figure. As a man misses his own childhood, Phenmir missed Hir. Part of him thought that Chenn was not prepared to be a captain, but he still knew so little about him. Everyone has moments of vulnerability and Phenmir had allowed the boy to express it.

Chenn's muffled sobs stilled, his breathing calmed, and he turned away from Phenmir's embrace. His eyes were still red, but he seemed in control. "I'm sorry, Thane Stolk."

"No need to apologize. I know when crying is the only way to solve your worries."

"But they haven't been solved."

"Do you feel better?"

Chenn nodded.

"Then that is all you need. You never have to solve all of your worries. You just need to learn how to live with them, how to show them that *you* are in charge, *Endower Captain Hult.*"

"What kind of captain cries before his people?"

"The best kind." Phenmir leaned forward, placing his forearms on his thighs, and looked into Chenn's eyes. "If a captain can cry, he still has emotions. He knows that there is a difference between right and wrong and that power is not the most important thing. Crying, expressing emotions, is what makes us human. Are you in control of your emotions now? Because I need you to understand something that is not easy."

Chenn furrowed his brow, clenched his jaw, and nodded.

"You are about to experience some horrible things. Some things no child should ever be forced to experience." *Are you telling him that he is going to fight? He will experience battle, won't he? There's no chance that the Endower captain will be spared from the worst.*

Perd this merciless world.

"What do you mean?"

"Are you ready, Chenn? For everything that will come?"

"Yes, but... I don't understand."

You've pushed him too far, making him fear what will come. Slow down until he is ready. "That is the difficulty with our roles as captains. We don't know exactly what we will face. This trip to the Middlelands shouldn't be something to worry about. I just want you to prepare you for the future."

Chenn nodded.

Stop treating him like your son. Treat him like an ally. "Mistakes are bound to happen. We are all still trying to figure out how war works. I'm only saying this because I think you will do great things, Chenn. These Endowers need you. Our *Court* needs you. And as the Thane of Harmony, *I* need you."

Chenn smiled as he looked out the window. The Chuss Dessert was becoming a yellow plain of reeds.

"So, please, don't be afraid to talk to me. With your parents back in Sliin, you can turn to me while we travel. I know how it feels to be handed an enormous responsibility."

"Thank you." He looked at Phenmir for a few seconds, then laid his head to rest on the shoulder next to him. "You can talk to me if you need to as well. It has to be harder for you to talk to someone about your worries when you are in charge of them. We are here for each other."

"Care is the Cr—"

Phenmir stopped breathing as he slammed his head against the carriage. The children hit him with their bodies as they were all thrown about the rotating carriage. All he could hear was cracking wood and screams as the carriage was thrown onto its left side and slid to a gradual stop.

He had seen something approaching the carriage window, but he figured they were moving closer to trees or hills.

The window was cracked and the carriage side had been dented in. He banished concern and looked to the Endowers.

"What happened?" one of them whimpered.

Another moaned as he touched his head and pulled back a bloody hand. Phenmir slid towards his side and held the boy's head in his hands.

He hissed as Phenmir palpated the skin near the wound.

"Can you tell me your name?"

"Kir."

"How old are you?"

"What happened?"

Phenmir moved the boy's head to look into his eyes. "We'll figure that out, but I need you to answer my questions. How old are you?"

"Seven."

"And where are you?"

"In a carriage to the Middlelands."

The wound was superficial. After his assessment, Phenmir felt he could focus on the other Endowers.

"Stay quiet," he whispered. A couple of them grunted, but no one had significant wounds as far as he could tell. They had survived thus far. He had to be sure their safety perpetuated.

He heard growls and coarse, accented commands outside of the carriage. The growls were ghete-like, but the voices that spoke did not remind him of any Chussman.

Phenmir looked towards Chenn, who nodded. *Well enough for now.* Phenmir raised a finger to his lips and moved beneath the carriage door that was now positioned above them.

His hands shook and his breath quivered as he pressed the door open to peek outside.

Two of the other carriages had been knocked over as well, most of their wheels broken into pieces. The fourth carriage remained standing but had been knocked off of their course and now stood a field's length away from the others.

The ghete who had pulled the carriages were either unconscious or dead. The power needed to topple such conveyances would require much more than ghete. He could not see the coachman who drove the still-standing carriage, but the three others had been tossed from their seats. There were too many people in need of a medical assessment, but a horde of beasts and riders kept him paralyzed.

The international ghete trade tended to use the green-scaled breeds due to their docile nature. Other breeds were less than cooperative.

Six silver-scaled ghete, each one larger than their green relatives, neared the standing carriage. Although Phenmir could not see them well, each one had a rider armed with a spear or blade.

One rider dismounted their steed and strode to the carriage door. They pulled it and pointed inside with the tip of their spear.

Phenmir's terror doubled as he did not see a Chuss guard exit the carriage, but a line of children held captive by the riders' blades. Even if the Endowers could overpower the riders, they were incompetent in battle and were likely more paralyzed by fear than Phenmir.

He closed the door and lowered himself into the cabin.

"Did you see anything?" Chenn whispered.

"We've been ambushed."

Chenn's eyes widened, his lips trembled.

Phenmir held Chenn by his shoulders and leaned in. "If you panic, so will everyone else. It's time to be an example, Captain."

Phenmir patted his shoulders and moved back to face the others.

Fearful eyes ate at his confidence. Each Endower looked at him as a beacon of hope. He wanted to bring an Endower with him, using one of their abilities to help resolve the problem. A Gorger could help defend the company. A Shiftling could act as the enemy. Chenn could read their thoughts to provide the best path forward. He couldn't use these terrified children to stop an ambush. *Cheric, help me care for these—*

His silent prayer was disrupted by shouting beyond their cabin walls.

"Stay quiet and still," he whispered and peeked outside of the carriage once again.

"Back away from the children!" a Chuss guard shouted. Blood ran down the side of his face.

A rider turned back to look at him and the other shouting Chuss guards as they exited the broken carriage.

The guards poured from the carriages until the two large companies stood by each other with weapons raised. They continued to shout and provoke the ambushers like a riotous mob.

Phenmir pulled himself up and leapt from the cabin. His stiff legs from hours of riding ached as he landed and ran towards his fellow Chussmen.

Three of the ambushers held Endowers at spearpoint. The others kicked their heels and the silver ghete ran towards the Chussmen. One wielded a halberd and raised it high, while the other two had spears pointed like lances as they charged towards the guards.

"Beastlings!" Phenmir shouted. Some of the Endowers turned to look at him, but the clamor of armor and pounding paws muffled his cry. "Stop the ghete!"

The three charging riders collided with the front line of the guards. They plowed through the company, trampling and knocking down rows of Chussmen. One of the spear-wielding riders impaled two Chussmen through their chests before abandoning the weapon and removing a sword sheathed in the ghete's saddle.

Phenmir ran back to the carriage and climbed on top. As the ghete riders continued to plow through the guards, Phenmir knew that his call to the Endowers was unsuccessful. He opened the door and reached down. "Are any of you Beastlings?"

A Chussgirl with a short braid moved towards him and took his hand. Their sweaty grips slipped upon first contact. He reached down again and held her arm higher, pulling her to the top of the toppled carriage.

He shut the door, leaving the rest to continue hiding in place.

"What's happening?" the Chussgirl asked.

"I'll explain later. I need you to stop those ghete." Phenmir pointed at the silver ghete. Nearly half of the Chuss guard force laid on the ground, some missing their heads.

"What happened to our ghete?"

He looked at the incapacitated ghete, then back to her. "Not sure. Just focus on the others."

Her eyes shot between him and the battle.

"Jump on my back. I'll keep you safe." *It worked in Kzhek with the kaesan, it must work now.*

She nodded. Her countenance was anything but calm. He lowered himself to the ground and helped her down onto his back, then ran towards the conflict.

"What do you want me to do?" she yelled over his left shoulder.

"Make one of them attack the others?"

"Only one?"

"Can you command them all to stop?"

"I think so."

"Show me what you can do. Start calling them when you think we are close enough." He gripped her thighs tighter and lifted her up higher. His back ached, but he chose not to focus on his pain as the raiders slaughtered his guards.

The Chussgirl roared over his shoulders. Her voice as the cry was a union of three roars at once, like a group of Chussmen shouting their ideal in unity.

The silver ghete stopped their prowling. Their riders twisted and turned, shouting for their steeds to continue, but they would not obey.

"Again," Phenmir commended, stepping closer to the violence.

She roared and caught the attention of the Chussmen and ambushers alike.

The silver ghete's agitation grew from discomfort to rage as they attacked each other. The riders fell from their saddles and into the clawed chaos to be shredded by their own steeds.

Of the three ghete riders who guarded the Endowers, two left to charge towards the rampaging steeds that had forsaken their riders.

The Beastling called again, causing the two charging riders to charge into each other as their steeds dueled on hind legs. The ghete trampled their riders with heavy, dirty paws.

The other three ghete had killed their riders and continued to attack each other until only one remained and was slain by the Chuss guards.

Phenmir ran towards the other Endowers. "Make the last one to drop its rider! We need one of them alive to figure out who they are."

She growled, catching the ghete's attention and causing it to stand still. She roared, and it stood on hind legs for a moment and shook like a wet dog until the rider fell to the ground.

Phenmir lowered her to the ground. "Go keep the remaining ghete calm."

As she roared, he ran towards the fallen rider and unsheathed the shortsword from his belt. He initially felt that the weapon was only another burden to carry with his title, but now understood its practicality when faced with an emergency.

The rider started to stand and reached for the spear at his side. Phenmir met him with a kick to the chest, knocking the man back with a gasp followed by a bloody cough.

Phenmir kicked the man's hand, tossing the blade across the ground. He stepped on the hand and shouted for any Endower Gorgers to come and hold his new captive.

Two Chussboys ran and held the man down on each side with the strength of titans.

Phenmir stared at the fleshy abomination before him.

To have a better look at the captive's face below his eyes, Phenmir removed a brown wrap. Beneath the worn cloth was a fleshy face that appeared to have been skinned and poorly healed. He was human, that much he could tell.

"Perd!" a Gorger shouted.

Phenmir paid the boy a brief glance, sharing his astonishment before looking back at the fiend below them.

"Free me!" he hissed. His mouth had only the remnants of cut lips that revealed yellowing teeth. If it were not for the frustrated tone of voice, it would have been hard to decipher his emotion.

Phenmir struggled to react. Were it any typical human, he would have been ready to interrogate them, but a face of red muscles had taken his breath away.

He turned back to see the Chuss guards resting on the ground, some exhausted, others mourned their fallen comrades.

"Who the perd are you? Why did you ambush our company?" Phenmir asked.

The captive twisted and tried to sit up. Drool dripped from the corners of his mouth.

The Gorgers pressed his hands down harder. Phenmir noted that the skin on his knuckles was intact and not flayed like his face had been.

"Your companions are–"

"*Perd* you!" The captive tried to spin in Phenmir's face, but the poor attempt only shot out a spray of phlegm and saliva.

Phenmir looked up at the Gorgers. "He's not going to speak. One of you is enough to help me keep him down." He pointed at the Gorger, who held the captive's right arm to the ground, then back at the carriage from which he had escaped. "Run back and bring Chenn to me. Tell him it's a command."

The Gorger nodded and ran. Phenmir shifted to the captive's side and continued to press him down as he continued to thrash.

Phenmir looked at the Chuss guards while he awaited Chenn's arrival. Amidst the sobs and cries of pain, he heard prayers to Cheric for mercy and for a blessing on the departed who had given their lives to protect the company. The past months in Sliin had been a luxury compared to what he had experienced in Kzhek. The reality of the continent's dwindling state was once again forced upon him. His title as the Chuss Thane of Harmony regained its terrible toll. Leading entailed suffering. Commanding entailed tragedy. As long as he fulfilled his duty, he would suffer with his soldiers. An expedition to the Middlelands had been too easy of a dream. Although he did yet know why their company had been ambushed, he could not help but attribute it to the war. He was again reminded that the war did not comprise merely the battles in Paiell and Kzhek, but was a widespread disease of hatred that caused people to assault each other throughout Facet.

Chenn arrived panting as he ran with the Gorger who retook his place holding the captive against the ground.

Phenmir placed a hand on the boy's shoulder. "I'm here with you. I need you to focus."

Chenn nodded and furrowed his brow.

The boy's confidence was a ruse, but one that would only help build his character. Phenmir knew this, having experienced it himself.

He had seen people die in battle and on the surgeon's table in the most gruesome ways. Despite his past terrors, he had yet to see something like a talking corpse. A memory surfaced, one reminiscent of the face before him, that of a Tchoyas mask changing ceremony. He let his eyes fall upon the face again. The resemblance to a maskless Tchoyasman was uncanny, though this one's skinless flesh had been dried and healed as much as it could without a layer of skin. Its vulnerability was still clear, as noted by the seeping cracks in the flesh. He could not fathom how painful it would be to live such a life.

Chenn stared at the corpse. The feigned confidence had dissipated.

"Chenn."

The Chussboy turned his head to Phenmir.

"Read him. Find out who they are and why they are here."

Chenn nodded and stared at the fleshy captive and studied him as if he were trying to comprehend a complex test.

"Where's Kaela?" Chenn asked.

"Why?"

"Bring her here. It's–I–just–" He squinted and shook his head. "There's a lot. Just bring her."

Phenmir pointed for the Gorger who had retrieved Chenn to return to the carriage. Phenmir shifted to hold the captive's arm down, though he had ceased his efforts to escape.

The captive's pale green eyes locked on Phenmir's. He had an urge to turn away but forced himself to stare into his enemy's glare. He was in control and would make that known. The captive turned away, his bloodshot eyes fixated on Chenn, who continued to read him with his Feelman ability.

Phenmir turned as he heard running footsteps nearing them. Kaela arrived and knelt at Phenmir's side, staring at the captive with no sign of discomfort.

"Do you know what this is, Kaela?" Phenmir asked.

"A Tchoyasman. Am I right, Chenn?"

The Chussboy nodded.

Phenmir's suspicions were confirmed. Their captive was a maskless Tchoyasman. How he survived without skin or a mask to cover his flesh, Phenmir did not know. "Have you seen these kinds of Tchoyasmen before, Kaela?"

"Not any that ride silver ghete and attack people, if that is what you mean. I just know what a maskless face looks like."

"Why would anyone want to live maskless?" Phenmir asked.

"The masks are tied to our Ideal and pledge of loyalty to our god. Besides that, I don't know who or what this man is." Kaela shrugged, then looked at Chenn. "You read him?"

"Yes."

Phenmir and Kaela looked at him in anxious anticipation.

He looked between them until he mustered the courage to speak. Whatever the boy had seen left him terrified. "They were sent by Krall Trhet."

The captive grumbled and shook.

Phenmir ran his hand through his hair. His eyes fell to the skinless Tchoyasman, who stared at him with a vile, lipless grin. He refocused on Chenn. "How did he know where we were? Do you mean to tell me he sent them *directly* for us to intercept our expedition?"

"I think so." The boy went silent for another moment as he stared at the Tchoyasman.

"Why did you want Kaela to come here?" Phenmir asked.

"I'm a Tchoyasgirl and should know about this, right Chenn?"

Chenn nodded. "Yes, but I wanted you to know something."

"What?"

"Like Thane Stolk said, these were sent by your Krall because he knew what we were doing." He pointed at the skinless Tchoyasman. "He doesn't know anything about who told the Krall where we were going. The Krall just hired them and didn't really say anything else except that he wanted us stopped. Someone on our side is working with the Krall."

"You *do* remember that I was the only Tchoyas Endower in Sliin, right?"

"Yes, but you're a Shiftling. You know how they work."

"So you think one of my Shiftlings snuck into Sliin?"

Chenn shrugged. "That's my best guess."

A terrifying guess. A Tchoyasman so bound to their Ideal of loyalty that they remain true to the Krall even after the atrocities that he committed.

The skinless Tchoyasman laughed and stared at Kaela. "You perding little traitor will suffer for what you have done."

"Keep him quiet," Phenmir told one of the Gorgers who still held the Tchoyasman against the ground. "Chenn can read anything we need to know. We don't need his prattling."

The Gorger moved one of his hands from the Tchoyasman's arm, clenched his jaw, and covered it. "Bite me and I'll rip your teeth out."

"Are you sure it was an Endower?" Kaela asked. "What if one of the Tchoyas Thanes that escaped Fayis is still working with him?"

Phenmir shook his head. "None of the Tchoyas Thanes have visited since we planned this expedition. Even if this informant is not an Endower, they have to be someone in Sliin."

They paused for a moment of uncomfortable silence.

"Won't the Tchoyasmen in the Middlelands know that we are coming?" asked Chenn.

Phenmir nodded. "I'm afraid so, unless they believe these raiders succeeded. Still, I think that they would watch for our arrival even if they are confident in the ability of these ghete riders." He sighed and clenched his eyes shut.

Had he been too optimistic in hoping that such a journey would be without difficulty? *Perding hypocrite. You claim that love is your Ideal, yet once again, you endanger a group of children for your gain.* His condemning thoughts had become more bothersome as of late. "Have you ever seen any Tchoyasmen like this, Kaela?

She shook her head. "I've heard stories, but like I said, it's a sin for one of us to remove our masks."

"What kinds of stories?" Phenmir asked.

She shrugged. "Some people talk about the maskless people. Some live in the wilderness to avoid punishment."

"Punishment? I thought Chenn said that they were hired by the Krall."

"He killed most of my Court's Thanes and now you ask why he is working with people like this?" She gestured at the Tchoyasman. "Do you have an answer, Chenn? I know that I'm a Tchoyasgirl, but I am just as confused as Phenmir."

"I think I might know."

"You know," Kaela said.

Chenn nodded. "They are members of a group that call themselves the 'faceless raiders.' They roam the Court without a city to call home and search for jobs like this one for the Krall. Someone pays, they hunt."

"Did any of the guards kill the leader?" Phenmir asked.

Chenn shook his head, and the Tchoyasman started to struggle under the grip of the Gorgers.

Chenn focused on him, squinting his eyes as he read the raider's thoughts. Chenn jumped to his feet and started to back away.

"What is it?" Phenmir asked.

"More are coming." His breathing sped up. "We need to leave. Hurry."

Phenmir placed his hand on the boy's shoulder. "Calm yourself. We can't leave right now. They destroyed our carriages and our ghete–"

"Poisoned." Chenn squinted at the Tchoyasman. "They shot poisoned darts at them before their ghete attacked our carts. They wanted to be sure that we couldn't escape."

Phenmir placed his finger over his lips to silence the boy's quivering. Kaela looked as if she too was about to panic.

Phenmir looked out to the horizon, listening. "I don't hear anyone coming. We should still have some time." He looked at the broken carriages, noting the lone standing carriage that had carried the other Endower. All of their ghete laid on the ground, though he did not know if they were dead or merely unconscious. Three of the silver ghete had either killed each other under the Beastling's command or had been killed by the Chuss guards. Three silver ghete remained sitting like docile cats, though two of them had plenty of bloody slashes across their scaled torsos.

"What are we going to do?" Kaela asked.

"We still have at least one carriage and three of the raiders' ghete." He looked over to see the Chuss guards. Their force had been decimated, leaving so many killed. "We can't fit everyone, but we can try packing in as tight as possible, maybe having some sit on top. Safety isn't our priority right now. Escape is."

"But if these raiders knew where we would be," said Kaela, "wouldn't the others be able to find us?"

Phenmir nodded. "We'll have to take another route, one unmapped and untraveled. One silver ghete should be enough to pull the carriage. We'll just have to figure out how to bridle them. We can send the other two forward with a guard and Beastling each to scout the path, making sure our carriage can travel there. If we don't have enough Beastlings for both, one should be enough if the ghete remain close enough." Phenmir nodded, feeling more confident in his plan as he thought it out. "This should work, but we have to be quick."

"What are we going to do with him?" Kaela pointed to the captive.

Phenmir stared at the Tchoyasman, asking himself the same question. He had the opportunity to teach the children a lesson on mercy or strict justice. Phenmir was a Chussman. She should never have questioned it, yet there were no clear Chuss doctrines on war, except to avoid it at all costs. That would no longer be possible. The vile Tchoyasman would have killed him without hesitation, for that was the reason they had ambushed the party.

"Phenmir?" Kaela asked.

"We'll keep him captive for now. Bind him to the back of the carriage if we have to." The Tchoyasman kept a stoic stare, but Phenmir thought that he noticed slight relief in his breathing. *Why do I feel obligated to spare him when we slaughtered so many Zhaesmen in Kzhek who only fought to serve their Court? They were without sin, according to Zhaes law. This faceless abomination forsook his land and god to pursue self-interest and bounties. This man is driven by bloodlust and greed.*

Chenn's timid smile suggested that he was relieved to leave the man alive. Children often scorned those unlike them, especially those with physical maladies that morphed their appearance. Despite this man's bare flesh, the Endowers still hoped that he would receive mercy.

"Thane Stolk!" a shout came from the party of Endowers.

He turned to search for the one who had called him and spotted a Chussgirl who ran towards him. Her eyes were fear-struck and her mouth hung open as if ready to scream.

"What is it?" He jogged to meet her.

"The hills!" She pointed up to the small rocky peak. "They're watching!"

Phenmir watched in horror as a party of faceless raiders sat atop their silver ghete mounts. Every eye in their small gathering turned to follow Phenmir's heart-stopping stare. The raiders stepped back from the rocky ridge after a moment and disappeared from their sight.

"Where are they going, Thane Stolk?" an Endower asked.

"What's happening?" Kaela asked.

"Keep him still, Gorgers!" Phenmir ran to the remaining Chuss guards. "Stand ready for a second ambush!"

"Where are they coming from?"

"What is happening?"

"Thane Stolk?"

"Thane Stolk?"

"Thane Stolk?"

Their questions and anxious cries bombarded him, but he was too focused on the Endowers, trying to find a way to use one of their abilities to defend against a second ambush. He took a breath, remembering that they had the Beastlings to control the ghete, yet part of him feared that they would have something to combat the Beastlings' abilities. He knew that there had to be a reason for only sending some of their party to the initial ambush.

How long have they been watching us?

He ran towards the Endowers. "Beastlings at the ready!" They stared at him, paralyzed with fear. "Now! Beastlings! Come here!"

Four of the Chuss children ran towards him. He crouched to meet their eyes as reached him. "Did you see what we did to the last silver ghete?"

They all nodded. *Perd, they are all shaking with terror. Why does the pride of the Courts subject these mere children to such torment?* "When you see them coming, do whatever you need to stop the ghete before they reach us." Tears welled in their eyes. "Can you do that for me?"

They nodded, bereft of enthusiasm. They had not chosen to take the organs as the Endowed did. Responsibility had been forced upon them at birth. Phenmir only stretched them further.

"Follow me." He waved and walked towards the guards. "Chussmen, I need these Endowers protected. Work that out amongst yourselves."

"Yes, Thane!" they replied in broken union.

Phenmir jogged back towards the captive Tchoyasman, not knowing what he should do next. Everything else depended on the next wave of faceless raiders.

The company fell silent. Everyone searched for a sign of ambush, yet there was nothing to be found. Vultures circled above like an omen for the tragedy that would be wrought. Hills and desert acacias covered the horizon, masking the arrival of any creature or raider. They had seen the faceless Tchoyasmen above them, but their ambush could come from any direction. Phenmir had a light set of armor, but it was designed to show his rank, not to protect. He, too, was vulnerable. Despite their armor, the guards were vulnerable to an ambush. The Endowers were the most vulnerable, and valuable, of them all.

A choking noise from behind caught Phenmir's attention. A child screamed, then grunted and fell silent. He turned to see what had happened. *Perd me.* The two Gorgers who were holding the captive Tchoyasman fell to the ground, one with a dart in his neck, the other with one in the temple. *The same used to pacify our ghete.* He wanted to rush over and help them but halted his ambition for running right into the enemy's target.

He crouched behind a large rock and peeked out. There was still no sign of the raiders.

The faceless Tchoyasman, no longer a captive, unsheathed a long knife from one of the Gorger's belts and held it out to fend anyone off who dared to pursue him.

"They have Beastlings!" the once-captive shouted. "Keep the ghete away from them!" He turned around, searching for a sign of his allies, then fixated on a certain point among the trees.

Perding fool. "There!" Phenmir pointed to the area, having seen the ghete riders hidden among the forestry.

A horde of what seemed like forty faceless Tchoyasmen ran through the trees, towards the group.

They left their ghete behind, yet the steeds were still somewhere among the trees. Their company would perish within a few moments against the armed raiders. Bringing a Beastling close to the ghete was their only hope for survival.

The Chussman shouted as they ran towards the raiders. They raised Chuss shortswords to meet javelins and flailing maces. As the parties neared each other, Phenmir could see that their guard force was less than half the size of the raider party. The guards had proved formidable in the past, but the prowess of the raiders was far beyond them. The guards were volunteer citizens compared to the trained mercenaries that were the faceless raiders.

Phenmir retained a fraction of hope. Four guards remained behind to protect the Beastlings. The defending guards had spread themselves wide, though fearfully thin, to protect the Beastlings at all costs. It was a hopeful strategy, though it would not last long.

"Glory to Cheric."

"Care is the Creed!"

The Chuss guards shouted, some cries cut off with blood curdling grunts as the raiders impaled them. Despite the diminishing Chussmen, they still felled plenty of the raiders. Phenmir spotted some making a last strike with their last breath after impalement.

"Follow!" Phenmir waved at the Beastlings and their guards and ran towards the ghete hidden among the trees. He spared a glance back. Three faceless raiders chased the Beastlings and drew closer every second.

Phenmir ran away from the conflict. He knew he was directing the defense by leading the Beastlings to the ghete, yet still felt that he was retreating from his responsibilities. He was a coward.

Chuss guards, mere civilians who were willing to give their lives for their Court, perished by the moment as they stopped to let the Endowers run onward.

"Thane Stolk?"

He stopped and waved for the Beastlings towards the ghete.

He let out a whimper. A childish cry for mercy. He stopped and stood still, facing the once-captive Tchoyasman. *How could we have forgotten about him for even a moment?*

He ambled towards the once-captive raider and held a hand out, pleading for mercy. The raider held Chenn with his right arm wrapped around the boy's neck. He held a blade in his left hand.

"Please" was all Phenmir could muster. He had to plead for mercy. Anything hostile or rash would only cause pain. Pain. Loss. *Guilt.*

"Call off your Beastlings and surrender or I'll kill this *perding* child for robbing me of my thoughts."

Hope was a butterfly that had landed so delicately in his heart, yet it was frightened away within a moment.

"Please."

The Tchoyasman shook his head and tightened his grip around Chenn's throat.

The boy grunted and stared at Phenmir with eyes that showed fear and betrayal. He felt as if the boy asked him, *"How could you let him take me? How could you forget about me? My father trusted you? I trusted you."*

"Make them stop!" the Tchoyasman shouted.

Once frozen by shock and fear, indecision had since taken him captive.

.

Little time remained until the Beastlings reached the silver ghete. It would be enough. It had to be.

Chen's lip protruded, and his eyes were red. The raider had stolen the boy's remaining dignity.

Ghete cries came from nearby, but Phenmir could not avert his gaze.

Chenn's mouth fell open as he wailed. He cried for mercy, for life.

A second chorus of roars came from the trees.

The Tchoyasman tightened his grip on Chenn's throat until he stopped screaming.

The roaring ceased and was replaced by deep growls.

Chenn shook his head, a last hopeless attempt to free himself from the Tchoyasman's grip.

Phenmir stood still. An impossible decision had paralyzed him. Cowardice had paralyzed him.

The Tchoyasman squeezed a weak whimper from Chenn as he turned to the trees.

Endowers and Chussmen sat atop the ghete as they ran to battle.

Phenmir turned back to the Tchoyasman. A silver blade had gone through Chenn's chest. The boy still whimpered but had lost his energy.

No.

The Tchoyasman stabbed through Chenn repeatedly, mutilating his body beyond the saving touch of a Eurythrin. Chenn's eyes were open with terror as he faced his final moments. The Tchoyasman dropped Chenn's body, soaking the ground with blood.

He wanted to shout some insult. Some vile line of words that would condemn Chenn's murderer, but only a painful yell escaped.

He felt the agony of a bereaved parent.

Hatred, the antithesis of the Chuss Ideal, filled him, yet the love of a parent fueled him to avenge Chenn.

The Tchoyasman held the blade in his right hand and crouched in a defensive stance as Phenmir ran towards him, with no weapon of his own. He swung his blade and Phenmir lowered himself to slam his shoulder into the Tchoyasman's gut and wrapped his arms around him as they fell to the ground.

A shot of pain shot through Phenmir's shoulder. He knew the raider had stabbed him, but he would not allow a second attack. He grabbed the Tchoyasman's arm and bit it, drawing blood. The Tchoyasman screamed and let go of the blade as his wrist contorted. Phenmir held the man's arm and turned the elbow up, snapping it like a branch.

Before the Tchoyasman could ask for mercy, Phenmir struck the faceless flesh with his gauntlet. He punched for Thane Hult, who had trusted him with his son. He punched for the Endowers. He punched for Court Chuss, for the horrors of war, for the flaws of mankind, for his own failures, for Chenn.

His fists throbbed as he stared down at the mess flesh that had once been a Tchoyasman. Rage compelled him to continue thrashing, but the thought of Chenn brought him back to reality.

He stumbled away from the Tchoyasman and fell at Chenn's side.

Clutching him in his arms as he would a babe, Phenmir looked into Chenn's eyes as the boy drifted away from consciousness. His heart warmed as Chenn smiled with an open mouth, but lost his joy as he realized the boy was merely frightened and trying to cry for help. A weak breath escaped Chenn's mouth, each one becoming weaker.

"Thane Stolk," he whimpered. A tear ran down to his mouth.

"I'm here." Was all he could think to say. He would not give the boy any false reassurance. Chenn would not live. Phenmir stared at him, forcing himself to accept that fate.

He had mere moments left with the boy. *What does one tell a dying child?*

Phenmir lifted Chenn's head to bid farewell. "See you in Cheric's holy halls." Phenmir smiled, hoping that Chenn would depart with a final joyful moment.

Chenn did not smile. His head shot back and forth as he coughed and shot blood at Phenmir's face, never drawing another breath.

Words could not describe the terror or sorrow. Only a painful cry could express Phenmir's frustration at his failure to protect each child. A weak thought whispered that it was not his fault. He banished the excuse like an exorcizing priest. The boy's bloody corpse felt symbolic of Facet's failures. A people so corrupted by pride had chosen to use warfare to reach a solution. Regardless of the victor, both sides of the conflict would leave with more that they had gained.

If Phenmir had the power to end the war and return to the little peace that they had, he would. He would have forsaken it all, but they were too far gone. Too many had died in pursuit of a collective dream.

He knew he had to continue. Chenn's death would not be in vain.

He knew he knelt with a corpse in the middle of a battle, but he could not pry himself from Chenn's side. He placed his head against Chenn's heart and wept.

"Phenmir." A hand rested on his shoulder after what felt like endless moments of tears. His knees ached on the rocky terrain.

"Phenmir."

He pulled himself away from Chenn's body and turned to see Kaela standing behind him. He stared at her and wiped his nose.

"It's over."

"Wh-what?"

"The Chussmen and Beastlings finished the Faceless raiders. They're all dead." Kaela fell at Phenmir's side, finally recognizing the corpse he held.

They wept together. Two Courts in unity mourned a fallen friend, for all soldiers who perish are friends to someone.

He still felt too weak to stand but looked around at the battle's aftermath. Six Chuss guards remained. He did not see any other dead Endowers but was afraid to discover their corpses.

Despite their self-proclaimed piety, the Courts of Facet had insulted their gods.

CHAPTER TWENTY-TWO

CRUCIBLE OF THE DUNES

G lowing stones blinded Hir. His eyes had grown so used to the dark after walking for what felt like an hour. He assumed passing beyond a certain point with the bronze on his staff had triggered the stones to glow, but he attributed every small oddity to the bronze ever since he entered the tunnel. He was lost in an ocean of questions. The bronze staff was the only drifting piece of debris that seemed to offer any clarity. The purpose of the Crucible had become no clearer.

His stomach burned from a day with nothing substantial to eat. He ate before leaving the chapterhouse two days previous but had quickly run through the food allotted to him and foraging was not a skill he claimed to possess. Until then, he had never considered eating moss. He held off, knowing the end of his trial was nearing. *Hoping, not knowing.*

He still heard occasional hisses in the dark ahead, but they had ceased bothering him. He never found the source of the sound, but they had become as regular as the chirping of stelcrested doves in the Vestning months before the heat of Letur set in.

More stones glowed as he walked deeper into the cavern. The tunnel had grown in size, but he was yet to find any exit. Certain corners and the triggered glowing stones make him wonder if the long cavern was the Patriarchy's creation. Despite his frustration with the Crucible of Dunes, he put his trust into the wisdom of the Patriarchy. He had not discovered enlightenment. He was yet to learn anything and only grew to hate himself more.

Is that the point of this? To reach some self-actualization that could have been better met in one of Cheric's temples?

The Patriarchy is a society, not a religion.

Why do they treat matters within the organization as sacred? Can anything temporal be sacred? Is it not Cheric's wish that we all seek knowledge?

What has the Patriarchy taught? What have you gained from them? Are you anything more than a servant? Do you actually believe that you can become one of them?

I am.

How do you know? Why do you even want to become a Scholar? Are you trying to prove something to yourself? Is this to satisfy your pride, showing others you are the genius you claim to be?

No. I want–

You are no greater than anyone else. You are less of a Chussman for wanting to place yourself above others, seeking praise like any Priessman.

No.

You think that if you prove your worth that all will be well.

No.

You want the title, the glory, the superiority of a Scholar.

No.

Then why are you here? Why have you chosen to focus on yourself while your father has dedicated his life to others in this war? What do you have to offer?

Then I, too, will dedicate myself to my people.

How? By revealing the Patriarchy's secrets?No, but by using my connections as a Scholar to serve the people as he does.

What will you do?

The tunnel opened up into a chamber like a river emptying into a pond.

What will you do?

It was not as large as he would have expected, only opening up into the size of the front room of his home. Still, the tunnel continued beyond the room. Was this some midway point or a final resting place before the ultimate conclusion of the Crucible?

The room glowed from a mound of stones in its center. The pile stood up to his knees and had a bronze sword stuck in the center. He sat down beside the pile, ready to take a rest and close his eyes, but he held off as he felt strange indentations in the oddly polished stone beneath him. Something had been carved into the stone and the images had been well preserved.

Hir stood to take a better glimpse and saw that the images circled the mound of glowing stones in a crescent with the ends not quite touching. He had studied ancient hieroglyphs briefly in his preparation to join the Patriarchy, but these carvings were much more modern. They had still aged, but he guessed by the polish and care given to them that they were created in his lifetime.

Is this trial something new to the Patriarchy? Had Scholar Sokov completed this Crucible of Dunes, a different Crucible, or any Crucible at all?

He almost fell into the pile of stones as he noticed the first image in the carved chronicle. It was that of a small, humanoid figure with an emotionless face and twisting lines for a body. The similarity to a

Middleman was uncanny, yet he questioned his conclusion. If this was a carving made by the Patriarchy–of which he was not yet sure–what interest do they have in the Middlemen?

The next image was a cloud with lines beneath it, a storm, and small leaves rising from the ground below. He continued to walk around, seeing that the next picture depicted a man in robes.

A Scholar. The next image was the same, except that the Scholar held a rod in his hand and the Middleman from the first image was laid horizontally against the ground. The next image was a small child, one with two umbilical cords. He stepped to the right to see the next one; three people stood in a line, each with a leaf over their navel. He reached the final image, one of a Scholar with a leaf over its navel and two images to its right. The upper was the same child, but its two umbilical cords floated next to it, or at least that was what he understood from the two lines at its side. The image below was covered by a glowing stone, one that had been carved into a square and was held in its place by small ridges around it.

Hir reached down and removed the glowing square, revealing a haunting image below. A carved figure laid beneath the image, humanoid, but gaunt like a skeleton. Although the other faces had little to no detail, this one had a screaming mouth in an upside down pear-shape. Three long claws extended from its arms. The image was unpleasant at the least, yet he found himself confused as he saw lines coming from the figure's abdomen. The lines had the exact length and curve as those floating near the child's image above.

The fear of that final carved image clouded the relief of finding a checkpoint in his journey. Never had he imagined that such a small caricature could frighten him so. Perhaps he was uneasy from the enigmatic quest, but something was unnatural about that drawing. He searched around the chamber, touching the walls and ground with his staff in search of some other secret, but there was nothing else to find. He tried removing the bronze sword from the stone pile, wondering if he was to use it, but it was as sturdy as the cave's walls.

The tunnel behind him remained lit, but the one ahead was dark with no promise of light. He would have stayed longer if he was not so eager to escape the Crucible. He prayed to Cheric for guidance and stepped into the dark.

A faint, rodentesque screech echoed from the beyond. He had heard the noise before, but it had not felt as close, as *real*, as this one. His hands started to ache from holding the staff with unrelenting tenacity.

He continued onward with no added light. With his staff tapping along the floor, he felt the tunnel turn, banishing the little light that he had behind.

He tapped down, noticing a step down before him. He knelt to feel the step himself, making sure that he did not stumble down any long staircase in the dark. It was only a single step, much to his relief, but one that was smooth and worn down like the polished stone that circled the pile of glowing stones. He felt the floor beyond. It was rough like the rest of the cave.

He descended the stair and continued for but a single step until the room lit with a circle of glowing stones around the chamber's perimeter. Unlike the previous chamber, this one was the size of a large house. The chamber was empty except for a large, murky pond at its center with a stone mound twice his side on its far bank.

Seeing no other escape from the cave, he worried that he would have to dive into the water to find an underground passage. It did not look deep, but the dirty water left him to wonder if it was a puddle or a pool. Fresh fish skeletons and other remains of unknown flesh sat on the bank or floated near it.

A sharp hiss followed by a deep eldritch groan pulled his attention to the rock mound as something walked up its back to the top.

A sickly, naked humanoid crouched atop the mound and glared back at him.

He gripped his staff and took a defensive stance, focusing on its gray face. *Is this what you have been training me for, Scholars? Is this the purpose of the Patriarchy? To rid the world of this hidden evil?* Recalling his failures when dueling his preceptor, Hir was terrified.

It reached the base of the rock mound and hunched over, wailing like a banshee with a maw that opened twice as wide as a human's. Boneless appendages hung from its abdomen, swinging like limp tentacles. His fears were manifested as he stared back at the thing whose terrible image was carved into the ground around the glowing stone mound.

Hir was a child. One cast into a beast's cavern with no apparent purpose except that of survival. He channeled his frustration and fear into his voice and yelled back at the beast.

Its dark eyes widened, and it dove into the pool between them. The murky water hid its image, but ripples on the surface told Hir that it was coming straight for him.

Thoughts of everyone that believed in him held him off from surrendering to fear. He could not retreat. Even remaining to fight could result in death, but he was ready. Ready to become whatever the Scholars willed him to be. *Whatever my parents believe I can become.*

He stepped back with one foot and held the staff diagonally, ready to strike or defend as necessary.

The water stilled. His heart felt as if it was vibrating. He tightened his grip.

The ghoul leapt from the water like a feral frog and ran towards him as it landed on two feet.

Hir held his staff with hands spread wide, hoping to knock it back, but it ducked and swiped at his legs, then across his face as he tried to react to the first swipe. Its claws tore his flesh like dull hunting knives that shred his flesh rather than cut straight through. The salty pond water still on its claws caused his injuries to sting, making his failure to defend himself even more impactful.

As he tried to ready himself for the next attack, it swiped upwards, tearing his clothes and drawing blood. His reactions were too slow.

The creature lunged at him, but he tucked the staff and rolled away, barely missing another strike. It grew frustrated and screeched, swiping with fury as it ran towards him. He rolled again, then switched directions with the next roll as it tried to follow. In the second he had behind the fiend, he swung his staff at its head and stuck its neck. The fiend choked as it roared.

He was not confident that he would be victorious, but he found a way to work around the creature's agility. The creature lunged and Hir rolled free from the attack again.

He continued to fight it with quick dodges and attacks, swinging when the creature stopped to catch its breath.

As the dance continued, he took more injuries than the fiend, but he began to understand its movement. It did not attack, defend, or move in a distinct pattern, but he felt he understood its style.

He was already thin, but the excess training and time without food had made his spine stick out even more, making the thin skin on his back feel raw as it scraped across the cavern floor with each roll. His shoulders pulsed, especially the right as he favored that side for rolling dodges. He was lightheaded and hoped that it was from exhaustion rather than blood loss. Even if he survived the fight, he worried he would die on the way out of the cave.

Hir had moved away from the creature as he tried to understand its attack style, but more so to have a moment to breathe. It showed no sign of fatigue. The only rest would be that achieved in victory. Training with his preceptor had trained him for this. Countless defeats had prepared him.

The creature hissed. He shouted back, and it ran for him.

Hir crouched, leaning onto his right knee as if ready to roll. He shot his shoulders to the right, but remained on his feet, remaining still after continuously rolling. His trick worked. The creature dove to the side and Hir swung his staff down into its ribs.

It screeched, and he struck its head before it had a chance to react.

Hir was bleeding, sore, and afraid, but he wagered everything and jumped on top of the creature.

He saddled its back and held on with legs crossed to squeeze. It turned and bit his leg, needle-like teeth into his thigh. He shouted, centering his rage into his attack as he shot the end of his staff down through the creature's back until it went through and hit the cavern floor.

The creature struggled and tried to stand, so Hir moved the staff, widening the wound and tearing the creature's flesh until it surrendered and lost consciousness.

Hir vomited on the fiend. He removed his staff with trembling hands and put it to the creature's side to keep himself from passing out on the mix of his vomit and the creature's black ichor.

He sat and waited for some revelation, ready for someone to congratulate him on the completion of his trial. No answer came. He had no one at his side besides a fiendish corpse. He laid beside it and lost consciousness.

CHAPTER TWENTY-THREE

BUDDING ANTLERS

"*Rasteen,*" Runith breathed the pattern that spoke the true name of the Middlemen.

The one who had given the name of its people to him shot its jaw forward twice in rapid succession.

"That's a nod." Golma said.

Runith did not openly speak about his devotion to the Zhaes faith, though he revered his god with all that he was. The same sacrality struck him as the Middlemen shared their true name.

"*Thank you.*" Runith breathed.

"*You are on the first branch of a tree of trust, beast man.*" The Rasteen breathed.

Beast man? Runith held his composure but was astounded by the Rasteen's insight. Had they seen him communicate with Lele? Did they recognize his ability or could they sense his organ?

"*What do you seek?*" it breathed.

Standing close helped Runith better understand the Middlemen–the Rasteen. Where did their moniker as the "Middlemen" originate? These were no mere myths, nor were they plants or some abomination. They were beautiful beings, statuesque masterpieces. The more he studied the vines, the more they seemed like strands of muscle that held their eggshell faces in place.

"*To know the Rasteen,*" Runith replied. He knew the response would only prompt further questions from the one he faced, but he did not have a better answer. He wanted to turn away from the Tchoyasmen and Zhaesmen. To know the Rasteen, their purpose, their culture, their reason for existence filled his mind with limitless curiosities. What *were* they? How were they connected to the Endower abilities? His old desires had dissipated as the spirit of nature flowered within.

"*What you desire is difficult to comprehend for one like you, beast man.*"

Runith smiled. "*I am not often turned away by difficulty. I can accomplish anything I set my mind to.*"

"*For one like you to know our kind not a task that one can accomplish, but it is a journey that one can begin.*"

"*This is what I want.*"

"*You alone?*"

Runith turned to look at the Tchoyas Endowers. They stepped towards him, then turned to face the Rasteen. They breathed in a single voice. "*We stand with him.*"

The Rasteen pontificated its jaw twice.

"*What do I call you? Do you have a name? Mine is Runith.*"

"*We are not known as Vibrations as you are.*"

Vibrations. Tones. Words. Names. "*Then how do I address you?*"

The Rasteen exhaled and inhaled in quick succession, like a frightened gasp.

"That is your name?" Runith asked.

"As I said, we do not have Vibrations–words or names by which we are known." The Rasteen gasped again. *"This is what I am. I have heard others call you by a name, but you are a beast man. I have called you beast man, for that is what you are. Your title is not relevant. Titles are descriptions, not identities."*

"Like a ruler? A farmer? You are this–" Runith mimicked the gasp.

"No, this is not my position in society nor is it a title to refer to what I do, I am–" it gasped.

He felt he understood it, yet it was difficult to fully grasp the concept. The first of many in greeting such an alien culture. He wondered if his ears and mind were not yet attuned to their form of naming. They still held the name Rasteen. A *Vibration*. It was a clear inconsistency, but only to him as an outsider. Assumptions were often gateways to error. He had experienced that enough times while trying to speak with them using his beastcalling.

Gasp continued to breathe. *"You want to know the way of the Rasteen? This is the beginning. You cannot think as a–"* Gasp hummed, almost moaning as if it was trying to say a word.

"You Vibrations do not think as we do." Gasp looked at the Endowers. *"The young already understand. You would be wise to follow them."*

Follow children? Runith found the children just as confounding as the Rasteen. *Since when has a child been more trusted than an adult?*

He nodded, still cautious to accept the advice.

"You come to know our people, but we already know the ways of yours," said Gasp.

"How? Are there other humans here?"

"Besides the company of invaders that you have brought, no. Our ties with your kind are ancient. Too often we have been betrayed."

Runith wanted to defend himself, but he could only do *that*. He could defend his stance, but not the desires of Royss and Krall Trhet, nor could he defend his ancestors.

"What do you mean by ancient ties?"

Gasp studied the Endowers, then turned back to Runith. *"There is much for you to learn, beast man."*

"I told you I have a name. It is not beast man."

"That is what you are."

Gasp stepped back among three other Rasteen. They breathed whispers that sounded like children trying to remain silent while hiding from a predator. They looked similar, with white faces and bodies made from roots and vines, but small characteristics set them apart.

He compared Gasp to the others, noting that the Rasteen had larger shoulders and thicker vines than some others. Of the four that stood before him, one other had a similar build to Gasp, while the other two were more feminine with less prominent chins and had small buds, even some flowers growing from them.

They have sexes.

He had worked with a Sprouten before and thought he heard about plants reproducing. Sproutens were not a common branch of Endowed or Endower, but one was prominent in Zhaes for her ability to coax plants to make the most spectacular flowers in the Court. When he asked how she did it, she said that she did not cause the flowers to appear, but rather used her ability to control their reproduction. Plant sex was not a topic too commonly spoken about. Runith did not like to think that he was perverted, but sexually driven topics tend to stick to one's mind like sap.

"Come." Gasp waved for Runith and the Endowers to follow as he turned away to walk down the road with the other Rasteen.

Golma brushed up beside him and reached for his hand. Runith had never wedded, never born children, yet he wondered if this was a glimpse into what it would feel like to have a daughter seek his comfort.

He took her hand. It was smooth and not yet callused like his. Neither of them spoke as they followed the Rasteen. Taer and the other three Tchoyas Endowers followed, with Lele hopping near the back.

"I'm still here, don't worry," croaked Lele.

Runith paused for her to catch up. *"Do you understand them yet?"*

"No, but it's pleasant to hear them speak."

Runith squeezed Golma's hand twice. "You're in charge." His mouth itched as he smiled. Weeks had passed since he trimmed his beard. "You heard the Middleman. I'm supposed to listen to you."

Golma shook her head and faced forward. Even if she was enjoying the encounter, it was obvious that the Rasteen unsettled her. Runith had met more beasts than he could count, many of them living nightmares. Perhaps that was why he appreciated the Rasteen's elegance. When one finds beauty in nature, it should be admired. *Protected.*

The roadway in the center of the Rasteen village was not paved, as were human cities, but they had laid out stone pathways, making their walk both smooth and on stable ground.

Rasteen emerged from small homes and stood from their gardens to watch the caravan through the village center. Golma reached around his arm with both hands and pressed against him. The other children noticed her unease and sped up to walk beside Runith.

The spectating Rasteen watched with no hint of emotion in their still gazes.

Rather than focus on the straight road ahead, Runith turned to the scenery. Most of the Rasteen buildings were rectangular, with domed roofs, not unlike the sandstone buildings in Court Chuss. Like the people, the buildings were covered in vibrant vines, some spawning fruit, others with flowers the size of a head. They had windows, though they were murky translucent panes that looked more like insect wings than glass. Large roots grew from the ground and swayed, though there was no wind. Bulbous pods that stood up to his knees were all around the village in a sporadic pattern, pulsing as if they were the hearts of the village. Unlike the Zhaes cities of stone and the remnants of dead trees repurposed, the Rasteen village was alive.

Gasp led the procession into a forested area. Trees twice as high as the largest trees that Runith had ever seen shaded them with gargantuan leaves. The biomes of the Middlelands were just as diverse as Facet itself, and he had only seen a small fraction of the territory claimed by the Rasteen. *Do they see the Courts as theirs? Are our cities their own 'Middlelands?' Is claiming land yet another foreign concept to them?*

The leafy covering opened up once again to allow a grand cathedral-like building to penetrate the sunny air. Unlike the other domed structures in the Rasteen village, this one had a peaked roof standing thin and tall. Once again, there were no glass windows, but panes of rainbow membranes that rivaled the masterful stained glass in Kzhek.

"Are we following them in there?" Golma asked.

The Rasteen entered the building as the vines on its hinges contracted like muscles.

Runith let his hand fall down to her back and he pressed her forward. "We go where they lead us."

"But what if–"

"Don't worry, Golma. I'm here with you."

She smiled through the open beak of her hawk mask. Runith was anxious, but he would not let his inhibitions steer her away. He did not think they were in any immediate danger, but he wondered how permitting they were of foreigners.

The other Endowers held close, but only Golma physically held on to Runith. Taer puffed out his chest, but Runith could hear the boy's shaky breathing through his beaver mask.

The Rasteen palace was a living organism, as if they had entered some giant pod. The windows looked like bubbles on the inside and were slightly convex. They walked on a leafy texture, the same one that the walls were composed of. Wooden and leafy furniture made it feel more inhabitable, and with the abundance of vines, it was like walking through an overgrown botanical garden.

Vines stretched from a second level and intersected to form a staircase that the company used to ascend. Gasp stopped and turned to face Runith and the children as they reached two giant leaves that stood twice as tall as him.

"*Where are we?*" Runith asked.

"*The Vineyard, one of many.*"

What does that perding mean? Runith was growing hungry and was becoming more temperate, but he held off from a biting reply. "*Is there anything we should know before going in*"—he pointed at the doors—"*there?*"

Golma squeezed his arm tighter.

"*Are you sure they will be permitted entry?*" another Rasteen asked.

"*The Branch will want to see the children,*" Gasp replied. "*But what about the beast man?*"

Gasp stared at Runith. The Rasteen's pupils seemed less foggy indoors, under the bioluminescent bulbs that hung from the ceiling. "*One of her councilors will read his intentions.*"

"*Are any in full flower?*"

"*Yes.*"

"*Very well.*" Gasp turned to lead the group past the large leaf doors.

Runith followed near the back of the procession, more perplexed than he had been all day. *Read me? Do they have Feelemen?*

"Budding?" asked Golma.

Runith shrugged. "Your guess is as good as mine." Some of the Rasteen looked at them while they spoke in Vibrations. *Can any of them understand us?*

The room beyond was reminiscent of a throne room with a large seat, but the walls made him feel like an insect in the center of a flower. They were made of multiple layers of plant fiber that reached up to the ceiling to form a dome. More of the bioluminescent buds hung from the ceiling vines and large bubble windows were spaced equally apart high on the walls.

"*Who are these Vibrations?*" a female Rasteen breathed atop a throne made from red leaves. Runith felt like he could finally understand the individual sexes in their breathing patterns. She looked just like any other Rasteen but had yellow flowers along her arms and a small crown made from the same red leaves that comprised her throne.

"*Branch of the North,*" breathed Gasp, "*we–*

She held a hand up to stop Gasp and leaned over to another Rasteen, this one covered in red flowers, who stood beside her throne. The other Rasteen's chest moved quickly, as if forcing a whisper.

The one they had called the Branch of the North leaned forward in her Throne. "*Are these truly children of the seed?*"

"*They are,*" breathed Gasp.

"*And the other?*" the Branch asked.

Her advisor leaned over to whisper again.

The Branch's shoulders tensed and the leaves on her crown twisted as if windblown. She shouted Gasp's name with a breath so loud that Runith thought he felt it. "*Why do you bring this desecration of nature to the Vineyard? His kind caused the fragmentation of the Korenod's Vineyard!*"

"*He stands with the children of the seed.*" Gasp stepped forward. "*This one is pure.*"

"*Then why has he come with invaders who seek to use us?*"

Runith felt a chill run down his spine. They had been watched. *Understood. Has an Endower been giving them information or are there some Rasteen capable of understanding the human tongue?*

"*He does not subscribe to their ideology,*" Gasp breathed. "*I believe he wants to advocate for us.*"

The Branch's leaves calmed. "*How do you know this? I see no bulbs growing on you. Did you have someone in your party that is flowering?*"

One of the Rasteen stepped forward and turned around to show the Branch that a small patch of red buds were beginning to flower.

"*Those are mere buds,*" the Branch said.

Gasp pontificated his jaw twice. "*But her ability has already begun to manifest. She could not read his thoughts, but she could see his intentions. If he did not want to advocate for us, I never would have brought him here.*"

A Feelman? Runith's thoughts had been read before, but never his intentions, namely the intentions that he hid in his subconscious. *Is that what I want? Am I choosing to advocate the Rasteen? Am I betraying my own people for this civilization that I am yet to understand?*

Return unto nature that which was taken from it. That which I have taken.

"*Is this true?*" the Branch asked. Her flowered advisor leaned over to whisper again, but the Branch pushed her back and stared at Runith.

"*He breathes as we do,*" Gasp said.

"*I do,*" Runith said.

The Branch's leaves on her head crown stood on end. "*I could accuse you of malintent and rebuke you for the sins of your people, but I will hold back my anger. It is too easy to scorn you, even though you are not responsible for their crimes. So is this why you have come? Do you wish to liberate us?*" She held up a hand to stop Runith from defending himself. "*We don't want your assistance. We are not victims nor a people in need of your services. Tell your Vibrations to leave our land.*"

"*I don't have any motive.*" Runith looked at Golma and the other children. They had come in search of hope while the continent warred. He thought about the organ of the dead infant that had made him a Beastling. Images of Krall Trhet's treacherous feast played across his mind. Life here could be simple, away from the murder and war that plagued Facet. He wanted to learn the Rasteen way of life. As far as he could tell, they were a peaceful people.

I'm not running away from everything. I just need some time away from the pain of human pride. In the Middlelands, an Endowed could stand near Endowers and count them as friends. *Come what may, it will be better than advocating Trhet's and Royss's schemes.*

Runith rubbed the back of Golma's hand with his thumb. "*Read my intentions if you need. I want nothing except to understand you.*"

The Branch breathed Gasp's name. "*Where did you find such a peculiar Vibration? This one stands with the children of the seed, whom he has violated with stolen power, and defects from his people to mingle with our kind?*" She faced Runith. "*You may not understand why just yet, but the fact that you can breathe as we do is an attestation that your soul is aligned with ours.*"

Runith breathed a sigh of relief, pausing to wonder if he had breathed a word in their language. The Branch remained focused on him. He wondered what her breath-name was.

She pointed to Gasp. "*Why have you brought this Vibration here? You've earned temporary approval. What else did you hope to gain?*"

Gasp touched him lightly on the shoulder. "*I believe he is a sign of the Era of Union. He is a harbinger of our lord's return.*"

The Branch's councilors whispered to one another.

"*Heresy!*"

"*Vibration pride is the very reason for which our lord was taken!*"

Runith did not feel insulted by the shouts of the councilors, merely confused by the depth of a history so unknown to him.

One of Gasp's companions spoke. *"He may not be as significant to the return of the lord, but he may be useful in connecting our people with other Vibrations like him."*

"And why would we want that?" one of the Branch's councilors shouted.

The Branch raised her hands and breathed out a hiss to silence the arguments. *"We will not say that he is here to fulfill any prophecy. Dwell with us for some time, Vibration, and we shall see what you have to offer. Just know that all you do will be observed and analyzed. You are not here to study us. We are allowing you to be here so that we might study you."* She breathed Gasp's name. *"We shall visit him soon. Do with him what you will until then."*

Gasp shifted and flared his nostrils. The Rasteen were odd, but even Runith could tell that Gasp was not revealing everything. Why had he taken an interest in Runith enough to bring him to the apparent leader of the village? Gasp sought the Branch's approval, but there was something more than asking for permission to have him as a guest.

Runith stepped ahead of Gasp to turn and look at him and the Branch on her throne. *"I understand we might be interesting to your kind,"* he focused on Gasp, *"but why would you take a stranger to your leader? Even if you think we can help with this 'Era of Union,' why are we here now?"*

The red flowered councilor breathed Gasp's name. *"His faith in the Era is more powerful than ours. He trusts the Vibration enough to take him through the Binding of Roots."*

"Is this true?" the Branch asked.

Gasp nodded. *"Even if he is not a perfect choice, our time is waning. The others who came with him, the invaders, are bringing our destruction. He is close enough to them to prevent our end."*

"Is he ready for the suffering that the Binding requires?" asked the Branch. *"Is he ready for the responsibility required by such a calling?"*

Runith almost laughed at the absurdity of the situation. *Are they trying to make me their savior? Is this more than just making peace between two people? What is Gasp perding thinking?*

He put his hand on Gasp's shoulder. "*Can we talk in private before we make any commitments?*"

"*Beast man, you are the–*"

"*I'm just some poor Vibration that wandered here–why do you–I just.*" He breathed Gasp's name. "*I feel lost and all of this only makes it worse. I need time.*"

"*I understand,*" Gasp breathed.

Runith felt as if he had shouted at a friend and was forced to face them. "*Thank you, your—grace.*" Runith bid the Branch farewell with a quick bow.

The Branch nodded. He left the throne room and continued outside to stare at the sky. Gray clouds covered the heavens, but rain had not fallen. Petrichor filled the air, reminding him of home.

Golma walked up to him and reached for his hand. He wanted to rip it free but held onto the patience that remained.

He looked down at her with a scowl. She held a silent smile. He knew he was making her nervous. *You're the adult here. Act like it.* He gave her a reassuring smile and rubbed the back of her hand with his thumb.

What is wrong with me? He felt like a beast slayer who had to forsake his past. Change was inevitable. He was no longer a guard meant to spend his days standing before a building and his nights in a tavern to sorrow over the mediocrity of his life.

Was that so bad? No one depended on me for anything extraordinary.

"*Beast man.*"

Runith turned back. Gasp and his company of Rasteen had followed him out of the building.

"*Did I make offense?*"

Runith was not angry at the Rasteen, but more at himself. Gasp had hope in him. *Too much for his own good.* He felt like he was disappointing his entire Court. "*No, I'm sorry, Gasp.*"

"*Then are you trying to offend me?*"

Blunt. They have much to learn about human impulsivity. "*No.*"

"*Then why did you leave? You came to understand our people. Why do you then turn away from my offer? Your desires confound me.*"

Runith slung his arm around Gasp's shoulder. "*I've been used as a tool by too many people. I came here for something new. We came to understand you, but instead of a friendly welcome, I'm told that I need to become your savior by helping your long-lost lord and uniting our people. I am nothing special. I would only fail you.*"

"*I see,*" Gasp breathed. "*Then I must ask for your forgiveness. Your Binding of Roots can wait.*"

"*I–*" Runith groaned, stilling his frustration. "*Why do you trust me? What makes you think I am some prophesied hero?*"

"*You are not a part of any prophecy. You are part of a reality that will come.*"

"*I still don't see a difference.*"

"*There is no single person meant to complete this task. You fit the requirements.*"

"*Requirements? Task?*" Runith breathed Gasp's name and shook his head. "*My friend, I think we both have a lot to learn about each other's cultures.*"

"*I see.*"

Runith patted Gasp on the back, but the Rasteen seemed frightened rather than taking it as a playful gesture. "*Don't worry, I'm going to stay for a while. I just want you to give me some time to take this all in. But enough of this confusion and contention. What do you have to eat? Anything for Vibrations?*"

"*What about those baskets you were carrying?*" Golma breathed. "*You were harvesting fruit, right?*"

Gasp looked at his companions. "*Those are not for consumption.*"

"*Maybe for you,*" said Runith, "*but they look edible for humans.*"

Gasp's eyes widened. "*No, you must not! They are for ritual—*"

"*Calm down.*" Runith patted him on the shoulder and chuckled. Now that he was the one making someone feel awkward, he felt his anger dissipate. "*We won't touch them. We'll try whatever you are going to eat.*"

Gasp stared back at him. "*We do not eat as you do.*"

Plants. Right. "Taer?" It felt nice to talk again. Runith's nostrils were raw, as if he had wiped it after ceaseless streams of mucus. "Do you still have that bag?"

The beaver-masked Gorger walked from the back of the group. He took off his backpack and handed it to Runith. He opened it and found the half-loaf of bread, nuts, and three apples that he had packed earlier.

"*This will do for now,*" he breathed, "*but we will have to find something more substantial later.*"

"*Of course, we would be pleased to assist.*" Gasp smiled. A rare sight from a Rasteen's typical dead glare.

"*Take us somewhere to rest for an hour. We can find something to eat afterwards.*" Eating anything wild would be a gamble, but Runith knew he could not yet return to the Tchoyas and Zhaes camp. Royss would arrive any day to assess their progress. Runith would not be present to greet the Thane.

"*We will rest with you,*" breathed another Rasteen.

"*I would enjoy that.*" He waved for the Rasteen to lead the way. "*Take us somewhere peaceful.*"

As the company continued forward, he took a moment to breathe alone, not speaking in the Rasteen tongue. The smell of rain was familiar, but the Middlelands felt more alive. He did not know how else to describe it, but the abundance of trees and plants made the air feel fresh, much cleaner than any place inhabited by humans. He felt as if he drank from a brisk mountain stream after years of tolerating polluted water. It was not only the air, but the environment itself. Even though the Rasteen had tried to force him into some role, they did it out of pure intent, or what seemed to be. These people seemed genuine, more hopeful than even the most eager child.

Their hungry hope suggested innocence, a people free of the guile and pride that tore the lands north of them apart. Still, their need for some redeemer spoke of their broken core. There was endless lore for him to explore. Runith only hoped that he could understand them enough to help without disappointment.

Something pressed against his leg. His mind returned to the present.

"Found yourself again?"

"Where have you been, Lele?"

"I stayed outside while you went into that palace."

"All of this drama must confuse you. Am I wrong?"

Her throat puffed out like an enormous bubble. *"Drama is a lot easier to avoid when you can't understand the language that you are speaking, or breathing."*

"I'll tell you about it later." He waved for her to follow him as they caught up to the group.

"You seem lost, Runith."

He chuckled. She didn't know how right she was. *"What makes you say that?"*

"Even though you smile, you don't look happy."

"Since when have you been so perceptive?"

"I can't read all of you humans, but I know you, Runith. You've acted differently since we left Fayis the last time, and when you left that palace just moments ago, you looked worse than ever."

"We all have times of happiness and sorrow."

She croaked. *"Deny it if you want, but if you need to talk to someone that is not a child or a plant—"*

"—you'll be there for me? A putle?" He smiled. This one felt genuine. She croaked again.

"Thank you, Lele. I'll let you know if I need anything."

She continued to hop beside him as they walked towards the edge of the village, but their conversation had ceased.

He knew some people struggled with mental battles, but he was not one of them. He was above that. Weakness was something he never needed to reveal. Every thought of self-defense felt like a lie. He had slain armies of beasts on his own. Killing them had been much more difficult than what he was going through. *What am I going through?* Depression was not the answer. He felt happy. Telling himself so was sure to make it manifest.

There was no easy way to explain the pressure that he felt, but in that moment, he felt humble enough to accept that he was uneasy. It was not the responsibilities required of him, he could do anything required of him.

The fear of failure. Those words felt right. Not of failing a single task, but of failing the expectations of all of those around him.

Golma walked a few paces ahead of him.

Will I fail her when I feel comfortable enough with Royss to return to my duties to Court Zhaes?

That is what I want, isn't it?

If I stay here to help these children, am I a failure to everyone who has believed in me? Am I a failure to my homeland, my people, my duty as a Zhaesman?

Laeih, am I failing you? What am I to do with my life? I stand on neutral ground surrounded by death. Is it better to remain so, or to give myself to some cause?

He longed for the days when his biggest concern was when he would be relieved from guard duty to spend the rest of the evening in a tavern. Those days were gone.

He bit his lip until it hurt more than his inner turmoil.

Laeih, help me.

CHAPTER TWENTY-FOUR

SCARRED CUB

The pinnacles were unsurmountable giants, needles compared to Kzhek's broad mountains. Even though the city itself was referred to as the Pinnacles, it sat in the center of the crescent-shaped range. Aerhee expected Voln to be excited, or at least impressed by their magnificence, but the boy had barely looked up since they arrived. His confident demeanor was dwindling. She would have taken that calmness from any other audacious captain, but it was an unsettling thing to see on a boy so young, especially knowing his personality. Her childhood had been traumatic, but his had the potential to be tenfold worse.

Zeir's hand was cold, but it was the thought that counted. He smiled and nodded, providing her with his characteristic silence that everything would work out eventually. She almost reached out to hold Voln's hand to offer him the same reassurance, but he would never accept it.

She adjusted her shroud as the hood fell over her eyes. Zeir put his hood up as they entered the more populated streets. Aerhee was thankful for the overcast skies and Zeemer wind that allowed their excess clothing to seem inconspicuous. She was not as recognized as the Thanes, but she remained cautious. She envied Voln's ability. He looked like a maskless Zhaesboy. She wondered if the face she saw was the one beneath his wolf mask.

Voln sighed, his shoulders lax. "Where now?"

Aerhee removed a piece of parchment from her pocket that had been crumpled, despite her best efforts to preserve it. The crudely drawn map had been given to them by an Allegiant scout who had found where the Reaper recruitment and council meetings were held. She did not know if they were going to pose as new or old members until they felt the atmosphere of the meeting. The scout's report was little more than a hopeful rumor, but it was the best they had.

She stopped and corrected their path before walking towards the center and pointed to the left. "Down there." She squinted at the parchment and moved it closer to her eyes. *Perding horrible handwriting.* "Look for a...I think it says a...textile house next to a blacksmith shop."

"Simple enough," said Voln.

"And the coin?" Zeir asked.

"Yes." Aerhee tucked the parchment back into her pocket. "Look for any coins with a hammer etched on the face. It might be some scratches with a rectangle and a line, but that is supposed to be a calling sign for other Holy Reapers."

"Look where?" Voln asked. "On the ground? Against the wall? Is someone going to hand it to us?"

"I don't know." Aerhee sighed and ran her hand through her hair. It was oily after weeks without a proper wash. "Just...look around."

"I'm trying," the boy replied.

"Are you alright, Aer?"

She squeezed Zeir's hand. "Just a little worried." She would never admit vulnerability to anyone except for her husband. Voln had heard enough, and she was losing her will to care about what he thought.

"And you have every right to be worried," he said. "Anything I can do?"

She shook her head. "You're already doing all that you can." She wanted help from someone who knew what they were doing. Zeir was as helpful as he could be, but he was no elite member of the Allegiant. He was a voice of reassurance. Even though that might not help progress their goal, it was enough.

"Did Colrig tell you anything else about this, Voln?"

The boy ignored her. He walked along the right side of the street, looking up and down at each building. He stopped to inspect anything small and metallic for mere seconds before continuing.

"Voln, where is Col–"

"I don't *perding* know!" It sounded like he spoke through clenched teeth.

Aerhee turned to look at Zeir, who shrugged with lips drawn thin. Her curiosity itched. Voln was often playfully hateful, but the animosity towards Colrig was raw. Before she could find an excuse to redirect their conversation, Vol stopped and pointed at an area cut out from the first level of a two story building. "What is it?"

"An anvil." Voln walked towards the next building and stopped before the large window. "Lots of fabric."

"Anyone in there?" Zeir quickened his pace to look inside as well.

"I can't see anyone." Voln stepped back from the window and inspected the outside of the building. "But I think I saw a staircase towards the back of the room."

Aerhee stood beside Zeir and looked in. For a Zhaes business, the shop was a shameful mess. She would not have been surprised to learn that the business had been abandoned months before. Shredded strips of fabric covered most of the floor and larger pieces were bunched up in disorganized piles on the tables rather than folded. "If anyone is there, they're probably the people we are looking for. It's late and most of the shops probably closed hours ago."

Zeir nodded. "You would think that they made their meeting places more obvious. With all that we hear about the Holy Reapers controlling the Pinnacles, I would have assumed that their opponents would be the ones in hiding."

Aerhee also wondered if the rumors caused her to overestimate the Reapers' influence. Perhaps they were not too far away from securing the Pinnacles to their cause.

"There." Vol pointed to a coin on the bottom right of the doorframe.

Aerhee stepped up beside him and crouched to see a coin that had been nailed to the doorframe. As expected, a rough etching of a hammer was on its face.

Voln tried the door. "Huh, no lock!"

She grabbed his shoulder before he walked in. "Listen first."

"Why? We're disguised."

"Just to be cautious."

Zeir squeezed her hand. "Do you want to stay out here, Aer?"

"No. Why would I? We came for this."

"In case they recognize you. We can tell you everything after."

Once again, she let ambition lead. "I'll be fine. I'll stay near the back." She stepped past Voln and peeked past the door. A preacher-like voice spoke from somewhere inside. Occasional affirmations to his words came as "yes" or "no" from a group.

"The meeting has already begun," she said.

Voln stepped inside. "I'm guaranteed not to be recognized. I'll lead."

"Are we sure that they allow children?" Zeir asked.

Voln already reached the staircase and started to descend.

Aerhee followed. "We'll learn soon enough."

The voice became clear as they descended the staircase. It was not angry, but it did sound controlling and manipulative, the type that promised large gains for little effort.

Voln stopped at the bottom of the staircase and faced a doorway on the right as he waited for her and Zeir. The staircase extended twice the length she would have expected from a small building. The room beyond the doorway was filled with people against each wall. Her fear of being noticed diminished. A couple of attendees looked at them as they entered, but they blended into the crowd within seconds.

"—the others must learn to accept that religion is a mere activity in one's life, not life itself."

Aerhee pushed past two people to have a better view of the speaker.

"Am I wrong to attribute this craze to religious extremism? People on both sides of this war believe that they are serving their god. All reason is tossed aside."

A man stood atop a platform with others behind him, though she could not see well through the sea of people before her. After taking a moment to comprehend what she saw, the speaker's words were meaningless when compared to his identity. She did not know who he was personally, but she knew *what* was. He was not only a Holy Reaper. His skin was not dark, but it did not have the pale complexion of a Zhaesman. His clothes were flamboyant and looked to be more expensive than even her official Caser attire. He paced across the stage with his chin held high.

This was a proud Priessman, no mere immigrant that had adopted Zhaes culture, preaching to Zhaesmen. Zhaesmen who agreed to the pontification of their Court's antithesis. She almost felt guilty for the hypocrisy of condemning someone who shared her birth nationality, but she had forsaken the Priess ways as a child.

Her breath shook.

"Aer," Zeir whispered. "Is everything okay?"

She nodded and kept her focus on the Priessman. The rumors about the Holy Reapers made her uneasy, but the fact that they were led by Priessmen *terrified* her. She knew then that the Holy Reapers were larger than some small group in the Pinnacles. Questions swarmed her mind. Anxiety broke her confidence. There was nothing else to do but listen.

"I was pleased to hear that we have had some success in opposing those who now control Kzhek, but that is not enough. We cannot remain stagnant while this war provides us with such a great opportunity. These two parties will continue to fight over harvesting. They treat this as a holy war. All of this is a large distraction. The people are vulnerable and need the freedom that we offer. Loyalist or Allegiant, it does not matter. We need committed members."

"We're trying!" a Zhaesman shouted.

"I don't want attempts," said the Priessman, "I want results. You repeat your past failures. This is not a message that people need to buy into, but an ideology that they must live. We are not searching for individuals who are looking for equality and unified Courts. We need organizations that might embrace these ideologies. Banks, governmental institutions, people with power."

Aerhee glanced at Zeir and Voln to gauge their reactions. Zeir squinted as he tried to focus. Voln was nowhere to be seen.

She shook Zeir's arm. "Where is Voln?"

His eyes widened after taking a second to focus. He stood on his toes, then crouched to look between the bodies before them and sighed.

"Did you find him?" she asked.

"He's a few rows ahead of us. It looks like he stopped trying to move forward, but I'll keep an eye on him."

The two Zhaesmen that stood before them turned back with a scowl. One of them placed his finger over his mouth.

Zeir whispered. "Just try to focus." His eyes shot back and forth between her and the Priessman.

She harnessed her anxiety to put on the mask of a stern noblewoman. She knew the domineering mask well, for it was the one that she put on every day.

"–we've told you about the advancements in our home Court. If you remain persistent, I guarantee you will reap the same benefits. Our service has already brought employment opportunities. As the battles continue, people die and cities are destroyed. This leaves us with clean slates upon which we can establish our way of living to bring unity to a land that has never been so divisive. Without division between Courts, Facet can be more unified than ever before. There will be no need for Courts, only a single union."

She wondered how many times this Priessman had given this speech. How many other Zhaesman were under his influence? That idea was absurd. This could not be the head of the Holy Reapers, merely a representative. She knew Priessmen well enough to know that any leader would be away from the streets in a comfortable room where he or she used these Priess preachers as pieces on a game board. It was not that idea that frightened her, but that the Pressman's ideas were not clearly evil. Neutrality and equality were great things if taken at face value. She did not fear succumbing to his ideas, but the fact that she found value in them made her realize why so many were willing to follow a Priessman. Aside from demolishing Court beliefs, he had a proper argument.

Aerhee crouched to make sure she could still see Voln. She breathed easily, seeing that he had moved no closer. The boy's ambition was both a strength and a weakness. He was destined to become the Krall or die young as a criminal. What did he think of this meeting? Did he harbor the same Priess hatred as did most of the Zhaesman?

She was almost the same age as he was when she left Priess. Those experiences made her who she was today more than any other event.

Her childhood still haunted her. She remembered her father under a different light cast by the Krall's revelations. The Holy Reapers were a significant threat, but they seemed a mere distraction when compared to the Bronze Seers. Could these Priessman be yet another branch from the Seer's wide influence? She wanted to justify focusing on them but striking them down now seemed as unrealistic as demolishing the Patriarchy of Scholars. They were a threat that had to be dealt with, lest all of Facet perish in their wake, or so her trauma and anxiety led her to believe. She wanted to toss aside everything and focus on the Seers but recognized that her bias stemmed from a need to avenge her father's death. The entire war on harvesting seemed a mighty facade that the greater powers of Facet used to enact their plans.

The Bronze Seers and Holy Reapers seemed larger threats than Royss and his loyalists. She would never again work with that manipulative swine, but she still needed to cooperate with the other Zhaes nobles to focus on their opponents. This was the reason why Sheath's cooperation was paramount to her Court's survival. Even the Krall wanted her to find Sheath. If Laeih was guiding her, this was a clear sign.

Sheath was not enough. Krall Vheen needed Thane Gromm. She banished the thoughts of that Scholar as soon as the memories of his unsettling countenance returned. Now was not the time to get lost in anxieties related to the Seers and the Patriarchy. The war against harvesting could be a front to their internal conflict, but now was not the time to face it. She had to take matters one step at a time.

She returned her focus to the Priessman's railings, hoping to gain something that they could use to win back the loyalty of the Pinnacles, or crush their rebellion before it infected the rest of the Court.

"–Kzhek will fall again. It is our responsibility to make the best of it."

Aerhee turned to Zeir. He stared forward with a stern glare.

"Until next time, do what you must, Reapers." The Priessman stepped down from the stand. He and the other Priessmen disappeared into the murmuring crowd.

Voln walked back towards them and bumped Zeir with his elbow. "Let's leave before anyone tries to talk to us."

The surrounding Zhaesman looked down on Voln with a scowl. Most of them were not lower classed Zhaesmen, as Aerhee would have presumed. They were dressed in fine ware, though nothing that compared to the costly apparel worn by the Priessman. These were typical Zhaesmen who had no reason to revolt. She feared she knew far too little about the common people outside of Kzhek. The war had shown her how poor a Caser she had been in representing her entire Court. She had been a piece of the nobility and little else.

The Tchoyasboy led them out of the building without stopping until they reached the end of the street.

"What was he talking about? What did he mean by Kzhek's fall?" Aerhee asked as they hid in an empty alley alcove.

"Are you so old that you couldn't hear?" said Voln.

Zeir held him back from leaving.

Aerhee was not taken aback by the insult's content, more so that it did not seem like a light joke. Was he still agitated from her asking about Colrig? She wanted to put her hand on his shoulder to comfort him but knew that it would have the opposite effect in his state.

"Stay here for a while, Voln. Let the crowd dissipate. Zeir, would *you* be kind enough to tell me what that last part was about? I was distracted."

She smiled at Voln, but he wouldn't make eye contact. That did not surprise her. She was taken aback by her *desire* to help someone who gave her anything *but* respect. *Since when have I been so focused on others' feelings? What am I doing? I don't even care about this disrespectful child.* She denied the maternal instincts, for they were feelings she had never experienced. They felt forced onto her from some external source. She was no Chusswoman. Caring for him was not her responsibility.

Voln shook Zeir's hand from his shoulder.

"Are you alright, Aer?"

"Yes, just tell me what they were talking about."

"Right. As they said when we first walked in, they want to use the war to their benefit. They expect the loyalists to return to Kzhek and instigate another battle even larger than the last. While both sides are weak, they'll step in to assert their dominance or 'provide a peaceful solution'. They will remain passive until the opportunity arises to gain control of Kzhek."

Aerhee checked around the corner. Fewer people walked the streets, but there were still plenty of attendees. "If they think they can do that, that must have been the smallest fraction of their entire membership."

"That," said Voln, "or they are too perding hopeful for their own good. I don't see why you are so worried about them. They seem as insane as any other group of rebels. We were crazy enough that everything somehow worked out for us."

Zeir looked at Aerhee with raised eyebrows. He knew her too well.

"Did you notice anything particular about the speaker?" Aerhee asked.

"You Zhaesmen look all alike to me."

"That is my point, Voln. That was no Zhaesman. He was a Priessman."

He grunted. She knew he was too prideful to admit that he did not grasp the significance of a Priessman leading a Zhaes sect.

"There are countless implications with this, Voln. We can spend some time here trying to learn more about their organization, but there is no longer a chance for us to win back the loyalty of *any* of these Reapers with the three of us alone. We have enough of a lead to help the Allegiant know what is keeping the Zhaesmen in the pinnacles away from the war."

Voln continued to scowl.

She sighed. "The Priessmen want to benefit from this war. They want to dissolve the Courts by attacking the systems that differentiate us. They want to dissolve religion."

"Aer, are you sure?"

"I don't like anyone controlling our population, least of all, Priessmen."

"These are probably just a few radicals," said Zeir. "I would wait before assuming that they are from the Priess nobility."

Zeir reached for her hand. She was neither in the mood for comfort nor placation. He knew that Priess involvement in the war had struck something deep within her. She could not help but make connections between the Seers and Priessmen. Even though she knew it was unlikely that they were allied, the fearful thought resurrected the crimes against her father. She accepted that there were good Priessmen out there, but this one did her native people injustice.

"I just think we should wait before making any conclusions," said Zeir. "You said that you were distracted during the meeting. Let's spend some time here to see what we can learn, then we can return to report to Kzhek. Alright?"

Aerhee nodded.

"Whatever," Voln said.

She shot him a frustrated glare.

"I'm sorry," he replied. "Maybe I'm a little exhausted. It's been a long day."

"Past your bedtime?" Aerhee said. "I forget how young–"

"Perd you." Voln sighed. "Please, don't treat me like I'm five."

Just a touch older than that. Don't wish away your childhood, it will be taken from you in an instant. "Then can you tell me–no, you know what, I think we all need to sleep. Let's find an inn, find something to eat, then rest."

Voln smiled.

"I was starting to think that you forgot how much Endowers have to eat."

She smiled too. It was a moment of levity that tossed aside the previous animosity. If they could end the night on pleasant, or at least neutral terms, the day would not be a loss. The thought made her want to laugh. *Perd, why am I trying so hard to impress a ten-year-old?*

Zeir pulled his hood forward to cover the rest of his black hair. He waved for them to follow. "The street is clear enough. Let's find an inn."

She trusted Zeir to find something best suited to their needs. Though she knew she would lean towards the finer establishments, he was more inclined to find something both practical and less expensive. They were in good financial standing, but with an unstable future, it was best to remain as conservative as possible. As their lives became more complex and dangerous, Aerhee was learning to accept discomfort. Her preferences did not matter as much as her success. War made her realize how privileged she was. Because of her humble upbringing, she never lost touch with what it meant to struggle for a livable life, but those thoughts had become distant the more she repressed them. As her home teetered on the edge of survival, she learned anew to appreciate her safety, health, and most of all, her relationships. Her membership in the Allegiant cost her many of her most treasured relationships. She only hoped that some were not beyond repair.

Moving away from the hub for an inn would do well to avoid the most intense parts of the politics in the Pinnacles. Rest and a break from responsibility were two things she learned to appreciate. As a Caser, she forced herself to give her role everything, forgetting what it meant to take time for herself.

Despite the unpleasant circumstances, she took a moment to appreciate the Pinnacles, both the mountains and the city in their center. She recalled visiting once or twice, but it was not an area many nonresidents visited. Perhaps that was why the Priessmen chose to focus their efforts on the city amidst the mountains.

As if to mimic the mountains themselves, most of the buildings were slim with high peaked roofs, especially the chapels. The clouds floated in a ring with the moonlight piercing its center. The rain had ceased, leaving the air humid and with a mineral musk.

To move away from the city and not directly towards the mountains, they had to walk straight through the city center. One side of the center street ended with the largest chapel in the city whose bronze peak almost pierced the low-hanging clouds. A cobblestone circle spanned wide before the chapel. In its center stood a statue of the Zhaes god Laeih, holding onto a miniature pinnacle mountain with one hand to keep himself stable as he stood on its steep side. In his other hand, he held a spear pointed upward. His peaked helm reached higher than the miniature mountain's peak and the spear, suggesting his authority over the power of men and nature. It was an unusual depiction, though not an unusual sight. The further one traveled from Kzhek, the more Zhaes religion followed personal interpretations.

The roads grew more rugged and the buildings more spaced out as they left the center. With fewer hanging lanterns to light their path, they became reliant on the moonlight until they reached a sign illuminated under a weak lantern that read *Northern Retreat*. The building's two windows were made from a distorted glass that hid the inside besides the light.

Without asking what they thought, Voln peeked his head in the front door, then stepped back, leaving it open. "There's a tavern and a staircase. Looks like an inn to me."

Zeir patted Voln's shoulder and moved him to the side to lead them in. Aerhee put her hood back on, having taken it off when they left the well-lit part of the city.

No one sat at the bar and the only person present was a Zhaesman with a thick mustache that connected to his sideburns. He sat behind a counter with a bottle in one hand, the other holding up his head. His eyes were shut and his snoring mouth hung open with a trail of drool reaching for the counter.

Zeir hit his boots on the floor, trying too hard to knock mud off of his mudless shoes.

The man behind the counter grunted and shook himself, blinking as he focused on his guests.

"Do you have a room?" Voln asked.

The boy could insist that he was an adult, but had much to learn about proper manners, especially by Zhaes standards.

"Sorry to disturb you," said Aerhee.

The man burped and spoke with a slight slur but conducted himself with decent sobriety. "Oh, it's no bother. Anything for a young couple and their child." He leaned over the counter. "A little late for you, lad, isn't it?"

"A petiir and a half."

She took out the coins from her satchel and added another zhon. "We would prefer not to be disturbed." She put her hand on Voln's shoulder. "He needs some extra sleep tonight."

He reached under the counter and took a shaky step, then stopped and shook his head. He handed the key to Aerhee. "Up the stairs, first–or–I mean last door on your... right."

It's just one night. She smiled and took the keys, keeping back her judgment. The Aerhee she was before the fall of Kzhek would have stormed out and demanded that they find somewhere where the innkeepers could stay sober enough to serve their customers. Even though she still harbored that impulse, she had developed the patience to control it. She knew that the war had changed her but was yet to recognize the extent of its effects. Patience, no matter how small, was a surprising result. Was her imprisonment in Fayis that resulted in such a change? She had an odd longing for that time alone in Krall Trhet's palace. She would not want to repeat it but had gained something invaluable while alone with her thoughts.

They followed the innkeeper's directions. She was relieved that his direction proved true, even if he struggled to speak to them.

Voln pushed to enter first but stopped right as he passed through the doorway.

"Is there something wrong?" Zeir patted the boy's back to prompt him forward, but Voln remained still. "Voln?"

"There's only one bed."

Zeir chuckled. "What did you expect?"

"I don't–"

He gave Voln a playful slap on the back. "Don't worry, you will fit between us. You won't go cold tonight."

The bed was smaller than theirs at home. Aerhee didn't know what to say. She hadn't tried to sniff Voln, but was convinced that he would smell just as bad as his wolven guise.

"I'll go ask the innkeeper for an extra blanket," she said. "I don't mind sleeping on the floor."

Zeir gave her a playful scowl. "Because you were so eager to talk to him before? Come on, Aer. It'll be fine."

"For once, I think I agree with her," said Voln. "I think the floor will be just fine for her."

"Fine," Zeir said. "You two can have what you want. I'll take the floor and you can share the bed."

"No–"

"But I–"

Zeir held his hands before him. "You two can argue over which side you want." He walked towards the door and laughed.

"Wait." Aerhee started to follow. "Where are you going?"

"We need something to eat. Stay here. You two can take that blanket, I'll grab my own on the way back."

"Zeir, really, don't worry about it. We can get something in the morning."

"No, we can't." Voln scowled at her. "Some of us like to eat, *Zhaeswoman*. Thank you, Zeir."

Zeir grabbed her hand. "Don't worry. I'll find something quick and hurry back." He kissed her cheek and lingered by her ear to whisper, "Learn to get along with him. This is your chance." He stepped out and peeked his head through the shutting doorway. "Love you Aer. Keep her safe, Voln." He shut it without a chance for them to argue.

Aerhee removed her boots near the door. Voln stared at her through the eyeholes of his wolf mask, having reverted to his Tchoyasboy form.

The cracked wooden panels were cold underneath her feet, protected only by her thin leggings. She sat on the bed and the mattress did not recoil. It was going to be an unpleasant sleep for more than that reason.

Voln had not moved. His gaze had not shifted from hers. Her eyes shot to his hands, thinking that she saw paws. *Perd, are you going to let a boy startle you?*

"Did your Beastlings find a drop off point for Sheath's letter?" she asked.

"Yes, but she wasn't in Court Tchoyas, like you said."

"Then where was she?"

"Ekscomos."

"I figured she was in Priess."

"Why?"

"I was with her and the other Zhaes Thanes who retreated before I came back to Kzhek. Your Krall was kind enough to keep me in his palace for a long while before they arrived."

"*Perding kulf.* I had problems with him even before his betrayal."

"I cannot say I'm too fond of him." She looked into his eyes. "So your Beastlings found her and delivered the letter?"

"Yes, that's what I said. Why are you asking twice?"

"Did she receive it?"

"Yes."

He stared at her.

Laeih's mercy. "Did she respond?"

"Not yet."

She glared at him. "Well?"

"I told the Beastlings that we would be in the Pinnacles and to have the bird deliver the message to the rookery here if Thane Leisa decides to respond."

"Thank you." She held back a bitter reply to his attitude. He did not seem his playfully rebellious self. He looked to be on the edge of tears rather than laughing. "We'll check in the morning."

Aerhee sat on the bed and felt the blanket between her fingers. It was a poor fabric, nothing like the silk that she was used to.

Voln continued to stare at her.

Her eyes fell back to her hands as she rubbed the blanket. She needed to say something. He was not going to. She had to face it. "I'm sorry if I've upset you." She looked at him again. "Whatever I did, forgive me Voln."

He sat beside her on the bed but remained silent.

"I'm trying to be a better person, especially to those who think differently." The humility required to apologize to a child, especially one as insolent as Voln, tore at her remaining pride. It pained her to submit to the boy's wallows, yet she knew she had to. If not for him, but for herself. "This war has been horrendous. You have seen terrible events that should never have been witnessed by a child. I'm sorry that my generation has failed you, and if I had any part in that."

She thought she heard him sniff and gave him a moment to speak, but he did not take it, so she continued to face the tension. The tension that kept back intimacy and trust. She thought about telling him about her past, but now was not the time to reveal her innermost weaknesses. Their trials, while both heavy, were different.

"Is there anything you need, Voln?"

Her heart ached from a need to console him. She imagined that was how a mother felt sitting beside a distraught child. If she could have erased anything wrong she had ever done to the boy, she would have. She would give anything to see him happy. Although she knew the boy very little, she felt the impulse to surrender her very being to heal whatever ailed him, whatever she had done to him, or whatever anyone else had done to him. Whatever the progressive Facet had done to him and his Endowers.

A thought returned to her of an offense she had made. A comment that had unsettled him more than any reprimand. A name that had ignited his temper. "Did Colrig do something to you?"

Voln grunted as if stung.

"I'm... *perd,* I'm here for you, Voln." She did not touch him but moved her hand closer to him on the bed. "Let me help you."

"There's nothing you can perding do." The last words came out as whimpers. He sniffed. His mask faced forward so she could not look into his eyes.

She let the silence linger. How she approached the sensitive topic would determine the future of their relationship. Intrusion did not intimidate her. It never had, until now. She felt as if she were treading on sacred ground that would be too easy to tarnish.

Another word might break him. The situation felt more dire than any diplomatic encounter she had ever faced. *Why do I feel this way? He's just a child. One that has paid me little to no respect.*

She thought about telling him about some sorrow of hers. Perhaps mutual wallowing could help soothe the ache, but that would not do. Now was not the time to draw attention to herself. She had spent years focusing on herself. The war was a terrible series of events that had forced her to care about others. The thought returned to her mind again. That same thought that contradicted her prideful–and she was willing to admit that it *was* prideful–personality. Rather than merely think that thought, she spoke it.

"I care about you, Voln."

"Why? What do I perding mean to you? I'm just a perding child."

I don't know why. I've known that you exist for a few months and have only known you personally for a week. "And I'm just a *perding* woman that people listen to because of a position I once held."

Voln wiped his nose under his mask with the edge of his sleeve. His voice no longer trembled, but he still sounded vulnerable. "A position in a government that fought to kill children like me."

Her voice turned from soothing to commanding. "We are not going to talk about harvesting. We are beyond that." She sighed, easing back her voice. "I'm here with you. That should tell you enough about where I stand. Either that, or I'm the worst Caser to have ever lived."

"A better member of the nobility than my Krall." Voln laughed and sniffed. He stuck his finger into his mask to wipe his nose..

Aerhee smiled. "You are one *disturbed* child."

Voln looked at her for a moment, then hung his head and shook it. "You don't even know. Colrig is a–" he grunted, "I respect him, but his ambition has killed more people than any harvesting surgeon has. Don't worry, I don't hate Phenmir. I did when I first learned about his past, but I knew that he was a great man. Colrig is a great man, but he is a perding sinner."

Aerhee remained silent, wondering if she would lose her faith in the Allegiant. *What kind of faith relies upon a leader? He is just a part of the system, not the system itself.*

"Colrig doesn't seem to care about his mistakes. He doesn't care who dies or what happens, as long as he gets what he wants."

Aerhee thought of Royss.

"Why do you care that I suffer, Zhaeswoman? What makes your life any better because you know what makes me sometimes wish they had killed me with a harvest?"

"Perd, Voln! Don't say–" she sighed. "I'm sorry. I ask because I want to help bear your burdens."

Voln's breathing became heavy. "You perding idiot. My parents were some of Colrig's first–" He stopped to shed a few tears. "–some of his first followers. They died before the war even began and cared more about his cause than they did about me. They left me to that perding Krall. He should have cared for me, Aerhee." He sobbed. "Perding Colrig took my parents away with his war. He didn't tell me when we first met. I didn't know that he was the one that recruited them until he apologized to me for their death right before we left. I'm alone because of him." He slammed his fists against the bed. "I don't want to lead. I want them back!"

Aerhee felt her own breathing shake. Her cheeks were already wet with tears. She felt that warmth, the connection to Voln, burn within her.

"It's not just him. I get that. I just–I can't–perd. *Perd. Perd. Perd.*"

She pulled him into an embrace to silence his tortured cries against her chest. Caring for him. Banishing the cold and careless woman she had been to embrace this boy and offer him the comfort of a mother that had been denied him for years.

She did not cry out as he did, but she wept as if her eyes were over-burdened storm clouds that had burst. Tears fell for her mother, whose memory returned to her. Tears fell for her father, sorrow clouding out her hatred of the injustice wrought upon him. She wept for herself and for her losses, but those only aggravated the pain that she felt for Voln. Here was a boy robbed of his childhood and parents because of the rebellions. Countless died, but casualties were easy to dismiss in pursuit of a greater good. Seeing Voln and hearing him speak was the purest form of the cost of war. Applying his pain to the countless dead, her agony multiplied.

Voln held onto her, tightening their embrace as he moaned through clenched teeth.

They held the embrace until they fell asleep, sorrow continuing on into their dreams.

❧❧❧❧❧ ❧❧❧❧❧

Voln stirred in the bed. She held her breath to listen, but he was no longer crying.

She blinked, waiting for her eyes to adjust, but the room was still dark. The candle she had lit had burned out. She guessed that they had slept for at least two hours, but Zeir was nowhere to be seen. Exhaustion overpowered worry, and she fell back asleep.

❧❧❧❧❧ ❧❧❧❧❧

Aerhee awoke to find Zeir asleep on the floor. She sat up and saw a small sack against the wall below the window. The sun had not yet risen, but a faint line of sunlight touched the eastern mountains.

Voln still held onto her. "When did he come back?"

She put her finger to her lips and replied in a whisper. "I don't know. It's still early. Let him sleep a little longer." She pointed to the sack. "Go see what you can find in there. Hopefully, he found something you'll eat."

He eased himself over the edge of the bed and walked across the wooden floor, his steps muffled by his socks.

Zeir stirred as Voln ruffled through the sack. He sat up and stretched with a loud yawn.

Voln lifted a handful of brown spheres from the bag. "What is this supposed to be?"

"Grain balls." Zeir threw his blanket from his legs. "They'll keep you full for a while."

Voln took a bite and coughed. "I need water. Perd, I'm never going to grow used to your food. Couldn't you have found–nevermind."

"They didn't have any of the bread that you like. It was hard to find something in the middle of the night."

Voln took a drink from a canteen in the sack, then ate another grain ball.

"We'll find something in the city," Aerhee said. "Why were you out so late, Zeir?"

"I was only gone for an hour. You two were asleep when I came back."

"I know we were," she said. "But I woke up and you were still gone."

"You must have woken up right after falling asleep. It took a while to find somewhere with food available so late. I walked around a while to see if I could hear something useful. The city was–"

Aerhee swiped her hand and shook her head. "Don't worry about it." *Better not to argue. We are stressed enough.*

"So, did Aerhee–" Zeir spoke to Voln, but she didn't grasp what he said. Her focus was clouded over by a panic that shook her from within. She held composure, but her mind was alight with terror.

Never before has Zeir lied to me.

She tried to maintain a smile but knew that it would look weak as she watched Zeir talk with Voln. Her perfect husband had a flaw. She did not know what it was, nor why he would ever hide something from her, especially in their circumstances.

Aerhee's world burned with hatred, but her home was always a sanctuary. She did not need a physical building, only Zeir at her side. Her reliance upon his stability made the cracks in their foundation ache more than a wound. She wanted to trust him, but the past few months had taught her to always be ready for the vilest of disappointments.

Just as she had felt after the death of her father and the gradual departure of her mother's sanity, Aerhee felt there was no one in the world to whom she could give her unwavering trust.

✧✧✧✧✧ ✦✦✦✦✦

As banter and rolling carts sounded from outside their window, they felt it was time to resume their day's duties. The sun was well above the mountain ridge and was hidden by the ring of clouds above the Pinnacles.

Voln gnawed on a chicken leg, relieved that they had found something he didn't complain about. He discarded the bones in an alley, having eaten most of the bird himself. Aerhee cared little about his discards. Now was not the time to focus on the boy's behavior.

"The innkeeper said it should be down there," Zeir pointed, "just past the altar."

Aerhee stopped before the altar.

"Come on," Voln said, paying the small bronze shrine of Laeih's bust a brief glance.

Zeir stopped and rested his hand on her back.

She looked at him and smiled. "I just need a moment. It's been a while since I—we've just been so—"

"Don't worry about it." He knelt before the altar.

She knelt beside him. She glanced back to see Voln leaning against a stone bench, his eyes wandering.

"Holy Laeih, the one true god," Zeir whispered. No one worshiped beside them.

Aerhee repeated the words. Zeir continued the routine prayer, but her mind was adrift. Worries about Zeir no longer directed her thoughts.

Rather, she said a prayer in her mind. It was no memorized prayer, but from her crying soul.

Laeih, what has become of us? What atrocities are we to turn against one another? Forgive my anger, for I know this is not thine doing. This is our mistake. This is our sin. Help me understand my path. Help me know what I am to become.

She wiped a tear from her eye.

When will this end? Help us. Please–"

"Whole is the Holy!" Zeir stood and performed the Zhaes salute to the shrine.

"Whole is the Holy!" Aerhee followed a moment after. Her legs felt weak, her chest unsteady.

Voln nodded down the street. "I can hear the birds from here."

The boy led them into a tall, but thin cobblestone building. The door was already open with a single woman inside behind a desk. Behind her stretched shelves with at least a hundred compartments, most of which were filled with envelopes or rolled up scrolls. Opposite the desk, a staircase rose to another floor with a missing center in its floor. A railing bordered the hole in the ground and as she looked up, Aerhee saw that the floor repeated itself at least three more times. She stepped to see it at an angle, noting that caged ravens lined the upper walls.

"Receive or deliver?" the Zhaeswoman asked. Her black hair was braided and cut to her shoulder. Though she was dressed in an elegant gray gown, she could not have a pleasant scent if she remained in the building. The musk reminded Aerhee of a ghete stable without the fishy odor.

Voln stepped up to the desk, his head held high as if he were the eldest in their group. "We are expecting a letter from Court Priess."

The woman sighed. "Which city?"

"Ekscomos. Now," he clapped, "on with it!"

She glared at Voln. "I assure you, Zhaesboy, that I–"

"Zhaesman will do."

Her eyes opened wide. "I–"

Perding Tchoyasboy. Aerhee placed her hand on Voln's shoulder. She was relieved that he allowed it to remain. "Forgive my son. He is quite the jester."

"Aren't I just!" He scowled at her with a forced laugh.

She squeezed his shoulder, only slightly digging her nails into him. She eased after he smiled at the woman. "Has anything arrived from Ekscomos yesterday or today?"

"I will check. What would the name be?"

Perd, did Voln tell her to send it to me under my name? Did she give her name? Aerhee had ordered hers to be sent by a Beastling-controlled bird directly to Sheath once it found her. No name attached. No major risk of interception.

"Zier," Voln said.

Zeir coughed. Aerhee sighed. It would still be traceable to her, but the name was less likely to be recognized.

"Any surname?" the woman asked.

"No." Voln replied.

Perfect. Zier was a common enough name. She should have decided on a better plan for the return message, but the rookery in a distant Zhaes city was not a poor option. When hiding their identities and navigating the city without a clear direction, it was a much better solution than having a Beastling-controlled bird find their exact location. Perhaps a rookery would have been better for Sheath, but she would have had no way of knowing that a letter was left for her.

The woman pulled an envelope from the wall. "Signed by *'Dagger'.*"

Aerhee smiled as she took the letter from the woman.

She paid the woman six zhon and left the rookery and opened the letter.

They never worked outside of the Zhaes law, for to do so was a sin, but she and Sheath had occasional opportunities in which it was best to work in a surreptitious manner. To anyone who took the time to think about the name 'Dagger,' the connection to Sheath was clear. Aerhee smiled, hopeful that their friendship endured.

Wind,

Despite the terror and division that surrounds us, I was pleased to hear from you. I, too, fear that there is more afoot than we previously assumed. This is no simple war. Harvesting is but a fraction of the conflict.

I hope to meet you, but I fear the cost of our meeting.

Aerhee's chest ached. Without Sheath, Court Zhaes would be lost. They needed to reunify it. The Allegiant grip could only hold on so long with the rising influence of the Holy Reapers.

Zeir looked at her with a sympathetic, yet oblivious, smile. She read onward.

But that does not mean that I think we should avoid a meeting. You were wise to go about this discreetly. I have so much to tell you, but it is best that we leave the more delicate matters for our meeting.

Her chest felt light again. Hope endured, but she was not yet ready to trust in the future.

Your request arrived at a time that could only have been chosen by Laeih himself. We will depart in a few days, once the opportunity arrives. We are not held captive by the Priess Thanes, but–

Sheath scratched the next line out so much that Aerhee could not even guess as to what she had written. It was unlike Sheath. She would have started over again. It was Sheath's handwriting. Aerhee was sure of that. *She was rushed. Discreet.* She read beyond the blotted out portion.

Meet us south of the Pinnacles, across the Priess border, in Unin. I'll be in the northmost inn.

She used 'us' and 'I.' Sheath was still trying to plan the rendezvous.

Priess is– She scratched out the next line again.

Whole is the Holy,

Dagger.

"Is she going to meet with us?" Voln asked.

Aerhee nodded, folded the letter, and tucked it in her pocket. "We need to head south."

Zeir frowned, his eyebrows tensed.

"Back to Kzhek?" Voln asked.

"No, not southeast, directly south, past the Priess border."

"You perding Zhaesmen are going to kill me."

"Aer, are you sure it is safe?"

She forced a laugh. "Are you kidding me? Of course not. Nothing is safe, especially with this war. Still, it will be safer than remaining here."

"But–"

"But what, Zeir? Do you want to remain here? The Reapers will only grow in power."

Zeir looked away from her.

"I'm sorry, Zeir but–I–we just have to do this. The Krall." She swiped her hands in the air. "Nevermind that–"

"Shouldn't we report back to Colrig and the rest of the Harmony Allegiant in Kzhek?"

"We need to work with Sheath. We only have a few rumors to work with here, but her presence in Court Priess could help us identify their connection to the holy Reapers. She won't betray us and–"

"Are you sure?" Voln asked.

"I'm sure. She only wants what's best."

"Voln is right to worry," said Zeir. "As long as she is with the enemy, she is a risk. She is a *Feelman*. Any secrets we hope to keep are forfeit."

"What do we have to hide at this point? When we meet her, we will have been away from the Allegiant leaders for weeks. The only thing on my mind will be preventing the spread of the Holy Reapers. She is adept, but nothing compared to the Endowers we've met since joining the Allegiant. I feel better equipped to face her after some of the Feelman defense trainings Colrig has put me through. The Reapers are not a threat to harvesting, but they *are* a threat to our freedom to worship, something Sheath still stands for." *At least I hope.*

He sighed.

She looked up at the darkening clouds. A storm was imminent. "Why are you arguing with me now? You supported me when I first sent the letter. You agreed that working with her would be wise. It's Sheath, Zeir. You trust Sheath. You *know* her. She would never hurt us."

"The world is changing," replied Zeir. His face was even more insecure. "You would have never rebelled against your nobility, but here we are."

Voln's impatient slouching turned to discomfort as he stepped away and pretended not to listen.

"You!" she held back her reprimand.

She told herself that she had improved, for life was a journey based on change. She was not ready to assess herself. Now was not the time for condemnation. Zeir was right, after a manner, but now was not the time to admit it. *Perding hypocrite. I'm a perding hypocrite.*

Zeir's shoulders raised. He stepped back.

Do you think I am going to hit you? Perd me. What have *I become?* "I'm sorry."

"I understand."

For once, stand up to yourself! You're not my servant. She held the argument back. "We can't–" her words trembled.

He stepped forward and embraced her.

She rested her head on his shoulder. "We can't break now. We've come too far." *Where have we come?* She silenced her doubts, but knew they would return soon. "I need this Zeir. Like you said, I've failed. Our people will die with our religion if we allow these Holy Reapers to continue. I don't care what Sheath thinks about harvesting." She looked at Voln with a sympathetic frown. "But I know she wants to preserve our people. The Holy Reapers are Priessmen. If Sheath is in Priess, she is the best person to help us. Please, Zeir." She would not cry. She held herself. *Yet I broke last night as I embraced a child.* "Please."

She felt him nod. "I trust you. We'll do it." He let go of her. "I'll go find some food for the journey."

"Oh, perding under realms, not you again."

They laughed at Voln's complaint.

"I'll find a better variety this time," Zeir laughed. "We'll need some other supplies. More clothes, a canteen for each of us–"

Aerhee kissed him. "Voln and I will worry about everything else. Meet us back at the inn when you finish. We'll leave before evening."

He stared at her for a moment. The corner of his mouth turned up. He kissed her on the forehead. "Not more than we can carry, but not too little that will make us struggle to survive."

Their hands slid across each other as he left towards the city center.

Voln's gaze wandered. He tried to distract himself whenever they were intimate.

She waved for him to follow her in the opposite direction, where she remembered seeing a used clothing market. She now recognized the need for such establishments while in their unusual circumstances. With most Zhaesmen believing that poor clothing was as good as begging for spare coins, it was a wonder they were in every city and village, or so she had once believed. Seeing the frustration towards society that burned within the Reaper recruits, she learned more of her blindness. Court Sleff was not the only court with poverty plaguing its people. She had never forgotten this and its impact on her childhood, but it had been pressed to the side of her mind.

Voln was silent.

"Something wrong?" she asked.

"Can you forget about last night?" he mumbled.

"Voln, I–"

"Please." He spoke forcefully, then pulled back on the aggression. "I don't want you to think that I'm so vulnerable. I'm not like that. I'm not weak."

Preding child. "Crying doesn't make you weak."

"Just, please, I don't want–"

"Voln, you need to know that it's healthy to express yourself." *Because I'm so emotionally well. I should take my own advice. He caught me at my single vulnerable moment.*

Aerhee liked to think of herself as unwavering, an emotional fortress unyielding to any opponent or circumstance. Once again, she caught herself in a lie. She was not impervious. The past few months had taken her foundation away. She was just as vulnerable as anyone else if caught in these circumstances. Despite that acknowledgement, she would continue to force her unbreakable personality upon herself. She had to be stoic. If not for herself, for those around her. She could accept private tears but would try her best to hold them back when others needed her.

"That's what you think. Please, just don't talk about it. It will only make it all worse."

She swallowed her need to make him what she thought he should become. He was a Tchoyasboy. She was a Zhaeswoman. Division existed for a reason. *Does it have to?* She banished the Reaper ideals from her head. Division does not mean the disbanding of diversity. It is when unity is forced upon someone that they lose any aspect of originality.

"Aerhee?"

She refocused on him. The world was filled with endless worries, but he was all that mattered in that moment. His well-being. His safety. His sense of worth. The odd feeling of devotion returned to her. She felt a burning impulse leading her to give Voln all that he needed to live a beautiful life. *Just like the one taken from me in my childhood.*

"Of course," she said. "Unless you want to talk about it, it never happened."

"Thank you."

She held her chin high, smiling as she wiped away a happy tear.

CHAPTER TWENTY-FIVE

WISDOM OF THE CROWD

"You are already familiar with games of deception." Thane Kelm stopped his pacing across the wide tent. He smiled at Semi. "Unless I am mistaken, Shiftling?"

"No."

"No, you are not familiar or no, I am not mistaken?"

"You are correct."

Since identifying her hesitancy, Thane Kelm had become more demanding. His voice did not assault her with the same hypnotic power he used against the Terpels, but she still felt his authority paired with his swelling condescension.

"Of course I am," he muttered. "I hope you know how pleased we are to have you."

"What do you mean?"

"We've spoken with plenty of the Court's Endowers in search of the best. While you may not be the greatest Shiftling in Thusk, many speak highly of you."

Not only demanding, but demeaning. She would have bitten back, but her training in the Gruth military had taught her more than physical resilience.

"Can I see you use it?"

She scowled.

"Your ability?"

"You haven't seen it yet?"

"Have you even used it in your training?"

"Why would I? It does nothing against the Terpels."

"Is that it, or are you afraid to use it now that the opposing Courts are on the hunt for your kind?"

"They aren't hunting Endowers."

He scowled at her.

"You know that, right, Thane Kelm?"

"The war is viler than you believe."

But I have seen it. "They don't want to kill us, they want to use us. I was in–"

"Enough."

He spoke in a peaceful tone, but she felt as if her throat closed. She had no choice but to remain silent. He stared at her and sighed. She was free.

"How long are you going to keep me here? I should be training."

"Oh, dear Semi, I am not here to prattle on until you scream for mercy." He laughed. "The Krall will join us soon enough to relay your assignment."

"Where are you sending me?" *Which Allegiant leader will become my enemy?*

He shrugged. "If I would have known, you wouldn't be here listening to me. Our dear Krall Plath likes to relay commands himself." He ducked his head, making his hunch even more pronounced. "He likes to make sure he seems important."

She smiled. Thane Kelm still had his amiable quirks, but he vacillated between pleasant and cruel.

"In truth, I don't think he is ready to send you anywhere outside of Thusk just yet. I would guess that he has some specific training in mind."

Her skin prickled. Her chest felt cold.

He seemed composed, but his pacing suggested otherwise. She was less intimidated by the Krall than his Thanes were, but she was not under his command. Perhaps this assignment would change that. People often learned too late that the most pleasant leaders were the best manipulators.

The door opened, and two Terpel guards entered before Krall Plath.

"Heloath! Firm is the Foundation!"

Thane Kelm and Semi repeated the Krall's greeting with the Gruth salute.

Each guard wore shimmering silver armor, untouched by combat, unseen among the beaten leather of those who trained. She would have assumed that they were ordinary Gruthmen if not for the eel brand on their cheeks. It was a small mark, one a simplistic rendering of the leviathan eel on the Gruth sigil, but it entailed possession. Thane Kelm insisted they were more than tools for the Court. She wondered if they would soon speak the same lie about her diminishing freedom.

"How has the training been so far?" said the Krall. "Enjoyable?"

"She still has aspects that require improvement."

"I don't need your opinion, Thane Kelm." He stepped towards Semi.

How can preparing for war be enjoyable? It's a necessity, something I have chosen to do. What fool would call that pain 'enjoyable?' "Fine."

"That bad?" he laughed.

One of the guards pulled a chair out for him to sit at the wooden table in the tent's center. The chair wobbled on the uneven red stone. He tried to adjust it to stabilize but gave up and sat with his legs wide to maintain balance. He waved for her and Thane Kelm to sit.

She tried to stop the wobbling chair as well and placed her arms on the table to keep herself still.

The Krall waved for his guards to leave the tent. She could still see their shadows as they stood against the entrance flaps. After they closed them, the heat choked even more. The wind from the sea only paces outside offered no grace in their tent under the open sun.

"No need to defend yourself," he said.

She hadn't. She remained silent.

"I know Thane Kelm makes any situation worse. My condolences, Semi."

She smiled. Thane Kelm forced a servile chuckle.

"But he has at least told you about our hope for you, right?"

"Assassination," she muttered.

He frowned. "It is much more than that, Semi, just as this war is much more than a massacre. Reason is everything."

She stared at the table and focused on the sound of the waves outside, lest her thoughts compel her to shout disagreements.

Unlike the political state of Facet, the tumultuous waves were calming. They would have been unsettling, even frightening to any sailor caught when the waves were their mightiest, but they soothed her. Perhaps that was why the nobility was not distraught by their crumbling society. The tumult only reassured them of their power. The cries of their people made them feel valued. Such a luxury would not last as the waves of war crept inward, tearing more Thanes and Kralls from their Cantons and thrones.

"Semi?" He dragged out her name as he spoke.

His pale blue eyes pierced her like an eel's.

"There she is."

She gave him a weak smile. If Thane Kelm would have treated her like this, it would be patronizing. Krall Plath seemed insincere, but as far as she could tell, he was a natural people-pleaser. Even if his desires were of the best nature, she knew he was blind to the suffering around the continent. It would reach him soon enough. She had seen and could not forget the stain it left in her mind.

"Sorry, I'm a little tired."

"As you should be. That makes me feel like you are actually benefiting from this training.!" He sat back against the chair and folded his arms. "As I was saying, this is not mere assassination. No one should rejoice in killing others. If anything, your reluctance makes me feel better that we have chosen the right Shiftling for the job."

"Which is?" she was relieved that her voice did not shake.

"We will get to that later, but your training is not complete. I have something prepared to test your prowess in a situation requiring both stealth and dexterity."

"Have there been any advancements, Your Grace?" said Thane Kelm.

"You're commanding the army. Have I sent you anywhere?"

"No, you–" Thane Kelm took a deep breath, "*outside* of our Court."

"You are too easy to rile." The Krall grinned.

"You seem rather pleasant for being at war."

"The Priessmen have aided the Sleff loyalists in securing Paiell."

"So I have heard."

"Then we are still silent as to matters in the other Court. You are the Scholar, shouldn't you be just as well informed as I am, if not more?"

Thane Kelm paused, tapping his fingers against the table.

What does *he know?*

"Have you sent my chosen representatives to Fayis?"

The Krall nodded.

"What was in Fayis?" Semi asked.

Thane Kelm turned towards her. "The Zhaes Thane of Scholarship has requested a meeting of the Courts' highest Scholars. I trust it was significant, but nothing is more demanding than the Terpels."

The Krall spoke before she had a chance to ask questions. "Thane Kelm, you knew about the captured Sleff scouts, unless I am mistaken."

"I heard about them in passing, Your Grace."

Semi scowled.

"And I take it you failed to relate the information to Semi?"

"I apologize, I–"

The Krall raised his hand. "No need. As I expected."

"Your Grace, please *listen*."

Semi felt the chilling compulsion to listen to Thane Kelm, but the Krall shot him a glare, impervious to his demand. The Thane stared at his own hands as if they were the most fascinating thing he had ever seen.

"A few weeks ago, patrolmen in two villages northeast of Doot happened upon Sleff scouting parties. As you might have assumed, these were not Sleff loyalists, but members of the cult that seized Kzhek. Had we not found them, they could have been detrimental to our operation. Much of the Terpels' worth comes from their hidden existence. The same reason why the Sleff Gorgers were so impactful in Kzhek, according to the Zhaes Thanes' report. Even our most loyal allies are unaware that we have an army at our disposal, let alone an army of Endowers."

Semi shifted uncomfortably. She knew her Court was prone to invasion but expected nothing of the sort until they attacked another Court. Scouting parties were dark clouds that warned of an incoming storm. "What did you do with them?"

"We've brought them here."

"You–" Thane Kelm clenched his teeth. "Forgive my *blatant* confusion, Your Grace, but why would you bring them here if you do not want them to be aware of our preparations?"

"They will not return to their home Court, at least until all of this has cleared."

Thane Kelm tapped the table with his fingers and took a deep breath.

"Don't worry about him," the Krall told Semi.

"What have you learned from them?" she asked.

"Little of worth. Rather than waste more time with interrogations, we are going to use them to test your skills."

She nodded but knew her fiddling fingers gave away her lack of confidence.

"You could use a break from your routine training," the Krall said.

That much she could agree with, though her routine had changed since she had requested to work with trainer. Thane Kelm took that request and returned the reverse, never allowing her to work with the same person for more than one session. He did not allow her time for her cathartic swimming, but she found ways to circumvent his control.

"How long will we be there?"

"Depends on your performance."

"Where are we going?"

"West of Thusk, just outside of the city's boundaries."

"Farmland?"

"What once *was* farmland."

She glared at Thane Kelm. He looked at the Krall unshaken by this revelation.

"What have you done to it?" she asked. "Is it–what–I'm sorry, what do you mean what once 'was' farmland?"

"You are smart enough to understand me, despite my northern accent."

"So it's just–you wiped out the land for this display?"

"Do not belittle the Krall," Thane Kelm demanded.

"She has every right to be concerned. Semi, if you want to be a greater part in this war, you need to learn to see the conflict as a whole, rather than minor undesirable occurrences. With half or so of the Courts in opposition to our stance on harvesting, they have made themselves our enemies. We do not feed our enemies. Decreasing production and export will not only strangle our opponents, but it allows us to focus on our military. The Terpels are only a single army, more of an elite task force. The trade embargo may not damage the enemy now, but it will in due time. If anything, it is another means of bargaining."

How long do you think this war will go for? What if you have taken so much away that we can no longer support our people? Are you so blind that you think we are the only food supplier? We may be the agricultural leaders, but that does not make us the sole contributor. What about the farmers, those whose land was stolen for your campaign? Regardless of your opinion, their lives will have been worsened by your actions. How many of these choices were yours? Arguments and faults to his argument filled her mind. She held them back. Thane Kelm had taught her that. The Zhaesmen had taught her that. She did not want to be "a greater part" in the war. She wanted peace. Solitude. Silence. She longed for a silent seaside with only the waves to make sound.

Her thoughts were bleak and terrible as of late. Given her circumstances, she felt it was impossible to think otherwise. She did not blame any of it on her god, only on her reluctance to turn to him.

"Semi."

She looked up at the Krall.

"Embrace your doubts. They will only make your knowledge even stronger once you understand their flaws. Every choice we have made came from a chain of agreements. Do you trust your people?"

If they strive for war with such zeal, then no. No, I no longer do. We've lost ourselves. "Yes."

Krall Plath smiled. "Then I think you will be pleasantly surprised by what we have in store for you."

She didn't smile. Her will to please him had perished.

They left the coastal district in the Krall's personal carriage to make the short journey through Thusk to the once lush farming district to the capitol's west.

When Semi exited the carriage, she was more shaken than "pleasantly surprised."

The remains of crop and livestock fields were nothing more than ghosts under the new buildings and paved roadways.

"When was this built?" she asked.

"Before the fall of Kzhek." said the Krall. "It has been months since it was established, but Terpels and Gorgers are godsent laborers when they are compelled to work in haste. Once the Terpels finished, we sent them to the coast to begin the training that you witnessed."

"And the Gorgers?"

"Sent elsewhere."

Thane Kelm was unmoved by the notion.

The district was silent. Although large white buildings with teal domed roofs were packed close together down the street, no one entered, left, or stood beside them.

Semi remained silent, accepting that nothing had been *normal* for months and that nothing would be *normal* until the conflict ended.

The road ended with two paths diverging. On the left rose a tall building of marbled white with veins of emerald that reminded her of a temple or Canton. Voices shouted from the right street, which curved, obscuring the end. The city had occupants, merely too much space for them. The Krall seemed to have ambitions for the area which were yet to be fulfilled or were vastly overestimated.

Krall Plath led them to the right. The buildings were filled with people, though they were not the bakeries and merchants typical in Thusk. All looked like bureaucrats and servants. There was no middle ground.

Semi turned to look back, noticing that Thane Kelm had left them for the building on the left.

"Don't worry," the Krall said. "We'll meet him there soon enough."

"What is it?"

"The Gruth Canton of Defense."

She had heard rumors of the rebels creating a new Canton to lead their military, but this was the first she had heard of the loyalists' attempt to do the same. A new part of Thusk, a city of its own, dedicated to such a purpose aimed at permanence. War would be cemented into the Courts as a part of their governments, regardless of the victor.

The Krall remained silent. It surprised her, especially noting his high chin and perfect posture that spoke of how proud he was of the city, or district. She was yet to conclude what the area was.

The winding street felt like walking into a mirror. The buildings stretched in a continual row of the same height and width.

She spared the Krall a glance. He offered her a relaxed smile and a delicate nod.

She was uncomfortable being alone with him. It was not that he seemed predatory or as manipulative as Thane Kelm. She was relieved to have left the Scholar behind. His intimidation seemed to come from his expectations.

Her discomfort arose from the realization that she would fail him. She was not the leader nor warrior he hoped she was or would become. Her foundation had never been more infirm.

They turned a corner and the line of buildings came to a sudden end, as did the paved road. A field spanned before her and countless workers crouched beside stout, scaled trunks that stood at knee-height. Leaves sprouted and fell from the top like unkempt hair. Large silver flowers bloomed from the verdant bushes. As they approached the cultivators, she could see that they used small blades to trim the inside of the flowers. Very few moved as they cut, only a few shifted from one flower to the next to repeat the process.

The Krall stopped and observed the laborers. His hands held behind his back, he straightened his shoulders and puffed out his chest. "Most flowers take at least a half hour to harvest. Newer harvesters can take hours on a single flower. The process never ends."

So you kept some fields? Who are these people? More slaves. She held her questions back and played along with the Krall's game. "Most of those plants have only two or three flowers. Wouldn't they finish within a day?"

"We only had enough space to keep one."

"Then what do you mean 'the process never ends?'"

He pointed to four Gruthmen who walked between the rows of crops. Each occasionally bent down to touch one of the plants, holding their hand against it for a minute before continuing.

She looked up at him with a scowl.

"Endowed with the ability to grow plants."

"Sproutens."

He nodded. "They keep the plants growing so the harvesters continue to harvest. With how rare they are, we only have four, but they serve us well."

She nodded, not wanting to know if they were employed, indentured criminals, or slaves. *Just like the Terpels.* She accepted that there was nothing she could do to change their predicament. There was no choice. If she chose to mourn them, she would only be burned by her inability to change their circumstances. *What a terrible realization it is when one allows injustice and suffering to perpetuate.*

"What are they harvesting?" She had expected the Krall to smile now that she had finally let her curiosity get the better of her.

His reply was solemn. "You've never seen it, have you? It's Pough Nettle."

She furrowed her brow.

"Better known as *brush* by the addicts."

"You replaced all the fields with buildings *except* for this one? Instead of feeding the people, you thought it better to enslave them? *Perd*! Forgive me, Your Grace, but what has happened to your sense? Does Thane Kelm know about this?"

"Of course." The Krall shook his head. "It was his idea."

She stared at him with condemnation.

He shook his head and stared at the ground as he kicked a pebble. "Do you think I am proud of this?"

"You seemed awfully proud walking here."

"It's terrible. I hate it as much as you do. More than you, knowing what it is doing. If I don't force myself to keep that false positivity, I'll only make matters worse."

"Who told you that? Thane Kelm?"

His silence was enough of an answer.

"But the man almost follows you on his knees! He fears you!"

"It's all a farce. His idea and its perding taxing. If he suspects I gave up the act for you, we will both face consequences."

She was silent.

"I sent him to prepare your training and insisted that you should see this. I needed a moment alone."

"A moment alone, or one to show me this without him to justify it?"

"Both, I suppose. I shouldn't have to tell you what so many already have, but be wary of the Patriarchy of Scholars, especially Thane Kelm."

"But... you're the Krall. Shouldn't your authority be above his?"

"The Patriarchy is higher than everything. If this war has taught me anything, it is that I am just a piece in their game. I think we will all learn soon enough how insignificant we are in their wake."

Silence fell between them. Her thoughts raced, worrying as they did about the inevitable.

The Krall remained still, in no apparent rush to leave.

"What is his justification, then?"

The Krall raised his eyebrow.

"For the brush. Why is he growing it? Even if his reasoning is flawed, he has to have some purpose."

"Control. It seems that is all the Patriarchy is ever after, but this one seems to be aimed at benefiting our Court rather than the Patriarchy themselves. Perd me for trying to understand those mystic kulfs, but I think most still remain loyal to their home Courts. If he isn't lying, he said that this is for Gruth's control."

"Over whom? The Court's citizens?"

Krall Plath shook his head. "Thank Deilf for that mercy."

"Even though Thane Kelm has a dominant influence, I still have authority over the Court." He paused, furrowing his brow as if to question that. "I would never allow such a plague to ruin our Court."

"I've seen plenty of brush smokers in Thusk."

"Yes, but none of their brush comes from here. Brush and other addictive substances will always find their way into society, but nothing quite as potent as those grown in this field. The Sproutens ensure that much and ours last much longer than most. Their durability makes shipping it to Priess and Sleff much easier."

"I get the Priessmen, but, Your Grace, how could you—I'm sorry, I know this was not your doing, but the Sleffmen? They're already a broken Court!"

Some of the harvesters looked at Semi.

The Krall placed his hand on her back and turned her away from the field. He pointed to the Canton of Defense and began to walk. He waited until they were further away from the laborers before speaking again. "Why do you think I brought you here? Something needs to be done about this, but not just yet. We need the aid of the Priessmen."

"But you're—he's controlling them. Does he want to make them an enemy or just a less valuable ally?"

"From what I can tell, his purposes with the Sleffmen and Priessmen have a slight difference. As you would assume, he continues to press brush into the Sleff streets through the Patriarchy. I assume they use some higher criminals to distribute and control the addicts."

"But they can't gain any money from them, can they?"

"Like I said, money is not the purpose. Dependence is. With the riots starting in Court Sleff, how do you think we were able to persuade the majority of Sleffmen to change their conviction to pro-harvesting? The brush is only used by a small portion of the population, but it serves as something more powerful than any currency. The Sleffmen are stricken by their skewed humility so much so that they submit to the opinion of the majority of their Court."

Semi nodded. They were close to the Canton, but still had a few minutes alone. "And the Priessmen?"

"Given directly to the nobility to use it on their people, as we do with the Sleffmen. They gain more control and our alliance with them strengthens. This has been implemented for only a few months but has proven to strengthen our ties with the Priessmen."

"But we are both loyalist nations."

"True, but you know how opposed most of us are to working with the Priessmen. Before the war, our relationship was less than amiable. A poor irony it is that war brings us together in unified hatred towards our enemies."

"Are there really that many addicts in Priess?"

"Enough, but the nobility uses it more in Endowed Row."

"And that is?"

"Pure debauchery." Krall Plath pulled open the Canton's metal door to let her in before him. He whispered. "Enough of that for now. Thane Kelm should know that I only flaunted his achievements."

"And a fine field it was."

She tucked her elbows at her side to give the Krall a Gruth salute as she passed him.

The dusty aroma of freshly cut stone gave testament to the building's youth. Natural light shining in through the emerald veins in the stone and the massive windows gave the large chamber a light green glow. Two halls extended onward on each side of a marble staircase ahead. She looked down the halls on the left and right sides as she walked forward, noting that they were lined with identical doors.

Just as it had been with the city, the massive chamber felt empty with only a few Gruthmen saluting the Krall with hushed "heloath"s as they passed, walking to the hallway on the left side of the staircase.

She felt as if they were walking through a temple with the pressured silence, yet the building itself was the opposite. Nothing is less sacred than war. She would never see war as anything the pinnacle of human savagery. Still, she recognized that some saw this war as a holy crusade. Regardless of how others justified the war, she would never see it as anything more than a desecration of the gods' creations.

Krall Plath led her through a series of hallways and three doors until they reached their destination. After each door, voices became more prominent and the illusion of solemnity dissipated.

They entered a capacious chamber with dark wooden paneling along the walls. Lanterns burned high on each of the eight walls. Thane Kelm stood in the center, conversing with three others. Two had the white and gold robes of a Scholar and bronze circlets around their wrists. Krall Plath stared at them with contempt but said nothing of the matter.

Semi ran to greet the third individual, whose wrinkled face seemed more exhausted than ever.

Thane Gett chuckled as he patted Semi on the back. He coughed with the eager strength of her arms around him. "Heloath! It's a pleasure to see you, Semi."

She let go and gave him the Gruth salute. Her cheeks flushed at her childlike impulse to hold on to the Thane. It was unlike her to jump to embrace anyone, even family members. Thane Gett was an old associate but felt like the closest friend at that moment. Ever since she began training, she had felt isolated. Thane Kelm was the only person who seemed to have a mind of his own among the Gruth Thanes. Her opinion of the Krall had improved, perhaps it would even more, but no other nobleman or woman compared to Thane Gett.

She tried to focus again by saluting the Scholars.

"Why are you here?" she asked Thane Gett.

"I've been working with the Gruth Scholars and the other Gruthmen on some innovations for our war effort."

"More visions?"

"Something of the like. I was in another building down the street but came when I heard you were here."

"That eager to see me?"

"I'm more interested to see what Thane Kelm has made of you."

"On with it then." Thane Kelm walked towards a pair of doors at the back of the room. "Best not waste time. You're here to observe, Thane Gett, not to distract my pupil."

The Scholars nodded and followed Thane Kelm. Thane Gett smiled and walked forward with Semi. The Krall followed from behind.

Thane Kelm pulled the Scholars closer and whispered with his shoulders hunched. They nodded and uttered no response. He pushed them aside and approached Semi with his left eyelid twitching. He smacked the side of his head, but it continued. "Are you ready?"

"How can I be?" she replied. "What is this? What am I supposed to expect? Do?"

He stared at her until she was silent. "Are you ready to listen?"

She nodded, and he opened the door.

They entered another octagonal room, this one twice as large and with a door on every second wall. Skylight lit the room from a window on the ceiling. Four unlit torches hung on each wall in between the doors. The walls were plated with a dull metal that bore a few scratch marks.

She knocked her knuckle against the worn metal, then turned back to him. "What is this?"

"It's had little use so far, but we hope to observe captive enemy fighters against our best to assess the technique they've been taught."

"Sparring? Surely you're not wasting the lives of our people to understand some foreign techniques."

"It is not so simple."

How very like him to avoid guilt. "How so?"

"In war, we cannot study the minute tactics of the masses. This allows a closer assessment. Espionage at its finest."

"But war is yet to reach Gruth!"

Thane Kelm waited until she calmed. "We are preparing for the future."

Is he a fool, or am I too dull to see what he is doing?

"Those are not the only purposes for this room, this *observation* chamber." He pointed to the slanted panels that connected the tops of the walls to the octagonal window above them. "Do you see the shimmer there? Those too are glass panels. The coverings behind them will be removed for us to observe you."

"Me? You want me to fight?"

"Not exactly."

"Then what?"

"Deceive." He waved for her to follow him to the middle of the room. "Do you recall the captured Sleffmen we mentioned?"

She nodded.

"We've divided them into six groups, each standing behind one of these other doors, not including ours and that one." He pointed to the door opposite the one they passed through. "We have conducted few Feelman interrogations but have learned that one of the Sleffmen from the two captured groups ranks high above the others. He is under direct command of their leader, while the others are mere scouts. In a moment, we will leave and dress you in their Sleff garb, taken from one who will be removed from this *assessment*. You will remain by this door while we ascend to the higher chamber. The doors will then open and you will enter the chamber with the other Sleffmen. The room will be in complete darkness for a minute, after which we will uncover the top window. Your assignment, *Shiftling*, is to alter your skin to match that of a Sleffwoman's."

"How is that supposed to test my–"

Thane Kelm held his hand up.

After weeks of his scorn and forced combat, she wanted to *display her progress* by assaulting him. She wanted to strike him. Strangle him. But she knew she never would.

If you value life and abhor the shedding of blood, then why are you here? How foolish are you to join a war in the hope of saving lives when each life protected requires another taken?

She accepted that she was lost. She wanted peace, but the words of her leaders echoed in her mind. "*We cannot have purity without prior cleansing. Justice will reign. It is our responsibility to determine whose justice will prevail. Will it be yours or your enemy's?*

"You need not fear that they will wonder who you are," said the Krall. "These groups were captured separately and will probably all assume that you are a part of the other group."

She smiled and thanked him with a nod.

The Krall stepped towards her. "But that does not mean that they will not note non-Sleff mannerisms. You must not only change your appearance, but the manner in which you act. *This* is the test."

He waited for a moment to see if she would interrupt. He smiled as she did not. "Find the leader and kill him or her without the others knowing what you are doing. Conceal the attack. Blame it on another Sleffman. However you choose to do it, it does not matter. All that matters is that you can complete your assignment without being noticed."

She felt her lip start to quiver. The Scholars watched her with dead glares. The Krall seemed neither happy nor sad. Thane Gett turned away from them and stared down the hallway.

She almost broke. He knew how this assignment was tearing her apart. Regardless of how much he cared for her, he still had his duty. Whether that was to the Krall or the Scholars, she could not tell.

Thane Kelm broke the uneasy silence. "Very well, on with it then." He waved the group forward, and they left the chamber.

A Gruthwoman stood outside the door with folded brown clothes in her hands. "This first," she said as she handed them to Semi. "Then those." She pointed to a bench behind her. Light leather armor laid across its wooden top and boots of the same stain sat at its base.

"You have ten minutes," Thane Kelm said as he led the group down the corridor. "Be quick. Enter as soon as the doors open."

She watched, hoping Thane Gett would turn back and offer some hopeful platitude. Any acknowledgement of her pain would have helped.

They left, no one turning back to wish her well.

Panic was a luxury she could not afford.

She tossed her clothes across the room and put on the Sleffman garb. It was made of rough fibers, but itching was a pleasant distraction from her fear. She donned the leather armor and tied the boots too tight for comfort. They were inflexible and already too small for her otherwise wide feet. A small sheath was fastened to the inside of the chest-piece. A stiletto knife with a blade as long as her hand rested inside, running down the left side of her sternum. Fearing that she would be unable to retrieve it without being noticed, she took the knife and slid it up her sleeve. She pulled on her gauntlet's straps, securing the blade against her wrist.

Her heart pounded and her breathing felt louder than ever as she faced the door.

Why, Deilf? If I am to serve my people, why must it resort to this?

Her good intentions had been twisted. She saw how they had treated the Terpels like weapons. Now, she felt their pain. She knew what it was like to be used to harm others. She told herself that she would not, could not, follow through with the assassination of some Sleffman. Regardless of his or her intentions, she could not be the one to end a life for some performance to appease a Thane.

Perhaps the Terpels were better off having forgotten who they were. Many, just like trainer, would soon head into battle without moral constraints.

I'm cursed to face this with the knowledge of what I am doing. My conscience will not be censored. Guilt will strike uninhibited.

The door opened, and she entered. She was alone. It slammed behind her and the window above was covered gradually, like an eclipse.

Her body was still while her hands shook.

Confused speaking–then shouts–filled the room with the sound of opening and closing doors. Bodies bumped into her and she moved towards the closed door behind her.

"The perd is going on?"

"Gaeth?"

"Phora?"

"Shan? Shan? Shan, where are you?"

"Help! Lord Heitt help us all!"

Semi resisted covering her ears. Espionage and deception were no novelty to her. She had served the nobility in such matters ever since her graft. She knew how to attain her goal. All of her past assignments as a Shiftling, no matter how far they drifted from morality, never required murder. Times were changing. Like the great leviathan eel on the Gruth sigil, she must adapt to the changing seasons or perish.

Just as any other crime starts, she began to justify her actions.

Listen.

"Shut your perding mouths!"

"Calm down!"

"What is happening?"

"Mercy on high! Heitt bless us!"

"Commander Laen!"

"Laen! What is happening?"

"Laen?"

"I'm here! Now calm the *perd* down!"

She held onto that voice. It had been a woman. The way she said the *"al"* in calm suggested that her tongue was higher in her mouth. *Southwestern Sleff.* The location itself was not important. All she needed was to locate it again.

A crescent of light shone from above, expanding until the whole window was uncovered.

Semi repressed her fears, calming her quivering hands, now as pale as a Sleffwoman. Her heart slowed as she controlled her breathing.

"Shan!" a Sleffman ran across the room to embrace a Sleffwoman. Similar reunions followed, though many still looked around, searching for an escape or explanation for their captivity.

Semi spared a glance up to see the Gruth Thanes and Krall observing through the slanted glass. Thane Gett was out of view, but she saw the others through a small portion of the darkened glass. No one else seemed to notice them and she did not blame them. If she had not known that they were being observed, she would have never focused enough to see the noblemen.

Semi started to move about the room. Her breath was even more controlled now that she heard others asking each other who they were. She hid as a member of each group and no group at all.

"They're all locked." a Sleffwoman said, though a Sleffman continued to pull on the door in front of her to no avail.

"Where were you?" a Sleffman asked.

She turned around to listen in on their conversation but continued to walk and look up to avoid attention.

"Some village east of Doot," replied another Sleffman. "They wanted us to look into the crop embargo. You?"

"We passed through a couple of villages south of Doot, but never made it to our destination."

"Where were you heading?"

"Thusk, maybe? Not sure, you'd have to ask Laen. I'm just a follower doing my duty."

An unsteady breath shook Semi's chest. *That name again.*

"Aren't we all?" They shared a laugh.

She moved on to the next conversation. Wandering through cries for help and grunted profanities, she found it hard to locate anything worth listening to.

No one appeared to be dressed like a commander, though her guess as to what that would be was little more than a hope of finding some golden emblem or insignia. Everyone was dressed just like her; rest garb and leather armor that would not withstand even the dullest of blades. She was grateful that Thane Kelm provided her with that much.

Wandering in crowded circles reminded her of past assignments in Court Priess. She was comfortable dressing in many clothing varieties but was yet to find herself comfortable in armor. She had spent most of her time training with the Terpels in similar armor but felt just as much a fraud as she did when on a Shiftling assignment.

The Sleffmen pulled away from the door, resorting to tears rather than anger. These were mere civilians. Even if scouting or soldiering was their role, it was one they had been thrust into because of the state of Facet. There were no true soldiers, only those brave enough to hold a weapon or unfortunate enough to be chosen for battle. They were vulnerable. She did not see this as an advantage, but as a realization that they were just like her. Her guilt was multiplied, knowing that anything she did was not to some sadistic warlord, but a human as simple as her. People throughout Facet perished because of their circumstances.

Part of her wished she could grow numb to the moral constraints and simply follow through with the Thane's assignment. She chose otherwise. If she was to harm another, she would face the burden on her conscience. If she chose complacency, there might be no return.

The Sleffmen stopped wandering and formed into small groups. She had to be swift before anything she did would be too obvious.

No one had spoken the commander's name for a few minutes and she could not locate the woman's voice amidst the crowd.

She walked past a short muscular Sleffman and listened to his voice, noting the slight garble that came from years of smoking brush.

"–I can't imagine why. I see no sense in it."

The context of his words did not matter, only the intonation. She walked past again.

"–you think so? Can't say I didn't think of it myself, poffin' noble-men."

The accent was typical for a Sleffmen. Poffin' or *poffing* seemed to be the equivalent of perding. This was at least what she had inferred, the colloquialism deriving from Dotrift, the Sleff city just north of the Gruth borders. This much she had concluded after spending time in some of the Gruth villages near that border, noting that they found the word an enticing one to add to their artillery if curses.

"–if we see the end of it and by Heitt, I hope we do."

She had his voice. She felt her vocal chords stretch to match his. It felt as natural as moving her fingers to make a shaped shadow behind the light of a fire. She had to move them just right, but when she did, the picture was clear.

"Captain Laen." She spoke with his voice not too close to him, but close enough that if the commander heard, she would turn.

No one turned to the call. She tried again. No answer.

"Captain Laen!" she shouted and was sure that at least half the room had heard her. Even though enough people were talking, a few were still yelling, it turned plenty of heads.

"Lenneth? Where are you?"

Breathe.

She passed him and shouted. "Here!" Using one of the lesser known Shiftling skills, she projected her voice a few paces away by further manipulating her vocal chords.

The man who she assumed was Lenneth turned his head but returned to his conversation.

A woman with a shaved head stood just higher than the man and placed her hand on his shoulder.

"You called me?" she asked.

He turned around and scowled. "Commander! Can I help you?"

"What did you want?"

"Excuse me?"

"Was that not you, Lenneth?" She laughed.

He chuckled, but it was just as shaky and forced as hers. "I'm sorry, you must be confused."

She nodded. "Only a few minutes in here and we're losing our minds."

He shrugged. "Who can blame us? Poffin' Gruthmen keep us locked away then give us some false hope by tossing us into another prison."

Semi passed by and noticed the Commander's heel turn.

Breathe. She wanted to scream for how anxious she had become. *What has happened to you? Have you forgotten your training? This is nothing compared to the Priess balls.*

No previous assignment required murder. No previous assignment was so obviously a transgression against Deilf's laws.

Perd you, Thane Kelm.

She let the stiletto fall from her sleeve. The cool flat of the blade rubbed across her forearm until she caught the handle. She hunched over and crossed her arms as if bracing for a typhoon.

The Commander shrugged and turned around. Lenneth turned back to his conversation.

Semi hid in plain sight.

Breathe. She couldn't. She held the burning breath as she neared the narrow gap between the Commander's and Lenneth's backs.

I don't have to do this. I won't. Perd you, Thane Kelm. I'll do what you need me to, but I won't kill for show. I'll show you my worth without the loss of an innocent life.

But she is not an innocent Sleffwoman. She came here to–

She lowered her arm and slid the stainless stiletto into the back of the Commander's thigh near the hip and tripped her.

Once ahead of the gap, Semi projected her voice–Lenneth's voice–back towards the fallen Commander. "It's your fault we're in here, you *poffin'* kulf!" She amplified the voice and caught the attention of the entire room.

"Commander Laen!" Two Sleffmen at her side crouched beside her with faces as bloodless as a Zhaesman's.

"*Perding*–" hissed the commander. "*Perding* Sleffman! Lenneth you bloody kulf!"

He turned around and scowled. Semi knew it was in confusion, but his glare looked like incriminating contempt. "The–I didn't–"

"Lenneth tried to murder Commander Laen!" one of the Sleffmen at her side shouted.

"What? I never–"

A Sleffman seized Lenneth's hands and pulled them behind his back.

"Let me go, you *poffin'* kulf!"

Another moved in to help keep Lenneth still.

"He's lying!" someone shouted.

"I heard him shout at her when he did it!"

Semi held her composure and pressed into the gathering crowd. She shouted with the voice of a woman twice her age. "I saw him do it! He stood right by her!"

"Me too! It was in plain sight!"

"I saw him do it!"

When trying to justify the punishment of the crowd, it is much easier to lie. When one believes in their conviction, lying is a mere means to an end. How easy it is to persuade a crowd seeking an immediate solution to conflict. Their reaction was exactly what she had hoped for.

It terrified her.

Shouted incriminations came to an abrupt halt at the sound of a fist pounding against flesh.

Semi moved away but could still see Lenneth touching his bloody lips.

He grunted and wretched as someone punched his abdomen.

"Please," he moaned, as bloody phlegm dripped from his mouth and held on until the mucus tail reached his waist.

Another Sleffman punched Lenneth's cheek and moaned with him as he held his shaking fist covered in the man's blood.

Semi peddled back and looked up at Thane Kelm and shook her head. *I've done what was needed. This is enough. Stop the unnecessary violence.*

The others stepped away from the dark window.

Thane Kelm kept his gaze on Semi.

"Finish the bastard!"

Semi turned to see two Sleffwomen and a Sleffmen brutalizing Lenneth on the ground, never giving even a second between their punches and stomps.

"Enough!" Semi shouted multiple times in a variety of voices.

The crowd would not yield their justice. Hatred and bottled political frustration let loose on a scapegoat.

The sound of fists hitting skin became more wet with intermittent cracks.

Deilf have mercy on me.

Lenneth's cries, then gurgling moans, had ceased. Sleffmen left his side. Semi glimpsed their bloody fists, but looked away from the dark red blur on the floor in her peripheral view.

She bit her fist. Whether it was to hold back her screams or regret, it was the same to her.

The doors opened behind her. *"Everyone remain still!"* Semi recognized Thane Kelm's voice not at first by his tone, but by the power that paralyzed her and everyone else in the room. *"Semi, come here!"*

She left the room. The doors closed behind her.

She wiped blurry eyes to see Thane Kelm applauding. The Scholars joined with less enthusiasm. Krall Plath followed their support with a wide grin.

Thane Gett stood a few paces behind the others. She and he locked eyes. He held his arms behind him and nodded.

He's the only one that understands.

"Excellent performance!" Krall Plath saluted Semi.

She could not return it.

"You surprised me," said Thane Kelm.

Because you knew this was something I never wanted? You thought I would fail you? Why do you want to see me suffer? She shrugged.

"Killing the commander was an easier choice, but instead, you killed her through another! Twice the success from a single effort! I should have known you would have taken the challenging route, seeing what you did back at the seaside."

"But I–" she stopped. *Does he think I killed her? I couldn't have. It was only her thigh. She couldn't have bled out. She couldn't have. He can't know. Any hope to let her live. He can't know that I've failed.*

He widened his eyes, but one eyelid struggled to open all the way. "You?"

"She needs some time to rest and eat." Thane Gett stepped forward. "Even though you were in there for a short time, I am sure you must be quite famished."

Semi nodded. She longed for her shore-side swims. She wanted to spend every last bit of mental and physical energy until she collapsed into numbness.

The Krall focused on Semi. "We're proud to have you. Thane Kelm has been working wonders."

"None of this was his doing," mumbled Thane Gett.

Thane Kelm shot Thane Gett a piercing glare, then smiled as if nothing had happened. "We'll see you tomorrow, Semi."

Semi mumbled what sounded like "you too" and "let me go" blended so much that even she did not know what she said.

Thane Kelm ignored it and waved for the Scholars to follow. Krall Plath saluted her and followed them.

Thane Gett approached her but kept a cautious distance. After the footsteps of the Scholars and Krall were no longer audible, he met her eyes.

She felt her lip shake.

"I'm sorry."

"Did you see it?" she felt her voice shake. "Did any of your visions show what he would do to me?"

He shook his head and left.

Foretellers are imperfect. All Endowers are imperfect. Their abilities never work to the extent they would like. Never to the extent the public would like.

Thane Gett was enough. He was no Feelman. He didn't need to be to know that she needed time alone.

She leaned against the wall and slid down, burying her head between her knees. The sound of a closing door opened her emotions. She was alone. Her tears were free. Her throat burned with long, agonizing groans.

Lennth's face was branded into her mind. His unkempt beard and scar across his forehead lost all intimidation in sight of his smile and joviality. She did not know the man but knew that his honest convictions had brought him here.

Why him?

Not only had she condemned him a traitor, but she turned paranoid zealots against their own. How terrible a fate it would be to have one's last moments be those of their friends and allies turning against them.

Murderer. As corrupt a judge as Thane Kelm. Perd him. Perd the Patriarchy.

Guilt did not sting, it strangled. She coughed and felt her vision blur as she struggled to breathe. Physical pain seemed a soothing alternative to the mental anguish.

She slammed her fist against the marble wall, finding it another cathartic relief.

She wanted to focus all her anger and hatred on Thane Kelm. He did not do this. She did. She thought she had reached the peak of suffering.

This is only the beginning.

The thought burned. Her eyes stung. Her head pounded with pressure.

You've shown them what you can do. This is only the beginning. You've invited more.

Nothing would alleviate the pain. This was her existence, damned to pursue the desires of vindictive warlords who will use anyone they need to achieve glory. Control. Sovereignty.

She heard the clicking of a door handle. Footsteps followed. She didn't need to look up. Her appearance was as shameful as her existence.

"Semi."

She would have ignored it if the voice belonged to anyone else. She almost laughed, wondering how delusional she had become.

"Semi."

Hearing the voice again, she returned to reality and looked up.

It was him. No mere memory but living flesh.

Yetrik crouched at her side and held onto her with the warmth of a new morning sun.

CHAPTER TWENTY-SIX

FOR A MOMENT WE WERE JUST FISH IN HEAVEN

Holding her was a whirlwind of joy and sorrow. Yetrik wanted nothing more than to see Semi. He had expected a joyous embrace. What he received was tragic, but much more intimate. He cast his wishes aside and gave himself to her.

A war waged outside but she was all that mattered.

He almost laughed as he struggled to take a deep breath. She held him tighter than the grasp of a giant crab. She rubbed her head against his chest. He ran his fingers through her tangled hair that smelt like the ocean. Both pleasant and fishy. It was home. Sanctuary.

She stopped crying after twenty minutes and waited just as long to speak to him. Her voice was firm, unshaken by sobs. "Why are you here?" Her head still rested against his chest.

"Am I no longer welcome in my own Court?"

"Please, Yetrik." She still sounded vulnerable. Humor would have to wait.

"I have a lot to tell you."

"I figure."

He lifted his head to look around the room. His attention was drawn to two large doors with intricate carvings. "And I assume you have just as much to tell me."

He felt her shoulders raise against his chest with her shrug.

"Are you here to stay?" she asked.

"For a while, at least. Best not make any promises with everything going on. At least Gruth seems peaceful."

She didn't reply.

"Come on," he stood. His knees ached. "I want you to meet some people."

She shook her head and pulled him back down.

"Alright, but we'll have to go eventually. They'll wonder where I've been."

"Then why can't you tell–" she stopped talking with her hand against his abdomen.

He had left the armor outside and only wore a light tunic with patches of sweat. The Gruth humidity made the return home an even warmer embrace.

She rubbed his abdomen, then reached under his shirt.

"Semi! What are you doing? I want–I mean, not now! Really this isn't–"

"They did it to you," she whispered. Her hand ran along the scar.

"It was my choice."

"Was it really?"

"Yes, of course... Are you mad at me?"

She didn't reply.

"Semi, you're an Endowed too. What have I done wrong?"

"Nothing."

Yetrik felt the distance between them return.

She stood. "Let's go."

He stood with her. "Semi, if I've done anything..."

"No."

"I'll explain it all later. There's more to it than just me becoming an Endower." She started to walk. He grabbed her hand and turned to face him. Red rings circled her eyes. "I've seen war, Semi."

"We all have."

"No, you don't understand. I was on the front lines."

"Was it as glorious as you would have hoped?" she sneered.

"It was horrendous! Worse than I could have ever imagined!"

"I'm sorry." She turned away from him and hung her head, but did not walk without him. "I just–I..."

He embraced her. "We've both had a lot to handle."

She nodded and stepped away from him. She rubbed her eyes.

"Do you need more time?"

She shook her head and walked towards the exit.

They walked side by side, but he felt as if he still embraced her. Their hands swung in unison, a finger's length apart. She turned her head and smiled.

She looked much better than she had moments before. She was healing, but still needed more time.

"Who came with you?"

"A Priessman, a Sleffwoman, and a zlatog."

She laughed and shook her head. "You're a Beastling then? It fits you."

He chuckled and a tear fell from his eye. Her shift in attitude was sudden, but it felt good to see her happy again.

He wanted to hold her. Nothing sounded better than crying together in joy, weeping for the little goodness that remained in life. Not everything was dark. Light would prevail. He held onto that notion through worry and sorrow. *Deilf will prevail in the end. Goodness, whatever that means, will triumph.*

"The Priessman and Sleffwoman aren't a surprise?"

"You've been away for some time. It doesn't surprise me you've found some friends."

He opened the last door and they left the building.

He squinted, taking a moment to adjust to the cloudless sky. They were a fair distance away from the coast, but the salty aroma was still present. Court Gruth felt, and smelt, more alive than any other Court.

Gruthmen mingled with Kevlen and the Sleff Krall.

Semi's arm touched his. It almost felt as if she was trying to hide behind him.

A loud screech silenced the chatter.

"*Calm down, Avra!*" Yetrik hissed through his nose.

Talons clicked on the ground as Avra crawled forward, containing her excitement.

Yetrik looked over his shoulder. Semi was smiling.

"This is the Shiftling I was telling you about, Your Grace." said a hunched, impish man in a long cloak. Thane Kelm looked just as uncomfortable as ever.

Krall Pensa left the crowd and held her hand out to shake Semi's hand. "Lhaen Pensa, Krall of Court Sleff."

Semi took her hand and shook it with a limp grip, then bowed. "Heloath. It is an honor to meet you, Your Grace."

"Likewise. Thane Kelm speaks highly of you."

Semi turned to look at Yetrik.

He took a moment to answer. "Ah, yes–right. So... dear Deilf, where do I begin?"

Krall Pensa had no problem filling in the information. She exaggerated Yetrik's heroism and told Semi about her desire to meet with the Gruth nobility. She had already spoken to Krall Plath and Thanes Gett and Kelm about the matter.

"And when are the Priess Thanes or Krall arriving?" Semi asked.

"Gruthwoman," Krall Pensa leaned in and whispered with a sneer. "You know the Bloated Krall cannot come." She turned back and waved Kevlen over. "This is the Krall's son. He can tell you what to expect."

Semi shot Yetrik a worried glare.

He smiled and put his hand on her shoulder. "Don't worry, he's one of the good ones. He's a friend."

She drew her lips together and nodded, then facing Kelven as he jogged over.

He bowed to Semi.

She nodded, not knowing how to react.

"Kevlen Phanos. It's a pleasure to meet you."

Semi smiled. "No title?"

"Just because I'm a Priessman, I have to flaunt it?" Kevlen chuckled. "Captain of the Priess Beastlings, rider of zlatogs, son of the Krall."

"So, you're the one who recruited Yetrik to become a Beastling?"

"You overestimate my influence, Gruthwoman."

Yetrik's chest felt light again. Not only was Semi happy, but she seemed to be getting along with Kevlen. He knew of her resentment towards Priessmen, based on "past assignments," but he knew Kevlen would be an exception. His charm and humorous pride set him apart from any title attached to him.

Semi's eyes moved to look at the zlatogs, then back to focus on Kevlen. "If your father is not coming, then who is?"

Semi seemed more confident than when he had last been with her. Kevlen was no Thane, yet he felt the circumstances were similar.

"I sent the letter to our Thane of Diplomacy. Whomever he invites is his choice. "

Yetrik felt the tightness in his chest return at the mention of Terin.

"A letter? From here?" Semi asked.

"We sent it while in Paiell," Kevlen replied.

"That's not much better. Are they coming by carriage? We could be waiting here for weeks!"

"The Thane has his ways," Kevlen replied. "I wouldn't be surprised if they have some Beastlings fly them here by zlatog."

"Is that one yours, Yetrik?" Semi pointed at Khoga.

He shook his head and moved her hand to point at Avra. "That one. The other is Kevlen's, but they aren't *ours*. It's a partnership."

"If anything, Khoga owns me," Kevlen chuckled.

"And what is yours named?" Semi asked Yetrik.

He couldn't hold back his smile from hers. "Avra."

She nodded. "Can I touch him? Her?"

"Avra is a she, but," Yetrik gave an awkward laugh and scratched his head, "you might as well ask Krall Pensa if you can touch her. I know some domestic animals might appreciate touch, but most of them find it just as weird as you asking to touch another person."

Semi smiled. "Well look at you, already a Beastling in all his glory."

Memories of the battle in Paiell played across his mind. Agony and blood. Joy was easy to lose. Senseless killings at his hands for the sake of triumph, whatever that triumph meant. He prompted her forward.

"Still, I want you to meet her." Despite the horrors wrought by his hands and her claws, he loved Avra. *How much of the fighting was her will and how much was what I forced upon her? Am I responsible for making her seem like a monster? Does she care for me or just obey without choice?* He squinted to banish his thoughts once again and held onto the joy he felt with Avra.

Semi moved her arm forward but held it back as she reached Avra. Giant eyes with yellow irises stared back at her, then shot to Yetrik.

"*She's a friend,*" he patted her.

"Oh, so you get to pet her?" Semi raised her eyebrow.

"No, it doesn't work like that, its–"

She put her hand on his shoulder. "Settle down, Gruthman."

"Yetrik! Semi!" Krall Plath waved them over to join the others. Kevlen left Khoga with a few pats and joined them as well.

The Krall nodded at Yetrik. "Krall Pensa is insistent that we move forward with planning our advancement."

"Best not waste time," Krall Pensa said. "War needs no rest."

Kevlen stepped forward. "As I've told you, Your Grace, I do not anticipate that my Thanes will arrive so soon."

"Which is why I want to begin now. I'll deal with the Priessmen when they come, but the Gruthmen are kind enough to accept my presence."

"Never a burden," said Krall Plath.

She shook her head. "No need to pander. We're all responsible adults here, and neither will bribery do."

"Yes, yes, indeed. Follow me." Krall Plath led the group into the Canton of Defence. Rather than return to the same place where Yetrik had found Semi, they ascended the stairs to the third level.

They entered a room with two large windows on each wall and tapestries on the other two. Each was faded with depictions of Thusk prior to the establishment of Courts, one of the only things he had seen in the building that predated its erection. The group gathered around a large square table in the center of the room, leaving one side open.

Krall Pensa was the last to sit and slapped her hands on the table as she did so. "What do you have to offer me, Gruthmen?"

Thane Plath laughed but lost his joviality as Krall Pensa remained silent.

"Humorous, is it?" she said. "What about you, Scholar? Do you and your followers find me just as humorous? Any Sleffman makes an easy target for a joke, especially when we ask for something! We're just *perding* beggars in need of your help!"

"Forgive me–"

She slapped her hands on the table again to stop Krall Plath. "No, I don't want your forgiveness. 'Are you serious?' Of course I am! You and your campaign have split my Court in two!"

"That was not our doing," said Thane Kelm.

"Now you're being the humorous one!" She shook her head. "Your Court might not be responsible, but I know you Scholars are doing more than we can see, especially the likes of those two." She pointed at the two Scholars beside Thane Kelm. "Maybe I am the one who should be asking for forgiveness. You must understand my predicament. Regardless of who started the war, two parties are tearing my people apart. Frankly, I *do not care* about harvesting if the policy's fate requires the lives of my nation. Both sides are fighting over an organ while *living* people are forced to sacrifice themselves. I will help whichever side will bring this to an end. So, I ask you again, what can you offer? Why should I help your side? I don't want to argue about harvesting." She pointed at Thane Kelm. "We both know that this war is *much more than that.*" She turned her finger to Krall Plath. "And I am quite aware of the Pough Nettle you are using to sway certain parties in Paiell. I will not be persuaded by such simple means."

Yetrik turned and whispered to Kevlen while Thane Kelm tried to defend his brush distribution. "Was she this frustrated with them before?"

Kevlen looked at the Thanes and Krall's to make sure he wasn't disrupting. "What do you mean?"

"Before Semi and I came outside."

"Oh, they didn't talk about any of this until now. Your Krall just told her about how they built this area to prepare their military. You didn't miss much."

He turned his attention back to a frustrated Krall Pensa. "—keep insulting my economy and I'll continue to talk about your Court's failure to evolve. Endurance does not always mean success if you are built upon a flawed foundation."

"Enough of this," Thane Gett.

"Agreed," Krall Plath replied. "Let us return to your original request. What can we offer you? That depends on what you require. We all have limited resources, noting that the war will only become more burdensome on our respective populations. We would appreciate your loyalty, Krall Pensa, and will do what we need to achieve it, but you must know that you came here on your own terms. It was the Priessmen and Zhaesmen who originally pleaded for your commitment. They sent the Beastlings, not us."

"Then why do you plead their cause?"

Krall Plath laughed. "For the sake of harvesting, of course! Why else? Have you forgotten what this war is about?"

She ignored the Gruth Krall's reply and turned to Thane Kelm. "Why commit to a foreign war while your Court remains peaceful, Scholar?"

Thane Kelm shook his head. "Do not presume to know the Patriarchy, Your Grace. Our machinations are beyond the scope of even some of the highest in our order. My Krall speaks the truth. Do you not have the same respect for harvesting as we do?"

"No. For one who holds the title of Scholar, you seem to have a poor understanding of simple words. I may appreciate what some Endowed have accomplished, I cannot focus on luxuries while my Court continues to kill itself under the pressure of warring ideals. *Again,* I want an end to the conflict."

"Then one side of the conflict must perish," said Krall Plath.

"Exactly, which is why I turn to you. At this moment, the harvesting loyalists hold power in my Court. A revolution in the opposite direction will double the mortality compared to the amount we would have if we retained this power. Help me retain it. Another attack is inevitable."

"What makes you so sure?" asked Thane Gett.

"Common sense," she bit back. "Of course they could redirect their efforts to focus on another Court before returning to ours, but I *know* that they will return to Paiell quicker than most would expect."

"Are you a Foreteller?" Thane Gett asked.

She shook her head. "But I have plenty who all warn me of an imminent attack that would render the Priessmen army in Paiell useless."

"You want our military?" Krall Plath leaned forward.

"I do."

"How do you know we have one to lend?"

"Your foretellers," said Thane Gett. "They've seen our army."

Krall Pensa smiled. "They haven't seen as much as we would have liked, but we know that you have something that no one else does. Tireless warriors. Peerless with blade and fist alike."

Krall Plath looked at Thane Kelm.

Thane Kelm furrowed his brow and forced a smile.

"You want my Court's allegiance?" said Krall Pensa. "I need your collaboration to help ensure that it remains mine."

Krall Plath leaned over and whispered to Thane Kelm.

He laughed and waved the Krall away. "We need them, Your Grace, not because of their power, but because of their title as a Court. You should know by now that titles have more sway than large groups of people." He knocked his ring against the marble tabletop and shook his head. He looked up to glare at Krall Pensa. "You want my Terpels, is that it?"

"If they can help hold Paiell, then yes, I want nothing else."

Thane Kelm smiled, but still glared at her. "Oh, they will help hold your Court. As you said, they are peerless. They will do much more than merely hold your Court, Your Grace, they will win us this war. Wouldn't you agree, Semi?"

Yetrik turned to her. He saw the discomfort, then the fear from before returning to her. Her lips were not quivering.

She nodded.

I've only been away for a few months. Have we always had an army?
Thane Kelm looked more confident than ever. This was his game.

Memories of Thane Gromm returned to him. *What is he doing in Fayis? Is he still there? Are we a part of his game? Is all of this some cover for the Patriarchy to play their own game?*

"Paiell is all I need," said Krall Pensa. "If I have the capitol, I have the people. The rebels will perish or flee. Without the support of the state, any who oppose it will fall. This is not a threat, but a fact. With our economy and policy of humility, one cannot survive without the Court's resources."

"Do you–" Krall Plath cleared his throat. "Do you have any idea when this... attack might come?"

"The first month of Vesting."

"That is mere weeks away!" Thane Gett pressed his fingers against the wrinkles of his forehead.

Krall Pensa leaned back in her seat and folded her arms. "Which is why we should leave as soon as possible. Is the army ready?"

The Krall turned to Thane Kelm, who smiled. "We cannot send our army just yet! We are just as vulnerable to an attack as the Sleffmen. If anything, we are at a higher risk. Our Court has more to offer its conqueror."

"We shall send them," Thane Kelm said.

"Is their allegiance so significant? She does not care about harvesting. You must understand–" Krall Plath clenched his fists. Yetrik thought he heard his teeth grinding.

"Oh, I understand, *my Krall*. I understand much more than you do. It would be best to listen. As she stated, harvesting is not the problem here. It has become something much larger and we need *complete* trust with the Sleffmen."

"What do you mean? This began with harvesting and it is a war on the policy itself!"

"And you know this because you have been directly engaged in the war?" Thane Kelm laughed and shook his head. "With whom have you spoken about these matters? Krall Trhet? The new perding Krall of the Chussmen? *No!* You have been wandering our Court with your chin held high while I have been communicating with the Scholars all throughout Facet. I am done with any false apprehension I had kneeling before you. It is due time that we Scholars receive the respect we deserve. Without us, Facet *will* perish."

The Scholars beside him smiled, their bronze wrist circlets clinked against each other as they gave him the Gruth salute.

Krall Plath forced a laugh. His eyes shot from one person to another, never taking hold. "Well, if we must make accusations, why should I believe the Sleff foretellers? Court Zhaes had plenty of Foretellers. Did that save Kzhek?" He pointed at Thane Gett. His scowl looked humorous amidst his poor accusations. "Where are your visions? Why are we hearing all of this from the Sleff Krall rather than one of our people?"

Thane Gett sighed as if speaking to a child eager to blame anyone but himself. Still, he held back a tone that would shame the Krall, unlike Thane Kelm. These subtle differences won Yetrik's respect. "Your Grace, forgive me, but you hold to a common misconception. Foretellers cannot *will* foresight or vision. These visions are gifts, often given infrequently and without clear reasoning. If we could see the future at all times, there would have never been a war. The enemies would have perished long before they had the time to rise."

"So you have had no visions regarding the war?" Krall Pensa asked.

"I said nothing of the sort, Your Grace. Because of my visions, we sent Yetrik and Semi to Kzhek. These were not visions of victory, but of defense. Some...higher being, whether it be Deilf himself or some other governing force regulates what we see."

"Of course Deilf sends the visions! Who else would?" scoffed the Krall.

"How little you know!" laughed Thane Kelm.

"Me?" The Krall put his hands on the table, almost pushing to stand.

"Of course *you*, you fool! Thane Gett seems to be one of the few noblemen with any sense! If it was simply Deilf, then why would he not grant us victory? All other Foretellers, and I have met *plenty*, experience the same thing. It is erroneous to believe that they are mere visions of the future at all! These are visions implanted by a sentient being, one that wishes to control the outcome of this conflict."

"Shouldn't we take that as a warning?" asked Kevlen. "If this *being* allows the Harmony Allegiant to control Kzhek, is that not a clear sign of its intentions?"

Krall Plath laughed. "Who is to say that this being is benevolent? If it isn't Deilf himself, I would be cautious of such visions."

"Nothing but superstitions," said Krall Pensa.

Thane Kelm scoffed. He turned to Kevlen with a condescending grin. "Why are *you* here, Priessman?"

"Because she requested us." He pointed to Krall Pensa, who grinned and shook her head. "What? Did I say something wrong?"

"Why do you think I was so eager to start this meeting?" She winked at Kevlen. "Poor Priessman. You should have known that our direct flight to Gruth was aimed at seeking *their* help. You heard what my Foretellers saw. I plan on leaving before your Thanes' arrival."

"You–" Kevlen stopped himself with a clenched jaw. He sighed. "Why didn't you tell me?"

"Because I needed the help of the Gruthmen. You provided a route for me to reach them. You two insisted on me meeting with your Priess Thanes. What can they offer me in comparison to the Gruth army?"

Kevlen stared at her, eyebrows arched in disappointment.

"Not to worry, Priessman," said Krall Plath. He smiled at Kevlen like a pitiful mentor. "We will benefit from their visit. It is due time we consult with them over this war."

"I don't care," said Kevlen. "She could have asked us to take her here. My disappointment will be nothing compared to the anger of my Thanes."

"Oh, I did not intend to toss aside anything they could offer," said Krall Pensa. "I just realized that now. Why wait for some past enemies to come here when I have the power I need to maintain control in Paiell?"

"Still," Thane Gett cleared his throat. His age sounded more pronounced since the last time Yetrik had seen him. "I would not appreciate such flippancy if I were in his position. We are allies here and must treat each other's time with respect."

"Tell me you feel the same when your Court is in ruin," barked Krall Pensa. "It shouldn't surprise you. I still never committed to your loyalist creed. I am doing what I need to in order to serve the majority of my people. Marching to the capitol with an army will aid that, waiting around for some Priessmen will not." She stared at Kevlen. "Am I wrong?"

He shook his head, not meeting her eyes. "I told you, this is something that you will have to settle with my Thanes."

She stood and patted down her pants. It was odd to see a Krall in anything other than elegant clothing. Luxury lost its allure. Life and the preservation of culture were all that mattered.

"What are you doing?" asked Krall Plath.

"We've finished, have we not?" She stepped away from the table. "I need some rest and you have an army to prepare." She pointed to Yetrik. "Gruthman, take me to a room that I can call my own while I'm here."

You think I know what to do? I was at war while they built it! He kept silent and stood. He stared at Krall with wide eyes and shrugged.

The Krall grabbed the edge of his marine crown and used it to scratch his head. "Go down a floor. She can take the last room on the right side of the right hall." He looked up and found Krall Pensa staring at him. He sighed and turned to her. "I'll have someone sent to bring you something to eat. I'll visit you before the day ends."

Krall Pensa gave him the Sleff salute. "I appreciate the hospitality."

Yetrik patted Semi's arm with the back of his hand. He waved for her to follow.

Krall Pensa left the room paces ahead. Semi whispered an apology to Thane Kelm and put her hand on Yetrik's back to push him forward.

They remained behind as the Krall descended the stairs, but close enough to keep her in sight.

"What in the *perding under realms* was that?" Semi's whisper felt like a whirlwind.

He dug his fingernail into his thumb to keep himself from laughing. As frustrated and perplexed as he was with the eccentric Sleff Krall, she knew how to entertain. "I've known her for a few days and am yet to find a different side to her personality."

"Why are we following her if Krall Plath told her where to go?"

He shrugged.

"I've had enough politics for today." She sighed. "I'll take the excuse to leave."

"You know it will only grow worse."

"Until it's over."

"And you think that is soon?"

She nodded. "I may not have seen the battle in Kzhek, but I've heard about the catastrophe it was."

"Of course it was. War is synonymous with catastrophe."

"No, it's more than that. They say it looked like two armies of uncoordinated children running at each other. Neither army was trained enough for war."

"What do you expect? No one has been training for war for decades." He put his hand on her back to catch up to Krall Pensa as she neared her door.

"That's my point. No one has trained until now. Our army is full of trained Endowed that cannot experience fatigue."

"You'll have to explain the army to me later. This is the first I have ever heard of it."

"You'll be familiar with them soon enough. They'll change all of this for the better or worse"

They stopped as the Krall shut her door a few seconds before they reached it. The sound of the lock engaging hinted at their lack of invitation. He sighed and put his hands on his hips. "But that's what we want, right? And end to this?"

She shrugged. "That depends on who controls them in the end. Our Court, or Thane Kelm and the Patriarchy."

He chuckled. "You're a believer, too?"

"What do you mean?"

"You're scared of the Patriarchy. You think that they run the world and will control us all."

"If they don't already."

He lost his smile. Silence hung between them as they walked away from the Krall's chamber. "What now?"

She turned to him with her eyebrows raised.

"You're the one that's been here for a while."

"A day in this new city is hardly a while," she stated.

"Still, I have no idea where we are. You don't want to go back to the noblemen, so lead the way, Gruthwoman."

She looked at him with a cold stare. He worried that her lip would quiver again. She blinked and shook her head. "Maybe some other time."

"I'm sorry?"

"There are things you should see in this district, but I don't want more burdens right now."

"Are you sure? I–"

"No, we both need a break from our responsibilities. Even if we only have an hour, it will be worth it."

He nodded. "Yes, of course. We deserve it, right?"

She wasn't looking at him, so he risked a touch. He touched the bottom of her chin and tipped it up to look at him.

His chest shook with each heartbeat. Warmth filled him more than the cloudless Gruth sky.

She blushed. His cheeks mirrored hers. He dropped his hand, but her eyes remained on his.

She brushed her hair behind her ear. It had grown down to her shoulders. "While you were away, or rather, while I was with the training army, I spent time in the sea."

"Doing what?"

"Swimming."

"I didn't know you were a swimmer."

"I wasn't, but I needed something to take my mind away from the repetitive training sessions. Now, I want nothing more than a swim to let my worries drift away in the waves."

"How poetic."

"But its–"

"Why not?"

"Yetrik, the sea is a long carriageride away. We can't just take some ghete or walk there. We have responsibilities. Even if I want a break, we can't abandon everything. What are you doing? Why are you smiling at me like that? Am I that foolish?"

"Let's go there."

"Yetrik–"

"No ghete or carriage needed. We can be back in an hour or so."

He continued to smile until her eyes went wide

"Yetrik–no, we shouldn't–"

"Bad excuse, Gruthwoman." He grabbed her hand. It was cold, yet the touch warmed him again.

She shook her head but followed him outside.

"*Are you up for a flight?*" Yetrik screeched.

Avra ran towards him and lowered herself. "*I almost left you for a flight of my own.*"

Yetrik jumped atop Avra and reached down towards Semi, his other hand gripping the horn of the saddle. "Come on. All you have to do is hold on. I'll handle the rest."

She swung her legs around the saddle and reached both hands around his waist in a tenacious embrace. He reached for the leather straps and pulled a belt around himself and Semi to secure them to Avra's saddle.

"You ready?"

"Just go!" she said.

Yetrik patted Avra. "*Fly east, towards the sea. You shouldn't have trouble seeing it when we're higher.*"

Semi pressed her face against Yetrik's back as Avra shook her wings.

Avra ran and took flight.

Semi screamed. He laughed.

She would learn to love it once she relaxed. He had been just as frightened the first time–and plenty following that. It was a privilege few humans would enjoy. Despite the controversy of harvesting and the associated costs, he was grateful for this opportunity. He set every political tie aside to enjoy the moment. Consequences would follow, as they always did, but this was time for Avra and Semi.

Semi pulled her head away after a few minutes of coasting. Her hands remained as tight against his waist.

"Feeling better?"

"Almost!" she shouted. "It's a lot better like this."

"Yeah, the coasting helps a lot."

"How much longer?"

"Look down and see."

"No!"

He leaned over to see past Avra's wings.

"Don't do that?"

"What?"

"Move so much!"

"You're fine, Semi." He leaned back over and felt her grip tighten. "Not much longer. Avoiding the roads and taking a direct path makes the trip a lot shorter."

The heat of the sun overcame the wind's cooling effect. Paired with the thick leather fit for flying in frigid climates, his sweat was more than enough to get him excited for the sea. He swam often when he was younger, but struggled to find the time amidst his studies as the years went on. Thoughts of plunging in the teal, salty water were a comforting nostalgia.

"Hold tight, we're about to descend."

He felt Semi's head press against his back again. *"You can drop us,"* he screeched. *"We both have a secure grip."*

Avra hummed an agreement and dove at a steep angle.

Semi screamed. He let go of the saddle horn with one hand and pressed the other against his abdomen on top of her hands.

They reached the beach in a matter of seconds. Semi shook as Yetrik helped lower her to the sand.

"Sorry, I should have had her make a more gradual descent."

"You perding maniac."

"Oh, come on. You didn't have fun?"

A smile cracked her stoney glare. "Now that it's over, I guess it was a little exciting."

"A little?"

"Don't pride yourself too much, Gruthman. I don't want to see that Priessman rubbing off on you."

"Kevlen? Oh, don't worry about him."

She began removing her boots. "He's an exception? Fails to live up to the ideal of his Court just like the rest of us?"

Yetrik followed her and started to remove everything except for his briefs. "He's plenty prideful, but it doesn't feel condescending. I feel like he is making fun of himself most of the time."

Semi placed her hands on her bare hips. She was naked.

Yetrik averted his eyes. "*Perd*, I thought you were from southern Gruth!"

She giggled. "More like southern Thusk. My name might be southern, but I've spent most of my life near the city and coast. Aren't you from Thusk? How can nudity bother you?"

"We moved around a lot when I was growing up. Still, I guess I've been away from home for too long. Do you want me to–"

"Do whatever you're comfortable with, *Priessman*. It doesn't mean anything to me. A body is a body, clothed or unclothed." She gave him a playful slap on the shoulder and ran into the water.

He slapped the sides of his face and removed his covering. "*Ignore it, Avra!*"

The zlatog snorted. "*You humans are the only beasts odd enough to cover your body. If you wish to mate with her–*"

"*Nothing of the sort!*"

"Something wrong, Yetrik?" Semi moved her wet hair from her face. Her smile had returned.

He shook his head and ran until the water reached his waist, then plunged. The tepid water breathed life into him. He swam deeper and felt the light touch of kelp brush across his legs.

This was home. His inhibitions and fear of nakedness dissipated. He was a child again. Memories of running across the sand and picking up starfish returned as if they were mere moments ago. He almost felt as if he could run out of the water and into the embrace of his parents. They were never the type to be concerned about him, yet he hadn't seen them since weeks before he first left for Kzhek.. He wanted to visit them, maybe introduce them to Semi, but Krall Pensa seemed insistent on marching to Paiell as soon as possible. Comforts fleeted at the thought of his immediate duties. Concern still clung to his mind, regardless of his attempts to vanish them. Despite his anxieties, he tried to focus on the moment. Pain and difficulty were inevitable, but they felt distant as he focused on Semi and the sea.

He swam to the surface as he felt her skin slide against his. He wiped his eyes and saw that she continued to swim, then made a quick turn back. She passed him again as he tread water. She came for a cathartic escape rather than leisure. Her timidity was faint and her determination had grown. They both had changed. More was yet to come.

He stopped following her as she treaded water to catch her breath. He felt that he could continue, and even wanted to with the momentum he had, but he came for her. Fear led him to believe that their time was limited.

"It's nice, isn't it?" she said.

"I forgot how much I love it." He swam towards her. "Maybe I should stay."

She didn't reply. He gave her time to breathe, blaming the silence on exhaustion.

"But I can't. Not yet. Someday this will all come to an end and we can swim together every day."

She smiled. "Yetrik?"

He swam closer to her. "Yes?"

She motioned her head to the shore and swam back. He followed and laid beside her on the warm sand. The setting sun filled the sky with a familiar pink and orange glow.

"How was your swim?" It was a hollow question that hurt as it came out. Her silence–brief though it was–frightened him. She could be dramatic. That was not unknown to him. Still, the anticipation forced him to imagine the worst.

He had grown comfortable sitting with her in silence, but his feelings were different when she addressed him with pregnant concern.

She did not answer. He let her sit for a few seconds before turning to her. He wiped away her tear and placed his hand on her back. It felt right.

"They want to send me to the Harmony Allegiant." She held still, more anger showing than sadness.

"To infiltrate them? Do they want you to act as a leader as well?"

She pressed her palms against her eyes and released her tension but kept her hands over her eyes. "They want me to assassinate the leaders of the Allegiant. One, many, I don't know. Perd me, I can't–" She turned to him with red eyes and told him about what she had done just before he found her in tears upon his arrival.

His eyes stung. After wiping sand from his hands, he wiped his tears. Both of them had become tools for those who would not fight themselves. Emotions became physical pain. He hurt both of them. "I'm sorry. I'm sorry I got you involved with this."

"It's not your fault."

"Of course it is. Thane Gett only sent you to Kzhek because he wanted me to go. Because I was so eager to see the world. What a perding fool I was. I'm still a fool."

"Better than most." She wiped her nose.

"What?"

She laughed. "You're better than most." Her red eyes stared into his. Their sorrow and vulnerability felt stronger than any joyful embrace they had ever shared. "It's no one's fault. Fate can be a crude kulf." She wiped her eyes again and pushed her wet hair behind her ears. "At least I have someone who knows how I feel. Someone to experience all of this with."

"Have you grown that fond of Thane Kelm?"

She laughed and pushed his shoulder. Her eyes found him again. "I mean it, Yetrik. We've known each other for a few months, many of those spent apart, but I don't know the last time I had someone this close. You've seen me at my highest and lowest. *Thank you*."

His chest burned as if he was having a spiritual experience. He felt like he was assaulted with anxiety and energy at the same time. Ice and fire filled his veins simultaneously.

He put his hands on the sides of her head and moved in, locking his lips with hers.

Joy, in its purest form, filled his soul.

CHAPTER TWENTY-SEVEN

THE SPOILED MILK OF INDULGENCE

Dessen and Port spent the hours following the feast in search of Tick, only to be rewarded by him wandering into their temporary residence after they had given up.

"Where the perd have you been?" Dessen shouted.

Tick played with a bottle and did not appear to be the least bit fatigued and sat against the wall.

"I asked where you've been!"

"Sit down, Dessen. Let him talk." Port yawned. His heart still pounded from Dessen's shout.

Tick shrugged.

Dessen laughed, but his furrowed brow showed his true emotions. "You're going to talk, you unreliable kulf. We spent our night looking for you—"

"Why?"

"Oh, now you're smiling? Couldn't keep your head straight when we entered the town, but *now* everything is well?"

Port sat up. "Dessen, please."

"Doesn't something about him bother you?"

Port looked at Tick. He wanted to defend the poor Sleffmen from Dessen's accusations–many of which had persisted since they met–but he found himself agreeing. Sunrise was nearing, yet Tick seemed well rested and had lost his perpetual frown. His cheeks were still gaunt, but his eyes did not seem as sunken in.

"Ignore Dessen. Can you tell *me* where you have been?"

Tick looked at Dessen as if he were about to laugh at him. He bit his lower lip and looked back at Port. "Around."

"*Heitt's mercy!*" Dessen said. He flung his hands, but to Port's relief, he did not strike Tick.

"Please, Tick," said Port.

"Am I not entitled to my own privacy?"

"No, you're not," said Dessen. "We're at war and our circumstances are more complicated here between the Chussmen and the imps."

Tick stared at both of them, shifting his eyes back and forth before laughing and shaking his head. "You make it sound as if I am a traitor! I went to see how some of the local Sleffmen live. Mere curiosity spent with my southern brethren."

Dessen grumbled.

Port nodded and laid back down. "Fine. We can discuss it tomorrow if we must. Get some sleep, Dessen."

Dessen sighed and extinguished the lamp. Port heard him lie down, but no sound came from Tick.

The moonlight cast a gray glow in the room.

Port rolled to face the other wall, not wanting to acknowledge Tick's smiling face staring at him. The man was odd, that much was not new to Port, but he has never seen Tick so confident.

⁂

Port's heart raced as Dessen shook him awake.

"Move already, Sleffman!"

Port scratched his face up and down. "What–"

"He's gone again."

"Well, he could have wanted an early start to the day." He sat up and looked out the window. The sky began to brighten, but the sunrise was still a while away.

"This early? He was always the last to wake up on our way here. Something is wrong with that jittery kulf. Don't tell me you didn't notice something last night."

"Yeah, he was different. Why are you so worried?"

Dessen sat back and sighed. His shoulders relaxed. "I can't put my finger on it. I would just ignore him if I didn't feel... something off."

"Yes, you already said that."

"I know, I know."

"What do you want me to do about it, Dessen? Yes, I'm the Thane. According to Colrig, I'm the perding captain. Do you want me to toss everything aside to focus on the change in personality of one of our men?"

"So you see the change?"

"Sure–yes, of course I noticed that something was odd with him. When has anything ever been normal? I'm sorry, but I can't give him all of my attention right now." Port put on his boots and light armor.

"Go search for him if you want to. I have more important things to deal with."

Imps roamed the streets. A few sat outside of the buildings to watch Sleffmen laborers start fires, set up tables, and lay out goods for the day's business. The imps stared at him in unity as he passed by. His armor, though simple compared to the Chussmen, was a stark contrast to the brown-stained rags worn by the local Sleffmen.

He walked towards the hall where they held the previous night's feast. To his surprise, the doors were open and Chussmen filled the rows as they broke their fasts.

Few Chussmen turned to look at him and even fewer cared about him entering and roaming the rows until he found the Chuss captain.

"Captain Lonik." He tapped her shoulder and forced his shoulders to straighten.

Khenna set down a half-eaten sausage. "Heloath, Sleffman! Sleep well?"

He nodded and smiled, though found himself still in a poor mood. "Well enough. What is on your itinerary for the day?"

She wiped her mouth and swallowed. "Conserve energy."

"No training?"

"I intend on marching to Paiell as soon as your troops arrive. I'm still perding perplexed as to why we didn't meet halfway. They might be exhausted when we make it back to Paiell, but I don't intend on pushing my soldiers any more before the long road ahead. Victory and survival are all I want. They have nothing to prove to me here by senseless drills."

Why didn't we meet in the middle? Is this halfway between Sliin and Paiell? Perd, we're as babes taking our awkward first steps. Too little time to plan. Too little time to learn.

Khenna returned to her sausage. Port's stomach grumbled, but the thought of food made him want to retch. War was just as mentally taxing as it was physically. Anticipation was worse on the mind than the battle itself. In combat, one could not think and worry about anything other than the battle itself.

"Would you rather we leave today and meet the others on the road?" Port asked.

Khenna pounded her chest and grunted before swallowing. "No, it's best that we stay here. The imps, though conniving kulfs they are, are talented healers. Their alchemy, from what I've seen with some of our injured men, rivals that of Eurythrins. After hearing about the slaughter—sorry—unfortunate loss in Paiell, it's best we tend to any injuries before we leave. Every soldier matters." She took a drink from a large wooden mug. "Regardless, even if we left now, we risk losing them along the way and running into the battle with half of our army. Knowing that your company took an alternate route, I wouldn't be surprised if some of them did."

"Fair enough." He nodded.

"Go eat. I don't care if you want it. You look fresh for a vulture's meal. You need food to heal." She clapped him on the side and turned back to laugh with her soldiers.

Port walked away. No one spared him a glance as they ate and laughed together. These were his allies, yet they were strangers. Dessen was lost trying to find Tick. Even with them, Port was alone. He thought of the troops who would soon arrive. They only thought of him as a commander. He longed for Kzhek and his closest comrades, if any remained. More people died each day, especially in the battles that were decimating Court Sleff. He prayed for an end yet called to Heitt in faithless pleas. The destruction would continue as long as humans were unwilling to change. He was a part of the problem, as was every person tied to the war. Still, he held on to hope, no matter how frail his grip was.

Four days of wasted time passed before the remaining Sleff forces arrived from Paiell.

Tick remained missing. Port had not seen Dessen since the previous morning.

Aside from Port's personal dilemmas, the arrival was better than he had expected. The debilitating wounds were few, and most of the soldiers felt well rested by the end of the day.

Port slept another night alone. He found the only way he could soothe his concerns, or the greatest of them, was to ignore them.

"Thane Kamen!"

Port turned over, the sun shining in his eyes from the open tent flap. Captain Khenna Lonik stood in the doorway, fully armored.

"Wha–" he cleared his throat as he was forced from his sleep. "What are you...doing? What–"

"Preparing, sir!" She approached him and slapped her hand on his shoulder, shaking it in her grip. "Your troops are as prepared as they'll ever be."

"Today? We haven't–"

"Sleffman, we've been waiting for their arrival for too long."

"But they need more time. Don't you think?"

She shook her head. "They'll be well enough. The imps took care of most of their wounds, as you surely know. The days on the road will give them time to heal."

"I thought *you* wanted more time?"

"My troops speak louder than I do. I would have insisted on another day or two, but your men seem well enough. The Chussmen grow anxious. Come on, time to rise." She moved over and took his blanket from him. "There won't be any beds on the road. Best get used to it."

He slapped her arm away as she grabbed it. "*What* are you doing? I'm the perding captain here!" Declaring so this time did not require courage. Anger was fuel enough.

She placed her hands on her hips. "So we're turning to that, are we?"

"I'm sorry, I just–"

"Still can't find your friend?"

He sat up and swung his knees over the edge of the bed and scratched his head. He already missed the warmth of the holey blanket. "It's not just him. Dessen's gone too."

She smiled and opened her mouth as if to make another jest. She sighed and sat beside him. "I'm sure he's caught up with the excitement of the new arrivals."

Port shrugged.

"Do you think he left with the other one?"

"I have no idea. Perd, what kind of captain am I?"

She looked into his eyes and bumped his elbow with hers. "A new one. It will work out."

"What? The war?"

"All is in the hands of our gods. It is our duty to fulfill their wills."

"That doesn't help, Khenna."

"We'll find them before we leave." She stood and waved for him to follow, which he did with reluctance. "Don't worry about searching on your own. I'm sure you will find them lined up with the other troops."

He stared at her for a moment, then shook his head and followed her out of the tent.

Chussmen loaded carts and others donned their armor. Their plating was light, but still much better than anything the Sleffmen had. Local Sleffmen helped the Sleff soldiers prepare food and materials for along the road. Port was not used to sleeping so late and felt a sting of guilt.

"Who's going to pull all of that?" Port pointed to a group of three Chussmen who struggled to push a loaded card aside for the next one to be loaded. "Do we need that much? We came here with nothing but the clothes and armor on us!"

"And how did that do for you?"

"What do you mean?"

"You lost, Sleffman. We need more than just more soldiers. We need weapons, heavier armor when we arrive, shields, sustenance."

"That still doesn't tell me who will pull it. Very few Gorgers remain in my company. They cannot do that on their own. Regardless of their strength, it would be torture to assign all of that to a few Endowed." He scowled. "Are you laughing at me? Perd, am I that sorry of a kulf?"

"Don't you think we had this resolved before coming here? The Beastlings assign the task to whatever beasts they find. Camels served us well in Chuss, but we had to switch to drivers more suited to your climate when we arrived. While two camels were enough for one of these wagons, the eldeer of your forests are strong enough to pull two in tow. Still, I would have preferred Zhaes eldeer. I wager they could pull three or four on their own."

Port nodded and walked onward, not giving Khenna the satisfaction of admitting that she was right. "Does the imp duke require anything of us?"

"I worried about that as well. He's been quiet, but I have been cautious of any final requests."

"Have you dealt with imps before?"

She shook her head. "I've been fortunate enough to avoid them for most of my life. We Chussmen don't take such a liking to them as you do. We are rather fond of our own belongings."

"You know I'm not like these fanatics who dedicate their lives to serving the imps, right?" he whispered to her.

"Right. You are just a fanatic who dedicates your life to another Sleff zealot." She stepped ahead of him and led them to the left.

"Couldn't I say the same about you and Thane Stolk?"

She smiled and shook her head. "I suppose neither of us is so simple."

"We each have our reason to serve."

"Some are holier than others."

Silence hung between them for a moment. *Is my purpose to serve myself? Am I anything more than a blind follower? What will I become when this ends? Someone perfected or tainted because of my choices?* Port grew uncomfortable with his own thoughts. "Why did you need to wake me up so early?"

"Your Sleffmen need you."

"But they already look busy enough."

"What kind of attitude is that, captain?" She was paces ahead of him and waved him forward. "It will make sense in a moment."

Perding Chusswoman thinks she's so clever as to treat me like a child with some surprise waiting. He saw how she greeted her men, waving to all as they saluted. *When did I become so resentful?*

Port never claimed perfection but recognized that the war's stress had taken a toll on his enthusiasm and kindness. He followed her and saluted his men as they passed. *Care is the Creed. Wise words for all people, not just Chussmen. We could all learn a little from their striving charity. If we all would have seen each other like valiant Chussmen, this war would have never happened.* He envied her. Both of them were new to their callings in leadership, yet she was greater than he. She earned more respect and did not force it through any means of intimidation. She was what he wanted to become. He had cast aside his timidity for ambition but directed said ambition in the wrong direction. *Charity wins.* He felt the antithesis of what he had been the year before. If he held onto any Ideal recently, it was the Priess Ideal. Pride had infected his Sleff humility. If he did not act, the pride would become terminal.

Lord Heitt on high, forgive your wayward servant.

His view of Khenna was no longer bitter. He watched her with admiration.

She led him around one last corner that left the city's alleys and opened to an extensive field of trampled straw. Sleffmen applauded him as he approached. They wore pristine armor, untainted by battle. Each member of the company was twice his size. He counted fifteen of them in the same armor and one with a larger Sleff sigil with the spinerat in silver rather than black.

"A late arrival," said Khenna, "but timely enough for what we need."

Port's throat felt light and thought he felt tears well in his eyes. *Heitt, am I worthy of such a mercy? Small though the company is, this is truly a blessing.* "The call to retreat from Paiell mentioned another company, but... I thought–mercy on high, it is a splendid gift to have you all here! I am sorry that you must join such a terrible crusade, but you... thank you. Thank you for being willing to come, Sleffmen."

The Gorger with the silver sigil saluted Port and stepped forward. "Pious is the Giver, Thane Kamen."

"Have we met?"

"No, but we are well aware of your achievements. My name is Shoge. Colrig named me captain of this Gorger company."

Aware of my achievements? My losses? My failure in Paiell? "How does Colrig fare?"

"Well enough. He still manages Kzhek."

Port nodded and patted his thighs. "Well, I suppose we should move forward with all of...this. The Chusswoman captain tells me you are ready to march?"

Shoge nodded. "I know that we have just arrived, but we would rather not lose momentum."

"Of course. Well then." He turned to Khenna and raised his brows.

She faced the Gorgers. "Follow me. We have some more carts to load and you can help line them up at the northern gate. The sooner we can leave, the better."

Port's smile remained, yet the lingering anxiety for Dessen and Tick kept him unsteady. During the battle of Paiell, he did not have time to think about each missing soldier. Later, he had come to recognize the humanity in each soldier through Tick and Dessen. Pairing that with the countless losses in the Sleff capitol—many from men who were likely better people than his companions—almost brought him to vomiting.

Khenna patted him on the back. "Better days lie ahead, Sleffman." It was a senseless platitude, one inspired by his uncertain smile. Regardless of her forced assurance, he felt better.

She stopped and pointed towards a gathering of carts. "Head there and help them finish, Gorgers. They'll have plenty of work for the next few hours. When you're done, we'll meet at the northern gate and depart when everyone is ready." They left after saluting her and Port with fingers making a crown.

"I thought you wanted to leave later in the evening?" he asked.

"Oh, it will be later in the evening, I assure you. You're working with Chussmen. *Care is the Creed.* We give plenty of care to our work, often too much. This company has held me back too often with near-Zhaes perfectionism. Once they see your troops gathering, they'll follow soon after."

"And me?"

"What about you? You're the perding captain. Do what you will." She peddled back towards a gathering of Chussmen. "I'll see you at the northern gate."

I'm the captain. Why do I fall back to sheepishness once again? One moment condescending command and the next shrinking before my equals? You're a perding mess.

If asked, he would prefer the humble commander, just like the one who followed Colrig, Phenmir, and now Khenna. The one who attaches to his superior like an anxious child. *The passive captain accomplishes nothing. Perhaps these impulses to follow another are mere humbling gestures from above. The balance between pride and humility is an ever delicate game.*

He shook his arms and slapped his cheeks, then left to help corral his Sleffman as a captain that they could count as a friend. He was meeting many for the first time. Each encounter was a chance to become a new captain.

❧❧❧❧❧ ❧❧❧❧❧

Port handed the final shortsword to a soldier from a cart dragged by a local Sleffman. His soldiers conversed, some jesting and others silent in fear, but they held in line just as he had commanded. It was a promising beginning, though the battle itself was yet to come. He cast off the trauma of war and tried to focus on the present.

"Why do we need this now?" asked the soldier, hefting the blade in his rather small arms. He could not be older than twenty. He was so similar to Port, only slightly younger and had been handed different circumstances. Following Colrig had changed everything that Port was and everything he would become.

Images passed through Port's mind not only of fighting his once-brothers and sisters in Paiell, but of the fiends that he had encountered in the abandoned fishing shacks before they took the river south. "Best be prepared. Enemies may come at any point. I'd rather have you carry that now than have to scramble for swords in the case of a mid-journey ambush."

He nodded and looked down at the blade. He wore a familiar face of discomfort. Port clapped his shoulder. "If that's too light, you're welcome to don some heavy armor and pick up a shield."

The boy smiled and shook his head. "This will be enough for now."

"*Pious is the Giver*, Sleffman."

"*Pious is the Giver*, Thane Kamen."

Port stepped back to observe the lines of Sleffmen and the Chussmen who followed. It was a small army, yet one large enough to bring him hope.

After another hour, the rest of the Chussmen filled in their lines, though there were more of them than Sleffmen.

Khenna approached him. His hands and chest felt uneasy. *The rest has come to an end.*

"Are your troops ready to march?" she asked.

He extended his neck to peer over the company. It was impossible for him to know how many he should expect. He had lost so many in Paiell and never found himself willing to total the fallen. "No one has joined us in nearly an hour. It seems like this is the most we will ever have."

She nodded and raised her hand, ready to signal them forward.

"Wait!" someone shouted from the Sleff side of the army.

"We cannot leave yet!" another pleaded.

He tried to find the source of the calls. Khenna stepped closer to him.

"Who said that?" Port shouted.

"We're missing at least ten Sleffmen!"

He pressed through the frontmost soldiers and found a sizable gap in a line of Sleffmen. He scowled, looking at the neighboring soldiers for an explanation.

One stepped forward. "There were twenty of us that have been close on this journey. Half of our company has been missing. We lost some a few days ago, some yesterday, even more today."

Khenna pressed through the crowd to stand beside him. "What is this?"

He repeated what the Sleffman had told him.

"Deserters?"

Port shook his head. "Remember my companions?"

"You think there is a connection?"

He looked at the Sleff soldier, then back to Khenna. "I am not usually a superstitious man, but there is something *uncanny* afoot."

She looked as if she were going to laugh, but refocused as Port held his stern glare.

"Is this worth our time, Port?"

"I'm no Feelman, but I feel like something dire may follow if we do not prevent it now. I would rather resolve this now before we arrive in Paiell with most of our company missing."

"Do you really—" she placed her fists on her hips and stared at him. "What would lead you to believe that such a thing would happen?"

"Intuition." He wouldn't have believed himself, but he felt a greater impulse than he had ever experienced. Something demanded that he did not leave this unresolved. *Heitt, is this a blessing? A warning?*

She sighed. "I'll give you two hours."

He felt no need to challenge her. Authority was not his problem at that moment. "Anything longer would be absurd."

She nodded. "I'll send some of my soldiers to help search." She turned and pressed through the crowd towards the Chussmen. He heard her garbled shouts lose volume as she pressed onward.

The Sleffman who had spoken before approached him. "Thane?"

"Take the rest of your company and sweep the town. We have two hours to locate them."

"What should we do if we find them?"

"I'll be with the imp duke to see if he has any solution. If not, I'll remain at his side until the time passes."

"Why?"

More intuition? Suspicion? "He is in the city center. Why not work with the head of the city in the city's heart? I am sure he is eager to be rid of us. The more successful we are, the less we trouble him."

The Sleffman nodded and took a step back.

"Wait. Organize the search. Send anyone else here you want to help with the search. I want as many of us on it with as little chaos."

The Sleffmen left and commanded his company, then jumped to the next to point them in another direction.

Port felt that he had exhausted Heitt's mercy, yet he uttered another silent prayer for aid.

꙳꙳꙳꙳ ꙳꙳꙳꙳

"Do you blame me for this?" the imp duke hissed.

"By no means!" Port stepped closer to him in the stable.

The duke held a hand up as he leaned over to suck from the teat of a goat as large as Port. He sighed and whipped the gray milk from his thin lips. "Nothing like drinking fresh from the source, eh? Do our differences make you so cautious as to blame us for the men whom you fail to parent?"

"I am requesting *aid*, respected duke, only advice. You are the mind of the city. Perhaps you have eyes about as well that might have seen anything?"

One of the imp's guards leaned over to suck from the goat but earned a backhand from the duke. "After a week in service, your superiors should have taught you well enough."

The other guard spoke. "Priess goats are for the high imp and his kin only." He pointed to a small goat in the next pen. "Suck from the weaker Sleff breeds if you must."

The guard did not even glance at the goat and remained by the duke's side with shoulders tense.

"Your followers do not concern me. Bruten is for my Sleffmen and imps, not your kind that believe themselves greater than your kin here. You preach humility, yet these seem to be the only people capable of understanding what that truly means."

Port held his tongue. There was no use in arguing with a man who saw his kind as slaves and potential slaves.

Rage births enemies. *Now is your chance to prove your humility. Don't let pride destroy.* "Forgive us if we have been a burden. We'll be gone by the end of the day."

The duke's sniveling stare held onto Port for a few silent seconds. The duke sucked one last time from the goat, then waved for the stablehands to lock it up. "Whether you wish to serve us, your missing men may have been convinced to join their fellow Sleffmen in service here."

They couldn't be so simple as to succumb to the imps, could they?

He thought of Tick's hesitancy upon arrival and his odd interest he had taken in the imps. He recalled the final confidence prior to Tick's last visit. It was not characteristic of one swearing off life as they knew it to become a servant. There was intention there, but Port had difficulty interpreting it.

An imp left the duke's residence and approached them. "High imp, one of this man's followers has requested entry."

The duke looked at Port's, raised a hairless brow, and turned back to the newcomer. "Only one?"

"A company waits out in front, but we only permitted one to wait within your—"

"*Fool*! You relay his invitation when you already permitted entrance?"

"High imp–"

Port stepped away from the duke. "No need. I'll leave and see to him."

The duke shrugged and waved for him to leave with cold ignorance. He glared at the imp who had relayed the news as he scurried back inside.

"Thane Kamen!" exclaimed a Sleffmen who stood by the door. He moved as if his bladder was about to burst. He waved for Port to follow.

Port followed him from duke's property.

Five other Sleffmen outside shared the Sleffman's anticipation.

"What is it?" Port asked, following them as they waved for him to continue down the street. "Have you found them?"

"Hurry, sir, please!"

Port's heart dropped as he followed them. The terror in the man's voice pulled him with the pain and strength of a fishing hook.

"Where are we going?" he asked, hoping to blunt the reveal. Whatever it was, he knew it would be disheartening.

"Almost there!" The leading Sleffman pointed down an alley to the left and ran down it.

They continued on, crossing streets and turning until they reached a dark stone sepulcher. It was much newer looking than most of the other buildings in Bruten. Its style was unlike any other in the city except for the faint resemblance it bore to the duke's residence.

The Sleffmen unsheathed their short swords and surrounded Port. More filled in from behind.

"What is this, a raid?" Port asked. "Heitt's mercy, *please* someone tell me what is happening."

"They're inside," said a Sleffman at his side while their leader peeked inside the building.

"Tick, Dessen, and the others? Are they being held by imps?"

The Sleffman shook his head. The leader waved them inside.

Port enjoyed his brief second of ignorance. The grotesque sight beyond the entrance hall and in the main chamber stole any hope for a simple departure that he had.

Tick stood in nothing but a loincloth and a spinerat pelt over his head. The missing soldiers stood around the circumference of the room with imps between them. An imp shaman dressed similarly to Tick, but had an entire spiked mask made from multiple spinerats with only small holes for his eyes.

"Tick! Wha–why–the–" Port's words failed him as he stepped to the side of a Sleffman to see the altar before Tick. Dessen was bound facing up, with his back against the stone altar. He was granted only a loincloth, revealing the red wear on his skin of the leather bands that fastened him.

Port felt the physical and mental pressure increase as two of the Sleff-men he had come with pressed him between them with their short swords pointing at Tick.

Dessen groaned with closed eyes. Small punctures covered his bare chest in patterns that fit the size of an adult spinerat's back. Bloody sputum fell from the corner of his mouth.

Port's eyes shot to the gilded dagger in Tick's hand. He held it at his side but hunched over Dessen as if ready to attack.

The surrounding soldiers-turned-traitors smiled with more menace than the imps between them.

Dessen sounded like he was choking on his own bloody saliva, unable to let out a proper scream. Tick plunged his knife into the top of Dessen's chest and pulled downward with jagged and sluggish movements.

All watched in awe. Dessen was gone. There was nothing else he could do.

"Perd you, you freak!" a Sleffman ran into the center of the room and tackled Tick. The ceremonial knife fell to the floor.

The peace between the groups has been cut. Dessen's comedically cynical affect was one that had grown on many of the Sleffmen. Losing him was a greater cost than a faceless death. The other Sleff soldiers ran into the chamber and raised their swords against the imp-seduced Sleffmen, who attacked them like starved wolves.

Port backed away, though he knew it was the caution of a coward that tamed him. Imps and rabid Sleffmen alike fell in a slaughter.

"Enough!" Port shouted, stepping into the chamber. "Let them live!"

The screams died down as the Sleff soldiers captured their remaining crazed counterparts in an array of painful holds.

"Pull them against the wall!" He pointed to two Sleffmen who held Tick. "Bring him to the center."

Port stepped towards his former-ally. *The imps did this. Tick would not do this. Do they possess some form of sorcery? Have they given him something to forsake his allegiance?*

Footsteps clattered behind him.

"What happened?"

He turned around to see Khenna enter the room with heavy breathing. Her eyes widened as she saw the dead half-naked Sleffmen and imps.

Port gave her a brief explanation of what he had witnessed, though they both had too many questions preventing them from understanding what had caused the odd gathering.

"He's gone, Port." She pointed at Tick. "You must kill him alongside the others."

Port stared at Tick, whose odd confidence had dissipated. He looked like the wary vagabond he had met weeks before. His eyes screamed innocence and fear, despite all he had done.

"Sleffman!" Khenna shook Port's shoulder and waited for him to look at her. Her voice fell to a whisper. "He's gone, twisted by impish incantations. Look at what he's done."

"Please, Captain Port," pleaded Tick. Tears wet his cheeks. The artificial confidence that he had worn upon his short return nights before had vanished. This was the real Tick. The vulnerable Sleffman too often mocked by his peers, stared at him with shaking hands.

"Do not let them hold you!" hissed an imp.

The Sleffman who held the imp slit its throat and kicked the writhing corpse forward.

Port shook. Flashes of confusion showed through tense eyebrows and his twisting mouth as uttered senseless whispers.

Port shook his head. He blinked away a tear. "Tick, what have you done?"

Tick no longer mumbled but tried to bite his captors like a rabid beast. They pulled his arms taut, each holding him from a safe distance. Tick lost his anger and his lips quivered. "Help me, Port."

Khenna stepped forward and shook her head. She turned back to Port just before reaching Tick. "If I have learned anything in war, it is that some forms of love are brutal. Whatever has become of them, be it their choice or not, is an enemy to their past selves. Your man cannot survive. He must be–"

Tick kicked one of the guards at his side, then spun like an acrobat to knock out his other captor. He pounced onto Khenna, his knife back in his grip. "Free them," he hissed.

Port could not be paralyzed by analysis once again. Time meant lives. He locked eyes with Khenna's, then looked at the soldier standing opposite him and behind Tick. He nodded.

Tick turned around, but the soldier remained still, only stumbling once Port glared at him. Tick looked at Port, then back to the soldier.

Port dashed forward in the second of distraction he had while Tick watched the anxious Sleffman from behind.

Port tried to say, "forgive me," but the words came out as shaken as his nerves as he plunged his shortsword into Tick's mouth. His old friend's jaw clicked as he pushed the blade through and pulled it out.

Khenna flung Tick's bloody corpse from her back and stood. She placed her hand on Port's shoulder. "It had to be done." She turned around to look at the other soldiers. "Finish them." They did so with haste. The last body fell, still gurgling blood. She pushed Port towards the door. "Forget that this happened. It will only weaken you." She pointed forward and commanded the soldiers. "Leave before any resident Sleffmen or imps notice. We will join the others."

Port dropped his shortsword with the sudden commands. He almost fell as he reached down to retrieve the crimson blade. He followed the others out, but his mind remained within the chamber.

Tick's broken smile had branded itself into the backs of Port's mind. He never would have murdered a friend. *That is what you are, what you have become in pursuit of glory.*

His days with Dessen had ended tragically. Whatever persuasion or sorcery had been used to corrupt him, and the other Sleffmen, was beyond him. He thought of Tick's initial worry and dark curiosity that had followed ever since seeing the first spinerat nailed to the tree. A small worry whispered that he would face similar circumstances again, but the tragedy was all that mattered.

He followed his soldiers back to the lined troops. He delegated the control of his army to Khenna for the rest of the departure. Her words and the rushing of the troops seemed silent amidst his self-incrimination. Despite Khenna's camaraderie, Dessen and Tick were the only two he had counted as close friends. The other Sleff troopers were followers, not friends.

He was alone, marching toward death as they tread northward towards Paiell for a second time.

CHAPTER TWENTY-EIGHT

LORD OF THE CICADAS

P henmir grinned and chuckled as tears fell down his cheeks.

The remaining Chuss Endowers followed Kaela and ran through the green grasslands. They fell to drink from the clear water that flowed through the southern Chuss grasslands. They were closer to the Middlelands than he had ever been. To see the children experience joy again after endless nights of pain, grief, and hunger was one of the most wholesome things he had ever witnessed.

Happiness dissipated as he thought of Chenn. The boy would have loved to see the small piece of forestry that his Court had. The boy remained like a resident ghost in Phenmir's mind, reminding him of the cost of war.

He had grown close to the six Chuss guards who survived the ambush of the faceless raiders. Without the Endowers' parents to offer solace, the soldiers had served as proxies. Nothing was perfect, but it was sufficient for what they had. No Endower had died along the way, but three others perished alongside Chenn during the attack. Many of the children were still processing the loss of friends that they counted as family members. Phenmir could not blame them for their perpetual grief. He, too, carried the burden of each fallen warrior, but the weight of a fallen child was almost overbearing. His longing for the Middlelands relied on his hope for reverie. The lingering hope that he would know peace again was enough inspiration to continue. He did so not for himself, but for the children. If they did not survive, all the agony to save them would be an ironic and blasphemous disgrace.

"How much longer, sir?"

Phenmir turned to the Chussman at his side. The man's clean-shaven face had grown a beard since their initial departure. Phenmir felt his own silver facial hair, noting that his beard was becoming more prominent. "A few days, I hope. Any sign of food yet?"

"We sent out one of our men with two Beastlings and Gorgers in search of any wild game. They are yet to return."

Phenmir nodded.

"Without carriages, will we be stuck there? Should we have a Beastling call for a bird to send a message to Sliin for a caravan to follow us?"

Phenmir shook his head. "We'll arrive soon enough. I would rather tell the Krall about the attack on us after we arrive in the Middlelands. If we send anything back too early, I fear she will call us back before we can complete our journey."

"Sorry to ask again, but what are we going to do when we arrive?"

Hope for peace. "Reignite old relationships." *Vague enough to suggest confidence, though only Cheric knows what we can do with such a broken company. We are at the whims of ancient allies.*

The Chussman nodded, though his mouth hung open as if he had another lingering question.

Phenmir walked into the grass to join the others and neared Kaela.

She looked up at him from the small creek, the chin of her mask still wet from drinking.

He crouched beside her and whispered. "How have the others held up since Chenn's passing?"

"Sad that we couldn't bury him. Letting wolves take his body made everyone angry except for the Beastlings that called them."

Phenmir thought of the journeyman's burial he had called for months ago with her and Voln on their scouting mission to Kzhek. She was much less frightened this time. War had aged her. Hardened her. Numbed her. "We couldn't wait to bury him. We were lucky no other Tchoyasmen followed. Are they fine other than that?"

"They have been worse."

He sighed. "What else?"

"Arguments."

"Over what?"

"They are trying to find blame for our failure."

Phenmir cupped some water into his mouth. It was cool, though not frigid. He had forgotten his thirst after it became so usual for him. "None of them are responsible."

"I know. I've told them that. Why don't you go tell them?"

"I can try, though I know it will do little. You–" *You children are the same. Stubborn and eager to force the blame onto another.* He stopped himself. *Adults are the same, even worse.* "We need to keep them focused. What has happened has ended. There is no way to change it."

"It's worse every day."

"I'm afraid, even if I speak to them, that it will do very little until we arrive."

"Then let's keep moving." She arched her back.

"Are you holding up well?"

"Better than you. I've heard you complain about your back more than once."

He chuckled, though even that hurt. His lumbar spine throbbed as if held in a flaming vise. "Neither will that get any better if we stop."

She stepped away from him and turned her head back. "Tell your soldiers back there to follow. I'll tell the Endowers that you're ready to keep going."

He stood and arched his back as well, sighing with the little relief that came through a simple stretch.

Kaela had matured. He wondered if Voln had changed but held a guilty hope that the boy remained the humorously cantankerous child he was. War scarred all, not only the warriors and rulers, but every witness to its atrocities.

The group managed to light a fire two hours after sundown. An hour later, they made a second farther away to split the increasing contention between certain Endowers. Each night, the soldiers improved their fire building technique, though it was clear that none of them were bred for wilderness survival. Privilege had crippled them.

Shouts erupted from the other fire. Phenmir turned to Kaela. "I thought you separated the worst of them?"

"Exactly, *the worst of them*, but there are some who will try to argue with anyone."

Phenmir let out a breath and ran his hands through his silver locks. They were greasy and covered in lingering orange dust from the desert. "Do you want–" he stopped himself from asking her to intervene again.

A smack stopped his thoughts. Another followed, as well as a shout and a scream. *Perd*.

He stood and jogged towards the other fire. The fist-to-flesh sounds of punching and grunts forced him into a sprint.

Two Sleff soldiers shouted for them to stop. One approached two shouting Gorgers but was thrown away at a tree.

"Stop!" Phenmir shouted as he halted before two Chuss Gorgers, whose fists were bloody from the child on the floor between them.

"Perding traitor!" the Gorger to the right shouted as she continued to beat the youngling. The other Gorger held the child down, blood splattered across his face.

Phenmir grabbed her shoulders to try to hold her back. She was almost as tall as him, though she was clearly no older than nine years old. He was pulled forward as she went in for another punch. "Show the Thane what you are!"

The child cried out as he was struck again, but his face was distorted by more than the punches of enraged behemoths.

Phenmir's action defied logic. He let the Gorger go and observed her punch.

The Chussboy's skin shimmered like a mirage. Part of his ebony face wavered from his natural skin tone to one golden and inhuman. Another punch caused his eyes to phase away for a second. They looked just like Voln's. Not in color, but that they were surrounded by gold-painted wood.

"Enough!" Phenmir pushed the Gorger, though she did not waver, and crouched at the child's side. "Let him go," he commanded the one who held the child down. He lifted the limp body and felt the child's face. His skin was swollen and bloody, though smooth.

He turned to look at the Gorgers, keeping the child tight in his grip. "Explain."

"You saw it," the Chussgirl panted as she massaged her bloody knuckles. "Didn't you, Thane?"

"I saw something."

"Sir," said the other Gorger. "We didn't mean to–"

"I don't need any excuses. Tell me what happened." Phenmir looked at the Chussgirl. "What was wrong with his face? It morphed."

"Can't you tell? He's a perding Shiftling. A *Tchoyas* Shiftling."

An answer, but no reason to beat an ally senseless. He closed his eyes and sighed before opening them again. "And what did he do to deserve this?"

"Traitor!" an observing Endower shouted.

The Gorger, who had held him down, smacked his unconscious face.

The shimmer of a Tchoyas mask, one humanoid though exaggerated features, flashed over his face. The guise of a Chussboy remained, but faded as with his consciousness.

"Where's a Eurythrin?" Phenmir stood and repeated himself twice until one stepped forth from the Endowers.

The Eurythrin looked to be five years old. Phenmir calmed himself before reprimanding the shaking child. "Place your hands on him and keep the blood moving away from the surface. Keep it inside."

The child nodded. The blood flow from the Shiftling's battered face stopped moments after the Eurythin touched him.

Phenmir lifted his hands to run them through his hair but stopped before covering it in blood. He would assess the Shiftling after some time with the Eurythrin. In the cruelest form, his profession regained relevance to his new position. Some form of brutal justice had been dealt. He turned to the Gorgers to gauge whether the crime was worthy of the punishment.

They glared at him, rage still billowing in their fierce eyes. His teeth were clenched as he spoke. "Have you forgotten that one of their leaders here is a Tchoyas Endower?"

"You don't understand what he did," one of them whined. Anger had fled in pursuit of self-defense. No matter how advanced their minds proved to be for their age, these were still children with every flaw that carried into their personalities.

Phenmir felt his shoulders grow lax. "Scaring people into submission is not how you win."

"Isn't that what you did in Kzhek?" the Chussgirl asked.

Phenmir shook his head, shying away from an outburst of anger or laughter. *It's more than that, isn't it?* "Please, tell me why–"

The Chussgirl had no hesitation in speaking. "He was the one who told his perding murderer of a Krall where we were going."

Phenmir felt his mercy for the beaten child waver. He stared at his still breathing, mutilated face. Anger told him to push the Eurythrin away, to let the child bleed out. Reason alone held him back. The child had to have a reason for his betrayal. Even if the child only acted in fear, it was better than the treachery he imagined. Had it been an adult, he would have found himself hardened, thinking their actions selfish beyond reason. He could not find himself in the right mind to pray for Cheric's mercy. The god was all knowing and all forgiving. Phenmir was not ready for forgiveness, yet his stillness suggested that his will would not succumb to rage.

The crowd watched Phenmir. His beating heart felt louder than any of their heavy breaths.

"Punish him!" shouted a child in the crowd. He did not look up to see who had spoken.

"It's all his fault!"

"He almost killed us!"

"He killed Chenn!"

Phenmir recoiled, clenching his teeth until they felt like breaking. He had to divert his thoughts. "Take him away to heal."

"Where?" asked the Chussboy Gorger.

All places beyond the campfires were too dark under the moonless sky. He became aware that the entire company's attention was focused on him and the Tchoyasboy. The group from the second campfire had gathered around to see what had occurred.

He shook his head and stood. "Eurythrin, keep healing him. Guards, keep watch here. Gorgers, follow me. If any Feelmen helped them out, you can come as well." He looked at the rest of the company and shouted. "Leave us be." The group dissipated, but Kaela stood still in their mists, staring at Phenmir. He nodded. She ran to his side.

The Gorgers, though temperamental as they were under his command to follow, helped wave off any Chussmen who tried to follow. Phenmir led the company with his head held high towards the other fire. The stars were as dim as his hope. Regardless of his inner turmoil, he would show no weakness. He was the Thane of Harmony. Though the Courts split, his people would hold.

The Gorgers waved for the remaining few around the second fire to leave. Phenmir called for them to sit. He tossed a few branches onto the flames and positioned himself between the two Gorgers. Looking to their sides, he noticed Kaela and a Chuss girl. "You're a Feelman, I take it?"

She nodded.

He turned his glare away from her and focused on the fire. *She has done no wrong. Without her, the secrets would persist.* He shot a quick glance to the two Gorgers, then once again focused on the fire with a pensive stare.

Phenmir kept his eyes on the fire. The girl was intimidated enough. "Feelman, tell us what you read."

"In the Shiftling?"

Patience. She's just a child. "Yes."

"He's a perding—"

"I asked her," Phenmir placed his hand on the Chussgirl Gorger's shoulder. He stared into her eyes. "Not you."

After a few seconds of tense silence, the Shiftling spoke.

"He arrived not long before we left, though I couldn't figure out how. We have known Gik for years.. He just did what he was told to do, but we think that some servants of the Tchoyas Krall took our Gik and made this Shiftling act like ours. We felt he was different, but we never would have guessed that it wasn't our Gik. We just didn't think about things like that, until yesterday. Some people noticed him doing things that we don't do. Tchoyas things, like making binding deals... whatever that was supposed to mean, and... I don't know, but it wasn't like him. Some of the others wanted me to read him, so I did, and these two Gorgers attacked him when I told everyone who this boy was."

"Did he ever say *why* he betrayed us?" Phenmir asked. "Did you know anything about this, Kaela?"

"No! I want nothing to do with that demon of a Krall! You know me, Phenmir. You know–"

"I trust you more than any of these children, Kaela, which is why I asked you."

They smiled at each other. A simple bit of joy in the madness of their situation warmed Phenmir. Hope would prevail. Righteousness, *his* righteousness, would prevail. This was a mere detour along their journey. He set aside his optimistic reverie and refocused on the Shiftling. "Well? Did you find out why he did it?"

"The Krall threatened to kill his family."

"Probably already has by now," said the Chussboy Gorger.

The Shiftling shrugged and continued. "He cried when I read that from his mind. He thinks that because the faceless raiders failed, he is going to come for him and do worse than killing his family."

He can't find us. The perding tyrant is too far away. His scouts have been slain. We are off course. Please, Cheric. Please tell me we are safe.

"He said, or his mind said, that there are more like him."

"In our company?" Phenmir's wide eyes burned from the smoke.

The Shiftling shook her head. "No. We checked and read every mind in the company. But there are more out there among the members of the Harmony Allegiant. More Endowers. More families are being threatened."

"What are you going to do with him?" the Shiftling asked. Her voice whimpered with concern.

At least one of you lives by your Ideal.

"Wait," the Chussboy Gorger pointed at Kaela, "you're a Tchoyasgirl. Why didn't his mask break when we—we hit flesh? I even saw the mask flash for a moment, but it never felt like hitting wood."

Kaela changed her face to match his. "The masks are as much a part of our body as any other. Although it is wooden in his usual form, he made it his flesh to stay hidden, not even changing it to defend himself. He kept the disguise even though you knew what he was. He is a true Tchoyasman. Loyal to the end."

"Loyal to that traitor of a Krall," the Gorger Chussboy scoffed.

"Loyal to those he defended under the Krall's threat," said Kaela.

"Are you a sympathizer too?" The Chussgirl tensed. "How can we trust you to be any different from him? If you're such loyal people, you must follow your Krall, right? You–"

"Enough!" Phenmir demanded. He looked at Kaela and noticed the fire's reflection in her wet eyes. "We need to move on from all of this. Gorgers, you two are the only ones deserving punishment."

"It was her–"

Phenmir raised his hand to silence the Chussboy. "You should have come straight to me. Justice is not your responsibility." He expected another biting response, but was relieved to have earned their silence. "What are we going to do with him? Pray that he'll survive." Phenmir stood. "If you want to grow up to be true Chussmen, you better learn to understand mercy."

"Chenn wasn't offered mercy," said the Chussgirl.

"If we aren't better than them, this war will end in failure. Why are we heading to the Middlelands and into more battles? Because we need to find another solution other than war."

"But weren't you hoping to use the Middlemen in war?"

I don't know what to hope for anymore besides divine intervention. These children cannot become like us, so focused on resolving issues through manifestations of power. "Never hope for war, only to escape it."

Kaela and the Feelman followed him towards the other fire. The Gorgers remained to murmur. He could not blame them for the inevitable scorn, only hoping that they would mature beyond forming a grudge. *How can I expect such maturity when the continent is filled with childish grudges?*

Though Kaela did not embrace him, she held tight to his side. Her pace slowed as he neared the Tchoyasboy. She kept her distance as he knelt down to inspect.

"What are we going to do with him?" Kaela asked, though she found the sky a more comforting sight.

Live your Ideal, you perding hypocrite. Now is your chance to change, to make a proper example for these children. Care is the Creed. "Love him." The words were awkward, as if from a poorly written children's tale, though there were no truer words he could speak. "Regardless of what he was forced to do, he is one of us. We'll see that he is made well."

"Couldn't have a better captain to take care of him."

He looked at Kaela, who smiled at the stars.

"I'll do my best." He looked at the Tchoyasboy who still wore the guise of a Chussboy. Cracks, like those in wood, split his right cheek and branched out. Dried blood covered his face and sealed the cracks.

The Eurythrin remained at the Tchoyasboy's side with hands on his chest. Phenmir laid a hand on one of her's. He felt the slow and shaky rhythm of the boy's breathing. "How is he?"

"Weak."

Phenmir chuckled, though it came out nervous and almost sorrowful. "I can tell."

"Everything is flowing as it should. I had to reroute some of the bleeding in his head near the brain and eyes. I'm not sure I saved the left eye, but the right one is fine. Do you need me to check anything else?"

"As long as his brain is undamaged, he should hold. You'll have to stay close to him to make sure that he heals."

"I planned on it," she said.

"Any signs of consciousness?"

"Do you want me to wake him up?"

"No, he needs the rest."

"It's not like I'm going to slap him or shake him."

He furrowed his brow.

"I forget how used to Endowed you adults are. They can control blood, some have control over a few other parts of the body, but natural born Endowers have much more. I can't make him dream or say something, if that is what you wanted, but I can wake him up for a moment. Trust me, it won't hurt his healing."

Phenmir nodded. "Just for a second, even if he doesn't remember it."

She flexed some of her fingers on his chest and the Tchoyasboy opened his right eye. He groaned.

"What is your name?" Phenmir asked.

The boy moaned and tears slid down his cheeks.

"You're safe. Lose the Chuss mask and let your own face show. You need to conserve energy."

The boy continued to groan. Phenmir repeated himself three times until the Tchoyasboy's mask showed.

The skin of a Chussboy faded into a cracked wooden mask shaped like a ghete cub.

Phenmir smiled despite the blood that had seeped through the mask's cracks. "Let him sleep again."

The moaning ceased as the Eurythrin flexed and relaxed her fingers again.

"Thank you," Phenmir whispered. He stood and waved for the others to come near. "We'll spend the night here. Take the time to rest well. We'll leave in the morning."

Chatter arose amidst the company as they prepared to rest. Some ventured out to pluck brush and large leaves for padding against the ground. Despite their hardships, they were still city Chussmen.

Kaela approached him.

"Did you see him yet?" Phenmir asked.

She nodded. "I knew him. His name is Fenk. He's a quiet one. Not the kind who would ever expect to betray his friends."

"They said the Krall held his family. Family means much more than friendship."

"To those that have one."

"And you don't?" He regretted his blunt tone as the unthoughtful words fell out.

She was silent for a moment. "Most of those who are a part of Voln's circle do not. Do you think so many parents would allow their children to roam free?"

Thoughts of worried parents had visited him often on their journey, but he tried to banish them. The emotional cost of war is easier to bear in ignorance. The parents had sent their children with him, trusting that they would be unharmed as they merely helped serve the armies who would preserve the proliferation of Endowers.

I'll have to face Chenn's father. May he be the only bereaved parent when we return.

"May I ask–"

"Of course you can, Phenmir. You've become as much a father to me."

He admired that she still called him by his name and not his title in intimate moments. "What happened to your parents and the parents of the others?"

"Not all are the same, but they are similar enough. Voln's story is different. You'll have to ask him about that yourself. My parents thought I was a freak, a monster. Seeing the war that has now come, they were right. They gave me to the Krall after Voln started to gather others like us. The Krall gave the authority, but it was Voln who welcomed us. Some were orphans, but most wanted a way to rid themselves of conflict. Tchoyasmen are not as loyal to their kin as you would expect. They live their Ideal with a flawed aim. They saw giving us to the Krall as the best form of loyalty. Most of our parents abandoned us at birth, but I was older when my parents gave me up."

Phenmir felt nauseous. Equal with Meira, Hir was everything to him. Hir was the reason he fought for the children of others. One need not be a Chussman to realize the crime done against love for these children.

"I'm sorry."

She nodded. "Like I said, I'm better off with you."

He reached for her hand and stroked it with his. Some of the Tchoyasboy's blood flaked off as he did so. "Until the end of this war and beyond, you will always have a place with me."

"Then let's make it to the end."

The company rose the next day and left with few words spoken. Rest would not come until they reached the Middlemen. Reliant upon hope for the crop people's mercy, the company hobbled south, each guard taking a turn carrying the recovering Tchoyasboy.

CHAPTER TWENTY-NINE

THE NATURE OF THE PATRIARCHY

H ir woke to a throbbing thigh and his heart pounding as if he had awakened from a dream of an endless fall. He sat up to find himself still living his nightmare. The fallen fiend had gone stiff at his side.

He stood, though the pain in his thigh felt like it had been scorched by hours under the sun.

No one was there to heal him. No one congratulated him on his victory over the beast. Once he came to his faculties, pushing himself through the unrelenting pain and fatigue, he swam across the cavern's pond to find a small bronze tablet on the floor near the back of the room. The Scholar's tongue had been written out with a nonsensical line, but a translation had been inscribed below.

Conquerors the Patriarchy rose, rulers they shall remain.

He swam back across the water and limped through the tunnels and out into the desert. Despite his struggles, he was confident in his findings.

Cryptic, yet an assurance true to their character.

It is finished.

He used the staff to carry him along the trail back to Sliin. He would return a victor–a Scholar in the Patriarchy–or a fool for misinterpreting the entire Crucible of Dunes.

No one congratulated him as he entered the desert under the night sky. No one came out of hiding to provide him with food or drink. He felt abandoned and worried that he would feel the same when he returned to the Chapterhouse. Only Scholar Sokov had made him feel welcome, yet Hir knew that the man would still be in Fayis for his gathering of higher Scholars.

Dust filled his nostrils as he dragged his weak leg across the fine sand. The pain became more tolerable as he walked onward, yet it ever remained. In this moment, his tenacity and stubborn pride were the only forces keeping him on the path to Scholarhood.

Is it over, or is this merely the beginning?

<hr />

The sun had reached its midday point by the time he arrived in Sliin. He did not feel that his Crucible had placed him so far into the desert, but his returning journey felt eternal.

He passed through a residential district and was given a camel steak and water by the first Chussman who saw him. Hir was not the type to beg or bother others for aid, but he found himself without a choice, as hunger compelled him forward.

The Chussman sat across from him at a wooden table with more dents than a tavern bar. He took a pull from a glass of pale mead, which Hir had refused in place of pinefruit juice. The blue citrus stung his cracked tongue, but breathed energy back into him.

"You've had some time to eat. Now, why don't you tell me what you were doing out there alone on the dunes?"

Hir almost choked on the meat. He spent little time chewing, and the steak was overcooked. The smokey flavor and pepper flakes helped compensate for the meat's poor quality. He took a sip from his drink to wash away the pepper burning on his tongue, though it still lingered. "Camping."

"Perd, you cannot be that poor a camper to end up like this. Your tattered clothes are too expensive looking for a beggar's style. Come on now, boy, I'm just trying to help."

Hir shook his head and stuffed his meat into his cheek with his tongue to speak. "I don't need anything. This is enough."

The man shook his head and took another drink. "Don't make me an improper Chussman. I can't let you roam the streets like that."

Hir stood and finished his juice to wash the rest of his steak down. "I can pay you back for this."

"You're making this difficult, aren't you?"

The man stood.

"I should be leaving."

"You can't! I can see the blood seeping through your pants!"

"Do you have a wife? Maybe she could help."

"Just a moment." The man ran into a room down the hall.

Hir limped as fast as he could towards the door and left the house with it still open. He hobbled down the street and sat in an alley, taking a moment to breathe as his food settled. He couldn't risk more questions. After the trial, he wasn't sure what he could say. The Patriarchy was quiet enough about their dealings. He had never heard of the Crucible of Dunes until they sent him out to complete it. The less he said, the safer he would be. After nearly perishing on his first true assignment in the Patriarchy, he understood how well earned the Patriarchy's fearful presence was.

His stomach was painfully bloated. He felt nauseous, yet it caused him to smile.

He was away from immediate danger and well fed. That was enough.

Hir left to roam the streets after what felt like fifteen minutes had passed. The surroundings felt familiar and became more recognizable as he ventured towards the city center. His home, now that he was a brother of the Patriarchy it had become his merely his parents' home, was not far. His mother would appreciate the visit. He could rest. Concern would dissipate in the comfort of someone who actually cared about him.

Despite his longing, he could not return. Home visits had been denied by the Patriarchy unless they granted explicit allowance. Every emotion within him called for him to abandon their rules. Family was the most important thing in life, was it not? Once again, stubborn pride and an underlying sense of duty trampled his inner longings. The Crucible was finished. Whether he had succeeded was to be determined by the Patriarchy.

Reason told him to abandon his childhood dream. How blind he had been to pursue such a path. How naïve he had been to wish for the life of a zealous Scholar. Against all, he remained. His journey had begun and would end with success, whatever that entailed.

Hir limped onward towards the Chapterhouse, ignoring the solace of his childhood home.

Court Chuss lived for charity and love, but these were not tenants of the Patriarchy of Scholars. Despite his disheveled appearance that called for aid, he was ignored by most as he entered the Chapterhouse. No congratulations came. All passing Scholars kept to their own duties.

Have they all experienced this? Is their ignorance a ruse to teach me some principle or perseverance?

Hir shook his head, once again banishing self-pity, and descended to the Chapterhouse's lower level.

As he had feared, Scholar Sokov was still absent.

"Hir! It is great to see you back, brother."

Hir turned to see his preceptor, Dumek, who spoke to him with an unforeseen joviality. He wondered if this was the first time he recognized him as anything other than a worthless lackey, let alone a brother.

Have I earned such a title? Does he know if I've succeeded? How would he? How would anyone?

"You returned earlier than expected. Well done! Noting Scholar Sokov's absence and the occupation of the higher Scholars, *I* have been designated to help you walk through becoming an Accepted Scholar."

Hir felt his world turned upon itself once again. "What are the Scholars doing? Is it the war? What has happened since I left?"

"Look at you! You are by no means ready for your acceptance ceremony." He started to walk away and waved. "Come, we'll have you washed and clothed in appropriate wear. You deserve the change for... how long was it? Three days? A week?"

"I–"

"Long enough," Dumek chuckled. "I'll show you to your new quarters. No need to dwell amongst the lowly apprentices anymore."

Hir should have been thrilled by the promotion, yet his mind forced forward the worries of what he had experienced during his Crucible.

They ascended to another floor, one higher than his previous room. He was delighted that even though his room was the same size, it was no longer shared between him and another apprentice Scholar. The inside was well lit, no longer by a dim candle, but by a tall window made of a light blue glass. It made him feel as if he would live underwater, which he was yet to determine if he enjoyed, but it was a welcome change.

Dumek opened a door inside the room, which Hir had thought was a closet, to reveal a bath chamber.

"No more common bath chambers. The first of many improve-ments."

Hir would have agreed if he was not met by two bald men with skeletal complexions near the steaming basin. Each wore a tight robe, held together in the center by a black belt.

Dumek peeked his head around to look at Hir's unsteady glare. "Is this your first time with the Patriarchy's Fools? Don't take that to be an insult. I was not the one who gave them the title."

"They aren't Scholars?"

"By Cheric, not at all!" Dumek walked forward and slapped one of them on the back. The Fool did not make any redaction besides a controlled wince. "Now that you are to become a brother, a *true* Scholar, you will meet plenty of the Fools in our service. Don't shy away from them when they bathe you. I understand you are not used to it yet but think of them as nothing more than statues. These eunuchs have just as much emotion as stone."

Hir found it impossible to hide his discomfort. He almost missed the privacy of the barren dunes. "Can I not bathe myself?"

"No. You're not familiar with the ceremonial washing process."

"So I have to do this 'ceremonial washing' every time I bathe?"

"No, only for certain occasions." Dumek walked through the doorway and grabbed the handle. "Don't expect to have all your questions answered. Such is the way of the Patriarchy. Always questioning, always learning. They'll escort you to your Acceptance after you finish." Dumek placed his hands in a circle over his chest to salute and closed the door.

"Enter the basin," one of the Fools spoke.

Hir removed his clothing with his gaze focused on the floor. Once naked, he entered the basin and submerged himself in the warm water. He sighed as his head rose above the water. He remained with the water at his neckline.

One of the Fools lifted a blue glass bottle and leaned towards Hir.

He lifted his hands up. "Wait, can I have a moment to relax?"

The Fool nodded and moved back a few paces.

Finally, ignoring the probing stares of the Fools, Hir felt comfortable. He was warm, satiated, and away from immediate danger. The latter aspect of his comfort felt fleeting, but he banished all to relish in the small gift he had from Cheric. It was a relief to see Dumek's apparent respect for the Chuss god. He was not surprised to have learned that many of the higher Scholars treated the Patriarchy as their own god. Others too easily forgot that the Patriarchy bound the Courts and was not a Court itself. Hir committed early in his life to follow Cheric and would allow nothing to change that. *Even if it means departing the Patriarchy in pursuit of my faith.*

The Fool approached him with the same bottle. Hir complied and sat up, letting the water rest near his abdomen.

Whatever would come seemed requisite to his complete Acceptance. He complied and felt cold liquid drain down from his head.

"Oil, with which you are made wise," the Fool spoke as he finished pouring the bottle on Hir's head.

"Cleanse," said the other in a dry tone as he dumped three cups of water on Hir.

The first Fool took another bottle and poured it on Hir's head.

Hir ran his fingers through his tight silver curls. It felt as sticky and viscous as honey.

"Leave it be," said the second Fool.

The first Fool finished pouring the substance, which now reached Hir's shoulders in its slow drip.

"Sap of the lords, with which you are made mighty."

"Wash."

The first Scholar poured another substance, though this one was red and fell from a large goblet.

"Solemn wine, with which you are raised above the foolish."

"Submerge."

Hir looked up at the second Scholar, who ducked his head. He nodded and followed the Fool's prompting, sinking below the tepid water and trying to remove anything that stuck to his hair or body.

The Fools grabbed his arms and lifted him to stand in the basin. They poured cups of fresh water on him until it ran clear.

A Fool grabbed Hir's arm to help him leave the basin. The other approached him from behind with white clothes rimmed in bronze. He helped Hir put on similar pants and brown sandals while the other removed a decedent white robe with bronze embroidery from a closet.

Hir was surprised to find how light it was as he adjusted the robe on his shoulders. He ruffled his hair but found the tight curls smooth and dry as if he had never been washed with sap.

"Are you ready?" one asked.

Hir nodded and followed them from the room.

They accompanied him to two wooden doors twice his size and left without further explanation.

Hir pressed the doors open and entered the grand hall of the Chapterhouse.

As anticipated, Dumek stood at the end of the hall upon a dais that rose three steps. Dumek had changed into similar robes, though with red embroidery winding throughout the fabric.

The company was underwhelming, including only two other Scholars, one standing below Dumek on each side of the procession. They wore the white Scholar's robes but were at least ten years older than him.

Hir's heart froze as he noticed that one wore a bronze circlet around his forehead and the other wore two smaller circlets around his wrists. Scholar Sokov's warnings of the Bronze Seers returned to him. He wished for his mentor's presence like a frightened child.

Are they trying to recruit me? Is this an induction into their order?

Regardless of their intentions, he was a victim of the Patriarchy's secrets. Evil or benevolent, he knew not what they would turn him into.

He stopped in line with the Seer Scholars and knelt on the red carpet that led to Dumek. Fear perpetuated, but he was somewhat relieved that he could not find any *visible* bronze on Dumek.

"Rise," said his preceptor. "You are one of us now and shall stand with us."

His legs felt weaker as he stood. He clenched his fists to still them.

"While this is a formal ceremony," said Dumek, "it does not mean that you must be so stern. The higher Scholars are away, Hir. Intimacy takes priority here. Speaking of which, tell us, how does it feel to have completed your Crucible? Let it be known that the Patriarchy believes the Crucible of the Dunes to be one of the most difficult Crucibles in Facet, second only to Court Gruth's Crucible of the Reef."

"How are you sure... how am I sure that I have completed it?" *Am I saying this to prove some failure? To find some escape? Perd me, what happened to my confidence? Has the Patriarchy succeeded   in making me a servant?*

"Your tattered clothing and leg injury, among others, seemed evidence enough that you did more than merely survive the desert. Sure, there are plenty of vicious beasts out in the desert, but very few leave the marks that you have on your thigh. Were you unable to defeat it? I've never known any who fail their trial before reaching the final goal and return so... lively."

I feel anything but. "I defeated it—yes, I was sure to do... that."

"As I expected." Dumek smiled.

"But what was it?"

Dumek stepped closer. "It is the reason you are here." He stepped towards one of the Seer Scholars. "Show him the scroll."

The Scholar removed a scroll from inside his robe and unfurled it for Hir.

Dumek stepped forward to stand beside Hir and pointed to the scroll. "Do these look familiar?"

Hir nodded. The scroll bore illustrations similar to those he had seen in the cave. The caricatures of the screaming creature and personages were much clearer and surrounded by written in illegible, yet beautiful calligraphy..

Dumek pointed to the creature that he took to be the fiend from the Crucible. "And this?"

"The end of the Crucible."

"Exactly. This is a record of what those *beings* are and what they represent. Do not expect to understand everything. This is but another step on your path to understand the very core of the Patriarchy of Scholars. Though we bind Courts through Scholarship and diplomacy, *this* is the Patriarchy's essence."

Dumek motioned for the Seer to take the scroll away and returned to his spot on the dais. "Adorned in the robes of a Scholar and anointed by the sap of lords, you have ascended beyond apprenticeship." He moved to the back of the dais and sat upon a decadent padded chair of red leather on golden wood.

The Seer Scholar to Hir's left stepped forward. "Your knowledge of harvesting is limited, but you must know this much: it began with the Patriarchy. Since the year of manifest, the Patriarchy has worked towards wielding this power."

Dumek chuckled, noticing Hir's astonishment. "Do not worry, Hir, this is merely a piece of history. We Chussmen still oppose harvesting."

The Seer nodded. "Nevertheless, you must recognize that this process originated within the Patriarchy. While our people do not condone harvesting, we show our reverence for this ability by respecting the Endowers."

Does the harvesting debate divide the Patriarchy as well? Is this the cause of the Seers rising? Are they the harvesting advocates within the anti-harvesting Courts?

Dumek spoke again. "Do not try to ask every question you think of. You do not need to understand as much as you wish. All you need to understand now is that the Patriarchy is tied to the organ abilities."

Hir nodded, though questions continued to bombard him.

The first Seer Scholar stepped back, and the other stepped forward.

"With this knowledge comes the significance of your trial. You finished the beast at the end of your Crucible. You survived and conquered an organ fiend. Your journey symbolizes the Patriarchy's dominance over the powers of nature, those powers that grant us with these abilities. These beings are the offspring of our failures. In becoming the greatest roots in the world's garden, we hone the powers of nature in the organs of our people."

"As you are a conqueror, so are we," said Dumek. "We are to rule beyond the dictates of Krall's and Thanes. You have begun your path. Knowledge is dominance. Scholarhood is might."

Hir nodded. *Are these the purposes of the Patriarchy or the Seers?*

CHAPTER THIRTY

CLEANSING THE VESSEL

Runith grimaced as he bit into a thick orange vegetable, reminiscent of a potato with a taste more like squash. The Rasteen stared at him as they sat across him on the floor of a hut just beyond the village boundaries.

"*Is the food to your liking?*" asked Gasp.

"*I think it would be better cooked,*" replied Runith. He reached for a basket containing leaves the size of his hand and just as thick. "*These are good enough for now.*"

Some Endowers continued to wear away at the potato squash, many unable to eat the thick cuts through their masks. Golma followed Runith, switching to the leaves whose taste reminded him of a savory watermelon with a hint of rosemary.

The Rasteen had been kind enough to offer a wide variety of semi-edible plants, though few had been worth the effort of eating. The large leaves were growing on Runith, though they did not keep him satiated for more than an hour.. So far, he had been unsuccessful in finding anything that resembled nuts or beans.

He still was unprepared to become their supposed harbinger, yet he felt comfortable enough in their midst. The respiration speaking felt nearly as comfortable as his natural tongue.

"*Are you prepared for the ritual, beast man?*" asked another Rasteen whose name resembled a wheeze.

They were well aware of his reluctance, yet still insisted on his participation in their "Binding of Roots" to save their lost lord. All he hoped was to avoid disappointing them, as he had surely disappointed his Court and Royss.

My participation means nothing. It's only a show of respect, not acceptance. "Are the children allowed to join me?"

"*Their reverence to the Korenod would be appreciated.*"

Runith nodded. While the Branch of the North and her associates referred to their lost leader as their Lord, most Rasteen referred to him as the "Korenod," a title whose meaning was unclear.

"*All right, shall we begin?*"

The Rasteen shook their heads.

"*This is no place of respect,*" breathed Gasp. "*We must first lead you to a temple.*"

The Rasteen stood with simultaneous focus and departed. Runith waved for the Endowers to follow as he made haste to keep up with the Rasteen. His knees ached and beds of leaves were poor substitutes for even the humble beds they had at the loyalist camp.

The village Rasteen had grown used to their presence. Even the Rasteen who had never seen them, paid no heed to their presence. Their gradual accommodation caused Runith to wonder if they held councils without his knowledge or if they had some system of communication.

Lele hopped alongside the group, having waited for them in a small pond while they ate.

"How's your skin?" Runith asked her.

"Better than it has been. Resting in the ponds while you have all of your gatherings has been convenient."

If only I could rest. He held his complaints back, knowing they would serve no one. With the children reliant on his confidence and the Rasteen unable to understand his humor, Runith felt himself quieter. Feelings high and low were often kept to himself. He would occasionally express his feelings to Lele, but didn't care much. Her focus was on survival, not the emotions that caused Runith's mood to change.

Golma walked beside him and smiled through her hawk's beak.

Strong for her. Strong for the Children. A deeper voice whispered within. *For all of them. All of the Endowers. Strength and justice for everyone like Golma.* His stomach felt uneasy as he recalled his duties to Royss. He knew he would have to return to Royss and the loyalists, yet those responsibilities felt so distant out in the Middlelands. His mind warred between his duties to his people and those who he had come to know as his people. The Endowers revered him like a father. Having heard from Golma that so many had lost touch with their parents when they joined their leader, Voln, Runith appreciated their trust even more.

Are you going to betray that trust, Runith?

After a few minutes of walking beyond the village, they reached a large clearing surrounded by a wall of trees, each one as wide as ten people. A holy castle sat in its center.

Unlike what one would assume by his outspoken personality, Runith counted himself as one of the more pious Zhaesmen in his inner circle, or what had been his inner circle. Despite his bias towards buildings dedicated to Laeih, the Rasteen temple made the Zhaes cathedrals and temples look like a cold and soulless institution.

As it was with the other buildings in the Rasteen village, the temple felt alive. It was shaped like a large bulb, with multiple stems rising to more bulbs and spires. Leaves created staircases with thin balusters, roofs, and all other decor in a variety of green, red, and yellow hues. Clear membranes made large windows, though these were more translucent than the others throughout the village.

Gasp led the company to doors that curled open with no action on their part.

Runith was once again astounded by the inner decor. Large roots throughout the room twisted in the shapes of Rasteen statues, some sprouted crowns of leaves and other flowers across their bodies. Stairways of leaf and vine twisted upward and led into a variety of hallways. Instead of paintings of past saints, tapestries of colorful moss grew on the green walls depicting unknown histories that he wished to explore. It was easy to see the novelty of the Rasteen and forget that they, too, had existed throughout human history. Runith longed for a knowledge that would remain beyond his reach. He wondered what pieces of their knowledge he would be granted if he dared complete their "Binding of Roots."

Gasp and the other Rasteen stopped before a twisting stalk in the middle of the grand chamber. It rose up to Runith's waist and had a white basin in its center that seemed to be made of the same marble-like substance as the Rasteen faces.

Few others occupied the temple, ten to Runith's estimate. Each one kept to themselves, some breathed what he thought to be prayers. One noted their entrance and came from the back wall to meet them with a basket in hand.

He, for Runith thought it was a male, noting its absence of flowers, handed a spherical white object to each member of the party. As he received his own, Runith noticed it was very much like the fruit had seen the Rasteen harvesting from the field upon their first arrival.

"*Do not eat it,*" Wheeze warned an Endower who tried to take a bite. "*Beast man, gather with the children around the basin.*"

He nodded and stepped up to peer into the basin. Rather than water, as he had expected, a dark honey-colored substance filled half of the basin.

Gasp stared at Runith. "*Are you prepared?*"

"*What is this?*" He toned back the harshness of his breathing, hoping not to offend.

"*We cannot–*" breathed Wheeze before he was interrupted by Gasp.

"*While the finer details are to be understood by one's inner roots and worship as they ascend, we can offer but the smallest explanation. I do so lightly, for this is of the most sacred nature.*"

He set aside his questions and listened to Gasp continue, knowing whatever he might experience, it could be no worse than the mighty beasts he had tamed in the past.

"*This is done in reverence for the Korenod.*"

"*Lord of the vineyards,*" the other Rasteen breathed in a forceful whisper.

Gasp continued. "*Though she has been taken by the prideful, we shall see her triumphant return. Though she is not among us in body, she bonds us internally. She has endowed us and shall continue to be our strength. In this, we become one*"

The sacredness of this figure felt distinct following Gasp's words. He wondered if this capture was more symbolic, as if humankind had done some unforgivable sacrilege to the Rasteen that had caused their division. Runith never took an interest in the history of Facet prior to the founding of Courts, but he was struck with a newfound interest. Perhaps the Rasteen and humans had been closer in eras past.

He decided it was best to ignore the influx of questions, knowing they would only continue to obscure his focus. His understanding of his own religion had been gradual. It would be the same with the Rasteen beliefs, perhaps slower because of the cultural rift.

The Rasteen nearest the children nudged them closer to the basin, which lowered itself to their height as the stalk retracted into the floor.

"Follow our actions and promptings. Speak no questions lest you disturb the Cleansing Promise."

"I thought this was the Binding of Roots?" an Endower asked.

Runith's heart dropped at the child's irreverence, but only one Rasteen reacted with a quiet reply.

"That is yet to come. The Cleansing Promise is but a requisite step on the road to the Binding."

The Rasteen passed small wooden cups around for each member of the circle.

"Drink some, but not all," Gasp breathed and did as he said.

Runith had never seen the Rasteen drink or eat anything until this moment. Their throats did not move to swallow, as if the absorption was immediate.

"Dip."

They followed Gasp's lead and dipped two fingers into the basin, scooping some of the viscous substance and placing it in their mouths.

Runith was the last to touch the substance to his tongue as he stared at the Rasteen's fingers. They had the same joints as humans, with five on each hand. Even the bending of their vine-fingers seemed to suggest a tendon underneath the outer plant layers.

Gasp stared at him and the others followed until he finished sucking the substance from his fingers. It was indeed reminiscent of honey, though less sweet and with a taste of pine. *"Is this sap?"*

"Sap of the Korenod, through which we taste of her might and mercy."

Literally or symbolically? Runith kept his question to himself and followed the others as Gasp called for them to take another drink of the water in their cups. It carried a similar aftertaste to the sap, though with a hint of salt.

The Rasteen raised their fruits in the air. Sunlight from the membranous windows reflected off of the white spheres, making them appear as holy orbs in the temple. *"Press."*

The Rasteen lowered their hands and held the fruit over their cups. They moved the cups and fruit above the basin and clenched the fruits in their hands, draining a vibrant red juice into the cups with the excess drops falling into the sap basin.

Runith managed to squeeze a few drops, but relied upon the Rasteen to help him and the other Endowers complete the process.

"Juice of the wise, for the Korenod grants us wisdom and truth." Gasp drank the juice as he had the water. All followed. Runith was happy to wash away the piney aftertaste and the thick lining the sap had left on the inside of his mouth. The juice was greater than any he had ever tasted. It was as sour as an orange, but sweeter than any dessert. As a Zhaesman, he had never tasted something so strong in flavor and would have turned it away, but the sweetness was not overwhelming as he had expected. He drained the cup, longing for more, though everyone else had finished theirs. He understood that this was a spiritual practice for the Rasteen, but it was greater than any feast.

Wheeze left the circle and approached Runith, though the other Rasteen remained focused on the basin. *"Beast man, how do you feel?"*

"Like I'm burning inside, but... it's a good burn. Warmth. Joy. By Laeih, better than I have ever felt." Childhood safety. His first success as a Beastling. Love without loss. Every pleasurable feeding was small in comparison. *"What is this? What happened?"*

"You will understand."

Runith blinked. His ears felt open. His mind was opened. He felt an unexplainable connection to the Rasteen. Their language was clearer than it had ever been. He understood more than the breathing, but their souls.

"It will become weaker with time. For this reason, we must continue to refresh our connection with each other, with the Korenod."

Runith was pleased to hear that he could re-experience what had already begun to dissipate, though he worried about the implications. *Surely this is not blasphemous, is it? Is this Korenod a false idol?* All intuition led him to believe that this was a distraction from worshiping Laeih, yet he felt so pulled by the Cleansing Promise. He wanted to forsake all to achieve it once again. *Laeih guide my choices, guide my weaknesses should I fall to temptation.*

A Rasteen with small red flowers covering her body approached Runith. Her eyes were wide with slight worry. Her breathing was still and peaceful. *"I see that you worry about the worship of one god over another."*

He was stunned as he recalled that the red flowers indicated their equivalent of Feelmen. She made his deepest concerns bare, those he would have never spoken to a Rasteen. He nodded, knowing that there was nothing he could hold back.

"Do not fret. You do not forsake your god by aiding the Korenod, for the gods of the land labor in union."

He scowled, somewhat relieved that he was not a blasphemer, but no closer to his answer.

"All benefit by seeking the Korenod. For this reason, we plead for your cooperation, should you become the harbinger of the Era of Unity. You see more than others, beyond the blindness of others. Your closeness to your god brings you closer to the Korenod."

Runith nodded and felt himself retreat from the conversation. He looked for Golma while the Rasteen Feelman continued to stare at him, pensive eyes read the thoughts he dared not let surface.

"*Remain as such, beast man. Becoming a blind spirit is too common among your kind.*"

Runith pressed forward, not responding to the Rasteen, yet he held to her words.

Golma left the circle and breathed to a wall. The leafy membrane pulsed and moved as she commanded a hole to appear and close.

"What are you doing?" Runith asked. He changed to the Rasteen language, thinking that he would rather not have them believe he was keeping secrets. "*Be careful. I don't want this place ruined.*"

"*Since when have you been the respectful type?*" she replied. She commanded the wall to open a hole twice as big as the previous one.

"*Please, Golma–*"

"*Don't you see, Runith? I'm a Beastling, but I can* speak to plants!"

"*I don't care what you Endowers can do that I cannot. I get it, you're better than me.*"

She chuckled and stepped away from the wall. "*No, it's not like that. I could never do this before. Don't you feel differently after their ritual?*

"*Yes.*"

"*Have you tried to speak to plants?*"

He laughed. "*Why would I try that?*"

"*Because!*" She moved the wall again. Some of the Rasteen noticed her, but their gazes did not linger. "*And it's not only me. The others said that they felt stronger, smarter, like they could see with more eyes than they had.*"

A terrifying scream caused them to turn their attention away from the wall. Thren, the Tchoyasboy foreteller, screamed through his mantis mask. He fell to his knees and pulled at his hair.

Runith ran to his side and crouched while the others, including the Rasteen, watched with frozen fear.

"Hey, hey." He turned the boy's face towards his and tried to speak in a calm and collected tone. Memories too familiar passed through his mind of consoling beasts as they perished to unmendable wounds. "Look at me."

The boy had calmed his cries, but still whimpered. His eyes that had rolled back now showed constricted pupils, though they were yet to focus on Runith.

Runith felt the surge of power that Golma had mentioned. He felt compelled to channel it towards Thren. "*Calm down.*" He spoke, though it felt like another tongue.

Thren's breathing stilled and his eyes focused on Runith, who was now holding him like a parent consoling their child after a nightmare.

"Heloath." Runith smiled and gave a relieved laugh. "Welcome back. Are you here with me?"

Thren nodded, reaching his fingers into his mask holes to wipe away tears.

"Can you tell me what happened?"

The boy remained silent for a few seconds before speaking. "I saw them, but also felt what they wanted to do. They did not have nice thoughts. They want to hurt us... and the Rasteen. They're coming."

Relief fled once again. "What do you mean?" Runith returned to the Rasteen language. "*Who is coming?*"

"*The bad Krall.*"

"*Krall Trhet?*"

Thren nodded. "*He's coming with your Thanes. Royss and the Scholar Gromm.*"

"*You know them?*"

"*No, but I do now. The visions have shown me who they are. Bad men, especially the Scholar.*"

"*What are they doing?*" Golma knelt beside Runith and clung to him.

"*I don't know. I can't see that much, but they are with the others here in the Middlelands.*"

"*The base camp?*"

"Yes. Bad things are happening in the Courts and they want to... use us... or the Rasteen... I don't know." Thren started to cry again. *"I don't know."*

Runith pulled him in tighter. *"It's okay. I'm here. I won't let them hurt us."* He and Golma caressed the Foreteller's messy hair. It was greasy and tangled. These were children, yet Runith had grown so used to working with the oldest among them. Thren felt like a child. He spoke and acted like one.

This is what they are fighting for.

Perd me, Laeih. What have I become? What have we done?

"Might we assist?" Gasp approached and extended the vine from his finger to touch Thren. It was an odd gesture, yet the intention seemed welcomed by the boy. He gripped it as would a babe its mother's finger.

"We need to speak with the Branch," breathed Runith.

"Their people threaten ours!" Wheeze breathed with a powerful gust. *"The beast man is no harbinger! He repeats the treachery of his predecessors!"*

"No!" Runith breathed with the same power that had calmed Thren. *"We will not leave you! Take me to the Branch."*

Until this moment, he had never seen the Rasteen anxious. The leaves and vines that made up their bodies twisted as if blown by a forceful wind.

The red-flowered Rasteen that had read his theological crisis stared at Golma. Her flowers opened wide. *"The beast man is right to be concerned. His desires indeed remain in line with ours. Come, Vibrations, the Branch will see you now."*

❧❧❧❧ ❧❧❧❧

The village was calm as dusk fell. Fireflies and luminescent buds on buildings gave a peaceful light to the otherwise anxious company.

Runith did not hear Thren shout the first few times as he paced headstrong towards the Rasteen palace.

"Runith!" Golma pulled on his coat until he stopped.

"What now?"

He turned to see a company of figures obscured in the dim light, approaching from the open plains to his right. *From the north.* "*Perd, they're here!*"

The Rasteen fell into stances with wide legs. Staffs, leaf blades, thorned maces, and all manners of plant weapons grew from their arms. Some sprouted shields of thick oak and moved towards the front of the company.

Runith's fright almost dissipated in awe of their unforeseen defense. He grabbed Golma and pulled her behind him. Without a weapon to bear, he had only his body to protect against the oncoming assailants if the Rasteen failed to stand.

"*Forward steady!*" Wheeze hissed in a forceful breath. He led the company as one of the bark-shield bearers along with four others.

Runith stood higher than all of them and peered at the incomers. They showed no sign of attack, rather, they condensed and slowed their approach.

The Rasteen shield-bearers continued to press onward. Branch spears stood out through the cracks between them.

The unknown company peddled back.

"*Charge them before they escape!*" Wheeze commanded. He seemed the most dominant among the Rasteen, yet Runith did not expect him to demand an attack.

The frontline Rasteen charged while Runith remained behind with the Endowers and two armed Rasteen.

Shouts came from the company. They turned to retreat, though one of the smaller members of their group stood their ground. The charging

Rasteen came to an abrupt halt right before colliding with the lone opposer.

Runith walked forward and beckoned the Endowers to remain in place.

"*What is happening?*" he called out.

No answer came, though he heard faint breathing from the Rasteen. Runith ran towards them, seeing that the Rasteen had retracted their blades and shields.

The opposing company returned to their position and approached the Rasteen. As Runith neared them, he could see that the company comprised a few adults and many Children, all of which were Chussmen except for a masked child.

"Kaela!"

Runith turned his head as Golma ran past him to meet the Tchoyas child among the others.

Runith jogged towards the group and was passed by many of his Endower followers as he did so.

"Golma!" He pressed through the Rasteen, who had moved to block his view.

He saw her standing among the Chuss children who spoke with the Rasteen. A company of Endowers had arrived, though he wondered why there was only a single Tchoyas child. *Where is the Krall?*

"Royss?" he shouted, though no answer came. He doubted the Thane could commit so many Chussmen to his cause. *You Perding fool. These are not our people. The enemy–the others–have found us.*

Golma embraced a Tchoyasgirl with the mask of a hawk.

The Endowers' allies. The so-called Harmony Allegiant. Perd me. I no longer have a choice, do I? Is this what you want from me, Laeih?

Runith broke from his reverie as a Chussman approached him. He had silver dreads, as did most of Chussmen his age, though the man was dressed like a captain with tattered clothes after a long-fought journey.

CHAPTER THIRTY-ONE

WIND AND DAGGER

The time spent in the city amidst Pinnacles was cold, even frigid, but paled compared to the mountains themselves. Aerhee's fingers were numb and her face burned. Despite the pain of the journey, Voln's complaints seemed to be about everything except for the temperature.

The young wolf of the Tchoyasman shifted his skin to fulfill his namesake. He walked on two legs and kept his human head but had changed the skin beneath his clothing to that of a direwolf's pelt. The clothing that they had found for him in the Pinnacles puffed out with the compressed fur underneath.

"How much longer do we have to walk?" groaned Voln.

Zeir, who walked a few paces before them, turned back and pulled down his scarf to speak. "No more than a day. The Priess border is near the base of the mountain. Unin is just beyond it. The town is filled with hunters who frequent the mountain, so it—"

"I don't care. Why couldn't we have taken a carriage the whole way? The carriage drivers don't need an explanation of where we are going to drive us."

"Look at the ground, Voln," said Aerhee.

"Looks solid enough to me."

"Did you ever think about the rocks we've had to climb?" she asked. "The thin trails that move back and forth up the steeper parts of the mountain?"

"If Zeir can do all of this, so can ghete."

"And the carriage wheels?"

Voln grumbled.

She laughed. Zeir paid them no attention and only heard them if they shouted due to the wind.

"Other than that," she whispered, "are you well? Do you feel–"

"I feel perding fantastic." the boy blurted with his face forward. His tone did not impress her.

"Voln, are–"

"I told you I don't want to talk about that, woman." Voln ran up to Zeir's side. She heard him say something about food.

They all slept together and held tight to keep warm under the humble shelter of branches they made each night. Zeir would lie behind her and she would keep Voln in her embrace. Would it not have been necessary, the boy would have refused, which he did initially. Though he muffled his sobs, she heard them each night as her head was pressed against his.

Aerhee was repulsed by how in tune she was with her emotions as of late. Emotions weaken. Emotions make one vulnerable. Yet, she could not deny her concern for the wolf boy.

She chose to support the Harmony Allegiant because it was the logical choice. It took imprisonment and the deaths around her for her to admit her erred thinking, but she finally felt comfortable as a member of the rebel union. No society should allow the massacre of children to perpetuate. She continued to argue for the logic of their plans, but each victory had been a miracle. Divine intervention was something she was growing to recognize as truth. Logic propelled her, but it was her hidden emotions that gave her reason. She worried Voln would continue to cause her emotions to surface. Regardless of her fears, she would not hold off from helping him. *Perd me. Whatever drove me to care for such a horrible child?* She knew "horrible" was an improper word. She insisted on thinking about it, but the boy was tender within.

With her thoughts clashing between stern logic and sound emotionality, she ran to walk beside Zeir and Voln. Solemnity reveals what one is otherwise unwilling to face. She abandoned such thoughts.

Whole is the Holy. Zhaes law. Do all in righteousness, let nothing waver against the frail feelings of the human mind.

Zeir turned to acknowledge her with a weak smile.

"Why are you in such a rush?" she asked.

"Are you serious, Aer? What reason is there *not* to rush?"

"I know–I just meant–you have been walking ahead of Voln and I since we left the carriage."

"Best to keep pace."

"We both know that I'm the one who usually keeps us moving. Since when have you been so anxious?"

"Aren't you concerned? What makes my diligence irrational?"

Her heart felt colder than her extremities. Her husband was growing distant. She would have blamed herself, but he had not left her in the past when she was sterner. She was still the same Zhaeswoman, but the recent happenings in Facet had reawakened her to her responsibilities as a wife. He did not prefer the emotionally blunt side of her. He reached intimacy more through subtle gestures.

Ever since the Pinnacles, since she had woken up late that night without him, she had noticed a hardening of his character.

She realized that she had forgotten to respond, lost in her reverie, but he took no note of her silence.

Voln dragged a stick through the snow opposite her. He was content enough. Despite her marital concerns, they were well for the time being. She cast aside her fears. He was safe for now. That was all that mattered.

✻✻✻✷ ✷✷✷✷

Aerhee woke up to the sound of a wolf growling. Voln was no longer in her embrace. She threw the few blankets they had off of her and wiped her eyes to see under the pale moonlight.

A direwolf faced away from her and barked into the darkness.

"Voln?"

"*Stay back*!" the wolf growled. He backpedaled towards her, though remained facing forward, ready to pounce.

"*Perd!*" Aerhee hissed under her breath, almost shrieking as a tall and thin humanoid ran through the trees. "What was that?"

Voln barked louder than before.

A growl came from the trees, opposite from whence the gaunt being had run.

A large brown bear, twice Voln's size, moved from out among the trees.

Aerhee gasped as Zeir embraced her from behind.

Voln altered the shape of his body to look more like a cross between the bear and a wolf. He growled towards the large bear, who then turned to focus its attention in the direction of the gaunt being.

Voln and the bear roared and moved closer to their target.

Aerhee felt for a blade but found no weapon to comfort her.

Zeir pulled her back, and she complied.

The gaunt being ran from the trees and jumped atop the bear like a dexterous imp. It raised its hands, long fingers–or claws, she could not tell–plunged into the back of the bear, who roared in agony.

The bear calmed and quieted, slowing its bucking. The creature sat atop it like an unholy jockey as it turned the bear to face them.

"Voln! Don't–" Aerhee's command fell flat as Voln reverted to his wolf form and charged.

She was unable to breathe as the meager wolf charged the bear twice with the rider on top.

Voln pounced higher than she thought possible and flew directly into the rider. His body slammed into the creature, his right arm moving with humanoid joints to grab the enemy, while the other paw turned into a single claw that found a hold in one of the bear's eyes and out the side of the head.

Using his claw in the bear's head to hold himself, he swung around like an adept journeyman, knocking the rider free and taking his place. He transformed his other arm into a long spike and slammed it through the top of the bear's head.

Voln jumped from the bear as it stumbled and ran into a tree. Now a hybrid between man and wolf, he ran towards the creature as it stood from its fall.

Aerhee turned back, noticed the shortsword in Zeir's hand, and took it as she ran towards Voln. *I don't care if you can handle this. I can't leave you alone.*

You cannot be alone. Not anymore.

You never will be. Never again.

The creature swung its claws at Voln, though he deflected their strikes with an arm that looked like a tortoise shell. His other arm, still shaped like a giant claw spike, stabbed below in the creature's berserk attacks into its stomach. Voln moved his arm as if punching with an uppercut, pressing his spiked hand up through the creature. His spike erupted through the creature's neck in an explosion of black gore.

Still holding onto the moments of life it had, it clawed at Voln, shredding deep gashes in his back.

Aerhee shed all caution and ran in with her blade. The flailing creature was too occupied with Voln to notice her as she ran and stabbed it up into its head. With the creature moving and standing a few heads taller than her, she could not push the blade through its skull but managed to bring its malevolent existence to an end.

Voln removed his arms from the creature and reverted to his natural Tchoyasboy shape. "Perd!" she shouted. He stood with his back against a tree and slid down, panting.

Aerhee let her sword drop along with the creature as she ran to him. She heard Zeir approach, but did not turn back.

"No," Voln grunted as she reached for him. He hissed as he tried to stand.

"What are you doing?" she shouted.

"Move, woman, I need to make sure the bear is taken care of."

"Stay," Zeir shouted.

She turned to see Zeir run after the sword and shake it free from the creature's head. Zeir ran to the bear, which moaned as it stirred. He stabbed it in the head repeatedly until it fell silent and still.

She turned back to Voln, who hissed as he touched his back, then looked to find blood on his hand.

"Zeir?" She looked at her husband. "Do you have anything for this? We need to hurry! He needs–"

"Enough," Voln grunted as he stood. "It stings perding bad, but I'll get over it."

"No, Voln, you need–"

He stopped and pointed at her with a bloody finger. "You need to listen to what I say! I know more about me than you. You think you know what I am because we spent a few days together? Nice perding chance. I've been through this before you decided you were *holy enough* to bow down and join us. Let's go."

"Wait a second," said Zeir, "I want to see what that thing was."

"Be my guest. I saw its ugly face when I killed it. You two can take care of it while I skin the bear. You two moan enough from the cold at night and could use an extra layer."

Zeir waved for Aerhee to follow him towards the creature's corpse.

She knew he was in pain. Pain aggravated him but his words still hurt. *Perding weakling.* She condemned herself. *Why don't you grow some thick skin?*

Still, to think that he wants to keep us warm... I think we might see more of you than you want us to believe. Stubborn child, you'll be a great man someday if you can learn to speak to others with respect.

Zeir held close to her and whispered as they walked away from Voln. "I *did* want to see what this was, but I figure we could use some time to force him to see if he needs some rest." He chuckled. "You know, he reminds me of you a little."

"He's a stubborn child who won't accept help from anyone."

Zeir grabbed her hand and smiled.

His hand was icy, yet it warmed her with such power. The tension between them was only an illusion cast by their difficult circumstances. She was ready to move past his brief disappearance and reluctance to address it while in the Pinnacles. She harbored enough secrets of her own. Though she doubted he had anything of significance to hide, the thought of his secrets continued to itch.

She squeezed his hand and smiled, though it dropped to a frown as they stopped before the creature's corpse.

She turned away for a moment of relief but found the sight of Voln skinning the bear with one of his small hunting knives no easier to observe.

"*Holy Laeih*, what do you think it is?"

She turned back to look at it. "I–" she struggled to speak. The gore was unsettling but frightened her little compared to the body itself.

Zeir spoke where she couldn't. "I almost want to say it's an imp because of those sharp cheeks and fangs, but the features are almost too humanoid. It's like a demented beggar who"—he pointed to its abdomen—"failed to receive an organ graft."

Aerhee grabbed a nearby stick and probed its stomach. A nest of organs twisted out as if an explosion had burst them free from the abdominal area, though they were quite dry and looked as if they had been dead for weeks.

She turned back to look at Zeir. "Voln never attacked its abdomen, did he?"

He shrugged. "I couldn't see much."

She stood and waved for him to follow. Its image would haunt her, though not as much as Zeir's seemingly random words that found too much purpose for comfort. They lingered, playing across her mind regardless of how much she tried to ignore them.

"It's like a demented beggar who failed to receive an organ graft."

Voln dragged the bear's pelt across the ground towards them with the bloody side up. "We can clean the bottom later. It needs to dry."

There was no sign of the head and only two arms remained after his asymmetrical cuts. It was no professional piece, but it would serve its purpose.

"How do the injuries feel?" she asked.

"*Perding Zhaeswoman*," he dragged out as if reprimanded by his mother. "I told you, *it's fine*. I don't want you to even think about trying to stitch anything up. This isn't my first injury, and it's far from the worst. Endowers heal a lot faster than you would think. Even though I'm no Eurythrin, it'll all be healed over before we reach Unin."

"Voln, really? We shouldn't push you–"

"Now you, Zeir? Come on!"

Aerhee shot him a glare.

"*Don't worry,*" Zeir whispered to her, "*I'll keep a close eye on him.*" He stepped towards Voln. "*But,* what I really want to know is why you can't be more original."

"What do you mean?"

Zeir chuckled. "A wolf? Really? That's the first thing you choose? Couldn't you choose anything other than the thing on your mask?"

Voln laughed. "You don't know me, do you? I'm the perding young wolf–"

"Of the Tchoyasmen," Zeir yawned. "I've heard it enough. More of a serious question, were your hands swords? I thought you could only change into other living beings."

"Swords? I wish! The hands were kaesan claws, which I think is pretty noble." He turned to look at Aehree. "In honor of you, Zhaeswoman."

She laughed, and he turned back to Zeir.

"The straight 'claws' were actually the prongs of eldeer antlers. I've heard they are as durable as steel and so far, I believe it. The shield that I used to block that *thing's* attack was a modification of my skin to match that of a tortoise shell."

"And you couldn't change your shoulders and back to match the shell? That would have saved you from that *pleasant* back scratch."

"You think I don't know that? You old people don't understand anything about us, do you? It takes a lot to shape yourself. I had the shell hand planned out for a long time but had no time to think about my back. The back would make me too heavy so I couldn't dodge another attack and if you want another reason, hands are much easier to change than my back, especially because I can see them. Enough about that, though. If you take any lesson from today, you should know that using my ability drains me more than anything you could ever do."

"What do you mean?"

"I mean the energy I burned doing all of this is the same amount you would need to climb four of these mountains."

"I think that sounds like an exaggeration."

Voln walked away. "I don't care what you think. I need to eat. A whole bear *might* be enough for a few hours. If you start the fire, maybe I'll leave a leg for you two to share."

⚘ ⚘

"We went uphill for so long," sighed Voln, "that I never thought we would go down. I'm so sick of walking. Now that we're here. Maybe I should throw myself down the mountain. It would be a lot faster, right?"

"Please don't," sighed Aerhee.

"*Perding Zhaesmen* can't take a joke," he mumbled, then stopped. "Do you see *that?*" He sprinted through the trees.

"Voln! Be careful!" She ran after him. Twigs snapped in her wake and pine needles scratched all bare skin. *I sound like my perding mother.* She chose to face the brief memory of her mother with ridicule rather than grief.

Voln had stopped just beyond the wall of trees and stood near a rocky ledge that overlooked the land south of the mountain. He pointed ahead. "Is that it?"

Aerhee turned back to the sound of rustling branches as Zeir pressed his way through, not allowing any branch to break or swing back at him.

He had insisted on carrying the bear pelt, which had weighed on him even though they discarded half of it.

"Look already!"

Aerhee stepped up beside Voln. While they still had much of the mountain to descend, a small village sat in a forest clearing. A road stretched onward from its southern side. No church steeple rose above the buildings. They had found their destination.

Aerhee nodded, taking in the view.

Voln stepped back. "That better be it. I'm ready for some food that I don't have to kill myself. Still, I don't know if I can last too many days in Priess, especially in such a small town."

Aerhee lost herself as she thought of meeting with Sheath, noting the political complexities of such a reunion after her retreat.

Zeir pulled her arm.

"Don't worry," he told the boy, "we won't stay for more than a day."

"What do you mean?" complained Voln.

"It's not safe."

"And the mountains are? You two would have died without me, and I thought I had a problem with Priessmen."

"It's not that."

"Then what is it? Where would we go?"

Zeir looked at Aerhee.

"That depends on what Sheath—Thane Leisa—tells us," she replied.

Voln exaggerated a sigh.

She was grateful that he kept further complaints to himself. Justifying working with someone who had become, by definition, her political opponent was difficult enough on her own psyche. Arguing about it with an insolent child did not make it any easier on her.

She stepped towards him. "Can you trust me, Voln? Please."

He mumbled and shrugged.

"What was that?"

"What do you want, woman? Do you need to bow to you? Sorry, your role as Caster matters as much to me as my Krall's withering nipple."

"Voln."

He slammed his side into her. She saw a smile as he turned his head for a second.

She smiled as they tread onward. Her thighs throbbed. Her stomach hurt even worse. She felt like passing out after restless nights.

Against all, she was happy. Despite hardships and fear, she had found a reason to continue, a reason to hope for a better future.

❧❧❧❧❧ ❧❧❧❧❧

Voln cheered and punched his fists in the air as they saw the first buildings of Unin only a few steps ahead through the dense forest.

Zeir placed his hands on the boy's shoulders. "Shh. Calm down, *young wolf*. If you can manage, try not to be the center of attention for one day."

"And get rid of the mask," Aerhee added.

"Are you trying to kill me? You know I can't survive without it!"

She sighed. "You know what I mean."

"Good enough?" He turned back with spread arms and gave her an insincere bow.

Though she was never blond, it was a common enough sight among Priessmen. His blond curls and skin a healthier color than the Zhaes pale reminded her of her cousins, who she had not seen since her childhood. She couldn't even remember their names.

"Good enough." Zeir walked past him and waved the group forward.

Although they entered Court Priess, Unin did not remind Aerhee of her childhood. Its Priess influence was apparent in the tall and slender architecture, but it was very much a rural town with more markets rather than established shops.

Townsfolk seemed to know their merchants well, some even embraced their produce sellers as they met. Away from the affluence of their capitol, Ekscomos, Unin seemed humble and homely. Companies of miners left the town from the northern road, waving to the merchants and townsfolk as they passed.

As they oriented themselves to the town in relation to the mountains' curve, they realized they had entered from a northwestern passage. Zeir led them to follow one of the mining companies towards the northern gate of the city. Just past a garden planted next to a crumbling northern wall as tall as Voln, stood an inn. A wooden sign hung out onto the street with the title *Pinnacle Base Inn*.

Aerhee stopped a few paces before the entrance. Zeir grabbed Voln by the upper arm before he could enter without them.

"Come on, *Caser*," Voln groaned. "You've complained enough when I wanted to stop. Now you can't keep me back from whatever they're cooking in there." He nodded towards the rectangular, two-story inn. Smoke billowed from two chimneys above, though the windows were too murky to see if any food awaited them.

"Is something wrong, Aer?" Zeir stepped closer to her and grabbed her hand. They were cold and dirty, but she appreciated the comfort.

"Someone who I think I would count as my closest friend waits for us beyond that door."

"Let's hope she is," Voln added, "or I am going to perding... perding... punch... something... or–"

Aerhee ignored him and looked at Zeir. "Do you think she will hold it against me, Zeir? My betrayal? What I did–"

He pumped her hand. "I think she'll understand that you are the least selfish person we know and that you only did it for the sake of Facet. For your Court."

Court Priess. The thought frightened her.

He seemed to read her thoughts. "For Court Zhaes and for Laeih himself."

"Enough of the preaching, now–"

They both ignored Voln. "Thank you, but I still ran away from everything that I promised to her."

"And what was that?"

"To serve my Court."

"And you *are*, Aer. Right? Regardless of what the other Thanes believe, you hold to what *you* think is true."

"I hope so."

"Come on," let's go.

Aerhee tried to banish her fears as she patted Voln's shoulder. "Keep your thoughts clean, Voln. She can and will read anything that's on your mind."

Aerhee stepped ahead and entered the inn. Any vulnerable thoughts remaining filled her mind. Sheath would see all she had done for the Allegiant. While her secrets were few, she trusted her friend would not use them against her.

Still, war changes one's values. It had done so for Aerhee. If Sheath saw this as an opportunity to exploit Aerhee for the benefit of the loyalists, so be it. Aether had given too much and come too far to retreat. She was desperate. She was vulnerable yet retained the little faith she had in an old ally.

The tavern smelt of smoked meats and old wood, with hints of mead. More people filled the room than she had expected. Each of the ten tables was filled, most visitors beginning their morning with slices of bread and cuts of red meat with blackened edges. She searched for but a moment until she found her.

Sheath broke away from her conversation with two Priessmen, each dressed like miners with plenty of coal stains on their coats.

Sheath placed her hands on Aerhee's shoulders as she met her, looking at her for a few seconds before speaking. "I don't need to read you to know that you missed me." She pulled her into an embrace that forced Aerhee's breath out. "By Laeih's grace, how can you still look like a stunning noblewoman with torn clothes covered in mud and blood? Come, let us find somewhere private."

Sheath stopped and smiled at her and Zeir, then bowed to Voln.

"What kind of noblewoman has an eye patch?"

"Voln!"

Sheath laughed and placed her hand on Aerhee's shoulder. "It's fine, Aer."

"I only say it out of respect," Voln muttered.

Sheath winked, then walked over to speak with the innkeeper.

"The Perding noblewoman will hate me," grumbled Voln.

Aerhee eyed him. "If you act like that, she will. Be civil."

"Come on, Zhaeswoman. You don't know me at all, do you?"

Sheath returned with a smile. "He's lent us a room on the upper floor. Follow me."

Aerhee followed with the other two in tow. "Don't you have a room here?"

"I spend the nights elsewhere in town. With how much time I have been spending here over the past few days, I would rather not give any pursuers an easy chance to go after me at night."

"Are you being followed? Is it that bad? I'm sorry, Sheath. I didn't mean to cause you any trouble."

Sheath slid the key into the lock and let Voln and Zeir in. "You are the least of my worries. Even if our opinions differ, at least I can rely on what you say."

They entered, and Sheath shut the door behind them.

Aerhee turned back to her. "But couldn't you just read anyone you work with? Anyone that knows you, knows that it is literally impossible to hide something from you."

Sheath sat down next to Aerhee at the small table, while the other two sat on the bedside. "If only things were as simple as they once were. Loyalist or Allegiant, it does not matter. No one knew how complex this war would become. If it had been merely over harvesting, matters could have settled on simple terms. Unfortunately, we have a longer battle ahead."

"Will you get to the point?"

Sheath turned to Voln with a sneer, then laughed. "Now who are you–"

"I don't want to hear 'boy, youngling, child,' or anything of the sort. Is that offensive *in my culture*? You bet your perding mother it is."

Aerhee sighed. "This is Voln." Sheath looked at her with a raised eyebrow. "Of course, go ahead and read me. I wouldn't expect anything else."

"Sorry, Aerhee. I know how sensitive this meeting might be. I'll try not to pry too much." She turned to Voln. "'*Young wolf of the Tchoyasmen?*' Quite the title. You must think you are *smart* to come up with that one, Shiftling."

"You–"

Sheath held up a hand to stop him. "All jests aside, I think it is an admirable title. Aerhee holds a high opinion of you, though she might not show it."

Aerhee's face flushed. She spoke before Voln could react. "If you are worried about being pursued, can we get to the point of this? You know I am happy to see you, Sheath, but there is a lot at risk here?"

"It suffices to say that this is *all* connected. My struggle to read others and your meeting with the Krall. I haven't read everything from you yet, only enough to get a brief understanding."

"Do it."

"What?"

"Read it all. It's no secret of the Allegiant. That meeting with him is purely about the livelihood of our Court and Facet as a whole. I trusted you could solve it when I invited you here. I trust you enough to read it."

Sheath nodded. "Very well, but I will tell you about my problems reading others."

"As long as you can read me, I don't need that answer right now. I need you to understand what we have seen. All in due time, *Dagger.*"

Sheath smirked. "If you say so, *Wind.*"

A tense silence fell as Sheath stared at Aerhee. Occasional twitches caused Sheath with intermittent squints and eyes opened in surprise. "I'm sorry I doubted your worries with Thane Gromm. I assumed... assumed that it was related to... other *experiences* you had."

"Oh, it was," said Aerhee. "But the meeting with Krall Vheen only resurrected my hatred for the Patriarchy."

"But the Krall said that they weren't the problem. It was the sect within their members that caused your father's pain."

"Please!" moaned Voln.

Aerhee hushed him.

He pushed her hand away from his mouth. "Please *stop* being so–agh–we can't *all* read Aerhee's mind.

Sheath looked back and forth between Aerhee and Voln. "I have a complicated past with the Patriarchy of Scholars."

He shot a puzzled glare at Sheath.

"She's been wronged by some of their more *zealous* members."

"What Scholar is *not* a zealot?" Scoffed Voln.

Aerhee gave a nervous laugh.

"The boy–"

"Voln!" he corrected.

"*Voln* is right. Let us begin with a clear purpose rather than moving around points of interest. You invited me because the Krall requested we meet."

Aerhee nodded.

"I want to help avoid conflict. Of course I do, but I am sorry to say that I can no longer focus on the war."

"What do you mean?" asked Voln. "The war is *all there is*."

"You are not wrong, but you and the Allegiant are focused on the battles themselves. I have...perd, there is so much to address. I have seen things, met people, done things that made me realize that most of this war is a ruse."

"How can that be?" asked Aerhee. "People are *dying*, Sheath. Cities, even Courts are on the brink of collapse."

"Perhaps *ruse* is not the right word. People are using the war to benefit them. Not to change the laws of harvesting, but to change the entire politics of Facet as a whole. There are individuals who would wish to dissolve Courts in favor of a single government. Organized religion and cultures nearly abolished for some idea of world peace."

"You speak of the Holy Reapers?" Aerhee asked.

"Who—wait, may I?"

Aerhee nodded and Sheath read her as the memories of the Reaper gatherings in the Pinnacles played across her mind.

"*Holy Laeih protect us*," Sheath gasped. "The connection is uncanny. It cannot be. No, no–" she looked up to see everyone staring at her. "Just give me a moment to process this."

Aerhee's heart raced. Zeir and Voln fixed their gazes on Sheath, but neither of their hands shook as much as hers.

Sheath nodded. "Alright, I need you to know what has happened since we were separated. You should know about my time in Court Priess." Her eyes moved between Voln and Aerhee.

She leaned in and whispered into Aerhee's ear behind a cupped hand. "Please tell me you've told Zeir by now."

"Of course I have," Aerhee said, drawing confused looks from Zeir and Voln.

"And the boy?" Sheath whispered.

He's seen enough and might as well know. He's even opened up to me about his past. With everything that is happening, is there even a point to hiding it any longer? "Voln, I was born in Court Priess."

"*Perd me*," Voln dragged out his words and looked as if he was about to laugh.

"We can talk about it later," Aerhee shook her head. "Now, Sheath, why must we talk about this right now?"

"The crime against your father may have a connection to all of this, as Krall Vheen has said. Back to Priess. Have you ever met Thane Terin Trosh?"

"You know I left as a child, right?"

"Of course." Sheath adjusted the cloth around her head that covered her missing eye. "I merely meant–"

"Yes, the Priess Thane of Diplomacy. Not as–" Aerhee held her hand out and lowered it.

"Small in stature, but you know he is a Gorger, right?"

"I've heard something in passing. What about him?"

"I have no proof of any connection, but he has a 'personal vision' for Facet. It just so happens that his vision sounds uncannily similar to the Holy Reapers' vision. You wondered why I panicked as I read that? Now you know."

Zeir spoke with a blend of fear and excitement. "Just like you said, Aerhee, they have Priess ties!" He pointed at Sheath. "Do you think that these Reapers who are trying to benefit from the war are his people? Is *he* the one who is trying to use the war as a tool?"

"One of them." Sheath replied.

"What do you mean?"

"Come on, Aerhee. You cannot believe that a single man would lead this."

"No, but he has the support of the Holy Reapers, does he not?"

"He is one cunning kulf but cannot handle the entire Court-removal movement on his own."

"And you know this because you read him?"

Sheath took a deep breath. "Again, to reach the significance of this, we need to move back to my time in Priess. Hold your assumptions. I think everything will make much more sense. Aerhee, do you remember Yetrik, the Gruthman?"

"The one who wanted to go to the Middlelands?"

"Yes, and he did. Thane Gromm took great interest in his journey, though he did not accompany him. Remember this, it may be significant later. Before their middleland expedition, I left with some others to Court Priess, where I met with plenty of Priess Thanes. While I had met Thane Terin Trosh on occasion in the past, I need not remind you that our relationship with the Priessmen are not close as of late. Terin, unlike Royss, does not like to puff himself up and draw attention. Yes, I know, quite odd for a Priessman. As I met with him concerning the war, I discovered his disinterest, and therefore his interest in his *vision*. Yetrik later visited us and though he seems like an intelligent young man, I think Terin saw him as something to mold, just as Royss did."

"So is he tied with Royss?" Aerhee asked.

"No. I have reason to believe that he is closer to another Thane. Thane Gromm."

"Why?"

"I read some of his associates and found that he has been communicating with Thane Gromm over the past few months. I couldn't read back far enough to tell how rooted their relationship was, but I know their recent communication has increased. The Thanes of Scholarship–"

"But Terin Trosh is the Thane of Diplomacy," said Aerhee.

"Yes, but as I said, I think there is more to him than we would like to believe."

"Did you read Terin's mind?" Voln asked."Of course she did," said Aerhee.

Voln shook his head. "She said that she read his associates, but never the man himself."

"You misunderstand–"

Sheath stopped Aerhee from continuing. "No, the boy is right. This is what I have been trying to get to. I hope your faith in me does not diminish. I must confess that I am somewhat prideful with my status as a Feelman. No need to laugh, Aerhee. Despite my prowess, I cannot read the mind of *every* person I meet. I have reason to believe that there is a way one can learn to shield their minds from the sight of a Feelman. One group of people seems to have mastered this mental fortitude, for they are the only ones in whom I have seen this shielding. Those people are the Patriarchy of Scholars. I know nothing more about Thane Gromm than you do, Aerhee. I should have told you this long ago. Forgive my pride. I have read the minds of early Patriarchy apprentices, but there is something that follows their acceptance ceremony that bars their mind from me. Unfortunately, it is after that ceremony that they learn the truths held by the Patriarchy."

Aerhee nodded, looking down and scratching her head as she pondered. She looked up at Sheath after a moment of silence. "And what does this have to do with Terin?"

"Can't you see? He's a Scholar! He neither dresses like one nor does he claim the title, but he *must* be one! If this barring of my reading does not convince you, he was invited to join Thane Gromm in Court Fayis. I was able to work this information out of his underlings as well as the fact that Gromm invited all of Facet's major Scholars, including the anti-harvesting Scholars."

"And that is when you came here?" Aerhee asked. "When he left, you took the opportunity to visit me. Is he truly that focused on you?"

"I am not sure if he suspects me of taking an interest in him, but I did not want to let anyone else know about my intentions. With people like him and Gromm manipulating the Holy Reapers, I struggle to place my trust in anyone. Yes, I came here during Terin's absence, but he did not go to Fayis. He left with another Thane to Thusk. Apparently Krall Pensa of Court Sleff has agreed to make an official stance on the war on the side of the activists under certain conditions, rather than favors granted by Courts Priess and Gruth. I know little else except that the invitation was made by the son of the Bloated Krall, who leads a Beastling force."

Aerhee tensed as she recalled memories of the Beastlings and their kaesan used in the failed defense of Kzhek. There was so much to process. Zeir and Voln seemed to struggle to comprehend everything that was happening. Aerhee had more insight than either of them and still struggled to piece everything together.

"Is everything alright, Aerhee?"

"Why are you telling me this? You sided with the loyalists and you're telling us what your leaders are planning."

"I have told you only what I can to help."

"But why?"

"Because I can no longer trust anyone that stands at my side. If I cannot read the Scholars, how am I to know who works towards collapsing Facet as we know it?"

"Just read them," Voln said. "Whoever you can't read will be a Scholar and then you know they are your enemy."

"It's not that simple. I could read some things from Thane Gromm, but a blockade would arise whenever I tried to read deeper. If I read other Scholars, I may mistake a Scholar for a simple mind that simply blocks the Scholar parts of their mind. We also must clarify, Voln, that not all members of the Patriarchy are our enemies. Only those who support this ploy by Terin and his associates to dissolve Court individuality."

"The Bronze Seers," Aerhee uttered.

Sheath nodded. "I believe so. The Krall told you that there is a division among the Scholars. We know too little to make any major movements against them, but *I do* believe that this division among the Scholars is the root of the Facet's ills. Their implicit connections to the Holy Reapers' goals when aligned with what the Krall has told you are rather frightening. I would go as far to doubt that the 'criminals' that Royss works with are more than mere thieves that liked the title of Bronze Seers. The Seers have likely grown beyond their Patriarchy membership. I've heard mentions of them, rather read them in the minds of others, for years now. If I am correct, then this war is a tool used by the Seers to make Facet a clean slate upon which they can build their ideal foundation."

"You think they started the war?" asked Zeir.

Sheath shrugged. "It is probable. To understand its origin, we must go to the beginning." She focused on Aerhee. "Where have your people made their base of operation?"

"Kzhek."

"Then it is time we return home. I need to meet the man who started this."

Colrig.

Voln clapped. "Perd me, so you really are leaving the enemies to join the righteous! Good for you, Zhaeswoman!"

"It is not about that. This war has become nothing to me. Endowers live or die? It doesn't matter what we decide if these anarchists triumph."

"What do you mean?" Voln asked. "I don't see what is so bad about these people. What is so wrong with removing Court boundaries? You privileged Zhaeswomen should learn to appreciate freedom. You may forbid yourselves from it, but it's still something we enjoy in the other Courts."

Aerhee placed her hand on Voln's shoulder, then quickly removed it. "You're a smart boy, Voln, but you have a lot to learn about politics."

Sheath nodded. "Everything I have heard from Terin and his associates frightens me more than Krall Trhet"—her eyes shot to Voln—"they are worse than anything I can imagine. To even *achieve* this vision, he will have to destroy the order in each Court, crumbling all governments until they subject themselves to his new order. Loyalist or Allegiant, it doesn't matter. What would this *new era* look like? Regardless of his purposes, should he be a Bronze Seer, Scholar or Holy Reaper, Terin is an enemy to Facet. He does not want to merely dissolve Court lines, but he wishes to remove all differences until we become one united under a single government."

"I still don't understand."

"Facet's beauty exists because of the Courts and their religions. I could no longer worship Laeih as I desire. I would be subject to the government that they make their god."

Voln continued to stare.

"What matters to you, Voln?" Sheath asked.

"Myself."

Sheath stared.

He looked at Aerhee, who gave him the same stare that pleaded for him to be serious.

"My friends."

Sheath leaned in closer. "The Endowers?"

Voln nodded.

They are all he has.

Sheath placed a hand on his knee. "In a world controlled by those who strive for a power, you and your friends will become tools. You think your Court uses you now? You will become like ghete to serve them."

"But you are using me.""Look at it this way. Your Gorger friends would no longer be effective workers, but slaves to build society. *Slaves* Voln. No life. No friends, only fellow sufferers. I do not know what the Gruthmen have yet, but Terin was too eager for my liking to fly to Thusk because they have already begun to do something along these lines. You still have your freedom. You will lose it in Terin's Facet. Not only the Endowers, but *everyone* will be subject to their tyranny. This is only what I could glean from some of his followers. More lies in store. Greater consequences. *Supernatural* consequences will follow if we do not prevent Terin's people from destroying society as we know it. You will be a piece in their system or die with Facet as we know it."

Aerhee leaned to look at Voln's face through his mask holes. His lip quivered.

Is she exaggerating? Our religions dissolved? Is Priess philosophy derived from the Bronze Seers? How sure are you? Assumption is a dangerous practice, Sheath.

"But it doesn't have to be like that, Voln. We will do all–"

Sheath's voice drifted away from Aerhee as she continued to console Voln. Aerhee found herself focused on Zeir, whose gaze was distant and far too pale, even for a Zhaesmen. He had grown quiet the more Sheath talked about the Seers and Terin's supposed ploy.

She placed her hand on his thigh. He turned to regard her, his lost gaze finding ground in her.

Sheath and Voln shared a laugh, though his joy was frail.

"Everything all right?"

Zeir looked up at her, struggling to maintain eye contact. He nodded.

"Are you sure?"

"Aerhee, I said I'm fine."

His reply demanded that she cease asking questions. Zeir was never blunt and demanding.

She turned back to Sheath.

"This is a path we should not *pursue*," he whispered.

A chill ran through Aerhee's spine and down her arms.

"Well then," Sheath said. "I'm glad to hear that you will accept my guidance. Rest for the remainder of the day. I have sufficient coin to hire a carriage back to Kzhek. We leave in the morning."

CHAPTER THIRTY-TWO

WHEN EELS HARMONIZE

Yetrik woke up to Avra's screech. He sat up and looked out the window to his borrowed room in the Canton of Defense. The sky was just beginning to light up with a pink glow. His back ached from sleeping on the stone floor. The spare clothing he found in adjacent rooms proved somewhat helpful beneath him, though a blanket was unnecessary in Court Gruth's eternal heat. He thought for a moment that he would thrive in Court Chuss, but reconsidered. He had forgotten how much he loved the sea.

Semi had helped him rekindle love for his home. It felt good to be back, despite the brevity of his stay.

Two jackets moved as Semi turned to look at him. Her shoulder-length hair was only slightly ruffled. Her eyes were heavy. She smiled and closed them.

He ran his fingers through her hair. She smiled, keeping her eyes closed. He reached over to put on his clothes and laid two more jackets on Semi as he left the room. Regardless of the temperature, she would want him to stay. He wanted to but had no choice. He could not leave Avra alone. Her call had been direct.

Yetrik scratched his head as he continued to wake up. Pinches of sand fell from his hair from their brief visit to the sea.

No one else seemed to be in the Canton. He was reminded of Krall Pensa and wondered if she would still insist on leaving so promptly after a night to consider the pleas of others to wait. They still had much to prepare to maintain control of Paiell. Images of the first battle in Paiell raced through his mind, causing his heart to pump in fearful anticipation of the imminent battle. More would perish. More death for the sake of some political endeavor. He cast aside worry in favor of thoughts of Semi, then for Avra, as he left the Canton to heed her call.

"Heloath! A pleasure to see you again, Beastling!" Terin stood outside the Canton of Defense, stroking Avra. Two more zlatog riders stood with their own steeds.

"Didn't expect us so early?" chuckled Thane Sairee Phemus.

Mixed feelings of his stay in Priess returned to him. He tried to not be a quick judge of character, but Thane Phemus looked as pretentious as ever.

"No 'how are you here so early.' Gruthman?" She took a step towards him.

Terin shook his head and stepped away from his zlatog escort. "How dull do you think he is? He's not blind to the giant beasts behind us, not to mention that he has one of his own. How is yours holding up, Yetrik?"

Yetrik walked towards Avra and stroked her mane. Despite his nervousness in the presence of the Priess Thanes, Avra made him feel safe. "Wonderfully."

He patted her side. "*When did they arrive?*"

"A few moments ago," she hummed. *"You were quick. I appreciate it."*

"Always. Until I leave this life—"

"Do not entertain such thoughts, Yetrik."

"Where is the Krall?" asked Terin.

"Which one?"

Thane Phemus laughed. "Two Priess Thanes, a Sleff Krall, and all the noblemen Court Gruth has to offer. And the public says that the war is dividing our nations? Perd me, this is a *healing* conflict!"

Terin did not acknowledge her. "Krall Pensa, though I assume we will be meeting with all the others. We can wait if that is what they would prefer. You Gruthmen enjoy sleeping late, don't you?"

Do I owe Krall Pensa anything? Am I wronging her for inviting them to join before she can escape? No. I am a Gruthman. My loyalty is firm. Whatever Krall Plath desires, whatever the Gruth—"

"Yetrik?" Terin asked.

Yetrik pulled himself from his reverie. "Krall Pensa wanted to leave as soon as possible to secure her control of Paiell."

"That woman has always been impulsive."

"You know her?"

"I knew what I was walking into when we sought her aid." He smiled at Thane Phemus. "It seems we have arrived just in time."

"Are you coming with us to Paiell?" asked Yetrik.

Terin chuckled and shook his head, patting Yetrik on the back. He pointed towards the Canton's entrance and started to walk. "I may be a Gorger, but this body is not fit for war."

And mine is?

"Well then," said Terin, "if she is eager enough to depart, best not keep her waiting. Show me to her."

Thane Phemus caught up with them as they entered. "Wake her if you must. I have no doubt that the impulsive kulf will leave without us if she has the time."

Yetrik led them down the hall. "When we came with the request for aid, she said she wanted to help your Court. As soon as we sat down to discuss our alliance, she pledged to help my Court if we helped control return to hers in Paiell. She didn't seem to care about the war, only about peace in Paiell, regardless of who that peace favored."

"As we should have expected," sighed Terin.

"I still think it was worth it. She agreed to help after we secure Paiell for her." *If we can manage to do that much.*

Terin scoffed. "Her message from Kevlen promised her allegiance. This would not be the first time Krall Pensa changes the wording of a promise to benefit her and cost as little as possible."

Thane Phemus moaned. "Terin, I told you that you should have worked with the Sleff Thane of Scholarship."

Terin laughed. "Perd, no. That man is a coward and a disgrace to the Patriarchy. He is too conservative for the loyalist movement. I haven't spoken with him in at least a year and would not be surprised to learn that he has sided with the Harmony Allegiant."

Yetrik turned back. "You work with the Patriarchy?"

"I work with everyone, Gruthman. Tis the responsibility of a diplomat. There are better Scholars in Court Sleff than the Thane, though they are few. At least Krall Pensa has power. We just need to see that her *intensity* is directed productively. Are you sure you know where she is, Gruthman?"

"Yes, sorry, I took a wrong turn early on. We're almost there. With all of this talk of control, are you taking over for your Krall?"

Thane Phemus chortled. "Oh, he wishes."

"I am not taking the throne, but you could say that I speak for the Court."

"Is he unwell?" asked Yetrik.

"Might as well be," scoffed Thane Phemus.

"What do you mean?"

She scowled at him as if he had no common sense. "You *do* know who our Krall is, right?"

"The Bloated Krall." Despite how close he had grown to Kevlen, Yetrik knew little about his friend's father. Whenever Yetrik asked, Kevlin found any other topic much more interesting.

She smiled. "The reviling *kulf* himself.

"A reminder to keep our pursuit for power under control," assured Terin.

Thane Phemus tucked her voluminous blond hair behind her ears. "We're talking humility now, are we? You perding blasphemous Priessman."

Terin sighed.

He slapped his shoulder. "I jest. Say what you want about the perding Krall. I'm satisfied with one graft. It's his fault he was foolish enough to go for a second."

The door at the end of the hall was open. Shouts echoed out of the room.

Thane Phemus chuckled. "The humble whore herself."

Yetrik tensed as they approached. His already sweaty hands felt even hotter.

They stepped inside to see Krall Pensa shouting at a Gruthman who was hunched in fear.

"I don't want you touching my perding things! I don't care about hospitality or whatever your perding Krall wants. No! Don't fix my sheets or even refill my goblet. What do you not understand, you servile kulf? I leave for a moment and return to find some imp desecrating my room."

"Krall Pensa," Terin stepped in. "He is only trying to serve Your Grace. Are you so *prideful* that you cannot accept a kind gesture from the Gruthmen?"

She turned toward him as the Gruthman scurried away with a wheeze. She shot Terin with the same glare as she had the Gruthman. "Don't insult me–"

He stepped towards her and held out his hand for her to shake. "Then learn to live your ideal and be humble, Your Grace."

She swatted it away. "What do you want?"

"Well, *you* were the one who invited us." He bit his lower lip as if holding back another insult.

"I no longer need your aid," she waved him away and started towards the door. "The Gruthmen have offered me sufficient help for my needs. Thank you for your concern."

He followed her. "You misunderstand, Your Grace. This is no exchange between two Courts–"

"As far as I'm concerned, it is."

Terin waved for the other two to follow him as he chased Krall Pensa, holding his robe to his side to seem regal and collected. "Then you have been misinformed."

"Krall Plath had no issue agreeing to my terms."

"Ah, I see where we err. This is not *his* deal to solidify."

She turned her head back for a brief glance but continued to press onward. "Then whose is it?"

"The loyalist coalition."

"An official title for the pro-harvesting noblemen?"

"Again, you err. This is beyond the harvesting policy, it all—" He paced ahead and stopped before her. "Please, Your Grace, might we address this in a more civilized manner? I would appreciate your attention."

"You have it for now. Walk. Let's be productive."

Yetrik and Thane Phemus neared them.

Terin clenched his fists and let the tension slowly release. "Krall Plath, though I still pay him his due respect, is not the proper representative for this. He is a late addition and has limited knowledge about what led to the collapse of Facet."

"And you do? Were you not in your own Court?"

"Oh, I assure you I was much more involved than you would believe. Ask Royss or Thane Gromm. Those Zhaesmen will attest to my claim."

She laughed. "Need I remind you I came here for help from the Gruthmen, not requesting to join your *coalition?*"

"The Krall does not command the Court's military power. Legally, he may, but the power itself rests in the hands of Thane Kelm. I have close ties to Thane Kelm as well and know that his aid depends on your commitment to the coalition. Pledging your stance once your capitol is safe will not suffice. We need the power your Court can offer."

"Which is?"

"Devotion not only to harvesting, but to the coalition's designs for a *lasting* government. The system in which we now live grows frail. Kzhek should be evidence enough."

She sighed.

Terin scoffed. "Forgive me, Your Grace, have I overwhelmed you?"

"I want to take this a piece at a time. Let me focus on my people before I bring the rest of Facet into my mind."

"Of course. Everything will be simpler when you have your people under your feet."

"I am not talking about power and domination, Thane Trosh."

"Neither am I."

"Where are we going?" Yetrik asked. He could tell that Terin was dissatisfied with the Krall's blatant distraction. Her promises were hollow and her intentions were loyal to only herself. Did Terin see his mission to Sleff as a failure?. He had brought them together. Was that not enough? This was a game of royalty. A game of power and control in which he had neither. The further the nobility pulled them into their war, the more insufficient he felt.

Krall Pensa stopped to look down a hallway, then proceeded to the left. "Before I returned to meet an unwelcome guest in my room, I left to call a morning council with the Gruth nobility."

Thane Phemus scoffed. "You realize that you need time to prepare the army before departure. The might of an entire Court cannot jump to your...*brisk* whim."

"How much experience have you had, Priesswoman? Need I remind you that this is the second time I am managing a war in my Court, and that does not include the countless preliminary riots? We may not have had an army, but I had to be *patient* with the 'loyalists' in my Court who rose to defend their city. Councils, dear Priesswoman, are key to moving armies. If we do not begin preparing now, we will make it to Paiell in ruins when the rebels assuredly return to wreak havoc in Paiell. I know what I am doing. Learn your place, Thane."

Thane Phemus straightened her shoulders.

Terin chortled and waved her forward. "Now is a better time than ever to build friendships, Thane Phemus."

She shot him a sour glare. Krall Pensa remained ignorant.

He scowled and hissed a whisper. "*Make an ally out of her.*"

She rolled her eyes and paced forward to walk beside the Krall.

Terin drifted back and relaxed his posture.

Yetrik gravitated towards him. "Forgive me, sir."

"What is there to forgive?"

"Kevlen and I... our terms must not have been clear to her." Terin chuckled. "You have done your best, Yetrik. Clarity doesn't matter when you try to speak to ears clogged with pride. Trust me, I should know. All that matters is that we are all together. Councils are too often filled with wasted arguments. It is my responsibility to ensure that is not the case today. With Thane Kelm to help, I am sure we will have her complete alliance soon enough."

"I didn't realize that you knew Thane Kelm so well."

He turned to Yetrik with a grin. "As I said, I *am* a diplomat."

Yetrik knew there was more to what he said but chose to ignore it.

"Do you know him well?"

Yetrik turned to see a pleasant smile on Terin's face, one that seemed to flaunt untold knowledge. "Not very well. Do you know–I mean, I spend most of my time in the service of Thane Gett when working with the nobility and occasionally the Krall."

"Krall Plath is an amiable and wise man, but he is young for the throne. He–" Terin shook his head. "None of it matters. You'll see."

Terin sped up to mingle with the other two.

Yetrik followed. "Your Grace?"

She turned back and raised an eyebrow.

"I'll join you and the others in a moment. I have a small matter to attend to."

She dismissed him with a wave. He could not deny the disappointment at her disinterest. True, he was no official nobleman, but once she found herself surrounded by the others, he was no longer significant. He was a mere stepping stone used to help bring her here. Self-doubt ate at him.

He ran back inside to find Semi still laying in their room.

"Hurry and get dressed!"

She turned over and gasped.

He calmed his breathing. "Sorry. I didn't mean to startle you. The Priess Thanes have arrived and Krall Pensa is already gathering the others."

"The Priess–how?"

"They came with zlatogs. Must have expected that Krall Pensa would want to leave before they could do anything about it."

She sat up and stretched her arms. "Smart of them." She wiped her face and opened her eyes more. "How many?"

"Just two. The same ones I spent time with while I was there."

She reached out her hand and clapped her thumb and fingers together as she pointed at her clothing near his feet.

He tossed it to her. "Did you sleep well?"

She giggled as she stood and dressed. "In the few hours of *actually* sleeping, yes. The best sleep I've had since all of this started."

He reached down to help her up.

She took his hand and caressed the back of it with her thumb.

He ignored the blood under her fingernails and thought of more pleasant things. Her affection soared. He was thrilled yet distracted. He wanted to give her all the attention he could muster, but a dying nation took priority. Regardless, he no longer felt alone.

He pulled with a light tug. "Come on. We don't want to miss it."

She rose and squinted her eyes, taking a moment to still herself. "Trust me, I'm plenty *eager* to meet these Priess friends of yours."

"They're not bad people. At least one of them isn't."

"During a time of war, you never can tell who is *good* or *bad*, can you?"

❧❧❧❧❧ ❧❧❧❧❧

Yetrik smiled as he panted. They had run to the courtyard after Semi had taken her time to wake up and prepare. Much to his surprise, they were not the last to arrive.

Krall Plath was yet to arrive. More Gruth Thanes had joined them than the previous day, though their yawning and baggy eyes argued against their supposed desire to attend. They were eager to meet Yetrik after hearing about his and Semi's work abroad. Being appreciated felt nice, even if the stories of his glory were stretched truths and told by faces he had never seen.

Yetrik took Semi's hand. "Come on, there's someone I want you to meet."

She was slow to follow but gave in as he won her smile with his.

Terin and Thane Kelm conversed outside of the crowd's center. Their hushed mutterings were a starkly different tone than the excitement of the others.

It was not until Yetrik called Terin's name for the third time that he turned away from the Gruth Thane of Scholarship. Both wore disgruntled faces, though Terin smiled after a sigh. "This is her, then? The Shiftling I've heard so much about? Heloath, Gruthwoman." He extended a hand. "Yetrik has told me so much about you."

Yetrik smiled at her, expecting her to blush or even smile. Though she did smile, it was unsteady, as if about to fall into a frown.

"Where are my manners? Even if Yetrik has introduced me, you deserve to hear a proper introduction from myself. Thane Terin Trosh, Priess Thane of Diplomacy, official spokesperson of the Priess loyalists."

Yetrik looked at Thane Kelm. They exchanged a Gruth salute but avoided any eye contact longer than a second.

Terin patted Yetrik's arm. "I appreciate the introduction and look forward to meeting her, but don't occupy yourselves with us now. Thane Kelm and I have uninteresting matters to discuss. We wouldn't want to bore you with bureaucracy. Have you introduced your friend to Thane Phemus?"

"No, I haven't. I–"

Yetrik stopped speaking as the crowd turned to salute Krall Plath as he entered. His hair looked greasy, disheveled, and he wore no crown above it. He dismissed everyone with a wave and continued to walk through the midst of guests with a countenance more stern than usual. His palace guards followed close behind. "Where are the Priessmen?"

Terin approached him. "Is something wrong, Your Grace?"

"No." He smiled and shook his head, looking at the ground then at Terin. "It is a pleasure to have you here with us, Thane Trosh. Other matters have kept me unsettled. Please, forgive–"

Terin gave him the Gruth salute. "We have come to assist. Apologies are due on our part for arriving after Krall Pensa. Is there something I can do for you?"

Yetrik and Semi shared a glance. He reached for her hand again and gave it a squeeze. Her face was uneasy, but the slight gesture helped her smile return. His world was collapsing around him. In Deilf he would trust, but he grew wary of any government. He had found his Firm Foundation. First in Dielf. Second in Semi.

"Not at the moment, thank you. Where is Krall Pensa?"

A clamor of mumbles held for a few seconds until Krall Pensa walked out of the crowd. "What is it? Perd, a little too much to drink last night? This is not the time for—"

"Neither is it the time for your jests or complaints. Your people are no longer the only ones in danger. The perding Chussmen have scorched the farming fields in the villages east of Doot. Some villages have capitulated to allow Chuss troops to infiltrate and hold ground there. We need to take care of Paiell and storm Chuss before they advance any further."

Krall Pensa smiled and rested a hand on his shoulder. She chuckled. "Dear Krall–"

He swatted her hand away. "Is this entertainment to you?"

She shook her head. "I am just pleased that you finally understand my urgency. It is not too pleasant to have your Court in danger, is it?"

"Where's Kelm?"

He raked back his whips of hair as he waddled towards Krall Plath. "Yes, Your Grace?"

"Have the Terpels ready to march." He looked at Krall Pensa. "We'll ensure domination in Paiell then head south directly for Sliin. I've sent some of my eastern authorities to control the raiders in the meantime. I will fulfill my promise to you, but as soon as victory is secured, I must show the Chussmen that we will not kneel."

"Oh, you will not be disappointed," Thane Kelm assured. "The Terpels need not march to Paiell when they can sprint."

"You would treat your soldiers so poorly?" said Thane Phemus.

Yetrik turned to her with surprise, only to realize after a moment that she had only spoken the words to seem sympathetic. His time with her, though brief, had taught him that she was the type of woman to fake a tear as she ate a steak, having secretly told the butcher to beat the cow well before death to tenderize the meat.

Thane Kelm grinned. "Worry not, Priesswoman. Terpels do not tire. Any rumor you've heard of them needing rest is a lie."

"Under certain conditions," Krall Plath added. "They still need food to propel them forward."

"Is this true?" Yetrik whispered to Semi.

"It's not that simple. They're still humans, but I think any mental fatigue has been blocked from their mind as well as their emotions. Something is wrong with them."

Is that a mercy, preventing them from recognizing the horrors that will be wrought by their hands? He turned back to Thane Kelm.

"–that will all be accommodated for. Ghete carriages will follow, taking any commanders we choose to appoint. We'll fill the carriages with enough food to feed them along the way, though we will spare little time to do so. The sprint to Paiell and conquest should not be long–"

"Be cautious, Thane Kelm," added Krall Plath.

The Thane took no note of the Krall's remark. "I'm sure Krall Pensa and her people will accommodate the needs of the Terpels for a brief reprieve before heading south to Sliin."

"Are you leaving Sliin to act unobserved while we focus on Paiell?" added another Gruth Thane. "I fear they may use our focus on Paiell against us, no matter how short it may be."

Krall Plath turned to Thane Kelm. "With the new arrivals from Court Priess offering their service, I would not want their charity to go unused. Thane Phemus?"

She shot her head to him, the only time she ever seemed displeased at hearing her name.

"Yes, come here."

She looked from side to side, though no one was there to save her.

Thane Kelm placed his hand on her mid back and pointed to Semi. "Let me introduce you to our finest Shiftling in Thusk."

Yetrik knew she was an exceptional Shiftling, the best he had ever seen. Despite his bias, he knew that Thane Kelm exaggerated to achieve what he wanted, as did all other successful politicians.

Thane Phemus nodded, and Thane Kelm beckoned Semi forward. She obeyed without the Priesswoman's reluctance. Yetrik wondered what else she had done in his time away. She had wept at her calling to become their assassin, but her glare spoke of compliance.

Compliance is the first step towards submission.

Yetrik was no guiltless soldier, still he feared for Semi. *Were my actions on the battlefield crimes? What constitutes a crime in this era of moral ambiguity? Deilf save us. We will all need forgiveness when this ends.*

Thane Phemus nodded at Semi.

Semi flinched forward as Thane Kelm placed his hand on her back, then on Thane Phemus'.

He took no note of it and kept his hand on both of them. "Yes, a fine pair you will be. Thane Phemus, you will manage the operation in Slinn. Semi will provide the insights needed to form a plan as she works her way into the Sliin's members of the Harmony Allegiant. You two will identify their weakest point and relay the message to help us assure dominance. Likewise, any threats you become aware of should be relayed to us immediately."

"Who else is joining us?" asked Thane Phemus.

"Only you two, besides your Priess Beastling escort with a Zlatog. Paiell needs the attention of our army. I do not want to startle anyone before we arrive. The Beastling can relay any message should they be necessary. Be swift, I don't expect to be in Paiell for too long."

Semi shot Yetrik a glance, then turned to Thane Kelm. "So Yetrik is joining us?"

"No, another Beastling will. He is needed in Paeill."

"Why?"

Thane Kelm scowled. "I should not need to justify myself, *Gruth-woman*."

"He has experience in Paiell," said Krall Pensa. "I requested his aid."

Semi's gaze returned to Yetrik.

His soul ached for her. He did not want war. He did not want to leave her side.

He banished any thoughts that this could be their last day together. Everything would turn out well. He could not think otherwise. To do so would damn him from any hope of future joy. His longing for her over-powered all other emotions, causing him to wonder why he continued to help others bring death to their enemies when he learned how valuable all life was.

There is no choice. We are both Endowed. Regardless of our choice, this has become our war. To battle or surrender, both welcome death.

Thane Pensa cleared her throat until everyone noticed her. "So the Shiftling and Priess Thane will depart for Sliin tonight? Tomorrow? A week's time? It does not matter. The Chussmen may be advancing, but my capitol is *already* in peril."

Thane Phemus chuckled. "Paiell is currently under loyalist control, or am I mistaken? Did our legion of zlatog riders mean nothing to you?"

"Everything in due time," Thane Kelm said before Krall Pensa could offer a rebuttal. "I will not allow contention between us while it runs rampant throughout Facet. My Proctors and I will accompany the Terpels to Paiell, for they rely upon my commands."

Thane Phemus scoffed. "Proctors? Why would we need Scholars?"

"Thane Kelm offered his service to serve as the Thane of Scholarship *and* Defense," said Krall Plath.

Murmurs spread across the crowd.

"And you would do well to trust him!" demanded Krall Plath.

"The Canton of Defense was erected during the war," said Thane Kelm. "A burden it has been, but not one that I am unable to carry."

The murmurs grew in volume.

"Listen!" Krall Plath shouted.

Thane Kelm bowed before the Krall before returning his attention to his audience. "I have provided Krall Plath with instructions for directing the scouting mission to Sliin. It will commence shortly after our departure."

"Shouldn't Krall Plath be the one giving *you* commands?" asked Thane Phemus.

Krall Plath did not respond. He held his hands behind his back and his posture tight.

Thane Kelm smiled and paid no further heed to her words. "Krall Pensa, prepare for a departure tomorrow."

She scoffed. "Tomorrow? Every minute we wait—"

"Has been accounted for, Your Grace." Thane Kelm grunted as he readjusted his posture. He winced but spoke as collected as ever.

Thane Phemus moaned and rolled her eyes. "How can we trust your handling? Your opinions?"

"They are not only his," said Terin. "If you do not think my opinion a valid addition, dear Priesswoman, then let me assure you that Thane Gromm of Court Zhaes—hold your bias against the Zhaesmen aside, for he is an exception—has coordinated control with the recently pledged loyalist, Krall Trhet of Court Tchoyas."

A wave of whispers passed through the crowd.

"Thank you, Terin." Thane Kelm opened his arms. "Let us remember that we are still a mere part of the whole. Our allies wage similar battles in the west to ensure that our new era prevails. Now, you would all be so kind, I will attempt to relay the plans once again for those who have been *less attentive*." He glanced over the crowd in silence. "The Terpels will march ahead of our carriage caravan. *March* is a poor word. They will *sprint* to Paiell. We have planned on three intermissions for them to replenish themselves, the lattermost occurring right before we enter the city. Captain Kevlen and the Beastling Yetrik will fly ahead of our army to meet with their fellow zlatog riders who are still stationed in the city. Our approach will differ depending on if the enemies have advanced to retake the city. Once the Beastlings relay their report, we will continue onward to seize the city. Regardless of the Allegiant's position, we have a strategy prepared. After we secure the city, we will reconvene to see how many need to remain in Paiell while the rest of our forces head southward to decimate our opposition in Sliin. Anyone who has questions about Semi and Thane Phemus' scouting assignment should reach out to one of Krall Plath's representatives after our departure. I will not be troubled further."

Terin joined him as he left, whispering.

Everyone had a different question, more born from anxiety than curiosity, but they were forced to obey. Answers—should they be permitted—would come following the execution of Thane Kelm's strategy.

Yetrik turned as he heard a heavy sigh.

"Are you ready to do it all over again?" Kevlen fiddled with his gauntlets.

Semi stood further away. She looked at him with a frown and eyes that warned of tears.

"I think... I just..." Kevlen's confidence had fled. "I don't want to. I don't know what I'm trying to say."

Semi looked at the ground with crossed arms.

Two friends in need. Both were on the edge of a breakdown. Yetrik was not the firm foundation they hoped for. He was just as worried as both of them and kept his feelings in a shell of control. He was not that foundation, but he would be. There was no other choice. His concerns were not theirs, but theirs had become his. *Deilf strengthen me.*

He put his hand on Kevlen's shoulder. *Perd, what do I say to him? There is no Preiss god for him to pray to. Is it insensitive to offer the help of mine?* "I am here with you, brother. Nothing will change that. Even in death, my soul will remain."

He did not know how Kevlen took that as the Priessman nodded. The words were awkward even to Yetrik, but it was the best he could offer.

"I don't know how you do it," Kevlen said.

Yetrik glanced at Semi. She was watching him. "Do what?"

"Usually I'm the confident one, but you make me look like a poor kulf. If I act like this, so broken from deaths and.... I can't be like this when we see the others." He pointed to the zlatog riders. Both focused on their steeds. "What kind of captain would I be to lose my composure in front of them? I'm only telling you this because you helped me pick myself up after we met Krall Pensa. I've *never* been like this. Never so vulnerable. Never...I've never acted like such a child."

"We've both seen terrible things and have been forced to do terrible things for the sake of some *greater good*. I would be worried if you weren't so put off by the atrocities. War is horrible. *Evil*. Evil for the sake of good. Perd, I don't understand it myself, but I'm putting my trust in those who know better."

Both of them looked at Thane Kelm and Terin, who had stopped in the distance and spoke with one another.

Kevlen gave a pitiful laugh. "How can we be sure *they* know better?"

We can't. Follow in blind trust and hope for the best result. Perd, what am I thinking? "I accept that I do not understand everything, but we need time. Give me a moment, Kev. I need to talk to someone. We'll have plenty of time to talk about all of this over the next few days." He patted Kevlen's back and started towards Semi. "I promise."

"I'm sorry, Yetrik."

He turned back.

"I'm sorry I'm putting this on you."

"Don't be. Like I said, You're my brother. I mean it."

Kevlen laughed and sniffed. He wiped his eyes. "You don't know how much that means to me, Yetrik. Perd the other Beastlings. Perd the nobility. Perd my imp of a father. I've been among so-called allies and you're the first one that feels true. I appreciate you. You're a good person."

Yetrik hated how he doubted that statement. "You too, Kev. We're going to prove that." *Even if we must abandon orders.*

Yetrik reached for Semi's hand.

She swung her arms around him and squeezed him, all past social inhibitions set aside.

Though his concern focused on her, he still found himself worried about the implications of their relationship becoming more intimate. His death would hurt her more the closer they became.

Some looked at them, but most remained ignorant of their emotional embrace. The nobility paid no heed to the dangers of war, for they were too distant. These Thanes would remain safe while their servants perished. Even Thane Kelm was confident behind the force of his army.

Countless lives would be lost. Despite the strength of the Terpels, many among them would perish. None of this concerned the nobility. They would remain in safe ignorance while others fought their battle.

Yetrik found himself frustrated, but more so envious of them. He hated that selfish thought, but it would have been much easier to forget all the surrounding suffering. He would experience history uncensored. Bare, naked violence would scar him, changing him evermore. He hoped that any change would be for the best, that he might learn to value any life given to him. In the nobility's ignorance, he worried he would only grow numb, as numb as they were to see soldiers as commodities to achieve their vision of a better nation.

Yetrik came to himself and rubbed Semi's lower back.

"I don't want to go." Her whisper was treasonous, but only he could hear.

Neither do I. He lifted her head. She did not cry. She still held herself. He could too. "That's not my choice."

"Of course it's not, neither is it mine."

"No, I meant none of this is our choice. We have to do as we are told."

"I know. I don't want to leave. I don't want to be alone... surrounded by enemies."

"You've done it before, right? Espionage for the Court before the war began?"

"*Before the war.* Before we were all trying to kill each other. I was an agent of the Court then, not an *assassin.*"

"But it's a scouting mission. Isn't that what Thane Kelm said?"

"If you take anything from this day, let it be that the Patriarchy is no coalition of saints. I've known very few in my life, but if Thane Kelm is like the rest," her nails dug into his back as she whispered with lips nearly touching his ear, "then they're a cult of tyrants and heathens."

He shook as she let go of him.

"I want to be with you Yetrik, but... I'm sorry. I need time. We'll have one more night together before you leave. You better be there."

He touched her cheek. "Where are you going?"

"To talk to Thane Gett. One of the few old men I can actually trust." She gave him a playful slap on the shoulder. "Tonight. Not a minute after sundown. The same place."

Fear, confusion, and love intertwined in his mind as she walked towards Thane Gett.

Kevlen stood beside Thane Phemus. The Priesswoman rolled her eyes and wrists like a jester as she complained to Gruth Thane who could do nothing but nod.

Yetrik cocked his head when Kevlen spotted him. He did not wait before leaving Thane Phemus.

Kevlen jogged to meet Yetrik as he walked away from the diminishing council. "What?"

Yetrik looked back, relieved that they could leave without being followed. "If you want to stay with Thane Phemus, be my guest. I've had enough of *this* for the day."

"At least she's entertaining."

"So you want to stay?"

"Perd no," Kevlen chuckled. "That woman is the living embodiment of every *evil Priessman* stereotype that you other Courts have against us."

"We don't–"

"Perdling liar!"

Yetrik smiled, happy to see that Kevlen was not taking any offense as his charisma returned.

"Come on, Gruthman. Gossiping, carnal, lust-filled, and vain."

"I'm sorry if we act like that. We're a bunch of sanctimonious kulfs who could learn something about tolerance."

"Oh, don't worry. I was just listing Thane Phemus' qualities. Regardless, one of the few lessons I've learned from this war is that I'm more like some of you foreigners than I am my people. Take you, add a little more confidence, and better style, and you have me."

Yetrik thought it best to not mention Kevlen's breakdowns in lieu of his self-proclaimed confidence. He was pompous, but all pride lived to hide a hidden weakness. "A little Gruth could do you some good. I have my parents to thank. Teach a child well and they will parent themselves." Yetrik thought of his parents. He felt guilty for not visiting them during his stay, but he had distinct responsibilities. *And newfound intimacy.* He promised himself that he would see them when he helped bring peace to Facet. He couldn't let his mind consider the alternative. "Can I ask you about your father?"

"You know, Yetrik, I'm in a great mood right now and I would rather not ruin it." His smile was forced, his jaw tense. "I heard about your trip to the sea."

Yetrik's cheeks felt warm. "What do you mean?"

Kevlen laughed. The tension from mentioning his father had fled. "Avra told Khoga. Khoga hides nothing from me." Kevlen laughed even more as Yetrik shook his head.

"Perd, Priessman, can't a man... perd me, we sound like children."

"I'm happy for you."

"Sure you're not jealous?"

"Are you jesting, Gruthman? Have you forgotten who I am?"

"Pompous, prideful, and noble born."

"My posterity makes things a lot easier, but seeding out the best ones is hard. I'll find a woman when this is over."

"Good idea." *The fewer relationships you have, the less grief.* "It will make things less complicated."

"She seemed pretty distraught. Are you going to be fine without her?"

"Yeah," he shook his head, then turned to Kevlen. "We'll be together soon enough. She did something odd, though.."

"And that was?"

"She told me not to trust the Patriarchy, especially Thane Kelm.

Kevlen turned to him with a raised eyebrow. "Perd me, Gruthman, you have a lot to learn, don't you?"

"What do you mean?"

"If you're just now growing wary of the Patriarchy, you've been ignorant too long. Wait, where are we going, anyway?"

Yetrik pointed ahead. "I wanted to prepare Avra for the morning's flight."

"Good thinking. Some people think the nobility are the ones you shouldn't trust. Sure, some Thanes are self-serving kulfs, but at least their motives are clear. It's when they get involved with the Patriarchy that things become complicated. Take your Krall, for example, your Thane of Scholarship owns him."

"How do you know?"

"Because I've seen it too many times. He's a frightened sheep next to that Thane Kelm, but none of your other Thanes seemed to be as controlled by him. It's nowhere near as bad as Terin. That man is a serpent and a perding puppeteer. He practically owns Priess."

Ice ran through Yetrik's veins as he thought about his plethora of conversations that he had with the Priess Thane of Scholarship. Kevlen was right, but Yetrik did not want to face the consequences of liking Terin. Ignorance made things easier, just as pushing a mess to one side of a room to clear up the other half. His choice would have delayed consequences, but he was too much of a coward to face them.

⁂

Yetrik woke the next morning covered in sweat. Semi's warm body pressed against him. She continued to sleep as he sat up with a pounding pulse.

Avra beckoned him. Her call was unsteady. Despite her predatory skill, he was pleased that she, too, hated to kill.

Who bears the greater guilt? Our commanders, or me, for compelling her to comply with their vision of justice and order. Who am I to force her to obey the same orders that I question?

He stood, leaving Semi with a kiss, before joining Avra and the Terpels on their flight to Paiell.

CHAPTER THIRTY-THREE

THE BATTLE FOR PAIELL - PART III

T he burn of the icy rain was almost lost to Port as he stood among Sleffmen and Chussmen, facing the dilapidated southern wall of Paiell as they hid along the forest's edge. He had never wanted to leave his home more than in this moment of painful anticipation.

The eldeer bulged their eagerness to continue. He turned back to see the Beastling Endowers atop their tavern-size steeds whose antlers of countless prongs seemed to glow like pale blue moonlight under the dark clouds above.

It was no optimal day for a battle. Then again, no day ever was.

Port turned back to see three more Endowers emerge from the verdant woods, each one atop a new eldeer recruit.

A Sleffman, burly and in worn leather armor from the first battle of Paiell, ran from the army. "That's the last of them, Thane Kamen!"

Khenna approached from the right. "All the Endowers and Endowed have been well-fed to last the rest of the battle."

"Are your troops ready?"

She nodded. "Those here are. Once you sound the call, the eastern and western troops will charge in to take out the surrounding forces."

"Any reports from the scouts?"

"Nothing within the city. Zlatog guards have been posted near most of the major watchtowers. They'll notice us when we enter the clearing."

"And the Beastlings?"

Khenna nodded. "All with their steeds. You're sure they can call the zlatogs and eldeer simultaneously?"

"We hope so. Most of them can speak to multiple animals of the same species. They think they can manage two species, though we will see how it fares."

Khenna shook her head. "Perd, Sleffman, they know that the zlatogs have a humming language, don't they?"

"I believe so. The Beastlings have managed to work with fish. I imagine it can't be too different."

Khenna scowled.

"We cannot be sure about *everything*. This is a perding mess. I like that as much as you do. We're fortunate enough to have any help. Those zlatogs were sent from the under realms themselves, but they aren't invincible."

"Neither are we."

You know nothing, Chusswoman. We are as early snowflakes, melting until the future layers find a hold on our remains.

The eldeer bugled again.

"Enough of this, Chusswoman. The zlatogs will notice their calls. Take your legions. It is time."

She nodded and walked over to mount her ghete. "I'll be with the east legion. My seconds will man the west."

"I thought you were going with the west?"

"I'm following an impression. If the gods can't help us, no one can."

Port nodded. "I'm staying on the path to the southern wall. From what we can tell, the walls, or what remains of them, allow for the most people to enter at once. We'll give you some time to meet your legion in the east. Have some of your eldeer bugle when you've reached it. We'll sound ours and march at the same time."

"See you in the center, Sleffman."

"And you, Chusswoman. Care is the Creed."

She smiled and made a crown with her fingers in the Sleff salute. "Pious is the Giver, Sleffman."

Amidst the vice of cold, a warmth filled Port. The feeling lingered as she ran through the forest to meet her legion, though it dissipated as his mind returned to the battlefield.

He turned and spoke to the nearest soldiers, who then turned to their peers and relayed the plan to the entire southern army of Sleffmen and the few Chussmen among them.

The forest sounded like a cemetery of ghastly whispers, though they were yet to perish. Their breathing was hushed as clouds of warm breath rose.

The eldeer moved back and forth, ready to prance when called. Gorgers stretched near the front lines, large hammers clenched between gauntleted fists, ready to destroy any wall that stood in their way to reach the city center.

The rainfall slowed.

No sobbing could be heard, though Port knew many held back tears. Some whispered good wishes to each other while others said what they believed to be their last prayers.

Port shook, as did many others, as a zlatog screeched in the distance. One flew above the city and descended into its center.

Silence returned. The continual pulse of his heart filled Port's mind. Every limb shook as he was ready to sprint into battle. He would remain behind enough to shout commands and stay as safe as possible, but he would not let others die as he remained a coward.

"Perd," someone whispered.

"Come on already."

"I'm ready to die."

The whispers of restless warriors continued. Port tried to ignore them as they became more profane and cynical.

He focused on his goals. Achieving two was simple enough. Trying to manage the entire battle in one's mind was sure to cause disarray and chaos. *Kill the zlatogs.* He took in a deep breath of humid air. He felt as if frost coated his lungs. To the side of the city, he saw the broken remains of the collapsed Tower of Alms. They had destroyed one monument, despite the failure that accompanied it. Their next goal was just as simple, though much more politically significant. *Take Krall's Hill. Control or destroy the palace. Whatever is viable. Kill and destroy.*

Humans were made to create, but too often chose the opposite. Beauty is admirable. Destruction proves strength.

Oh lord Heitt, holy and high are—

His prayer was cut short as the eldeer in his legion joined their bugles with those in the east and west.

Some of the newer recruits shouted as they charged, but lost their motive as the veterans of Paiell ran in silence. The experienced troops ran in the back of the company, many limping from injuries that they had taken in the first battle for Paiell

Port's chest burned. Exhaustion and cold squeezed him.

Rain returned as they reached the southern wall.

The screech of zlatogs sounded from every direction. One ascended before them and was soon lost in the dark rain.

The procession continued into the city.

A screech took what little breath Port had as he was knocked to the side. Soldiers fell to dodge the zlatog reaper whose talons took out a row of unsuspecting Sleffmen.

Eldeer bugled as they ran towards the zlatog. It looped high above like an eagle ready to strike at a calculated moment. Its predatory gaze watched the eldeer, the army no longer its concern.

Port found himself among the weaker soldiers in the back, with most of the army now beyond the wall. Impulse told him to run ahead and join them in the bulk of the battle, but he had to know how the Beastlings fared against the zlatogs.

The Beastlings began to screech, mimicking the zlatog's insidious cries.

The zlatog ascended and dug its claws into the back of an eldeer, tearing its rider from its back with a chunk of the steed's flesh. The eldeer cried out in agony as it ran in circles, blood dripping down its back.

The zlatog dropped the Beastling from the clouds. The child called for the zlatog to save him, but no rescue came. Port screamed as the child slammed against the ground with an eruption of mud.

He remained back, unwilling to see the cost that the battle had already taken on the youth. The other two Beastlings ceased crying after the zlatogs and coordinated the movements of their eldeer.

The zlatog ascended in a steep drop.

One of the Beastling let out a higher-pitched bugle, and the eldeer remained still. The zlatog's talons opened, ready to capture another Beastling.

Justice charged its price for the creature's bloodlust. It screeched as the eldeer's antlers impaled its body. The antlers had spread out from its ball of thorns into barbed vines that had captured the zlatog just before it reached the Beastling.

The zlatog screeched as its rider pounded on its side with their hands. The Priess Beastling's last commands proved futile.

The eldeer's antlers kept the zlatog immobile and rolled it back into the ball atop its head, squeezing the bat-drake like hands wringing out a rag. The zlatog and rider screamed together as they were crushed in a mess of unbreakable antlers and prongs as sharp as any sword.

Port ran forward to understand what had happened as the eldeer unfurled its antlers before itself to free the gory remains of the zlatog and its rider.

"What perding happened?" Port screamed to the other Beastling who had witnessed the execution. Her steed lowered to let her meet him.

"I don't know," she whimpered.

He turned to the sound of trotting and falling. The first-attacked eldeer had fallen near its rider. Blood continued to seep out as its cries ceased. The bloody-antlered eldeer let its Beastling down to approach them.

He ran with the younger Beastling towards the older one as she ascended her mount, covered in blood from the crushed zlatog. She was bereft of emotion while the younger Beastling sobbed.

"It didn't work," the younger Beastling said between sniffs.

"Of course it didn't work." Her voice was mature and cold. "We should have never lost Hae."

Port held the gloved hand of the younger Beastling in his. "What was the problem? Where their riders better–"

"*Perd,* no. All Endowed are weaker in skill than any Endower. Like we said, the battle, the zlatogs have their own humming language. I think the rider used that to override any command I gave."

"So we can't defeat them?" the younger Beastling whimpered.

"Didn't you see what I just did? Kill those perding zlatogs like that. Don't worry about trying to control them or you'll end up like Hae."

The younger Beastling nodded.

"Now you get it? Good." She slapped the younger Chussgirl on the back. "You ride west, I'll take the east. Don't enter deep into the city yet but go tell the other Beastlings what we have learned."

"Don't you think they've figured it out by now?" asked Port. "The zlatogs were posted around the city's circumference. If they don't know yet, they'll learn before you reach them. Head into the city and search for more zlatogs. We need to eliminate them as quickly as possible before they take out too many of our ground troops."

The older Beastling stared at him, mouth agape, like he was a punishing parent.

"I'm the commander here. Don't forget that." He hated saying it, but knew what it would take for her to obey. "Do you understand, Chusswoman?"

"Yes, Thane Kamen."

He squeezed the younger Beastling's hand. "And you too?"

"Everything will be alright if we do what you say, right?"

Perd. I can't lie to you, either.

"Come on," the older Beastling said before Port would come up with an excuse. The younger Chussgirl turned and followed her as they ran towards their steeds. "Have your eldeer extend its antlers and roll them back to protect anything that comes at you from above and you'll be–"

Her words faded in the rain.

Port shook slushy rain from his armor and jogged towards the city, only to collect more as it fell from above. He found himself among the injured and continued to run with the adrenaline that he had until he reached the newer recruits. They fought enemy Sleffmen and Priessmen in untouched armor a few streets away from the center.

The familiar clamor of battle cries and clashing metal rang in his ears. His eyes shot from side to side, looking for an opportunistic point of entry. The battle line pushed forward, each step moving slowly but faster than the last.

He looked up to see the Sleff banner waving high in the dark storm clouds. Krall's Hill hid behind the gradual rise of buildings. Still, the banner atop the palace remained visible for all. The goal was in sight. They still had a long while to go before they reached it, but it was closer than Bruten. That was enough.

Port almost fell over as an overzealous Sleffman hit his shoulder in pursuit of combat. *Do you know what you are doing?* He straightened and shook his head. *I am weak for not doing the same?*

The Sleffman continued to run with a distinct limp. His leathers had large slashes and burn marks across the back.

He was with us the first time. He knows exactly what he is doing.

Port readied himself to run alongside the man but halted just behind the front lines as one of his recently appointed captains shouted commands with his sword raised and pointing towards the tower.

"Captain!" he shouted as he approached, having forgotten the man's name, even though he too was there for the first battle of Paiell.

The captain stepped down from the remains of a stone bench and turned back. "Thane Kamen?"

Amidst the chaos, Port still found himself worried about a matter of self-worth. *I am a coward. I have become prideful, unworthy of bearing such a title.*

"What has happened?" the exasperated captain said.

"What has–"

"Are you injured? Have the others fallen?"

Port shook his head. "I was with the Beastlings, it's not–tell me what's happened." He looked past the captain, noting that the army had advanced a street further. "Where do you need me?"

He laughed and wiped his forehead with the back of his hand. The leather glove left a bloody streak. "You're the Thane! You should be the—" He stopped speaking and looked past Port.

Port turned around to hear the unified bugle of two eldeer, both now had bloody antlers curled into brambles atop their heads.

The Allegiant troops who noticed them in time ran out of their path, while the others continued to slay their opponents.

Port was far enough away and was frozen in awe as he watched the magnificent beasts. The eldeer pranced and jumped over the nearest engagements, landing atop enemy soldiers. Port was sure that some Allegiant soldiers had fallen, even perished in their wake, yet he knew it would be worth the cost.

The eldeer lowered their heads, making only their backs visible as they seemed to sweep the enemy lines with their antlers. As they lifted their heads, Port could see that they had stretched out their antlers, impaling entire companies and twisting them back up in their crown of prongs.

Energy rather than ice filled Port's lungs as he charged forward with the army. He followed a group that ran to the right of the eldeer as the Beastlings continued to wreak havoc in the center of the street.

An eldeer bugled, capturing his attention for a second. Port shook and cried out as a blade slashed his cheek. He turned, the pain growing worse, surprised to see that no one had attacked him, but an ally had fallen against him. The man had fallen on him with a raised sword, but it did not cut too deep. Once he regained focus, he saw that the man stood no more and screamed as a prong of a fallen eldeer held him against the ground.

One of the Beastlings ran further into the city while her steed remained standing. Sleffmen loyalists climbed atop the fallen eldeer and repeatedly stabbed it, blood dripping with the rain that ran down its body. Its rider was nowhere to be seen.

A group of Allegiant soldiers climbed up the beast's side to wage against the enemies, who were fixated on eliminating any remaining chance it had to survive. The captain, whose name Port had forgotten, decapitated a loyalist and prepared for his next target behind him. Two Allegiant soldiers stood to protect the incapacitated Beastling who was tangled up in the makeshift saddle they had created for her with leather straps.

Two loyalists ran towards the captain, one parried his strike and the other kicked him from atop the eldeer's head into the antlers. He screamed and twisted, unable to escape impalement.

Port's instincts kicked in and he ran to join the fight to ensure that the Beastling would survive, if she had not yet perished. One of the Allegiant soldiers left her with the other and joined Port as he ran to meet the approaching loyalists.

Running across the dead creature felt like a desecration of its glory. With each step, he felt his foot press into fat. Any rib or muscle was a gift of stability.

One of the loyalists slipped on the rain-slick fur and caught himself halfway down its side as he plunged a sword into it. The Allegiant soldier stabbed him before he could find his way back up. The loyalist fell into Allegiant soldiers below, leaving his sword in the Eldeer's side.

As Port's blade collided with that of his enemy, he found himself more practiced against the loyalist's uncoordinated movements. Still, he recognized his weakness.

The loyalist struck Port's shoulder, though it only shook his armor. He felt himself sliding to his right and crouched to grab a weak hold of the eldeer's fur. It was not an ideal grip, but it helped him slide slower and catch his opponent off guard. He swung his sword at his opponent's leg near the slope of the eldeer's chest. As he expected, it did not injure the man but caused him to stumble and slide off just like his ally.

Port had no time to risk seeing how the loyalist landed. He moved back to the beast's side and pressed on towards the loyalists.

Two Allegiant soldiers fell, but the remaining three helped Port knock off four loyalists before they could reach the Beastling.

Port gasped as he crouched beside her, her body lying prostrate on the beast's back. "Is she–"

"She's fine," said the first Allegiant soldier to reach her, a Chusswoman. She pulled the Beastling up and into an embrace, then moved the girl's brown hair from her eyes to reveal a face half-covered in blood. "Just a little startled. She's got a cut on her forehead, but nothing too bad."

Port stepped closer and heard her cry. "Are you sure?"

"Hey," the soldier turned the Beastling's to face Port, "your Thane wants to know if you are alright."

"They killed him!" she cried. "We have to kill them all! They killed my friend!" She kicked free from the soldier's grip and grabbed the eldeer's fur, pressing her face against it.

"Come on!" the Soldier said as she pried the Beastling back up and into her arms.

Port placed his hand on the Chussgirl's shoulder. "We have to keep moving." He knew not what else to say. He had treated Endowers as children and other times as adults, but both felt incorrect.

"I'm going to kill them for what they did!" She bugled, but no Eldeer answered her call. Each Beastling had their own steed, their own companion. *They will fall just like this one, a commodity for war.*

Her cry to kill everyone who stood against them pained his strategist's mind and conscience alike. *Perhaps this is the greatest crime of all. We did not harvest from these children, yet we turned them into vessels of hatred. Innocence stolen for the sake of continual death.*

She let out another bugle and was answered. The reply was not that of an eldeer, but by that of a zlatog, screeching from above.

"Perd," the Chusswoman said under her breath. She looked back and forth between the Beastling and the sky. "Do something about it!"

She let out a bugle, one with a wounded moan to it.

She shook the Beastling. "No, not–gah! Your perding eldeer is dead! What don't you understand? Control the perding bat!"

The Beastling started to cry.

"Perding–" Port cut the Chusswoman off with a gauntleted slap. He held back, but it still left an imprint.

"*You* don't understand." He grabbed the Beastling and helped her stand. "Is there anything you can do?"

She let out another pained eldeer cry.

The soldier rubbed her cheek. "See! Perding girl doesn't understand anything!"

The zlatog screeched as it descended as fast as the rain. Port grabbed the girl and rolled, aiming to follow the path down the creature's leg towards the ground. They rolled off the edge of the eldeer's knee and fell the height of a person, tumbling down as they landed on a pile of stone rubble.

His head spun and pulsed as his aching back seized. "Are you okay?" he grunted.

He followed the Beastling's gaze upward just in time to see the zlatog release the soldier that had been with them from its grip. His limp body joined allies and enemies alike in the eldeer's antlers.

Port covered his ears as the Beastling let out yet another eldeer cry. His headache turned to an agonizing migraine.

Before he could beg her to stop, she did of her own accord. A distant eldeer let out a powerful, reassuring bugle that grew louder by the second.

The zlatog's screech joined the cacophony.

Each sound drew closer. Port felt a child himself, covering his head as titans clashed around him.

The ground rumbled. The Beastling held onto him with unrelenting tenacity. He pressed past the painful sounds and overwhelming atmosphere, daring a glance up. Another eldeer had answered the young Beastling's call and stood above them with the zlatog caught in its antlers. It wailed and tried to flap its way free, but the eldeer's antler vice continued to tighten and twist.

Port's attention snapped away from the creatures and to the fallen eldeer's legs as something slapped onto its drenched fur. A body had fallen onto it and slid down, then fell with a metallic crash near Port.

A heavily armored Priessman, though he wore no helm, pressed himself up from the ground. Before Port could think how to react, the Priessman let out an Eldeer's bugle.

The eldeer tossed the zlatog corpse aside. It let out a call, then shook its head and started to lose balance.

Just like the kaesan.

"Can you do something?" Port held the Beastling's arms

"I-I–"

"Anything! Please!"

She copied the other Beastling Endower's call as she tried to control her steed.

The eldeer stilled and stared at the Priessman, targeting him, then ran and pounded him with its massive hooves. All that remained was a mess of twisted metal and blood that steamed in the cold.

Port felt an impulse to shield the child's eyes, yet they were the ones to commit such an act. Maturation or death. There was no middle ground. They paved the way so that there might be a choice in the future.

"Come up!" the Beastling who had saved them shouted. The eldeer lowered itself. Its head twitched as if a fly continued to land on its nose. He couldn't imagine what it would be like to be controlled by a child, let alone torn between conflicting voices and forced to kill one.

She extended her hand to help the younger Beastling climb up and sit behind her. "Are you coming, Thane Kamen?"

He looked towards the battle lines. They sounded like a storm moving away and had passed multiple streets while he was otherwise occupied. He couldn't see much of the battle, but knew he had to join them.

The older Beastling let down a hand. He took it and rode behind the two girls as the eldeer took them back to the heat of battle.

The Allegiant front had spread out, following three different paths that forked out, but each led to the center.

"Take me over there."

"Where?" the older Beastling asked.

He pointed to the street. As they approached the clash of soldiers, his suspicions were confirmed. At the end of the street, just beyond the loyalist troops, he spotted a company of Chussmen in their silver armor and red leathers. The size of the loyalist company rapidly diminished as it was pressed between Sleffmen from the south and Chussmen from the north.

"Where exactly?" she asked. "You won't do anything. Just *look* at what's happening!" Joy filled her voice after being deprived of it for so long.

Chussmen and Sleffmen trampled over loyalist corpses as they closed the gap.

"Go back and to the left. The others will need our help."

The Beastling sighed and pulled back to lead the eldeer to the middle road. She pointed down. "Is that what you want? Do you want me to drop you off in the middle?"

He held back from biting at her patronizing tone. He *had* to do something. They needed him. He was the Thane of Harmony. To stand and observe was betrayal while they waged the war.

Where is your humility, Sleffman? She's right.

The eldeer could toss him into the heat of battle, but what difference would that make? What would he gain besides aggrandizing himself as a savior, if not only to perish a moment later? He had given commands and their strategies were proving successful. What else was he expected to do when the soldiers led themselves?

Still, I am no greater than them. Pious is the Giver. Pious is the one who gives his life for another.

He achieved nothing while waiting atop the eldeer and knew that was enough motivation to act. He had fulfilled his duty as captain. If he fell, another would take his place. *One much better.*

He commanded the Beastling to let him down. Though he would make little difference, he felt his conscience soothe as he joined his fellow Sleffmen.

Dropping onto the battlefield felt like plunging into a half-frozen lake. His nerves seized and his head ached as he found himself amidst the heat of clashing blades.

"Thane Kamen!" a soldier shouted. "What are you doing here? You should not—"

The words drifted away by the shouts and grunts as he pressed closer to the battle line.

Doubts continued to bombard him. He pressed onward, reciting in his mind a psalm from the *Tome of the Meek.*

"Pious is the Giver. In all shall I give."

Perding fool! You are not irreplaceable. You've had to learn so much to come here. Colrig invested too much in you! You've already given enough for this battle.

"Never shall I shirk, for Heitt has given all."

Perding fool!

"I defy the wisdom of the flesh for that which is holy."

He unsheathed his blade and stepped forward, finding himself standing between two Sleff soldiers. One had lost an eye. Half of her face continued to drip blood. The other held a sword before him to block, his other hand hung limp and bloody at his side.

Port jumped back as a loyalist rammed a spear into the limp-armed man's chest.

A coward and a fool. As prideful as a Priessman.

"As my brethren have given, so shall I. This I give as a final gift, my life and soul."

Port grabbed the shaft of the spear before the loyalist could pull it back through the soldier's body. The loyalist stumbled forward. Port stepped closer and grabbed the loyalist's shoulder pad, throwing him down to the floor.

Port plunged his blade into the exposed area below the back of the loyalist's helm. Before Port could toss the body aside, his vision seemed to be an explosion of black and white as the force of a ghete in pursuit slammed into his side.

He was tossed, rolling across bodies, both living and dead, before he stopped atop a mound of corpses. How many, he could not tell, nor did he care, for his side burned. Burning became a searing. A blade had found its way into his side.

He screamed and rolled over, pulling the dagger from his side. Out of pure chance, the dagger of a fallen soldier had found its use without anyone wielding it.

Port sat up and saw an armored Gorger, three times his size, charging at him to finish his kill. Port had no time to react himself. Two Allegiant soldiers pushed him aside and out of the Gorger's wake.

The Gorger ran not only at the Allegiant soldiers, but he had impaled both of them with a claymore, one in each of his hands. The Gorger continued to impale more Allegiant soldiers until the weight of bodies became even too burdensome for him.

Port's head pounded. His vision was blurred, and he could not focus on his side enough to see how badly he bled.

"Get him out of here!"

He turned to see who had shouted, but could not find them as others joined in.

"I'll take him!"

"Hurry, he's bleeding out!"

"Is he going to die?"

"Perd!"

"Save the Thane!"

"The Thane is dead. Look at him!"

"Where's a Eurtythin?"

He found a moment of clarity atop the shoulders of a giant shoulder. An Allegiant Gorger ran him away from the battlefield. As the sound of battle seemed more distant, though ever loud, he could hear his grunting. He wanted to command the Gorger to return him, but he knew he would die. It was true. He was a fool. He would die, accomplishing nothing but wasted effort.

"Find me a perding Eurythrin!" the Gorger shouted. He slowed to a heavy-footed trot. "Hurry! The perding Thane is about to die!"

"Put me down," Port moaned.

"We can't find any!" someone shouted.

"What do you mean? How can you lose them?"

"We're using them all across the battlefield! Some of the Beastlings were injured while fighting–"

"I know! I mean, just hurry!" The Gorger lowered Port into a cradled grip.

"Bring him here," an unfamiliar voice said. "Let me take a look."

"You a medic?" the Gorger lowered Port to the ground before a Sleff-man.

"I saw enough after the first battle here to know what kind of injury means death."

Port hissed as the man moved his armor and clothes to expose the dagger wound.

"Perding lucky kulf," the Sleffman chuckled.

Port sat up, hissing as he did so. "What?"

"Get up, Thane, you're fine." The Allegiant soldier was an older man who wore less armor than most. He looked at the Gorger and pointed down the street. "Get back out there! They need you."

"Not for long," the Gorger replied. "I would've had a couple of unendowed bring him back, but the Chussmen are closing in. They'll be done any second now. You're sure he'll be fine?"

"The Thane? Won't even need to stitch it up. You overreacted."

"Perding Sleffman. *He's* the one that acted like he was dying!"

I didn't. Did I?

"Whatever." The Sleffman soldier waved him away. "You go do something else. I'll keep him here before he is foolish enough to try to kill himself again."

Not a coward, a fool. You almost wasted your life for nothing more than to show what you thought you could do.

Their words stirred his thoughts that stung worse than the wound. *If I shirk with such a minor injury, how much more are those who die giving?*

The old soldier tore a piece of cloth from a corpse and wound it around Port's chest, placing more atop the wound.

He recalled the soldier who still fought with a limp arm and the other who fought, even though half of her face was useless.

I retreated after a scratch. They continued with a foot in the under realms.

Forgive me, Heitt, for I have given so little. I will give enough. I promise thee.

I have not yet given enough.

I'll give it all.

All that remains.

"There," the old soldier tucked the end of the fabric in.

I will become worthy. In the end. Nothing will remain. I am yours, Lord.

"Feel better?"

Port turned to see the man, finding it much easier to focus. "Yeah. It still stings."

"Of course it does. No matter how small, it was still a cut."

Port stood but held onto the soldier's shoulder. He was lightheaded. Hungry, even thirsty. Fatigue settled in.

"At least we've scared away the civilians." noted the old soldier. "I've spotted a few from their windows. Can't imagine how terrified they must be. Then again, we're the ones throwing ourselves out to die. A little fear could do us well. Sorry if I was too hard on you, Thane Kamen."

Port saluted the old soldier, then turned to the battle, which had indeed diminished. The sound of clashing swords and armor echoed in the west, but it had ceased ahead and to the east.

The old soldier stood and placed his hands on his hips. "Not too bad, right? Good call with the Chussmen entering from the side."

You should be thanking Khenna. Port nodded and left the soldier behind.

He started back down the road toward the city center.

A limping soldier waved at him. "We've done it, Thane Kamen!"

"We've only taken a step forward, Sleffman. Keep pressing forward."

"Yes, of course."

The same conversation repeated as he walked through the soldiers towards the Chussman who had pressed the enemy forces from the other side.

Their responses became more congratulatory, each one pressing Port's guilt further.

"Well done, Thane!"

"This is your victory, Thane Kamen!"

"Praise the Sleff Thane of Harmony!"

"Even *he* fought alongside us."

Lies. I am not enough. I never have been. Perd you Colrig, why did you think I was worthy of this?

He held his composure, ignoring the cacophony of praise, but knew he would lose it if called to fight again.

"Thane Kamen."

Port pressed past the soldier.

"Thane Kamen!" the same voice shouted.

He turned to look at a Chussman.

"What is it?"

The soldier scowled. "Do you not recognize... nevermind that. Now that we've reached your legions, you should speak with Captain Lonik, she–"

"Who are you to tell me what I should do?"

The Chussman's mouth hung open in silence. His eyebrows arched rather than drawn to anger.

What was that for? Just because you are in pain does not mean you should lash out on an eager ally.

Port looked down. The Chussman was missing two fingers that still bled from the stumps. *Perd.* "Forgive me, Chussman, I'll seek her out."

"No forgiveness required, Thane Kamen."

Chuss charity. We could all learn something from each other. How can I focus on another Ideal when mine is so fleeting? Where is the balance between humility and pride for one meant to lead?

Perd me, Heitt. Forgive me for what I have become.

When this all ends, let me leave as a worthy representative of thy name.

The Chussman stared at him, but Port remained silent for a moment longer. His faith burned, though he knew his request would come at a price.

Humble me, Lord Heitt. Be it in life or death, I will give enough. Whatever thou desirest, let me give it.

"Is she looking for me?" Port asked

The Chussman shook his head. "She told all of her seconds to search you out when our troops met. I suppose I was lucky to find you."

"So where is she?"

"She was with us, but left to help clear the western passage as soon as we drew closer to victory here. It should be safe to head there. By the time you arrive, they should have cleared it, if your troops have continued to press forward from your side."

Port nodded and offered the man the Chuss salute. His eyes opened wide and he returned the gesture. He smiled with bloody teeth and an eye that could not quite open all the way.

The Chussman called the two nearest Chuss soldiers. "Help escort Thane Kamen to the western legion. He is to meet with Captain Lonik. Ensure that they meet safely."

Port wanted to refuse the offer, but realized how disgraceful it would have been. Humility was returning to his heart, though it was gradual and could be easily frightened.

The two Chuss soldiers walked a step ahead of him, each with their sword at the ready. He almost stumbled as they crossed over bodies, Sleff loyalist and Chussman alike. Though they had found victory on this street, it had come with a cost. *As does every battle. All the more reason to end it as soon as possible.*

They passed through the southernmost part of the central square to reach the western passage. Chussmen obscured his view. They stood still, ignoring the corpses at their feet, ready for the next order. He focused on the guards as they turned left.

The metallic clatter continued but combat in the western passage had also ended. Sleffmen and Chussman marched towards the central square, many stumbling in fatigue as he did over the mass of bodies spread across the cobblestone street. The cracks between stones would forever be stained with the blood of the city's inhabitants over their disagreements. How could a Court expect the aid of their god when all the vilest atrocities were wrought by their own hands? The war was no divine punishment, but a tragedy wrought by humankind itself.

Port lifted his gaze from a crushed head down the street at the sound of an eldeer bugle. A Beastling marched their steed forward from the back of the street. Victory had been called. Though it was a small step towards a greater triumph, it still deserved recognition.

"Captain Lonik!" Port turned to see a Chusswoman shouting, a dented helm in the crux of her elbow. "Thane Kamen has arrived!"

A head higher than the rest of the Chussman caused the limping crowd to split. Captain Khenna Lonik slowed her ghete's trot as she neared Port, who raised his sword to hail her.

"Perd, even you've taken a beating. Good on you for joining the efforts."

He forced a chuckle. "You as well."

She touched her cheek, wiping off crusted blood. "The armor may look pitiful, but nothing worse than a few bruises." She patted her steed's head. "She took worse. Some slashes on the side and the perding kulfs took her tail as a trophy. Little it did for them as she mauled them down in retribution. Maybe you should hold back next time. Can't have our general dying in a minor scuffle."

I have not yet given enough. "And you'll still join them?"

"Of course! Why else would I have the ghete? I suppose you could make an argument that—no none of that matters. I'm the captain of just my share of the army. You're the perding Thane of Harmony. You don't see Thane Stolk here, do you?"

"No, I suppose not."

"Be careful, Sleffman. We're just as vulnerable as those who have fallen."

He nodded but cared not to think further upon her words. He had been too reserved, too weak, and would not allow for that to repeat.

Logic was fleeting for the sake of honor, and he was fine with that. "I saw that you've already occupied the center. How many did they have positioned there?"

"Very few compared to those around the perimeter. We cleared it within a few minutes, though I noted that many fled to larger groups of their soldiers to even the odds. How was the south?"

"Sizable, as we expected. Despite our losses, I anticipated that it would have been much more difficult to reach this point."

She nodded. "As you should. The eastern and western passages were well manned, but we caught a glimpse of some of the northern areas as the city rises. The palace, at least, is surrounded by a vast number of soldiers, many of which seemed much larger than the others."

"I should have assumed they would leave most of the Gorgers to protect the nobility. It's a shame so many remained loyal when they were all made for the Allegiant." He sighed. "With most of the Cantons in the northern districts of the city, we can anticipate that it will become even more difficult."

"Keep your hopes high, Sleffman."

"I'm trying."

"I trust the Beastlings and their eldeer fared well?"

"We should have sent more with you. The zlatogs almost worthless with the eldeer on our sides. Did the zlatogs trouble you?"

"We lost a fair amount of soldiers to some, but a colony of them retreated."

"Retreated?"

She shrugged. "So we suppose. At least three flew to the east. A blessing indeed."

"I would think otherwise."

"Why? With how easily our eldeer took them out, it would make sense that they would avoid wasting them."

"While they continue to 'waste' the lives of foot soldiers?"

"Then what do you suppose, Sleffman?"

"While they have sufficient forces to challenge us, there are few compared to before. There is a reason we retreated rather than mere zlatogs. Even if we assume that they have more in the northern districts, I doubt that is all."

"You think they are marshaling troops elsewhere?"

He nodded. "I would be wary of the east. With the Priess Beastlings resting there, we should expect that they'll recruit eldeer or any other beasts in place of their zlatogs."

Khenna nodded and cursed under her breath. "Perhaps we should find some loyalists on the edge of death. Those in pain may give information in exchange for mercy, or do we have any Feelman?"

"Not that I know of."

She shook her head and stared at the ground. "Despite all of our preparation, we still fall short."

"Is anyone ever prepared for war?"

She chuckled. "Before all of this began, to do so would have been cynical."

"Cynical or realistic?"

"Who can tell these days?

"I suppose that depends on one's faith in humanity."

"And your faith?"

He gripped the hilt of his sword. "In my god? Ever present. In humankind, ever diminishing."

"Let us do our best to change that."

I have not yet given enough. "I know I will. I pray others are willing to do the same."

He found optimism a difficult feat, but even Khenna seemed to have lost her ever-present smile. She spoke after a moment of silence, each of them staring off into the distance. "To the north then, Thane?"

"Let's hold firm before we send everyone there. While you have a ghete"—he pointed to the eldeer down the street—"would you mind running to have the Beastlings scout around the perimeter to ensure the eastern and western districts have been taken care of?"

"Of course," she pulled on the ghete's reins.

"Care is the Creed, Chusswoman." He made a circle with his hands over his chest, forming the Chuss salute.

"Pious is the Giver." She returned the Sleff salute and departed.

As he made eye contact with passing Chuss soldiers, they too saluted him with the Sleff sign.

How odd that years ago such a display would have seemed treasonous. In the Harmony Allegiant, it had become so commonplace to exchange salutes as mingling with foreigners became more frequent than it had been in decades previous.

The platitude, so often spoken by leaders of the Harmony Allegiant, returned to his mind. *It took us a war to realize the need to love one another.*

Though the members of the Allegiant grew closer, the division between them and the loyalists grew evermore pernicious.

CHAPTER THIRTY-FOUR

THE BATTLE FOR PAIELL - PART IV

Yetrik almost fell off of Avra as Kevlen dove before him towards the forest below. He recalled flying past the large clearing below them and knew that they had at a fair distance ahead before they reached Paiell.

Avra hummed her confusion. He patted an assurance and conveyed his trust in Kevlen. Learning that he could trust a Priessman, someone he had been raised to detest, had done much to shift his ever changing view on Court identities. He had met imperfect Zhaesmen and quickly understood that a Priessmen with a touch of humility was not so absurd.

He patted her again and she dove after Khoga and Kevlen.

As they descended below the thin layer of clouds, Yetrik saw that Kevlen had led them to a village, or rather than an empty clearing. He tried to save his questions, but recognized Kevlen's maneuver. A zlatog below flapped its wings as Khoga and Avra slowed their descent.

Avra landed with the grace of an uncoordinated boy jumping from a wall as she raced alongside Khoga to meet their unknown relative. The three beasts screeched in unison, then began humming.

Yetrik placed his hand against Avra to feel her hums as she communicated with the other Zlatogs the language most intimate to them. He shot a quick glance at Kevlen, who did likewise.

At a glance, the zlatogs were identical. Some had distinct characteristics, such as Avra's right ear, that failed to stand, but that was nothing compared to what their rider could sense. Yetrik's soul had bound itself to her. He could recognize her as well as his parents. Without Kevlen, he found it near impossible to know which zlatog was Khoga.

"*Who are you?*" Avra hummed.

The zlatog hummed.

"*Gholl.*" Khoga and Avra repeated.

Yetrik did not understand the name until he felt the vibrations spoken by Avra. Though he understood the zlatog hums as well as his native tongue, their names had a deeper significance, one translated into simpler sounds by Avra.

Avra pounded the floor with the claws on her wings. "*You were with the colony in Paiell. Why did you defect?*"

"*I do not defect but have come to warn!*" Gholl screeched.

Khoga hummed. "*Yet you depart the colony.*"

"*I did nothing of the sort!*"

Avra hummed as well, despite Gholl's screeching outbursts. "*You have a companion? Invite them out. Let the humans settle this matter. Only their matters, those related to their war, would trump your reasoning for departing your station.*"

Gholl screeched, the same pitch that Avra had used to awaken Yetrik too often as of late.

Yetrik patted her. "*Why patronize your kin? If Gholl has come to warn us, I don't see why you and Khoga should be so... I cannot think of the concept to percuss. You speak to offend.*"

"*You misunderstand zlatog emotions, Yetrik. Humans are too quick to take offense. Zlatogs do not find it a crime to speak in such a manner.*"

"*Gholl sounded quite frustrated with your accusations.*"

Avra kept her focus on Yetrik. "*Statements, not accusations. As I said, this is how we speak. Neither party is a coward that shrinks away because of the directness of one's voice.*"

Yetrik hummed his agreement.

"*You still have much to learn, Yetrik. You are wise enough to recognize that we are not bound to serve you in this war because we side with your politics.*"

"*Then why do you help us?*"

"*I ask myself that same question too often as of late. We have our own matters to deal with, yet we let your human quarrels triumph. This is all because of our bonds with you.*"

"*I'm flattered.*"

"*Though I have developed an affinity for you, not all zlatogs take such a liking to their riders, despite their soul bonds.*"

How much of the bond is their choice? Are we imposing our will upon them? Do you actually care for me, Avra? He wondered how well she could read his thoughts, for he often understood her unspoken feelings. "*You said you have personal matters outside of our war.*"

"*Of course we do. Life. Culture. All that you have. Does that surprise you?*"

"*No, I... I just never thought about it. Is that why you reprimanded Gholl for leaving Paiell?*"

"*In a way. We will learn why her rider brought her here. She left the colony in Paiell. I feel you do not understand why this is such a dangerous thing. I do not expect you to. You may be bound to me, but you will never be a zlatog. This is but a small contradiction of desires between my kind and yours. I do not expect it to cause any problem. Then again, I remain ever cautious."*

"Captain Phanos!" a Priesswoman shouted as she ran past Gholl and stopped before Khoga.

Kevlen dismounted. He raised his furrowed eyebrows. He ran to her and they spoke.

"Do you hear what they are saying?" Yetrik patted.

"He is your ally. Why did you not join him?" Avra hummed.

"I'm still learning where I stand in the ranks of his Beastling corps."

"You seem to run back and forth between confidence and cowardice."

"I know. I'm trying to improve."

"You have done well maintaining humility amidst your prideful companion."

"He is humbler than most of his people. I suppose they would count that as a weakness where I see it as a virtue."

"Yetrik!" Kevlen waved him over.

Avra lowered herself for him to dismount. *"Even he seems to trust you more than you do yourself."*

Yetrik caught his balance with a hand on Avra as he jumped down. He ran to meet them and recalled having seen the Priesswoman before, though he had forgotten her name. He popped his ears as they continued to readjust to the rapid drop in elevation. "Yes?"

Kevlen sighed. "Paiell has been attacked. The Harmony Allegiant returned."

Yetrik's eyes shot to the Priesswoman, who now stroked the side of Gholl. She nodded.

"How long ago? How bad was it?"

"Three days ago," she replied. "I fled to post here to warn you before the city fell into their control. I sent some falcons to scout and have learned that they still fight with some of our forces that from the surrounding villages, but the city is practically theirs."

Kevlen and Yetrik exchanged glances.

"Forgive me for leaving the city, Captain Phanos, but I knew you were coming from the east. Three other zlatog riders left with me to await any sign of your company in some other villages nearby. I was just lucky enough to be the one you found."

"If your zlatog had not been out in the open," said Kevlen, "we wouldn't have. With how close the city is, we would have reached it without a warning." He looked to Yetrik. "We'll have to fly back and alert Thane Kelm before he and the Terpels reach us." He returned his focus to the Priesswoman. "Were our initial reinforcements so feeble? Why did you and the zlatogs flee when you could have helped turn the tides? How large were their armies this time?"

"Most of the zlatogs died. Knowing you and Khoga would likely lead a counterattack, I could not let you go in blind."

"Gorgers?" Yetrik asked.

"Some," she replied, "but they brought Endower Beastlings on eldeer."

Kevlen chuckled, though he had started to sweat. "And what did they do? Trample the zlatogs? Were you perding kulfs foolish enough to stay on the ground the whole time?"

Her frown became more pronounced. "They used their antlers to capture any zlatogs who attacked them and wrung them dry with their riders like bloody cloths."

Kevlen chuckled. He moved his fingers in quick repetition at his side just as he did before breaking down in panic.

"What do you mean?" asked Yetrik. "Are you sure these were eldeer?"

"Of course!"

"And their antlers... moved?"

She nodded. "Like thorny tentacles."

Kevlen's face relaxed. "Antlers are not malleable."

"Fine, I'm lying. Is that what you want to hear? You've seen similar things happen when you control beasts. What about the percussion-speak we use with our zlatogs? I know you've seen animals and beasts behave strangely, sometimes manifesting a new skill when you use your beast call."

"Yes, but nothing of this scale."

She almost spat on him with the seething frustration in her voice. "These Endowers are more than we could ever hope to be. The sooner you learn that Endowers are more in touch with their abilities, the better. Sometimes we need to set aside pride to see the truth. Call me a traitor to our Ideal, I don't care. The war is changing more each day, and not in our favor."

Kevlen let out an exaggerated breath, shook his head, then looked back at her. "Then what should we do?"

"What about the Terpels?" Yetrik asked.

Kevlen swatted the air. "We'll get to that. I'm sure we'll win on the ground, but *she* insists that we don't use our *beloved* steeds."

"I never said that. I just meant that you cannot go for their eldeer with your zlatogs. Perhaps bring something else to use or stay away from the eldeer."

"Despite our troop numbers, I would like something large if we have to take out those behemoths." He turned to Yetrik. "Do you want to search the forest for some beasts to use, or would you rather speak with Thane Kelm?"

"Why can't the zlatogs just avoid the eldeer?" asked Yetrik.

"You would think it would be so simple," said the Priesswoman, "but the eldeer are quite fast when controlled by Beastlings. I would have thought we could just attack around them, but the eldeer follow the zlatogs well below and caught too many of our Beastlings off guard, following throughout the entire city like moving bear traps. Unless we take them out first, we're better off without them."

Kevlen shook his head.

"Now you see why we retreated. Why don't you two leave the eldeer recruitment to me?"

"Are there any other beasts that might be better to use?" asked Kevlen.

She shook her head. "None that I have found. Plenty of bears and large cats, but nothing that would prove a challenge to the eldeer. Let me handle that part while you two focus on the army. Gholl and I will alert our other Beastlings in the nearby villages to do the same. We will all leave our zlatogs in a village and meet you with the eldeer on the eastern side of Paiell before you begin the complete invasion. How far out would you say the Gruth army is? A few days behind you?"

"Hours," Kevlen said. "The Terpels are sprinting the entire way."

Yetrik heard Avra's hum. He dismissed Kevlen to tell the Priesswoman what the Terpels were. Yetrik had not even known what they were until some few days before but had not the time or will to question Thane Kelm about them. More Endowed types continued to reveal themselves, though all seemed to be equal harbingers of death. He feared the unpleasant surprise that would soon greet the Harmony Allegiant. Though they were enemies, they were all mere people who believed in something. He ran to Avra and shook his head before he could think too much about the children who would perish only to defend their Endower livelihood.

"*What is it?*" Yetrik patted.

"*Do you not feel it?*"

"*Feel what?*"

She pounded her claws against the ground. "*You may be able to percuss with me, but your senses need to grow. The rest of your colony, the footsoldiers, are nearing.*"

"*How close?*"

"*If your friend does not end his conversation soon, they will pass us.*"

Perd. He patted his gratitude and ran back.

The Priesswoman scratched her head. "What is a Scholar doing with an army of–"

"Kevlen, we have to move now!"

She and Kevlen turned to Yetrik.

"Avra felt the Terpels. They'll be here soon."

Kevlen shrugged. "I don't feel them."

"Trust me."

Kevlen pointed at the Priesswoman. "How far away are the other zlatog riders?"

"A few minutes' flight north and south, if I push Gholl."

"Then *go now*. Find the eldeer on the way if you have to. The zlatogs are smart enough to stay where they are told. Send them here if you need. I don't care. Just hurry."

She placed her hands on her hips. "Why so sudden? Can't your army wait a little longer until we are sure we are ready?"

Kevlen shook his head. "Too many reasons to count. It's difficult to conceal an army so close to the city. At this point, we have to continue if we are to catch anyone unprepared. Aside from that, no village nearby will be sufficient to feed them."

"Feed them? This is war! Not a feast!"

"You're a perding Beastling. You should know how much using your ability drains you. Imagine sprinting across Facet and only being fed a few times."

"What are they going to do? Pillage?"

Kevlen and Yetrik held a somber gaze.

"Perd me! We are the terrible people they claim we are, aren't we?"

Kevlen shook his head. "It won't be too bad. They'll take what they can find while they fight. No need to sit down and eat. I doubt many of the merchants are in their shops anymore."

She ran her fingers through her hair as she stared at the ground. "The more I hear about this woman, the less she seems fit for the throne."

"You're not wrong," said Kevlen, "but we'll handle the politics when this ends."

"What little can *we* do? This is their war, not—perd, I'm sorry. All of this is just... so much. What about the eldeer? What if we can't find any before you reach the city?"

He placed his hand on her shoulder. "I know you're worried, but it will work out."

"How do you know?"

"I'm not worried about the eldeer as much as you are. I'm sure the Terpels can take down the behemoths. Having our own will help us minimize losses, but we can fare without them. Yetrik and I will watch from above until the eldeer have been cleared, then we will fly in and help finish the battle."

"Perd me–"

"Enough. If you're so concerned about the eldeer, leave now to take care of it."

She cupped her ear and raised her other arm. "Mighty is the Free, Captain."

He returned the Priess salute.

She mounted Gholl and left forthwith.

"Perding woman." Kevlen's hands shook. "Is that how I sound when I'm unstable?"

Yetrik chuckled.

"Are you ready to leave, Gruthman?"

Yetrik nodded. "Should we tell Thane Kelm what she said?"

"Do I want to? Perd no, but we probably should. Like you said, those Patriarchy Scholars have too much going on that we don't know about. I'd rather not cross him." He moved towards Khoga and prepared to mount. "We'll head back, inform him of what has happened here, then fly just ahead of the army for some observation."

"Kevlen?"

He turned back before climbing up atop Khoga. "Last minute doubts?"

"Something like that."

"I hate killing people for the sake of politics as much as you do. Like I said, we'll stay out of conflict and above until they need us and our zlatogs. Maybe the Terpels will be enough. Thane Kelm seems confident enough in those things of his."

"Not just that. I mean—even if we aren't the ones to do the killing, people still die. I know they are dying everywhere, but some of them—"

"Yes, the women and the children. Avoid them at all costs."

"No, not just the civilians and, well... yes. The children. The civilians might be safe in hiding, but their Endowers will be in the heart of the battle."

"A little too late to doubt, Gruthman. If you're worried about them, you're on the wrong side of the war."

I tell myself the same too often. What a poor soldier I am, doubting my reason for war. "I don't mean it that way. The Endowers. The ones they brought to fight in this war. She said they have Beastlings. Who knows what other kinds have come? Imagine their *terror* when our army arrives."

Kevlen winced as he focused on Khoga's mane, raking his fingers through it. "I would rather not."

"That's *exactly* what I mean. Sure, we can justify harvesting at birth. Perd, even justify killing our opponents like we do for the sake of some *greater good*. I don't care how you see the war or even if you see those children as weapons here. They are just a piece in this system that has no choice but to cooperate."

"Sounds familiar, doesn't it?"

"Besides us, they have their whole lives ahead. Toss aside all justifications of harvesting and politics as well. Even if you want to say that we take these children and use them for our side, do it. I–I just... when this is all over, when the battle in the city has settled–perd, I don't know what to say."

"If we can spare any and take them elsewhere," Kevlen looked up at him and smirked, "we will."

Yetrik furrowed his brow and struggled to smile.

"Is there something wrong with what I said?"

"No, I just expected you to be angry."

"With you? For doubting what you are doing? You comforted me over nearly the same thing before we left Krall Pensa's palace. Different subject, same idea. Sure, I'm frustrated. Not with you, but–"

"I know."

"If we can do something, we will." Kevlen climbed up to mount Khoga. "As long as it doesn't go against our cause, I'll support any act of mercy you choose to pursue. I wouldn't recommend talking to him, but if you could ask my father, he would tell you I've always been a problematic child."

Gregor limped. His leg throbbed with each step, and his knees were reluctant to comply.

Still, he smiled.

He headed towards the eastern gate of Paiell with a basket of bread in his hands. His family had hidden inside their bakery for two days since the battle began. Having nearly lost his life supporting the Allegiant, he returned home for a day of idle recuperation.

Now, three days since the battle had begun, townsfolk had started to leave their houses for necessities. Battles in the north still waged, as did other smaller conflicts outside of the city, but Gregor did not mind risking himself to feed some soldiers who guarded the gates next to his home, doing what he could not.

He pressed one of the loaves between his fingers with hands still covered in flour. It was stiff, having been baked a few days prior to the battle, but no signs of mold showed. They would have taken it regardless. All Allegiant Soldiers were gracious for any form of support, especially anything edible.

Gregor grabbed a loaf and waved it as he neared a group of Sleff and Chuss soldiers who stood by the gate.

A thunderous sound rumbled in the distance. Everyone looked up to see a sky with few clouds.

"Do you think they took down one of the Cantons in the north?" a Chussman asked.

The rumbling continued, increasing in volume.

"Something like that," a Sleffman said. "Best ignore it until we see something."

"That sounds like poor advice," grumbled an older Chussman.

"Anyone hungry?"

They turned to Gregor, who passed out the five loaves he had. "Make sure to share it with some others."

"Thank you, Sleffman!" one of the Chussmen gave him the Sleff salute.

"It's the least I could do. I wanted to be sure—"

"Does that not bother you?" one of the Sleff soldiers shook his neighbors' shoulders and shouted. "Perd, I can barely hear myself talk!"

The Chussman who had thanked Gregor turned back to him. "Best head back to your family now. Don't want you to be caught in a surprise."

One of the Chussmen shook his head. "I wouldn't worry about it. Probably just something happening in a village."

"Oh, and you were so sure it was a Canton falling moments before?"

Gregor stepped away and thanked them again for their service. Their complaints drowned out in a quaking clamor.

Gregor smiled, knowing that he would be safe in his home. It was built well to withstand the occasional heavy storms that passed through Paiell. It was nothing to worry about. The Allegiant would prevail.

The sound of metal against metal and breaking wood forced him to look back.

The half-rebuilt eastern gate fell again. A flood of Gruth soldiers sprinted into the city.

Gregor uttered a prayer for mercy, but was cut off as a Gruthman ran into him.

❧❧❧❧ ❧❧❧❧

Terpel, for that was what he knew himself by, stood again after tripping over a corpse. A Sleffman with the remains of a basket and a bloody baker's apron had been reduced to a faceless mound of trampled red flesh.

Terpel ran, his mind connected to the other Terpels around him. He ran near the back of the army and could no longer hear Thane Kelm's commands, yet he felt them within.

A command split the army down various streets. Terpel continued down the street ahead of him. Those before him cut down any who stood in their way. He held his unsheathed sword, moving in with his swinging arms in perfect synchronized movements to not hit any of his allies in their dense sprinting pack.

They entered a wide square and dispersed like sand falling from the middle of an hourglass.

Sleffmen and Chussmen screamed as the Terpels stabbed, sliced, and trampled them with fluidity and calculated grace.

Terpel held his blade at the ready, though it remained clean as those ahead of him handled their opponents.

The ground shook, and an animal called out, but Terpel did not stop. Some of his allies fell as they plowed through the city.

The animal called again. A large leg stomped from above, crushing a few Terpels in its wake.

"Take out the legs first, then kill it when it falls," Thane Kelm's voice rang in his mind.

He stopped before the blue furred leg and stabbed into it repeatedly. Others joined in, many using their blades to stab and climb until the leg shook.

The mighty beast fell like a collapsing tower, crushing many Terpels in its wake. The nearby survivors climbed atop the fallen beast, stabbing and slicing until the ground was flooded with its blood.

"Well done. Repeat if any of you meet another. Press westward."

Terpel and his fellow warriors abandoned the fallen eldeer and continued their run towards the western side as commanded. Once again, their group split into smaller packs as the thin streets divided their cluster.

Terpel found himself near the front of the procession. Only a few others stood between him and the Terpels who clashed against unprepared Allegiant soldiers. While some of his allies fell, only one would fall for every three Allegiant killed. Any who were knocked down, perished soon after as they were trampled like crops under a herd of cattle.

Cattle. Faint image played across Terpel's mind. Cattle training as he reached out to milk them. Others were with him. A woman and a young child. He felt he should know them yet could not recall their blurry faces.

His mind returned to the battle a moment too late as he tripped over the body of a fallen Chussman. He pressed up on him and stared at the bloody mess that had once been a man's face. The other soldiers moved past him like a river moving around a rock in the middle of a stream.

He joined the rushing army once again as they fought with the ferocity of starved hounds. They slowed as they met their enemies, though some continued to run past the enemy lines.

The battle was no longer kept to the front lines as each group filled in the gaps of the other. Terpel stabbed any who came at him, kicking their limp bodies down to join the corpse-covered cobblestone.

He plunged his blade into a new opponent, who did not shirk away with a sword through his chest. The Chussman coughed and spat blood as he grabbed the hilt of Terpel's blade with one hand, the other holding his sword.

Terpel tried to free his sword from the Chussman's grip, but the man only pulled it closer to him. The blade slid through the Chussman, causing him to hiss and grunt as he pulled himself closer to Terpel. With one final effort, the Chussman stabbed his sword up through Terpel's chest, the tip erupting from the back of his neck.

<hr />

Terpel, for that was what she knew herself by, heeded the command spoken to her by Thane Kelm. It was the most piercing demand he had sent in the three hours they had spent retaking the city from the Allegiant invaders.

"A group of Sleffmen have started to horde the Endowers that they brought into the battle. Kill them before they can escape or use them against us."

Children are the enemy. Children like these were a shame to her existence as a Terpel. This was what Thane Kelm had taught them. Terpels were simple-minded. Thane Kelm was wise, for he was a Scholar. Terpel trusted, for this was all she knew. Her memories were few and her knowledge limited. *Children are the enemy.*

Vague thoughts echoed from afar. *Three children. Two boys and an older girl.* For a moment, Terpel felt as if she were harvesting yams with them. Images of carrots, yellow and blue, paired well with those of smiling children.

She wanted to be with them. It was the only desire stronger than Thane Kelm's commands. Greater than hunger or thirst, yet as impossible to retrieve.

The images dissipated.

Her shoulders collided with her allies as they all tried to run into a smaller alleyway. All set towards the western gate. All heeded Thane Kelm's command. They did not care for each other, only for the command. Feelings were something long lost.

She breathed deeply as she pressed through the bottleneck into an open area. The buildings were smaller, yet it was still part of Paiell's central district. Thin and nimble as she was, she pressed herself to the front of the charging party.

Without other Terpels obstructing her view, she could see her target.

A group of children stood behind a wall of Allegiant soldiers, one behind them wore little leather and a Sleff yellow covering. No Terpel grew wary as they approached their enemy in such a small group compared to the scattered legions throughout the city.

Her bright vision darkened as if the sun was swallowed.

⁂

Port's breathing shook as the eldeer pranced from a small fortress to land atop the first wave of Gruthmen. The image of the confident Gruthwoman who stood in front of them burned into his mind. Her blood was the first to splatter the eldeer's hoof.

"Hold firm!" he commanded. He turned back to see the Endowers in tears. He grabbed onto the arm of two Beastlings. "Keep calling for them! Please! You have to–"

Everyone turned back to the Gruthmen at the sound of the eldeer's bugle. Swords stuck into its legs, some of the Gruthmen clung to the fur and stabbed repeatedly.

He turned back to the children, shaking from the increased intensity of their screams.

"I don't want to bring more into the city! They'll just kill them!"

"Please don't make us do it!"

One of the Chussmen turned back. "What's going on?"

"They won't call any more eldeer," Port said. "They don't want them to die! And what are you doing, Chussman? Focus!"

"The eldeer corpse is keeping them back."

Port turned to see that the eldeer's body had fallen into the alleyway. "That won't hold long."

"All the more time to have the Endowers call some more!"

Port shook his head and knelt beside the Endowers. "Turn back. You see that broken wall?" He pointed to the western wall that their party had been pressed against. "All you have to do is run into the forest and call out for *anything*."

"Captain, we can't–"

The Chussman dropped his sword and grabbed the Endower's shoulders. As he shook the terrified Sleffboy, his fellow soldiers filled in his gap, bracing for any surprise. "If you don't find a beast to take us out of here, *we all will die*."

"Are the perding children whining again?" one of the Sleff soldiers shouted.

"Please," Port repeated.

"Will you come with us?" one of the Beastlings asked.

"I can't."

"The Thane must command," said the Chussman. "I'll come with you."

Bravery or cowardice? Likely a blend of both, but it will do. Whatever we need.

Port coughed. His entire body ached. "Take them."

The Chussman stood and waved the children towards the wall. "Come on now. Start calling for any animal that can carry us away faster than those Gruthmen can run."

"Why can't we run?" one of them asked.

"I just told you. Without an eldeer or something of the like, we will be chased down. I can guarantee they don't want any of you left alive."

Their whining continued as they left. The Chussman was blunt, but his words held true. The children needed to know that if they could not escape with some steed, their hope would be trampled by crazed Gruthmen. He did not know what had been done to make the Gruthmen so ruthless. Their intensity seemed to match that of a Gorger, though they were smaller and did not seem to tire.

Port did not overwhelm himself with the ever-evolving threats. Information did not matter when they were already giving all that they could.

I have not yet given enough. Now is my chance.

His dagger wound, though small, had grown worse over the three days of battle. It leaked pus and was inflamed. *Enough self-pity. I cannot be the only one with such problems.*

He moved forward to stand among Sleffmen and Chussmen in the small line of defense that they had around the Endowers they had gathered. They saluted, accepting his contribution. No need to protect the Thane anymore. The children took priority.

The city no longer mattered. From what he had seen, they stood no chance against the Gruthmen. Victory was no longer a concern. Survival, not his own, but that of any who he could save.

If I perish so that one other might live, so be it, for this is perfect humility. I may harbor pride within, but I give it all to thee, lord Heitt. Let me become thy vessel. I will serve thee until the very end. If that is soon, so be it. I will have given all for the sake of thee and thy children. Pious is the Giver.

⋙⋙⋙ ⋘⋘⋘

The sight of victory was a harrowing abomination.

Yetrik turned to Kevlen, each of them sitting atop their zlatogs on the roof of the highest building they could find in Paiell. The Priessman stared down on to the city below, his eyes in a similar abhorrent awe.

It was not pleasing to see his friend in such anguish. Still, he was relieved to see that Kevlen did not rejoice in the massive deaths below. Regardless of one's conviction, they were still people doing what they believed to be right. He trembled, wondering what his life would have been like on the losing side of the conflict.

The losers today may be the victors tomorrow. With annihilation such as this, we can only hope for mercy should the tides change. If war has taught me anything, it is that mercy diminishes as cruelty increases.

He turned to the bugles of two eldeer, the only ones the Priess Beastlings had managed to find, as they locked antlers with the Allegiant eldeer. With the Terpels attacking from below, the enemy steeds were quick to fall.

Kevlen pointed to the battle below. "Should we join now that the eldeer have been taken care of?"

Yetrik starred as the Terpels climbed atop the eldeer like ants atop food scraps.

"Yetrik?"

"Huh? Oh, I–" He took a moment to refocus. "Why risk it? What good would it do? Just look at what is happening! It's a massacre."

Not a victory. A massacre. The perfect word for the tragedy below. The flood of Terpels had entered from the east and filled most of the city, leaving only some of the north and west districts unoccupied. They ran, uninhibited by enemies as they plowed through them.

"So you just want to sit here and watch it all fall to ruin?" Kevlen asked.

"Perd me, I don't know! What can we do?"

Kevlen pointed to the eastern wall. "Do you see that?"

Yetrik moved his head to see. "I can't see it very well, but it looks like some Allegiant soldiers are trying to escape. Perd me, Kevlen, you want to go and finish them off? The city is ours. Do we have to slay every last Allegiant soldier?"

"Let's just fly over and see what is happening. I can't see any Terpels fighting with them, but they seem to have found everyone else in the city. Even if we just look. I don't want it to seem like we sat and watched the whole time?"

"You want your name tied to what happened here?"

Kevlen shook his head. "I never said that. Just follow me." He patted Khoga, and they flew from the building's edge, descending gradually towards the collapsed western wall.

Yetrik commanded Avra to follow. As they drew closer, he could more clearly see a semicircle of soldiers surrounding a smaller group of people. *With the open wall behind them, why not flee already?*

His question remained, though he admired their tenacity. Whatever their reason was, they remained. Rather than risk running through the woods to be pursued by relentless Terpels, they held onto whatever last wish they had. Convictions and politics set aside, Yetrik revered them. They stood against death, not surrendering when defeat was inevitable.

A whirlwind stirred as Avra flapped her wings, slowing to descend by Kevlen and Khoga atop a much smaller building.

"We talked about it. Now it's perding happening." Kevlen gave a nervous laugh.

"What do you mean?" He looked over Avra's head to see the courageous few. "Sleffmen and Chussmen side by side. What do you want me to say?"

"No." He pointed behind them. "Next to the wall. Do you see that? Those aren't injured soldiers being protected by some brave few. They're awfully small for that."

"Perd me."

"Exactly."

Children, Endowers judging by their small soldier's armament, huddled together in the pouring rain. Some of them kept fixed gazes on the forest beyond the broken walls.

Yetrik clenched his teeth. *Treason and mercy or loyalty and cruelty.* "What—perd, I don't know what to say. Why did this have to happen?"

"Your perding god must have thought you a diligent boy to put you here."

"So you want to help them?"

"We said we would, right? We can leave the soldiers to die, but the children should at least be spared."

We could spare them too. Would that be so wrong?

"Do you agree, Yetrik? I'll lie my way through whatever complaints they raise if we are caught, though I doubt anything will come from it. Those perding Terpels are as dull as rocks."

Yetrik turned to Kevlen. The Priessman's face was drawn in stern determination. Wavering emotions had been solidified. Kevlen was fragile when pressed to act against what he saw to be true. Yetrek's admiration for him grew as he saw his friend become firmer in his foundation, having set his mind on something honorable.

"Come on, Gruthman. Are you with me? I'll have my perding father defend me if need be."

Yetrik shook his head and chuckled. "Consequences are no problem. I can suffer if it means those children don't."

Kevlen smiled with renewed vigor. He bent his elbows in the Gruth salute and took flight.

Yetrik took a deep breath, half wondering if it would be one of his last and followed.

The descent lasted less than a minute. They landed atop the remains of the fallen wall and jumped down, stumbling down its rubble until they were steadily on the ground.

All the children faced them, huddled like frightened mice before him and Kevlen. The guards broke their silent terror, some moving from their semicircle to run at them with raised swords.

A charging Sleffman with a greatsword in his hands screamed as if he were a father giving himself to defend his child.

"Stop!" Yetrik shouted, to no avail.

Kevlen hissed to Khoga, whose screech blasted a sonic wave at the charging Allegiant soldiers. They all fell on their backs and were slow to rise in their daze.

"Stand down!" Kevlen shouted. "I'll do that again if I have to! We're not here to kill you, but those *things* are." He pointed back to the eldeer corpse wedged between the alley's walls. "They are going to come through any minute. I don't care if we are on different sides of this war. These children do not deserve to die here. Help us help you esca–"

"You *perding* hypocrites!" a Sleffman shouted. "You decide that now is the time to change your stance on the war? Took you long enough to–"

"Enough!" the frontmost Sleffman commanded as he stood. He wore no helm, only a yellow cloak and light armor. "Why–I–I don't care. How can we trust you?"

The Chussman groaned. "Come *on* Thane Kamen! We cannot so blindly trust these Beastlings."

The so-called Thane turned back to Yetrik and Kevlen. His sorrowed eyebrows framed his exhaustion.

If you're a Thane, why aren't you dressed like one? "What do I need to say to convince you?" Yetrik asked. "Do you have a Feelman?" he pointed to the Endowers.

The Thane shook his head. "No, we didn't bring any along. Only Beastlings and–perd, I'm sorry. Even if you want to help, I can't risk it. These children–"

"Will surely die without help." Kevlen blurted out. "You have nothing to lose. If you think we will kill them, it couldn't be worse than being run over by those Gruth fiends."

"We have help on the way!" one of the Endowers poked her head out of the group. "The Beastlings went to find some animals to help us run away."

"Keep the perding child quiet!" a Chussman shouted.

Yetrik turned back to the forest. "I don't see anyone coming. Looks like we are your best chance. Our zlatogs can take all the children and a couple of you soldiers."

"*Oh*, now you are going to save us?" a Chussman shouted. "How fortunate are we?"

Kevlen threw a rock at the man's feet. "Pretty perding fortunate and your luck is about to run out! I'll take the children, force them from you if I have to! I'll take them wherever they need to go, but I swear on the perding banner of Priess that I will not sit and watch them die!"

"Please," Yetrik stared at the Thane. "I don't claim to understand what you have experienced here, but it's horrible. Let us–"

They all turned towards the city as enraged shouts erupted from the corpse of the eldeer. Terpels covered in dark blood had burrowed their way through the fallen eldeer and sprinted free from the alley towards them.

"*Perd!*" the difficult Chussman shouted. He and the other Allegiant soldiers moved back into their semicircle to defend.

"Wait!" Yetrik ran forward and grabbed the Thane. "Please, just a moment!"

"What? If you want to help, go kill them!" he pointed towards the Terpels.

Kevlen ran forward to help hold him back. "We can't overtake a perding army with two zlatogs. We're just trying to offer a little mercy."

A roar came from the forest as three great bears, each thrice the size of a black bear, ran towards the group with Endowers atop their backs.

"Perfect timing!" one of the Endower Sleffgirls shouted.

The Terpels were mere moments away. Yetrik shook the Thane. "Those can only hold a few children each. You have to let us help, or all of you will be slain and trampled."

⤜⤛ ⤚⤝

Port's arms fell weakly at his side after he sheathed his greatsword. He looked at the zlatogs, to the Gruth army, then back to the Gruthman who held his arm. *Heitt have mercy.* "Take them. As many as you can."

The Gruthman nodded. "I promise we will deliver them to somewhere safe and far away."

Port nodded and pointed to the line of Allegiant soldiers. "Take them too. Any of them if you can."

"Hurry!" The Priessman had overheard them and had called his zlatog forward to load the children on their backs.

"We don't have enough time!" one of the Endowers shouted. He pointed to the Priessman. "Stop them so we can all climb on!"

Port shook his head and ran towards one of the great bears. He climbed atop and held the Beastling on his back.

"Are you coming with me?" the child asked.

"No." Port pointed to the zlatog. "The others will use the other bears. I want you to climb onto a zlatog with the others."

"Why?"

"I need you to listen to me. We don't have time."

The Beastling nodded. "I need you to step off and mount the zlatogs with the others or jump on another bear to run away. I don't care. You decide, but I need you to tell this bear to run to the enemies with me on top of it."

"Why?"

"Just do it! I'm your Thane, now obey!"

The child nodded and jumped down to join the other children.

"Priessman!" Port shouted.

He turned as he lifted another child onto the zlatogs back.

Port pointed at the Beastling whom he had commanded. "Make sure that one sends this bear to ride with me into battle."

"What are you perding doing, Sleffman?"

"Buying you a few more seconds."

The Priessman shook his head, then lifted his hands into the Sleff salute. "May your god bless you!"

May he bless us all. The bear charged. It hopped over the semicircle of Allegiant soldiers. He heard his name shouted with pleas to stop, but he could not.

The few seconds he had before reaching the line of Gruthmen felt like minutes. Seeing their ferocity, he knew the soldiers behind him would last a second each against the Gruthmen, unless they escaped.

Is this it? My final gift. Have I achieved piety in this, Lord Heitt?

The bear met the Terpels and mauled them with paws the size of shields. He swung with one hand on his greatsword, the other holding onto the bear's fur.

Sharp pain seized Port's leg. He knew a Gruth blade had struck him. Similar pain continued to strike him all around his body.

He turned back to see children still climbing atop the zlatogs.

The Gruthmen had slowed, focusing on him.

Please Heitt, let this be enough. If I give myself, let it not be in vain.

Memories returned to him.

He was a boy. Colrig asked him to join the Allegiant.

He was a boy. Phenmir accompanied him to Kzhek.

He was a boy. As a captain, he failed to save Court's capital.

He was a boy. He fostered friendships and learned to lead in Bruten.

He was a boy. He marched back to Paiell, ready to save the city he had lost.

He was a man. He sat atop a bear, giving himself so that others might endure.

The world was unjust and dark. He had failed to enlighten it, yet he held his candle high, offering the little light he could.

Let this be true, for it is my last request.

I have given enough.

❧❧❧❧❧ ❧❧❧❧❧

A Chussman lifted up the final Endower onto Avra as Khoga took flight. Yetrik spared a moment to glance at the semicircle of Allegiant soldiers who could not stand longer than a second against the wave of Terpels.

Yetrik patted Avra, who lifted from the ground right as the last Chussman was trampled and slain. The Sleffman and his bear had given them the smallest amount of time, but his sacrifice proved successful. The few seconds they were granted were invaluable. Yetrik looked back as Avra flew west. The smallest lump of fur remained, but he could not see the remains of the Sleffman, whose corpse had been trampled by countless Terpels.

He knew the man for a moment, yet he had earned Yetrik's admiration.

He turned back to focus on the flight. Khoga was only a few seconds ahead. They saved every child. No soldiers had made it onto the zlatogs and the bears proved a wasted effort. *Except for one last sacrifice.*

Yetrik felt disgusted by any harm he had done, any selfish act, for he would never be as noble as the sacrificial Sleffman. Despite his doubts, he was determined to become a worthy comparison.

CHAPTER THIRTY-FIVE

PARASITE

W rought with exhaustion worse than she had experienced training with the Terpels, Semi collapsed into the seat across from Thane Phemus.

Why the woman insisted on finding the finest tavern outside of Sliin was beyond her. The twenty minute ghete ride to the Sred, the next city east of Sliin, was a waste of time. Thane Phemus wouldn't take any village or city small enough to deprive her of every convenience she could request, even though any smaller village would have been a better spot for her to hide in. They were far enough out from the political excitement in the Chuss capital, despite the occasional Allegiant party that passed through Sred. Semi was not worried that they would be arrested. Outside of Sliin, foreigners were common, which tended to be the opposite of most Courts and their capitals. What shredded her nerves was Thane

Phemus' indolence paired with her need for convenience and comfort, never thinking about the opposite effect her so-called needs had on Semi.

Thane Phemus took a petite sip from her slender glass of pink wine. "So, tell me what you–"

Semi smacked her hand on the table. "You couldn't have ordered me a drink? Really? It's the least you could have done."

"Cannot have you inebriated on the job."

"Perd me, woman–"

"Mistress or Thane will do."

"You're an Endowed, aren't you? You should know that intoxication is never a problem if we don't want it to be. Besides, I'm done for the day."

"That is your decision to make, is it?"

Perding insufferable Priesswoman. Live beyond your stereotype and maybe people won't detest you as much as I do right now. Aside from her frustration, Semi felt the smallest satisfaction that her usual hesitancy with new members of the nobility had dissipated. She wondered if her new attitude towards the Priess Thane would cost her.

"You have no–" she sighed. *I'm better than this.* Semi waved the barkeep over and requested the largest amount of Middleman's bane they would allow. She ran her fingers through her hair, disgusted by the grease that clumped her locks together. *I've become too used to convenience.* She accepted her state, embracing all that she was and loving herself for it.

Thane Phemus cleared her throat.

Semi tried to look at the Thane with as little abhorrence as possible. Despite her training in espionage and lying, she couldn't stare at the Priesswoman with even the most artificial admiration. "As expected with the recent raids on the western Gruth villages, they've fortified the eastern cities, but surprisingly little focus on Sliin itself."

Thane Phemus raised her eyebrow and sipped from her glass. "So the advancement to your Court was a natural progression of their expansion. Perding *'pacifists'* are as hypocritical as the rest of us." She forced a laugh and shook her head. "Still, I find it hard to believe that Sliin is as unprotected as you would assume."

"You question my skill?"

"No, no, nothing of the sort...well, perhaps I merely question the source of your knowledge. Where did you obtain this information?"

After pursuing my own path, having wasted most of the day following your pointless suggestions. 'Royal gatherings' are a Priess construct born of luxury. "I found it quite easy to blend in as an Allegiant high guard."

"Did you have to do away with one of the high guards to obtain their gear?"

"There are other ways to obtain what one needs."

She nodded. "Go on."

"I found my way into an Allegiant meeting that included the new Krall among—"

"How is she?" She ran her finger along the edge of her glass, her eyes passing between the few remaining drops of her drink and the barkeep.

Semi stared at her, waiting for her to invest her attention in Semi's report. It never came. "She's quite polite."

Thane Phemus scoffed. "And that will be her downfall."

Really? Pride and self-service were the attributes that attracted the last Krall's death. "Their attention is focused elsewhere. Of course they have prepared for an inevitable attack on their city, but their attention has been more focused on strengthening the rebels' hold on Kzhek."

"The head of the bronze empire is only going to become more important as the war progresses."

"What is that supposed to mean?"

Thane Phemus shrugged. "Something Terin continues to tell me. I trust him, you should too."

"I've never met him."

"I could have sworn you spoke with him in Thusk."

"I had other matters to attend to."

Thane Phemus grinned. "I see. Well, let's keep our minds focused on the present."

Semi had to clench her jaw to prevent it from dropping.

"As I was saying, though their fortifications are yet to be finished, they have been focused on fortifying the eastern cities, hence the activity here in Sred, with some focus on the north. They obviously anticipate an attack from Court Gruth, but an attack from Court Sleff would not seem too out of place. If the Terpels can keep a steady pace, they should be able to attack the city before any messages are related to Sliin as they near. Even if the Chuss Endowers have Beastlings send a message, I have faith that the Terpels will arrive before the message can disperse."

"So we attack from the west?"

Semi nodded. "If we can have them reroute to attack the city from the south-western corner, that would be the most ideal. Regardless of their preparation, I am not worried about the performance of the Terpels. Attacking their vulnerable points will merely save us time, lives, and resources."

"You have a lot of faith in these Terpels."

Semi held back her response as the Chussman barkeep placed her drink on the table. He did so with delicacy, still the overflowing glass spilled a few drops onto the worn table. He smiled, no sign showing that he had heard them speak. She reached for her drink and was once again aware of her darker skin tone. She had grown so used to her Chuss form that she forgot she maintained it, though her hunger was starting to reveal the cost of her ability.

"I spent enough time with them to know that they are reliable."

"We shall see." She pushed her empty wineglass aside. "Are they more focused on Court Gruth or maintaining Kzhek?"

"Their attention wasn't set on any single matter. We must also recognize that these focal points are more so directed by the Chussmen, or at least their branch of the Harmony Allegiant, rather than the entire Allegiant themselves."

Thane Phemus shrugged. "They want to overthrow harvesting. What else is there to know? They sound disorganized, which will only leave them more vulnerable. I'm surprised they have even lasted this long."

"Maybe I wasn't clear. They were not disorganized, rather spread wide."

"Is there a difference?"

"Yes, a significant one."

"It would do you well to speak your full thoughts, Gruthwoman. Your leading statements only cause dissonance."

And you could learn something about speaking to someone that does not bow before everything you say. "Aside from their clear Allegiant-based motives they have sent a party to the Middlelands."

"Ah, following our ideas because they can't form any valuable ones themselves. So they hope to take advantage of the Middlemen as well? Krall Trhet's party will not take well to that. How many did they send?"

"Only a small group, from what I could infer."

"*Infer?*"

"I'm not a perding Feelman. What do you expect? Asking questions will only–" she stopped as Thane Phemus' sneer drifted towards a laugh.

"Forgive me. Let us take a step back. How *small* of a group?"

"Plenty of Endowers, some members of the city guard, and their new Thane."

Thane Phemus' eyes lit up with a feeling other than self-love. Semi had her attention and something to bargain for it.

"Do you know him?"

"Thane Phenmir Stolk, once the most renowned physician in all of Court Chuss, particularly known for his skill in harvesting, until he defected to lead the Chussmen in the rebellion movement. Thane of

Harmony is the title they have chosen to adopt, though it has only been assigned to a Sleffman and this Chussman, as far as we can tell."

"And *I* am the one tasked with finding secrets when you are so obviously aware of them?"

"These are not secrets, mere tenants of their organization. Terin was the one who told me about the 'Thanes of Harmony,' but I have known Phenmir for quite some time."

Semi squinted.

"Have you forgotten who I am? I am the Priess Thane of *Haleness*. I may not look the scholarly type but I know near all that you can about the human body, especially noting my status as an Eurythrin. Much of my research has been conducted on myself, but that is beside the point. This man served when assigned to harvest, but by the Priess banner, he was gifted... *is* gifted. Mind and body alike, I would have swept him from his wife if we were closer acquainted, though he would never accept. We need to find him."

"We can't. I already told you that he is in the Middlelands."

"Or en route, though who knows if he will ever arrive." She bit her lip and rubbed her finger across the table. Her eyes turned back up to look at Semi after a moment. "Find out where he lives. Speak with his wife on the matter. He has a son as well. Search them out–"

"Wait, what are you talking about? This is about attacking Sliin, not focusing on what some self-proclaimed rebel leader is after."

"From what you have told me, I am not worried about attacking Sliin, in fact, I never was. Your Terpels will outmatch any challenge. I'll alert the Beastling to tell Kelm's army to approach from the southwest. That insight is enough for now. Leave that to me and you can look further into this. While they focus on the battle, we can focus on the entire war. Phenmir is too wise to pursue some ghost chase to the south without purpose. Whatever Krall Trhet or the Zhaes Thanes saw in the Middlelands, Phenmir has now seen it and wants it."

"Are you sure?"

"As sure as I can be. Aside from my suspicions, Terin has made it known to me that the Middlemen are the key to our victory. I do not think he merely subscribes to the Zhaesmen's favor for the Middlelands, rather this seems like something he must have thought about long ago with them. Most see the nobilities of Courts Zhaes and Priess as enemies, but there are some who are closer allies with each other than they are with many of their allies at home. Royss and Thane Gromm have been known to visit Terin often."

The implications of Thane Phemus' revelations started to spin her head, but it was caught on the assignment. "So you want me to invade this Chussman's house and interrogate his wife and son?"

"Yes."

Semi was struck by the Thane's unwavering bluntness. Her mind was wiped of any clever remark.

"Will this be a problem? Entering a single home cannot be any more difficult than wandering into a gathering of the Court's highmost Allegiant representatives."

Where my presence can be ignored. A single household. One woman, perhaps a son as well, to deceive. "The setting is more intimate in this situation."

"Then find someone his wife would expect to visit. Adopt their visage and make it seem ordinary."

"Don't you know anyone he is close to?"

Thane Phemus scoffed. "You overestimate our familiarity. If you cannot find anyone, pose as an Allegiant representative or perhaps a member of the Krall's personal guard. From what little I know about his wife, she has ties to the new Krall. Terin was unable to provide me with little else on their relationship. You know," she ran her finger across her chin, "your build is not too different from that of Krall Dhera Kost. Perhaps you could don a fine dress and take her image."

Semi laughed. "I cannot pass as the Krall."

Thane Phemus shrugged. "I suppose my opinion of you was too great."

"If they are close, she would recognize me in an instant. Specific individuals are the hardest to replicate. My appearance may be the same, but my personality remains my own. It is best to act as a non-existent Chusswoman. The more freedom I have to create a guise, the better I perform."

"Very well, do as you must, but I want this taken care of. Find out why he decided to go to the Middlelands. Learn without asking too many questions. I trust you will find a way. If he follows the same path as we do, they must be doing more than we expect. Their military power is already proving to fail against ours. At this point, our only true threat is if they have discovered what Terin and the Zhaes Thanes wish to keep hidden."

Semi scowled.

"It would be best for you to learn now, Gruthwoman, that you will be better off serving without asking questions. Curious minds often lead to treachery."

❧❧❧❧ ❧❧❧❧

Semi spent the remainder of the day searching for the best guise to adopt before visiting the Thane of Harmony's house just after sundown.

She was unable to locate the Krall, if even only to observe her mannerisms. She chose to spend the time she had left observing the members of the Harmony Allegiant, blending their Chuss mannerisms and rebellious attitude to form a representative for her disguise. Finding the Thane of Harmony's home took little effort, much less than she would have presumed, as she was deferred to the small infirmary that was a part of his home.

Semi's hands sweated from more than the heat of the Chuss night as she knocked on the door.

No one opened after her first attempt. She felt a touch of hope in thinking that she could abandon her duty but knew that Thane Phemus would not relinquish the lead. Semi preferred not to break and enter, but she had the experience needed to do so, should it be required.

She attempted again. The door opened before she finished her series of knocks.

"Forgive me, I was in the bedchamber tidying up–" the tall Chusswoman stopped. Her sharp cheeks became more prominent as she stared at Semi with a scowl. "Who are you?"

"I'm with the Harmony Allegiant."

"As we all are." She made no sign of welcoming.

Semi stared at her, knowing that she had but a second to process her thoughts to seem credible. The Chusswoman had the glare of sharp discernment and was dressed in with an elegant dress and shawls as would a noblewoman.

I have done this before with people higher than her. This is what I have been trained for. For this purpose I was created, born again as a Shiftling. As if removing her hood, she cleared her mind and became the deceiving Shiftling the Gruth nobility believed she was.

"Forgive me, Lady Stolk, I've come as a messenger for Captain Tesik."

"Who?"

Semi took a step forward, but the Chusswoman still gave no sign of welcoming. *Fine, let's be brief.* "Your husband appointed him to lead the eastern fortifications."

"He made no such thing known unto me."

"Do you require validation?" Semi reached into her pocket. "I have–"

The Chusswoman raised her hand. "No need. Just get to the point."

"Captain Tesik has requested a report on Thane Stolk's labors. Before you turn me away to one of his seconds, Tesik requested it specifically from you. He finds it difficult to trust others, noting the enemy Shiftlings."

She scowled. "Let me see the documentation."

Semi removed a rolled scroll and handed it to the Chusswoman. She took it and unfurled it, reading the approval from Dhera Kost, one meant to clear suspicions. Semi held back her smile. The Chusswoman's confirming nod was all she needed. The Allegiant outposts had plenty of similar clearances from the Krall to allow captain's access to certain information. It just so happened that the message contained within this scroll aligned well with Semi's assignment. If the Chusswoman would have been more pensive, perhaps she would have some questions to raise based on inconsistencies. Semi had questions prepared to defend herself but was glad that she had none to answer. Her aptitude in thievery was proving to be quite useful, though she did not warm to that recognition.

"Forgive me, it's been a long evening. Sometimes I think I am the one working on Phen's campaign while he is out exploring."

"The fault is mine. I would have come at a different time, but our labors are delicate in the east."

"What does the captain wish to know?"

"A brief report will do, whatever you think Thane Stolk would want him to know."

"Then I fear I will leave you disappointed. I should have expected someone to come to me for a report on his whereabouts when no report arrived. I have been left with the same suspicions as your captain likely has. I have received nothing since he reached Sonnek."

Semi felt her scowl betray her.

"Don't worry, I don't expect you to know. I had never heard of it until now. It's a hamlet halfway to the southern border. All was well then, but I have heard nothing since. I know I should trust him and that he has already reached the Middlelands. It is like Phen to be too self-occupied when he finds a new trove of intrigue. Let your captain know my concerns and that he should inform me if he receives any reports. Only let this be known to him. I do not want people to believe that Phen is lost. Too many people doubt the worth of his southern journey. Reporting our lack of communication will only aid the seeds of doubt that are throughout the Court."

"I am sorry to hear that, Lady Stolk." *New route.* "Is there anything we can offer? I recognize that we are all well-occupied with the present conflict, but we should not leave the head woman of the Allegiant unaided."

She chuckled. "You flatter me. No, besides that, everything is quite well."

Risk it. Leave nothing behind. "And your son? I trust that he fares well despite his father's absence."

"Oh, most assuredly. Hir is thriving, from what little we can be told. We receive occasional messages from the Chapterhouse, little assurances, but enough to help us maintain hope."

Perd. Chapterhouse? Their son is a perding Scholar? How did I not know? Her mind was a whirlwind of connections and theories. The coincidences were too uncanny to ignore. *Thane Gromm of Zhaes. The Patriarchy. Could this Thane Stolk have gleaned his information on the Middlelands, whatever those secrets entailed, from a Patriarchy informant? Is his son nothing more than a watchbird in the Patriarchy?*

It was a small lead, one born more from suspicions and feelings, yet it was one that would not leave Thane Phemus empty handed.

Days of preparation passed, each one more stressful that the previous as Semi labored diligently before the Terpels arrived. Balancing order and chaos had become difficult enough. Bringing an army to Sliin was sure to tip the scales in favor of disorder. Based on the few messages Thane Phemus had received, Paiell had been an easy victory and they were well on their way to claim the Chuss capitol.

As one would expect when investigating a member of the Patriarchy, Semi was unable to learn very little about Hir Stolk. While she learned enough about him outside of his life as a Scholar, almost nothing was known about his experience within the Patriarchy. He was new to their order, and that was telling enough. He was vulnerable. Whatever his conviction, he would not have developed the cold loyalty like that of Thane Kelm.

Semi approached the Sliin Chapterhouse of the Patriarchy or Scholars just as the rising sun cast an orange glow on the already rust-colored desert paradise.

She stepped into the courtyard, the hem of her stolen apprentice robes caressed the sand. While she had faith in her ability to procure what she needed, she never aimed to steal the robes of a Scholar. Having located a recent inductee, she took advantage of his wide-eyed obliviousness and took his robes. One would expect much less from an apprentice, still she hoped her fragmented guesses about the Patriarchy would let her pass.

She followed a trio of Scholars into the Chapterhouse's back entrance and walked alongside another youthful Scholar. Everyone was silent from their morning meditation walks, making it all the easier to pass by unnoticed. She had taken the face of a generic Chussman, one around her age with no distinct features. While she had fragmented knowledge about the Patriarchy, she still could not understand why she had never seen a female Scholar. Some said they were a misogynistic society while others said that the females were the true Scholars hidden within the society and the men were mere servants.

She had come to learn about the Middlemen, the Thane of Harmony, and the connection between him and his son. These were already difficult enough questions to answer that she need not burden herself with greater mysteries.

As she entered, she wondered how many Shiftlings had done the same thing. If there had been many, what secrets had they discovered? Why had it not been made public knowledge? To what extent will the Patriarchy go to protect their secrets?

The halls were of the finest marble with masterful statues and paintings along the way. Lanterns kept the halls well lit, making it feel like she walked through a grand athenaeum rather than the cultish crypt she had expected.

The hall opened into a capacious chamber with tables of refined orange acacia. The floor looked as if it was sandstone, though it had a pristine finish as if glass had been poured atop.

"Are you lost, brother?" Semi turned to see a bald Chussman in the robes of a high Scholar. He smiled as he approached. "Others may condemn you for forgetfulness, but I remember well how it felt to be an apprentice."

She gave him the Chuss salute accompanied by a light laugh.

He held his hand up before she could speak. He leaned in to whisper. "Again, I tell you this so that you might avoid the stern correction of others. *Remember*, we do not salute here, for within the Patriarchy, we are all one."

Be careful. "Yes, sir, forgive me sir."

He patted her on the back as he turned to leave. "'*Brother*' will do just as well."

Perd me. "One more thing, brother?"

He turned and nodded. "I seem to have lost my fellow apprentices."

He scowled.

"I am looking for brother Hir Stolk."

"Ah." He nodded. "I see where the confusion is. Have you not heard? Brother Stolk has completed his Crucible. He has been accepted as a full brother. Perhaps it would be good for you to see him. You could learn a thing or two from his diligence."

"I thought the very same."

"I would look for him in the mess hall. If you have been following him, you must be working with Scholar Sokov, yes?"

"Of course."

"Then I suppose he would be pleased to speak with both of you following the meal."

He bowed and she followed.

He left her pondering on how she would feign association not only with the Thane's son, but a high Scholar as well.

She continued down the hall, hoping to appear more confident as she searched for yet another location on her trail of risks and frail hope. If all should fail, she had ground claiming that she served Thane Kelm.

All Scholars are of the same conviction, are they not?

CHAPTER THIRTY-SIX

BINDING OF ROOTS

U ntil Golma ran to embrace the other Tchoyasgirl, Phenmir thought that the barbarian of a Zhaesman was about to ambush him.

"Are you with Trhet?" The Zhaesman demanded as he stepped before the Tchoyas Endowers. His disheveled beard and stained clothing spoke of his stay in the Middlelands.

Phenmir tried to keep his eyes away from the man's blade.

"No, that perding kulf has caused nothing but torment. Are you?"

The Zhaesman relaxed his shoulders. "I didn't think you were, after what he did... but that's beside the point."

Phenmir scowled. "Are *you* with him?"

"Perd no, that wretched kulf is someone I would like to keep at a distance."

"Then who are you?"

The Zhaesman chuckled. "I suppose I am trying to figure that out myself."

Phenmir squinted.

"Sorry." He gave the Chuss salute. "The name's Runith."

Phenmir felt his anxiety wane. The simple gesture of greeting him with the salute of another Court told more than words could express. He made the Zhaes salute. "Phenmir. Are you a member of the Allegiant?"

Runith shook his head, then looked at the Tchoyas children. "I suppose I am somewhere in between. Have you met them yet?" A putle hopped beside the Zhaesmen. He had seen too many oddities as of late to question the amphibian's presence.

"Who?"

Runith pointed to the plant people behind him.

Phenmir froze as the Middlemen stood, unrelenting with weapons held and shields, ready to defend.

Runith turned back and breathed in a pattern. The Middlemen relaxed and turned back to their village.

Phenmir's eyes were wide and his mouth open

He chuckled. "You have a lot to learn, Chussman. He waved for Phenmir to follow the Middlemen back to their home. "Come. I am no Rasteen, but I'll tell you what I've learned. First of all, that is their true name. Middlemen is our term, not theirs."

Phenmir looked to Kaela as they followed Runith and the Rasteen. She spoke with Golma, but still spared him a glance. Though difficult to see under her mask, she smiled. He felt he should be the one consoling her, but he was a stranger in an even stranger land. Runith was jovial and welcoming, but only earned Phenmir's trust thus far because of affection the other Tchoyas children had for him.

"Kaela?"

She turned back to his call. He waved her to him and she left the Tchoyasgirl after a few words.

Phenmir walked beside her.

"Yes?" she asked.

"You know them?"

"Of course! Golma is like my sister! She and I have been through a lot together."

"With Trhet?"

She nodded and shrugged. "Most of us have been, some worse than others. You saw what kind of man he is with how he treated Fenk. Golma had it worse than most of us."

A chill seized Phenmir's back and pierced his heart. He had suffered on the journey after Chenn's death, but did not expect that his remorse would continue to expand.

"It's in the past. Like you say, hard times help us grow."

"Right." He did not recall telling her anything like that, yet it was so on character. Having so much time with the younglings at the height of war was the perfect opportunity to share his endless platitudes. He doubted they would remember what he said and only wished that they would remember his character. *Is my character admirable? Have I become a worthy rolemodel or has my honor drifted too far? Oh Cheric, make me a worthy vessel to dispense thy charity.*

His mind turned to Hir. He had given his son all that he could, any wisdom or lesson he thought worthy. He not only wished but prayed that they would find fertile soil in his son as he continued to grow. Perhaps it was narcissistic to hope that his son valued what he had taught him. Phenmir was a man of many mistakes, only hoping to leave behind a legacy of some admiration. He would never draw close to perfection but would do all that he could to bring others as close as possible.

"What does she think about the Zhaesman?"

Kaela pointed at Runith. "Him?"

Phenmir chuckled, making sure he did not sound rude. "I don't see any others besides him."

"She wants you to meet him for yourself."

He scowled.

"You can't make allies through other people."

"*Allies?*"

"She said he's a good person. Why else would he be here with the Endowers."

He patted her on the back and walked ahead, keeping pace with Runith.

The Zhaesman kept his face forward. "I don't blame you for the wrongs wrought by your people, Chussman."

"What? Why would you even bring that up?"

"Because I know you blame me for the crimes of my people. The Zhaesmen, not merely the loyalists."

Phenmir scoffed. "I know many great Zhaesman, especially since this war began."

"Then why do you look at me like I'm your enemy? We should be more like these children. It can be a risk to trust so easily, but I think we could gain something by starting off well. Judge me for who I am, not for where I come from."

Memories of harvesting flashed through Phenmir's mind. *Perd, you have no idea how deep your Court has scarred me.*

Runith looked at him, then continued to speak. "Neither of us is responsible for the crimes of our people. Blaming each other for such tragedies will not end well. Blame is a game of blind archers. The arrows never land on the responsible target."

Phenmir nodded. "Forgive me if I gave off that impression. It's been a long journey here, to say the least. I only assumed you would be with Trhet and the other Zhaes Thanes after finding you here."

"Perd those kulfs."

"So you're not with them?"

Runith chucked and shook his head. "I stand for order and peace between all living beings, whatever that entails."

"That is no longer an easy choice, Zhaesmen."

"And I suppose you are due for an explanation. Don't worry, we'll get to that. We need to speak with a Rasteen leader. They need to know that the Krall and some of the Zhaes Thanes have returned."

"Which ones?"

"Agriculture and Scholarship, do you know them?"

Phenmir shook his head.

"I've lost touch with them recently. All that matters is that the Rasteen and children are safe. Is anyone in your company injured?"

"Some minor injuries, but we've handled most of it."

"Good. Let's have you fed."

"You read my mind."

Runith hung his head and smiled. "I'm no Feelman, but you should know that I am an Endower. I lead the Zhaes Beastling corps."

Phenmir's chest froze again. "Did you have any involvement in the battle of Kzhek?"

"The kaesan? Sure, that was one of my orders." He turned to stare at Phenmir. "But come on now, you should know that a nobleman's command is not always the servant's wish."

Phenmir nodded, hesitant to maintain eye contact. He tried not to process the death the man had caused with the beasts, but knew that they caused similar atrocities, all for the sake of a 'virtuous' victory. In war, no victory is ever virtuous.

"Keep that chin up, Chussman, I don't want you readying your arrows to play the game of blame once again. Don't forget charity and love, your own virtues. You of all people should believe in a change of heart."

⁂

Before reporting to the Rasteen whom Runith had referred to as the "Branch of the North," he invited some of the local Rasteen to feed Phenmir, the Endowers, and his Chuss guards. They ate foreign fruits and what meat Runith's Beastlings had found on their hunts.

While Runith's party of Endowers joined them, the Rasteen chose to distance themselves from Phenmir's party, nevertheless remaining to observe. He thought he would have been more astonished by the language of the Rasteen and the fact that the Zhaesmen spoke with them as well as *all* the Endowers, but he had grown used to change. With the crop people around him and the continent split by war, normalcy was but a distant memory.

While they replenished themselves, Runith told Phenmir of his life since the fall of Kzhek. He felt better about the Zhaesman as the story progressed and felt he could trust him when he told his defection from the loyalist camp. Phenmir likewise told him about their journey and the faceless raiders but avoided the details of the still open wounds from the tragedies wrought.

"What did you do with the Endower?" asked Runith.

Phenmir pointed to Fenk, who sat silently next to Kaela and Golma. "Kaela has vouched for him and is keeping an eye out. I doubt there is little else he can do, but I would rather eliminate the threat before taking any further measures."

"Perd me, Chussman, I thought you were defending the Endowers? These are just perding children!"

"No, of course not. I meant Krall Trhet. You told me that you despise what he did, but how far are you willing to go? Do you want to side with the Allegiant? We could use your expertise."

Runith shook his head. "I want to avoid politics."

Phenmir tried to hold back his frustration. "You must realize that *everything* that we are facing in Facet *is* politics."

"*Must I*, Chussman? Since when has harvesting and the wars tied to it been part of us? What happened to our Ideals, or religions, our spirituality being the center of our existence? I will not oppose you and I ask you to do the same for me."

Phenmir took a drink of the juice given to him in the hard shell of the fruit from which it was derived. It was pale and had the taste of grape with a touch of lemon. "That depends on what you are going to do, Zhaesman."

"Free these children from the political ties that we force upon them. Half of the continent sees them as crops for harvesting"—he pointed at Phenmir—"while the other sees them as weapons."

Phenmir sighed. "We are not using them as weapons, but—"

"Maybe you aren't but Kzhek was all the proof I need." Runith's eyes shot to Phenmir's clenched fists. "Now, Chussman, I will not oppose you. Our motives may differ but let us at least help those who cannot help themselves. I am not talking about overturning harvesting. Politics are beyond me now and I want to change that which I am capable of."

"Alright."

"Part of that includes helping *this* vulnerable population. Trhet and the other Zhaes Thanes that sided with him are trying to take these people from their homes and use them in war. I accompanied them with one of the Rasteen back to Fayis and my Thane of Scholarship *cut* himself and offered his bloody hand to one of them. I don't think anything happened, at least from what I saw, but he then invited more of the Patriarchy brethren to observe the Rasteen. Who knows what other tests or trials have been done to them. They plan on forcing these innocent people in fight their war. How *vile* is that? Have we not committed enough sin in waging war that we need to involve these peaceful people? I don't know how they wish to do it, but after Thane Gromm's revolting self-injury, I wonder if they have more sinister means prepared to force the Rasteen to act against their will. Do you see what I mean?"

Phenmir tapped on the table.

"Perd me, Chussman, did you come with the same intention? Did you hope to use them for your side as well?"

"It's not as simple as that."

"I hope not! Perd, maybe *I* can teach you something about charity and love."

"Please, it's more than–"

"We had to try something before being crushed by them." Kaela approached from behind. Golma stood at her side. "Regardless of what you call 'good' and 'evil,' someone was going to use them."

Runith shook his head. "You've made those children into cold hearted politicians right after they finished nursing from their mother's breast!"

"We are capable of more than you think," Kaela said.

Golma stepped forward and spoke. "They don't want to control them like you think, Runith."

Kaela nodded. "While you told Phenmir about what happened, Golma told me about your time here." She placed her hand on Phenmir's shoulder. "Thane, our best hope is in helping these people achieve what they need rather than fighting our war."

Phenmir sighed, then nodded. "And what do they need? I'm sorry, Zhaesman, Tchoyasgirls, but even if I could help these crop people, I *can't*. We are in the middle of a war." He moaned and pulled at his hair. "Perd me, what have I done? I've wasted all this time for what? People have *died* for us to come here and find support. I only hoped that we might have their help to achieve peace."

Kaela patted his back. "We can. We just have to take a different route."

He looked up at her with arched eyebrows and a frown reflecting his inner turmoil.

"I've learned things here," said Golma. "These people have a *deep* connection to Facet and its people."

"What kind of connection?" Phenmir asked.

"I'm not sure, but I can *feel* it. We can speak with the Rasteen *because* we feel a connection to them. Our endowed organs, the war, all of it is somehow connected."

"I'm sorry, but I can't rely on suspicions." Phenmir said.

Golma neared him. "Then let it be on faith. There are steps we have to make and goals we need to follow. I believe they want to help us. Or more specifically, Runith."

Phenmir looked at the Zhaesman with a furrowed brow.

"Perd, I forgot to tell you about the ritual. We'll get to that soon."

He looked back at Golma.

"Our first step: we need to get rid of Trhet and the Zhaes Thanes."

"I figured that was obvious."

"We need to remove any threat of them being used by humans. That includes the Patriarchy of Scholars. If Thane Gromm's meeting with them went as he planned, I think they might force them to help the loyalists."

Phenmir nodded. "Cut their ties with the loyalists."

"Banish them from the Middlelands–"

Runith leaned in. "Then we go to 'free the Korenod'."

"What is that supposed to mean?" Phenmir asked.

"I'm close to finding out, but we need to speak with the Branch of the North."

Phenmir stared at him.

Runith sighed. "I want to help these people and get that perding Tchoyas Krall away from these children. You want power. You help me get those perding tyrants out of the Middlelands. My goal is achieved. I'll offer you any intel I have on them. Zhaes secrets? They're yours. I'm done with all of that. I want peace, even if that means I spend the rest of my life here, away from your politics. Not enough for you? Just wait until you see what these Rasteen can do. That ritual did something to the Endowers, doubled their power, I don't know. Maybe the Rasteen won't fight your war. I pray they won't, but who knows. Even if they don't, I am sure they have something to offer you and your Endowers to make your journey worthwhile."

"Even if they can offer me some new 'power,' it–"

"Quit whining, Phenmir!" Kaela shouted. "You are fighting your war out here. Do what you can and don't pout because you aren't at home sitting in councils. Like Golma said, we will weaken the loyalists by preventing their connection with the Rasteen."

"I'm sure they'll grow on you once you give them a chance," said Runith.

Grow?

"Please, Phenmir," Kaela said.

He chuckled. "This is not the first time a child has been wiser than me."

Runith clapped Phenmir on the shoulder. "Yes, Chussman! Let us both be like these Tchoyasgirls, patient for a great reward. Once you see what the Rasteen are, you are sure to have an open heart. Let's see some of that Chuss love!"

Phenmir smiled and shook his head. *Care is the Creed. Learn it already, you perding kulf, Phenmir.*

"I want to end this war as much as you do," said Golma.

"Let us all have such faith. Now, let's report to the Branch, then"—Runith stared into Phenmir's eyes—"we are going to rid the Middlelands of the human pests you call '*loyalists.*'"

❧ ❦

Golma walked before Runith into the Branch's palace. "*Ever since the Chussman arrived, you seem so sure about becoming the* chosen one *for the Rasteen,*" she breathed to him. "*They'll be happy to hear about your commitment.*"

Runith shot a glance back. The Chussman and his party remained close behind. Lele jumped into a nearby pond, avoiding politics as he wished he could. *"I don't know what happened to me. It's like a parental instinct. He came wanting to use them, and I had to defend them."*

A doorway of leaves opened before Golma. *"I doubt he wanted to abuse them."*

"I know. Something struck me."

"You feel it too?"

"What do you mean?"

"Like I told him and Kaela. I know that they are connected to all of this. I think it's all connected to the Ritual with the juice. You feel it too, right?"

"A little." He recalled the *Binding of Roots* that they had mentioned. *But I do not think the connection is complete.*

The Branch's throne chamber sounded like they had entered a rainstorm as every Rasteen inside breathed a greeting, some greetings more pregnant with concern and emotion than others.

"Beast man!" the Branch rejoiced. The leaves on her crown danced as if blown in the wind as she stood. Three Rasteen stood on each side of her with different colored flowers and buds covering their bodies. *"Have you come to prepare for your Binding? We felt your loyalty before you even completed the Cleansing Promise. The Korenod will be pleased to have a—"* A vine extended from her finger as she pointed to the Chussman and his party. *"Who are they?"*

Runith was happy to avoid the need to declare his loyalty to them just yet. He felt with everything inside, just as he felt Laeih's touch on his life, that he needed to help the Rasteen. Despite his assurance, doubts and feelings of inadequacy tried to hold him back. His depressive thoughts of entropy vanished as the need to serve filled him.

Before Runuth could introduce the Chussman's party, the Branch breathed again. *"More children of the seed have come to join! Praise the Korenod, for she will rejoice in her new devotees."*

Phenmir stopped at Runith's side. "Translation, please?"

"She is happy that the Endowers have come, but wants to know—"

"Why?"

Runith smiled. "They call the Endowers '*Children of the Seed*.'"

"And you've already pledged yourself to them? Perd me, Zhaesman, you really don't care for your Court, do you?"

"It's not that simple."

"Runith!" Golma smacked his leg and pointed to the Branch. "*Would you care to explain what is happening?*"

The green-flowered Rasteen at her side was three times as large as any he had seen before. The vines on the Rasteen's body twisted as if she were flexing as she took slow steps towards them. After Runith explained their sexes, he felt more comfortable knowing that they at least had that in common with humans.

"*They are no threat!*" Runith expelled snot as he breathed as forcefully as he could manage. He pointed at the red-flowered Rasteen. "*Has she read him yet? She will know that they are here to offer help.*"

The Branch lifted her hand for her green-flowered guard to stop. She gestured to her guards. "*They only use their gifts according to my command.*"

"*Then command it and you will see!*"

"*No. Reading others is not without cost. She does not wish to connect her mind to him before they have spoken. Entering the mind of a stranger can be dangerous. One should always be cautious of what enters their mind. I would like for you to extend that branch, beast man.*"

Thane Leisa could learn something from that warning. Runith nodded, then felt awkward, realizing that the gesture had no meaning in the Rasteen culture. He pontificated his jaw twice. "*They have come to help banish those with whom we traveled here. Those people to the south wish to use your people and we would like to prevent that.*"

"*This would not be the first time. What do they request in return?*"

Runith relayed her question to Phenmir.

"Tell them that we merely benefit from removing the threat of the loyalists."

Runith repeated the message in terms the Rasteen would understand.

"*I sense there is more,*" breathed the Branch.

He turned back to Phenmir. "Not enough. They want more."

"What do they expect? We had a long conversation settling this matter. You tell them."

"What else is there to say? You hope they will join your fight?"

"*He struggles to relay his desires,*" breathed the branch. "*I do not feel with my mind as she does,*" she pointed to the red-flower guard, "*but I would have reason to believe that he wishes the same as those to the south.*"

"*No,*" breathed Runith. "*Perhaps he did at one point, but I have told him about my desire to help your people outside of the war fought by men in the north. It's all–*" he shook his head and pointed to the red-flower guard. "*Have her read me. I plead it of you, Branch. My innermost thoughts can speak better than my breathed words.*"

The Branch breathed her agreement and extended her finger vine towards the red flower guard and twisted into her body.

Runith squinted.

"*I sense your confusion, beast man,*" the Branch breathed. "*Worry not. Soon you will understand the intricacies of interconnected roots. As my guard reads you, so shall I see what your mind holds.*"

The red flower guard stepped forwards. A faint yellow glow brightened her ghastly eyes. The flowers on her opened and closed as her emotionless gaze became flustered.

She let out the Rasteen equivalent of a scream. To his ears it sounded steam escaping through a small hole in a pot of boiling water.

"What is happening?" Phenmir shouted. He was the only one in the room unable to understand the Rasteen language, yet he was no further than anyone else from understanding what had happened.

The Branch whipped her finger with the speed of a snake flicking its tongue. She fell back onto her throne.

Runith ran to help, though the flower guards remained still. The only one who moved was the red flower guard, who had fallen to her knees and held her head between her hands.

The Branch held her hand up to Runith. "*I am not unwell, physically at least.*"

"*What happened?*"

"*We saw what you witnessed in the place you call Fayis.*"

"*What do you mean? What hurt you?*"

"*I am not injured, merely overwhelmed by the implications of what I saw. This 'Gromm' knows more than he should. The Korenod is in more danger than we assumed.*"

Runith scowled and scratched his head. His heart pounded.

The Branch straightened her posture and looked up at him. "*These 'Scholars' are more of a threat than you realize.*"

"*Why?*" He gave up trying to defend Phenmir, realizing that they had seen something within him that warranted much closer attention. "*What did you see?*"

"*Blasphemy,*" breathed the red flower guard.

"*This self-proclaimed Scholar, Thane Gromm, must be executed.*"

Runith felt his nerves surge. "*Why him? Did you not see what Krall Trhet has done?*"

"*That is little in comparison to what this Gromm has done.*" The Branch's leaves shook, then stilled as she took a deep breath. "*You were correct in saying that he wishes to weaponize us. His people have attempted in the past, but now they go further, violating our most sacred matters. All of them must be punished.*"

"*That is what we are trying to do!*"

"*So you will commit yourself to us, beast man?*"

"*Yes, was that not clear?*"

"You will lead the era of union?"

"We can address that later. We are talking about something else."

"No. Everything is one. We need your commitment now to complete what we ask."

"And what is that?"

"That you begin your Binding of Roots now."

"I still don't know what that is. I–"

The Branch spoke with the force of a Zhaes typhoon. *"Will you save us?"*

"I cannot promise."

"But you will give yourself."

Runith stared into the Branch's pale eyes, seeing the faint yellow glow behind them grow. *How can I do it if I do not know the cost?* Visceral memories of commanding the kaesan in Kzhek returned to him as fresh wounds. His work had killed countless soldiers on each side. *Countless people trying to save their own.*

"Beast man."

His eyes remained on hers, though he wanted to pull them away. More memories returned, this time of his beast hunting prior to receiving his graft. Prior to recognizing the cost of taking any life. *If I don't act, these people will lose their freedom, their lives.*

I must return to nature what I have taken. *"I will."*

The Branch pointed to her blue flower guard. *"Come forth, ready to cut and bind."*

The blue flower guard stepped towards Runith, her hands forming into the shape of a wooden blade that looked sharper than any sword he had seen.

"What is happening?" Phenmir shouted, fueling Runith's unease. He breathed. *"Branch, what is this?"*

She placed her hand on the blue flower guard's shoulder, stopping her.

"*Scholar Gromm tried to force Rasteen power from one of our sisters. He attempted that which we would never grant him. That which would never be granted to a prideful Vibration such as him.*" She gestured for the blue flower guard to approach. "*Hold out your palm, Runith.*"

His choices to obey had been his own until that moment. His hand shot forward with the Branch's command.

He was under her control and could not scream as the blue flower guard sliced open his palm and touched the flesh with her viney finger.

The Branch stared into his eyes as she breathed. "*The false Scholar Gromm attempted to force the Binding of Roots. This power will never be his, but it will be yours. We can no longer wait. Your trust has been pledged and we must accept it or become slaves to the followers of this false Scholar.*" She looked at her blue flower guard. "*Let his roots become ours.*"

The vine dug into his flesh, tunneling like a worm.

CHAPTER THIRTY-SEVEN

ALL FLOWERS MUST WILT

Aside from the turmoil that rent the land, Aerhee held on to peace. She climbed into the carriage after Sheath with a course set for Kzhek. Even though she worried about riding through Priess' most traveled roads, it beat repeating their journey from the pinnacles.

Her cares dissipated. Sheath sat across from her. Zeir sat beside her, warming her with his coat that he claimed to not need. Voln, the crude child with a soft heart behind his hard front, sat beside Sheath. Even he smiled through his wolf mask. She had detested the violent mask the day she met him, but it had grown on her.

As with his personality, the fierce wolf face masked the frightened boy within. Part of her wished she had never seen his vulnerability. Their relationship would have been simpler, free of responsibility. She valued how close they had become but felt guilt for having brought him on an arduous journey, one vile enough to peel away his innocence.

The carriage shook with the shout of the coachman as the ghete began to pull them. The cabin was slow to warm and their breaths were all too visible. She valued Zeir's proximity more than ever, though the comfort he offered was more of an emotional warmth than physical.

"How long until Kzhek?" Voln asked.

"The more you ask, the longer it will be," said Sheath.

"That makes no perding sense."

"Try to sleep," Zeir said. "It'll pass faster."

Voln sighed, making sure that it was loud enough for everyone to notice, and turned to stare out of the frost-covered window.

Zeir looked out as well, though they could only see through the small hole that Voln had scratched in the frost before entering. Sheath pulled out a travel sized version of the *Tome of Measure.* Her lips moved slightly as she read.

Since traveling, Aerhee had missed most of her morning study sessions. She would have thought herself a poor Zhaeswoman, yet she was occupied with matters dearer to Laeih than reviewing the holy scripts. If she failed to prevent the domination of the Holy Reapers, she might not have the chance to worship as she wished. Still, that was no excuse for shirking her studies.

She reached for Zeir's hand. It was just as cold as hers. He smiled, though his gaze remained on the window. His demeanor had calmed since the previous night.

"*This is a path we should not pursue.*" His words played across her mind. She could not understand his doubts. What was there for them to lose? If the Seers did not plant Colrig to sow the seeds of war, they would merely have a pleasant conversation. Regardless, they were returning home. Kzhek would welcome them, but Zeir acted as if they were heading down a treacherous path. She chose to ignore her concerns. Ignorance is often the easiest path to peace, yet the most temporary.

She rested her head on his shoulder and closed her eyes. Her intimacy had grown while his had shrunk. Once again, she chose the fleeting salve of ignorance and closed her eyes. In sleep, all was well.

⁂

"Is that Ekscomos?"

Aerhee woke up to Voln staring out the window.

Sheath and Zeir stirred after he asked a few more times.

"What do you mean?" Aerhee swallowed her dry throat. She looked out the window, noting the sun's position to see that a few hours had passed.

"Do you see it now?" Voln tapped the glass. "That's a big city, right? I don't know, maybe all Priess cities are larger than Fayis."

Aerhee looked down at the passing buildings. They were the large architectural feats she knew well from her childhood. "It can't be. We haven't traveled that far and Ekscomos is out of the way."

Sheath blinked her eyes slowly. "What?"

Aerhee pointed to the window. "Look outside."

"You should know, Aerhee."

"I haven't been here in decades."

Sheath looked out the window. "It doesn't look like Ekscomos. The architecture still has the slender Zhaes influence, but we didn't have any major cities on our path."

Aerhee turned to Zeir to see if he was awake. His eyes were wide and his breaths were quick and shallow.

She placed her hand on his chest. "Zeir? What is going on?"

He reached his hand out. "Sheath, do you have a map? Go tell the coachman to correct the course."

Aerhee felt her breaths shake. "Zeir, what is–"

"Now!" He never yelled, but he did now. "We need to go to Kzhek as directly as possible. Switch carriages, hire a new driver, walk, I don't care. Please, we need to–"

Voln turned away from the window. "Why are we going *into* the city?"

Sheath and Aerhee moved over to the window, but Zeir's stare was stuck to the wall.

Sheath sighed and groaned. "Open the door, Voln. I'll ask him what is happening."

"Can't you just read him?" Voln asked.

She shook her head. "I need to see him. Don't forget that it isn't exactly 'reading minds.' It is an analysis of facial, expressions, the aura of emotions, and–"

Voln scoffed. "I've met Endowers that can do it."

She scowled. "Just open the door."

He shook the handle, to no avail. He slammed his shoulder against the door, but it did not budge. "The kulf locked it."

"Try the–"

"What is his problem?" Voln pointed at Zeir. "Come on, Zhaesman, we can try the top latch. Quit whining."

"Zeir?" Sheath asked.

"Just go!"

Aerhee shook his shoulders. "Zeir, what is wrong?"

He shook his head.

Voln forced a worried laugh. "Just read the Kulf, Sheath."

She stared at Zeir, but his panic persisted with his lost glare. "I–I can't."

"What do you mean?" Aerhee asked.

"I–he–"

Voln groaned. "Perd me! Come on, Zhaeswoman, have you never read him?"

"I have, but—I can read him, but his mind shows that he is as calm as ever. I can't read any worries or fears. He is–or something–is blocking me."

Aerhee shook her head. "He's not an Endowed, I would know."

"And I don't think he is," she replied. "But maybe he is being used."

Aerhee shook him. He looked at her with a quivering lip. Tears fell from his bloodshot eyes.

"Open the top, Voln," Sheath commanded.

He stood but fell over as the carriage stopped.

Aerhee tried to collect herself. "Sheath. Where are we?"

They looked out the window, then moved to look out the other side. The carriage had ridden into a small cobblestone square surrounded by buildings.

The door unlocked and opened.

Sheath was the first out. Before the others could follow, she stopped and turned back. "Aerhee."

"What is it?"

"Keep calm," she whispered.

What are you talking about? She pushed her way past Voln and stepped out onto the road. A circle of Priess Patriarchy Scholars circled the carriage. Many wore armor over their shortened robes. All had a weapon, whether it be a spear at the ready or a knife sheathed in their belt.

Voln jumped free from the carriage. "What is perding–" he lifted his head up after a clumsy fall "–happening."

The boy's ever present confidence faltered.

Aerhee shot a quick glance back to the carriage. Zeir remained frozen in his seat. She faced the Scholars, forcing the confidence that she had held for such a moment. She knew she would face the Patriarchy again, but did not expect it to be so soon and on their terms. Then again, few seek the Patriarchy of Scholars themselves.

Three of the Scholars wore bronze armor and no helm, in contrast to the others who wore silver armor and helms with the faceplates down.

The Scholar in the center of the trio stepped forward, adjusting the bronze circlet around his head as if flaunting a halo. "Zeir, do not disappoint us more than you already have."

"What is going on?" Aerhee demanded. "What have you done to him?"

Sheath whispered. "I can't read them either, Aer."

The Scholar scoffed. "What have *we* done? I suppose not enough, dear Priesswoman."

Her heart fluttered and her mind froze.

"No need to play coy. We know about your past. But why should we speak when your husband can offer better insights into his failures?"

Aerhee's rage took place of fear. "What are you talking about?"

"Oh, I am sure you have plenty of questions, many of which are beyond the sight of even your dear friend Sheath Leisa." He took a step forward and raised his hand. "Come now, Zeir."

"Zeir!" Aerhee shouted.

The carriage shook as Zeir stepped down, his head hung low.

The Scholar took another step forward.

Voln jumped in front of Aerhee. His hands turned into wolf claws and the wood of his mask shaped itself into an actual snout. "Back *the perd* away from her, you *kulf* or I'll–"

The circle of guards closed in on them with blades pointed at Voln.

"I wouldn't risk it if I were you, Tchoyasboy." Scales flickered across the Scholar's forehead and his pupils became slits for a mere second. "Many of us here are blessed."

"Perd you!"

Aerhee tried to push him back, but his clawed feet had dug into the ground. She hung her arms in front of him and held her hands by his sternum. Despite her expectations, he remained still and returned to his natural form.

The Scholar waved for the others to stand down. He cleared his throat as they lowered their weapons. "Now, Zeir, please come forth. You Zhaesemen know well that confession must follow every mistake, or in your case, series of mistakes."

He walked forward and spared Aerhee the quickest of glances. A faint whisper escaped his lips. "Forgive me."

The two Scholars next to the apparent leader came to Zeir's sides. Each one grabbed one of his arms, their wrists each bearing a bronze circlet.

"What is happening?" Aerhee pleaded.

The Scholar's attention turned away from Zeir and to Sheath. "Right guards, take the Feelman."

Aerhee cried out as four guards seized Sheath.

The Scholar sighed. "Left guards, take Aerhee and the boy. This will be easier with them still."

They did as commended. Two held Aerhee. Two held Voln with their blades at his chest until he stopped struggling.

"Aerhee!" Sheath shrieked. "This one is–"

The head Scholar shouted over Sheath. "She is reading one of you perding kulfs! Kill her before she reads more!"

"Ae–" Sheath's dying cry became a choking gargle as the Scholar at her side thrust his dagger into her throat. He shook it inside and removed it with a most unclean cut, sure to mutilate her vocal cords.

"Sheath!" Aerhee wailed but cut her cry as the Scholars tightened their grip, one clenching her throat.

"Order now!" the head Scholar Shouted. He pointed to the Scholars who held Sheath's bleeding body. "Take her body elsewhere. I need Aerhee's attention *now*!"

They scurried away, leaving a bloody trail.

Aerhee would have fallen if the Scholars did not hold her up. Shock had stolen any tears from her eyes. Pain left no room for sorrow, though it would surely follow.

"Excuse that unpleasant sight," the head Scholar said. "We have delicate matters to discuss and I could not risk a Feelman's readings, even if most of us could have prevented her probing. Very well—sha—co–if–"

The Scholar's words scrambled in her mind. She became numb and her vision unclear.

Sheath could not be dead. The rational part of her knew that denial accompanied every loss. It had been the same with her father. Sheath's death was sudden and cruel. Everything had been going according to their plan. Sheath recognized the errors in the ways of the loyalists. She couldn't have been taken.

Her blurry gaze focused on the head Scholar. Her head throbbed and her cheek burned. The Scholar holding her had slapped her face.

"Do I have your attention now, Aerhee?" The head Scholar leaned over to her as the Scholars at her side lifted her up after her legs had fallen weak.

He patted the side of her burning cheek. "There she is. Now, where were we? Ah, yes, Zeir, come here."

"What do you want?" Her words shook. Tears stung her eyes.

"Stay focused and I will tell you. After all, we had your carriage driver bring *you* to us."

"Then let the other two go."

"I am afraid that isn't possible. The boy is a liability and complicates matters more than we would have liked. Zeir–" he shook his head and smiled. "Oh Zeir, why don't you tell your dear wife what you have done? Rather, what you have failed to do."

Zeir remained silent, his head down.

One of the Scholars holding him punched him in the ribs.

"Come on now, Zeir," said the head Scholar.

"I never meant to hurt you, Aer."

The head Scholar scoffed. "Oh, you still speak with affection? I have to say, Zeir, we were fond of your work. That is, until you failed to keep her on the right track."

"What are they talking about, Zeir?" Aerhee shouted.

Please, don't take him too. He's all I have.

He looked up at her. His frown spoke of regret. "I only wanted what is best for you."

The head Scholar paced back and forth. "The words of all manipulators. How unoriginal. Still, you remained by her side until the end." He stopped and looked at Zeir. "Enough with the banter. Are you going to tell her, or do I have to?"

"I love you, Aerhee. I always have."

"So the lies persist?"

"They're not lies!"

The head Scholar shook his head and walked towards Aerhee. "Your husband will learn the consequences of crossing the *Bronze Seers*. Does that name frighten you? There is no reason for us to hide anymore. You've followed our trail. Well done! After all, we'll need your help going forth."

Aerhee had no room in her mind for objection. The head Scholar *owned* her attention.

"Your father used to be a friend of mine. Most friendships that end do so because of death or betrayal. I suppose in your father's circumstances, it was both. *'How does Zeir have anything to do with this?'* I can see the question behind your quivering lips."

He fixed the bronze circlet on his head and resumed his pacing. "Your father was a Scholar. Before you shout your doubts, you must know by now that the highest Scholars hide among the populus rather than remain in the Chapterhouse, despite some exceptions. I was not as high in the Patriarchy as your father, but we worked together. That is, until he chose to betray his people. The Bronze Seers and our offspring in the citizens of Facet, the Holy Reapers, seek none other than equality among all in Facet. Your religions divide more than any war. Your father, while he was interested in the Zhaes religion, did not leave to become a Zhaes convert, as you might have assumed. Did you note that he found himself busy laboring in the Cloven Gleff while you and your mother worshiped?"

Aerhee gave him a blank stare, but she knew it told him enough.

"Your father labored in the Gleff not only for money, but in search of an ancient faith that was buried for a good reason." He stopped and stared at her. "Your father was a believer in the old god of Court Priess."

A new world opened in her mind.

"As the Seers rose within the Patriarchy, your father turned against us in pursuit of the very thing our Court banished eras before. If your father pursued his path without intervention, he would have caused a war within Court Priess. Some secrets are best left alone. Those counterfeit coins with a clear connection to the Seers were planted on your father. Even though he knew they were counterfeit, he never knew where they came from. His assassination was completed because the Zhaes Scholars saw him as a Seer invader. Knowing his rank, he seemed that much more of a threat. For years they have tried to destroy our people within their Patriarchy, but our roots are too deep.

"After your father was dealt with, the old Priess fanaticism was put to rest. Still, we knew that some of your father's knowledge was valuable. *Dangerous* in the wrong hands. He harbored secrets we could never obtain. They must be used for Facet's good rather than old rituals fueled that will only divide our people. Hoping to keep an eye out for the remnants of his knowledge, however it was passed down, we kept eyes on you. Ever since the day the statue of the Bronze Transgressor was formed, you have been under our watch."

He slapped his arm on Zeir's back, causing him to grunt. "Enter Zeir, your *perfect* companion. Before you ask, no, he is neither Scholar nor Seer, but a tool. Have you ever wondered why he remained so resilient despite your insufferable criticism and dry love?"

"They forced me, Aerhee! They used me to gain Allegiant secrets as well! I was the one who told them that you were going to take Paiell! Priess soldiers defended Sleff because of what they made me do! Some of them can force someone to—"

"Enough!" The head Scholar calmed his heavy breathing.

Denial offered no respite from the sting.

"Zeir served as your husband and our eye, always monitoring you and remaining by your side despite everything. Your husband's false perfection was an act."

Zeir sobbed. "I love you—"

The Scholar at his side covered Zeir's mouth and squeezed.

"Your father was a Priess traitor, we did away with him, and Zeir has been our eyes on you. Now that he has failed, he is no longer of use."

The head Scholar snapped his fingers and the Scholar holding Zeir broke his neck.

Aerhee tried to scream, but the Scholar at her side covered her mouth with an iron grip.

The head Scholar approached.

"You will come with us now. New powers have swept Facet and we need to dig into that mind of yours to see if there is anything left of your father. We have means of digging deep. No need to worry about your weak memory. Your father always said you were gifted. Let's see how true his words remain." His head snapped to the side. "Take the Tchoyasboy as well. We have a cell ready for them in the Chapterhouse."

CHAPTER THIRTY-EIGHT

WHEAT AND TARES

Despite his confusion and persistent discomfort following his acceptance, Hir was excited to share the news of his advancement with Scholar Sokov. After keeping the news for a few days, he was relieved to hear about his mentor's safe return from Fayis.

He ran towards Scholar Sokov's study but stopped halfway as his stomach cramped. He was still recovering from near starvation in the Chuss desert and struggled to reach satiety. With a little movement right after eating double portions, he felt the weight of his meal. Perhaps forcing down his food right as he heard about Scholar Sokov's return had not been such a wise option. Still, he could not delay.

He reached the door and clenched his side as the cramp dissipated. He gave it a light knock, but it opened with each movement, never having been shut.

The room was empty, but the sound of ruffled papers and dropped objects came from his large closet. Before Hir thought to walk back there or announce himself, he stood still before the mess of a room. Books had toppled from their piles and shelves. Papers were tossed in every direction in complete disarray. Ink vials and a jar of quills had fallen to the floor, yet the vials retained their caps as a small mercy.

Scholar Sokov almost stumbled from the closet with a stack of documents held against his chest. "Hir, what are you—excuse me, I–"

"Is something wrong?" Something most certainly was, yet did not want to seem intrusive, despite his intrusion.

Sokov shook his head as he set the papers on his desk. Some slipped free and joined others on the floor. "If you think my study is out of order, you cannot imagine how scattered my mind is."

"Then what are you doing?"

"Looking for... things. Documents, though I suppose that is obvious. Would you shut that door?"

Hir jumped to follow the command.

"Sit, Hir." He shook his head. "It's worse than I imagined."

"What is?"

"I shouldn't bring you into this, then again." He looked at Hir. "Everyone will know soon enough. I am sorry to have burdened you before with talking about the Bronze Seers. Their movement within the Patriarchy is worse than I could have imagined."

Hir thought about the bronze circlet that Dumek had worn during the acceptance ceremony. "I think I might understand."

"You–no, I'm talking about Fayis."

"What happened?"

"The Zhaesmen and some of the Priess Scholars, many of them are Seers. I learned this recently, but the gathering was a flaunting of their power over the true Scholars."

"What happened?"

"Most of the Seers side with the loyalist movement."

"Why did they invite you?"

"Despite the division in the Patriarchy, we still try to share our findings. Thane Gromm of Court Zhaes requested my knowledge on a particular point of the Patriarchy's foundation." He shook his head. "I didn't expect the meeting to be so politically charged. They spoke of it as if it were a study, but I could read the vile intentions behind their actions. The Seers will manipulate anyone and *anything* for power."

"*Anything?*"

"They brought a perding Middleman... by Cheric's mercy, I cannot put this all on you right now."

"Why not?"

"Because you have only been an Accepted Scholar for but a moment. I cannot toss you into boiling water when you are not yet used to the heat. If you read every tome in the Chapterhouse about the Patriarchy's history, perhaps you could understand. We do not have the time for that now. The Patriarchy is in danger, Hir."

"Then let me help save it! I've been accepted! I completed the Crucible and the acceptance ceremony."

"Until I learned how deep within our ranks they have dug, even here in Chuss, I wouldn't have been so worried to hear that."

"What do you mean?"

"Who led your acceptance ceremony?"

"Dumek."

"How did he explain the crucible?"

"What do you mean?"

Sokov pounded his hands on his desk and shouted, "What did he say?" He took a deep breath, pushed the books from his chair and sat down, speaking in a collected voice. "What did he say was the purpose of the Crucible of Dunes?"

"He called me a conqueror. Said that it was a metaphor for the Patriarchy's dominance."

Sokov's face fell into his hands. He squeezed it and groaned. "The Patriarchy is not meant to *dominate*. We are to unite in faith. The *Seers* aim to conquer. They aim to dominate with the power of humans, not of gods."

"I knew he was a Seer."

"For how long?"

"I only learned during the acceptance. I saw bronze."

"Your trial. You faced the organ fiend?"

Images of the vile shadow of a man played across his mind. "I think so."

"Those are a mistake. Errors from failed harvests, though they are much more than unsuccessful experiments. They are a sign from nature, a warning against trying to use the power of the gods against their will. There is so much to explain to you, more so more questions that can be asked. I have but a mere crumb of understanding the Patriarchy's history, but I know that the Seers betray its purpose."

"Then what is its purpose?"

"To let the holy prevail. To maintain peace through–"

The door cracked open. Scholar Sokov shot to his feet.

A Chussboy with his short silver dreads tied atop his head stepped in. He adjusted his apprentice robes. Hir knew all the apprentices, for they only joined once a year. He had never seen this boy.

"May I help you?" asked Scholar Sokov. "We are occupied at the moment."

Hir squinted at the apprentice, then looked at Scholar Sokov. Their eyes met and Hir nodded.

"Shut the door behind you," said Sokov. "Take the chair against the wall."

Sokov returned to his seat. "Well, what is it?"

"I've been looking for Scholar Hir. I have a pertinent message for him from his mother."

Hir's eyes shifted between Scholar Sokov and the apprentice. "What does she want?"

"Perhaps we should leave Scholar Sokov alone. I sense we are disturbing his studies."

Scholar Sokov scoffed.

Hir felt that nothing had changed following his acceptance ceremony except for increased confusion. Despite his incessant self-doubt, he felt comfortable enough with Scholar Sokov. "Right here will do. I am sure Scholar Sokov would be interested in hearing the message as well. He oversees all that I do here."

Sokov scowled at him and he nodded. "Yes, as Scholar Hir said. Be on with it now."

"She has not heard from your father in some while and wanted to know if you had heard anything from him."

Hir looked between the two, realizing that he had to stop lest he give his suspicion away. He tried to ignore the concerning news about his father, doing all that he could to tell himself it was a lie. "And why did she send you? I'm sorry, I don't believe we have met."

The Chussboy furrowed his brow. "I almost want to take offense that you do not recognize me. Then again, I can't expect you to pay too much to those who train right after you and Dumek."

Hir shrugged. "It's hard to stay conscious after working with him."

Scholar Sokov glared at him as if to say, "*Must you bother me? I have too much to worry about right now.*"

"Have you met this apprentice before, Scholar Sokov?"

He shook his head. "I rarely spend so much time with apprentices. Not everyone *seeks* attention as much as you." They shared a laugh, but not one of them seemed sincere.

Hir stared at the apprentice. "Now you have me concerned. Have they heard anything from—first of all, who sent you?"

"He looked like one of the Krall's guards, but who can tell with the Allegiant soldiers everywhere? He was running around and I was the first Scholar he could find, poor Chussman."

"Why was he in a rush?"

"Said that a storm was coming, and it sounded like a bad one." The apprentice shrugged. "Who knows where he was running? I didn't see any storm clouds, but I heard the thunder."

Hir folded his arms. "And you're supposed to report back to him? After the storm? After he has fled?"

The apprentice smiled and shook his head. "No, but I figured–"

Hir raised his hand to stop the apprentice from speaking. Voices shouted in the hall. Irreverence was never permitted, nor known to happen in the halls of the Chapterhouse.

Scholar Sokov's gaze filled Hir with terror.

"What is that?" the words struggled to leave Hir's lips.

The apprentice adopted a similar terror.

Sokov rushed to the door with a slight limp. Hir offered his hand to help, but the Scholar swatted it away. They peeked outside.

"Do you think it is about that storm you were talking about?" asked Hir.

Scholar Sokov scoffed. "You should know better than that, Hir. Sandstorms are common enough that they would not cause this kind of panic."

Hir looked at the apprentice, almost asking if he had seen any dust clouds, then recalled the words the apprentice had spoken moments before. "*I didn't see any storm clouds.*" *No Chussman looks above for a storm. Rain is too rare to be one's first suspicion. Any true Chussman would look for dust clouds, not storm clouds. Outsiders are too quick to attach thunder to rain. Chuss sand storms always come with thunder.*

It was the smallest observation, yet the inconsistency bothered him. If his study of people as a Scholar had taught him anything, he knew this Chussman was not from Sliin. This Chussman had tried to cover something. That was not the only inconsistency in his words. Perhaps this was a Chussman, *but this was no Scholar.*

"Who are you?" Hir asked.

"Wha-what? What are you talking about?" The apprentice pointed at the Scholars running through the halls. "Can't you see there is something happening?"

Set aside suspicion. Do not bury it.

Scholar Sokov had left the room and approached one of his fellow high Scholars. The other was much older than Sokov and relied on two canes to hobble as fast as he could manage.

"–attack?"

Hir ran to Sokov, hoping that his hearing had failed him.

"The Allegiant soldiers came with a message."

Sokov shook the man's shoulders, then stopped as the older Scholar almost fell. "Then *tell* me already!"

"Gruthmen! An army of them! Smaller than Gorgers, but much faster! They've destroyed the Western wall and have been rampaging through the city! Come, Scholar Sokov! We must descend to the shelters below!"

Hir turned back to the apprentice, whose attention was down the hall. Hir grabbed his shoulder, pulling him along.

"What are you doing?" the apprentice whined.

"Didn't you hear Scholar Sokov? The city is under attack! We have to find–"

The apprentice's false surprise failed him. The Chussman knew the city would be attacked. He looked as if he had been told that the Krall had just arrived, rather than a foreign army. The poor reaction lasted for but a moment until believable terror took over.

My father did not seek shelter as the war raged on. He left his shelter in pursuit of what was needed. What is needed now?

He looked at the apprentice again. *If they have just entered the west, we still have time. The Krall's palace is only a quick sprint away from here.*

"You were right. I need to relay what I know about my father to the Krall. You're coming with me."

"You–what?"

He grabbed the apprentice's robes and would not let them go. Even if force was required, he would give Dhera the so-called apprentice. Perhaps the city would fall, but they at least had to know why. This Chussman was the only piece of information he had.

"Where are you going?" Scholar Sokov shouted.

Hir pushed past other running Scholars as he forced the apprentice to follow. Sokov would understand. A Scholar's best pursuit is the one that burns within them.

Hir picked up the pace as he saw some Scholars pushing furniture towards the door to block the entrance. His grip remained tenacious on the apprentice. He had failed too often as a Scholar. Cheric was giving him a chance to redeem himself, so he took it with faith.

"Move! Let us through!" He pushed past a divan and bookshelves. He risked losing his fingers but gave the door all that he could to open it. A small crack opened between the giant wooden doors with more noise than he could have ever expected. Screams and shouts mixed with the sounds of shattering glass and breaking wood. Before the doors could shut again, he peeked through the crack to see a plume of smoke coming from the area towards the Krall's palace.

He turned back and pulled the apprentice with him.

"What are you doing?"

"If you want information, you need to follow me. If you want safety, you need to follow me. Leave me"—he pointed back towards the door—"and whatever is out there gets you."

They ascended the spiraling staircases and made their way to the top floor as quickly as possible. Hir was as obedient as the ideal Zhaesman, yet he knew how to step outside of the rules if necessary. He had found the hidden ladder to the roof of the Chapterhouse once before. Between his wishes to remember it and forget it at the same time, his mind sided with the former.

"You first." He pulled the apprentice's sleeve and forced him to grab a rung.

Hir followed, hitting the apprentice's feel each time he reached for a rung to keep moving.

"Slide the latch to the left and push up and to the right."

The apprentice did as instructed. They climbed through and onto the roof, back into the turmoil of Sliin falling apart.

Hir followed him out onto the roof and moved to the side of one of the domes to have a clear sight of the city. They were frozen in awe and terror as smoke rose in the distance. Many of Sliin's most prominent buildings were missing from the skyline. Sprinting soldier companies charged through the streets like a flood, destroying markets and monuments as it passed. Allegiant Soldiers fled after seeing their allies trampled by the racing Gruthmen.

"Perd me, what is this?"

The apprentice looked up at the orange sky of the setting sun. Hir followed his gaze, suddenly becoming aware that not only was the city full of screams and destruction, but the sky was filled with screeches.

Zlatogs.

Some flew above in circles like vultures looking for meat rotting under the sun. Others dove to the street and flew up into the sky again, dropping as many Allegiant soldiers as their claws could carry to their deaths.

To seek the Krall would be a fool's errand. Any help she could offer could not be much better than the advice the Scholars could give in the shelters below. Hir knew his quest would yield little, if anything, but he found it more reassuring to focus on duty rather than impending doom.

Sliin was falling, but he would remain standing.

He tugged on the apprentice's sleeve. "Come on, let's go back!"

The apprentice looked back at him, then jogged to the opening, closed it and remained on top.

"What are you doing?"

The apprentice stood on the panel and looked upward. He shouted loud enough for the entire city to hear. *"Yetrik! Semi is here! Priessman, take me to Yetrik!"*

Yetrik? Who? Priessmen? Semi? Is that his name? All the questions were worthless when placed against what was necessary to produce such a loud call.

Hir grabbed the apprentice's shoulders and shook them. "You're a perding Shiftling? Who is Yetrik?"

Hir let go and covered his ears again as the apprentice repeated his cry for Semi and Yetrik.

"Perd, Chussman! Tell me what is happening!"

His ears rang, and he tried to force the apprentice from the panel. The apprentice repeated the call again and pushed Hir away.

"Tell me what is *perding* happening!"

The apprentice glared at him.

Hir's eyes darted up to see a zlatog swooping towards them. He ran away from the apprentice, whose skin changed from a Chussman's to the slightly lighter tone of a Gruthwoman's.

Before Hir could shout another question, he was in the grip of a zlatog, soaring above Sliin.

CHAPTER THIRTY-NINE

A RIGHTEOUS GENERATION

For the second time in the span of a few days, Yetrik stood atop a building with Avra, staring at the fall of a Court capitol.

Sliin was dying.

Kevlen's scolding face spoke nothing other than disgust.

"What are we doing here?" asked Yetrik.

Kevlen shrugged. "They don't need our help and we're perding lucky that they never caught us dropping the Endowers off in that Sleff village."

"Maybe they did, but Kelm didn't. Why would mindless murderers care what we did? All they know is to obey."

"Are we not doing the same? Perd me, Yetrik, I can't just sit here and watch this. Paiell was something else, at least the first time. Those were soldiers. Sure, there are a couple Allegiant zealots below, but most of these are civilians. People."

"And so are the soldiers."

Kevlen shook his head. "I'll repeat what we did in Paiell if you want. Go find some people in need, take them to a safe village, and camp out there. I'm the perding captain of the Beastlings. I'll do what pleases me."

Yetrik pointed at a zlatog diving into the city. "Are you going to turn your Beastlings to help follow us as well?"

"Those kulfs are as dull as the Terpels and too prideful to turn away from their commands. Maybe I am too, but *this* is Thane Kelm's choice. Perding kulf must have used the same tricks he uses on the Terpels to control the other Thanes into complying."

"I think he uses more than mere tricks."

"What do you mean? How well do you know him?"

"I told you I worked with Thane Gett."

"Yes."

"With that comes interactions with the other members of the nobility. Some more than others. I don't know him too well, but as it is with most Scholars of Scholarship, he has a reputation. He is not as feared as most Scholars, who deem him a weakling, almost an outcast. I knew he was an Endower, just not what type. Semi told me more about him before we left Gruth for Paiell. She said he commanded the Terpels as if they had no choice. She knew it was tied to his ability because she even heard a *difference* in his voice when he commanded them. Despite this, his voice was of little worth in convincing other people to obey him."

"I've heard of some people like this, some call them Breathers, others Pressists. Must not be enough of them to be well known."

"I've heard the term Pressist as well, but it's often associated with someone who can do what Kelm does to more people, though even they have limits to their power."

"It's just like Beastlings. You're talented, Yetrik, but you have a lot to learn."

"Oh trust me, I know. Sometimes I wonder how connected all of these organ abilities are. We speak to animals while the Pressists use the same persuasion for humans. Where is the line of power drawn?"

"I suppose we will never know."

Perhaps.

Kevlen pointed ahead to a zlatog flying towards them. "Get ready. They may need backup."

They each climbed atop their steeds and grabbed onto their reins. Yetrik leaned forward, trying to see what the zlatog held in its claws as it reached the roof.

He dismounted and ran to the zlatog, who dropped two people onto the roof before landing next to them.

"What—who are those?" Kevlen shouted as he approached from behind.

The zlatog rider dismounted, but Yetrik did not hear what he had to say. One was a Chuss Scholar. The other held him with hands behind his back and his face pressed to the roof. Yetrik ran towards the captor, a Gruthwoman in Chuss Scholar robes.

"Kevlen, come take him!" Semi shouted.

Kevlen and the other Priess Beastling ran over to keep the Chussman down.

Semi ran into Yetrik's embrace, then pulled his head down to repeatedly kiss his forehead.

"You got the message?" she asked.

He still held onto her but pulled back to look into her eyes. "To attack from the west?"

She nodded. "At least that worked." She turned back to look over the city.

"Who in Deilf's name is this Chussman?"

"Let off of him a little, Kevlen. He's not dangerous, but we can't let him go."

The Chussman grunted as Kevlen pulled back his pressure. He whispered to the other Priessman and waved for him to take his steed back into battle.

Yetrik raised his eyebrows as Semi turned back to him, her hair swept by the gust from the departing zlatog.

"He's the son of the Chuss leader of the Harmony Allegiant," she said.

"Oh, wow. Why is he here?"

"Phemus wanted me to investigate his father. He has been missing in the Middlelands for some time."

What have I done? Were my desires to see the crop people an invitation of war into their land? Perd me. Deilf forgive me.

"What are you going to do with him?"

"I don't know. He was taking me somewhere–I think he realized that I was not a Chuss Scholar."

"Even I know that."

She chortled and shook her head. "There's no point in letting him die down there with everyone else."

"There's no point in leaving *anyone* down there. This is a cruel massacre, Semi. Can't you see it?"

"Can't I see it?" She pushed his chest back. "Couldn't you see it when Royss wanted to destroy his own city? This is all a mess. It has been ever since we entered Kzhek."

"Settle down," Kevlen said. "You two are on the same side. Quit fighting."

Yetrik stroked her arm. "I'm sorry."

"Me too. We're both trying to do what is right. I think we all want to help decrease suffering and restore order."

"What do you want with this?" groaned the Chussman. "Are you hoping for surrender? You won't have anyone left to surrender once you destroy our home."

Kevlen looked at Semi, acting like he was going to push the Chussman back against the ground, but she shook her head.

"We *want* to help." Yetrik proceeded to tell them about the rescue of the Endowers in Paiell. The image of the Sleff captain would forever be branded into his mind. He looked at Kevlen. "I don't want Terin's *new Facet*. I want all of us to return to our Courts and live as things once were. Perd harvesting, end it all if it means that we end this."

The Chussman laughed.

"What do you want?" asked Kevlen.

"We are all too much alike, aren't we? I want the same thing as you said. You want to help?"

"We're not joining your rebel force, if that is what you were implying," said Kevlen.

"No, not that. If you want to change the outcome of this war. You have to go after a different target. The Chussmen aren't your problem."

Kevlen tightened his grip, and the Chussman hissed. "Speak clearly, Scholar."

The Chussman scoffed. "I'm hardly even a Scholar. I'd probably lose my privileges as a Scholar for telling you their secrets, but the Bronze Seers are your true enemy."

"That petty groups of criminals?" asked Kevlen.

"No, they are only a front to the real threat. These Seers want to conquer Facet. Not for harvesting, but for power and what else, I don't know. They are a sect of Scholars that have broken off to misuse the authority of the Patriarchy."

Semi and Yetrik exchanged glances. "Yetrik."

"Perd me."

"What do we do?"

They looked at the Chussman.

"Can you let me stand?"

Semi nodded, and Kevlen obliged.

He brushed the red dust from the roof off of his robes. "If you saved those Endowers, you have more of a heart than most of the continent. I'm risking everything on you, but even then, I have no choice." He spared his city a glance. "Are those two zlatogs yours?"

Kevlen and Yetrik nodded.

"Can they take the four of us? Two on each?"

"Yes." Yetrik said.

"Wait." Semi stepped in front of Yetrik. "You are just going to let this Scholar tell us what to do? He could be just like Kelm, but even worse! What if the Patriarchy is the one that wants power?"

Kevlen shook his head. "Where is a Feelman when you need one? She's right though, Yetrik. We have to be careful. Captives will go to desperate measures to live. He's smart enough to try to stay with us while his city falls."

"I'm sorry, Chussman," Yetrik said. "I'm sorry that this is happening to your city." Sorrow and regret compelled him to do whatever he could to help this man.

"Bind me if you want. I don't care." The Chussman pointed at Semi. "You wanted to know where my father is? Let's go find him."

"So you just want to leave your city behind?" asked Kevlen.

"What choice do I have? I want to survive. If I stay, I'll be just another casualty."

Kevlen nodded. "But what would going to the Middlelands do against these Seers?"

"The Middlemen are connected to the Seers, the Patriarchy, and I think much more than we realize."

"Semi."

She turned to Yetrik.

"I've done it before, but this time we have a reason."

"You want to go back to the Middlelands?"

He looked at the Chussman, then back at Semi, and nodded. "If the Allegiant are down there with Royss and his party, it will only turn the Middlelands into Paiell and Sliin. I told Royss to go there first. I cannot be responsible for their destruction. Perd responsibility. Perd the loyalists. We all realize that this war has gone beyond harvesting. Kelm must be stopped before he and his Terpels destroy Facet. If he is one of these Seers like the Chussman said, then I am willing to bet my life and honor on going to the Middlelands. I will not stay and watch the massacre continue. I will not participate in this slaughter. I will not be killed as a traitor for turning against Kelm's army, that is, until we know how to strike them at their center. If this Chussman has even the smallest hope that we can see order return to Facet, I trust him. A flight to the Middlelands will be shorter than a trip to Thusk from here."

Semi nodded.

"Kevlen?" he asked.

"Get me out of this perding mess."

Yetrik smiled and looked at the Chussman. "You better live your Ideal, Chussman."

"My name is Hir."

Yetrik grabbed Semi's hand, then pointed Hir to Kevlen. "Jump on with him. Let's fly to the Middlelands."

CHAPTER FORTY

STEADFAST IS THE HONOR

R unith gasped as the vines entered his organs. He breathed along-side the plants as they became part of him. His arm contorted as the Rasteen continued to give of herself until she collapsed.

Her fellow Rasteen rushed to help her. One of them cut the vine connecting her to Runith. The rest of the vine finished entering his hand. The wound closed as a rooty twine came from forth from his skin to bind the sides together.

He was on the edge of collapsing, filled with weakness and power all at once. Every one of his senses was amplified and new senses opened in his evolved consciousness. He felt the blood running in his body and a new humor filled his veins. He heard the plants around him and saw the life they exuded. Every new sensation was overwhelming for but a moment until it became as usual as breathing. He had a mind of his own, yet he felt connected with every Rasteen in the room.

Even those outside of this hall. Our roots are bound.

He could not quite grasp the meaning of all he felt and knew, but he was at peace. His mental storm had quelled.

"Perd me! What happened to you?"

He turned to Phenmir, whose gaze was a mix of terror and awe. He could feel the Chussman's emotions, not quite reading them as a Feelman, but as if he were the most perceptive inquisitor.

He looked down at the blue flower guard lying supine on the floor. He rushed to her side, to join two other Rasteen who knelt beside her, vines coming twisting from their hands and into her body.

The Branch of the North held him back. *"Do not give your energy, beast man. She gave hers for you to bind your roots. She will be well, give her time."*

Runith looked down at his hands to see that he was reaching towards the blue flower guard with *vines* that had erupted from his palms. His fright followed up his arms as he saw the vines twisting around them. He was not becoming a Rasteen, or so he hoped, for bare skin remained. He counted four vines twisting around each arm and four more around each leg. The vines from his hands retracted into his skin, while those around the arms remained. He peeked under his clothes and found some around his chest. He felt his face and followed a vine on each side, coming from his clavicle up his neck, around the corners of his mouth, along the sides of his nose, across the eyebrows, and out like a horned owl.

Anyone with more sense than him would have fallen into a panic. He laughed, joy filling his chest just like it did when he drank the juice during their Cleansing Promise ceremony.

Perd me. He wanted to curse with happiness but knew no equivalent in the Rasteen language. He understood their language to a higher level after the vines entered his body. Their culture filled his mind. A lack of understanding was not the problem, Rasteen simply had no curses. The idea was foreign. He found himself caught between two civilizations, each so unlike each other, yet with beautiful similarities.

He smiled, seeing the blue flower guard regain her strength.

He turned to Phenmir and extended a vine towards him. "Perd me, Chussman, I think I might be a Sprouten now."

"No more beast calling?"

Runith hissed. The plants on the wall danced to his call. He croaked as loud as he could manage. Lele hopped in. Her giant eyes somehow seemed even larger as she hopped closer to observe.

Runith chuckled. "Still have that."

The Endowers shouted their questions at him and swarmed him, each reaching out a hand to feel the vines around him.

"*They take pleasure in it,*" breathed the Branch. "*Do you?*"

"*Is it sad to say that I feel happier than I have ever been? I love myself. I loved what I was, yet this is... its beyond words. My soul wishes to praise–*"

"*Praise the Korenod!*" Every Rasteen in the room breathed.

He repeated their shout. Just as one of the Rasteen had told him before. It did not feel blasphemous. He felt like he praised an ally to his god, perhaps a prophet. He found comfort in the idea of their spiritual truths uniting. It reassured his faith. Despite any questions or doubts that lingered in the back of his mind, he knew he was on the path destined for his soul.

Runith pointed to the blue flower guard as she stood with the aid of the Rasteen at her side. "*Did she grant me her power?*"

"*In a way, yet so much more.*"

Runith scowled. He felt the vines around him twist with his changing expression. He looked at the other Rasteen, noting that their still faces were no longer emotionless. Their faces had not changed, but his perception had.

Their vines twisted. He saw joy, unease, and even fear in their verdant expressions. *"We have a name for those who can speak to plants. Have I gained this as a second ability?"*

"No. You Vibrations compartmentalize. It is true that those with the gift of the seed can wield a single power, but it is not so with the Rasteen. No longer is it so with you, Beast man. The abilities of the seed are one great round of interconnected light. The colors of each of my guards' flowers show their strength. Their compartments, as you speak of with your kind. The colors of their flowers show how they manifest the light they receive. How they receive light is manifested by their gifts. You have ascended beyond that."

"Paladin," the Rasteen in the room hissed with quick breaths.

The Branch of the North continued to breathe. *"Your talent will always be beast calling, for this has found its way into your soul. No longer are you limited by that part of your stolen intestine, for the vines have spread throughout your body."*

The Branch studied him for a moment, then reached out and touched the vines wrapping his arms. *"I see you are still troubled. Think of the gifts of the seed–these talents–as pools of water connected by a river. Each pool represents a single talent, but occasionally, the water will flow from one pool into another. Your talent for beast calling will likely flow into the pools of calling plants and Vibrations. You are no longer a being with talent, but a vessel for the holy. Your god or ours, the purpose is the same. You have become a holy knight, a harbinger of the Era of Union. You have joined those who brought such unity to the northern Vineyard, our brothers and sisters who once dwelt among your people."*

"The Rasteen lived among us?"

"Not as widespread as you imagine, but our ancestors worked with the scholars and rulers, uniting our holy orders for the gods of this continent. You are now like these holy Rasteen knights. You have become one of them, a Paladin of the Harvest. As you become, so shall they return."

Runith spared a glance back to see Golma whispering translations to Phenmir. He waited to see the Chussman's reaction. Surprise and confusion colored his face. The Chuss guards stepped closer to hear as well.

"Runith!" one of the Tchoyasboys called. He switched to breathe. *"Shouldn't we hurry? We're giving the Krall and your Thanes too much time to work against us!"*

"He's right," Phenmir said with a delay for translation.

Runith turned back to the Branch. With his perception of senses so improved, he felt her burning hope ignite within him. *Am I taking advantage of their naivety? Do I wield this only to enact justice against the tyrants of the human world?*

No.

I feel their pain. Their need. Their sacrifice given and the cost of their faith so that I might, in the slightest chance, return glory to their name and their faith.

The Branch breathed as if she was impressed, as if basking in his glory. *"Redeem what is lost. Make retribution for the abomination attempted by the foolish one who calls himself a Scholar. He attempted to become as you are now, but for the unholy reasons of pride and using our people, rather than seeing us grow."*

Not only could he see them, but Runith felt the eyes of the Rasteen stare at him with hope. Their emotions filled his vines, sending pulses of trust that he felt he did not deserve. Perhaps they were not so naïve, only desperate as their race became subject to the war between humans.

"I will do as you say, Branch of the North," he breathed.

She hummed her appreciation. *"I will prepare a guard force to accompany you whenever you are ready to depart."*

He looked back to Phenmir, waiting for the Endower to finish translating. "How much time do you and your Chussmen need?"

"Give us a few hours," Phenmir replied. "Can the Middlemen attack at night?"

Runith nodded. "Bioluminescence is one thing they have on humans."

"What?"

"Some of them glow at night."

"Yeah, I get that, but... won't that give us away?"

Runith shrugged. "An ambush will be more noticeable if you ask me."

Phenmir shook his head. The hint of a grin betrayed his glare.

Runith chuckled. "I think invading their camp after sundown is a great idea. It'll give your people some time to rest and us time to strategize."

Phenmir nodded.

Runith gave him the Chuss salute. Phenmir returned the Zhaes salute.

"*We invade their camp at nightfall,*" he breathed to the Branch. "*Justice will be served for the false Scholar's act and justice against the tyrants that lead their company. We will remove the parasitic Vibrations from your land.*"

"*You are welcome here among us, as is your company, beast man.*"

"*What about the Korenod? Shouldn't we leave to serve...them?*"

"*We shall discuss your duty to her following the banishment. Return to us upon your success, beast man.*"

Runith knew not how to pay deference, so he resorted to a bow. The Branch made no reaction. He dismissed himself before further embarrassment.

A Rasteen approached him, though it had neither flowers nor buds. "*Come with me beast man, you must learn to care for your vines.*"

Runith furrowed his brow, shrugged, and waved for his company to follow.

❧❧❧❧❧ ❧❧❧❧❧

The sun was setting, casting an orange and pink glow across the swampy pond. It was the size of a Canton's plot and the water was dark as a Tchoyas bog.

Phenmir sat on the grassy edge just above the waterline. Runith waded in the water up to his knees alongside the other Rasteen who would accompany them. He enjoyed, rather took part, in the first non-human practice since his vines had grown on him. His vines, as well as the vines of the surrounding Rasteen, absorbed the water. It was muddy yet filled with nutrients that breathed more energy into Runith than the best night of rest he had ever received.

Endowers splashed nearby, enjoying the water for the sake of entertainment. It did not bother the Rasteen, rather, their breaths resonated with pleasure at seeing the innocent play. Lele hopped by him in the water where she would remain until the next day. She was not meant for war. It was a tragedy that the Rasteen, living nature, had to be brought into it. Perhaps it would be the only battle they needed to take part in. He hoped yet doubted.

Runith smiled. The Endowers took a rare moment to relish in something that had been stolen from them by the war.

They were being children. Play. Laughter. Joy unmarred by duty. Pain and duty would return before they would have liked, yet this was a greater mercy than Runith could have asked for them.

Phenmir plucked the grass and pulled the long blades into individual strings. "How much longer?"

"No rest for the captain of the Chussman?" Runith asked.

Phenmir shook his head and plucked another handful of blades. "Can't. Until the night is over and that Krall and his prodigy associates have been taken care of, I will not rest."

Runith could not blame him. If it hadn't been for the novelty of his transformation, he would have sat beside the Chussman, doing something to occupy his mind. He put his hand at the level of his eyebrows and looked at the horizon. "How much longer do you think? An hour? Two?"

"If that. Maybe we should pull the children out of the water. I don't want them complaining about being cold when they don't have the sun to dry them out."

Runith nodded but did nothing to act upon it. "Do we need the children with us? You have your guards, I have the Rasteen. Shouldn't that be enough?"

Phenmir tossed the grass into the water, though the wind carried most of it away. "Your company was the first that I saw since leaving Sliin. I never saw the base camp. How many would you say were there?"

"When I left, very few, but that was prior to the arrival of Krall Trhet and the Zhaes Thanes. Judging by their usual manner, I would be surprised if they did not have a fair amount of guards with them. Still, not enough to warrant the children."

"No amount should be enough to make us use them," Phenmir mumbled. He sighed and stood, brushing the dead grass from his armored legs. "Let's take a few with us to stay in the back, only if we need them. Gorgers, maybe a few Beastlings to control their ghete if they have any."

"Not a bad idea."

"What about you?"

"What do you mean?"

"You have the abilities of a Sprouten, obviously the skills of a Beastling. You said you can sense people's emotions, so there is some Feelman in you. What *can't* you do?"

Runith stepped from the water. His vines pulsed with the same sensation as a full stomach. Other Rasteen followed. "Not much more that I could do before. My senses are sharper, but I cannot exactly read minds like Feelmen. I guess I could read through a lie, but I am far away from a multi-talented Endowed. I have the vines, but I can't say that I feel much else besides that."

"I'm sure you'll pick up a trick or two, *Paladin*."

Runith smiled. "I guess I have to clean up my act if I am to become their holy knight."

"You have a whole new world to learn. If things go well with the Middlemen–the Rasteen–after this, all of us will have to learn something about their culture."

"Perhaps we could take the time to learn about each other."

Phenmir folded his arms and stretched his back. "Maybe if we would have done that before everything happened, we could have avoided a war. Failure to understand your fellow man is the best fertilizer for hatred. Love is found in patient understanding. Even if one does not agree with another, respect can be found."

"Spoken like a true Chussman."

Phenmir shrugged. "It would have done me a lot of good to learn all of this beforehand. I think we are all starting to understand that this war is more than a conflict harvesting."

"Which is why we must do our best to make that known."

"And remove those who instigate hatred."

Runith nodded.

"So, Zhaesman, you know our targets and their camp. What is the plan?"

A foreign general, one who should be his enemy by the political state of Faect, offered him more camaraderie than he could tell in that single statement.

"The Rasteen are most perturbed by Thane Gromm because of his desecration of their binding ritual. I think we would be best off with them by delivering him to them."

"I agree."

"Everyone else is a mere servant besides Thane Trhet and Thane Royss Belik."

Runith scowled. "I know of the Krall's treachery, and I have heard other rumors about Thane Belik's manipulative character."

You don't know the least of it. "Both are threats we cannot leave alone."

A moment of tense silence built between them. Runith felt Phenmir's emotions pulsate with the same hesitancy as he had.

Is execution the answer?

"Both must be punished. The Rasteen did not seem quite as interested in them. I would hate to make their usefulness go to waste. Should we have them taken to your people?"

"The Harmony Allegiant?"

Runith nodded. "Could they benefit from having them as prisoners?"

"It's worth a try. Don't forget that I am just a piece in their game. I figure it's worth the try. They're better off as resources than dead. As long as we can safely detain them."

"Agreed. If they try anything radical, safety is our priority."

Phenmir nodded. "If they become too dangerous, I can deal with them."

"As will I."

"Let us pray it does not come to that."

"If I have learned anything about living under constant threats, Chussman, it is that we should never stop praying."

Torches and camp fires flickered just over the hill. Loud shouts and laughter filled the unsuspecting loyalist camp.

Runith looked to Phenmir, who crouched at his right. They hid beside the Rasteen and Chuss guards, all armed and ready to charge at their command. The plan had been relayed several times, though Runith's senses warned that the worst was bound to happen. Anxiety and intuition were divided by an almost nonexistent line.

He hoped that all the loyalists would submit to be held and later delivered to the Allegiant. Whatever Phenmir decided to do with them was his problem. Runith did not need to pledge his allegiance to their rebellion. His responsibility lied with the Rasteen. He tried not to think about all that would come from that service, lest he become overwhelmed.

"*Are you ready, beast man?*" one of the Rasteen guards breathed.

As ready as I can be. Lord Laeih be with us. If this Korenod is your ally, then let thy servants succeed. "One moment."

He turned to Phenmir. "Are you and your men ready, Chussman?"

Phenmir nodded. "Let the Rasteen bind Gromm and we'll take care of the guards, then move to the other noblemen."

"And we'll help once Gromm is secured."

Phenmir nodded. "Give the signal and we'll lead."

"*Follow the Vibration captain after me,*" Runith Breathed. He tapped Phenmir's shoulder. "On your mark."

Phenmir ran forward in a crouch, guards at each of his sides, all following him as they hid in the tall grass.

They moved from the tall grass into the clearing. The Chussmen went directly to the largest tent, pursuing those who celebrated their naïve inebriation only to be taken out before they could grasp what was happening.

Runith veered to the right with the Rasteen towards the command tents, where he hoped to find Thane Gromm.

Guards interspersed between their tents took notice of the approaching Rasteen and readied their weapons. Some shouted out but were quickly subdued.

The Rasteen stuck their viney fingers in the ground. Moments later, rooty vines erupted from the ground beneath the guards, securing them to the ground with smaller vines across their mouth to keep them from making any clear warnings. As soon as a guard was bound, the Rasteen would pull their vines from the ground, leaving solid dead roots holding the captives against the ground.

He thought to try, but dared not risk stumbling. This was no time to practice.

Shouts came from behind. Runith spared a glance behind to see torches raised. Shouts turned to swords clashing. Runith prayed that it would end. There had been few guards and armed soldiers when he arrived, but he knew their numbers had likely doubled since the arrival of the nobility.

Runith picked up his pace to stay with the Rasteen after falling behind.

The sound of a hawk's cry, one not native to the Middlelands, pierced the air. Golma and Kaela had insisted on accompanying them to the camp. Runith was reluctant to agree, but Phenmir tasked them with making sure the other Endowers in the camp were safe. Golma's hawk call signaled their safety, allowing him to feel somewhat soothed, until the sound of more fighting washed it away.

The camp was alive. Civil servants and researchers screamed as they ran to hide. Anyone armed and brave enough to defend ran towards the Rasteen, though their charges were short-lived.

Runith kept to the center of the party, staying within the protection of the Rasteen guards.

Their company slowed as a group of Zhaes loyalists ambushed them. No Rasteen fell, though many lost limbs that quickly regrew.

As their momentum picked up, he breathed to one of the Rasteen guards on the right flank. *"Bring me one of them?"*

"The Vibrations?" a Rasteen replied.

"Yes. Did any of them shout commands?"

The Rasteen breathed to all others around her. Before Runith could hear what they were saying, a Zhaesman in Scholar's robes was delivered to him on a moving bed of thick vines. Even though the man was not Thane Gromm, he was not in the least bit disappointed in their quick adherence to his request.

"Remove the vines from his mouth." Runith breathed.

The Scholar twisted and tried to rock free, to no avail. He gasped and coughed, exaggerating his struggles as the vines retracted from his face.

Runith bent over. "Where's Gromm?"

"Beastling Runith?" the Scholar gasped. "By Laeih's holy order! What has happened to you? Have these crop men—"

"Answer the perding question, Zhaesman!"

'I-I–"

"Tighten the grip," Runith breathed.

The Rasteen complied.

"Tell me before they press your sides with thorns."

"They can do that?"

He didn't know. The Scholar did not need to know either, if he was willing to talk. Sometimes suspense is the best intimidator. Silence can be a powerful catalyst.

"Is he expecting you? I-I–"

"Perd! Just tell me where he is!"

The Scholar tried to point with his chin. "That way!"

"Let one of his arms go."

The Rasteen followed his command and freed the Scholar's right arm, though vines still twisted around to constrict if needed. "It's a large pyramidal tent, lined with fur and better looking than any tent here!"

As expected. "I appreciate your service." He nodded to the Rasteen and signaled them forward. He hoped they had picked up on his nodding by now. Even though he hated to force his culture on them, he hoped they would at least pick up on some parts of it for all he was willing to do for them.

The vines around the Scholar severed from the ground and kept him tight with the dead roots still twisted around his body.

The sounds of battle had slowed from behind, but the shouts persisted. He heard the occasional battle cry in the name of Laieh, but they were growing fewer as time went on. War had taught him to fulfill his purpose and ignore what was beyond his control. Each person had their duty to fulfill. Until that was accomplished, one could not worry about others, lest they fall.

They slowed their pace as they reached the aforementioned tent. It was as the Scholar described and the walls glowed with inner illumination. Before Runith could enter, two Rasteen guards used their vines to pull the ropes binding the door flaps, tearing the tent wide open.

"*Stand down, Beastling,*" Thane Gromm hissed in the human tongue, though it shook with power. He sat on a seat behind two heavily armored Zhaes guards.

Runith shook away the discomfort from the Thane's command. "Perd you, Gromm."

Thane Gromm's eyes were wide in surprise, a reaction Runith had never seen from the sniveling Scholar. Runith felt the Thane's emotions. Gromm had known that his command would force Runith to obey. Runith proved the Scholar's knowledge incorrect.

The Guards ran forward with halberds ready to defend. Their efforts and armor proved worthless as the Rasteen tied them to the ground with larger vines than usual.

Gromm pulled a bronze blade from his side and ran at one of the Rasteen.

Runith shook his head and crossed his arms, waiting for Thane Gromm to meet similar disappointment.

Runith found himself to be the one disappointed, rather appalled to see a Rasteen fall weak before Gromm, almost surrendering himself to the Scholar Thane for a decapitation that could not be healed.

Perd.

Gromm laughed. He stepped back and pulled a bronze helm from the tent. *"Stand down, Beastling."*

His words pulsed through Runith's vines. They tighten against him like living rope. He banished doubt. Banished pain. Banished apprehension and charged.

Thane Gromm raised his sword. Runith felt his vines tighten even more, slowing his pace.

Forgive me, brother. Desperation, too, is a great catalyst. He grabbed the head of the fallen Rasteen and threw it at Thane Gromm's head. His strength had failed him, but his aim was precise.

Gromm hunched and grabbed his face after the head hit him right in the nose. Blood trailed down its peak and drops flew as Runith tackled him.

The sword had fallen, but the bronze helmet still pulsed through his vines like a sun burning his veins. He pushed beyond the flames and tossed it from Gromm's head.

Life returned to his vines. Gromm was vulnerable. Gromm was his. Runith had no time to think about the power that bronze had. He shook free the history of bronze's value that tried to creep in. He had much to learn. Now was not the time for learning.

Runith breathed out his call but kept his eyes on Thane Gromm. *"Can you bind him now?"*

He jumped back as vines twisted over Thane Gromm's body.

The Scholar had lost, yet his grin remained.

Runith smacked his face. "Enough."

Gromm's teeth were bloody as his smile returned. "You've given your-self to them, Beastling? I know well the power you seek. It will not last forever. Your hunger will grow and they will end it before you achieve your full potential."

Runith shook his head and stook. *"Have the vines take him back to the center of the camp. He'll see the Branch before the night ends."*

"I know how you feel," Thane Gromm breathed a reply.

"How–"

"Many Scholars used to speak what some called 'the Scholar's tongue. Even if the Rasteen will not obey my commands, I still retain the talent."

Runith's heart pounded. He wondered how much his shock showed through his glare.

"You may have the upper hand now, but more is afoot than you believe. All shall know the power of the Seers. What is there to hide now that you have seen Facet's greatest tool?"

Now is not the time for learning. Runith reminded himself. *Fulfill your duty, then questions can be asked.*

⁓ ⁓

Phenmir steadied his breath as he stood before the treacherous Krall of the Tchoyasmen.

"Serves you right for what you did to him," Royss laughed at Krall Trhet. They sat back to back, bound by vines lent by a Rasteen who had followed some of the wandering Endowers. Few had trickled in since the complete capture of the camp, despite Phenmir's commands for them to stay hidden.

"*You* did this to me!" Krall Trhet shouted. "You perding *manipulative* Zhaesman!" He turned his owl mask towards Phenmir. "I had no con-trol! He forced my will, Chussman!"

"Enough!" one of the Chussman shouted as he pointed his sword at Krall Trhet.

Phenmir had lost his rage. He had held it since Krall Trhet assassinated the Tchoyas Thanes. His hatred grew to its fullest potential after they were ambushed by the faceless raiders. That final wound was exacerbated by the Krall's usage of the Endower in their company who betrayed them by revealing their location.

The Krall weaponized a child.

So had Phenmir. He had never threatened a child as the Krall had. Perhaps Phenmir's crime was worse for convincing the children that warfare was the answer.

The Krall, regardless of if his claims of being manipulated proved true, was just another person trying to make a wrong world right. By no means did Phenmir agree with him, but he saw past the evil owl that lurked in his mind.

Phenmir saw himself in the Krall, as he did in Royss. Both were extremes he would reach if he failed to focus on what mattered.

He fought to show the children a better world.

In understanding, hatred dispersed. Their ideals were flawed, yet they only tried to do what was best.

Despite their attempts at doing good, they had failed. Failure entailed punishment.

Phenmir was a piece in the system. A piece in Facet's command. Krall Trhet's fate would be placed into the hands of the granddaughter whom he betrayed. Royss' fate would be given to Aerhee, the high most Zhaes representative in the Harmony Allegiant.

"Thane Stolk?"

He ignored the voice, taking a moment to appreciate not only their victory, but how it had been accomplished.

Soldiers or nobleman, it did not matter, all had been apprehended, with only a few having perished. He looked at the final guards, who were held to the ground by Rasteen vines. They, and the many others, would be dealt with after their leaders.

"Phenmir!"

He shot his attention to one of his Chuss guards, who pointed at the Krall. "Take care of her!"

Her? He looked, but the soldier was not pointing at the Krall, rather right next to him. *Perd.* "Kaela! Step back from him!"

He ran, as did she. She had come out of nowhere. Her assignment elsewhere was designed for more than her personal safety. Endowers were rarely the lesser power in a contest, especially Shiftlings like her.

"Stop! Kaela please!"

She spared him a glance, and her hands turned into paws with claws as long as his fingers. The mouth of her mask had formed into a toothy maw, the fangs well exaggerated as well.

Phenmir had learned to control his rage. He would struggle with it in days to come, but he was well in that moment.

He was calm. Kaela was not.

"Perd you!" She shouted as she pounced onto the Krall and Royss, tearing at her former ruler in a frenzy.

One of the Chussman shouted and pointed a Rasteen towards Royss as the shredded vines fell off of them in Kaela's wake. The Rasteen seemed to understand and caught Royss in his own vines before he could escape.

Phenmir returned his focus to Kaela and the Krall and ran to intervene. His safety was less important than her sanity. Rage fueled her now, but the withdrawal paired with future remorse would cure emotional wounds with ugly scars.

He reached to pry her off of him, but she turned and gnashed her bloody teeth until he stepped back.

He watched, as did all others, the Krall's execution. He had killed half of her nobility. His machinations had manipulated her and her friends into becoming tools for his purposes. The punishment was just.

Silence returned as she finished shredding him. She tossed his bloody owl mask at Phenmir's feet and reverted to her Tchoyasgirl form. Crickets and struggling prisoners were but white noise against the intensity of her slow, shaky breaths.

Phenmir was caught between wanting to run to comfort and pure disgust.

"Save me Laieh!" Royss shouted with a prayer that cried for attention rather than in sincerity. "I'll give you what you need, just please—"

"Enough!" Phenmir commanded. His eyes remained locked with Kaela's.

"His honor was not steadfast." Kaela spoke. "He failed to fulfill his ideal. *I* have returned honor to him. May Klen's justice serve him well in the under realms."

Phenmir nodded.

An evil day has come when children are forced into adulthood.

EPILOGUE

"Not the way you wanted to come back home, is it?"

Aerhee lifted her head up from between her hugged knees. Her back ached, yet it was only physical pain. That she could withstand. The alternative had been laid upon her too much to bear.

Still, Voln smiled. The candlelight shined just right in the cell for her to see his cracked lips.

"Priess is not my home," she said.

"Sorry I said so."

Was that an apology? He has never *apologized. Even in insincerity, it was* still *an apology.* Even his cocksure charisma had dwindled. Days–how many had been lost to her–spent in a Patriarchy prison could damage even the brightest of souls. The deaths associated with their captivity were thorns around the punishment.

"Don't be, Voln."

He nodded. She could no longer see his smile as he hung his head.

Perd. I cannot become weak now. He needs me now more than he ever did in the wilderness.

She looked up at him. She felt—

She started to cry. Again. He did as well.

Perd me, Zeir! You were too perfect! All lies are too perfect! How could I have fallen for years of–you! You only cared to serve your assignment! You didn't betray just me, but the Allegiant as well! Your lies cost the lives of Paiell! You only cared to—perd. In the end, you cared for me. Didn't you? You perding kulf! You learned to love the most unlovable person to have ever been born! I was the worst spouse and you—even aside from all my poor behavior. I don't care if you did it for them.

In the end, you did it for me.

Didn't you?

I know you did.

I loved you Zeir.

I still do.

She tried to mourn Sheath, yet her mind could only hold to the only love she ever knew. Voln cried. She let her sobs call out louder than ever as she pulled in the lonely Tchoyasboy as tight as she could.

I love you Zeir. I love you. I love you. I don't care if I'm delusional or in denial. I know you. You dug deep enough to know me. That's all I could have ever asked for. You loved me. You truly did.

I'm sorry, Zeir. I'm sorry.

She slammed her fist on the stone floor and cried out.

I love you.

She pulled back and looked into Voln's red eyes. The rims of his eye holes were almost dripping, having absorbed his tears.

She looked at him, seeing the vulnerable boy. One as alone in the world as she was. Zeir was gone, but her love could continue in a new way. They had wanted children, though duty never allowed.

"Voln, I'll be the mother you have never had."

The words seemed so awkward coming from her lips. He voiced no agreement as he embraced her as she had embraced her mother so many years ago in the very same city. His embrace was enough of an answer.

The cell doors opened, they both turned to see a trio of Scholars standing in the doorway.

"Well, isn't this touching?" a Scholar chuckled.

His words had no effect.. She felt joy again in the most miserable time in her life.

"Come." He directed and the other two Scholars picked up Aerhee and Voln, leading them from the cell and placing manacles on their wrists.

They walked with the Scholars down the dank hallway to another cell. The Scholars unlocked it, yet the cell held only a door.

He stepped forward and opened it. The other Scholars pushed Aerhee forward and kept Voln close behind.

Her joy dispersed in place of fear and confusion.

A skeleton of vines sat against the wall. Dead leaves covered its head like a haunted crown. It lifted its head. Piercing gray eyes stared at her from the white marble face that looked so much like a mask. It forced out a heavy breath.

"Perd me," Aerhee whispered.

"Well," the Scholar leaned forward, "I hoped that you would recognize her, but perhaps it was only your father who met her. Fear not, we will dig deep enough to learn how you two are connected."

"A Middleman?"

"Oh, dear Aerhee, she is more than that. This is the very founder of the Patriarchy of Scholars. Our bride, if you will, and we her *loyal* husband. This is the very Root Lord herself."

AFTERWORD

Thank you for taking your time to read this book! As an independent author, your opinion of this book can make a big difference. Please take a few moments to review this book on Goodreads, Amazon, and anywhere else you would like. If you enjoyed reading this, please tell your friends and family about it! Thank you for taking your time to read Duet, a Hymn will come soon...

ACKNOWLEDGEMENTS

My author career finally unfolded as I wrote this book simultaneously with the first year of Elegy's release. I want to thank everyone who has read it and shared your love for it. With the support and love I had from readers, I had the drive to continue to write.

As always, thank you my dear wife Sima for helping me figure life out as an author. Your art and growing love for fantasy gives me more energy and hope than you realize.

As mentioned in the dedication, I have to thank my author friends who have helped me in my first year of publishing. Please go read their books.

Thank you to all the booktubers, bloggers, and reviewers who have helped my little book see the spotlight. Thank you Daniel Greene, Petrik Leo, Andrew Watson (again), and everyone else that has helped my series see some light.

Thank you to all of my @Svetlingpress (instagram) followers and Love & Lore subscribers. By watching me talk about books, I've been able to share my stories with more people than I could have ever imagined.

If you are reading this, thank you. I love you and your time means more than you could ever know.

ABOUT THE AUTHOR

Kaden Love currently resides in Salt Lake City, Utah with his wife (and illustrator), Sima. When he isn't reading, he juggles running marathons to audiobooks, writing, and living out his own adventures.

@kadenloveauthor on Instagram, X (Twitter)

@svetlingpress on Instagram

Kadenrlove.com

www.ingramcontent.com/pod-product-compliance
Ingram Content Group UK Ltd.
Pitfield, Milton Keynes, MK11 3LW, UK
UKHW031930310125
454496UK00005B/406